Julian Hawthorne

Garth

A Novel

Julian Hawthorne

Garth
A Novel

ISBN/EAN: 9783337002503

Printed in Europe, USA, Canada, Australia, Japan

Cover: Foto ©Andreas Hilbeck / pixelio.de

More available books at **www.hansebooks.com**

GARTH:

A NOVEL.

BY

JULIAN HAWTHORNE,

AUTHOR OF

"BRESSANT," "SAXON STUDIES," ETC.

NEW YORK:
D. APPLETON AND COMPANY,
1880.

CONTENTS.

GARTH.

BOOK I.

URMHURST.

CHAPTER I.

A BIRD-PROLOGUE.

EVERY clear morning, for more than two hundred years past, the rising sun had thrown across the broad hip-roof of Urmhurst the shadow of its eastern chimney. The earliest beams, though fresh and pure from their ocean-bath, yet scrupled not to embrace the weather-worn old shaft, or to kiss warmly its smoke-blackened mouth.

The chimney, for its part, seldom suffered these kind greetings to pass without due recognition. In the winter months its reply was a jolly puff of blue smoke, odorous of the pungent spirit of the great pine-log which had been kindled on the hearth below. But its summer response was livelier and, perhaps, more poetical. First would be heard a mysterious, soft rumbling and twittering, as though the venerable structure were cleaning its sooty throat to say good-morning; and anon, like cheerful thoughts born of an aged heart, forth would flutter, from their abode in the cavernous interior, a rejoicing flock of chimney-swallows.

There were dozens and scores of them. Hardly in all New England, and certainly not in New Hampshire, could be found such another chimney for swifts as this eastern one of Urmhurst—so tall was it, so roomy, so full of convenient holes and crevices.

Here had they builded through generations innumerable; each head of a family, at his decease, jealously transmitting the chosen ancestral cranny to the eldest son. But even the largest chimneys have a limit to their capacity for accommodating lodgers; and, during the last century or so, there must have occurred in the swift colony many sad but unavoidable family partings. Every year a certain contingent must go forth to seek their homes elsewhere. They would cluster together upon the brink of their old dwelling; and perhaps the less experienced among them would ask why they need go farther than just across the roof, where the western chimney, to all appearances the very twin of the eastern, upreared itself in silent invitation.

"Ah, my dear child," some wise old cock would reply, whetting his beak against a brick, and then tipping his head sagely to one side, "that site is not so eligible as it looks to be. Not a bird of us all has ever settled there. The air thereabouts is very feverish and unwholesome. In short, as I said before, it's not so eligible as—"

"But what makes the air unwholesome, grandpa?" the youngster would break in.

"Well, you see, it's called the kitchen-chimney; and wherever, in your future career, you come across a chimney that is called a kitchen-chimney, don't go near it. They are never wholesome; and what makes it a greater pity is that half the time they're the largest chimneys in the house."

"In my opinion, then, it's an outrage; and, if I live, I'll see it righted. What! are not chimneys made for chimney-swallows? Does not our very name demonstrate it? And, if so, why should not one be as good as another?"

"But men build them, you know," begins the old cock, whetting his bill apologetically; "and perhaps they may sometimes want to use them for some purposes of their own. You see there are two sides to every question; appearances are deceptive, and, at all events, we ought to allow men to plead their own cause before condemning them."

"I disagree with you. You are old and timid. For me, I hold no parley with injustice—I crush it. Men build chimneys, perhaps; but that is nothing to their credit, they are obliged to do it in order to accommodate us. Under what pretext, then, can they usurp the use of them? I say no injustice ever was more flagrant. It should be a standing heritage of indignation to the swift colony until it is righted; and, for my part, I am ready to begin the good work at once!"

"Tut, tut!" says the old one, "you are young and hot-headed; but what can you do? Do you suppose you are the first bird that ever was indignant? No, nor will you be the last; but the chimney will remain ineligible, nevertheless. At all events, don't begin your reforms with Urmhurst; for one does not meet every day, as you will by-and-by find out, with a human family so uniformly considerate as these Urmsons of ours. For example, in my younger days," continued the patriarch, beginning the story for the seven-hundredth time at least—"in my younger days, Garth Urmson and I became quite intimate. The friendship originated, you must know, in his setting a fracture of this leg—"

"Yes, yes, yes!" is the unanimous twitter of the conclave; "don't tell us that old yarn again; we know all about it, and how kind Garth always has been to us. Why shouldn't he be? Yes, yes, yes!"

"Quite so!" rejoins the patriarch, pretending not to mind the interruption, though in reality quite put off the track of his ideas by it—"quite so. Garth has always been

kind to us since that time; it is out of the regard he feels for me. When I am gone you may find a difference; I hope not, but you may! Yes, and the old gentleman, Mr. Cuthbert Urmson, he is very obliging also. Often and often has he put crumbs on his study window-sill out of regard for me, you understand; and has smiled and nodded very pleasantly when I came to carry them off. A charming old gentleman; I feel a sympathy for him. I should not wonder if that book he is writing were a history of chimney-swallows; supplemented, perhaps, with allusions to his own family records, and to the vicissitudes of Urmhurst itself. Now, is it reasonable to suppose," adds the patriarch, suddenly getting his cue again, and raising his chirp (for his audience was betraying symptoms of inattention)—"is it reasonable, I say, to accuse persons, otherwise so friendly, of wantonly—*wantonly*, mark you!—infringing upon our rights in a matter so vital as this? No, a thousand times no! Depend upon it, some hidden causes are at work here. This old house is full of mysterious and sinister traditions; and who knows whether there may not be some occult connection between the dinners of our good friends below there, and this unwholesome atmosphere of the kitchen-chimney?"

"Then," twitters the irreconcilable, skimming away, "here goes for knocking soot into their broth-kettle!"

CHAPTER II.

LEAVING the annals of the swifts to good Mr. Cuthbert Urmson (if such be really the subject of his labors), let us observe with how comfortable a familiarity the sunshine disposes itself upon the gray-green lichens of Urmhurst's shingled roof, and weaves golden fibres into the ponderous oaken logs wherewith the ancient house is built. Ancient—yet it seems to wax more massive and stalwart year by year. Here is no sagging of the ridge-pole, nor leaning of the uprights, nor settling of the granite foundations. This oaken framework is stanch as a mammoth's skeleton; and these log-built walls as enduring as stone courses. Perhaps the sun, during the two centuries that he has shone on Urmhurst, has imparted to it, along with his heat, something likewise of his immortality. These great, unpainted boles, that sleep so snugly one on another, have acquired a ruddy lustre suggestive of living flesh and blood; but to the frailties and infirmities of humanity they seem to own no kinship.

Urmhurst faces the south; and thus its venerable front, rich in projections and unevennesses, takes the sun's rays obliquely, and generates a carnival of shadows of all shapes, sizes, and gradations. The curt hip-roof is here modified by the addition of a steeply-shelving curb, veiling the bareness of the upper story, as though the house had pulled its hat-brim low down over its forehead. Through this curb project the hooded gables of three dormer-windows, the central one cut down so as to form a glass door, whereby access is had to a balcony surmounting the porch. The eastern, known as Eve's window, is framed in a climbing vine of small pink roses. Below, the impending eaves cast a contemplative shade over the deep-set casements of the ground-floor; the dormers project pointed shadows aslant; but the profoundest obscurity always collects beneath the porch. This is partly due to the fact that the pillars and canopy, instead of being carpenter's work, are fashioned of living trees—a couple of gnarled and stunted oaks, planted generations ago on either side the wide doorway. At the height of about twelve feet from the ground their upward growth has been arrested, and the strength of their knotted limbs spread out horizontally above the threshold stone. Thus interlocked, they appear to grapple each other like a pair of misshapen wrestlers. They support the balcony appertaining to the second floor, and their dark and sedate foliage lets fall, on whomsoever passes beneath, a transparent veil of gloom.

This gloom has been deepened by tradition. The death-grip of the two trees would seem to typify a sinister deed said to have been done on the spot, which was after-

ward covered by the still-existing granite threshold, but which, at the primitive epoch referred to, was the consecrated grave of a mighty Indian warrior and sachem. After his death, his tribe had migrated to a tract several hundred miles to the southward; but his descendants (in obedience to some pious superstition) were in the habit of making occasional pilgrimages to his tomb. What mystic rites they observe there we have no means of knowing, but it is believed that every year, for more than three generations, the two wisest and bravest chiefs of the tribe were chosen to make the long journey through the trackless forest; and, so great was the awe wherewith the deceased sachem was invested, not only in the eyes of his own people, but also in those of other tribes, that the pilgrims never once met with any hinderance on their sacred expedition, nor ever found the solemn privacy of the tomb disturbed.

But at length there came a year when the appointed twain arrived to find a strange company there before them. The grave-mound was situated near the centre of an opening—a natural glade in the mid-heart of the primeval forest. Around it was now assembled a troop of twenty or more white-faced personages with steel caps on their heads, and wearing bright accoutrements, which glistened in the sunshine. A number of wagons were drawn up near at hand and fresh-faced women were seated on and among the medley of household goods wherewith they were laden. Upon the consecrated mound itself a short, strongly-built man, dark-browed, and bearing in the centre of his chin a deep scar or cleft, had taken his stand and was haranguing the assemblage. Close to him sat on horseback a stately young woman, holding an infant in her arms. She listened to the man's harangue, her dark eyes fixed sadly but lovingly on his face; and when he ceased speaking she turned to the steel-clad company and uplifted before them her babe, uttering at the same time words of earnest encouragement, to which they of the steel head-pieces responded with three loud shouts and a waving of their weapons.

Up to this moment the two Indians, hidden within the leafy verge of the forest, had looked on in mingled awe and amazement. These were the first white men they had seen, and they perhaps supposed them to be a kind of spirits, come from heaven to do honor to the illustrious dead. History, however, bids us recognize them as that sturdy band of pioneers whom Captain Neil Urmson, the Puritan soldier of Marston Moor and Naseby, led, about the middle of the seventeenth century, into the unknown wilderness west from Portsmouth. Captain Urmson was a man of undoubted pith and ability; and, had it not been for the singular restlessness of disposition which drove him forth from the restraints of the Portsmouth colony, he would have made a deep mark in the first pages of our New England history. Though harsh of aspect and unequal in his moods, he seems to have been possessed of a peculiar power over the wills and judgments of those with whom he came in personal contact. Wealthy, and endowed with a physical strength and energy exceptional even in those iron times, he might have risen to the highest place in almost any community. But an uneasy devil possessed him; and, after causing him to abandon the prospect of a brilliant career in England under the Protectorate (which he had helped much to establish), it haunted him even in his self-imposed exile over-seas. Scarce four months after his disembarkation at Portsmouth, he already showed symptoms of discontent. Much was done to appease him, for the little colony could ill afford to be at odds with so rich and able a member as Captain Urmson. But it was all to no purpose. Imperiously rejecting advice and reason, he packed his wagons, collected his people, and departed northwestward. Nothing more was heard of him, and he was soon given up for lost. But boldness and sagacity were his safeguard through the wild difficulties and perils of the forest. He managed either to awe or to conciliate such Indians as crossed his path; and when, some months after leaving the colony, he and his followers halted at last on the site of the sachem's grave, not a man of them all was missing, or had suffered in health or limb.

At this point, however, blood was spilt.

Captain Urmson, in haranguing his retainers, had bade them look upon this forest-glade as the nucleus of their future home; and his wife Eleanor had cheered them by showing the undaunted front of little Ralph, a pioneer less than a year old—for he was born at sea. Thereupon the captain, snatching a pickaxe from the hand of one of the men standing near him—John Selwyn by name—and with the words, "Here, in this virgin soil, where are no dead bones or blood-stains of the past, will I set the threshold of our new life!"—with this singularly infelicitous exclamation, he raised the heavy pick above his head, and then drove it deep into the green turf of the unsuspected grave.

Before he could uplift it for another stroke, a wild yell broke startling on the ears of all. All recognized the Indian warwhoop, and, fancying themselves attacked by a whole tribe at once, they fell for a moment into something like confusion. Meanwhile, two dusky figures, with long black hair and brandished tomahawks, had bounded forward from the concealment of the trees. One of them sprang at Captain Urmson, and wrenched the pickaxe from his hand. The suddenness and audacity of the savage apparition increased the dismay of the white men, not one of whom stirred in defense. But on Neil Urmson's swarthy face there was at once a smile and a dark frown. Eleanor, who had seen that expression once before at a momentous epoch in their lives, turned pale and tried to restrain him as he was drawing the heavy pistol from his belt.

"Do not, husband!" she said. "Remember our wedding-day; defile not likewise this first hour of our new life with blood!"

Tradition affirms that Urmson did hesitate for a moment, with his hand on the butt of the pistol. And then was heard the stentorian voice of the Reverend Anak Graeme, who had accompanied Urmson from England, and was rumored to have been the officiating clergyman at his marriage, "Verily, methinks it were well to parley with the heathen before slaying them!"

"Well said!" cried John Selwyn, a slenderly-built man, with bold eyes and careless bearing. "Give the devil his due, captain. For aught we know, these red-skinned sinners may have better right here than we!"

But, even as he spoke, the second Indian, who was younger and presumably less steady than his companion, drew his bow and let fly an arrow. It glanced harmlessly from the captain's polished helmet, and pierced Eleanor's shoulder, and the face of little Ralph was smeared with her blood. As quick as thought Neil leveled his pistol and fired right into the heart of the first Indian, who was close in front of him. The tall savage leaped from the ground, and falling prone, his brawny arms hugged the grave of his dishonored ancestor, and his teeth bit the turf. Eleanor, though sorely wounded, clasped her child to her bosom and strove to support herself upon her frightened horse. Scarce a minute had elapsed since the first alarm of the war-whoop.

By the time the smoke of Captain Neil's pistol had cleared away, his retainers had formed to resist as best they might the expected onslaught. But they waited in vain. Only the dark trunks of the mighty oaks and hemlocks surrounded them, and there was no sound save the twittering of scared birds, and the rustle of the leaves in the summer wind. No avengers came; or, if any, not then, nor for many a year thereafter. The second Indian had fled, silently as a dream, toward the distant wigwams of his tribe, there to keep alive, as tradition would have us believe, an hereditary memory of the sacrilege and a purpose of requital. A neighboring stream, which rushes headlong over a jagged bed of rocks and empties into a lake some miles away, is still pointed out as having been traversed by the fugitive in his desperate canoe.

Having assured themselves of their safety, the colonists had leisure to take thought concerning the dead and wounded. As to the former, it was resolved, in accordance with Captain Urmson's suggestion, to bury the heathen on the spot where he had fallen, and to make his gravestone the threshold of the projected edifice. "For it is fitting," said the grim Puritan, "and an emblem of what shall surely come to pass throughout this land, that in entering our new home we plant our foot first upon the bones of the red-man."

In digging the grave, however, the relics of the ancient sachem were revealed, and the mysterious attack of the two Indians thereby explained. The grave-diggers hereupon shook their heads, and were reluctant to proceed; and John Selwyn threw down his spade, and flatly refused to have anything more to do with the business; declaring, with sundry strange oaths peculiar to him, that no good would come of stealing dead men's ground, and that, rather than live there, he would part from the colony and seek his fortune alone. Captain Urmson, then, having resolutely confronted his enemies while they were alive, was not inclined to be squeamish about them dead. Taking Selwyn's spade, and thrusting the other men aside, he finished the grave himself, and pitched into it the body of the slain, and covered up the corpse with the earth-stained skeleton of the original occupant. He stamped the earth level with his booted feet, and looking with glowing eyes into the faces of the silent group who had stood watching his ill-omened toil—"It is my deed," he said, "and thus do I trample down this blood, and all superstitious terrors!"

CHAPTER III.

THE GENERATIONS.

SUCH is the gloomy legend that underlies the threshold of our story. Selwyn was as good as his word, and departed with what few possessions he had; being the first of Captain Urmson's followers who had ever had the hardihood to desert him. Nevertheless, Urmhurst was built, and a huge slab of rough-hewed granite, heavy enough to have kept down the most athletic ghost, pressed its weight above the nameless remains. It so happened, however, that the frost of the ensuing winter, or some other less obvious agent, cracked the ponderous stone across its entire breadth; and this cleft, from a variety of causes, became afterward so much widened that, at the epoch of which I am to write, there were two distinct thresholds instead of one, with a gap of two or three inches between them. This accident was interpreted by the sagacious as a sign that the blood which Neil Urmson had so arrogantly trodden into the earth would one day rise against him; and for many years whatever misfortune befell the family, whether or not really ascribable to the Indians, was by such sapient persons unerringly referred to a birthplace beneath the cloven threshold.

Urmhurst was built; but, at least during its builder's lifetime, it could hardly have been a cheerful dwelling-place. Eleanor never recovered from the effects of her wound. She lingered through several months; but, when the house was at last completed, she had to be carried to her chamber and laid upon the bed which she left only for the graveyard. Hints have come down to us that her death was hastened by mental disquietude; and her reference, when trying to dissuade her husband from bloodshed, to something which had happened on their wedding-day, has been quoted in support of this notion. Furthermore, attempts have been made to trace a connection between the purport of these words of hers and the sudden self-banishment of Captain Urmson from England. His family had been a prominent and powerful one; the English Urmhurst was a valuable estate; and the Cromwellian party, of which the captain was an adherent, was just establishing its supremacy when he exiled himself. Had he remained he must presumably have filled a high office under the new government. Why had he fled? Not, surely, from religious motives, since he had never been a religious bigot; and though after his emigration he was occasionally subject to violent fits of fanaticism, yet these had no root in his nature, and generally left him with a tendency toward reaction. The explanation therefore must be sought elsewhere; and, putting what was known and what was surmised together, the conclusion was reached that Captain Urmson had done some deed rendering himself alike odious to his own and the opposite party; and that his marriage with Eleanor

had somehow been either the incitement to this deed or the occasion of it.

To button-hole the captain and ask him the simple question whose answer would put an end to conjecture, might seem a simple matter; but there were serious obstacles to this course. The first master of Urmhurst would certainly have knocked down whomsoever had presumed to catechise him, and possibly would not have been contented to stop even there. He had never been distinguished for affability, and after his wife's death he became uncompromisingly savage. He shut himself up in his fort (for Urmhurst was really little more than that in his lifetime), and devoted himself to the education of his son Ralph, who is said to have strongly resembled his father, even to the cleft in the chin. The captain had no near neighbors, Urmhurst standing then, as always, alone. The other members of the colony built their huts on the banks of the rapid stream to the westward, thus forming the germ of the prosperous little village of Urmsworth, which exists there to-day. This secession may have been owing to those superstitious terrors which Urmson himself had professed to despise; but it is as readily explained by the circumstance that, although the situation of Urmhurst itself is unapproachably fine, there happens to be no other site in the vicinity even tolerably eligible.

The house, as we behold it now, rises from the summit of a smooth, grassy knoll, barely half an acre in area. This knoll is itself the culminating point of a long and gradual acclivity, ascending by almost imperceptible degrees from the broad southern valley. The real loftiness of the site can be realized only by considering how wide a sweep of prospect it commands over a scene of beauty at once noble and peaceful. The wooded slopes trend majestically southward till they merge in the broad gleam of a lake some three miles away. Beyond appear at intervals the white reaches of a placid stream, winding onward through miles of level cranberry-pastures, which themselves resemble a gigantic green river, slumbering between wooded shores. The farther extremity of this valley is sentineled by a mountain—or rather a group of high hills—having the ap-

pearance, from the point of view of Urmhurst, of a crouching lion, whose shaggy
head rests ponderously on his fore-paws.

The Indian name of this mountain is Wabeno—the Juggler; perhaps in allusion to
the protean changes which the seasons and
the variations of the weather cause him to
undergo. In spring he acquires a dark-blu-
ish tinge, especially in the early morning,
when the moist haziness of the atmosphere
is supplemented by the fleecy mists which
ascend from the meadows and clamber up
his headlong sides. In summer his coat is
shadowed purple, with greenish lights; and
monster thunder-clouds sweep and burst over
his crest, letting through broad, slanting bars
of gauzy light. In autumn his mane grows
tawny, and the clear air magnifies him, so
that he appears nearer by several miles than
at other seasons. In times of drought he
occasionally takes fire, and lies swathed for
days or weeks in mysterious clouds of shift-
ing smoke, which by night are illumined
with a dull russet glow, like that reflected
upward from the profound pit of a volcano.
Winter makes him gray and ghost-like; and
when in long December nights the white
moon hangs above him in the frosty sky, he
seems in truth no more substantial than an
horizon cloud. In snow-storms he vanishes
quite away; but when the northern winds
have cleared the valley, there he looms as
before—a lion in the path! After all this
phantom show of life and activity, behold!
he crouches impassive and motionless, his
shaggy head upon his paws. There he lies,
and seems to watch the old house, that
watches back from its lonely station twenty
miles away.

It has been fancifully affirmed that Wabeno is in fact neither a mountain nor a lion,
but an incarnation of the spirit of that incorrigible old sachem whose dust lies underneath Urmhurst's threshold-stone. And it
is further stated that when Urmhurst shall
step down from between the two tower-
like chimneys to which it has been moored
during so many generations, Wabeno will
spring up and emit a roar which shall make
New Hampshire tremble. If we grant the
first act of this drama, we might admit the
second; but the ancient mansion budges

not! It has rested so long on its granite
foundations that it has almost become a part
of the continent itself. Like some immemorial oak-tree, it has thrown out roots far
and near and on every side, so that its up-
heaval would tear open the ground for a
quarter of a mile in circuit. It is the eye
and key of the landscape, harmonizing so
justly with its surroundings that any alteration would seem tantamount to the viola-
tion of a natural law.

This semblance of spontaneous growth is
enhanced by the devious footpaths which
lead this way and that from the doors, and
journey in time-worn furrows down the
slopes. We cannot call them artificial, for
they were honestly worn by the footsteps
of generations, and therefore fill precisely
their natural places. Yonder, where it goes
up the acclivity, the track is narrow but
deeply worn; whereas, above, it broadens
and throws off a lighter sideway parallel to
itself. See again how deftly it avoids that
jut of rock; and here, how sagaciously it
slips beneath the shadow of the great elm.
In a similar manner do the other accessories
of the dwelling conspire to fix it more intimately in its place. The antique well-
sweep, poised like a giant's fishing-pole, in
the crotch of a tree; the barn, which looks
older than the house, though in reality its
junior by near a century; the great orchard
in the rear toward the north, containing
trees off which old Neil himself might have
gathered apples—all these things are mar-
riage-tokens.

And finally there is the graveyard, indis-
solublest bond of all, since it is a moral as
well as a natural one. It lies about a hundred paces eastward, and takes the earliest
sunshine. It is well populated, this little
inclosure, for although the Urmson race has
ever been a turbulent and adventurous one
—many of them followers of the sea, or
fighters against whomsoever there was to
fight, Indian, Frenchman, or Englishman,
as the case might be—it has, nevertheless,
happened that most of them wandered home
to die. The burial-ground was consecrated
by that same Reverend Anak of whom we
have already had a glimpse—he who married Eleanor to Neil, and came with them

to the New World. This worthy man of God lived to pronounce another than the marriage service over the pair: they are buried in one grave. The imaginative moralizer will observe that, although Eleanor's epitaph is still legible, in that of her husband, who died nearly forty years later, only the single word "died" has survived obliteration.

Near at hand stands the tombstone of Ralph, who, if report be true, inherited all the bad and gloomy traits of his father, with few of his virtues. But he was gifted with the same peculiar personal influence over the minds and wills of others that Neil had possessed. It was remarked, however, that as often as the Urmsons had their way in a matter (and they seldom failed to have it), it turned to their disadvantage. Their luck, in other words, was their misfortune. Now, if there be a certain crisis in the life of every man, when a depraved or impious passion engages in final contest with better knowledge and purer instincts, could the latter's defeat be more fitly punished than by dooming the sinner to act successfully out, forever afterward, his unrestrained and unrepentant self? So may it have fared with these dark-browed, hot-hearted Urmsons, who often seemed to carry all before them at the very moment when they were being hurried to their own destruction.

We search in vain among the tombstones for the record of any daughter of the Urmson name. For it is a remarkable fact that, since the epoch of their emigration, no woman-child has been born to them — as though the family nature were too harsh and gloomy to produce a feminine flower. Not a daughter in seven generations? Yes, one there has been, and within the present century; but there is more of sorrow than of joy in the mention of her name. Eve Urmson was the daughter of Garth's grandfather—old Brian, of Revolutionary renown. She is described as having been a peculiar but fascinating child, and the old warrior is said to have taken boundless pride and delight in her. When she was ten years old, Eve disappeared, and was never afterward heard of. It was conjectured that a party of Indians, who were known to have been

in the neighborhood about the time of the child's disappearance, had kidnapped her; and such of the old wives and village oracles as had kept alive a memory of the legends, maintained that the kidnappers were no other than the lineal descendants of the sachem and his murdered defender, who thus wreaked their revenge. Be that as it may, Urmhurst's greatest blessing was thus changed into its saddest misfortune.

A lack of the feminine element is noticeable about the house; its features and aspects, though for the most part picturesque, are too massive and masculine. Eve's chamber is the only exception; it has been preserved nearly as she left it, and the rose-vine, which her childish hands planted, clambers unrestrained over her window. But there is need of a living and loving woman in these great, old-fashioned, wainscoted rooms. Garth's mother died while he was in college; and latterly he and his father—who is a son of Brian Urmson by a first marriage, and half-brother to the lost Eve—have lived here pretty much by themselves, each immersed in his own chosen pursuit, and putting the maintenance of the farm in the light of a recreation. The only other member of the family known to be alive is an own brother of Eve's named Golightley—the name of his mother's family, old settlers of Virginia. Golightley was remembered in Urmsworth village as a talented and affable youth, whose delicate constitution unfitted him for the pursuit of any hard-working profession, and who went to Europe in quest of health and of that æsthetic culture which his soul craved. Apparently he must have found what he sought, for he had already been absent more than twenty years without betraying any inclination to return.

But it is time to bring this preliminary chat to a close. Urmhurst still stands in the woods, though now the primitive forest-glade has expanded into a clearing of thirty acres, chiefly comprising the profile of the southern slope. Part of this land is used as a vegetable-garden; there are corn and potato fields, and ample pasturage for cows and horses. As for the interior of the mansion, it is chiefly remarkable for an antique spaciousness of hall and staircase, a suggestive mystery of garret and cellar, and a noble extravagance of hearth and chimney-corner.

But it is rather with the Urmsons than with their dwelling that we are presently concerned.

BOOK II.

THE FATHER OF THE MAN.

CHAPTER IV.

THE MAN.

A BROAD-BUILT young fellow, about twenty-six years of age, but looking older, stands on the cloven threshold of Urmhurst, with his feet apart and his face bent downward, as though in reverie. His eyes, however, are rather outlooking than introspective; and, considering how fair a prospect lies before him, it would be strange if they were otherwise. The sun shines level through the October oak-leaves on the eastern side of the porch, and casts a russet glow on the young fellow's swarthy check.

Like most Urmsons, Garth is shorter than the average of men; but, to make up for it, he is chested like a bison, and vigorous and compact all over. His dress this morning differs little from that ordinarily worn by the New Hampshire farmer. His dark, shaggy hair pokes itself through the torn crown of a battered straw hat, which he has clapped on the capacious back of his head. In his left hand is a tuft of maple-leaves, the splendid scarlet of which causes his red-flannel shirt to appear dingy by contrast. A rough sack-coat (the pockets bulging with crimson and yellow apples), and corduroy trousers tucked into cowhide boots, complete his costume. He carries, strapped to his back, a sort of shallow knapsack; and in his right hand a bundle of something neatly tied up in a linen case, like a jointed fishing-rod. From outward appearances, therefore, he might be going angling.

The famous green door of Urmhurst forms an agreeable background to this sturdy figure. It is a massive structure of six-inch oaken timbers, clamped and bolted with iron, and scarred by many an ineffectual dint of tomahawk and bullet in Indian fights of yore. On the upper part of the framework may still be deciphered the date and initials, "N. U., 1648," deeply cut in old-fashioned characters. This redoubtable door, besides enjoying its present green old age, passed a verdant youth and prime likewise. It got its latest coat of emerald so long ago as the War of 1812; but the forty years or so which have elapsed since then have so mellowed and enriched the original tint that, at a few paces' distance, we might fancy the hard surface overgrown with a thick coating of soft moss, like that which cushions tombstones in the damp church-yards of Old England.

Though the sun is but half an hour out of the Atlantic, Garth has already made the rounds of the farm. His bedroom being on the ground-floor, he had only to lift the sash and swing himself out ankle-deep in the thick grass which grows just beneath the eaves. He went first to the barn, pushed up the long wooden latch, and entered. The interior was dark, but sweet and comfortable with the breath of cows and hay. The farm animals, one and all, greeted him with hearty brute courtesy, which he returned with a tender human indulgence, being on the kindest terms with them all. It is wholesome for a man whose demeanor toward the world is reserved to unmask himself to these jolly, unceremonious, soft-hearted creatures, whose regard, because it cannot help being sincere, is the most cordial flattery. Garth might well prize his horses and oxen, his cows and his hens; for their use was not to be measured by eggs, milk, or draft. Men are caskets compact of a score of metals, in which the cunning workmanship disguises the material; animals are the virgin ore, frank and simple, and to be loved or loathed only for their intrinsic qualities. But men would be mere outlines without them—fine bits of draughtmanship, devoid of color or substance. The material value of beasts and birds can at most be but symbolic of their actual use—or such was Garth's opinion. It was pleasant to behold what a fund of innocent playfulness was developed between the two parties: the young man had his private joke with each four-footed or feathered compatriot, and many was the humorous smile or sympathetic guffaw that they enjoyed together.

The morning compliments being over, Garth opened an eastern shutter, and let a stream of morning fall aslant the manger. The picturesque effect seemed to strike him, and he stood observing it for several moments. Presently, he bethought himself of the crimson horse-blanket which lay folded up under the seat of the old sleigh; he fetched it out and hung it over the lower rounds of the ladder which leaned against the hay-bin, half in and half out of shadow. Further consideration led him to stir up a little more dust to spin in the sharp-drawn light-beam. He was now the possessor of such a Rembrandt as might have been dreamed of, but was never painted—gloomy, rich, luminous. A human countenance would, perhaps, have been an addition; but, after all, what could be finer than the dark head of that bull, with his white horns illuminated from the window, and the hairy edges of his ears softened by the light? The human being might be left to the imagination, and improve thereby; but the bull could be omitted on no pretense whatever. The picture being arranged to his satisfaction, Garth studied it with a pithy, efficient musing, which never seemed to wander vaguely from the point, but to be determined by a constant and conscious purpose. This purpose,

whatever it might be, could have had very little to do with practical farming; and, were it not that young Mr. Urmson owns a visage singularly deficient in aimlessness, he would undoubtedly have been open to the suspicion of wasting his time.

When he had done studying the Rembrandt, Garth lingered not purposelessly about; though he seemed to be never out of leisure, yet did his times and seasons fit snugly into one another, without either gaps or crowdings. He passed from the barn westward to the vegetable-garden. The Indian-corn had been harvested, but the stalks, bound together in eccentric pyramids, stood in dry, rustling rows along the dusty field. Adjoining this was the potato-district, many of its hills already despoiled of their ill-complexioned treasures, and the greenery of the rest withered and drooping. Next came the pumpkin and squash plantation, and here again the farmer made thoughtful pause. The yellow squashes, with their long, twisted necks seemed to be alive and striving, in a ridiculous panic of would-be modesty, to hide their glaring nakedness beneath their shriveled leaves. Meanwhile the mighty pumpkins reposed serene and complete, with a broad, golden smile of full content, each one swelling his yellow sides at the sun, and looking at least as big and solid as that luminary. Garth put himself to some trouble to select the goldenest and snakiest of the squashes—as though the curves and color of the great vegetable were of more importance to him than its succulence—and, carrying it back to the house, conveyed it heedfully through the pantry-window. Then he bethought himself of the orchard, and proceeded thither forthwith, whistling as he went.

In its prime, a few generations ago, this had been accounted the finest orchard in New Hampshire—no small renown in that American garden of the Hesperides. Most delectable fruit, in eight or nine varieties, could still be eaten there; and of late years an attempt had been made, by dint of pruning, grafting, and setting out, to bring back again the ancient repute. The present season's crop was a fine one; and Garth, strolling about beneath the trees, his hands thrust in his sacque-pockets and his hat on the back of his head, rejoiced in the tall scarlet and yellow heaps which were gathered together beneath the low branches. Fascinating, likewise, were the grotesque contortions of the trees themselves. Apple-bearing, one would suppose, must be the painfulest of all vegetable processes. Some of the old limbs were the incarnation of twisted agony; and there were few trees but had eaten their ancient hearts out in voiceless torment, and now harbored blue-jays and woodpeckers in their hollow bosoms. Nevertheless, the sweetest fruit often grew on the ungainliest boughs; and, in spring, Garth had not failed to admire how well beauty and fragrance and freshness assimilated with old age, deformity, and decay.

Having stuffed his pockets with lusty crimson baldwins and firm-fleshed russets, he turned homeward. An elderly crow, which had been contemplating the sunrise from the top of a lofty hemlock, accosted him with a single taunting, "Caw!" as much as to say, "I would much rather be what I am than what you are!" Garth picked up a worm-eaten pippin, and flung it at the contemptuous fowl with so true an aim that, had not the latter been wary, there might have been a catastrophe. But it was not unacquainted with the red-shirted man and his ways, and, entering at once into the spirit of the thing, it pretended to be seriously alarmed, and pitched flapping from its perch with a volley of hoarse objurgations. The cry was straightway taken up by the whole indigenous community of crows, and in another moment thirty or forty of these sable humorists were wheeling their black bodies aloft and clamoring their harshest ostensibly in vast consternation, but really for their own and Garth's amusement.

A little on the hither verge of the pine-forest grew a large sugar-maple, its autumnal foliage showing against that gloomy background like a bonfire. Halting here in his pursuit of the crows, our transcendental farmer gathered himself a great bunch of flaming leaves. With them he returned to the house; and, finding that neither his father nor old Nikomis, the cook, was yet stirring, he clambered in by the window as quietly as he had come out. Ten minutes

afterward he reissued through the front-door, and paused a moment within the porch, where we first caught sight of him. Anon he stepped briskly forth from shadow to sunshine, casting aside his preoccupation, and appearing so alert that it would have been difficult to believe his proper mood a contemplative one. Action seemed the truer sphere for him, so soon as he became active.

He followed the grass-bordered path that clung to the eastward declivity, enjoying the morning clouds, while his shadow undulated long and slim behind him. Arriving presently at the little graveyard, squared within its compact stone fence, he went in and paused beside the latest grave, now several years old. Here lay buried the mortality of Martha Urmson, Garth's mother, and daughter of old Parson Graeme, who was still above-ground after near a century of earthly existence. The little flower-bed which crowned the grave had ceased to bloom, and Garth plucked away the withered leaves and stalks, and emblazoned the brown strip of earth with his splendid maple-leaves. No breeze was astir as yet, and they lay motionless there, though seemingly aglow with life. But to the young man's mind the life of autumn was of a kind to harmonize well with tombstones. There was more heart-break in her deep-toned sunshine than in the gloom of conventional mourning, and her gayest painting could but make the seer thoughtful and often sad. For her pomps presaged decay; and the strand of pathos was subtilely inwoven with hers as with all mortal beauty.

But, however alive to these perceptions, Garth would have been guilty of an affectation alien to his temperament, could he have faced the rich phantasmagoria of the valley otherwise than delightedly. Surely, thought he, it looked its best to-day. The thin-spread mists were dissolving like a happy dream, and mellow ranges of red and yellow awakened to vividness near at hand, and lapsed in violet cadences far away. Autumn was the holiday—the Sunday of the year. She reclined at ease, ripe, voluptuous, sweet-breathed with new-mown hay, robed in crimson and crowned with gold. She was more tender, than the working seasons—with a pensive tenderness infinitely winning. Cheerful in her embrace could no one be; but she wooed her love far below the trifling surface-ripple of emotion, and taught him the neglected wisdom of repose.

Garth had so loving an eye for color, and had so often brooded over the autumnal aspects of his native woods, that it would be wronging him to suppress all allusion to such matters. And he was a man endowed with deep susceptibilities, which yet were seldom able to find utterance in speech. If he indulged in soliloquies, therefore, they were of a kind not immediately quotable on a printed page. But this solitary walk of his (which should be taken as a type of many similar walks, and indeed of one complete phase of his life at this epoch) possessed a sort of significance which it would not do entirely to neglect.

CHAPTER V.

AN OCTOBER VIOLET.

AFTER leaving the graveyard, the path continued its unobtrusive journey down the slope, Garth striding downward with it, eating a cool apple as he went, and rejoicing in the dew which abundantly glossed his cowhide boots. In a few minutes he had entered the forest which infringed upon the southern extremity of the long pasture. The trees grew thickly, but shadow there was none. A golden glow lingered in the densest coverts, for the density was itself an illumination. The black trunks and branches appeared overstrong for their ethereal sunshiny burdens. The greenness which had not yet forsaken the grass in sheltered situations—the greenness which summer cheapens—now seemed rare and strange, the superfluity of pomp giving a new worth to simplicity.

It is well, after all, that the autumn glories of New England should be so transitory. These sunset tints of foliage exalt the beholder's spirit to a pitch which could not long be sustained. Green is the color that lies nearest to human sympathies, and no diviner one could be suffered permanently to usurp its place in Nature. Indeed, it is remarkable that Yankees accept the magic transformations of their October so philosophically as they do—that they are not startled or even incredulous, as they doubtless would be were the matter one of hearsay. But throughout this apparently reckless splendor there runs ever a saving element of economy; the reds and yellows are all variations of one theme, and differ among themselves not more than do the greens of summer. There is no gaudiness; and thus no one remembers to be astonished at the display until it is over.

The footpath, beyond the pasture limits, merged into a forest lane: in the centre a narrow channel, worn by horses' feet, flanked on both sides by deep wheel-ruts, while thin ridges of green turf intervened. From its work-a-day, business-like aspect, this lane might have been supposed, by the unwary, to be the introduction to some country road, and, becoming more and more public-spirited and practical as it proceeded, finally to attain the dignity and social position of a turnpike or highway. As a matter of fact, however, it had no more end than beginning, and could properly be said to exist only as to its centre. New England woods are full of such deceptive lanes, beginning without apparent reason, and fading out of sight just when the lost traveler is expecting to arrive at something. They are, in truth, created and used by the wood-cutters, whose carts and sledges have worn these ruts; and since the ends of wood-cutters differ from those of other men, though their means are the same, we must not wonder at their leading us to a pine-stump when we had made up our mouths for a village.

As for Garth, he numbered wood-cutting among his own accomplishments, and was rather pleased than disconcerted when the path ran up a tree and the forest grew trackless before him. Had he lived in colonial times he would have plunged into the primeval wilderness with all the boldness and fervor of the original Captain Neil; not, like him, from a morbid distaste for society, but with masculine zest for the charms of virgin

Nature—savage and hard to tame. His spirits dilated as he left civilized boundaries behind him, until at length even his dilapidated hat grew irksome, and he pulled it off, and threw back the broad collar of his shirt. The woods were almost utterly silent; cold nights had chilled the loquacity of insects, and the birds seemed to have sung all their songs for that year, and to be meditating what next. Now and then a chattering squirrel darted from apparent non-existence into intensest life, and after a noisy minute departed into nothingness once more. Far off somewhere sounded the drumming of a partridge, or close at hand one suddenly whizzed from its covert. But the Midas's touch which had transmuted the trees to gold seemed to have stricken existence almost dumb.

Presently, however, Garth began to whistle, mellowly as an Arcadian flute-player. The sound melted sweetly into the forest distances, like a bird-note; and he pursued it along the glowing vistas with a grave jocundity of step and countenance. The land tended by long gradients downward, and occasionally his foot sank in swampy ground; the vegetation became more untrammeled, and carmine sumach-leaves burned here and there in the jungle. Anon approached the silver gurgle of a brook, new-born from some hidden source, babbling its transparent secrets beside the pathway, and continuing to gossip even when its wayward course had taken it temporarily out of hearing. Great painted toadstools, generated overnight from the fruitful union of vegetable decay and dampness, clustered in fantastic groups beneath the yellow shade; and not a few dandelions and asters foolhardily tempted the frost. All these things Garth felt by a kind of sympathy rather than saw in detail; he was not of the quick-eyed breed of men; his glance was leisurely, but comprehensive and penetrating.

This faculty of observation, at once enjoying and effortless, marked him as one who was not only accustomed to meet Nature in private and alone, but content to let her monopolize him during the interview. Yet I would not have you infer that a young man of his aspect, who must have known the vicissitudes of at least five-and-twenty years, had missed all acquaintance with that finer solitude which is attainable only through rare human companionship. There was nothing of the ascetic in Garth's face or figure that he should be deemed insensible to the love of woman. And though there might be neither nymphs nor hamadryads in the New Hampshire woods, and though the young farmer's dress and habits might seem to raise a barrier between him and fashionable society, yet something there was in his look and bearing that indicated a wider culture than that of the farm and forest.

Indeed, the more narrowly you observed him, the greater would have been your doubt whether the agricultural element was really vital in him at all. His hands were certainly not those of a farmer; their form was at once powerful and elegant, and the texture of the skin was fine and soft. And where did he acquire that firm carriage of the shoulders and that easy precision of tread? Not surely from the plough and the scythe. And though his features seemed at the first glance rugged and almost harsh, they were in fact moulded with singular force and meaning, every part responded sensitively to his thought. In spite, therefore, of his rough garb, early hours, and familiarity with barn-yard stock, it would have been rash to write him down a country bumpkin. There was an indescribable flavor of distinction about him, such as is only given by travel, thought, and conversation with the world. Admitting this, his quiet assumption (or resumption) of rusticity argued a freshness and independence of nature unusual in traveled youth nowadays.

But what was his present destination? for a man, especially a young gentleman of culture, does not plunge into pathless forests before breakfast for nothing. Would it be allowable, in the absence of any trustworthy information on the subject, to indulge in a little fanciful conjecture? Let us suppose, then, that, while Garth was traveling in Europe, he met a noble and lovely lady, who, like himself, was a stranger there. In the rich heart of the Old World they met, and

2

neither knew the other, nor was it granted them ever to speak together, or to exchange a pressure of the hand; but once, in a strange room full of antique jewels and precious works of art, their glances had met in a crystal mirror, and had read in one another a mutual revelation. For one deep moment they gazed, and knew they loved; then time and space rolled between and parted them. But for years thereafter, as they moved along their separate paths, visions would rise before them of that unforgotten moment, until at length, by much dreaming over it, the event itself began to take on the semblance of a dream; and Garth, returning home, pledged himself to another woman; and the lady promised, against her better instincts, to become the wife of another man. Shall our romance end here, or shall that picturesque providence, which watches over lovers only, bring them once more together, ere the last irrevocable steps that fix their destinies be taken? Yes, let them meet, since all is imagination! And, by way of accounting for Garth's early presence in these woodland solitudes, be this the morning of the meeting, and the place, the shores of the little lake whither his steps now tend. Of course the encounter must be accidental on both sides—a genuine providential interference. We need not indulge our fancy further. If, being met, they do not succeed in freeing themselves from their entanglements, and living together happily ever afterward, they are not the romantic lovers we take them to be.

Truly, for so extravagant a flight of imagination as this, the splendid witchery of the autumnal trees is hardly valid excuse. And yet there was about Garth that which might lay a strong grasp on a woman's heart, though little were said on either side. Perhaps he inherited something of that peculiar power which tradition ascribed to his forefathers, and on the other hand there was a glow in his eyes which indicated ardent receptivity and keen appreciation, qualities which render shallow people what is called "susceptible." We might imagine Garth beguiled by a beautiful face into postulating a beautiful soul to it; but sooner or later he would know whether he were mis-

taken, and then the issue might be tragical. Intensity of belief has always a germ of pathos in it; and, if its trust be betrayed, the flower of tragedy is at once full blown.

But, to prolong these hap-hazard speculations regarding a man who has thus far given us no practical evidence of a specially wayward or portentous disposition, would really be doing him injustice. It is probably his very undemonstrativeness that gives such loose rein to our conjecture. The world is apt to put a tongue of its own into the heads of those who do not speak for themselves. To an indifferent eye Garth would appear simply as a young countryman who had risen betimes in order to enjoy a quiet angle for perch and pickerel in the pond. It was a likely enough sheet of water for such sport, and, as its gleam reached him through the belt of dark pines that bordered its northern shore, Garth stopped whistling and hastened his step a bit, as though anxious to be at work.

On the hither verge of the pine-belt was planted a lichen-covered rock, girdled with a crimson growth of huckleberry-bushes. Beneath the bushes, amid a cluster of round green leaves, lurked a meditative little flower—retired enough, one would think, to elude all ordinary eyesight. Nevertheless, Garth saw it as he was passing by, and, stopping, threw himself at full length on the ground to examine it at his leisure. It was a violet—a rarity in that month, and the sweeter for its strangeness. Garth lifted up its dewy downcast little visage with the tip of his forefinger, and looked—not botanically but lovingly—into its tiny golden eye. Perhaps from conscientious scruples, he did not pluck the flower, but was content to gain only the better part of it. By-and-by he gently withdrew his finger, rose to his feet, and walked on. No violet could have desired a more considerate admirer.

But, before he had gone far, this chivalric lover turned abruptly back and deliberately plucked the poor violet after all, together with one of its green leaves. Was the act merely wanton? or was there something so much more worshipful in his eyes than an October violet as to justify him in making a sacrificial offering of the flower?

It is a pregnant question, but we must be content to let time give it answer. Garth carefully disposed the offering, if such it was to be, in his hat-band, and then, continuing on through the pines, he shortly brought his three-mile walk to an end on the sandy beach of a little cove which commanded an outlook over the greater part of the lake.

About a quarter of a mile southward, in the mouth of the bay, rose a small island densely tufted with red and yellow foliage. Far beyond, between the island and the western promontory of the shore, towered the misty shape of Wabeno, glowing in the sunlight like a dim heap of jewels. The water of the lake was perfectly still and pellucid, and reflected each painted leaf of the myriad trees that pressed to the margin, as if to behold their own magnificence in the clear mirror. And the reflection was better even than the reality—it had a charm like that belonging to an idealized remembrance. The sky, pale and cool at this hour, set off the sumptuous coloring of the earth. The sun was not yet too high to throw tall shadows of the eastern trees across the quiet mystery of the liquid surface. The charm of the scene was so complete as to warrant the belief that it must have been less beautiful a moment ago and would begin to deteriorate a moment hence. There needed only a poet or a painter, cunning of hand and loving of heart, to collect these points of loveliness and recast them in the symmetrical mould of some noble and profound idea.

Judging by appearances, Garth has come here with the intention of remaining some hours, and, perhaps, during this interval of enforced leisure, we cannot do better than angle in the waters of the past for whatever stray facts concerning him and his may chance within our reach.

<hr/>

CHAPTER VI.

THE CHILD.

CAPTAIN BRIAN URMSON, the old warrior of the Revolution, had nearly completed his seventieth year when Garth began the world. His little daughter Eve had then been lost some ten or twelve years, during which time the captain had led a sombre and lonely life; lonely—despite the fact that Golightley, the son of his second marriage, was living with him. The grim soldier had never understood this young man's æsthetic aspirations, nor sympathized with them; and he, moreover, had what he chose to consider reasons for positively disliking the young man himself. As for his favorite, Cuthbert, the only child of his first love, he had gone abroad the year of Eve's disappearance, and he staid away an unconscionably long while.

However, he came back at last, safe and sound, and then the captain's gloom began to lighten. The sky was further cleared by Golightley's departure, which took place a month or two later; but the crowning gratification was Cuthbert's marriage with Parson Graeme's daughter. And when, in due time, sweet young Mrs. Urmson began to grow indolent and languid, and her husband consulted her lightest wish with anxious solicitude; and when, finally, a strange female made her appearance in the house, with noiseless step and despotic authority; then did Captain Brian become as cheerful and good-humored an old gentleman as any in the county. He would sit for hours beneath the porch in his high-backed armchair, his stern visage softened with flitting smiles, and his wrinkled eyes half closed in pleasant reverie. Anon he would arouse himself and beckon Cuthbert and the strange female mysteriously aside, and question them in hoarse whispers;

"How soon may we expect—eh, ma'am? I'll bet ten to one it'll be a girl, Cuthbert! —Ay, by God, a little girl—like Eve, boy—like my little Eve, eh?" This with a half-appealing intonation, accompanied by a gruff, nervous little laugh that sometimes brought tears to Cuthbert's kind gray eyes.

Doubtless these last weeks were the happiest of Captain Brian's life, which had been a violent and irregular one, and not altogether above suspicions of something worse than irregularity. Happily, too, he died before knowing that his anticipations of a granddaughter were not destined to fulfillment. For one night, after a long talk with Cuthbert, in the course of which the old man had opened his heart on many subjects more than he had ever done before, and had spoken at some length regarding his two marriages, and about the lost Eve; after this, and after bidding his son an affectionate good-night, he shut his door, and was found the next day on the floor, by the bedside, in a kneeling position, dead. So far as was known, it had never been his custom to pray, but it is to be hoped that death came up with him in a first effort heavenward, being mercifully desirous not to let so rare an opportunity pass unimproved.

In the same hour that the dead body was discovered, Garth first saw the light. The nurse looked at him, prepared, as usual, to pronounce him the image either of his father or of his mother, as it might happen; but the formula stumbled on her lips, and, after a pause, she declared in a tone weighty with conviction:

"Ef the child ain't the living image of his dead grandpa!"

This verdict was subsequently confirmed by that of other persons esteemed wise in such matters, but most of all by Garth himself; who, as he advanced from infant jellydom to the solid flesh of babyhood, showed over more and more unmistakably the miniature form and features of the deceased warrior.

Parson Graeme, the gigantic minister and patriarch of the parish, was a frequent caller at Urmhurst, where he sat in council with the young father and mother, giving them the benefit of his vast experience and enormous wisdom on all subjects, but generally with special reference to the character and education of little Garth. Young fathers and mothers do not as a rule take this kind of interference in very good part; but, if any counselor could claim justification for counseling, Parson Graeme was surely he. Not only was he the descendant of the Puritan divine who accompanied Neil Urmson from England, but he had officiated at both of Captain Brian's weddings, as well as at his funeral. Not only this, but he was Mrs. Urmson's father, and, by dint of marrying her to Cuthbert, had constituted himself the latter's father-in-law; and if anything more were wanted, he had performed the rite of baptism upon that most important of personages, Garth himself! With such an array of credentials as this, a man of far less personal charm than the venerable parson possessed might have obtained a hearing. But the best of it was, that the Reverend Mr. Graeme was at least as entertaining as he was wise; and, come when or wherefore he might, he was sure to be, not only tolerated but welcomed.

"Genuine old Urmson—no mistake about that!" the old gentleman would bellow forth in his big bass voice, after a chuckling inspection of the small, red-faced bundle reposing in Mrs. Urmson's lap. "Not a bit like you, son-in-law! I recollect, when you were born, folks said the Urmson type was dying out—that Captain Brian had been the last of them. But not a bit of it! Your younger brother, Golightley, some folks thought, was going to be one of 'em; well, he had the cleft in the chin, to be sure, but not the eye, not the head, and not a bone of the figure! Ay, the captain should have seen this little chap before he died; just a few hours more would have done it—think of that now! But the Lord knows best, of course; and maybe the old man would have been mad because the lad wasn't a girl! Ay, the Lord knows best—no mistake about that!"

"Do you think Garth so very much like his grandfather?" inquired gentle Mrs. Urmson.

"There was jealousy in that question," said Cuthbert, smiling. "She wants him to resemble me, with my sharp nose and bald forehead and consumptive tendency—don't you, Cotton?" (Her name was Martha; but her husband, in recognition of her skill and diligence with darning and knitting needles, and also out of compliment to the memory of the distinguished colonial divine, had dubbed her Cotton Martha, and diminutively Cotton.)

"I would like him to have your eyes, at any rate," returned she.

Cuthbert had the pleasantest, kindest gray eyes in the world, and his other features kept them well in countenance; for his slightly aquiline nose was beautifully shaped, the point being particularly delicate; and his mouth (although there was sometimes a touch of satire in its fine curves) was in sympathy with his eyes.

"Like him? he's the image of him!" rumbled in the ponderous tones of the gigantic pastor, ignoring this minor prattle of the young people, and taking up the original question; "and of his great-great-grandfather, and of his great-great-grandfather's father before him—and that's Captain Neil himself. Why, Mattie, girl, I recollect my father (he died only thirty years ago, at over a hundred) — well, I recollect his telling Brian, in my hearing (we were both lads at the time), often and often he told us that Brian's grandfather, Ralph, was as like Brian as two hymn-books. My father knew Ralph Urmson well in his younger days, a hundred and twenty years back; and it used to be said at that time, 'Ralph's his father's own son!' Well, Ralph was a sad dog; he was more feared than Captain Neil had been, and liked less. He had but one friend, 'twas said, and him he killed in some mad quarrel or other. And, for that matter, the saying is, that every true Urmson will kill the man he loves best."

"Father!" exclaimed Martha, horror-stricken.

"Hand me down the old pistol from above the fireplace, my dear," said Cuthbert, in a tone of quiet determination. "I will shoot both your father and Garth, for fear of making a mistake between them."

"Haw! haw! haw!" laughed the stentorian pastor. "No, no, son-in-law, you're not the sort of Urmson the saying applies to; but as for your boy there, I wouldn't like to answer for him!—You must look sharp after him, Mattie, girl—ha, ha, ha! Well, but there's something in it after all. There was Neil, you know, to begin with; then Ralph; and after Ralph—let's see—well, the next out-and-out Urmson after Ralph was Captain Brian, and it would be hard to say who his best friend was. But there, forgive me, boy! No one loved your father better than I did, and I'm sure he didn't kill me!"

Cuthbert's face had become graver, and

he presently said: "I have heard the saying before; and, Cotton, it was with that same old pistol up there that these several tragedies were accomplished. Captain Neil brought it over from England, and my father carried it through the Revolution. I wonder whether it's loaded now?"

Sweet Cotton Martha shuddered and clasped Master Garth impulsively to her bosom, thereby awakening him from the nap which he had been enjoying for the past half-hour. In his philosophy, to be awake was to be hungry; and he began to seek, with imperious cries, the bounteous source of food and happiness. That attained, he relapsed into the enjoyment of his sensations; and the talk went on.

"Don't you fret your little heart, Mattie," said the Reverend Mr. Graeme, noting the disturbed expression which still dwelt on his daughter's naturally serene face. "It was but a jest, my lass. If the babe looked twice the Urmson he is, the Lord has given him a soul of his own; and a good mother, though I say it!"

"Cotton, don't suffer your just anxiety to be cajoled by any such sophistry," Cuthbert interposed. "When I was a little boy your father taught me my lessons, and I had a good opportunity to find him out. Although not a bad man, socially and humanly speaking, his philosophy is defective. In those early days I often argued with him, and exposed his fallacies; but as fast as I converted him at one end he would relapse at the other. I suppose there's no hope of producing an impression on a man seven feet high, and weighing twenty stone!"

"Haw! haw! haw! and what has that to do with it, I'd like to know?" demanded the venerable stentor.

"You hear, Cotton, that your father doesn't know what that has to do with it. He has never read Dr. Combe's 'Phrenology,' but pronounces it humbug at a venture. He fancies that body and soul have no necessary and intimate connection, but have come together in an entirely accidental and illogical manner; in short, that any soul may pop into any body it happens to fall in with, in the same way that the body may afterward go to a tailor's shop and jump into a ready-made suit of clothes, which, ten to one, would have fitted somebody else better.

"Pooh! a great way you have of putting an argument!" growled the parson.

"He thinks," continued Cuthbert, with a mischievous lifting of one eyebrow, "that spirit and matter, having through some ill luck run foul of each other, are making an awkward job of their enforced companionship. That is the reason why he sees no connection between his twenty stone and his rejection of rational arguments; and that is why he tells you that the fact of Garth's looking like his ancestors need not imply his being like them."

Martha, who had been watching her baby's face with all a mother's rapt enthusiasm, until she had forgotten the existence of anything else, here stooped down and kissed it, and whispered: "O-o mother's pet!" The two men smiled apart to themselves, and Cuthbert continued:

"For my part I rejoice that the Urmson coil has lain fallow in my generation, if it therefore produces a full-flavored crop in this. I not only think that Garth resembles Brian and Neil, but I hope and believe that his leading traits of character resemble theirs; that he has the same imperious will, the same pugnacity and vehement temper." Cuthbert had spoken these words with more than his usual earnestness, and after a pause he added, "I hope he has in him every evil trait of the Urmsons in its strongest form."

Both his hearers were startled. Martha, always reticent and undemonstrative, only fixed her eyes upon him with a gentle consternation; but the parson wheeled round in his chair and bellowed out: "What d'ye mean, Cuthbert? Are you crazy?"

"Why, no," replied he. "A family is a man of larger growth and more complex character, but of individuality as distinct as yours or mine. It is young; it grows up, prospers, and dies; its years are generations; each one inevitably moulding the next. At last comes a year when all its evil is arrayed against all its good. Then must the great battle be lost and won."

"You've been a heretic ever since you could speak," grumbled the old gentleman;

"but it's a new heresy to wish evil to one's children."

"Well, let me have my heresy out. When a man has the making of a thorough devil in him, he has the possibility of an angel in him too—for angels are bare survivors from the deadly struggle of man with his inherent devilishness. In that struggle, both sides use the same weapons; and the stronger the weapons the greater the final victory or defeat."

"What weapons do you mean, dear?" asked gentle Martha.

"I mean the powers and passions of the mind and heart, which may be used either for good or for evil. Now, in our own family history, the Urmsons have generally been worsted by their old Adam; yet no one of them was ever utterly wicked, and hence I infer that the decisive battle has not yet come off, and that there is still a chance to vindicate the angel. He in whom the struggle culminates must be thoroughly Urmson—a compendium of the race—no diluted alien like myself. The more stubborn the devil in him the better worth the victory, should that fall to the angel. Am I an unnatural father, my little Cotton, if I pray that Garth may turn out our champion? The loftiest good can exist only on the overthrow of the deepest evil."

Martha smiled forgivingly upon her husband, while two tears rolled down her comely cheeks, and fell upon the plump visage of the unconscious babe. But the large pastor scratched his head (whereon white hair grew as thickly as the brown had done in the heyday of youth), knitted his brows, and growled:

"You're a queer chap, son-in-law! Humph! takes a devil to make an angel, is that it? Maybe it does; but, though you're as poor a show for a devil as any man I know, if all Urmsons had been like you, it might have been better for them!"

With this ambiguous utterance the Reverend Mr. Graeme uplifted his towering figure from the bench in the porch, where the discussion had taken place, and having resoundingly kissed the mother and child, and grasped the father's hand, he swung off through the late August afternoon, carrying well his seventy years. The little family stood watching him till he was hidden within the westward forest, and then, with a lingering glance at hazy Wabeno, they entered the house in great tranquillity of spirit.

CHAPTER VII.

THE BIRCH-ROD.

DESPITE the presages of a momentous destiny, the infant Garth acted as though eating and sleeping were the chief ends of man, and he grew strong and wholesome accordingly. One of his earlier exploits was to cry for the American flag which Captain Brian had brought home from the wars, and which was festooned over the nursery fireplace. For a long time his wishes were not understood; but as day after day he persisted in his inarticulate demands, with many explosions of resentful wrath, his mother, being at her wits' end, finally pulled down the historic bunting more in despair than in hope; and having shaken the dust of thirty years out of its folds, she surrendered it to the despot. He graciously received it, and wanted no better plaything, clutching at the bright colors with his little fists, and emitting guttural exclamations of approval. The flag was afterward draped over the hood of his crib, and appeared to soothe both his dreams and his temper.

Mrs. Urmson maintained that his pleasure in it was based upon a refined love of beauty. But the parson, whose interest in the young compendium of his race looked forward to different issues, explained it otherwise.

"Love of beauty? Ho! ho! ho! Do you take Garth for a young lady, to be tickled by a scarlet ribbon? Tut! he's no such molly-coddle. Garth has his grandfather's spirit—the spirit of Seventy-six, that smote the oppressor hip and thigh, and made us the greatest nation on earth. Patriotism!—that's it. He loves the Stars and Stripes because they're his country's flag."

"In my opinion," remarked Cuthbert, "you both of you misapprehend the matter, and do injustice to the profundity of Garth's meaning. He recognizes in the Stars and Stripes an allegory of the philosophy of existence. He would intimate to us his belief that the higher ends of life are never to be attained, unless by enduring the stripes of adversity."

"That is to say, you'll flog him to make him a good boy?" rejoined grandfather Graeme.

"Oh!" deprecated Martha.

"Why, if he asked my help in that direction, I shouldn't feel justified in withholding it," said Cuthbert, arching his eyebrow. "Being his father, I am bound to serve him until he is able to serve himself."

"And of course he'll always be begging you not to spare the rod," threw in the ironic parson; "it's a way boys have!"

"Seriously, I shall take pains to explain the matter to him. Once let him know that naughtiness is the parent of punishment, and the great end is gained. Despotism would be of no use with a boy of his make; he must bring himself to bear against himself; he must be delivered over to the jailership of his own conscience. I shall encourage him to apply to me only in extreme cases; but, whenever he does tell me that he wants a whipping, I shall lay aside all personal considerations, and drub him soundly!"

"He'll be no such fool, depend upon it!" said Mr. Graeme, nodding his white head at Martha and chuckling.

"I hope otherwise," returned Cuthbert. "Look at his head. Cerebellum large, and great bumps behind the ears; but well-arched crown, and square, solid forehead. He will have reverence for law, as well as for his own free-will."

But the parson always threw ridicule upon any allusion to phrenology; and even Mrs. Urmson was secretly pleased to hear that her beloved son was to be his own disciplinarian. She argued from her own tenderness, which denied the use of suffering, and ever aimed to enlarge the boundaries of mercy. And, so far as she was concerned, Garth was spoiled as long as she lived.

Nevertheless, Cuthbert's plan was not unsuccessful. Garth was violent, passionate, and headstrong, long before he was reasonable; but his nature was essentially reverential, and, when he found that his liberty was respected, he began to take an interest in the progress of his moral emancipation, and to listen to such quiet hints regarding the best ways of fighting the old Adam as Cuthbert from time to time let fall. It was a triumph for the father when Garth made his first spontaneous request to be put in the corner; and by degrees the small warrior found out that there were no pangs like those of conscience, which were sure to become worse the longer the antidote was withheld. As he grew older the penitential corner gave way to other prescriptions, proportioned to his deeper needs. At last came the turn of the rod. This grim instrument of regeneration had been confided to Garth's care by his father, when the former was five years old, the gift being accompanied by a grave explanation of its use and properties; and the little man was further enjoined not to allow any mistaken tenderness for the parental feelings to hinder a demand for its application, whenever necessary.

"It will hurt us both, Garth," concluded Mr. Urmson, "but we must not forget that the wrong would hurt us more."

Garth listened in solemn silence, and was evidently much impressed; but the day of execution did not arrive until nearly two years afterward. Some grievous sin—history does not specify what it was—had been committed, and straightway a dreadful struggle began between Garth and his conscience. Conscience declared that the delinquent ought to be whipped; the delinquent rebelled, and the contest prolonged its awful length from the morning of one day to the afternoon of the next; Cuthbert, Martha, and the parson, all looking on in silent suspense. At last Old Adam got the worst of it. Obedient to an appalling summons, Cuthbert repaired to the nursery, leaving Martha in tears and the parson puzzled and silent; nor was his own composure by any means unruffled. He found Garth standing in the centre of the floor, excited, flushed, ashamed, but resolute, holding forth the rod. It was a trying moment, and the father's heart almost faltered. Nevertheless, the thing must be done; and,

inwardly resolving to do it as gently as he dared, he was making the few simple preparations for the ceremony, when the victim said, breathing quick through his clinched teeth:

"Hard! papa—do it hard!"

Abashed at what seemed a rebuke of his faint-heartedness, the unhappy executioner obeyed. The pain was much sharper than Garth anticipated, but though he gnashed his teeth and curled his little toes and fingers in anguish, he made no attempt to escape, or to curtail the proceedings. When all was over, the father, with an irrepressibly guilty feeling, helped the little man to adjust his toilet, amid a silence broken only by the spasmodic sighs of yet tumultuous emotion. But, as they were leaving the scene of the tragedy, Cuthbert felt his sleeve pulled, and looked sorrowfully down at the crimson little phiz upturned to him.

"Papa," said the smaller sufferer, in such broken accents as his mental and physical disorder permitted, "I'm—sorry you—had to do it!"

"So am I, Garth—"

"Yes, papa; and—it isn't fair—you should have to do it; I didn't—know how to do it—before; but now I—know, I'll—do it for you next time, papa!" And with this the heroic tension gave way in a flood of tears.

Cuthbert had not expected this, and at first failed to grasp the full significance of the matter. But in a moment he comprehended the chivalrous truth, and stooping down he kissed the boy's hot cheek with a feeling akin to reverence, though, at the same time, his irrepressible sense of the humorous came near making him laugh.

"You are a fine old boy!" said he. "Let's see what grandpapa will say to that! and mamma may spoil you now if she can!"

It is pleasant to be able to record that Garth's ingenuity and constancy were never called upon to compass a self-inflicted flogging. The birch-rod hung for many years in the closet where he kept his playthings, as a sort of *memento mori;* but no sufficient occasion for using it ever again arose. Cuthbert, indeed, was wont to lay it, in a figurative sense, across the parson's shoulders, whenever the latter criticised his theory of education. The parson could only scratch his head and grumble out that Garth's letting himself be imposed upon was no argument in favor of phrenology; to which Cuthbert's answer was an arch lifting of the eyebrow, and a general air of irritating complacency.

CHAPTER VIII.

THE FAËRIE QUEENE.

However, there were still many wry strands in the composition of the youngest Urmson. In spite of a sensitive conscience, and a fine sense of honor, the bugbear of study darkened his sunshine, and the habit of taciturnity grew upon him. The open sky attracted him like a magnet; he knew the woods far better than his lessons. In summer, he loved to lie on his back upon the grass, with the torrid sun pouring its light and heat straight down upon him. He had a gift of laziness, a talent for preoccupation, and a genius for wonder. In short, he caused his grandfather continual anxiety.

"Teach him the deaf-and-dumb alphabet," growled the old gentleman. "He's quicker with his fingers than with his tongue, any day."

"Garth has sense, father, I'm sure," said Martha, quietly darning.

"Why can't he talk, then? A little nonsense would do him no harm, to set his sense going."

"Perhaps he's silent from policy," was Cuthbert's suave suggestion, "as negroes say that monkeys won't talk lest they be forced to work. He values the few ideas he has too highly to betray their whereabouts by speech. Only those who imbibe the world readily find much to say."

Martha glanced covertly at her husband's mischievous mouth, and continued her darning, with a smile. The simple pastor answered:

"Wrong principle, son-in-law! Good talking never spoiled an idea. I'm eighty last birthday, and I guess I've done as much

talking as most folks, and I'm none the worse for it that I know of. Hold your tongue for fear of losing your ideas? haw! haw! haw! Might as well stop planting grape-vines for fear of spoiling the grapes."

"I only give Garth's probable argument. But, to tell the truth, I'm afraid Garth's silence is nothing but pretense."

"Ha! well, now you're beyond me," said the parson, shaking his head.

"Why, for instance, there are people who talk from morning till night, and yet actually say less than Garth does. That sort of silence is really silence, but merely to abstain from uttering words is silence only in appearance. Garth, in my hearing, has often held his tongue in such a way that I thought he was talking to good purpose."

"Send him to school!" exclaimed the parson, as briskly as if he had never given the advice before.

"I dare not assume the responsibility; he would corrupt the scholars. You don't half know him. Why, last Sunday afternoon he disappeared, wearing the new clothes that Cotton had just made him. About sunset I found him on his back in a swamp, with his head underneath a rhodora-bush. He said the flowers looked prettier from that point of view; and he wouldn't pluck any, for fear they'd be homesick. You can't send a boy like that to school."

"Humph! very odd," muttered the parson, gravely.

"That is a trifle. But the other morning I woke up about four o'clock with one of my toothaches, and went into his room for the medicine-chest. There He was in his night-gown, his head out of the open window, and so absorbed as not to notice me till I went up and asked him what had happened. He pointed to the eastern horizon. It was near sunrise, and the sky was covered with yellow, red, and purple clouds. He had got out of bed on a cold May morning just to see that."

"Well, now, think of that! doesn't sound much like an Urmson—eh?"

"You know that kaleidoscope of his," continued Cuthbert, delighted with the effect he was producing; "he never was without it until quite lately. I supposed he had broken it; but yesterday I missed one of the glass prisms from the old candlestick, and this morning I found Garth sitting in the sun, throwing the seven colors on a blank leaf of the 'Faërie Queene.' He was delighted with the thing, and thought it was a discovery of his own."

"The 'Faërie Queene'—what's that?"

"A book of antiquated poetry, which I believe the boy knows by heart. But what could our schoolmaster make out of a fellow like that?"

The good pastor sighed, and rubbed his bewildered brow. "Well, trust in the Lord, son-in-law; maybe he'll outgrow it. I'm glad to see you don't lose heart about him, although seeing his faults as clearly as a stranger might. He's a stout, broad-shouldered lad, anyway, and as sweet a disposition as any I know of."

Upon this Martha arose and kissed her father; and Garth coming in at the moment, with his dark tangled hair and his scarlet boating-shirt, even the unsympathetic Cuthbert looked at him with a certain tolerance, notwithstanding the prism and the "Faërie Queene."

The "Faërie Queene" had first revealed herself to Garth about a year before, and he was now completely under the spell of her enchantment. The sway and music of the verse and rhyme charmed him, he knew not why; he lived in every champion, from the Redcross Knight to Sir Calidore, engaging with tragic sympathy in each adventure, putting his whole heart into each sword-stroke and lance-thrust, and trembling over the fate of every wronged and lovely lady. The fable was to him more real than the actual circumstances amid which he lived; and he saw giants and enchanted castles in his rocks and trees, and followed the steps of nymphs and satyrs through the woods. He never left the house, but with the expectation of encountering such perils and achieving such knightly deeds as would take a week to recount and a regiment of Arthurs and Arthegalls to rival. No event of his daily life so trifling, but a touch of imagination lifted it into the region of romance and chivalry. Every true boy is a Don Quixote at heart, and acts out the character according to his capacity and opportunity.

Garth happened to be well furnished in both respects. He could imagine anything; his time was more his own than any one except his parents thought good for him; and in the vast garret which extended all over the top of the house there was enough old armor to equip half a dozen knightly Garths. Here were the steel caps, breastplates, and battle-axes, which had glanced so brightly in the sunshine of two hundred years ago, when Captain Neil Urmson and his band first stood on the site of Urmhurst. They were rusty now, but enough of the original brightness remained to show how resplendent they must formerly have been. The dusty sunbeams which slanted through the cobwebs of the garret-windows tried with ill-success to reflect themselves from the corroded surface of the steel. Garth had at first mistaken this red rust for blood, and lost himself in awful imaginings, till grim spectres in mortal combat peopled every corner of the dark garret.

But in process of time he took courage, and set to work furbishing up the ancient harness, with a view to entering the profession of knight-errantry forthwith. For a time the forest and the sky knew him no more, and it was several days before even his father found him out. Cuthbert, too, in his boyish days, had spent many an hour in the old garret, being attracted thither not by the armor, but by a great mountain of quaint and dusty literature, the heedless accumulation of unknown Urmson generations: from which the studious youth had extracted more information concerning the past history of his race than was possessed by any other person then alive. But Garth, who was at once more matter-of-fact and more imaginative than his father, deemed a helmet and buckler to be worth all the musty parchments in the world. He scrubbed away, therefore, and the faded arms shone once more, reviving under the influence of a chivalric spirit. Garth, in the purified armor of his forefathers, his young fervent face glowing boyishly heroic beneath the steel head-piece, the battle-axe heavy in his guiltless grasp, must have been a fair sight, which it had been churlish of the old garret to keep to itself. Among many secrets it had known none pleasanter than this.

Had the secret been left to Garth to reveal, it might have remained hidden to this day; for within the boundaries of his ideal realm he was shy of human presence and criticism, mankind being less amenable to the transforming wand of his imagination than anything besides. But his father, who divined the boy's condition, climbed the garret-stairs in the character of Sir Guyon, and plunged with such zest into enchanted lore that taciturn Garth was soon in arrears. None the less was he gladdened by the revelation of a kindred spirit—one who not only honored his knights and ladies and shared his high hostility against magicians and giants, but who was learned in the laws of chivalry and the etiquette of knighthood—matters whereof Garth knew little. That was a happy afternoon that the two passed together in the garret; Garth told himself that he had never known his father till now. A whole new vein of companionship was opened up between them. The universe was deeper and wider than of yore, with glimpses of harmonious meanings underneath. And when Cuthbert, trusting to the innate symbolism of the boy's mind, ventured to raise a little the veil of the faërie allegory, Garth's eyes glowed, and he lifted his head. The best that he had dreamed was true—and more than the best. What a noble, valiant world was this that men lived in!

Thus encouraged, Garth had little hesitation in following his father down-stairs and making knightly obeisance at his mother's footstool. But gentle Cotton Martha, with her feminine timidity, was half dismayed at so warlike an apparition, and could scarcely divest herself of a misgiving that it foreboded some peril to the beloved boy himself. In time, however, maternal pride and admiration got the better of alarm; and soon she could notice that, though his helmet fitted well, his breastplate was too big for him; and could devise and make such alterations as at last turned him out a well-appointed hero.

"But there's one thing you have forgotten, Sir Garth," observed his father. "You have no lady-love!"

"Mamma is my lady-love," answered the champion, with a sort of indignation that there should even be a question on the subject, and throwing his arm around her waist.

"I would do battle with you for her, were I younger," said Cuthbert after a pause. "As it is, I suppose I must resign her with what grace I may. Cotton, my dear, accept your new knight! Bind your favor upon his crest, and bid him be right faithful, brave, and true in deed and word, in his campaign against the powers of darkness. Garth, you have chosen your lady well; but take warning by the Redcross Knight, and let no false Duessa lead you astray!"

Garth looked proudly in his mother's eyes, while she fastened on his steel cap the blue kerchief from her throat. That ceremony over, he kissed—not her hand, as the etiquette of chivalry demanded, but her lips heartily. And then he sallied forth, for the first time since donning his accoutrements, into the open air and sunshine.

"The old boy makes quite a fine appearance, doesn't he?" remarked Cuthbert, smiling. "His arms, like St. George's, bear the cruel marks of many a bloody field, though arms till this time did he never wield. God bless him!"

"Is it wise, husband," questioned the mother, smiling but sighing too, "to train him to love such things? His forefathers were violent men, and he has so much of their adventurous and warlike spirit—does it need fostering?"

"It's the old story of the birch-rod again. Garth has those warlike traits, and the best thing to do is to enlist them on the right side. He understands the allegory of self-conquest—that Garth the unregenerate must be his sole enemy. I bade him lay on and spare not—to kill himself fifty times a day if necessary; and if this old Puritan armor, which has stood the brunt of Prince Rupert's Cavaliers, helps him feel the reality of the battle, it will be well worth the furbishing he has given it; not to speak of other good results."

Martha retired in-doors, but Cuthbert staid in the porch, watching the shadow of a great white cloud travel southward down the valley; now crossing the pasture,

now the wood beyond; presently darkening the bright surface of the lake; anon
sweeping slowly along the meadowed river-
basin, and finally mottling the distant flank
of slumbering Wabeno. All at once a flash
of reflected sunlight fell on his eyes, and
caused him to look round.

"Here goes your champion, Lady Martha," he called to his wife. "He has
mounted old Dobbin, and is riding off to
slay the dragon with a lance made out of the
handle of the hay-rake. You ought to mount
the castle-turret, dishevel your hair, and
pray that the dragon does not eat him up!"

Sir Garth, riding slowly (for old Dobbin
had abated much of his original fire), passed
gleaming beneath the shadow of the trees
and was lost to view; and his father resumed his meditations. Nearly an hour
went by; then the sound of hoofs attracted
his eyes once more westward.

"Cotton, come quickly!" he exclaimed.
"Your champion returns victorious; he has
rescued a fair lady from thraldom, and she
rides behind him with her arms about his
waist. The giant, the owner of the castle,
now vanquished and a prisoner, is forced to
accompany them on foot, and assist the lady
in keeping her seat. Do come out and look!
My poor Cotton, you have a rival already!
no Duessa though, let us hope."

"Oh, it's father; and who is that little
girl? it must be Madge Danver. Some more
medicine for her poor mother, I suppose."

"Haw, haw, haw!" bellowed the patriarch, as the group came up; "so you're
really alive? Madge and I lost our way after
leaving the village, and strayed into the century before last; and I was looking out for
my grandfather—ho, ho, ho! We met Captain Neil Urmson, here, instead, and he was
kind enough to let the third-cousin of his
great-great-great-grandson ride behind him.
If there wasn't a couple of centuries or so
difference in ages, I should be anxious about
the old chap's heart—eh, son-in-law? Oh,
ho, ho, ho!—eh, Mattie, girl?—ha, ha, haw,
haw, ho! There, jump down, my little
dear—that's right! Yes, Mrs. Danver has
her hip again, Mattie—wants your bryonia.
—Well, Captain Urmson," he added to Garth,
"when you come back from the stables,

your remote posterity will be glad of a chat
with you!" And with a final roar the jolly
parson led the way into the house.

—————

CHAPTER IX

CALF-LOVE.

SINCE the world grew old she has taken
to making fun of some things which formerly she reverenced; and, among other things,
of children. The deeds, thoughts, and emotions, of that part of the community, so far
as they affect us at all, amuse us; we find
them transient, and therefore laugh at them.
Yet the logic of the case seems defective; if
it be true that the aroma of heaven abides
with us but a few years, and that afterward
we come to smell of the earth, would it not
be wiser to grieve than to grin?

To a humane mind, one would suppose,
nothing could be more touching than the
spectacle of that fresh, wondering, purely
passionate homage of a boy for a girl—that
self-devotion of the new man, who obscure-
ly feels that human nature is twofold, for
the opposite side of the tender mystery, the
lovelier, diviner Eve—which the world has
agreed to call calf-love! It is a sentiment
refined beyond the scope of our common expression; something too delicate to be deliberately recalled and described. In finer
moments—in a happy strain of music or a
sudden insight into nature—we may catch
an echo or a glimpse of it; but the moment
after, it has vanished, ere we can say with
the memory of a memory, "Lo, there!"

There is a mute pathos about it. Your
boy is your only true sighing lover; he must
sigh whether his suit prosper or not. The
reason is, that boys know nothing of the
soul; soul and body are in them so soundly
united that they confound spiritual longings
with physical ones. At the same time, the
very refinement of those spiritual longings
inculcates the impossibility of their earthly
gratification; the gross body lies in the way,
yet the boy's philosophy declares the body
to be all. His love feeds perforce on dreams
and visions; even the beloved one herself

must not come too near. An actual embrace would degrade the imaginary one; it would be too much, because proving that there could never be enough. Later on in life we may temper such failures with gossip of immortality; but boys live only in the present, and regard death as the final annihilation of existence.

That Garth should be a victim to this melancholy passion was only what was to be expected from a boy of his character; and the grave intensity of his nature promised to render the attack a more than ordinarily prolonged one. Moreover, Madge Danver was a very fascinating little creature; quite able, on her own merits, to impose constancy upon a colder lover than Garth was likely to prove. Yet the growth of the sentiment in him proceeded slowly, and for a time without his even being conscious of its existence. From that afternoon when the dark-eyed little maiden clung to his steel-clad waist, the great horse bearing her and him onward to a common destination, while the reverend giant strode beside them, lending to their union the support of the church; from that hour to the one in which Garth finally realized that he loved her, was a period of more than three years. And, even then, the realization was brought about by an accident.

He had been acquainted with Madge, childishly speaking, as long as he could remember; and his earliest feeling with regard to her had been a slight boyish aversion. Her confident, self-possessed vivacity had jarred against his constitutional reserve, and, in a general way, he preferred her room to her company. But, after their woodland adventure, his attitude toward her suffered a change. The change troubled him, and his first impulse (as it often happens) was to misinterpret it. He persuaded himself that instead of passively objecting to her, as heretofore, he now actively disliked her—nor was this persuasion entirely without arguments to justify it. The beginnings of a powerful emotion—one destined vitally to influence the nature—are apt to be painful; and pain, in a child's estimation, is synonymous with evil. When Garth, therefore, found that the thought of Madge disturbed him, and that her presence threw him into a state of tremor and distress, and that the sound of her voice or the touch of her hand made him positively uncomfortable, it is not surprising that he should have looked upon her as an enemy. He could no longer be himself because of her; she interfered with his freedom, she had cast a spell over him; she was a witch—a malicious enchantress! She deserved to have her head cut off; but, alas! the executioner's arm was powerless against her, and the more she merited punishment the less heart had he to inflict it.

But, by-and-by, Garth began to ask himself whether, after all, Madge was really responsible for his disquietude. Was he not tormenting himself, and then laying the blame on her? Had he any reason to suppose that she was even aware of his sufferings? Was it her fault that when he fled from her he seemed to take her with him in his flight, insomuch that the remotest solitude was peopled with her? Could she help it that he met her eye in every flower, and heard her tones in every bird-note, or that all he thought and did had reference to her? It was unjust to assume as much without proof, and what proof had he? Was any proof obtainable? Well, it might be worth while to try. What if, instead of shunning her altogether, he were to watch her secretly, so that, if she were really a witch, he might some day surprise her in the very act of brewing her spell? The more Garth considered this plan the better it pleased him, and it was not long before he put it in practice. He climbed trees beneath which Madge was to pass, and peeped fearfully down at her from between the branches; he slipped behind rocks, and, with a beating heart, listened to her approaching and departing steps; or, from some distant coign of vantage, he would feverishly observe her playing about in her cottage-garden. But all this espionage failed to provide him with evidence in support of his injurious suspicions. Madge was not a witch; what, then, was she? If she was not something very bad, might she not possibly be something very good? It had by this time become a question of extremes one way or the other. If she were very good, how was it that he disliked her? Did he dislike her?

When once that question had been asked, of course it could be answered in only one way. Madge was an angel, and Garth adored her; not she, but his own blindness had been at fault. By the light of his present revelation, he reviewed his past experiences, and fancied that he understood them thoroughly. Nevertheless, it is open to doubt whether he saw his mistress, at this juncture, so clearly as either before or afterward. He endowed her with graces filched from the fairies. There had thus far been no actual intimacy between the two, such as might mould into definite shape the lover's fantastic hyperboles. Garth loved, but he loved an ideal; not, as yet, a creature of flesh and blood, and it is not improbable that, had he been left to himself, he might have gone on loving the ideal Madge until the real one had been quite outgrown. He was very shy, and, in the absence of any outside agency forcing him to identify the shadow with the substance, he might easily have suffered them to diverge beyond the point of reconcilement. It was a critical moment in the affair. Madge was prevented from influencing the issue simply by her ignorance of there being any issue to influence. Garth was the last boy in the neighborhood whom she would have expected to be in love with her; and he was the only boy of her acquaintance in whose presence she had ever felt embarrassment. She did not understand him, and was a little afraid of him; she saw that he was not ill-looking, but she was sure that he was disagreeable. It was evident, therefore, that the *dénoûment* would depend upon some accidental turn of events for which neither Garth nor Madge would be consciously responsible.

CHAPTER X.

GARTH's great-grandfather had been a farmer, and, during the second quarter of the last century, he had dealings with a certain M. d'Anver, an Acadian, who was likewise a farmer, and wealthy in land and herds. Afterward, when the expatriation of the Acadians took place, the D'Anver family directed their steps to New Hampshire, and finally arrived in a pretty destitute condition at the little village of Urmsworth. The villagers, with Mr. Urmson at their head, received the exiles hospitably, and presented them with a small grant of land on the outskirts of the town. In the course of the ensuing five-and-twenty years, the family managed to acquire a tolerable competence, and, as they took kindly to their new surroundings, no one had cause to regret their advent.

At the outbreak of the Revolution, Pierre Danver, son of the first settler, eagerly took sides against the English; and he and Brian Urmson (then a youth of nineteen) marched with Ethan Allen to Ticonderoga. A few months later, Pierre was permanently disabled by a gunshot-wound. His young companion-in-arms brought him home, and, before leaving again, was betrothed to Pierre's sister Marie. With her kiss upon his lips he returned to the war, and, after a series of wild adventures on land, he took service on board a privateersman, of which he subsequently became commander. When peace was declared, he reappeared at Urmhurst with the title of captain, and with a goodly sum of prize-money in his purse. His father having died meanwhile, Captain Brian took possession of the estate, which he considerably enriched by judicious investments. Marie Danver had remained true to him throughout the seven weary years of their betrothment, and he now married her in spite of certain obscure rumors as to some entanglement of his with a lady in Virginia. He lived happily with his wife for twelve years, when she died, having borne him one child—the Cuthbert of this story.

Captain Brian remained a widower seven years, and, for all that his neighbors expected, he would have remained one to the end of his days; but, one winter's morning, a mysterious stranger suddenly made her appearance in Urmsworth. No one knew who she was or whence she came. Though somewhat past the prime of life, she was still handsome, and had the air of a lady accustomed to luxury and refinement. She engaged lodgings in the village, and then sent a messenger to Urmhurst with a note for Captain Brian Urmson. The note was delivered, and, half an hour afterward, the captain presented himself at her parlor-door. His call was prolonged until late in the afternoon, and, on leaving, he repaired directly to the parsonage, and had a private interview with the Reverend Mr. Graeme. Two days afterward it was known that Mrs. Golightley and Captain Urmson were to be married, and, before the end of another week, the wedding had actually taken place.

The village was fain to deal with its astonishment and curiosity as best it might, for the captain never vouchsafed any explanation of this singular proceeding. He was passionately devoted to his new wife, and she to him; but their union was not destined to last long. She survived her marriage only three years, during which time she gave birth to two children—Eve and Golightley—dying in childbed when the latter was about three months old. Her husband, as we know, took her death very much to heart; but he had his little Eve to comfort him; and, though poor Golightley was never in much favor, Cuthbert, who was by this time approaching his twentieth year, was admitted by his father to a friendly, rather than a merely filial, footing. One reason of this distinction probably was that Cuthbert never showed any fear of the savage and morose old warrior, but answered him always with a respectful firmness that commanded equally his affection and respect. Among the villagers, however, Golightley was more popular than his half-brother, the latter being considered self-opinionated and satirical. Cuthbert graduated at Bowdoin, and then, in the same year that Eve was lost, set out on his travels, and did not come back till he was over thirty.

Meantime, the Danvers had been suffering reverses. Captain Urmson, after his first wife's death, had not been at much pains to keep up an intimacy with her family; and his second marriage widened the gap between him and them. Pierre's son was a man of some mechanical genius, and of an inventive turn of intellect. He sank a great deal of money in experimenting with his inventions, and gradually contracted the habit of solacing his disappointments with drink. To add to his misfortunes, he was of an uncomfortably sensitive temperament, and chose to take umbrage at the captain's neglect; and, when adversity came, his pride would not allow him to apply to Urmhurst for assistance. Shortly before the captain's decease, however, he married a young woman who was something of an invalid and a good deal of a shrew, but who brought him a dowry of several thousand dollars. The only offspring of this marriage was little dark-eyed Madge, who came into the world a few years after Garth. By this time, thanks to the kindly overtures of Cuthbert and his gentle wife, the old relations between the two families had been reëstablished on a friendlier footing than ever, and, the Danvers being again in a needy condition, the Urmsons were able to exercise their benevolent ingenuity in devising expedients for relieving them without offending their susceptibilities.

As for Madge, she was both mentally and physically precocious; she always led her class at school, and, though not a large child, was active and skillful in dancing, skating, and such-like exercises. She was the first of her race to be baptized into the Protestant Church; Parson Graeme officiated at the ceremony, and ever afterward took the little convert into his especial favor and protection. But Madge was almost universally popular among grown-up people. She possessed a charming vivacity and confidence of manner, tempered by a subtile tact which enabled her to steer clear of the vulgar conceit and self-assertion of most so-called clever children. Her face was rather French in type; long and dark, with large oval eyes and vivid scarlet lips; and in her earlier years she had a tendency to the use of French idioms in her speech. For the rest, she was good-humored, cheerful, neat, and possessed a flavor and accent of her own. Her very dress, without being conspicuous, could only have been worn by herself, and she attracted a half-amused, half-pleased attention wherever she went. Such attention never disconcerted her; she was not born for seclusion, and the eye of the world had no terrors for her. There was a touch of worldly wisdom in her composition, which, as often as it came to the surface, had an indescribably piquant effect. Her voice was endowed with a certain soothing or caressing intonation, employed only upon occasion, but which might have flattered an icicle or coaxed a flint.

But she was not quite so popular with the boys and girls as with the grown folks. In fact, most girls of her own age disliked her. Madge never was guilty of any of those intimate, effusive, mysterious, whispering, anti-masculine, girl friendships, which are less rare a sight than might be expected, in view of the wealth of sentiment pervading them. She could afford to do without them because of her undeniable ability to beguile the heart of any boy in Urmsworth. A boy might distrust her when he was not in her company; he might say bitter things of her behind her back; he might even warn other boys that she was a flirt; nevertheless, to spend half an hour at her side was to forget all his doubts and to abjure all his hard speeches. She was so naïve, so frank, so confiding, and so entertaining, that it was not in ordinary boyhood to resist her. If she were a coquette, coquetry was as natural to her as plain faces or slow wits are to other young ladies, and perhaps she was no more to blame for her failing than they for theirs.

Concerning this side of Madge's life, Garth knew nothing. He regarded her as a thing apart; and without a bit of self-conceit it had never occurred to him that any third person could come between them two. The sacredness which invested her in his eyes must impress itself upon others as well; but he alone could ever be privileged to do her homage. Unworthy of her though he might be, Providence had made her no other mate; the mystic thread of destiny had united her star to his earth, and not to another's. The trifling circumstance that he had never exchanged a single unconventional or sentimental word with the mistress of his soul could have, of course, no influence on his convictions. Like all visionaries, he liked his dreams better than facts; for facts are apt to make fun of visionaries. Madge was a palpable little fact, and no doubt she would have made fun of Garth, if she could

have peeped into his mind at this epoch. But, fortunately for the loves and friendships of mankind, such insights are seldom possible. The friend cannot read his friend's heart, even when the latter desires to open it to his perusal; nor can the lover reveal himself to his mistress, however great their mutual good-will. We are mysteries to ourselves and to one another; the last secret of our natures is still withheld from us, lest we abuse it.

It had for many years been the practice of the Urmsworth school-children to picnic every Michaelmas in a certain woodland tract some three miles up the mill-stream. It was a romantic spot—a natural landscape garden, beautifully diversified. The journey thither was made in farm-wagons, hay-carts, on foot or on horseback, with laughter, singing, and jollity; the day was spent as happily as are most fête-days, and the home return as much resembled the allegoric pictures of the "Triumph of Autumn" as real life can be expected to resemble unreal.

Old Parson Graeme had been the originator of these junketings, and was wont to be the most uproarious of the junketers; his stentorian "Haw, haw, haw!" being always the nucleus of the fun; and the picnic without the parson would have been like autumn stripped of its autumnal leaves. No such deprivation had yet occurred, and the reverend patriarch, though now in his eighty-fifth year, was almost as hearty and full as jolly as at any time during the last quarter of a century. Much as he enjoyed the diversion, however, one thing was yet wanting to complete his satisfaction, and that was Garth's presence at the picnic along with the rest. To be brought face to face with boys and girls of his own age was, in the good gentleman's opinion, the only cure for his grandson's shyness, indolence, taciturnity, and other failings. But Garth had thus far steadily declined to join himself with the revelers, and, Cuthbert refusing to interfere, the parson had year after year been fain to digest his disappointment. But year after year he renewed the attack, not so much, at last, in expectation of success, as from a conscientious resolve to do his duty in the matter. Accordingly, when the present Michaelmas-tide came round, he found an opportunity to collar Garth in the barn-yard, where he was feeding the hens, and addressed him as follows:

"Grandson, now listen to me. You're fifteen years old now, or pretty near it. Well, that's a pretty good age for a boy. But I'm nearly six times as old as you, and I ought to know what's best for you."

Here the parson made a sort of oratorical pause, clearing his throat and raising his finger to begin his exordium in earnest. But Garth looked up from his hens and asked:

"Do you want me to go to the picnic this year, grandpapa?"

"Ay, lad, that I do. What—will you go?"

"Yes," replied Garth, looking down at his hens again, "I am going."

The parson could scarcely believe his ears, so wholly unexpected was this spontaneous compliance. After a pause of astonishment, he laid his mighty hand on the boy's shoulder and bellowed out:

"Recollect—you've promised it. No backing out! Well, you're a good lad, and in future years you'll look back on next Saturday as the date of your first real start in life. You've only been playing till now. You're a good lad, and I hope to see you graduate at Bowdoin College, as I saw your father before you. But mind you, now—no backing out, eh? You'll keep your word?"

"I shall always keep my word, grandpapa," said Garth, gravely; and walked dignifiedly away, his hens following him.

The parson, however, was much gratified at the lad's conversion, which he ascribed to his own eloquence and perseverance. But the truth of the matter was this: he had consented to go to the picnic because Madge had previously asked him to do so. They had met in the forest-path that very morning; Garth had been too much agitated to attempt escape, and even she was so much taken aback as to say the first thing which came into her head:

"Are you coming to the picnic next Saturday, Mr. Garth?"

"I didn't— If you tell me to!"

Mr. Garth's heart was beating hard; but no knight that he could remember had ever refused a boon to his lady-love.

"Oh, yes, you must come!" exclaimed she, with a sparkling smile.

She thought this strong-looking young Urmson boy, with his flushed cheeks, wild hair, and glowing eyes, was altogether as nice as anybody she knew.

"But how strange he is!" she murmured to herself, as Garth bowed his head and hurried away to ponder his incredible adventure in deepest solitude. "Sam Kineo would not so have run away from me—I am sure of it. Garth looks like him a little; only Sam's hair is straighter, and his forehead less high. And Sam is more polite. But I like Garth; I will be kind to him at the picnic; and then Sam will be fierce, but Garth can be fierce too, I think."

This Sam Kineo was a half-breed Indian —a black-haired, swarthy, active fellow, with a quick, shining eye. He was accounted the best runner, skater, and hunter, in the neighborhood. He was about a year older than Garth, and tall of his age. He had first appeared at Urmsworth ten years before, when an Indian woman, who had carried him through the wintry wilderness on her back, sank down at the parson's door, exhausted with the weary anguish of a broken knee. She told a romantic story about the seduction of a daughter by a faithless white man, of a consequent tragedy, and of her own flight northward with the child. She was kindly cared for by the hospitable minister, and the child was taken in charge and taught the catechism, and afterward put to school. He was bright enough, but averse from steady work; or, as the schoolmaster put it, he was "deficient in application rather than in native intelligence."

The Indian woman, who was known as Nikomis, took up her abode in a wigwam on the borders of the forest, where she practised medicine and popular necromancy, and was esteemed one of the lions of the place. Sam, who lived with her, was at the age of thirteen apprenticed to a gunsmith. He accommodated himself to the social life of the village with a facility that belonged to certain aspects of his character, and soon became popular at dances, sleighing-parties, and such-like amusements. He was a handsome fellow, and his half tamed cleverness, physical powers, and mysterious origin, combined to lend him a good deal of prestige in some people's eyes—Madge's among others. She was not indifferent to physical attractions, and liked romantic irregularity.

Garth and Sam were acquainted, after a rough fashion of their own. They knew each other's names, had certain similarities of taste and knowledge, communicated with each other mainly by signs, and often went on hunting expeditions together. Sam surpassed Garth in the instinct and sagacity due to his Indian strain; yet Garth, with the higher part of his nature omitted, might have rivaled Sam more nearly than was the case as things stood. The intimacy of the two boys never got beyond a superficial companionship; any attempts to push it further would only have brought about a mutual repulsion. Sam, however, had sharper eyes than Garth, and was accustomed to study the latter much more keenly than Garth studied him. Whether he gained anything from his scrutiny is open to question; at all events, he probably fancied that he understood his companion more thoroughly than in reality he did. But, taking into consideration the character of these two boys, their respective attitudes toward Madge, and her disposition toward each of them, it is easy to see that a meeting between the three might have interesting results.

CHAPTER XI.

UP A TREE.

ON picnic morning Garth was up early, though he had slept ill during the night. Fantastic visions of the morrow had flitted through his brain, and tossed him in flushed discomfort from one side of his bed to the other. He had pursued a phantom Garth through all manner of grotesque adventures, and was distressed to observe that the spectre always contrived to fail, by an inch or a moment, of creditably acquitting himself.

Wishing that Garth incarnate might do better, tho' boy let himself quietly out of his bedroom-window at sunrise, and struck off through the awakening woods toward the picnic-grounds. He knew that some hours must elapse before the party would arrive, but he meant to employ this spare time in thoroughly reconnoitring the scene of the coming festival, and trying to accustom himself to the idea of facing so many people; for, although he might know every individual in the company, Garth dreaded confronting them in mass. Assuming, as he did, that every one would make a point of observing his slightest manifestation, and taking it for granted that he must appear to other eyes at least as transparent as he did to his own, it was not strange that his courage sometimes misgave him. On the other hand, there was Madge—or Miss Danver, as he must begin to call her, since their acquaintance was about to emerge from fairyland into the every-day world—whom to meet he knew not whether he most rejoiced or feared. To meet her, to be near her, perhaps to converse with her—oh, to think of it! After all, was not the real world a yet more marvelous place than fairy-land?

As he walked on, however, brushed by the leaves which had scarcely begun to be autumnal, and cheered by the lusty enthusiasm of the morning sunshine, his fears dwindled, and he felt brave enough to look his joys in the face. They were all Madge! The vistas of the wood, the glimpses of heaven overhead, the tonic breath of the pines, the stirring of the breeze, were beautiful because of her. He so delighted in these reflections and reminders of his mistress that the way did not seem long nor the time wearisome ere she should appear in her proper person. An older or more experienced lover would have found everything irksome save the actual beloved presence, but Garth knew as yet neither the sweetness nor the disappointment of living hands and lips. He looked back, nevertheless, with long-drawn breaths and reddenings of the cheek, at his several encounters with Madge thus far, and especially to that memorable evening when she had sat behind him on horseback, her small arm round his waist, and her face so near, that, when he turned to answer his grandfather, stalking beside them, he could feel her warm breath on his cheek. Ah! sighed Garth, would they ever ride thus again? At all events, he was resolved on making unheard-of advances to-day. He would go up to her as soon as she arrived, and take her by the hand in bidding her good-morning. He would sit near her at dinner-time, and persuade her to share the contents of his luncheon-basket. He would pluck off the burs from the chestnuts for her; and in the games and trials of strength and skill which were to occupy the forenoon, he would win every prize for her sake; even Sam Kineo should not prevail against him.

After proceeding a mile or two on his way, he came to a spot where the path branched off in two directions. Here, amid a cluster of moist and mossy stones, a spring bubbled up and flowed across the track and onward through the roots of the trees into the forest. The spring was overshadowed by a young rock-maple, whose foliage had forced the season, most of it being already yellow, and branches here and there clustered with clear red leaves which seemed adrip with living blood. The boy threw himself down to drink of the cold water, staring the while at the mysterious bubbling commotion at the sandy bottom of the spring, as seen through the reflection of his own brown face. Some time, he thought, in pursuance of the custom of pious knights of old, when they had had their fill of blood-shed, it would be well to erect on this spot a sort of temple or shrine consecrated to lovely Madge Danver, and affording her and him a place of meeting, or of refuge, if need were. Love and peace should reign here; all deeds and thoughts should be as pure and kindly as this beneficent spring. Urmhurst had been built upon a grave, and its foundation had been laid in strife and blood; but Garth would raise his edifice on innocent ground, and so keep his life blameless. The plan so took his fancy that, by way of securing the site against foreign appropriation, he pulled out his knife and cut his own and Madge's initials deep in the bark of the rock-maple, and drew a line round them. Pleased

with the conceit, which was as original with him as with the forefather of all lovers, Garth put his knife in his pocket, and resumed his way to the picnic-ground.

As he neared it, and finally looked upon the place where this assemblage of living and palpable human beings was actually to appear within an hour or two, the boy's apprehensions in a measure returned, and he was glad he had allowed himself space to compose his mind and fortify his resolution for the ordeal. He rambled hither and thither about the rocky and wildly picturesque glen, peopling it with imaginary picnickers, and endeavoring to make himself at home with them; while a shadowy Madge seemed ever at his side. At length he came to an enormous chestnut-tree, standing near the upper verge of the tract, and stretching its mighty limbs over a diameter of one hundred feet. The ground beneath was strewed with clusters of the burred nuts, and thousands more hung between the thick leaves overhead. After trying his teeth for a while upon the former, Garth began to turn his eyes upward, and consider the practicability of a climb.

Swarming was out of the question; the chestnut was eighteen feet in girth; but there were twigs sprouting here and there from the lower trunk, and a few promising knots and clefts which might be of use. Once ten feet from the ground and the lowest of the main limbs could be reached, and thence was a broad, winding staircase to the tiptop. It was a very tall tree, and no doubt commanded a large view: perhaps he could see the picnic-party on their way hither from the village. This last thought bound him to the attempt, and forgetting that enough time had already passed to allow of their being very near, he forthwith set about it. It was a slow and arduous job, and after working hard for ten minutes, and ascending about eight feet, it became necessary either to trust his weight to a certain dead twig, or to come down again. Garth paused to deliberate. In the midst of his pause a strange sound fell upon his ear—a throbbing, reduplicating, long-drawn note, dying away in a cadence, which would have sounded melancholy to one ignorant (as Garth was not) that it was the stentorian laughter of Parson Graeme echoing afar through the woods.

The party must be close at hand, and the climber, following his first and most natural impulse, committed himself to the twig, which cracked, indeed, but did not break, and helped him to a main limb of the tree. He rapidly clambered upward, and before the vanguard of the revelers had come in sight, he was safe among the topmost branches, whence he could overlook the whole ground, excepting only the space immediately beneath him, but was himself invisible from all points.

By the time he had recovered his breath and wiped the perspiration from his face, the picnickers were defiling with jollity into the glen, the gigantic parson in front, with Madge's hand in his, Sam Kineo not far off, upward of a score of grown people and children following on behind, and, last of all, an old hay-cart drawn by a venerable white steed, that had retired from active life and reserved himself for festive occasions like the present. The cart was beladen with provision-baskets, in charge of three or four elderly ladies, whose years entitled them to a ride, though it is doubtful whether the jolting they got was not a sharper trial of endurance than a three-mile walk would have been.

Garth had climbed his tree involuntarily, so to speak; but it now occurred to him that the opportunity of overlooking his company and familiarizing himself with their individual and aggregate aspect, before descending and mixing with them on an equal footing, was worth improving. He kept his perch accordingly, and held his peace, and enjoyed the aroma of affairs like a superior being, without having his appreciation dulled by a personal share in them.

The cart was drawn up beneath Garth's very chestnut, and the venerable steed was relieved of his harness and turned out to amuse himself, while the elderly ladies were severally lifted down by the gallant parson, who was provided with a flattering witticism for each one of them. The next thing was to take out the provision-baskets and select a site for the table.

"Why not have it here beneath the tree?" demanded the ponderous tones of the reverend Titan.

But somebody objected that the chestnut burs would render sitting down impossible; and therefore, after some discussion and much mirth, the place was fixed a few rods off, under the southern side of a lichened rock: entirely with Garth's approval, since he could now see all that went on, without overhearing conversation perhaps not intended for his ears. Whatever his grandfather said he must, indeed, make up his mind to be privy to; the old gentleman would have been audible at the top of a mimosa. But then his grandfather never talked secrets.

"Now, boys and girls," bellowed he, having left the elderly ladies to unpack the baskets and make dilatory preparations for the feast—"now, then, we must have our games. What shall we begin with? Speak up, somebody. Boys, you ought to give the ladies the first choice. Or what do you say to a boy and a girl being chosen to decide it, between themselves, for all of us? Very well; who shall they be? What do you say to—let me see—to Madge Danver and Garth Urmson?"

Garth started, and dropped a chestnut. Was he discovered? and did he hear his name coupled with hers? Oh, he must come down!

But hark again! "Why, where is Garth? —not here? no one seen him? That's odd —that's odd. He told me he'd be here. Well!—however, it's early still; he'll come yet, depend upon it.—What did you say, my dear?" to Madge. Garth did not catch her rejoinder, but it seemed to tickle the minister, whose mood changed from solicitude to mirth. "Ho! ho! ho! Oh, very well, if that's the case, we needn't feel anxious about him; he'll come sooner or later. I thought it was all on *my* account—ha! ha! ha!— Well, boys and girls, we can't wait for him, so whom shall we choose in his place? Let me see—what do you say to Sam Kineo?"

It was a foible of the good minister to be most autocratic under the guise of deferring to the opinion of others; so now, while appearing to choose Madge and Sam by appeal to the popular will, he in reality (though

unawares) pleased no one except himself
and his nominees. The girls were affronted
that the "Frenchified little thing" should
be put over them, while the boys were as
little flattered to play second fiddle to an
Indian half-breed. However, there was no
disputing the minister's vote, and Sam and
Madge were chosen, if not unanimously, at
least without a dissentient voice. They
walked apart mysteriously, and consulted.
There was not much to consult about; but
still Garth's eyes followed the pair with singular anxiety, and he was continually wondering how Sam felt, and imagining how he
himself would feel in Sam's place, and be-
rating himself for having been out of the
way at the critical moment. Not but Sam
carried it off well enough: indeed, Garth
could not help acknowledging that the half-
breed's behavior was more easy and gallant
than his own would have dared to be in the
circumstances. And Madge—Miss Danver
—seemed charmingly affable. For a moment
Garth questioned whether she would have
been so affable to him!

Nevertheless, he was not jealous: he
had too much refinement and too little experience for that. Madge was gracious as
a queen might be; and Sam's self-possession
was that of a courtier who knows his place.
With Garth it would be different; he must
meet the queen only as her destined lover;
and on those high terms it was no marvel if
the dapper forms of society should hitch and
stammer a little at first. He was not jealous, for the idea that Madge would receive
the advances of any one but himself, or that
any one except himself would venture to
make advances to her, never entered his
head. But he could not with equanimity
behold so much sweetness thrown away on
Sam Kineo—sweetness from which only
this unlucky chestnut debarred him. What
had possessed him to expend so much pains
in climbing out of the reach of his own happiness? Why had he not been content to
remain on the same footing with the rest
of the world, and take his equal chances?
Solitude and seclusion are good in their
way, but a body among the clouds while the
soul languishes on earth Garth found a
most unprofitable predicament.

Meanwhile the committee had decided
upon their programme, and the games began. Garth, sitting disconsolate like a deserted idol in his niche, was astonished to
see what a good time boys and girls had together. He had always taken it for granted
that enjoyment was in a direct ratio to iso-
lation; but here numbers seemed to be the
very zest of the fun. How they laughed,
shouted, ran about, and laughed again!
What a delightful game blindman's-buff
was, and hunt-the-slipper, and kitchen-fur-
niture, and pass-the-ring! Garth joined in
every laugh, and nearly fell out of his tree
in the heedless sympathy with which he followed the movements of the players. How
lovely Madge looked! how handy and clever
was Sam Kineo! A sigh surprised Garth
in the midst of his enjoyment. What right
had he to laugh? he was not playing. He
was like a forlorn ghost vainly attempting
to partake of earthly pleasures. He was resolved, if once he got his foot on solid earth
again, to give up tree-climbing. Meanwhile
it was plain that he must stay where he was
so long as the picnic lasted. To come down
now would be indeed a come-down, and
Garth's dignity and sense of the ludicrous
alike forbade it.

By-and-by the girls were tired, and there
was a pause. The minister, who had contributed more noise to the games than any
of the players, now revived the topic of
Garth's absence, observing that he the more
regretted it since, in the trials of strength
and skill which were to come off between
the boys, he was certain that his grandson
would have borne a distinguished part. But
at this Sam Kineo ventured to turn up his
nose, intimating that it might be just as well
for Garth's reputation to keep out of the
way. Sam, in fact, was generally admitted
to be a formidable athlete; he was a year
older than the minister's grandson, and, had
the two been matched against each other,
the odds must have been in the Indian's
favor. Garth, nevertheless, cramped and impatient in his tree, would gladly have descended to try his strength, had Sam's
prowess been double what it was.. In
Madge's presence, too, he could scarcely
have failed of success—so he fancied; and

now he was to lose this signal opportunity of proving himself worthy of her favor. Oh for a bout at wrestling with Sam Kineo!

Perhaps, to own the truth, something more than ordinary rivalry was at the bottom of that wish. Sam seemed to be eating Garth's cake and his own too. How easy it would be quietly to drop down in the midst! and yet how much harder it was to climb down against moral obstacles than up against material ones, and what a different kind of agility was requisite!

After a sufficient rest, the minister, abandoning all hopes of his young relative's appearance, gave orders for the athletic sports to begin. Madge was probably the only person who (for her own private reasons) shared the old gentleman's disappointment at Master Urmson's defection. She had laid plans which promised to bring about an exciting little episode or two; but Garth and Sam were both involved in the scheme, and its consequent failure made Madge rather captious. She was piqued at the former's implicit slight, but this did not prevent her taking his part against the latter, who probably found her less disposed to encourage his attentions than had Garth been on the ground.

Thus, when Sam jumped higher, ran faster, leaped farther, and wrestled better than any of his opponents, Madge only shrugged her little shoulders, and would have him to understand that matters would have fallen out otherwise if Garth Urmson had been there. Poor Sam could only scowl and secretly wish to tear his rival limb from limb; but then Madge would look so irresistible that wrath was perforce merged in adulation.

As for Garth, he would have been glad to be free of his leafy prison at the risk of being tomahawked and scalped as soon as he reached the earth. Mental irritation apart, his physical discomfort was most dolorous; he had tried every practicable position again and again, and not one was tolerable. The forenoon dragged past; there was a contra-dance, in which Madge and Sam were partners; then dinner was announced by the elderly ladies, and interminably eaten, under favor of a stentorian grace

from Parson Graeme; and it was Sam, not Garth, who kept Madge supplied with delicacies. After dinner the minister leaned back against the rock and went fast asleep; and the elderly ladies, when they had finished replacing the knives and forks and table-ware in the baskets, crawled under the hay-cart, and followed his example.

The younger part of the company, being thus left to their own devices, paired off and strolled away, each couple toward a different point of the compass, and at length only Sam and Madge remained. Between these two there seemed to be some misunderstanding, a state of things which Garth accepted more philosophically than his rival. The latter, after several ineffectual attempts to persuade Madge to accompany him, loitered moodily off by himself, and was presently lost to sight behind a clump of sombre hemlocks.

Madge sat still for a while, looking up into the chestnut-tree, apparently lost in thought; once or twice Garth could almost believe that their glances met. But before he could decide upon the propriety of then and there discovering himself to the mistress of his heart, she abruptly arose, tied on her broad-brimmed straw hat beneath her soft little chin, and walked demurely away, with her short steps and erect little figure. The direction she took, though not exactly opposite to Sam's, was at a considerable angle from it. Garth, having satisfied himself that whoever was not asleep was out of the way, descended his tree as fast as his stiffened legs would let him, and dropped to the ground with almost a shout of relief.

At last he was once more his own master, the owner of his own limbs, motions, and volitions; he had learned more than one wise lesson up yonder among the chestnut-burs; he had pricked his fingers, but it was his fault if he had not profited by a few solid kernels. The first use he made of his wisdom was to determine on pursuing Madge; but, looking about him, he found the aspect of the country so much altered from his new point of view as to put him in some doubt which way she had gone. He paused a moment to listen. It was a silent afternoon, the loudest noise being the snoring of his grandfather, which was reëchoed in a fainter key from beneath the hay-cart. Far off somewhere a boy was whistling a tune that sounded like "Yankee Doodle." A cat-bird piped from an alder-thicket near at hand. From another direction came a distant murmur of laughter. But there was nothing that told of Madge; so, having reconsidered his bearings as accurately as possible, the sturdy young lover set forth, and was quickly swallowed up in the inscrutable mazes of the forest.

CHAPTER XII.

FIGHTING.

ABOUT six hours later, weary in body and dejected in mind, ragged, hungry, and thirsty, Garth emerged at the cool bubbling spring amid the stones, at the meeting of the ways; and once more he threw himself at length beneath the crimson maple and drank a refreshing draught. He had not found Madge, neither had he seen a human being since leaving the picnic-ground; he had wandered on preoccupied, he knew not where; ever surrounded by a twilight of trees; sometimes fancying he heard a voice or caught a glimpse of a broad-brimmed straw hat, which would change to a festoon of moss or a bird-note as he approached. He made a vast *détour* of loneliness, and it was not till he came upon the fountain, and saw in the moss the imprint he had made in the morning, that he realized in what part of the world he was. He drank, and then seated himself upon a stone to meditate over his first picnic.

Hark! was not that the minister's laugh? some faint echo of it seeming to come from the direction of the village. The picnickers, then, must newly have passed by; a few minutes earlier, and Garth would have fallen in with them. He rose to his feet, resolved to pursue them, and put to the proof his late-learned doctrine of the value of society; at all events, to clear his character with his grandfather and Madge—Miss Danver; to show them that he·had kept his promise in

being at the festival, albeit veiled in the invisibility of a chestnut-tree. But before he had advanced two steps toward putting these good resolutions in execution he heard a foot-tramp from behind, and, turning, beheld Sam Kineo hastening toward him as if from the picnic-ground. Sam looked elate and excited, but on seeing Garth he stopped in surprise.

"Hallo, hallo!" said he, in his rapid way, eying the other all over, and finally fixing a sharp look on his face. "Where ha' you been, Garth? Been lost? Ha, ha!"

"Didn't you meet her either?" demanded Garth.

"Meet who? What d'you know about it? 'Meet her either?' what are you talkin' about, Garth? You weren't at th' picnic; you know nothin'."

"I was in the chestnut-tree," said Garth, reddening a little. "I saw Ma—Miss Danver—"

Here Sam interrupted him with a laugh, the undisguised offensiveness of which made Garth redden still more. Ha, ha! Up in a tree like a chipmunk! "Ha, ha! 'Fraid to come down, fear you'd be beaten runnin', wrestlin', jumpin'. Ha! very sensible. We didn't want you! Madge 'nd I rather be alone together. Ha, ha!"

"Sam!" exclaimed the reverential Garth, too much shocked at the other's light mention of the adored name to remember that he ought to be angry.

"Well, well!" rejoined the half-breed, coming forward a step, with a hectoring air. He threw the black straight hair from his face, and met the other's eyes with a keen, shining glance. He was certainly a handsome lad, as well as an active and well-grown one; but there was the hardness and superficiality of the Indian in his expression, and just now a savage suggestiveness in the gleam of his white teeth.

"D'you think she likes you, eh?" he continued, rapidly; "think she likes you, Garth Urmson? I tell you what, she likes nobody but me. She loves me, Madge does. She's my girl. You better not interfere."

"Stop!" said Garth, in a low tone. "You have no right—"

There was a tremor in his voice, which

caught Sam's ear, and caused him to make a grave mistake. He had been inclined to pick a quarrel from the first, and Garth's behavior thus far had rather fostered the inclination. But the quaver in these last words appeared to Sam to be due to fear, and determined him to proceed to extremities at once. He believed himself able to give Garth a thrashing, and there was more than one reason why it was desirable he should do so. He threw off all disguise.

"You hold your tongue—you Garth! Tell me I have no right? Ha! ha! I kiss her often as I please; she gives me half a dozen kisses, puts her arms round my neck, lets me carry her over th' brook! Guess I have a right. . . . Hallo! hallo!"

Garth had waked up at last, though this unexpected torrent of blasphemy (such he considered it) had made him powerless for a few moments. The words stung and rankled, and seemed to blacken the day. There could be no adequate punishment for them. Since they were spoken, all innocence and freshness were parched and blighted out of life. Had he believed them true, he would have wished to live no longer.

But he held them falsest of the false, and he felt that it rested with him to inflict whatever punishment was possible. That Madge was innocent, that her lips and heart were pure, was to him as certain as that she existed. Sam had lied as no one ever lied before. To be so wicked must bring a punishment of its own, but it was none the less Garth's duty to vindicate Madge's honor to the uttermost. He took Sam by the throat in the midst of his blasphemies, and pushed him backward to a level bit of turf beside the maple - tree. Here the half - breed wrenched himself loose, and the boys faced each other in silence for nearly a minute. Something there was in the moulding and play of their features at this juncture which almost amounted to a resemblance, each to each. The lines of passion are much alike in all faces.

"You don't deserve to live," said Garth, at length, drawing a deep breath, and with an air of profound solemnity.

In fact, there was a sternness and an absence of flourish in Garth's demeanor which

a little dashed Sam's spirits. It made him feel the need of bending his every physical and mental faculty to the work before him. He was puzzled, perhaps, at the sudden change in Garth's attitude from shrinking to aggressive; he lacked the refined insight which might sympathetically have fathomed the cause of it. He could easily understand jealousy on his rival's part; but of such wrath kindled at mere wantonness of speech he had no comprehension. It was to his disadvantage that he had not, since the loftier passion is ever the more potent and enduring.

"Now, then, what do you want?" blustered he, raising his voice.

"Fight!" whispered Garth, glowing, and doubling his fists; and the very atmosphere seemed to grow murky and heavy with the word.

"What for?" demanded Sam, hesitating.

Garth, whose every bone yearned for battle, could hardly command his voice to speak. "Was it a lie?" he asked, tremulously.

"D'ye mean about the kissing? You ask her—"

"Fight! or I'll kill you," hissed Garth; and the fight began on the instant.

It was a breathless, fierce, desperate fight enough, though the fighters were boys fresh in their teens. Not a scientific fight on either side: there were no rounds, no rules, no courtesies. There was no noise either, except the sound of the blows, and the quick gasping for breath, and the soft trampling on the turf. There is a concentration and an economy about affairs of this kind which are lacking in most other business transactions; waste, diffuseness, is suicidal.

A blackbird happened to perch on the top of the maple at the moment the fight began, and was its sole witness. At first the shorter boy got the worst of it; he was knocked down three times within as many minutes. Whoever has been knocked down once can tell what this means. But Garth was not beaten. He started up as if the touch of earth refreshed him. Such stamina a little disheartened his adversary, to whom, indeed, the other's deliberate fury was quite unaccountable, and gradually became appalling. Sam fought with his strength, but Garth put the annihilation of all evil into every blow. He got more and more terribly in a rage each moment, but it was rage that calmed and cooled the faculties, not blinded them. No enemy is so unpleasant to meet as one of this kind; only killing can beat him, and, if not killed, he is very apt to kill. Garth's face was fixed in a singular expression—a compound of a smile and a frown. He was bleeding from a blow on the chin. Two hundred years before, an ancestor of his, on his wedding-day, had looked precisely thus.

When Sam stopped knocking his opponent down, the blackbird noted a change in the aspect of the fray. The larger boy was now defending himself. He was tiring, and was lacking in the unquenchable passion which should take the place of strength. He was fighting for his life, yet showed less vigor than the attacking party, who, it must be inferred, was doing battle for something to which life was a secondary consideration. It was an ugly sight now; even a bird, one would think, might have felt the ugliness of it. Both the faces were bleeding and disfigured, the leaves of the maple looked dabbled with blood, the setting sun was swathed in a bloody mist, and the black plumage of the bird was dashed here and there with red. All of a sudden the larger boy fell heavily and loosely backward, and lay inert. It was the other's first knock-down blow; with the force of it he, too, fell on his enemy's body.

The blackbird flew away. Garth, with an effort, staggered to his feet, and set his foot on Sam's breast, gasping out, after the custom of the knights in the "Faërie Queene," "Do you yield?"

Sam neither answered nor made sign of surrender, but lay exactly as he had fallen. In truth, the boy was stunned by the blow and the fall. But Garth, who was well read in details of mortal engagements, straightway took him for dead. He snatched back his foot, and stared at the motionless body, with a strange feeling curdling round his heart. He had fought fair—ay, with the odds against him; he could plead justice, truth, honor, and all, on his side; barely had

he won the victory; he could reproach himself in nothing; and yet there lay Sam, who so lately had lived and breathed, dead by Garth's hand, and the deadness of him seemed somehow to have filled the world and the sky, and even to have communicated itself to the springs of his slayer's life, and made the better part of him dead too.

Garth raised his eyes, and they fell upon the trunk of the maple-tree just beyond, on which were cut his own and Madge Danver's initials. This was the spot which, twelve hours before, he had consecrated to the genius of love, and to peace and innocence, and such pretty things—had consecrated it at sunrise in order to pollute it at sunset, or rather to consecrate it anew to bloodshed, strife, and hate. Had he done wrong or right in this matter? He could reproach himself in nothing; and Sam, there, could not accuse him—alas! no—could only lie still and accuse by not accusing. All was a puzzle and a mystery except that awful unmoving thing that was, and yet was not, Sam.

Kneeling down beside the spring, Garth washed the blood from his own face and hands, hastily bethinking himself the while what was to be done. The deadly earnestness and reality of the situation purged his mind of the fantastic vapors and visions which had beset him heretofore. He was in fairy-land no longer; Sam and he were not knights, but two boys, one of whom had killed the other. Madge—yes, even she was disenchanted—was no longer Gloriana, or Una, or Belphœbe, but a little girl, in defense of whose innocent reputation Garth had compromised his own innocence and his life. For the boy knew that murder was punished by hanging, and, not being acquainted with the various gradations of manslaughter and justifiable homicide, he made no doubt that hanging was his due. Mindful of his early discipline, therefore—of that self-invited discipline of the rod—he considered it incumbent upon himself not only to be hanged, but to lose no time in putting his head into the noose.

Had it occurred to him to spend a few minutes in applying to Sam the ordinary methods for restoring suspended animation, he would have been spared half an hour or so of very tragic anguish. But Garth had a natural bent to tragedy—a tendency to regard the saddest aspect of a thing as the most likely to be true. That Sam appeared dead, accordingly, was reason enough for believing that he was so: it would perhaps have seemed disrespectful to the awful majesty of fate to believe otherwise. He did not look at the body any more, though he was conscious of it as it lay there, with one knee bent, and one arm thrown over its head. He resolutely concentrated his thoughts on the two or three questions which demanded an immediate answer. Must he set off for Haverhill at once, and deliver himself up to justice without bidding farewell to his relatives, or would it be allowable first to go home? and might he not see Madge before he went, and have the consolation of telling her that he was to die in her cause?

He answered the last question first, and said no to it. He was blood-stained; he carried a death-scent about him; and though the stain had been incurred for Madge's sake, it was not fitting that he should invade her pure presence with it. If she wished to see him, she would visit him in prison, and he could receive her there. As to his father and mother, he was in doubt. He felt that he belonged to them, and might approach them, stained as he was, without offense; but when he thought of his mother's agony at hearing that he was to be hanged, he hesitated and held back. Yet, on the other hand, it was scarcely practicable for him to get to Haverhill and tell his story there entirely unsupported. In the midst of his doubts he suddenly remembered his grandfather. He was the man for the emergency —wise, influential, energetic, and not too tender-nerved. He could give the advice and assistance needed, and to him Garth would go.

It was already twilight in the solemn woods as the boy rose to act upon this decision. He walked hurriedly away without a sidewise or backward glance. The burden of his deed was heavy upon him, and he could not rest until the penalty was paid. He had done what seemed to him right; but was any right right enough to warrant his taking a life? Garth feared not. He was ready to be hanged; and yet he would rather have been hanged innocent than in requital of this questionable crime. His soul was very heavy; and when he had left the polluted ground behind him he was presently seized with a nervous horror, and began to run; and then the misery of his plight overcame him, and he sobbed dolefully, still running and stumbling along the darkening pathway.

CHAPTER XIII.

LOVING.

WHEN he had gone about a mile, an abrupt turning brought him close upon a small figure seated on an old stump. It rose as he approached, and he saw that it was Madge. The encounter did not surprise him—he was too unhappy for surprise; yet it was strange that she should be there so late alone. She seemed to have been expecting some one—not Garth certainly. She must have mistaken him at first for another person, for on recognizing him she gave a start and an exclamation:

"Ah! it is not— It is Garth Urmson."

Garth, unready of tongue, stood silent, an unlovely object. Hatless, bloody, distraught, he looked anything but a squire of dames. But Madge, apparently embarrassed on her own account, did not immediately remark his disorder.

"The others have gone on," she observed, in an airy tone, smoothing out the strings of her hat and tying them again. "I—missed something, and had come back to look for it. Then it grew dark. O Mr. Garth," she continued, archly uplifting her small finger, "you were unkind not to come as you promised me. I was very unhappy. You forgot all about me!"

"Oh!" groaned Garth. Then, finding himself unequal to any protestations, "You must not talk so. I have just killed him. Will you say good-by to me?"

The little woman stared, laughed, checked herself, scrutinized the boy's face keenly, and finally began to whimper:

"Wh-what do you mean? Oh, don't look so—you fr-frighten me so!"

"I'm going to be hanged," said Garth, apologetically. "I didn't know you were here. We fought on equal ground—because he told lies about you."

"How—he told lies about me?" she exclaimed, forgetting everything in curiosity. "You did fight him? but who—who was it? Tell me, Garth!"

"Sam."

"Sam!" repeated she softly, clasping her hands. "O Garth! Good Heavens! really have you killed him? He told lies, but you didn't believe him, dear Garth?" She came close, and put her hand on his sleeve with a lovely, beseeching tearfulness. "It was wicked of him to tell—to say such things. What did he say about poor little Madge? I am glad he is dead!"

Garth was thrilling beneath her touch and the caress of her voice; and she had called him "dear!" But in the midst of his happiness her harshness toward Sam, whose ears would never be blessed by her sweet tones again, jarred upon him. He could not echo her words. He had not a heart which could at once melt toward his living mistress and harden against a dead enemy. Moreover, the anticipation of his own near dissolution disposed him to charity.

"Be sorry," said he; "he is dead, you know. When he said that he—that you—"

"Don't believe it. It was a wi-wicked falsehood!"

"He would not confess. I did not know I should kill him. He seemed to die of himself," exclaimed Garth, greatly agitated.

By this time Madge was clinging to him, and sobbing with her face against his shoulder. She did not half comprehend him; she feared him to the marrow of her pretty little bones; and therefore she admired him, as women do admire the enigmatic, the terrible, and the victorious. "Oh, don't leave me! You don't hate me, do you? You will take me home, won't you? Oh; you are so hurt, dear! I will nurse you."

"But I must be hanged," faltered Garth.

"No, no, you shall not. What! for killing an Indian? And nobody saw you do it, and—you need not say you did it."

"I must be," repeated Garth, half inclined to think that hanging, so sweetly mourned, was preferable to ordinary life. "And since I did kill him, I can't say I did not."

"You must! I will not have you die! I want y-you to live! You are the bravest and the strongest, and—Garth—*you* may—" She held up to his her tremulous, red, delicious mouth; and he—simple, unhackneyed soul—did!

Yes, it was at last no dream, but a concrete fact; and he would have resented the suggestion that the fact was not as good as or better than the dream. Nevertheless it is not too much to say that Madge was less overcome by the situation—possibly less a stranger to such situations—than Garth. The feminine nature seems to be better appointed for such predicaments than the male, and accepts them more easily and philosophically. Meanwhile, with those soft arms round his neck, it was hard to prefer the hangman's knot, and perhaps the boy's resolution may have wavered a little. At all events, before he had found time distinctly to vindicate both his love and his honor, the struggle was annulled by the apparition of the murdered Sam himself.

Madge was the first to hear the approaching footfall, and, with admirable presence of mind, she drew Garth behind the thick screen of an arbor-vitæ. Sam approached slowly, staggering now and then as he walked. When his late adversary recognized him, he felt a tumult of joy and thankfulness rising up within him like a fountain. Forgetting himself and Madge, almost, in his glad emotion, he thought only of leaping forth and hugging his bruised and beaten enemy. But Madge kept her wits about her, and resolutely held Garth back. For reasons best known to herself, she was determined to at least postpone a meeting. Sam, therefore, hobbled past, unconscious of spectators. His face was sullen, livid, and disfigured.

"I'm sure he's ugly enough!" whispered Madge, half to herself. "So—he is not dead."

"No, not dead!" repeated Garth, with a different intonation. "Why didn't we speak to him? We forgive him, and we are so happy!"

"Do you forgive him?" said the little creature, fixing her black eyes on her companion's face. "He is just as wicked as before you beat him. Perhaps, now he's alive, he will tell those falsehoods again. But you'll never believe him, will you?"

"How could I believe what is not true? But he will never say it again," added Garth, with a wholesome confidence in the moral efficacy of knock-down blows.

Madge, however, had turned pensive, and made no reply; but when the guilty Sam was some time gone by, she put her small warm hand in the boy's, and they walked along together through the gloom, Garth thinking he had never been so happy in all his life; and as for Madge, she too was single-minded: she liked the dark, shy boy better than anybody else. She believed in power that could be felt and seen, such as Garth had shown to-day. She had a feminine love of display, and of being allied with strength and conspicuous merit like Garth's. He frightened her, but she liked that sort of frightening. She scarcely appreciated, it would seem, the finer and really essential part of his nature. She was like Sam in supposing that he had fought out of common jealousy. She missed the far higher compliment he had paid her. She feared him as a force swayed by a rude impulse, not tempered and concentrated by delicacy, conscience, and reverence. She believed, and liked to believe, that on due provocation he would knock her senseless as well as Sam. Of course she would beware of offering the provocation; but there was to her mind a sense of security in the very danger.

If Madge was incomplete in her apprehension of Garth, she nevertheless got at him very shrewdly on some points; whereas he so entirely missed her that, so her outward semblance and tone of voice remained unaltered, she might have run the whole human gamut of temperament, character, and disposition, without a suspicion on his part of what was happening. The only Madge he knew was the graceful piece of flesh-and-blood sculpture that went by her name, the actual informing essence of which he quietly ignored, and substituted therefor a conception of his own. His attitude lacked the stability of Madge's. She built in the first instance on the tangible, and was thus both safe from falls and provided with a solid starting-point for possible flights.

Garth reached home that night by moonlight, tired, sore, and in an exalted mood of happiness. He went to his room and took from its drawer a blue kerchief, with which in hand he proceeded to the porch, where his father and mother were sitting. He was too full of his purpose to give orderly answer to the questions wherewith they greeted him. He pressed the kerchief into his mother's hands.

"I must not keep it any longer," said he.

"What is it, my dear?" inquired placid Mrs. Urmson, relinquishing her knitting and examining the kerchief in the moonlight. "Why, I declare, it looks like an old one of mine!"

"I love you as much as ever, mamma," continued Garth, too much preoccupied to notice this inadequate remark; "but something has happened, and it would be dishonorable in me to keep it any longer."

"Dishonorable, my child? Surely not. Keep it if you want it; it is too much soiled and creased for me to use again."

"Papa," said Garth, in a mortified tone, "mamma does not understand me."

"There is apt to be a misunderstanding about matters of this sort, my boy. For my part, I should consider it a fortunate circumstance if the lady-love I proposed deserting had forgotten our troth-plighting. You will find it does not always turn out so."

"I do not desert her. She is always mamma."

"But she is not quite equal to your new mistress."

Garth paused and hesitated. At length he said, "If mamma were not your wife, she could not be my mother."

"Cotton, my dear, you must be content with me alone for the future," said her husband, gravely. "Garth has hit upon the fatal argument, and is weaned henceforth. We are old people, of secondary importance at best, from this day forward.—Garth, when you are married and settled, you will not refuse us a place by your kitchen-fire?"

"How can you plague the dear child

so?" said Cotton, reproachfully, drawing Garth to her and kissing him; and she added to him: "I remember about the kerchief now. But has my boy really fallen in love? How did it happen?"

"His grandfather would make him go to the picnic," suggested Cuthbert, arching his eyebrow.

"It was after the picnic," said the ingenuous Garth; and being questioned, the whole day's history was drawn from him, with the single exception of what Sam had said about Miss Margaret Danver, which, in obedience to that young lady's request, was hinted at only in general terms. Cuthbert laughed a good deal, being one of those persons who can laugh at a pathetic tale more sympathetically than another could weep at it, so that Garth's sensibilities were not hurt. His mother was in such a tremor about the fight that she could hardly give due attention to the love-story, nor rest until she had poured wine and oil into his every scratch. "And poor Sam Kineo!" murmured she; "you should have brought him home with you, my dear. I'm afraid his grandmother won't take proper care of him."

"You forget that Sam had not yielded," interposed Cuthbert. "The etiquette of chivalry must be observed.—So Miss Danver is to be your mother's successor?"

"She is a beautiful child," said Mrs. Urmson, smiling with a wistful tenderness at her son; "not like her grand-aunt; but she seems good, and I dare say she is much sweeter than I know. We must see more of her. I shall love whomever Garth loves. Your mother is not a rival—remember that, dear. I wish you to be happier than I can make you."

Years afterward, when his mother was dead, Garth used to muse over this saying of hers, and over the whole episode of the silken kerchief; but for that night his head was full of the new elixir, whose potent flavor overpowered the older and subtiler aroma. Even his father's parting words seemed less significant at the time than afterward:

"We will call to-morrow on your late adversary, Sir Samuel Kineo, and try to conclude an honorable peace between the families. I understand he wishes to try his fortune at Newburyport or Boston; and perhaps we may be able to smooth his way thither. As for Madame Nikomis, I think of asking her to come and sit in our kitchen for the future; she knows both how to fry an omelet and boil a potato; and then mamma will have more time for her darning. By-the-way, Garth—"

Garth knew his father's tones, and turned quickly.

"Your ancestor, Neil Urmson, before he left England, standing with his bride before the marriage altar, killed the man who had been his dearest friend. A generation afterward, Ralph, his son, slew in a petty duel the man who had saved his life. Seventy-five years after that, your grandfather, Captain Brian Urmson, shot dead the brother of the woman to whom he was betrothed, and whom he afterward married. Then more than fifty years passed, and Garth Urmson accidentally failed to kill an acquaintance of his who had never been taught to fight against himself."

Here Cuthbert made a solemn pause, during which he and his son steadfastly regarded one another, the latter reddening and awe-stricken.

"I make no doubt," the former then continued, "that the next time he engages, he will kill his opponent in earnest. But, when that happens, I trust he will forget that he once bore his mother's favor and pretended to be her knight, because such feats of arms are not of a kind to do her memory honor. In fact, unless he can make up his mind to rest contented with his exploits of to-day, and forego all such indulgences for the future, I think he does well to disown her now."

Garth made no reply, except by the changes in his eyes, and a sort of inward movement of the lips, as if something were speaking within him. At length his mother bade him come and kiss her, which he did in so humble and penitent a manner that his father smiled. But when the boy had gone to bed, and Martha had gently upbraided the paternal severity which, she averred, had almost broken their son's heart, Cuthbert passed his slender hand through his soft grayish hair with something like a sigh.

"Perhaps, after all, nothing less than heart-break will save him. The old fellow meant something by that kiss he gave you, however.—Cotton, tell me something!"

She looked up.

"About Miss Margaret Danver. Do you suppose her indignation at Mr. Kineo's indiscreet statements proceeded from precisely the same ground as Garth's?"

"We don't know what Sam said," replied Mrs. Urmson, after some consideration.

"True. I forgot that! Well, Garth is a more attractive young gentleman than I had supposed. I should have pitched on Mr. Kineo as likely to be the favored man in this case—judging from my knowledge of the lady."

"How could she help loving Garth best?" returned tender Cotton Martha, with a mother's serene arrogance; and Cuthbert only arched his eyebrow.

BOOK III.

GROPING.

CHAPTER XIV.

ANTAGONISMS.

WHEN Sam had recovered from his bruises sufficiently to allow of his putting a decent face on the world, he went to Newburyport, where Mr. Urmson had obtained him an eligible situation. Garth had expected that his adversary would have honorably acknowledged the wrong to Madge of which he had been guilty, and would have bidden him a friendly farewell. But Sam, if he had any confessions to make, chose not to make them; so the breach between the two remained unhealed.

During the next year or two, Garth grew in more ways than one. It was his anomalous period; the child character was dissolving, and the elements were reforming into youthhood. He was unlike both his earlier and his later self; his manner was restless, his moods unequal, and he had occasional fits of something like talkativeness. Having cast off his faëric accoutrements, he was trying to accustom himself to the homespun of every-day humanity, and to determine his use and place in the real world.

The tendency to universal investigation is a perilous one; but Garth had a foreboding that he would one day be wiser than now, and hence he often suspended his judgment and bided his time, lest his future should ridicule his present. Yet he laid valiantly about him on all sides to find his own, and it was often amusing to observe in what incongruous directions his groping energies were put forth.

Besides a new diligence in book-learning (though he had the air of studying his lessons less for their intrinsic sake than in the hope of their opening up some hidden process or suggestion), he was zealous in chopping wood, digging potatoes, skating, riding, and canoeing; and he developed a fresh critical interest in flowers and forests, hills, streams, and clouds, until it seemed likely he might turn out a naturalist. Again, one of his main occupations during several months was housekeeping; and Urmhurst had seldom seen brighter days than under his administration.

Having learned from his mother the what and how of his duties, he thereafter did them with such conscientious vigor that they seemed to have never been done before. The steel knives looked like silver; pots, pans, and crockery, glistened and sparkled, and were never broken. The black oaken floors and wainscot, the brass candle-brackets, the huge andirons, the legs of the tables, and the runnels of the chairs, all shone beneath his potent rub. In the kitchen, Garth wore a white-paper cap and an apron, and rolled up his sleeves to the elbow. The dough which he kneaded rose up like Samson in the night, lifting the kneading-board on its white shoulders. The meat was roasted with all the warmth of his heart. Though his cookery was rather whimsical at first, it rapidly improved, until its worst fault was its lack of economy. While there still appeared to be a great deal to learn in the way of household lore, Garth pursued it unremittingly; but, once he had got the upper hand of it, its attractions began to pall upon him. Fortunately, his engagement as chief cook and housemaid had never been looked upon as other than a temporary affair—a means of filling the gap between the defection of one servant and the installation of another; so that, by the time he had exhausted the novelty of the experience, a successor was at hand to relieve him.

His intellectual diversions lasted him better; books enticed him by failing to satisfy him; but, after all, it was only in wooing Nature that he found both gratification and incitement. His lofty ambitions charmed his mother and amused his father; boundless were the worth and wisdom whereto he proposed to attain. About this time he got hold of the Bible, and read it through with reverential avidity. His mother, indeed, had instructed him in the psalms and gospels from as far back as he could remember; but he had listened rather to her tones than to what she said, and had been more impressed by the acknowledged solemnity of the hour than by the sacred teachings themselves. Now, for the first time, he approached the book independently, and drew his own conclusions from what he read. Probably they were unorthodox; and an experience of his, about this time, at the village meeting house, would seem to have confirmed him in his nonconformity. The boy had never yet been to church, his father always declining to force his will in the matter, and Garth being daunted at the idea of

facing a congregation. However, his grandfather at length gained his ear, and bellowed into it to such good effect that Garth was presently as eager as he had before been reluctant to sit in a pew, and on the following Sunday morning he accordingly took his place in one, and awaited what might happen in hushed expectation.

His notions of worship having always been associated with privacy, he was at first somewhat abashed by the openness of everything. How could he be expected to unfold his heart to the Lord with fifty or sixty people looking on? Just as he had made up his mind that the place he was then in must be a sort of antechamber, whence he would presently be admitted to some hallowed inner tabernacle, the white-headed pastor uprose tower-like in the pulpit, and, to Garth's amazement, began to rumble forth a prayer! Glancing hastily around, he saw that the congregation had hidden its face in its hands—a gesture which he attributed to their shame at the poor minister's irreverent conduct. No one interfered to stop him, however, and the prayer went on, Garth blushing anew at each fresh invocation. This ordeal over, a short pause ensued, and the neophyte observed a general coughing, rustling, and brandishing of handkerchiefs—efforts on the part of the scandalized hearers to recover their equanimity. But now the hoary offender rose again, to all appearance still unabashed, and proceeded to read a hymn, the sing-song piety of which was in as bad taste as the prayer, though on other accounts less offensive. It will scarcely be credited, but the assemblage, instead of signifying their disapproval by a unanimous sigh, or even by an eloquent silence, rose with one accord to their feet, and sang aloud to the accompaniment of music the very words that Parson Graeme had just read. After this rude shock, Garth began to realize into how ill a place he had fallen. He was solitary in the midst of a callous and unsympathetic crowd, and had the pain of being at odds with them, without the power of believing himself in the wrong.

It was a long session for him; even the physical discomfort of the narrow seat became almost intolerable. The sermon was a revelation, though not in the sense that its author intended. It was one of the parson's best, and probably the spectacle of Garth's emotion, which was manifest enough in its effects if not in its causes, spurred the wretched man to unwonted exertions. With the lusty good-fellowship of long familiarity, the worthy preacher rang the changes upon the Divine name, and critically interpreted the Divine acts and purposes. Garth was visited to his depths with the hot glow of shame, sorrow, and indignation. He dared not own even to himself his opinion of his grandfather; and knew not what to think of a congregation which could not only unresistingly endure this indecent profanation, but in several instances (or else Garth's eyes and ears deceived him) could go to sleep in the midst of it! For a moment, the boy mistrusted and abhorred his kind; and as for his grandfather, he intended to have an interview with him after service was over, and urge him to abandon the ministerial calling at once and forever.

Fortunately, however, the meeting was prevented. Madge Danver joined her young lover at the door of the meeting-house, and he, anxious to gain her sympathetic hearing for his wrongs, walked away with her to the rocky margin of the stream, and there spent a somewhat unsatisfactory hour in her company.

It was about the middle of March; the snows had been melted by a week of warm rain; the trees were already beginning to put forth small greenish-brown buds; the earth was moist and spongy, and the river was swollen beyond precedent, and rushed in tumultuous rapids over its headlong bed. The point at which the young people had stationed themselves was considerably above the lake-level, and the descent thither was in several places very abrupt. The stream, in fact, was a succession of low waterfalls alternating with irregular inclines; it turned two or three mill-wheels above the town, but for the last four miles of its course it ran unimpeded. During the dry months this portion of it was useful only from an æsthetic point of view, being highly picturesque; in the season of spring freshets the wood-cutters sometimes floated logs down

to the lake; but the rapids were at all times considered impassable by the skillfulest canoe.

On the banks half a mile below the village was a small shed, rudely constructed of four uprights and a thatching of twigs and bark. Here Garth, during the last few weeks, had been building a birch canoe, and had succeeded remarkably well in combining strength with lightness in its construction. It now lay on the stocks, complete save for a few ornamental additions. The youth and maiden, whose steps had insensibly brought them hither, had seated themselves by mutual consent upon the prostrate trunk of a hemlock near the shed.

"How shall you get the canoe to the lake, Garth?" the maiden inquired.

"Carry it on my head — it's light enough."

"If I were a man," she rejoined, glancing at him from the corner of her dark, provoking eye, "I would make it carry me!"

"It's well you are not a man: for man or woman either couldn't take a canoe down those rapids in a freshet like this."

"An Indian could do it, though! That Indian, long ago—when your first ancestor came over here—he did it. Do you believe that story, Mr. Garth?"

"If he believed he could do it, I believe he may have done it," answered the youth after a pause. "But I thought that was a private family tradition of ours, Madge. How came you to know of it?"

"Oh," said she, turning her head sideways and smiling, "the descendant of that Indian told me. But, no doubt, as you say, there was never a white man who could have done such a thing. Indians are more reckless and daring."

To this assertion Garth made no rejoinder, and a silence fell between the two. At length Madge jumped up impatiently, and declared that she was going home. Garth also rose mechanically, and prepared to accompany her.

"No—no!" she exclaimed, shaking her head waywardly; "no, I won't have you!"

"Why not?"

"Because—because you have been very disagreeable this afternoon, and you don't love me. And you wouldn't care if you never saw me again." She looked full at him as she said these words; as if watching their effect. Garth met her eyes with such an impetuous glance, that they wavered.

"Would you care, then?" she asked, moving a chip of birch-bark about with the point of one little shoe.

"I care too much!" exclaimed Garth, with vehemence. "I sometimes think I would rather be what you like than what —than what I ought to be!"

"What ought you to be?" demanded she, pouting.

"I ought to be what God likes!" said Garth, reddening up to his hair.

Madge averted her face, and shrugged her pretty shoulders. "Oh, well, if God doesn't like you to love me, of course that ends it. I think you might have told me before!"

"Do you misunderstand me on purpose?" exclaimed Garth, putting his hands behind him and clinching them together. "I meant, that you often seem to like me most when I am least what I care to be. And I don't know what to do."

"I think you'd better say good-by to me," returned Madge, stealing another look at him. "You will be happier not to see me again."

Garth struggled with his temper for a moment and forced it down, but his voice shook a little as he said: "Don't speak so, Madge. Do you wish to quarrel? it has seemed so, lately, and to-day you have done nothing but make fun of me for what I said about going to church. Forgive me for answering you so roughly!"

"Oh, I don't mind that, you foolish boy!" she replied, half relentingly. "I like you to be rough and savage—in the right sort of way! But it's so tiresome to have you always thinking about what your highest vocation is, and all that sort of thing. If you'd only just be strong and—and terrible, like some great hero!"

Garth kept his eyes fixed gloomily upon her, and shook his head, but answered nothing.

"Well, I'm going," she said, after a pause, beginning to move away. At the

distance of about a dozen paces, she turned and looked at him once more; he still stood in the same position, with his hands behind him.

"Good-by, Garth!" she called, in a tone of mingled reproach and affectionate regret. "Good-by, my Garth!" and she kissed her hand to him.

"Shall I come with you?" he said, advancing; but she motioned him back with the same hand she had just kissed to him. Nevertheless, he came close up to her, and saw that her eyes had tears in them.

"O Madge, forgive me!" he repeated, very remorsefully. "What shall I do?"

"No, no, it is all my fault," she said, brushing her tears lightly away and smiling. "I don't know myself what I want, and it's no matter. You mustn't mind all the nonsense I talk. Good-by!" She hesitated, glancing at him sidelong. "Tell me, Garth, what would you say, really, if you were never to see me again—if I were to run away or something, and never come back?"

"I should say it was my fault, I suppose," replied he, smiling also, though by no means with an air of being amused.

The answer did not seem to please Madge; she tossed her head, and muttered something to herself, and again walked away. Just before passing out of sight, however, she threw a parting glance over her shoulder. Garth had gone back to the hemlock-log, and was sitting upon it with his head resting on his hands.

"He won't care!" the girl said, half aloud; and she caught her breath with a sob as she hastened along beneath the trees.

CHAPTER XV.

A NARROW ESCAPE.

GARTH staid by the little shed for a long time, in a state of moody dissatisfaction with himself and the world. It was now about eighteen months since the memorable night of his battle with Sam Kineo, and during this time he and Madge had had several misunderstandings, more or less similar to the one which had just taken place.

Madge had grown more rapidly than Garth, and, though she was still early in her teens, she might almost have been called a young woman. Her beauty had now a distinct and definite character, and outdid even its childish promise. That so much feminine charm should be cooped up in an out-of-the-way village like Urmsworth, was an injustice to mankind, to which Madge herself, perhaps, was not altogether insensible. She had ambitions beyond her present lot, which occasionally made her restive and capricious, and almost ready to prefer an exciting and adventurous adversity to a commonplace and uneventful prosperity.

She and Garth had never been formally betrothed. Not that parental obduracy distinctly stood in the way; but Mr. Urmson had put it to them with winning gravity, whether, before settling their destiny beyond recall, it were not well to wait until a somewhat wider experience should render their choice a finer mutual compliment. Garth was captured by this logic, which suggested opportunities for self-sacrifice, for which (perhaps believing them to be of rare occurrence in this happy world) he had a lusty appetite. Madge likewise acquiesced, though whether on the same grounds as her lover did not appear. At all events, the sequel seemed to prove her better qualified than he to endure the freedom of the probation.

Indeed, Garth was not entirely responsible for the uneasiness which possessed him; Madge, in one way or another, fomented his disquietude. She wished him to be a hero, and heroism was his aim too; but their conceptions of the heroic not happening to agree, her influence rather agitated than directed him. It was not his seasons of mental exaltation that most impressed her; but when he was physically aroused—when, perchance, she had tempted him to an outbreak of glowing wrath—then would she rejoicingly tremble and deem him a man of men. On the other hand, Garth's early training, as well as his innate morality, bade him keep down the very phase of his nature which Madge aimed to stimulate. She was, in a sense, the embodiment of those tendencies against which his higher traits were

embattled. Perhaps neither of them saw their mutual position in this light; but its effect upon Garth must be to endanger the hardly-raised barriers of self-control.

Such spiritual turmoils in a person whose physical constitution was singularly healthy and robust often led him to put his nerves and muscles to a strain, by way of recovering his moral equanimity. It was a natural instinct, the slighting of which might have occasioned trouble of a more serious kind than would follow upon its indulgence. The feats of strength and daring which he achieved at such times would have made him the talk of the neighborhood, only that he never spoke of them, and, indeed, set no value upon them, save as they cleared his inward sky. Even Madge seldom found them out, though, had he realized how much they elevated him in her estimation, he might have waxed more communicative.

Madge was hungry for sensation; she wanted continual evidence that her lover was better than any other girl's, and, unless she got this, was prone to become intractable and coquettish. To-day she had been especially trying, and, had Garth been of a jealous disposition, he might have found warrant in some of her broken hints for grave anxiety. His unsuspicious temper saved him from this; but he began to foresee one of his hair-brained escapades, and was ready to improve the first opportunity that presented itself.

After a long fit of musing, the boy arose and sauntered along the moist wood-paths to Urmhurst, where he ate a cold dinner with philosophic indifference. His father purposely abstained from questioning him about his church adventure of the morning; but at last Garth said, leaning back in his chair and clutching the thick hair on either side of his head:

"Church is not good for me."

"What was the sermon about, my dear?" asked Mrs. Urmson from the window-seat.

Garth's only reply was a solemn shake of the head. Then, addressing his father:

"You never go to church."

"I heard all your grandfather's sermons when I was a boy, and can preach them now to myself."

Garth fell into a brown study; but finally emerged to inquire:

"Is there no way of going to church alone?"

"Why?" returned Mr. Urmson.

"Going to the meeting-house does not make me feel at church. But last winter I skated alone on the lake at night, and I came to a thin place where the water was deep. The ice broke behind me as I passed over it. Then—all at once—I felt as I thought I was to feel this morning. I understood all sorts of beautiful and holy things, and everything seemed to mean—it was like that nineteenth Psalm you taught me, mamma!"

Here Garth stopped abruptly; the silence that ensued appeared to reveal to him his unwonted garrulity, and, coloring uncomfortably, he got up and left the room.

"To think of the dear child having been alone on the thin ice at night! What if he had fallen in and been drowned!" exclaimed Martha, with a shudder.

Cuthbert laughed in his ambiguous, unexpected fashion.

"It's the thought of poor grandpapa that troubles me. His ill-success with Garth will make him prematurely aged."

"Garth is very strange at times. Sometimes I almost think I hardly understand him myself! And, think! my husband," continued Martha, laying her knitting on her lap, "he won't be a child much longer. It makes me feel old to remember it!"

The eyes of husband and wife met, and each realized, for the first time, perhaps, that the other's hair was getting gray. She was fifty, he fifty-five. They had wedded at middle-age, but with young hearts, and their love remaining youthful they had taken small heed of time. Cuthbert, who, as a boy, had been delicate, and had returned from his prolonged foreign tour only partly restored, showed more signs of age in his slightly bent and attenuated figure than in his face; which had an inward kindliness and serenity of expression that half neutralized the testimony of wrinkles and of grizzled locks. Martha was more bounteously made than her husband; she was a sane, quiet, wholesome soul, with dark, level eyebrows, and a tender, motherly,

comely countenance. She had mellowed rather than aged with time; yet the immaculate whiteness of her cap presented yearly less and less contrast to the smooth hair below it, and there was a growing dimness in her eyesight that told of spectacles not far off. Cuthbert's gray eyes still retained nearly the brilliancy of youth; and, perhaps, in spite of appearances, his hold on life was stronger than Martha's.

"Yes; it's time we stopped playing at being old people," said he, with the musing half-smile that was wont to curl up one corner of his mouth. "Let us in future lay aside disguise, and be the children that we are. How else can we have the face to put down in Garth his insolent assumption of being over sixteen years old?"

Cuthbert, in some of his moods, had always been an agreeable mystery to his wife; and she now resumed her knitting with no other answer than a smile.

"Cotton," began he again, looking fixedly at the page of his book, "Miss Danver will soon be of marriageable age."

"But Garth will not, for several years," returned Mrs. Urmson, somewhat eagerly.

"Why, then—poor Margaret!"

"But you know the children are not engaged, my dear." Here Mrs. Urmson shifted her needles. "Madge is very pretty, and always seems sweet, though somehow I can't feel as if I were thoroughly acquainted with her yet." Mrs. Urmson knitted a row in silence, and then added: "Not that I think she'd be likely to change her mind, of course!"

"Why, then—poor Sam Kinco!" said Cuthbert, laughing.

Mrs. Urmson dropped her knitting. "Has he come back?" she cried.

"Not that I know of. Oh, what a sphinx you are, Cotton! You never say half you mean. Do you think, then, that Garth had better go through college before making a Mrs. Garth?"

"Oh—college? But, my dear, have we thought of college before?"

"Why, to be sure; I don't remember our having spoken of it till now. But, as I was saying, there is no telling what you may be thinking about until you choose to open your lips! We'll mention the matter to Garth to-morrow."

"Garth in college—dear me! But perhaps, after all, it may be best," murmured Martha, over her rhythmic needles. Cuthbert smiled apart to his book, and for the present the subject dropped.

Meanwhile the youth in question went early to bed. But at midnight he arose, and let himself quietly out of his bedroom-window. The round moon, looking freshly issued from some celestial mint, rode above the thin black arms of the naked trees, and the gloomy masses of the pines. There was no wind; nothing seemed to move save Garth and his shadow. These two traveled along in company, occasionally losing each other in dark places, but always together in the moonlight. Proceeding swiftly, they were soon on the bank of the stream, at the shed where the canoe lay. Having slipped off his shoes and his shirt, Garth carried the canoe to the water's edge, and set it in the water below a projection of the bank, where an eddy set back against the stream. Then he stepped lightly into the round aperture amidships, grasped the paddle, and in another moment was away! The wind of his going blew his hair backward. The canoe seemed to be snatched onward by invisible hands.

A few yards ahead the uprooted stump of a great tree was sweeping along, rolling over and over, whirling round and round, and tossing its black, knotted roots toward the quiet moon like a drowning hobgoblin. Garth, in its wake, sat like an ivory statue, bending a little forward, the paddle dividing the water behind like a fish's tail. To himself he appeared stationary, while the world was in mad race and whirl around him: only the moon and he stood still. Of a sudden a glistening crest of rock seemed to rush toward him through the foam, to dash him in pieces; now it swerved dizzily from his path, and shot by him with a hiss. But the great stump had thrown out a twisted arm, which caught the rock for a moment—long enough for the canoe to get abreast of it; and then the two flew downward side by side. After a perilous minute the stump crashed into the branches of a fallen tree which lay half across the stream, and, before

it could disengage itself, the canoe was in advance. Thenceforward Garth heard the unseen monster splashing and rushing close astern.

Though keeping his eyes unswervingly to the front, he was observant of everything. He felt transcendently awake; every faculty was full of life and quietly in tune. The rush and tumult brought him repose, and he was stronger for the power that seemed to threaten him. He was not at the mercy of the waters, but they bore him as slaves their master. The river ran as he pleased. His apparent peril was but proof of his power. The boy felt no hurry of excitement, no confused throbbing of brain or tremor of muscle. He marked the white clots of foam that slowly fell behind him; the spinning eddies crossed without diverting his course. He was conscious of the reeling banks, their blackness cloven here and there by gleams of moonlight. The night air through which he dived downward smote cool on his naked breast, even as the water against the birchen bows of his canoe. His shadow rested palpitating on the boiling current to the right. He was at one with Nature, and therefore safe; a human being, and therefore above security. He was inwardly tickled with spiritual laughter; he sat at ease, while the earth buzzed for him like a top! Down—plunging downward through the ghostly forest, leaping unknown falls, slipping swallow-like athwart whizzing rapids! During the glancing ten minutes of his three-mile journey, Garth drank so deep a draught of the vigorous splendor of existence as sweetened and elated him for many a day thereafter.

Near the mouth of the stream, where it hurled itself into the lake, rose a rocky eminence crowned with hemlocks. It commanded a view of the latter half-mile or so of the rapids, and was nearly on a line with the last and deepest of the falls. At the moment when Garth, rounding the bend above, entered this stretch, two persons were standing on the eminence beneath the shadow of the trees.

"Look! look!" exclaimed one, catching her companion by the arm and pointing up the stream. "He has done it!"

Onward swept the slender canoe, now eclipsed in shadow, now leaping into moonlight which gleamed white on the arms and shoulders of its rider. As he came near, his face was distinctly visible. It wore an expression of composure which its youthfulness made impressive.

"I knew it was he; he is beautiful!" murmured the female voice again, excitedly.

"He'll be drowned—you see!" returned the other in a surly tone. "He'll never get over this fall alive!"

"He will! He can do what no one else does. And if he does do it—"

"What then, eh?"

"Then you may go to Europe alone. There will be no one like him in the whole world."

"You go with me if he gets drowned?"

"Yes!"

As she spoke, the canoe was within thirty yards of the verge of the fall. Her companion sprang suddenly forward, his breath drawn for a shout. But before he could utter it, the girl had wound one arm round his throat, and was pressing the other hand over his mouth. The cry was not entirely smothered, however; it reached the boatman's ears just as he balanced on the critical edge, half in water and half in air. It turned his glance aside a hair's-breadth, and the paddle swerved likewise. The canoe leaped the fall a trifle aslant, plunged, and emerged half full of water.

Recovering his balance, Garth hurtled onward in a half-sinking condition, and realizing for the first time through what deadly peril he had passed. He was jostled off the peak of exaltation, and was at commonplace once more. He knew nothing of the event that had broken the spell; but looking back upon his wild voyage, he knew that in a thousand trials he would never again accomplish so desperate a feat. Meanwhile, he had reached the lake, and, paddling hastily shoreward, foundered in shallow water. Leaping out, he drew the canoe to the sandy beach, emptied it of water, and then, resuming his seat, paddled quietly round the point out of sight.

The girl drew a long breath, and leaned her shoulder against the stem of one of the pines. But, after a short interval, she again stood erect and looked at her companion.

"You must go, you see," she said. "Get into your boat and row away. You might have known how it would be; I like him best; I always did. I shall stay with him. I shall never find a man equal to him, and I don't mean to try."

There was an ugly gleam in the eyes of the tall, dark-visaged youth that boded the girl no good.

"Do you know I could kill you where you stand?" said he. He stepped close up to her. She laughed in his face.

"You will never kill me; you are too much in love with me. You had better go, sir, or I shall hate you."

The other bit his nails and seemed to hesitate a moment or two. "If I didn't know you better'n you know yourself," he said at last, "I would kill you, love or not! But I know I'll get you some time. We'll see—we'll see! I'll get you at last, 'nd then you'll say you were a fool to-night. Oh, well, good-by now! But I know you better'n you know yourself."

CHAPTER XVI.

GETTING TO WORK.

GARTH showed the next morning a bearing so much more cheerful than that of the previous afternoon that his mother congratulated him on the improvement, and asked him what pleasant dreams had visited him during the night. But the young fellow, besides his aversion to rehearsing his own exploits, knew that to tell his mother what he had done would be to give her a fright which the sight of the narrator himself, devouring a huge plate of buckwheat-cakes, would only partially allay. Accordingly, he was resolved to say nothing about his late voyage, and it might never have become history but for Madge. This young person came up to Urmhurst during the afternoon in company with Parson Graeme, whose favorite parishioner she was; and when Garth and she were alone together she chanced, by an apparently accidental allusion, to lead up to the subject of the canoe; and thereupon was presently elicited the whole marvelous tale.

"You didn't see anything—not meet any one—not see any one, I mean?" asked she, after listening restlessly and with many sidelong glances till the end.

Garth shook his head; but, after a minute's reflection he said: "After I'd stowed the canoe away, and was just starting home, I thought I saw a boat far out upon the lake. But the moon dazzled so on the water that I may have been mistaken."

"Yes, or maybe the boat sunk!" exclaimed Madge, a sudden light coming forth in her face, and giving it a more vivid beauty. Then she laughed and said: "You strange boy! why didn't you tell me yesterday that you meant to do it?"

"I didn't think of it till after you went home."

"If I'd known you were going to do it, I'd have staid with you, and not have plagued you so. Well, now I mean to tell everybody."

"Pshaw! don't," said Garth, turning red.

"Now, listen to me," she said, taking hold of a button of his coat, and looking gravely up in his face. "What's the use of doing fine things if nobody's to hear about them? If you were the greatest man in the world, and never told of it, how could I be proud of you? Why, it's better to be over-estimated than under-estimated, you silly Garth! You don't know what you may lose by always holding your tongue."

"Nothing worth having!" answered Garth, intractably.

"That's very rude and unkind! So I'm nothing worth having, am I?"

"My dear, I love you," returned he, with a more manly earnestness than she had ever known in him before. "You speak without thinking. Yesterday you half made me think you had stopped caring for me."

"My Garth, you know I always loved you," she whispered in his ear, feeling very truthful and melting. She liked him to overbear her. "You don't know how much I have—would do for your sake, Garth."

"You could not do more than love me,"

answered he, and the observation was a just one. They kissed each other very tenderly, and then went into the room where the grown-up people were sitting.

"Here he is!" thundered the mighty parson.—"Come here, grandson. We've got a proposition to make to you. Now, what have you got to say to it? For of course, according to your good father's usual style, it's to be left to your own option to take it or leave it."

Garth was standing with his back against the door, hand-in-hand with Madge, and facing the company. As his grandfather spoke, the color mounted slowly to his face, and his eyes sought those of his mother first, and then his father's.

"What is it?" demanded he.

"Nothing very terrible, old gentleman," said his father, with a smile. "We were only wondering whether your worship would condescend to go to college next autumn."

"College?" repeated Garth, in an inward tone. He felt Madge's hand tighten on his own, and, looking round at her, caught a sparkle from her dark eyes. Evidently she was pleased with the idea: and, after Garth's less rapid mind had contemplated the prospect for a minute or two, he also began to kindle at it. He threw back his shoulders and respired a mightier atmosphere. College meant learning — scholarship — experience; the means of becoming wiser and better than he was. He had yearned already to get beyond his immediate horizon, and had even envied Sam Kineo his opportunities of becoming acquainted with the world.

"Do you wish to leave us, my child?" asked his mother, with a slight tremor of sadness in her voice, in spite of her effort to make it cheerful.

"I ought to go to college, mamma—I want to go!" answered he, eagerly. In the first glow of feeling he could not anticipate homesickness; much less enter into the misgivings of a mother's heart.

"Oh, yes, I think it will be splendid," Madge exclaimed. "Think of his being a collegian! And all great people have been to college, haven't they, Mr. Graeme? At least, I'm sure you and Mr. Urmson went!"

"Come, there's a compliment for you and me, son-in-law, eh? haw, haw, haw! —Well, well, Miss Maggie, if you're in favor of it, I guess that would be enough to settle Garth, even if he were less ready than he appears to be; ha! ha! ha! So that's all fixed, and I'm glad of it.—Shake hands, Garth, my lad; may the Lord bless and keep you!"

"Amen!" whispered Mrs. Urmson, with tears in her eyes, and a smile of love on her lips. Garth kissed her cheek, but he was too much of a man now to hug her, as he longed to do, before company. His father said:

"For my part, I shall be very glad to get rid of him. Four years of peace and quiet are not to be despised at my time of life.—I suppose your worship won't think of coming home in the vacations?"

"O Mr. Urmson! he must come back in the holidays," exclaimed Madge, so naively that no one could help thinking her charming. "And not having seen each other for such long whiles will make the meetings pleasanter," she said, with a foresight remarkable in so inexperienced a young lady. It made Garth feel a little uncomfortable, and he looked her honestly in the face; but all he could see there was a wondrous harmony of curves and colors. He sighed—a boy's sigh—for which he would have been puzzled to give a reason.

"But you're forgetting one thing, Miss Maggie," boomed forth the parson again, with elephantine playfulness; "the best thing of all—love-letters!—Ah! Garth, you rascal, you'd thought of it, I'll be bound! eh? the best thing of all—eh? ha! ha!"

Garth, thus rallied, turned an ingenuous red, while his beautiful little mistress's oval eyes sparkled in arch acknowledgment of the patriarch's refined humor. She had the self-possession which is like ballast to a fair vessel, and for lack of which many a fair vessel dare not spread her sails.

"But there's one thing he'll learn to appreciate while he's away," observed Cuthbert," with a gleam of mischief in his clear face, "and that's such a sermon as he heard yesterday. He'll hardly hear such a one from the Brunswick parson in all his four years."

"True enough, son-in-law," responded the guileless Titan, sobering down again; "though it's no doubt a good man they've got there, too. But you see it takes a man who has been in his pulpit for six-and-sixty consecutive years, and never missed a Sunday—it needs a man like that to preach a sermon. Bless the lad, I saw him! He didn't know what his old grandfather could do for him—eh, Garth? There, there—never be ashamed of it! I liked to see you warm up to it, and the tears in your eyes; it showed a right heart, and a right head, too! But then even I can't promise you a sermon like that every week—no! no!"

"Garth, have you shown Miss Madge that new tulip of yours?" Cuthbert asked; and, when the two young people had gone out, he resumed: "It's just as well you cannot, parson. Garth was rather too powerfully affected by your yesterday's discourse. He's more impressible than you might suppose from the build of his chest and shoulders. So I sha'n't let you loose upon him often. By-the-by," he added, before the other had time to bring himself to bear, "what were you saying when you first came in about there having been a fire last night? Not the meeting-house, I hope?"

"Ha! Oh, no. It was my old witch's place. Old Ma'am Nikomis's wigwam."

"It happens opportunely. I engaged her long ago to come and rule our roast here, so soon as she became weary of professional witchcraft. Garth will have to give up housekeeping for study now, so the old lady will just fill his place. But I forgot to ask the particulars. Has she fallen out with the black-man, or are they plotting new deviltries? or what is the secret of the conflagration? She was not scorched herself, I trust?"

"The poor old woman," exclaimed Martha, pityingly. "I suppose she must have set herself afire with that curious tobacco-pipe of hers that she is always smoking. I hope she saved some of her belongings."

"Why, here she comes?" remarked Cuthbert, who was seated in the embrasure of the southwestern window; "and, apparently, the bulk of her goods and chattels are in that bag on her back. She has saved her collection of scalps among other things, and has got them festooned around her person. Well, since adversity has at last brought her to her friends, I'll step out and welcome her home."

Accordingly, they all three sallied forth, and stood on the cloven threshold, awaiting the old squaw's approach. She was a grim-looking Indian, somewhat stunted of stature, with broad, high cheekbones, and narrow black eyes. Ugly and stolid though her outside aspect was, a keen observer might have detected signs of sagacity and purpose beneath it.

When she had come within a few paces of the porch she halted—a wild and savage figure enough, with her grizzled black hair hanging round her shoulders, her beaded and blanketed costume, her dangling scalps, and her bag of household goods slung across her back. She fastened her eyes first on the parson, and then on Mrs. Urmson; and, finally, without making any gesture of greeting, but with the air of some grotesque sovereign announcing herself to her vassals, she spoke in a harsh, guttural tone to Cuthbert.

"Nikomis a-come!" said she.

"You are welcome," replied Cuthbert; "we were expecting·you. Come in!"

"Come in, ma'am!" vociferated the gigantic parson, swinging his arm. "You're lucky to get into such good quarters, I can tell you!"

Nikomis paid no heed to this observation, unless it were to assume a yet more haughty bearing than at first. But, after a pause, she pointed to the cleft in the threshold, and shook her head.

"Nikomis not come this side," grunted she, "other side—other door!"

"She's heard the legend, probably," said Cuthbert to the minister, in a low voice," "and is superstitious about walking over gravestones.—Let me conduct you to the kitchen-door, madam," he added, aloud. "So long as you are content not to leave Urmhurst, you have your choice of entrances."

Nikomis nodded assent, and followed him round the house. On the kitchen-door-step were seated Madge and Garth in close confabulation. Garth rose in surprise, but

Madge started up manifestly disconcerted—as became a.young woman.caught in a tender predicament. The Indian stopped short, and eyed her in silence.

"I—thought I might meet you," said the girl, rapidly recovering herself. "You must let me come and see you some time. I could not help it!"

"Nikomis is your successor, Garth," said his father, at the same moment. "You are deposed; surrender your keys, and march!"

"We must be friends though, Nikomis," said the youth, holding out his hand with a smile; for, since his fight with Sam, the old squaw had seemed to cherish some resentment toward him, and he wished to improve this opportunity for reconciliation. The Indian, however, either did not understand the Christian practice of hand-shaking, or else was averse from friendly overtures; at all events, she passed in through the kitchen-door without appearing to notice Garth at all; and, during many months thereafter, she hardly vouchsafed a word to him.

"She is clean, and perfectly upright, I think," kind Mrs. Urmson would say of her strange domestic. "I only wish she wouldn't smoke that pipe while she is cooking dinner. But she cooks some things very well—especially vegetables and soups."

"Witches have always been renowned for their broth, you know," Cuthbert would answer. "But what captivates me is her authoritative bearing. She is absolute, and yet makes no fuss about it. I feel like a tenant, the recipient of her bounty. I am continually grateful at not getting notice to quit. I believe, Cotton, I should have been a happier man if you had always bullied me!"

"I shall have time now to knit Garth enough socks and mittens to last him all through college," would be Mrs. Urmson's conclusion.

Cuthbert was, in the old-fashioned sense, a humorist, and took pleasure in doing kind things which brought him neither fame nor profit. Nikomis was treated with consideration, and paid good wages, which she was never known to spend. By day she brooded much in the chimney-corner, sending puffs of tobacco-smoke up the wide flue along with the savor of roast-meat. At night she mounted to the garret, a compartment of which she had fitted up in wigwam fashion; but what she did there it would be rash to affirm. During several years following her domestication at Urmhurst, only one person was suspected of having visited her in her den, and that one was Madge Danver. But Madge was discreet, and, if she was made privy to aught strange or unlawful, had the wisdom to say nothing about it.

CHAPTER XVII.

ANOTHER ATTIC MYSTERY.

GARTH prepared for the college examination under the tuition of his father; he always got his lessons, but at the cost of much unnecessary labor. He could not learn things by rote, nor profit by the use of rules and formulas which he had not worked out for himself. He was better at classics than at mathematics, but could not be accounted great in either. He would sigh, and stretch his arms over his books, and twist his hair into a matted tangle, and anon would set-to afresh with stern, immitigable brow. Then a sudden burst of sunshine, or a bird-song, or a humming-bird at the lilies in his window, would sorely try his resolution.

Yet it was the methodism of books, rather than their intrinsic contents, that annoyed him. His mind did not lack capacity, but flowed not easily in the mould of other men's. His free habits, and a way his father had of making him answer his own questions, had given him independence, but, at the same time, hindered facility. Ladders only embarrassed him; he would prefer to climb the tree of knowledge as he had climbed the chestnut at the picnic.

Though he had plenty to do, Garth contrived to reserve the evening and the earliest morning to himself. The former hours he spent in society—that is to say, in the company of Madge, of his parents, and of the parson. His relations with his father had entered upon a new phase of late. The spontaneous confidences of childhood had ceased, and the youth, sensible of inward changes, whose nature and purport he did not wholly comprehend, had spun himself an instinctive cocoon of reserve, which the elder religiously respected. But, after a while, Garth began to discover that he remained essentially the same fellow, notwithstanding his development, and yearned for a wiser intimacy. Perhaps he doubted, at first, whether his father could any longer serve him as counselor and guide; persons at Garth's time of life being apt to think that their problems would puzzle anybody. Nevertheless, when Cuthbert still made shift to at least discuss such abstruse matters intelligently, the son would secretly marvel at the possible extent of human knowledge and experience!

Madge often accompanied the old minister to Urmhurst, and was charming there. Her mother was an invalid, her father overfond of Bourbon whiskey, and neither could be good company for a maiden so full of life, freshness, and innocence, as was their daughter. She had already graduated with distinction at the village school, and, most of the housework being done by a charwoman, her time was largely at her own disposal. Physically speaking, she would have been an ornament to any community, and, to all appearance, she was as good as she was beautiful; though, no doubt, there may have been certain narrow-minded persons in the village who entertained an 'unreasonable prejudice against her. But the parson was always her champion.

"Look how cheerful and steady she is!" he would bellow out. "Any other girl in her shoes would mope or get into mischief. Ay, there are gossips about; and, if they were in their pews as regularly as my Maggie, I guess I'd read them a lesson!"

"She is, indeed, of a happy temperament," Cuthbert would reply. "And she has too much self-respect to dismiss that charwoman as an unnecessary expense, and injure her hands, temper, and sensibilities, by doing the work herself."

"Well, son-in-law," said the parson, profoundly, "there are folks in this world who just seem made to make other folks happy by looking happy and pretty themselves. That's their work, and they're not called on to do any other."

"Oh! if only I had been born pretty and happy," sighed Cuthbert, "how I would have beatified mankind!"

In spite of his irony, however, he was, perhaps, almost as much captivated by Madge as the venerable minister himself. This ironical habit of his was mainly intellectual, often, no doubt, mechanical. His heart must not seldom have protested against the saturnine judgments of his brain.

Moreover, as regarded the Danvers, they were not too poor to afford the charwoman; and this was a fact which Cuthbert, who had latterly been intrusted with the care of their "estate," must have known. One of Mr. Danver's old, half-forgotten patents seemed all at once to have acquired new life, and now brought in a yearly sum of money that made the family income more than sufficient for their bare necessities. That they should lay up anything was not to be expected; nor was it reasonable that Madge, Garth's wife that was to be, should be asked to perform manual labor so long as it was possible for her to avoid it. Mr. Urmson's aspersions were uncalled for. He might be very learned and clever, and he was popularly believed to be very wealthy; and, if wealthy, then certainly he was economical, almost to the verge of stinginess. But America was a free country, and neither Mr. Urmson nor anybody else had any call to put on airs. Such, at least, was the opinion of the Urmsworthies, those of them who were wont to settle the affairs of the world at the corner grocery, between the hours of seven and nine every evening. And thus it may be seen that the master of Urmhurst, like other men of mark before and since, was not honored as a prophet in his own country.

Let us return to Garth, whose morning hours have yet to be accounted for. When the sun rose clear, he generally took his pleasure out-of-doors; but in inclement weather the garret was his customary retreat. He had a den there, in the northeast corner, which was kept even more strictly private than Nikomis's in the northwest;

not Madge herself could guess the secret of it. Garth would enter this den stealthily, locking the door behind him, and for two or three hours there would be neither sign nor sound of him. At length he would emerge, flushed with what might have been either shame or exaltation, and come down to breakfast.

Yet Garth was not naturally prone to concealment, and we can only suppose that he was indulging some fond weakness or other, which, though unworthy of him, had insinuated its roots so deeply into his affections as hardly to be denied. Such indulgences conceal themselves by instinct, and a more subtle person than Garth would have veiled even the fact that there was anything to veil. But he was frank in the midst of his reticence. Perhaps he relied on years to help him outgrow his folly, whatever it was. As the last weeks of his home-life slipped by, however, these solitary hours seemed to become more than ever precious to him. He would watch the sun set and rise with an eager look, as though there were to be no such things in college. His early love of the beautiful forms and colors of the world took on a kind of forlorn ardor, and he laid much to heart a sage remark of his grandfather's, that "boys never learned anything by doing what they liked!"

"I like to look at your face," he said to Madge, "and yet I learn something from it."

"What can my face teach you, I'd like to know?" returned she, not displeased.

"Oh!" said he, vaguely, and drove his heel into the log that smouldered on the hearth. It was a habit of his to answer inconvenient questions with that monosyllable.

"There is not much more time left for it to teach you anything," she resumed, unwilling to let so pretty a topic drop.

Garth sighed, and clutched his hair musingly.

"I wish I could have my picture painted for you," she remarked, presently.

"No, no!" he exclaimed, with energy, adding in a lower tone: "God made you; what man has a right to imitate your beauty?"

"Well, you are in a mood for compliments to-day, sir!" cried Madge, fairly flushing with pleasure.

"It is no compliment to say God made you, Madge," returned he, gravely. "But painting is irreverent."

"Irreverent? You strange boy! Why, Roman Catholics have pictures of God, and the Virgin, and Christ, and angels and saints —my father has told me of them. And I would like to have my portrait painted a hundred times. Wouldn't you paint me if you knew how?"

Garth kicked the log into a blaze. "I'm afraid I would!" he said, between his teeth.

"Oh, it would be lovely!" cried she, resting her folded hands on her lap and gazing wide-eyed into the flame. "Your painting it, I mean!"

He moved his shoulders impulsively, and presently said, "It might not be wrong for Catholics; but I'm a Puritan!"

"Then you might become a Catholic, I think—just long enough to paint me!" she answered with a laugh. "Now, tell me, Garth, have you never done what was a little wrong, because it was also very agreeable?"

"Yes!"

"Dear me, you needn't look so ashamed. For my part I think things are all the more delightful for being a little—"

She finished the sentence with an arch suggestive movement of the head and hand.

"You have felt it too!" ejaculated Garth, with a sort of dismay.

"Yes, my dear Garth, and so did Adam and Eve; and I'm sure I don't care to be better than they. But you are so funny!"

Hereupon Garth lapsed into a brown study that put an end to the conversation. But, from that hour, he abstained from his attic diversions; locking up his den, and putting the key in his pocket. His forbearance tried him severely, though he still admitted no one to his confidence. He studied more rigorously than ever, but with less cheerfulness. His manner became moody and apathetic; and, in short, if he had anticipated finding virtue its own reward, he was tempted to think that virtue was satisfied with very little.

CHAPTER XVIII.

AN EXPLANATION.

It was not often that Urmsworth sent a student to the university, and, for two or three weeks prior to Garth's departure, he was a prominent personage in the village, and Madge Danver loved him all the better for being so. A few days before the last, Mr. Urmson and the parson, assisted by half a dozen old examination papers, put the young candidate to a very searching test of his proficiency. He acquitted himself so well that his grandfather gave him a sort of preparatory blessing—a foretaste of the grand final one which he was to take with him to Bowdoin. That evening, after Garth had gone to his chamber and was pacing up and down the floor with his hands behind him, his father knocked and came in.

"Well, beloved Hottentot!" was his greeting, "are you sleepy?"

"Not a bit!"

"Nor I; but I thought that a little talk with an expectant freshman would probably make me so. Well—are you as glad to leave us as your mother and Miss Madge are to be rid of you?"

Garth's only response was a somewhat sorry smile.

"And what do you mean to do in college? Shall you stand in the first ten? or shall you do what you will find many of the pleasantest fellows doing—see life? that is, scrape an acquaintance with the devil?"

Garth thumped his foot against the trunk upon which he was sitting, and answered dejectedly that he didn't think he should do much, either good or bad.

"You know, old gentleman," continued his father, "that I have never interfered with your inalienable Yankee independence much, and I sha'n't begin now. But there is one point in which I shall have to impose a restraint upon you, and that is, your expenditure. I shall give you all the money there is to give, but you will often wish you had more than I can send you."

"We are poor, then?"

"I believe our neighbors think otherwise, and it's true that your grandfather,

Captain Brian, left a good deal of money. But all of it cannot be said to belong to us, exactly."

"Whose is it?"

Mr. Urmson picked up a window-stick, and with his penknife, which he always kept very sharp, he began to whittle, in smooth, slow strokes, as if the stick represented the topic he was about to discuss.

"You know, Captain Urmson, your grandfather, married twice. I was the only child of his first marriage. His second wedding came twenty years after his first; Eve and Golightley were born in the two following years, and Mrs. Urmson, never recovering from her second confinement, died within the year after Golightley's birth. The captain idolized Eve, as you have often heard; but he and Golightley could never hit it off together. Golightley was always as filial as pie; but he was rather a sickly youth, and not very robust in character. As he grew older he became rather a sentimentalist, and was apt to wax eloquent about æsthetic culture, and the True, and the Beautiful, and the Good; the captain called it all damned nonsense."

"What did you call it, father?" demanded Garth.

"I only heard of it afterward: I was in Europe then—went the same year Eve was lost, and only came back ten years afterward. I think your grandfather was harsh and unjust; but he had never been used to hide his opinions or pick his words. Well, when I was in London, shortly before my return home, I happened to win the very good will of a banker there, a ridiculously wealthy fellow; he offered to take me into his office, and put me in the way of making a fortune. I preferred to see old Urmhurst again; but I told him about my half-brother, and was allowed to accept the position in his behalf. When I got home and told him of it, he was delighted; as he expressed it, he had 'thirsted for Europe all his life.' So then your grandfather— Are you interested?"

Garth clumped an affirmative heel against his trunk, and Mr. Urmson, curling off a dexterous shaving, continued:

"The captain made no objections; but

he remarked that, since he would probably never see us both together again, he would read us his will. I expected to get the house and land, and supposed Golightley would have the ready money and securities. The value of the estate—the whole property—amounted to about one hundred thousand dollars. Of this the captain had bequeathed to Golightley ten thousand dollars, and the remaining nine-tenths, including Urmhurst, he had given wholly to me."

"Hullo! You didn't like that, did you?" said Garth, sympathetically.

"How do you know I didn't, sir? At all events, the captain would hear of no alteration then. He read a codicil to the will, however, providing for the chance of Eve's ever being found, or any descendants of hers in the first generation. In that case Urmhurst and fifty thousand dollars were to be given up to them.

"When the reading was over, Golightley declared himself perfectly satisfied, and said he cared not for money, but for beauty; and that as for Urmhurst, had it fallen to his share, he would have wished to be rid of it; for he could not bear to be tied down even in thought to one particular spot of earth. And no doubt," observed Mr. Urmson, arching his eyebrows, "your uncle was in earnest. I give you his words, so that you may draw your own conclusions. But he did not reflect how much beauty costs nowadays. If the world had only been arranged as he wished it, I dare say he would never have soiled his fingers with such dross as dollars and cents.

"He went to England," continued Mr. Urmson, whittling away at his window-stick, "with his two thousand pounds, and I married your mother. He wrote to me twice within the first six months; he had been well received by the banker; declared himself positively depressed by the prospect of vast wealth that loomed inevitably before him; envied me the philosophic calm that could endure riches, and looked forward with longing to the time when he might disburden himself of his own in my favor."

"Generous, wasn't he!" muttered Garth, with a glow of appreciation.

"I think he has always loved the beauty

of disinterested behavior; but inexperienced young fellows such as he was then are apt to take offense at the practical obstacles in the way of virtue. His second letter mentioned ill health, and talked of a vacation in Greece or Italy. Four months later came a third letter addressed to the captain. I never saw its contents, but they produced a violent effect upon your grandfather.

"He locked himself into his room and would admit no one for nearly twenty-four hours. We could hear him tramping up and down the floor and talking to himself. Once in a while he gave way to fits of rage—stamped on the floor till the house shook, and roared out oaths which, I presume, used to do duty aboard his privateer during the Revolution. At last he came out haggard and grim, with a sealed letter addressed to your uncle in his hand."

"Why did I never hear all this before?" demanded Garth, with a long sigh of interest, as his father paused to pare off a particularly thin shaving.

"Well, you are going to be a man on your own account now, and so are bound to hear of whatever concerns the family. But you will have to rely on your own ingenuity to explain some of the things that I shall tell you—at least I can't help you. But about this letter—I afterward had reason to believe that it contained a large draft in Golightley's favor. It was about two months after this that your grandfather died. The night before his death—he seemed as well as usual or better—he called me to his room, the same we are in now, and began talking about his second marriage. His wife, as you know, was a Golightley, and it appeared that he had met her in Virginia so long ago as 1781. He had landed at Jamestown after an unsuccessful cruise, at the time when Arnold and Cornwallis were ravaging the country. He organized a band of guerrillas, his lieutenant being a brother of Maud Golightley's, named Rupert, and their headquarters were at the Golightley mansion.

"Your grandfather had landed under an assumed name—John Dane—and he kept it carefully all through. He and Rupert became great friends. Maud, he soon learned, was betrothed to a cousin, who was also a Golightley. Nevertheless, she fell in love with John Dane, who, I imagine, was a splendid-looking fellow in those days—he was then about twenty-three. I don't know precisely the succession of events after this affair (which of course was a profound secret between the lovers), but at any rate there was suddenly a violent quarrel between your grandfather and Rupert—who had, perhaps, fancied some insult to his sister from something he may have seen—and the Southerner insisted upon a duel. So out they went—it was after dusk—to a plantation of trees near the house. Your grandfather told me that he shut his eyes when he fired, but that didn't prevent his shooting Rupert dead with that old pistol hanging over the fireplace."

Here Mr. Urmson pointed to the ungainly weapon with his window-stick, and Garth stared with awe at the antique relic which had rested in its place ever since he could remember. It had killed a man!

"When he had got to this point in his story," Mr. Urmson resumed, "your grandfather paused so long that I thought he was not going to tell any more. But at length he went on to say that the report of the pistol not only carried death to his friend, but seemed to have called into life a hundred enemies. In truth, the men had actually fought their duel in the midst of an ambuscade of the English, planned to sack the house. The concealed troops had witnessed the duel, and now rushed forward to take prisoner the survivor. But he so desperately laid about him with his clubbed pistol, that the redcoats had to shoot at him; a musket-ball grazed his temple and knocked him senseless, and, after he had fallen, he received a bayonet-wound in the leg. They left him for dead, and when, some hours later, he and Rupert were found lying side by side, they were supposed to have fallen like brothers-in-arms, fighting against a common enemy. Your grandfather with difficulty revived, and was told that the house had been sacked, and that Maud Golightley had been shot, whether accidentally by the enemy or by her own hand to escape violence was not known. He dragged himself, in agony of mind and body, to the house, and searched it from top to bottom. There were some relics of Maud in her chamber, but of her not a vestige. They had left him not even her body. He told me that in the midst of his agony he yelled for joy to think she would never know he had slain her brother. . . . How now, beloved Hottentot!"

Mr. Urmson had a marvelous voice, absolutely controlled by a highly-sensitive and delicate mental organization; humor, pathos, or appeal, came in a manner transfigured from his lips. But to-night, gradually kindled by his story to a mood he seldom suffered himself to attain, the flexible melody of his low-spoken words had filled the scope of else ineffable emotion. It had been too much for Garth's youthful imagination, apart from his being a descendant of the chief actor in the event. His heart was melted within him, picturing forth afresh the anguish which had passed long ago.

CHAPTER XIX.

GOLIGHTLEY.

"I suppose you think," remarked his father, after a pause, recurring to his ordinary tone, "that all this is a subterfuge of mine for letting you know why you won't have enough pocket-money in college. It is a roundabout explanation, I admit; but still it consists, as I will show you." He resumed his knife, which had dropped idle during the last few minutes, and, applying it to the other end of his stick, continued: "Your grandfather made his way to Jamestown, and reëmbarked there, leaving behind him (as he afterward discovered) not only a living and uninjured Maud, but a circumstantial account, which reached her ears, of his own death. She married her cousin a year or two afterward, and they had a daughter, who, if she be living, must be about my own age. I suppose she yielded to this marriage in the indifference of despair; besides, her husband was wealthy, and could afford her any kind of diversion. This, at all events, was your grandfather's

subsequent understanding of the matter, though he did not so account for his own marriage with my mother, which took place about the same time. Mrs. Golightley's husband did not live long, and the widow and her daughter remained together until the daughter was married, at the age of seventeen. It must have been about this time that Mrs. Golightley happened to hear that your grandfather was still living, and conceived the rather incautious purpose—though it seems to have been in keeping with her general character—to disappear from her own place and friends and hunt him up."

"Did she go without their knowing?" demanded the absorbed hearer.

"So it appears. She had already settled the bulk of the fortune left by her husband on her married daughter, and she came North alone and secretly—so secretly, indeed, that her friends believed she had been the victim of foul play. Luckily for her, she found your grandfather a widower, and disposed to marry her, even after nearly twenty years. I must confess, however, that the story has always seemed to me incomplete, and I think there must have been circumstances which have never come out. With all allowance for my step-mother's romantic flightiness, I cannot understand her abandoning the home of a lifetime merely on the chance that a man whom she had known but for two or three months in her girlhood, and had not heard of since, would be in a condition or a mind to become her husband. However, so it turned out."

"Did she know, then, that his name was Brian Urmson, not John Dane?"

"Yes, he had confided that secret to her. And, by-the-way, that episode brings to light a curious historical coincidence. Our old English ancestor, Neil Urmson, whose steel head-piece you used to wear, was in his boyhood on terms of friendship with a certain Reginald Golightley, son of the Golightleys of Hertfordshire. When the civil war broke out, they took opposite sides, still, however, remaining personal friends. But they quarreled about a woman, and after that they used the great war as a means to glut their private hatred. At last they met in the battle of Naseby, and our ancestor vanquished his enemy, and made him prisoner. He forced him to accompany him to the English Urmhurst, and there witness his marriage to this woman—who was no other than the Eleanor who afterward came with her husband to New England. Well, in the midst of the marriage-service, Reginald, breaking loose in his fury from the men who held him, snatched a battle-axe from one of them, and aimed a blow at Neil's head.. Neil had just time to interpose his pistol, which broke the force of the stroke and saved his life; nevertheless, the blade reached his chin, and almost cleft it asunder. Then Neil, with the blood streaming over his breast, leveled his pistol, and fired through Reginald's heart. Was not that an unceremonious manner of treating his groomsman? The scar of Reginald's blow Neil carried to his grave; not only that, but his son was born with it, and it has appeared occasionally in the family ever since. Yes, that is the history of the cleft in your chin."

Impelled by a sudden interest, such as he had never before felt, in his own countenance, Garth walked across the room and examined his reflection in the mirror with a kind of respectful curiosity, while his father, a half-smile curling one corner of his mouth, went on with his whittling.

"But are these Virginia Golightleys of the same family as Reginald?" inquired the youth, on returning to his trunk.

"They are descendants of Reginald's younger brother, who emigrated to Jamestown in 1648 or thereabouts; and the pistol, of course, is the same old pistol all through. Now, when your grandfather landed in Jamestown a hundred and thirty years afterward, and met Rupert Golightley and his beautiful sister, he probably thought he could not do better than keep his *incognito;* he had enough of a lover's cunning to see that it would be more than likely to prejudice Maud against him. However, when he was sure of her love, he avowed himself to her; but poor Rupert died in ignorance that the man who slew him was his hereditary enemy.

"Now we get back more to our own times. There can be no doubt that your grandfather was extravagantly fond of his

second wife, and one cause of his harshness to Golightley was that the boy had been the death of his mother, as the captain put it. Understanding all this as I did—and the captain made no concealment of it—I was puzzled by his final words to me, in this room, on that night before his death. He began abruptly to speak of Golightley, and of the letter he had lately received from him, and which, he said, he had destroyed. I asked him whether he would tell me its contents; he answered between his teeth, 'No! not if I'm damned for it!' which was only his way of saying 'No!' 'But I didn't manage right about the will,' he said; 'if Maud had been alive, she'd have had it different, no doubt. After all, he's her son, if he did kill her. I'm no friend of his, Cuthbert—you know it; but I should have made the will different. You can't bury the devil; he'll crop up somewhere! We must give him more money if he wants it—do you hear me?—we must give him more money. I didn't do right; I didn't—damn me!'

"I said, 'I shall be glad to have the will altered; but, from what Golightley wrote to me, I thought he needed nothing less than money.'

"'I won't alter the will!' he shouted out, stamping on the floor; 'I say I won't alter it. He may die before I do—who knows? sickly young dog! Ah, if Eve would come back, that would settle him! Need money? You'll see he needs it! and we must give it him—do you hear me?—and if I die first, you must send him what he asks for, send it without a word. No, I won't alter the will; I won't—damn me!'

"'But in that case,' said I, 'I won't let Golightley or any one else bully me into giving up what is mine. You shall give me some reason, sir.'

"At that the old soldier burst into tears. I was very much moved, Garth. I had not supposed he felt so much. I had seen him weep only twice before—once when Maud died, and again when Eve was lost. His sobs shook him terribly, my dear old father! He said: 'Don't cross me, boy—don't cross an old wretch like me. I love you, Cuthbert—I loved Maud; I ask you to give her son whatever he may ask of you. He may die soon—damn him, I hope he will—but don't cross me, boy! Don't ask me for reasons; I have none, sir; I have none. Ask your father for reasons? Promise me, Cuthbert—promise me, boy, that if he needs money, you'll send it without a word!'

"Said I, 'I promise it shall be as you say.' I saw that for some reason he was too much excited for any argument or question that night, and I gave him the promise, expecting to discuss the matter afresh next morning, and come to a better understanding of it. But your grandfather was dead the next morning, and who can tell what was his secret?"

"But does my uncle take advantage of such a promise—is he dishonorable?" demanded Garth, with an indignant flush.

"I fear," answered Mr. Urmson, quietly, "that wrong has been done whereby both he and we are sufferers. He cannot, I am sure, be a happy man. He has not the self-knowledge to correct his shortcomings, which are nevertheless a constant pain to him. He is always wanting to make his friends impossibly happy, yet destiny seems resolved to keep him their beneficiary."

Garth began to twist his hair reflectively. "He must be unhappy! And is he too ill to work for his own living?"

"He seems to have the malady of ill-success. He conceives vast schemes, and works at them enthusiastically for a while: they need money, but they haven't made any yet. The truth is, Garth—you are old enough to hear it now, and it is known to no one else—that your uncle has spent the greater part of our income for over fifteen years. Sometimes I have been hard put to it to make the ends meet. It is easy to consider this a hardship, and no doubt I might have derived a certain kind of satisfaction from doing so. But really, though it has probably benefited both sides, it has been much better for us than for your uncle. We have been vastly more easy than he. Your mother has had her heart's fill of knitting and darning, which wealth would have lost her. For my part, I have become quite a valued contributor to the English and American reviews, not to mention the diligence with which I have prosecuted my history.

As for you, you have learned how to sweep and cook and clean your own boots, and to plough, and to cut and pile timber, none of which things your uncle has had opportunity to learn, though affording it to you. So, under guise of being helped by us, he has been secretly doing us the greatest good."

"Ah, but he doesn't know it," said Garth, with a commiserating sigh. "If he did, he would be happier. Father, what do you think was in that letter he wrote to Captain Urmson?"

"I don't know, Garth, and I don't want to. As things are, I can love both your uncle and your grandfather. It is never wise to look too hard at our fellow-mortals. Few are entirely beautiful."

Garth immediately thought of Madge as a notable exception; but on deeper consideration he fancied his father might have intended something less obvious, and in this doubt he kept silence.

"So now," observed Mr. Urmson, whittling the perorating chip off his stick, "you know what has become of your pocket-money. Are you sleepy yet?"

"Father, are there any Golightleys living now?"

"Unless Maud Golightley's first daughter be alive, none that I know of. I believe she had another brother besides Rupert, but he must have died long ago. If he left descendants, I never heard of them."

"I hope he did; for our ancestors were always in the wrong, and if the Golightleys are dead, how can it ever be righted!"

"It might in that case be considered, at all events, settled," returned Mr. Urmson, with a smile. "But, even supposing a scion of that house alive, I don't see how he could pay off his debt of vengeance except by killing you and me with the old pistol, and eloping with Mrs. Urmson afterward. To be sure, if the descendant happened to be a daughter instead of a son, you might compound matters by— But no, on second thoughts. Well, good-night, beloved Hottentot, and good-by. I sha'n't bid you good-by again before you go; I shall leave you entirely to Miss Margaret. Think often of your mother while you are away. She will never forget you—and even I may remember you once in a while. Good-by."

They shook hands, constrained by a whimsical reserve characteristic of Yankees and Englishmen. But the next moment Garth, with a glowing impulse peculiar to the hot-hearted Urmsons, who could never be tamed to the temper of their surroundings, took his father in his stout young arms and hugged him hard. Many noble and pure pledges were given and taken in that silent embrace; and after it was over the two felt that they should sleep sound and peacefully.

CHAPTER XX.

NEWS.

AFTER two or three days of superficial hurry and bustle, oddly contrasting with an inward heavinesss and stagnation, Garth found himself established in Bowdoin College. At first sight the place impressed him as desolate, over-populated, and artificial; he fancied he never should become reconciled to it. He was continually shocked, moreover, at meeting faces wholly strange to him. Heretofore he had considered himself a stranger to many of the dwellers in Urmsworth; now first did he discover the difference between not recognizing people and not knowing them. He freshly realized the extent of his human dependence; and he could almost believe that he missed his own family less than he did those indifferent villagers.

At the moment of parting, good-by had been easily said; but afterward he perceived that his mood had been shallow, and he wished he had taken the occasion more to heart. That familiar circle at Urmhurst—how plainly it lived in his reverie! There sat his father, reading in the ancestral arm-chair, whose ponderous build contrasted quaintly with the slender proportions of the tranquil, keen, clear-visaged man. Here moved his mother, demurely cheerful, in her white cap, soft-handed, light-footed, low-voiced, with a sweet solidity of figure and aspect. Now enters the frequent parson, huge, rejoicing, with snowy summit and accents of thunder,

but bending a little of late beneath his eighty-seven stalwart years. Anon behold Madge, with her picturesque and piquant "toilets," as she styles them, her vigorous, symmetrical little figure, her slender, oval face, with its vivid hues, long, sparkling eyes, and mobile mouth; her self-possessed yet winning manners. Garth wished for her more than for the others, though whether it were because he needed her more, or because of an obscure misgiving as to whether he felt the loss of her enough, was a question which might give him pause.

By-and-by the harshness of the desolation wore away. It was consoling to find thirty or forty young fellows, his immediate associates, in no cheerfuler predicament than himself. Moreover, there was work to do, though not so much or so difficult as he had expected. The novelty of the situation, the fixed hours, the punctual bells, the rigid tutors, and the stimulus of the crowded class-room, long served to keep the son of the woods self-forgetfully surprised. At first he had stood apart by himself, in the persuasion that he was one unit and the rest of the university another, mutually repellent. Afterward he came into possession of two or three unprecedentedly sympathetic friendships, and from these advanced with naïve precipitance until he had met the whole class, man by man. They all liked him. Garth hardly understood this, or, rather, he took it for a matter of course that classmates must like each other. It was not that he was exceptionally attractive, but all the fellows were good and charming.

In fact, however, Garth was not long in becoming both distinguished and influential. As often happens, it was the oppression and insufferable arrogance of the sophomores that brought his more engaging qualities to the surface. At first his modest allowance of the superior claims of age and experience, and his cordial deference to legitimate authority, tended to put his temper in a false light. When half a dozen young gentlemen of the upper class visited his room, Garth closed his books and received his guests with respectful courtesy. He was flagrantly fresh —greener than he there was not; nevertheless, something in the set of his features, and

5

a kind of straightforward reserve in his manner, had virtue to keep the half-dozen within bounds for a while. They sounded him with fathoms of solemn fabrication, most of it time-honored stock; he listened with such grave acceptance and brief replies that they somewhat misdoubted the sincerity of his guilelessness. At length one of their number, who had an unfortunate talent for sallies of the Rabelais order, let loose a salvo, of which Garth understood enough sharply to disgust him.

He got up, with a glance at the offender of such plentiful dislike that the latter's countenance changed a little, and for a few moments there was a dramatic silence.

" I am sorry," then quoth Garth, " but you must go out."

" Hoity-toity, freshman! Keep a civil tongue for your betters, sir."

At this Garth glared round at the other faces; all seemed to support the cause of indecency. Despite his guilelessness, he was anything but thick-witted, and in a flash he saw through the sham of these tall-talking visitors, and reddened to the back of his neck with resentment. He stepped passionately to the door, hurled it open, and confronted the six—short, square, and darksome —but with a spirit in him that might have overtopped Parson Graeme's seven feet.

" Get out—all of you!" he growled, flinging back his arm toward the doorway, and imperiously stamping his foot.

Every youth rose to his feet. Some looked grave, others laboriously laughed; only the disciple of Rabelais—a youth scarce Garth's better in height, and far his inferior in brawn—fired up, and haughtily swore he would stand no insolence from a freshman. He made up to Garth, and aimed a hearty blow at him. It was partly parried, yet slightly touched the cheek. Garth's pulse beat murder once; but he had not forgotten the lesson of Sam Kineo. Suddenly griping the warlike sophomore by both arms, he faced him at short range.

" Don't fight for unclean words; they'd beat you beforehand."

Having driven this sentence into his antagonist, he loosened him; and the latter, whether admonished by the startling force

of Garth's clutch or by the solidity of his argument, did not strike again. His companions, who had hitherto looked on, apparently not unwilling to behold a fight, now espoused the cause of the invaded party.

" Better let that freshman alone, Jack Selwyn," remarked the biggest of them. " He could have shaken your head off if he'd wanted to."

" Freshy had the right of it, too," affirmed another, off-handedly. " No business to hit a fellow for not liking smut! "

" Guess we'll take our young friend's hint," exclaimed a third, cheerfully.—" Come on, men, we've plenty more calls to make this evening. By-by, Freshy; if you live long enough, you'll be a missionary and convert the heathen. Sorry we can't spend the night with you; try to some other time." Thus they filed out, peacefully enough; Selwyn last, and seemingly half inclined to stay and have it out with the grim freshman in private. But the others pulled him, laughing, away, and Garth was alone again. He too itched for battle, though in his first review of the affair he was not altogether clear whether or not he was justified in treating his guests so cavalierly. But, after lying awake all night to discuss the question, he came to the conclusion that he had not done amiss, and this honest conviction went far to soothe the sting of the blow he had received. But the restraint put on himself had wrenched his sensibilities; the unquenched embers of wrath fevered his blood. Though he might not regret his forbearance, he would shun the future exercise of so uncomfortable a virtue. Thought he: "I won't be so angry next time, no matter how much they are in the wrong; then I can fight without fear of killing them! "

This was satisfactory, and Garth attended morning recitation cheerful in the prospect of good-temperedly thrashing a sophomore ere nightfall. But he reckoned without his host. His adventure had already got wind, and he was puzzled to find himself a hero, a champion—the freshman who, single-footed, had kicked an army of tyrants out of his room.

" They went of themselves; I only told them to go," he explained to his admirers.

But his reputation was made, and the fact that the sophomores (whether by chance or design) uniformly kept out of his way confirmed it. Moreover — for college youths are especially susceptible to a vigorous example on the manly side — his classmates were inspired by his exploit to offer so intrepid a front to oppression that hazing that season had but a short and uneasy life of it.

Although this episode gave Garth a social impetus at first, its final effect was in a contrary direction. He began with opening his heart warm and wide to all comers; but he found out, earlier than most, what rare birds friends are. His circle of intimates was always contracting. He wanted his companion to be at least as fine as the landscape; and, after repeated disappointments, he became deliberately—instead of, as heretofore, involuntarily—reserved. His lovers found him on one or another ground impracticable, and gave him up. He was too quick to see that men were not pure gold, too loath to accept good working alloys. He was getting experience at once too slowly and too fast.

It is, however, noticeable (and it attracted remark at the time) that the only undergraduate with whom by the end of the year Garth distinctly fraternized was no other than the Jack Selwyn whose first interview with young Urmson had been so unpropitious. Some months after the scene in which he had played scapegoat, Selwyn renewed the acquaintance, and seemed to find his account in keeping it up. Garth, at first shy, later turned and met him half-way. So incongruous a friendship was generally ridiculed. Selwyn, who belonged to what was called the fast set, was rallied for Puritanism. Sad-browed Garth was analyzed as a secret libertine. But it may be conjectured that these diverse characters attracted each other's best side, and fattened upon mutual unlikeness. Selwyn was a fellow of fire and ability, and his eighteen years had seen a strange variety of life. He was cursed with a rakish devil which he could not control; but he had heights and lights as well as depths and blots, and the contrasts in him were picturesque. He loved Garth's pas-

sionate steadiness of character. Garth loved his swift light and shadow, his struggle, his weakness, and his well-told adventures. At all events, the friendship lasted.

Meanwhile books and recitations were not neglected. But Garth a little mystified his instructors. They were sometimes in doubt as to whether he knew more or less than was set down for him. He often seemed better versed in commentaries and parallel readings than in the lesson itself of the day. Parts of a subject would attract him, and he would follow them down to the root with curious zeal, merely skimming the surface of the rest. His translations from the classics were sometimes quaintly felicitous, though always very free and idiomatic. Algebraic generalizations were distasteful to him; he loved vivid particulars; and though the sublime developments of the higher geometry attracted him, he never could forgive the petty inductive steps which must lead him thither. He still abhorred formulas, and smacked his lips over individuality. He occasionally took strange liberties with the tutors and professors in class, but with so grave a front, and in general so aptly to the matter in hand, that they could not count it impertinence.

In fact, Garth was learning his college lessons least of all; but the black and white lore of the world was entering him at all points, and putting him in a manner beside himself. Life no longer seemed a private affair between himself and his God, but there were as many modes and opinions of life as there were men. It was amazing how widely human principles could differ! People begin with expecting harmony in those they meet, and discord is the saddest discovery. "To what end," wondered Garth, "does Omnipotence permit such a waste of force? Men thwart one another and misunderstand and run amuck, when a little economy and accord would bridge the universe."

But the young man had not the instinct of a reformer. If he preached, it was to himself, and the only affairs he undertook to regulate were his own. No doubt he believed that, as regarded fundamental moral principles, he was right, and all who disputed him were wrong. But Garth's principles had little to do with his intellect; he would never discuss a truth which he had felt—unlike Selwyn, who was for putting a why to everything. This bigotry as to the main axioms of conduct is not seldom the sign of a strong nature. It is called stupidity by volatile people, whose very sediment is stirred by all breezes. But deep-set men, whose foundations no storm can reach, who never seem to move, are the rocks whereby the world climbs upward. They play games with their intellect, but do their serious business by dint of something else.

"What are you going to be, after graduating, Urmson?" was frequently Selwyn's inquiry.

"If I knew," the other would reply, "I wouldn't wait to graduate."

"Lawyer, doctor, parson, grocer, pirate, president, gold-digger?"

Garth shook his head.

"You'd make a good pirate, if you once got started. I'd be your first-mate, and arrange the skulls and bones on the cabin-walls. Was chased by a pirate once, in the Pacific, and wished I was aboard her, with a knife between my teeth, and the devil for captain."

"It needs brains to be a devil," said Garth, "so I wouldn't do."

"Oh, wickedness sharpens the wits; it would clear you up wonderfully. The fellows say, now, that you're a good-for-nothing, lazy chap; that you're well as far as you go, but that the important cog is left out of you."

"The cog's left out," repeated Garth, abstractedly, clutching his hair.

"What do I think of you, backwoodsman? Let me smoke, and I'll tell you."

"Go ahead."

"Try a pipe yourself, Garth. Oh, very well; but you were born for a smoker, and you'll smoke yet, when your cog is in gear. That reminds me—it's not left out, only out of gear."

"That opinion isn't worth a pipe."

"I knew before that you were stupid and ill-mannered, and you don't deserve to hear it; and, if I thought you'd believe it, I wouldn't tell you. But, after all, they're said to be the unhappiest of men, as a rule,

and you'll hardly be an exception. So here goes!" said Selwyn, puffing away.

"What?"

"Hear me in all seriousness. You are a genius, my poor friend. The secret is out, Garth: you are a genius!"

"Genius for what?"

"That is your business; but you will do something as it has never been done before. Your stupidity results from unrecognized genius. Genius, my man, is a sort of magic tail, which, before you get the hang of it, trips you up, and weighs you down, and makes you disagreeable to everybody you meet. But once you learn how to wag it, and not all the kangaroos, beavers, and peacocks in creation can come near you. You understand me, of course, figuratively."

"I don't understand you at all."

"You are a genius—one of the best kind, the unconscious. There is an horizontal depression athwart the centre of your forehead. You believe in things, without arguing, more potently than I can after being logically convinced. You are not only an individual, but a unique; nothing comes out of you or goes into you the same as with other people. Now I'm a man of talent, the reverse of a unique. I see and do things in the hackneyed old ways, only better than most people. I can do a lot of things better than you can do anything—except that one thing you have a genius for. In short, your immediate ancestor was Adam, or Noah, or the archangel Gabriel—some one of those primal fellows; whereas I am what is called a supreme product of civilization. D'ye see?"

"When did you make this discovery?"

"When I punched your head, six months ago. D—— you, Garth Urmson, how you did hold on to me! When I was sixteen, in Madrid, and was in the midst of a flirtation (one of my first serious ones) with a fair señorita—well, one night the other fellow—there always is another fellow in Spain—jumped out at me with his knife. He pricked me in the arm the first thing, and afterward in the hip; but I wasn't a bit afraid of him, but sailed in and half killed him. Till you took hold of me that night I never was afraid of anything—do you hear? But when you set that infernal black face of yours in front of me, I felt as if I were melted sealing-wax, and you had stamped your own ugly features on me for a seal. It was horrible. There was nothing of me left in me, but I seemed changed into you; and still there was enough of me left to be frightened. I didn't get over it for days; I was always running to the looking-glass to see whether it was your head or mine that was on my shoulders."

"Well, Selwyn!"

"Do you suppose if you hadn't been a regular primeval devil, or angel, or whatever else you choose to call a genius, that I wouldn't have broken loose and thrashed you, if you'd been ten times as strong? But I saw your horns and tail, and your heavenly pinions, and I had to give in. I knew you then."

"Then why don't I know me?" demanded Garth, getting up with glowing eyes, and his hair on end.

"Because there's too much for a boy of your age to know. You'd run away with yourself, and tear yourself to pieces. Wait till you're old enough."

"Selwyn — you're in earnest?" said Garth, breathing deeply.

"Yes, by God, I am!"

"Genius!" continued the other, walking up and down the room in a kind of restrained tumult. "I have felt sometimes as though I—no, as though the earth were my body, and I saw through it, and lived through it, and understood it, just as I do my human body. It never lasted but a few minutes, but then I was as strong as the whole world, and as happy as heaven."

Selwyn smoked in silence.

"If that could last!" said Garth, stopping, and doubling his fists at his sides—"but afterward I'm as lazy and shapeless as a bag of sand. But if that was genius, I'll question it next time! All I thought was to enjoy it. But genius for what?"

"You seem to think," returned Selwyn, on being thus vehemently addressed, "that because I've given you a glimpse of your hidden treasure, I'm bound to tell you what you'll spend it for. What the devil is that to me? If you could benefit me with it, 'twould be another matter. But if you had

the genius of Solomon and Raphael and Praxiteles, all rolled into one, it would never benefit any one but yourself. No man ever helped another yet — not even helped to damn him! We're made selfish, and we're never so selfish as when we try to be generous. Good joke, isn't it? Ha! ha! ha!"

Garth looked with curious compassion at his friend, whose cynical outbursts were not unfamiliar to him, but neither smiled nor answered.

"A sensible fellow I am, to care for you," resumed Selwyn, amid his smoke; "tossing up my cap, and giving three cheers for your genius, and you can't wait for the words to be out of my mouth before you want to be off enjoying yourself with it. I wish I'd kept it to myself; I wish I could prevent your ever finding out what it's for; I wish you were as good-for-nothing a fool as I am, and then we might have some good times together. No, on second thoughts, I take it all back. If I could tell you what your vocation was to be, you should know before this pipe went out. I wish you did know it. The day you do, you see the last of Jack Selwyn."

"Where do you mean to go?"

"Oh, Heaven preserve me from a man wedded to his genius! I hope you don't propose committing bigamy with any innocent young woman? Yes, whenever you discover what you are made for, let me know. I know the kind of friend a man of genius wants, and I'm not one of that kind. No!"

"If you mean to hint that I could become so taken up in any pursuit as to slight you or any one I love, either you don't know what genius is, or I haven't any," growled Garth, in indignation. "I won't talk about it any more. We've said too much about it already. I feel little enough like a genius now."

"Well, slit my tongue, Garth, or, better still, cut my throat. Did you ever hear of such a sentimental, gushing young thing as I am? But, Garth, I swear by you, or, rather, whatever name I take in vain, it will never be yours. Good-night, old genius! Ah, you may turn out a great man, and I may kowtow to you, but you'll never be

great enough to do one thing, kotow or not
—save me from going to the devil! Ha!
ha! ha! Good-by."

CHAPTER XXI.

THIS conversation did Garth no ostensible good; he became graver and more
preoccupied than ever. The glimpse of hidden treasure which Selwyn had given him
seemed rather to bewilder than to enrich
him. He wandered about with a sprig of
witch-hazel, exploring his mind for what
might lie buried in it.

His searches resulted as most such
searches do. He discovered nothing, and
began to more than suspect that there was
nothing to discover. Meantime, his hours
and days were slipping into nothingness.
He could almost wish, like Selwyn, that he
had been an acknowledged fool, if so he
might be happier.

"I am an impostor, deceiving even myself," he would sometimes think.

Howbeit, the deception was often wondrous subtile. What was this power, this
clearness and facility, that ever and anon
surged and lived within him? Was it singular or common? Did everybody see and
feel what he sometimes saw and felt? At
all events, he knew no one who could reply
to him in such moods; indeed, there was no
one to whom he felt it possible adequately
to express himself. But, if his riches could
not be used and profited by, were they not
a misfortune? A genius who could make
his genius of no avail was especially pitiable.
Nevertheless, Garth could not wholly resign
himself to being commonplace.

He saw the world under two alternate
and strongly-contrasted aspects. Now, it
glowed and throbbed with color and rhythm.
It gleamed and floated, too rich and poetic
to be solid reality. These tints, and forms,
and motions, were beautiful, not in themselves, but by dint of transcendent significances shining through—significances which
trembled on the verge of expression. Could
they be expressed? If so, how blessed their

interpreter! The universe would flow and
be plastic in his hands; he could shape its
sublime generalities into lovely and wise
particulars; he could bring the ends of the
earth together, and cause them to enhance
each other's beauty. His abstracts would
suggest the truth of the whole, and bring it
to common recognition; and upon each abstract, each particular, would be stamped
the seal of his individual mind and nature,
lending to the wild page of Nature a human
interest which should endear it to men's
hearts. Yes, the great invisible world of
men and things was the security of an infinite treasure which it was the lot of the
chosen seer to take and spend for the weal
of humankind.

More often, however, the world wore a
less promising appearance. It was solid and
superficial: nothing short of a pickaxe or
chisel could discover an interior. It was
wonderfully painted, modeled, and arranged;
but with a little more skill and knowledge,
man might produce something nearly as
good. It had no meaning, except utility or
inconvenience. Its closest relation to man
was a chemical one. It was a monument
of divine power; but the human race was
only accidentally associated with it, and
might just as well have been anywhere else.
Creation was arbitrary, and it was an idle
vision, that of a comprehensive and logical
necessity pervading all.

"It is better to be an amateur than in
earnest," Selwyn would assert. "Whoever
tries to take such a stupendous joke as this
world is seriously, gets crucified for his
pains. Besides, it isn't dignified."

"At all events," growled Garth, after a
silence, "I shall worship the God who suffers from every doubt and evil impulse that
I feel, and fights against them with me, and
whom I crucify every time I reject his help.
Not such a God as you talk about—who
creates arbitrarily, and enjoys formal superstitious flattery, and can sit idle while I am
sinning and struggling and dying down
here."

Selwyn stared in surprise.

"I have my deaf and blind times," the
other went on, still eying his companion:
"I'm that way to-day, and the world seems

dead and dumb. But when I feel alive and clear, so seems the world too. It follows my good or bad humor. It is bound up with me, somehow; and if there is a God, he is bound up with me; at any rate, if he is not bound up in me, there is no Christ, who is the only God worth talking about."

"Well, Master Urmson, I have sometimes suspected my own orthodoxy; but what to call you— Do you know you have a way of staring me straight in the face? It's devilish disagreeable, and I wish you'd stop it."

"I wasn't thinking of your face: it's a handsome one, but too pale. Your hair curves about prettily, and has the right shade of brown, but it's soft as a woman's. However, it matches well enough with that straight, delicate nose of yours, and with—"

"Your genius is not for badinage, decidedly; you remind me of a dancing bear I used to know in Tyrol. By-the-way, have you found out yet what it *is* for?"

"Dancing, I suppose. Oh, my genius! Selwyn, if the universe is a joke, and God an experimenter, what is genius?"

"Ha! ha! ha! I don't think you can be responsible for your utterances to-day. If you were not Garth, I should fancy you'd had too much gin!"

"I don't know what you are laughing at," said Garth, rather grimly. "Genius is getting at God's meaning; but if he means what you say, the fewer geniuses there are the better. Are you a humbug, after all? What you say doesn't hold together. If you are only playing at skepticism, it's poor play, I think."

"Upon my word you are getting rather personal," exclaimed Selwyn, somewhat hotly.

"Oh, forget your person for a few minutes. Well, I beg your pardon. Do you remember hinting some time ago that when I found my vocation I might slight my friends? The danger seems more likely to come from my not finding it. I grow more disagreeable to myself and to you every day. Most of the tutors hate the sight of me. I've a mind to go before the mast. I can be a sailor, at all events."

"I am an effeminate brute, sure enough, to be angry with you, you dear old curmud-

geon. If you go before the mast, I'll go with you: I've seen a little of that life, already, you know. But that's nonsense. Why don't you write Milton, or paint Michael Angelo, or preach St. Paul? That's the sort of thing you are up to, if you only knew it."

"Painter!" cried Garth, raising himself from his chair, and reddening.

"What are you in a rage about? Yes, now I think of it, I shouldn't wonder if painting was your line. You'd be a sort of Beethoven of the easel."

Garth walked several times up and down the small dingy room, scowling at the carpet, and doubling and undoubling his fists. At length he stopped in front of Selwyn, and spoke with unusually bitter energy.

"If you knew what a time I've had for years past! When I was a child, with no thought of right and wrong, I was ashamed of it; afterward I began to see it for what it was, but the temptation was so strong that half the time I gave in to it. I used to sneak off to that room in the garret. I can't understand it! In what seem my best moments I feel the temptation strongest, and I'm never so happy as while I am yielding. Since I've been here, and have had no chance, I've been wretched."

"What has this to do with being a painter?"

"I believe Satan was the first painter. The Lord had given him power and insight —the noblest weapons—and he turned them against him, to mock him and parody his works. Those great painters, honored as they are, were either miserably weak or wicked. They used their genius to degrade this God-created world to their own level. Men praise them because such degradation flatters their vanity. I have the best right to call them contemptible. The better they paint, the worse they are. I believe they are less able or less daring now; but those old painters used to—Selwyn, they used to paint God himself and angels. It was blasphemy!"

"And beautiful blasphemy some of it was. I saw a big blasphemy in Rome, called the 'Transfiguration,' done by a famous devil of the name of Raphael. He and others have painted crowds of Virgins and saints, most of which are prayed to in churches. Oh, the works of the devil are all the rage in Europe, I assure you. And the best of it is they are called divinely inspired. But see here, Garth, I shall pull as long a face as your own for a few moments, and ask you some serious questions. You are the most perverse idiot for a genius that I ever heard of. Do you mean to say that you've ever painted anything?"

"I did what I could," replied the other, gloomily, resuming his seat. "I had no knowledge nor materials to speak of; only the desire."

"Did you ever see a famous picture?" Garth shook his head. "Nor ever mean to. It's enough to have heard of them—and I've seen copies of some in books."

"What a delicate moralist you are, to be sure! What does your father say on the subject?"

"I never spoke to him about it; never to any one except—"

"That was selfish of you; for you only being right, and all the rest of the world wrong, you ought to make converts and preach a crusade. Tell me one thing, is it as wicked to draw *Pons Asinorum* on the blackboard as to paint the 'Transfiguration?'"

"If I could jest about this, I should be yet more contemptible than I am. I've been thinking it over lately, and may as well face the truth now as later: my genius, if I have genius—at any rate, the strongest bent of my faculties and impulses—is to be a painter. I'm that or nothing; an intellectual pauper, or rich on devil's wages. Now you know why I'm ill-humored. I don't see why I was created fit only for an ill purpose. It makes me doubt. I'd better go to sea, as my forefathers did."

Here followed a pause of some length, both young men looking a good deal out of sorts. At last Selwyn broke out, smiting his hands against the arms of his chair:

"This is the most absurd tragedy I ever heard of. Shall I laugh or cry? What is the use of my talking? No one can confute you better than yourself. Your skepticism is so monstrous and irrational, it will end in

making me a credulous bigot. Garth, tell me one thing, did you ever fall in love?"

"Do you— Yes, I—"

"Oh, don't blush; you're no worse than the rest of us. But see here, did you go smash at the first look, or did you hold back at first, and only give in afterward?"

"I believe that was—but—"

"Ha! and when you'd given in, didn't you love her most for the very things you'd found most fault with at first? Didn't you?"

"Perhaps. You seem to know all about it—but—"

"There! Yes, I do know my alphabet, and part of yours into the bargain; and that's more knowledge than you can lay claim to, with all your genius. Don't you see how it is? Painting is your mistress, and you're madly in love with her—so much so that the mere thought of her makes you an irrational fool. You are bound to her, soul and body, so of course you can't hear argument or talk sense about her. She attracts you so that you mistake your *vis inertiæ* for repulsion, and babble what you fancy is abuse, but what wise men know to be abject love-talk. Blasphemy, forsooth! Painting is your mistress, and when you are come to years of discretion, if you don't marry her, and eat your blackguard words in dust and ashes—if you don't— Damn, there goes the bell! and my rhetoric all unlearned."

"You have your rhetoric by heart," muttered Garth, as his friend slammed the door and was gone; and he sat scowling at the carpet and scorning to be cajoled by words. Nevertheless, he presently discovered some abatement in his ill-humor. It was a satisfaction to have recognized the truth about himself, and to have spoken it out, once for all. Selwyn had ridiculed him, which was foolish in Selwyn; but it showed, at least, that the matter could be honestly regarded from two sides. He would gladly believe that those arch-sinners, Raphael, Titian, and the rest, were honest too. But that was not possible—hardly possible. Whoever had felt the temptation rage within him must have had insight to divine its impiety. Pictures could not be painted by fools, nor in fits of abstraction.

No, Selwyn was a better rhetorician than logician. What arguments had he used? Not one! only adduced illustrations, and forced ones at that. Indeed, what arguments on his side of the question were there? But why talk of argument? Argument about a matter such as this was out of place, undignified. The truth must be felt intuitively, and there an end. The only puzzle was, that the truth was not as manifest to the rest of the world as to Garth; whereas, as Selwyn had said, Garth stood alone. Could there be anything in the suggestion that one's very partiality to a thing might blind him to its merits? It had been so in the case of Madge, to be sure; but this was a moral, not a personal, question.

It here struck Garth as an odd coincidence that Madge (to whom only beside Selwyn he had mentioned painting) should have agreed with Selwyn in approving it. What if others—what if his father—were to do the same? Was any individual safe in setting his intuitive sentiment above the verdict of history and of his contemporaries? Might not one be too closely concerned in such verdict to feel intuitively at all, especially if he were a new-made collegian with little knowledge and less experience?

But now he drew himself up and sternly questioned his integrity. If incompetent to decide against his desires, much less dare he favor them. No majority of voices could make wrong right; while, on the other hand, his very unfamiliarity with current opinion might enhance the worth of his judgment. Moreover, Garth had a potent belief in his own sanity. On a matter of such large moment as this, juggling with syllogisms was out of place. A spontaneous conviction could be attacked only by another as spontaneous. It seemed most honorable not to think about the subject more than he could help. If his present position was just, time would confirm it; if not, time would bring the deeper insight to undermine it. Though this might seem an unpromising conclusion, it left Garth less heavy-hearted than of late, and disposed to question whether all of life lay between the horns of a dilemma.

CHAPTER XXII.

ARGUMENT.

MEANWHILE, in furtherance of his purpose to banish the matter from his thoughts, he strove doggedly to fill himself with study. His freshman year was nearly done; but he had already resolved to spend the summer vacation at the college. Perhaps, in thinking of home, the garret-chamber stood out too prominently, and he shunned putting his resolution to the test too soon. Moreover, home-ties having been cut, he may have wished the wound thoroughly to heal before returning. He had proved himself a better correspondent than might have been expected, addressing most of his letters to his mother, who, for her part, replied with sweet motherly phrases and inquiries and hopes and fears, one letter being nearly a repetition of the rest, and the dearer to Garth on that account. His father's injunction to think often of his mother might have been spared. He felt nearer to her than before their separation, and loved her more intelligently since learning something of the unloveliness of the outer world.

His correspondence with Madge was of a more fitful and less satisfactory sort. In the first place, he was at a loss what to write to her. A mere account of his haps and mishaps—though, no doubt, Madge would have found it acceptable enough—seemed to Garth too slight a theme, while he found huge difficulty in composing an ideal love-letter; for to soar to the ideal was to lose sight of Madge, and to keep her steadily in view was to miss the ideal. So, albeit he spent much more time and pains over his letters to her than on those to his mother, he did not like them nearly so well when they were done.

Madge, for her part, was punctual in her answers; but these did little to relieve Garth of his embarrassment. His mother's epistles, unstudied and simple though they were, seemed almost to hold her living image in every sentence; but Madge's rather obscured than brought her before him; he could not reconcile her written with her visible self. He thought she did herself injustice, was ignorant of her worth, and translated herself from a divinity into something approaching the commonplace. In herself he knew her to be only too captivating, but he fancied he could never have fallen in love with her through the post.

Meanwhile the fault was not in Madge's letters, but in her lover's unreasonable standard. There was no contradiction between what she wrote and herself; but Garth had never sufficiently separated his mind her appearance from her character. It is the misfortune of very beautiful persons that they are open to invidious comparisons between their outside and their inside. Nor did he sufficiently consider the necessary effect of her confined position upon her alert and ambitious spirit. Village born and bred, but with a disposition whose restlessness was calculated for a much wider sphere, she had dreamed from childhood of the pride and splendor of the outer world. And now that Garth had made his first step into this unknown and fascinating region, she constituted him her proxy, and expected him not only to take an interest in all that would have interested her, but to send her vivid and enthusiastic accounts thereof. She imagined him consorting with the dignitaries of the earth; engaging in an endless series of parties, receptions, picnics, and other dissipations; the companion of brilliant, wise, and witty men, and (which often prompted her to outbursts of fantastic and far-fetched jealousy) of lovely and aristocratic women. Endless was her curiosity on all social subjects; and despite continual betrayals of ignorance on Garth's part, both implicit and explicit, she could never bring herself to believe that he was really living the secluded and monotonous life which he pretended. Perhaps it was as well for his credit that she was thus incredulous; she might have found it hard to respect a man who cared nothing for what she considered the cream of existence. But she did not believe him; she thought he was concealing his triumphs from her; and while this supposed reticence tormented and piqued her to the last degree, she nevertheless, by a sort of feminine perversity, admired him more for keeping his own coun-

sel than she would have thanked him for the most circumstantial avowal of his proceedings.

She was very constant to him; perhaps more so than had he never worn the halo of absence. It may be doubted, likewise, whether her faith would have staid so well if she, and not Garth, had been the traveler, since even he, despite the stout sinew of his rugged principle, had felt the strain of new places and views. In fact, by the close of his first year he was not sorry to have been away from her. Not that he had met, or expected to meet, or wished to meet, other women in any respect preferable to her; indeed, so far as mere loveliness and winning manners were concerned, he might have journeyed much farther than Bowdoin College without finding any such. But he had never contemplated Madge from his present point of view; and the new aspect creating in him a sort of strangeness, not estrangement, he wanted to get over this and become familiarized with his mistress on fresh ground before returning to take up the old relations.

Moreover, his state of unsettlement regarding what use he was to make of himself might have disinclined him to the more active phases of love-making. Could he have discussed his prospects with Madge, then, indeed, a strong link would straightway have been forged in their chain of sympathy. But from this he was debarred, partly by a feeling that the selfish putting forward of such grave topics would never gain her interest, and partly because on the matter which lay nearest his heart she had already expressed an opinion—one which he did not wish to combat, and with which he feared to agree. Such was the state of his affairs on this side.

His communion with his father was of another color. Mr. Urmson's letters were not long, yet Garth thought there was a great deal in them. They were not frequent, but they never seemed to come a moment too soon or late. They were not given to asking questions, but appeared written from a vantage-ground of tranquil knowledge. There was, however, no assumption of superiority, but Garth found himself addressed as an equal in subtile essays, couched in a tone of cool and quiet humor, and treating of certain aspects of life and conduct such as happened to be just then engaging the young man's attention. At first he took this opportuneness for a singular coincidence; but when the coincidence had recurred more or less remarkably some half-dozen times, he began to suspect his father of being very wise, and of having appalling insight not only into the general ways of life, but particularly into his son's needs and nature.

Both in tone and substance these letters were a wholesome complement to the drift of Selwyn's conversation; they gleamed sometimes with irony, but were never cynical or loose. Neither had they anything of Selwyn's fitful vehemence and passion, but kept the attitude of even-tempered, observant criticism—criticism which Garth could hardly have appreciated at its full worth then, though it often armed his hand with the very weapon the crisis asked; but which inclined him to believe that there might be one man who understood him even better than he understood himself. Nevertheless, Mr. Urmson never referred to Garth's probable occupation on leaving college; and, since Garth himself shunned introducing it, there seemed no likelihood of this most important topic's being discussed. Mr. Urmson, indeed, was always shy of advancing his own opinion where another was as apt to be the true one. However, Garth did not mean to settle down in the world without having had it out with his father about painting. He held this purpose in reserve, and, without fixing the time or place of its execution, he looked forward to it as the finishing incident of this preparatory phase of his existence.

It was noticeable that his grandfather, who occasionally sent him weighty epistles, bearing all the outward and much of the inward aspect of sermons, generally enlarged upon the very subject which Mr. Urmson forbore to touch. The venerable gentleman was as full of sapient suggestions as Polonius, and sketched out, during this first year, as many as four or five different careers for his grandson, not one of which was lacking either in piety, propriety, or respectability, and which were unavailable mainly because of

the difficulty of making a selection from them. Each of these ponderous manuscripts was embellished with a stalwart blessing, and illuminated with one or two enormous witticisms, which recalled to the mind's ear the reverberating haw-haw-ho's of their white-headed deviser. And, altogether, the letters did Garth as much good as his grandfather had meant they should, only in a little different way.

The summer vacation, though spent away from home, was neither so dull nor so fruitless as might have been expected. One of the college professors who had taken an interest in Garth, partly on account of having met his father when at Bowdoin thirty and odd years before, now placed his library—a very comprehensive one—at the young man's disposal. At almost any other period of his life Garth would have profited little by such a privilege; but it happened to come at a time when everything seemed to be stagnant, and he caught at it with the zest of a famished outcast for a warm meal. There is no telling from what mischief this library may have saved him, but the good it did him was never questionable. The professor, besides being learned, was a man of the world, and his books embodied no one-sided or sectarian views. He had taken the measure of Garth's literary needs, and, without prescribing a course, he yet so directed and ministered to his reading as to save him from wasting his time. And Garth got up early, and read day after day far into the short summer nights. The professor—who was a bald-headed old bachelor, with eye-glasses, a stiff, gray beard, and an eagle's beak—sitting in his chair at the opposite side of the breezy library, would often watch, for an hour at a time, his shaggy-browed young visitor's strenuous progress through a book. "He's no taster!" the learned man would mutter to himself, "chews and digests them all—can see him do it!" Anon would he resume his own reading, with the low, stern chuckle which served him for a laugh. Again looking up, at a more than usually labored sigh from the absorbed youth:

"Look out, there, youngster; you'll get a stomach-ache if you swallow too much at a time."

Sometimes Garth would be too far rapt away to answer or hear; otherwise he would look up at first with a vacant stare, which gradually concentrated into intelligence, and ended in a smile.

"Mop your forehead, and pull off your coat; we'll try a drop of claret and a biscuit," the professor would continue, suiting the action to the word; and over their frugal lunch the two would chat together with mutual good-will and freedom.

"Professor Grindle, do you like being a professor?"

"Some parts of it, Mr. Urmson—some parts of it. I'm free to say that I'd rather see you drink my claret than hear you say your lesson."

"Is reading books anything like traveling?"

"A very uncomfortable kind of traveling, I can assure you, as the world is now. Not but the world is better written than most books, too. And yet no two human beings ever read it just alike. We each live in a world by ourselves."

"Then whoever truly tells what he sees, tells news to all the rest?"

"Right! and that's why good pictures are precious. Nature, digested by a great painter, emerges transfigured; his rendering endows us, so far, with his own nobler insight, and we rise so much nearer to a vision of the Creator, Mr. Urmson."

"What do you call Nature?"

"Ay, that has puzzled wiser heads than ours, young gentleman. 'Tis a background, a means, a negative, a compromise, between finite and infinite, a marriage between what makes you and me what we are and what makes God what he is. It's each man's looking-glass, Mr. Urmson; and, if a man's a fool, it's only a fool's face he'll see in it. In itself it's just nothing at all; and thence comes it—though how 'twould be long to explain—that the difference between angel and devil is mainly one of opinion. Pass the bottle, sir, and catch your breath."

"Is that in any of your books, Professor Grindle?"

"Ay; but in none that you've seen. Do you like the sound of it?"

"I want the books."

"Perhaps, perhaps, Mr. Urmson; though it's not every man one throws pearls to—you understand me! I'll acquaint you with one fact, however: 'twas these books brought your father and myself acquainted. He introduced me to them; and for that service I owe him much, sir. Much indeed. Fill your glass. Well, well—I'll see, I'll see. I'll be writing to your father before long, young gentleman, and maybe will mention the matter to him, just to see what he says."

"Who wrote these books?"

"A good man, Mr. Urmson, and a wise and a simple. But 'twas not his own credit he looked to, and his name is less known to-day than will be the case a thousand years from now. That's no matter. Here's to your better acquaintance with him at some future day; and, meanwhile, go ahead with your Johnson."

Garth resumed the world-renowned biography accordingly; but the most of that afternoon slipped away in reverie, and at night, in a pleasant dream, he seemed to make the acquaintance of the unknown reverend writer who had cared less for himself than for his work.

The vacation passed, and sophomore year began, and Garth fancied himself a much deeper and broader being, metaphysically speaking, than he was twelve months ago, and he eyed his classmates curiously to see whether they had grown so fast as he. At his time of life, this perception of increase is not unpleasant; the upward slope of age seems endless, and the expanding prospect exhilarates, while the ignorant plain of childhood lies so short a distance behind us that we can almost believe ourselves wise in the midst of innocence. Be that as it may, Garth had made some progress, and, thanks partly to Professor Grindle, with his books and claret, not altogether in a wrong direction.

He looked with eagerness for the appearance of Selwyn, as if some of his vacation studies had given him new subjects to talk about, or at least furnished new means to the old discussions. But Selwyn came not; and, when a week had passed, Garth received a note from his friend's mother saying that he was seriously ill with a fever. This fever and its consequences prevented his return to college during the first half of the year, and, before the friends met, Garth had seen Urmhurst again, and experienced deeper vicissitudes than even Professor Grindle's library could offer.

Meanwhile, whether reacting from the prolonged solitude of the vacation, or in pursuance of some new ideas concerning the propriety of human brotherhood, he showed himself much more companionable and public-spirited than heretofore. He was no longer either so heedlessly impulsive or so unreasonably fastidious as when stumbling amid the crudities of his freshman year; and, in resuming his former influential position among his classmates, he took his stand upon a more secure basis. Sophomore year is, in all respects, the busiest of the college course. More new things are begun in it, more old things ended, more novel sensations felt, than either before or afterward. Garth was again able to give the key-note of behavior to his class, and again he struck a manly pitch. The freshmen were kept sufficiently in awe, yet were generally permitted the freedom of their bodies and consciences; the societies bestirred themselves with a throb of more vigorous blood in their veins; the class consolidated and organized, and began to acquire a recognizable individuality; and, though it boasted no eminent scholars, yet the average of scholarship was fairly high. And Garth Urmson was the central figure in this respectable assemblage—a position which no amount of amiability and good intentions would have got him if unaccompanied by a certain impressive sturdiness of mind and body, which fails not to command respect and following, be the other qualities what they may. In Garth, however, was superadded a charm of manner not easily defined, and only occasionally exercised, but which, when present, was almost irresistibly winning. The fact that it seemed to be exercised unconsciously enhanced its effect; and, under more stirring conditions, it might have kindled the sort of enthusiasm which it is the prerogative of the Nelsons and Napoleons of the world to inspire, and which,

if report be true, had been lavished upon more than one of Garth's own ancestors.

As it was, by the close of the winter term he stood highest in repute among his classmates, if not in the studies. Popularity is never a very solid affair; but perhaps a college hero holds his position by purer title-deeds than are often attainable in later life. His heroship may be brief, but it was had in virtue of some honest and manly quality, not by dint of interest or intimidation. He is a genuine fact so long as he exists at all; though it by no means follows that his genuineness will avert his overthrow, or prevent his supporters from getting tired of him and idolizing some one else.

CHAPTER XXIII.

GAIN AND LOSS.

IT had been Garth's intention to spend the winter holidays in college, both because there were very few of them, and because the advent of a tremendous snow-storm had so blocked up the roads that a large part of his vacation would necessarily be spent in mere going and returning. But at the last moment he changed his mind. Perhaps the deciding influence was the tone of a letter from his mother, which came to hand a day or two before the term ended. It was written in a mood of yearning tenderness, and its ostensible cheerfulness could not hide from Garth's apprehension an undertone of pathetic complaint at the prolonged absence of the son who never before had been removed beyond an hour's recall. In rereading it he was suddenly overcome by an intolerable longing to see her again; the memory of her dear face came vividly before him, and he determined to be with her straightway, were it but for a day. It seemed to him that he had never loved her, never demanded her, so ardently as now. She was a woman of nature so mild and unassuming that only an intimate acquaintance could discover her profound worth, her very guilelessness and purity creating about her an atmosphere of feminine reserve which was impenetrable to whomsoever possessed not the gentle talisman to disperse it. In her letter to Garth she had not urged his return, but had concluded somewhat wistfully thus: "I shall send you by the first opportunity some things I have made you, to remind you that I love and think of you; and I hope they will add to your comfort this cold winter, too. Oh, dear, how pleasant it will be when the Christmas comes which will bring me the gift of your face! This Christmas we are not to meet; and yet we shall be together, for I shall be with you in spirit, though not in body. Do not forget that. Good-by, my dear son; I love and bless you. I have written a stupid letter, but my head aches to-day, and it makes me stupid, for you know I never have headaches. But I am an old woman now; my hair is quite white, and I wear spectacles all the time. Your father says I am getting decrepit, and makes great fun of me. He sends his love, and bids me tell you to punch a freshman's head on his account! Good-by from your own, ownest mamma."

"God bless her!" thought Garth, as he folded up the letter; "we'll have a merrier Christmas than she thinks for. Spirit is not enough; we must be together in body, too. To think of her blessed white hair and her spectacles! and I have been away from her a whole year and a half! She was my first lady-love—and she is still."

Having made his decision and his few preparations, time dragged till he could depart. He called at Professor Grindle's to acquaint him with his proposed journey.

"Is your mother ill?" the professor demanded.

"No; but I haven't seen her for a year and a half."

"Well, go ahead. I had intended having you take your Christmas turkey with me, en garçon. That's no matter. Remember me to your father. That was a fine thing of his in the last *North American*—'Public Benefits of Private History.' Should put the notion into practice. Good-by. Don't forget to come back again: we'll do something with you yet. Love to your father."

Early the next morning Garth set forth, and fought his way northwestward through the mighty snow-drifts. He had ever loved the snow, and, as a boy, enjoyed plunging into the thickest of it. But now he became impatient with it. It checked his progress toward his goal; the sport of his childhood was the clog of his elder years. The stout horses floundered and strained, and the buried sleigh-runners quivered in the white furrows. The sharp bells clashed and jangled, the driver whooped and swore; but, in spite of all, the pace was slow, and the delays and interruptions many. Under ordinary circumstances it would have been a glorious sleigh-ride, every check and mishap a source of fun and mirthful uproar; and at first Garth tried to regard them from the humorous standpoint; but after the first day the joke lost its point. At night he dreamed uneasily, oppressed with a nightmare notion that Urmhurst was escaping from him on sleigh-runners; that his mother called to him from her chamber-window, and waved her hand; that he struggled onward desparately, and at last seemed gaining; that now he was close upon the flying house—had but to burst throught this belt of black timber and he would be there. But when he emerged, breathless, there was a silent, white, open space, encircled with a serried ring of naked trees, and in the centre was a snow-covered mound. The house had vanished—whither? Above Wabeno drifted a gray cloud, which, for a moment, assumed the familiar outlines of his lost home; but where was his mother?

Starting betimes the next day, Garth had hopes of reaching home by nightfall; but a wind arose, accompanied by fresh snow, and progress was slower than yesterday. The young traveler sat muffled in his seat, winking at the flakes which whirled into his eyes, and envying the warmth of the toiling horses.

Occasionally, however, a vision of beloved Urmhurst and of those he would find there rose vividly in his imagination; he would brighten up and look hopefully to the horizon to see whether the cloud which shut down upon the white uplands were not lifting a little. He pictured to himself the vast chestnut-stump spouting fire and smouldering incandescent on the roomy hearth, its flickering blaze gladdening the dark wainscot and smoky ceiling of the well-remembered room. There sat his mother, with glinting knitting-needles, and white cap on white hair, anon turning her face toward the snow-drifted window, and thinking of the son whom she believes to be scores of miles away at Bowdoin. How joyfully shall she be disappointed!

His father, standing with his back to the fire, perhaps revolves the contents of Garth's last letter, wherein enigmatic allusion is made to certain pregnant disturbances which had recently occurred in the writer's mental domain, and threaten to overturn the present constitution and establish a new one, but the complete annals of which are to be reserved, adds the letter, until the meeting next summer. Destiny, however, has forbidden so long a delay, and Garth will bring forward the matter this very night, if Fortune permit. What will Grandfather Graeme say to it, and Madge? he wonders.

But, alas! day is already drawing to a close, and it is too evident that Urmhurst will not be reached to-night. An hour after dark the sleigh pulls up at the door of a wayside inn, and Garth, dismounting, with stiff joints, eats his supper before the kitchen fire, and, going immediately to bed, sleeps dreamlessly till morning.

At noon of the third day they jingle along the familiar wood-path, a keen sun sparkling through the snow-frosted boughs, and lighting up the dazzling landscape with exhilaration. It is a glorious day, fit to celebrate a home-return. There is no gloom or anxiety on Garth's face now, but unalloyed delight and genial anticipation, while the thought that he is wholly unexpected adds a fine zest to his enjoyment. Now, they draw near; yonder through the trees looms the dark side of the dear old house: how dear it is, how unchanged, how well remembered! Now some one has stepped out on the threshold. His mother? no; the hair is gray, but the face is dusky—not his mother; it is the old Indian woman, Nikomis, standing with her broom, on the cloven threshold. At the sound of the approaching sleigh she turns her head and looks beneath her leveled hand. Garth shouts and waves his cap joyfully. She looks, and then vanishes

within-doors. The sleigh comes fleetly up, and stops, and Garth springs out and meets his father at the door.

"How are you, father?"

"Garth!" Mr. Urmson opened his arms, and the two embraced, even as they had done at parting, eighteen months before. Then they looked at each other. Mr. Urmson had a flush in his usually pale face, and his eyes were bright. Garth thought he appeared unusually well. There was a little more stoop, another wrinkle, an unsteadiness, perhaps. Oh, but he was in good health and heart!

"You could not have got my letter?" said Mr. Urmson, after a moment's hesitation, still standing on the threshold.

"Mother's you mean. Yes, and it made me come. All at once I thought I must see her. Come in, dear. Where is my mamma?"

"Not here. You'll see her by-and-by, if you are a good boy. You did not stop at your grandfather's? Sit down.—You may go upstairs, Nikomis. I wrote to you night before last, Garth—I wrote you to come; so you anticipated us. Here's a joint of beef."

"I'll cut it. You're tired, your hand trembles. Oh, I'm glad to be at home! Nearly three days getting here, father! Is mother well?"

"I believe she is far better than she has ever been. So my friend Grindle has been having you in charge? Has he succeeded in getting any ideas into your head?"

"O father, I came partly to talk with you about it; but let us wait till my mamma comes. Will it be long?"

"What would Miss Margaret say if she knew you had not even mentioned her name yet? She tells me that she writes you long letters, and you never answer her questions. Wait, I'll get you the mustard. Now, beloved Hottentot, hadn't you better open your heart to your old father? Can't you do with me alone for half an hour?"

Garth laughed. "You see, since I've been away I've always thought of you and mother as one. It seems as though you could never be apart—when one of you goes to heaven, the other would too. Did you say she was at grandfather's, this snowy day? She must be strong, certainly! Well,

I'll begin to tell you—there's plenty of it, and yet there may not be many words about it, after all. You know I bequeathed you the key of my garret-room when I went away? I meant to send you word, as soon as I got pluck enough to make up my mind, to open the place and burn every thing in it. It's full of pictures and drawings that I made. I was ashamed to have done them, and yet I couldn't stop it—didn't at least. Now, father, I hoped you would turn up your eyebrow in that way you used to."

"I see you already have the artistic perception; but artists are not usually ashamed of what they have done until they have done something better, or at least something else. What have you painted since you were in college?"

"That was not my trouble. My idea was, since God made Nature, it must be perfect: so what business has man to make imitations of it—improvements on it, rather? for if he didn't think his version the better, what was the sense of his doing it?"

"Ah! you were very sagacious. But you think differently now?"

Garth settled himself back in his chair, and began fumbling with his hair.

"The fact is, father, I want to think differently so much that I'm afraid to. You know, grandfather used to say whatever a man most enjoyed doing was not the right thing. When I began imitating what I saw in this way, I only thought it a delightful discovery. But, when the idea of delightful things being wrong got in my head, I began to fear there must be something very wrong in my discovery; and, the more I reasoned about it, the more it seemed so. By-and-by, if any argument to the contrary suggested itself, I mistrusted it and put it away. Don't you see what I mean?"

"Why, I never heard you talk before. The matter has loosed your tongue, right or wrong. Let us hear the rest of it."

"I am it!" said Garth, dropping his hands on his knees emphatically. "I've tried to put it out of my mind, but all I do and think somehow relates to it. I was very unhappy about it: I believed I was possessed of a devil. At last Selwyn told me I had genius, and it came out what I thought about paint-ing, and he laughed at me, and said I was a fool. It seems to me I was glad to have him think so, though I didn't admit it. Later, Professor Grindle happened to say that Nature came transfigured through painters; and I found things about painting in his library, and also engravings of pictures. Perhaps I was wrong: painting is not irreverent? If you think it is not, and if you can show me why, I—"

He stopped, kindled to a high pitch of feeling.

Mr. Urmson partly smiled. "So, after all," he said, half aloud, gazing in the fire, "your grandfather did have a hand in your education. You are a queer instrument to play upon, and he struck a perilous note, though it may enrich the harmony at last. Painter! perhaps it's as well I did not think of that. What would she have thought?—perhaps it is as well."

"Father, do you sigh because I'm wrong?" demanded Garth, clearing his throat.

"Sighing, was I? Well, old gentleman, because there is a finer kind of gifts called bereavements; but gifts are gifts, too, in spite of your scruples. Painting irreverent? Why, is history—I mean real not written history—irreverent? History is the painting of time: it is Nature fused in man. I should call it worship."

"But history is not imitation."

"Not more than Nature and man are imitations, or approximations. The Lord is the sole original type. Man sees himself in Nature something as the Parthenon might see itself in the marble-quarry, and in God as the Parthenon might behold its ideal in some cloud-temple. A painter divines an interior human significance in hills, trees, and rivers, in flowers or in castles; he selects and combines them to the tune of his own best ideas—which are himself, as himself is his peculiar view of the Creator—and thus recognizes, and, so far as he may, assists the Creator's purpose. That is, he lets the Lord work through him; for the Lord is at the bottom of every man, and art is the divinity cropping out."

"Yes, yes!" cried Garth, half getting up, and sitting down again.

"If you declare war against painters, your hand will be against every honest man, yourself, let us hope, among the rest. Only evil is inartistic. As for paint and canvas, they are the least essential elements in a picture."

"Then ought they to be used at all?"

"Why, yes; they suggest a world of more harmonious forms and tints than human beings ever see. They are often misused to deceive the eye—as if the essential perfections of Nature could be copied! We can improve the world, and set it in a better light; but we cannot reproduce it. A true painter paints a heaven of his own out of materials earth affords him, but does not ask us to mistake the suggestion for the reality; so both he and we are the better for his work. However, if you are a painter, old gentleman, you must understand all this better than I do. Your scruples were not very wise; but, if you are otherwise gifted for the trade, I dare say you'll be the better for having had them. So this was the mystery of the attic?"

"I feel it now," muttered Garth, absorbed, and with his head in the air. "Men find their ideal selves in Nature, and paint that. Yes, it is a kind of worship. Father, I never was so happy in all my life. But what will mother say?—will she understand?"

As the elder man met the younger's eyes, tears rose in his own. He did not brush them away, nor attempt to keep them back, and Garth saw them as they rolled slowly down his cheeks. How old his father looked! What did these tears betoken?—profounder sympathy with his rejoicing than could be borne on a smile? Almost immediately Mr. Urmson spoke:

"Hold on to that happiness as long as you live: you have a right to it. You'll have griefs enough; but, if you are a painter and an honest man, the happiness of being useful in a high way to human beings must underlie any grief. Perhaps," he added, leaning his head on his hand, and looking at Garth with keen steadfastness, "the moment of greatest happiness can best bear a heavy loss."

"Father?"

C

The blithe jingling of sleigh-bells came nearer, and paused at the door. Garth got up excitedly. "There is mother!" exclaimed he.

There was a pause; then heavy steps and the low booming of a rugged voice; and withal a light step and soft, pleasingly modulated tone—all familiar to Garth. His grandfather and Madge came in, but, on seeing Garth, stopped near the open doorway. The latter came forward a few steps, and then stopped also, throwing a questioning, suspicious glance at each face in turn. Mr. Urmson remained motionless in his chair.

"Garth, dear lad," rumbled the venerable pastor, holding out both his aged hands, which trembled somewhat—indeed, the whole man seemed more infirm and ploughed with years than Garth had expected to find him—"Garth, poor lad, bear up: that's right; be like me and your father. The Lord giveth and he taketh away. Bear up, bear up, dear boy, like me and your good father. Here's the dear child—I brought her along. They said in town you'd just come back, and I didn't lose a moment. Ay, she'll kiss your tears away. Bear up, lad—be an Urmson. That's right! that's right!"

Madge had come close to Garth's other side, and taken between hers his heavy-hanging hand, upturning the while a lovely rosy face, buried warm in the furred hood.

"Oh, I'm so sorry!" she murmured; "and I'm so glad you've come back. How did you come so quick?—but you are always cleverer than anybody. How sad you must feel!—I'm sure I do. I cried so all last night."

Garth shook himself free from both his grandfather and Madge, and turned toward his father, exclaiming in a tone apparently of gruff irritation, "Has anything happened? —didn't mother come with you? where is she?"

"Oh, doesn't he know?—Why, don't you know, dear?" exclaimed Madge, with a kind of eagerness.—"Let me tell him.—Oh, how can I tell you! Oh, Garth, it is so terrible!"

Garth came over to Mr. Urmson's chair, and resting one hand upon it, bent toward him. "Father!" said he, in a low voice.

"I wanted you to see that I could bear it, Garth—it comes hard to me: and you have your happiness besides. Your mother died the day before yesterday."

"Did she?" faltered Garth, with an impulse partly incredulous, partly rebellious. No one spoke while he stood fumbling with a button of his coat, and staring at the wall. In a minute he walked to the door, half opened it, and turned back. "Has she gone up-stairs? I mean," he added, stamping his foot, impatiently, "where—where—"

"Oh, he doesn't know! Let me show you, dear: it's up in the east chamber."

Garth turned upon her with such a frown as frightened her into silence. "I'll meet my mother alone," said he. He walked quickly down the hall, and bounded up-stairs. At the door of the east chamber stood a dusky figure — old Nikomis. As Garth came up she threw open the door, and, when he had entered, closed it behind him and listened; but no sound came from within.

BOOK IV.

COLLISION.

CHAPTER XXIV.

TWO AND A PAIR.

It is not my purpose to invite the reader across the threshold of the room where the dead body lies. Let us rather take a new departure, and, forbearing to trace directly the events of the next few years, rejoin the square-visaged, dark-browed young man in farmer's attire, whom we left, many pages since, at his morning easel on the shore of the quiet lake. For Garth, as will already have been divined, was an artist; a fisher, not of fish, but of Nature and of man.

Here again are the level translucence of the silent surface, the golden islet at the cove's month, the glory of the October woods, the distant pomp of Wabeno, every-thing as before, save that the day is three or four hours older. The stillness of the early morning has melted into a voiceless-ness yet more profound, as though Nature were hushing herself to sleep beneath the overriding sun. When Garth trilled forth a snatch of mellow whistling, or tapped his easel musingly with the handle of the paint-brush, the sound went titillating across the lake, and sometimes tiptoed softly back

again. The young man preferred whis-tling to any other form of soliloquy. There was a satisfaction in the accurate phras-ing of a scrap of a tune which resembled that conveyed by a happy stroke of the brush.

At length he glanced at the sun, and told himself that it must be after eleven—too late for any more morning effects. How-ever, the sketch was nearly finished, and the meaning which he had meant to bring out was sufficiently indicated. His father would understand it. Madge would not; no mat-ter—it was there. By-the-way, where was Madge? Eleven o'clock, and she was to have been down there at ten to go on a nut-ting-expedition. She had been looking for-ward to it for some days; what could have induced her to change her mind?

Garth rose, and, going to the water's edge, picked up his hat, which lay amphibi-ously on the margin. He had put it there for the violet's sake, and, on examining the flower, he found it almost as fresh as when first plucked. "It will fade before she gets it, though," thought Garth, "and Madge doesn't care for faded things. Well, and why should she? She's young, and healthy, and beautiful, and happy, I suppose. I wouldn't have her morbid and sentimental, would I?"

He turned back to his easel, and began slowly to pack up his implements preparatory to going home. In the midst of this employment he was startled by a distant warble of song. It came from no bird's throat, nor could any man have uttered it. It was clear, elastic, pure, and full of exaltation, mingled with sadness; for sadness overtakes and sweetens the merriest sound that comes from afar off. Such as it was, it went straight to Garth's heart. He loved music profoundly, for he was a man of fine ear and deep emotional perception; but there was little music to be had in the village, and he was generally reduced to imagining symphonies of his own in the roar and murmur of the oaks and hemlocks outside his studio-window.

The outburst of song died away, and a few moments afterward Garth began to doubt whether his fancy had not played him a trick by developing the strain from some slight natural origin. As he debated the matter with himself, he was all at once inexplicably reminded of a face which he had seen a year or two ago, the image whereof had staid so persistently in his memory that at length, to be rid of it, he had put it on canvas. It was a face which few people would have pronounced beautiful, but for the artist it had a singular fascination. Its lines appeared at the first glance discordant and irregular, but presently an inner harmony and significance began to declare themselves, of a kind to which the ordinary gauges of female beauty could not be applied. Mr. Urmson, to whom Garth once showed his sketch, studied it a good while in silence, and finally said, with one of his kindly, penetrating smiles: "Well, old gentleman, it's an odd face, and, if I once happened to like it, I can imagine my not soon getting tired of it. But what does Madge think of it?"

"I haven't shown it to her," Garth replied, slightly reddening; "but I know she would think it ugly." And, whether for that or for some better reason, he never did show it to her, either then or thereafter.

It must not be inferred, however, that he now recalled the face merely because he was in the habit of brooding over it, and of associating it with all kinds of pleasant impressions, visible or audible. As a man of principle, whose affections were engaged elsewhere, he would not knowingly have allowed himself such an indulgence. It must be accepted that there was some genuine affinity between the voice and the countenance, that there was that in the one which might recall the other to a man of genius, say, in a particularly lucid and impressionable mood. Meanwhile, the melodious outbreak had been so unexpected, so charming, and withal so fairy-like, that Garth would certainly have laid it to his imagination, had it not of a sudden been repeated, this time sounding nearer, and unmistakably distinct.

He turned sharply round, and saw a woman's figure standing near the extremity of the tongue of land which formed the western side of the cove. Her scarlet jacket, and the peculiarly-shaped straw hat which she wore, left him no doubt as to her being Madge. But where did the voice come from?

"Have the morning and the autumn tints got into her throat?" he asked himself. "Madge has been anything except musical heretofore. Can she be a Jenny Lind without my having suspected it? No! It was that quarter of a mile of air and water that did it. But can mere distance weave such a spell as that? I don't believe it was her voice, after all!"

As if in answer to his denial, the figure in the scarlet jacket caroled forth a bar of melody for the third time. She seemed to be trying her voice, or enjoying the answering music of the echoes. Apparently she had not yet seen Garth; so he, after listening until the last pulsation of sound had died away, called out to her, and beckoned with his hand. She looked at him, and then, without making any answering salute, turned away and passed out of view. Garth fancied she moved with a more stately step than was her wont. Madge was always graceful as a panther, but she could hardly be called dignified.

The artist resumed his packing in a state of mind midway between exhilaration and perplexity. Every true lover believes that he believes the woman of his choice to be perfection. If, then, she dawns upon him in a new light, delightfully transcending his past knowledge of her, he feels bound to be jealous of his own former opinion of her. He must be displeased that she pleases him more than at the beginning: and yet how can he slight the new-comer without doubly forsaking her predecessor?

Entangled in this whimsical quandary, Garth all at once heard himself addressed from behind by a courteous male voice, which, despite its courtesy, impressed him with a feeling of distrust and aversion. He turned about with a kind of indignation, but what he saw so far modified his emotion as to make him bow very politely.

A lady and gentleman were standing together on the turf that sloped to the beach. The latter had much the advantage in years over his companion, though he still might have passed for forty. His appearance was rather prepossessing than otherwise, and his bearing was at once affable and polished. At the same time, his effect was slightly contradictory. His forehead might, with a trifle more arch and height about the temples, have been called noble. The brow was level and handsome, but the eyes were veiled behind a pair of bluish-tinted glasses set in tortoise-shell—which glasses had a polish of their own that was somewhat too obtrusive. The nose which they bestrode, though a trifle too long, was perhaps the most unexceptionable feature in the face ; it was straight and delicately moulded. The whole countenance had a Jewish cast, which enhanced rather than detracted from its cultured aspect. The lower part of the visage was undecipherable, owing to the fact that the stranger wore a mustache, a pair of whiskers, and an imperial, each of which grew independently, and were separately unimpeachable ; but, taken together, destroyed one another's effect.

The gentleman was dressed in a quiet but fashionably-cut suit of tweed, and held in his hand a soft, Italian-looking felt hat. In the other hand he carried a short, pliable cane, which the spurs on his neatly-fitting boots argued a riding-whip. These boots, which reached to the knee, gave the lower part of the figure a dapper air contrasting oddly with the unassuming elegance of the gentleman's upper half. How came the owner of so fair a forehead to be supported upon so sportive a pair of legs? The inconsistency would have been unaccountable but for that triple growth of beard, which somewhat prepared the mind for other vagaries.

The stranger's first address, while perfectly civil, had been couched in the tone of a superior. But on encountering Garth's glance he seemed, by some imperceptible process, to shift his standpoint. He smiled behind his glasses, tapped his boot with his riding-whip, and returned the artist's bow. "Pardon us, sir," he said. "We have intruded unceremoniously ; but, frankly, we—"

"Can you direct us how to get back to Urmhurst?" interposed the young lady, in a low but very distinct tone. She looked at Garth as she spoke, and their glances met. Garth so far forgot his manners as to stare for several moments without making any reply. At length the young lady turned away with a haughty movement of the lips and eyebrows, and seemed about to retire.

"I beg your pardon!" exclaimed the artist, immediately ; "yes, I can take you to Urmhurst, if you'll wait till I get this easel packed. I was going there myself."

"Ah, thanks," said the bearded gentleman. "Elinor, my dear, you'll wait? since our friend is so kind as to offer to guide us. I used to be familiar with these woods myself when a boy," he continued, to Garth ; "but, ah!" putting on his hat, and shaking his head with a melancholy smile, "one forgets, you know—one forgets. And yet it begins to come back to me ; yes, yes! I believe I bathed in this very cove thirty years ago, or nearly that ; and caught pike (or pickerel, as you would call them) through the ice in winter. You are an artist, I perceive—would you allow me? Ah, ah! by George, that's a fine effect you have caught there—wonderfully true and delicate. H'm! now might I ask whether you reside hereabouts, and happen to be personally acquainted with Mr. Cuthbert Urmson? Ah!

and how is he getting on? Is he quite well?"

The young lady here interposed again, in the same low tone: "Perhaps this gentleman is an Urmson himself."

"My name is Garth Urmson," acknowledged the artist, who had now finished tying up his bundle. He was thinking to himself that this indifferent and somewhat supercilious young lady had a good deal of penetration. "I have seen you before," he said to her, "in the crystal mirror at the Green Vaults in Dresden."

"I am Miss Golightley," returned the young lady, composedly. "I suppose this is your uncle—Mr. Golightley Urmson."

"My dear, dear boy!" exclaimed the booted gentleman, stepping hastily up, and tucking his whip under his arm in order to grasp Garth's free hand in both his own. His greeting was very warm. "My dear, dear nephew!" he repeated.

The three now walked on together for a short time in silence, this unexpected recognition seeming to have taken the breath out of conversation. Miss Golightley was a little in advance, and Garth took the opportunity to examine her narrowly. She was a trifle above the medium height, but looked taller, owing to her manner of carrying herself, which was unusually dignified. A loose scarlet jacket, fantastically embroidered round the edges, was thrown cloakwise over her shoulders. Her face was of a kind more likely to command interest than to show it. There was nobility in it, veiled, however, by an indifferent expression akin to cynicism. The eyes were gray, and the left one was a little smaller than the other; but their shape, and the manner in which they were set beneath the clear, delicate brows, were such as the artist knew how to appreciate. The high cheek-bones were rounded into somewhat undue prominence, and, though the nose was small, the chin had too much decision. The mouth was the only technically faultless feature; it was exquisitely curved and refined; but the lips were too pale, and there was a touch of disdain upon them. Especially noticeable to Garth was the gem-like purity of the facial contours; the lines were as smooth and

sharp as the cutting of a cameo. For the rest, her slight figure gave promise of full womanly development, and one of her small, ungloved hands was bleeding from the scratch of a thorn.

"It was your voice I heard across the cove?" Garth asked, breaking the silence.

"Yes; I was trying the echo. I didn't know any one was within hearing."

"I liked your voice very much."

"I sing very well. I have had the best masters," said this imperturbable young lady.

"Your hat and cloak made me mistake you for some one else."

"I saw in the village yesterday a very pretty girl with a hat like this, so I made over mine to resemble it. She must have a great deal of taste. Who is she?"

"I suppose you mean Margaret Danver," said Garth, his color rising a little.

"I have seen girls not unlike her in Normandy. But Margaret Danver is prettier."

"She's of French descent—Acadian."

"Danver? Yes; the good people with whom you and your mother thought of taking lodgings," observed Uncle Golightley, who had been walking along humming to himself in a preoccupied manner. "A lovely child, that Maggie, as Mr. Graeme calls her. By-the-by, my dear Garth, your mother was a Danver; yes, the same family. My mother, you know, was a Golightley; and Miss Elinor here is—how is it, my dear? —my mother's grand-niece. So we call ourselves cousins—don't we, Elinor?—But, Garth," he went on, resting his hand affectionately on the young man's shoulder, "tell me all about Cuthbert—all about your dear father. Is he well? Is he happy?"

"He has grown old, all but his eyes and voice. When did you arrive, Uncle Golightley?"

"Oh, yesterday—yesterday afternoon. We left Europe very suddenly, you see. Well, and this morning Miss Elinor here insisted upon exploring the forest primeval and getting lost in it. Yes, she takes to the woods like a native, she who is next thing to being a native of Europe. And I—you can never know, Garth," exclaimed Uncle Golightley, in a burst of confidence, "how I rejoice to find myself here once more. By

George! but to think that such a solid, flesh-and-blood fact as you are should have wholly come into existence since I was last at Urmhurst! You know I sailed for Europe the year you were born, and my good father died—dear old Captain Brian! You are very like him, your face and build. And so you're an artist? really a painter? By George! I envy you. Art was a dream of my youthful days, too; but I couldn't do it; hadn't the physical stamina. O for a year of your arms and chest, by George! And you're succeeding—that goes without saying?"

"I manage to live, if that's what you mean," returned Garth, gravely. "But that costs little here."

"Ah! Well, my dear boy, you are quite right to make your art an end, not a means," observed his uncle, stroking forward his hair above his ears. "That's what I have always longed to do—take what Fortune sent, and be rich only in the joy of creating."

"And in the money of other people," Garth felt tempted to add, but he forbore. He had long since settled it in his mind that his uncle had a moral if not a legal right to at least half of the property; and though of late years his drafts had swallowed up not only the income of the family estate, but the greater portion of the estate itself, neither Garth nor his father had hesitated about paying them. Golightley had accompanied each draft with the assurance that it would be the last, and that the profits from this or that speculation would place them all forever beyond the reach of want. Nothing could be further from his intention—so he had always declared—than permanently to possess himself of a dollar of the family inheritance. Doubtless he meant what he said; and if he were really aware of any moral claim to the money he spent, his conduct might be regarded as quite justifiable. Besides, during the last twelve months his applications had altogether ceased, and nothing good or bad had been heard of him. Perhaps the great fortune had at last been made, and Golightley returned to make the long-promised restitution.

But Garth did not feel inclined to continue this particular vein of conversation,

so he turned to Miss Elinor, and asked whether she had settled to lodge with Mrs. Danver.

"Mother was going to see her to-day," replied the young lady. "She seemed to me an honest and cleanly sort of person, and I am very much pleased with the girl you say is her daughter."

This speech, quietly as it was given, nettled Garth exceedingly. Who was this gray-eyed, self-complacent young aristocrat who presumed to speak of his future mother-in-law as "honest and clean," and of his betrothed wife as of some pretty animal? No doubt she regarded him as a country bumpkin, and would treat his father as an entertaining old peasant! If only she had been a man, Garth would have knocked her down without more ceremony. And yet he could understand that to a person of foreign education and prejudices, who had been bred to luxury and to a belief in caste, the ruggedness of country life and appearances might be indistinguishable from vulgarity. Having paused awhile, therefore, to give his resentment time to cool, he answered with grim simplicity:

"Honesty and cleanliness are great virtues; many people are well off with only one of them, and not many have both."

"I was speaking of Mrs. Danver in her capacity as landlady; excuse me for forgetting that she is a relative of yours," said Miss Elinor, ceremoniously.

"I've often warned you, my dear," observed Uncle Golightley, throwing up his chin and handling his imperial, "that we New-Englanders have democratic notions that will strike you harshly at first."

"I agree with what Mr. Urmson just said, though," rejoined she with some emphasis, and a faint pinkness in her clear cheeks. "I should be satisfied to be honest and clean myself, and that is all I shall require of other people."

"Brava, brava!" cried Uncle Golightley, smiling, and gently clapping his hands. "We'll make a Yankee of her yet—eh, Garth?"

Garth kept silence, but liked the supercilious young lady a little better. Suddenly his uncle turned upon him and asked:

"But didn't you say something, my dear boy, about having seen us in Dresden?"

"I saw Miss Golightley, and an old lady and gentleman—Mr. and Mrs. Golightley, perhaps."

Uncle Golightley placed a hand of gentle admonition on Garth's arm, and then laid his long forefinger on his lips. "You were misled by our dear Elinor's speaking of 'mother,'" said he in an undertone. "No; it was Mr. and Mrs. Tenterden. Elinor's father and mother died in Charleston, of yellow fever, upward of ten years ago. The Tenterdens, having no children, adopted her. Mrs. Tenterden, by-the-by, was a Golightley—only daughter of my mother's first marriage. You know, my mother was a widow when she came North and married Captain Brian?"

Garth believed he did know that.

"Yes. Well, then, last year came our great grief, Mr. Tenterden's death. Dear John! dear, good John Tenterden!—Ah! I shouldn't have mentioned this before you," he added, turning to Elinor, and drawing her reluctant hand tenderly under his arm.

"Mentioning does not make it worse," said she, with a peculiar compression of the corners of her mouth. In a few moments she quietly drew away from her cousin's affectionate support, and walked by herself just within the verge of the trees. Golightley, who seemed under a necessity of constantly touching somebody, leaned once more upon Garth's shoulder, and continued:

"Poor John! it was so sudden—heart-disease, you know. A trying time, Garth, I can tell you; of course, it all fell on my shoulders, and, by George!" shaking his head with a sad smile, "I don't know what they'd have done without me. But, of course, I'd willingly have done ten times as much; for John—well, frankly, my dear Garth, John idolized me up to the day of his death; and, not only that, he assisted me materially at a critical moment of my affairs. Poor John! his whole immense fortune went almost immediately afterward."

"And he died in consequence?"

"In consequence? no, no, no—no!" said Uncle Golightley, adjusting his glasses.

"Heart-disease—not heart-breaking; no, no!"

"So you brought his widow and Miss Golightley to America?"

"I'm; yes. But you say you have been abroad," returned the elder man, shaking off an apparent tendency to preoccupation. Tell me all about it—what, how, and why; that's a good fellow!"

"It isn't much of a story. After my mother died I left college and took a drawing-master. Then I went to Europe with a chum of mine, Selwyn. Staid there till a year ago. Now I have my old garret-studio. I shall be glad to show it you."

"Yes," murmured his companion, absently; "yes; thanks, thanks."

By this time they had reached the lichened rock on the border of the pine-grove, where Garth had found the violet some hours earlier. Elinor, walking close by the rock, saw the green leaves at its base, and stooped to search among them. Garth turned aside and joined her.

"I plucked the last one this morning," said he; "here it is in my hat-band. It isn't quite faded. Will you take it?"

"Oh, thank you!" she said, looking up at him with the first smile she had vouchsafed that day. She took the drooping flower from the artist's fingers, smelt it, and then fastened it carefully in the bosom of her dress. They walked on together, saying nothing. Garth was rather surprised at what he had done; for he had plucked the violet in ignorance of Miss Elinor Golightley's existence, and with the intention of presenting it to a very different person.

Meanwhile Uncle Golightley was out of sight round a bend of the path; but soon voices were heard, and Garth and Elinor, coming up, found him in affable converse with a very beautiful young woman in a scarlet jacket and an oddly-shaped straw hat.

"Your cousin—Miss Danvers," said Elinor, quickly.

Garth answered slowly: "I had forgotten her; or, rather, I thought she had forgotten me."

———

CHAPTER XXV.

A QUESTION OF PRIVILEGE.

"Ah! Garth," cried Uncle Golightley, glancing at his nephew with airy playfulness, "you see Miss Margaret and I have found each other out without your help —haven't we, Margaret?—By George! you rogue," laughingly tapping Garth's shoulder with his whip, "no wonder you stick to your woods if this is the sort of flower that grows there!"

Garth seemed at first inclined to take this badinage rather sombrely; but Madge wore to-day her loveliest aspect, and it was impossible to see her without delight. She was about Elinor's height, and her lightsome, roundly-moulded figure expressed vigor as well as grace. Her attire was piquant and original—quite at variance with the fashion, but artfully enhancing the beauties of the wearer's face and form. Her quilted satin petticoat was short enough to reveal a pair of slim, arched feet, and its blackness contrasted brightly with the red stockings. The light-colored over-skirt was gathered up and puffed out at the sides, and open down the front of the body; the sleeves were tight above the elbow and fell open below it. There was a V-shaped glimpse of a lovely neck, partly concealed by the sleeves of the scarlet jacket, which were tied loosely round the throat. The straw hat, courtesying quaintly downward over her smooth brow, completed the costume. Perhaps the influence of her artist lover had increased the girl's natural tendency to be picturesque; but few young women could have indulged in her solecisms either of dress or behavior, without making themselves ridiculous. Madge was privileged by dint of her genuine originality and fascination.

She was a brunette; and her beauty, great though it was, was intensified by the extraordinary vividness and mobility of her expression. Her dark eyes were of a long oval shape, and she seemed able to see all round herself without turning her head. Her face, without noticeable movement, could indicate a thousand subtile shades of meaning. Her manner one moment effer-vesced with gay audacity; anon it would become demurely undemonstrative; and yet again it would be graced by innumerable winning flatteries and caresses. A slight Frenchy flavor was still perceptible in all she said and did, and perhaps this, and an occasional touch of *naïve* rusticity, aided her escape from ordinary standards of criticism. But she had few detractors now, the villagers had come round to Parson Graeme's opinion—that her mere charm was her sufficient excuse for being. Madge Danvers grew not on every tree!

"Mrs. Tenterden came to see mother," said this lovely creature, addressing Garth a little shyly in the presence of his new friends, and at the same time half meeting Elinor's point-blank glance with a timid smile. "We've been showing her the rooms, and she's been saying which she would have. —And she says she'll come to us if Miss Golightley did not object," continued Madge, now turning more directly to Elinor, with a prettily apologetic air.

"And leaves me altogether out of the question," exclaimed Uncle Golightley, humorously counterfeiting indignation. "Ah, that's the way you women treat gray-haired old boys like me!—Well, Garth, you're a man and a nephew, you won't refuse a roof to your old uncle, will you?"

"It would be strange if you went anywhere else," returned the young man, cordially. "I expect a great deal of benefit, too, from your criticism and suggestions. Though, I tell you fairly, I have an opinion of my own on some things."

"Thanks—double thanks, my dear nephew," cried Uncle Golightley, laughing and turning his eyes from Garth to Elinor, and from her to Madge. "I should have had no peace of mind, you know, lodging in the same house with two such incomparable ladies fair. Even Urmhurst may not put me far enough out of the reach of temptation?"

Madge's mischievous dark eyes sparkled at this gallantry, though she kept her face otherwise demure. Elinor turned her head aside with a slightly contemptuous movement of the upper lip, which Garth, who happened to be looking at her, was glad to see; for he thought his unclo's sally was in rather poor taste.

"How soon can we come to you, Miss Danver?" Elinor asked, abruptly.

"Oh, you will come, then?" cried Madge, eagerly. "I'm so glad. Oh, to-day, if you like."

"Well, I do like," replied Elinor, smiling a little.

Madge pressed her hands quickly together, with an exclamation of pleasure. Elinor's mouth softened still more, as she continued:

"But I should ask you, first, whether you or your mother will be disturbed by my music? I play on the violin."

"The violin!" exclaimed Madge, in unaffected surprise; "oh, how — delightful! Why, I thought only men played on the violin!"

They all smiled at this, and Uncle Golightley said: "Ah, my dear child, you'll see the world some day, if I'm not much mistaken, and then you'll find out that you women are robbing us of our masculine prerogatives, one after another."

"I was expecting you earlier," Garth remarked to Madge.

"I was busy, you know," she answered, stepping close to him and twisting a button of his coat while she spoke. "Then Mrs. Tenterden said that Miss Golightley and—and Uncle Golightley," with a sidelong glance at that gentleman, "had gone to the lake; and I thought that if you all met, and you wanted to take your uncle to Urmhurst, I might show Miss Golightley the way to our house. So I came."

"Thank you—that is just what I wanted," said Elinor. "Shall we go now?"

Madge went up to the reserved young lady, took her by the hand as a child might have done, and said, "Come!"

Elinor had a momentary impulse to draw her hand back; but Madge's clasp was so soft and winning, and her eyes so soft and ingenuous, as not to be resisted. With a blush, therefore, and a corresponding relenting in her whole manner, she yielded.

Hereupon Uncle Golightley put his arm through Garth's, and affected to hurry off with him in despair.

"Let's get away!" he exclaimed. "I own myself beaten. That Margaret of yours has won over, in four minutes, the woman who's been intractable to me almost as many years! Witchcraft, by George! the witchery of a woman!"

But Garth was again unresponsive; the episode had touched him differently. He did not altogether like to see Elinor Golightley's reserve overborne, even by his own Madge.

The party were now at the fork of the path, one branch of which led to Urmhurst, the other to the village. Golightley faced round toward the two young ladies, and lifted his hat in picturesque salute.

"Addio, fair lassies! we part friends. A riveder-le! as the Florentines say." He stepped in front of them, and flowed on in his easy tones: "Elinor, tell mamma I'll be with her in the course of the afternoon to oversee the moving.—Margaret, you won't mind if an elderly, respectable Uncle Golightley . . . eh?" he bent forward and kissed her cheek.

She screamed "Oh!" and clung to Elinor's hand as if for protection. Golightley, however, did not read displeasure in her laughing eye; although Garth (who had his perversities, and was feeling rather fierce at such free behavior) was partly appeased by a lightning glance of comic repugnance, which she somehow or other contrived to dispatch in his direction at the same moment. Thus, in a very awkward predicament, Madge's nimble tact and self-possession recommended her to each of three very dissimilar persons. An ordinary woman would have offended them all, and made herself ridiculous into the bargain.

In thinking over this incident, Garth was puzzled to account for his own mental attitude. Instead of sympathetic indignation at maiden sanctities invaded (as just before with far slighter cause in Elinor's behalf), he had felt only anger at the infringement of his own rights. Yet, Madge, to his best knowledge and belief, was pure and modest as Elinor or any other woman could be. Was it possible, then, that she might, without detriment or dishonor, allow liberties which Elinor could not modestly have tol-

erated? And, if so, did it follow that Elinor's was the higher nature? or was Madge's
the fuller and more comprehensive, able to
think and do things which the colder and
narrower temperament must abjure? So
Garth would fain believe.

CHAPTER XXVI.

CHARACTERISTICS.

MEANWHILE he and his uncle were jog-
ging along the wood-path together with
every appearance of amity, the two young
women having turned off villageward. Golightley, after informing himself as to the
present condition of Urmhurst and the
neighborhood, began to talk about himself
in a manner which Garth, despite his irritation, could not but feel was humorous and
entertaining. It would appear that his companion had lived a life of no ordinary scope
and distinction. His creed smacked of the
companionship of gods: he knew them all
and called them by their first names, often
preceded by a pungent descriptive epithet.
He knew the politics of Europe, and his
counsel had given wealth to a Rothschild, or
saved the kingdom of a monarch. Many a
famous name in art and literature had he
helped to its renown. He touched lightly,
though ever with an air of authority, upon
æsthetic topics. Culture was his divinity,
he her high-priest. Beneath his unruffled
shirt-front abode in harmony the souls of
artist, author, sculptor, scholar, and epicure.
In sober earnest, Golightley Urmson was a
clever and even brilliant man, of observation
wide and hungry, if not always accurate;
shrewd and not without tact; hard to em-
barrass or put down. His style of narration, when he was in the vein, was engaging even when it moved the listener to smile
a little. He loved approbation, and when he
thought himself believed in he overflowed
with an airy kind of good-fellowship. He
manifestly, and not unjustly, prided himself
upon his astuteness and insight; yet a person
of less ability, who had been acquainted with
his foibles, might easily have mocked him
to his unconscious face. Self-centred men
too seldom take the precaution to look at
themselves from an outside point of view;
and can be skeptical about anything except
the sincerity of their companions' homage.

By-and-by some peculiar feature of the
landscape forced itself on Uncle Golightley's
attention, and led him to speak of his earlier
days.

"I never could decide, Garth," he remarked in his languid, superior, enlightened
way, drawing his hand down over his face
with a slow, self-admiring gesture—"I never
could quite make up my mind what place in
the world was worthiest for me to fill. My
father, dear good man that he was, wanted
me to go into business. No doubt I had business talents—splendid ones; but I shrank,
you know—recoiled from the idea of bind-
ing myself up for life in a ledger! Money
making, in the gross sense, was always hateful to me. What I craved, as I tell you,
was education—culture! Well, I had, at
one time, a passion for college; but, when I
came to look into it, I saw it was not for
me. I was a natural, a born scholar; but I
demanded first of all freedom, expansion! I
remember writing to the President of Har-
vard, and putting it to him whether that
place deserved the name of university where
each student might not study in his own
way and at his own leisure. But he was
too narrow to see the thing as I saw it, and
I was obliged to give it up! I saw then
that I must seek in the grand university of
the world all that our pygmy institutions
could not furnish. Well, I went to Europe.
There were some painful episodes connected
with my departure. My dear father was—
yes, Garth, why shouldn't you hear it?—he
was unjust, cruelly unjust to me. Yet I
never gave him cause for anger. Ah, well,
it's over now, forgiven if not forgotten.
But, by George! I've suffered!"

"But you're glad to be at home again?"

Golightley took off his hat and passed his
fingers wearily through his hair. "No one
can have stronger home-instincts than I
have," said he; "none could look forward
more yearningly to the rest and peace that
only home can bring. But a man who has lived
as I have lived can seldom feel what you young
people call gladness. There's too much bitter

knowledge—too much— But what am I about!" he exclaimed, suddenly altering his dejected tone, "piling the weight of my hypochondriacal philosophy on your young shoulders. Glad to get home? Yes, and I mean to stay here!"

"And the ladies too?"

"Now, old fellow," laughed Golightley, "not too much concern about my ladies, if you please! Great God! if your native ladies aren't enough for you, you are hard to satisfy. However, I'll tell you something about them. I met John Tenterden—crude, good-hearted, thick-bodied, old millionaire —in Germany. Got acquainted quite by accident, you know. A good old fellow, but no culture—oh, not a vestige of it, Garth!"

"Has Mrs. Tenterden got any?"

"Mildred—ah, Mildred is a fine woman! Naturally clever; Southern bred, and has her eccentricities, her little ruggednesses of speech and manner. Lovely to talk with, though, she has so much information."

"She is not a young woman?

"Oh, Mildred is all of sixty, perhaps sixty-five. · She and Cuthbert must be about of an age. But she don't look it; dark hair and eyes, erect, full bust, fine figure of a woman! But you should have seen her astonishment when I claimed her as my sister! Till that moment she had supposed that her mother and mine had met her death by accident or violence in the latter part of 1803. She had come North in that year, you know, to find Captain Brian, and had so contrived her flight as to lead to the belief that she'd been killed."

"Father told me that she had been in love with my grandfather long before; and had afterward married her cousin in the belief that he was dead. It's a strange story. Such constancy seems unnatural."

"A woman with a crotchet in her head is an unaccountable being," said Golightley, trimming his mustache. "Well, Mildred was about seventeen, and just married, when her mother disappeared. By-the-by, Mildred's marriage will show you the sort of woman she is. She wouldn't have John, though he'd offered himself half a dozen times, until one day he lost every penny he had in the world. Then what did she

do but offer herself and her fortune to him!"

"Very good of her."

"Oh, she's a darling! But I was going to tell you about Elinor. They'd come abroad chiefly to educate her. And by George! Garth, there never was a girl better educated, or with finer natural abilities, or who said less about them, than Elinor Golightley!"

"She looks rather cynical—"

"Ah! that kind of woman, that fine, sensitive organization, is so seldom at peace with itself. Until she met me she'd never known a human being who really understood her. Then, losing her father and mother just when she was becoming most passionately attached to them, you know, and coming among strangers, uncongenial in spite of their kindness; then, again, having no desire ungratified except the all-important desire for some being worthy of her love and able intelligently to sympathize with her—I tell you, I only wonder she isn't a greater cynic than she is. But under my influence she was losing all that, when poor John's death put her back a little temporarily."

"Music is her resource, I suppose?"

"Why, that voice of hers, my dear Garth," said Golightley in a confidential undertone—"that voice is simply—unique! Some of the first masters have told me that it is, in some respects, superior to anything else off the stage or on it. They were all wild about her, and there was one fellow in Dresden whom I thought I should have trouble with. He taught her for three months, and worshiped the very ground she walked on. One day he burst into the parlor where John and Mildred and I were sitting, and burst into tears. He said the thought of that voice being lost to the world was breaking his heart; and what was more, that he adored her, and would follow her round the world till she agreed to marry him! By George! you ought to have seen Mildred. She drew herself up like a regiment of cavalry. 'My good gracious alive, John! is the man mad?' Just then in came Elinor. She walked up to the writing-table with an air as if she owned mankind, and a devilish cold, sarcastic expression about the eyes and mouth. 'Come here, Herr Skalier,' says she. Down the poor devil plumps upon his knees, not knowing what was coming. She took out her purse. 'Our month is not quite up, Herr Skalier, but I'll pay you now, if you please. Count that and see if it's right, and then sign your name here;' and she dipped a pen in ink and held it to him. By George! Garth, I turned pale—I turned pale! Well, that's the sort of woman *she* is!"

"Quite unlike Mrs. Tenterden."

"Ha! ha! and only eighteen at the time, too. But she's a 'captain,' as Mildred would say. However, most people fall in love with Mildred before they do with Elinor. Well, she set her foot down that she'd have no more singing-masters; she'd been fond of the violin before, and from that time she took to it altogether; and to-day she's as supreme with that as she used to be with her voice. I tell you, Garth, she has but to say the word, and she might command a fortune from any director in Europe!"

Garth shook his head; the idea of Elinor on the public stage was repugnant to him.

"Of course, such a thing isn't to be thought of," resumed Golightley; "though she'd be as *safe* there, with that devilish cold eye of hers, as in her own boudoir. But oh," caressing his cheek, "we hope she's reserved for a happier, tenderer destiny than that!"

Garth drew his eyebrows slowly together; then, to change the subject, made some inquiry as to Mr. Tenterden's late loss of fortune.

"There was a mystery about that," replied his uncle, with a short laugh. "Nobody seemed to know what became of the money. John had asked me, some time before, to take charge of the estate for him. I told him I couldn't accept the responsibility. He said his former agent had died, and that he himself knew no more about business than a child (which was true enough); and he implored me to advise him as a friend, or if not that, then as Mildred's brother, since all the money really belonged to her. I was the more grieved to refuse, because I knew how much I might have done for him. Why, Garth, I remember standing in 1844 on the floor of the House of Commons talking with William Ewart Gladstone—one of the greatest financial geniuses that ever lived. I'd been dropping some hints about the forthcoming budget, and William was so startled by my insight into the thing that he turned to me and said, 'Mr. Urmson, if you were a member of this House we might look forward to the financial future of the country with confidence!' But as I was saying, just before John's disaster came about, a rather curious thing happened, which I was glad of on his account as well as my own.—Ah! what's that on the hill? is that our old Urmhurst?"

They had emerged from the woods, and there stood the venerable mansion, dark, solid, and square, against the sky, moored between its mighty chimneys; the many-paned windows glanced blue, while the dense oak-foliage of the porch wore a sullen crimson color. The projecting eaves and gabled dormers cast their shadows downward beneath the mid-day sun. Uncle Golightley made a long pause.

"Where is your studio, Garth?" he asked.

"In the northeast corner of the garret."

"In the garret—the old garret! Do you know, I spent a good deal of my time in that garret, when I was a boy. Pulling over musty old papers; I don't suppose there was a single document that I didn't examine."

"Did you expect to find some ancient deed of land, or forgotten will?"

"Ha! ha! Well, I dare say I was romantic enough for that. Odd, if you and I had both found our fortunes in that old garret—I with my documents, and you with your canvases. Tell me, Garth, you have good eyes, who is standing under the porch?"

"That's our old cook, Nikomis."

"Nikomis! an Indian name. Who is she?"

"No one knows much about her. She has lived with us more than ten years. I have taken her portrait; she's a picturesque old savage."

"How our forefathers would have stared to hear that an Indian would one day be domiciled at Urmhurst! Does the old lady know whose bones underlie that stone she's standing on?"

"She often looks grim enough to be the incarnation of their revenge," said Garth, smiling. "I'll christen my portrait 'Our Fury!'"

A silvery-haired figure at this moment turned the corner of the house, walking slowly, with his hands behind him, and a slight stoop in the shoulders. Golightley caught Garth by the arm. "Can that be Cuthbert?" he exclaimed. "Good God! is that white-headed old man Cuthbert Urmson?"

"Is he so old?" asked Garth, falteringly.

"Good God!" repeated Golightley, snatching off his tinted glasses, and thereby revealing a peculiar cast in one of his eyes; "my poor brother Cuthbert! Garth . . . what do you think he'll say to me?"

CHAPTER XXVII.

THE FIRESIDE.

AT Urmhurst, that night, there was an unusual scene. It had fallen suddenly cold after sunset, and the mighty kitchen-hearth had been cleared of the movable iron stove, kept to facilitate cooking operations, and the first great fire of the season had been kindled upon it. The rude stump of a hemlock-tree nearly six feet in girth, was brought in by Garth on a wheelbarrow, and cunningly built into place with a substructure and abattis of smaller logs, dry branches, brushwood, and shavings, and the whole set going by a skillfully-applied match. With much crackling and whispering the flames fastened hastily to their work, climbing from the smaller to the larger sticks with ever-increasing power and relish, until the underside of the hemlock itself began to flush red-hot from the multitudinous soft lapping of the fiery tongues, which corroded while seeming to caress. Anon came sharp, dry detonations, and a bubbling and stewing of sap from the ends of the huge stump; the

welded smoke and flame hurtled upward, and the spacious fireplace radiated such an abundance of heat that only one or two of the seven persons sitting round about could endure to face it steadily.

But love of a noble fire is so deep and universal in the human heart that it must correspond to some essential human quality. There is no better company, for it talks to each one in the language he loves best—helps the wit to be brilliant, and the silent man to hold his tongue with a good grace; is as fitting to a savage's cave as to an emperor's palace, and can never be in bad taste or out of fashion. It roars, and frolics, and devours, and tosses daringly aloft into the blackness of the chimney, even as the vital principle of existence flouts the hollowness of death. It humors our joy or sadness, but creates neither, being mere life without heart or soul; perhaps it suits best with that pensive mood which is often nearer to enjoyment than enjoyment itself.

The Urmhurst fireplace, with its room-like breadth and depth, must have been large, even for the age in which it was built. Standing within it, on a clear afternoon, and looking upward through the shaft of the chimney, stars could be discerned in the oblong patch of sky above. There was no mantel-piece, but, instead, a great hemispherical canopy of stonework projected outward, like a supplementary sort of roof; and there was some ornamentation in the way of old, smoke-darkened Dutch tiles, inlaid here and there, and, within the recess, half a dozen sooty iron hooks and festooned chains recalled the primitive methods of cookery.

The fireplace was built of brick, all but the hearthstone, a roughly-hewed piece of granite, its inequalities polished by the shuffling feet of full seven generations of Urmhurst cooks. As for the kitchen itself, it was large and lofty, and darksomely picturesque; wainscoted breast-high with black oak, and traversed as to the ceiling by two gigantic beams made out of irregularly-squared trunks of oak-trees, gradually narrowing in breadth from one end to the other. The half of the floor adjoining the front window was raised above the rest by a step some six inches in height; and the long, massive table, whose legs passed through the planking and descended into the cellar like the masts of a ship, was made with a corresponding joy half-way down its length.

Beyond the fireplace a narrow passage-way led to the back entrance of the kitchen, passing the head of the cellar-stairs on the right. The walls were diversified with shelves of glistening crockery, and here and there a closet-door. All these details, however, were but indistinctly discernible in the gamboling firelight, which, indeed, was less concerned in giving these prominence than in causing the seven shadows of those who sat so quietly around the hearth to dance an extravagant fandango—leaping from floor to ceiling, bobbing and beckoning to one another like grotesque goblins, and darting to and fro with superhuman agility; all this phantasmagoric *mêlée* being accompanied by a breathless stillness that rendered it oddly impressive.

"Ah! how it all comes back to me!" said one of the party at length; "bless you! I used to make just such fires as that, when I was a boy, on this very hearth. Delightful —isn't it, Mildred?—this primitive flavor about everything! I knew you'd enjoy it."

The lady addressed had been leaning back in her chair, posed in a stately, luxurious attitude that seemed natural to one of her statuesque proportions. She laughed good-naturedly, and answered, smoothing down her black dress with one hand:

"Oh, we have fires and fireplaces like this in Virginia, too: I dare say you know, Mr. Urmson? This is splendid, though, I'm sure, and I suppose the people here need great fires more than we do, the winters are so cold."

"But she never saw a hearthstone like this in Virginia—did she, Cuthbert? Come, you're our historian, tell us about it! It's a component part of New Hampshire, isn't it?"

"It goes down through the cellar, at all events," said Mr. Urmson. "When the foundations of the house were digging, this great bottomless rock seemed very much in the way, and the faint-hearted ones, who were terribly afraid of the ghost of the dead

Indian, wanted to abandon the site and go elsewhere. But Captain Neil would not, and by turning the plan of his house a little more to the southward, he brought the top of the rock into the kitchen fireplace. Then he reduced it to the proper level by cutting a thick slice off it, and so killed three birds with one stone; for there was a hearth ready made, and as for the slice, it served both as a tombstone to keep down the ghost, and as a threshold for the house. But Mrs. Tenterden will think she is living in a ghost-story if she hears any more Urmhurst legends to-night," added he, looking at her with his keen, grave smile.

"Oh, mercy!" exclaimed Mrs. Tenterden, more good-naturedly than ever, "I'm sure I don't mind it at all."

"It was good enough to make a hearth-stone of a piece of the solid earth," observed a low, sober-toned young voice from Mr. Urmson's right hand.

"I think so too," said he, turning toward her. "It's like a bond between the heart of the house and the heart of Nature. I like to believe that to the end of time this savage old rock can never quite forget the years it spent amid us, with our joys and follies, and griefs and deaths. Here it will stand when Urmhurst, and even this famous Yankee nation of ours, has dissolved into dust and vapor. But something human will have melted into it, and that is better than engraving inscriptions on obelisks for strangers to be curious about five thousand years hence."

"Now, Cuthbert, lad, do you tell the stories, and leave the preaching to me—haw, haw!—it's my business—haw, haw, ho! I don't believe this good lady here, nor miss there beside you, understands how a bit of granite can remember folks, any better than I do! and I was ninety-five last birthday, ma'am, so *that* needn't trouble you—eh? ha, ha!"

No one could resist the hoary geniality of this gruff-spoken old colossus, who seemed himself more ancient than the rocky womb of the land that bore him.

Mrs. Tenterden laughed heartily, and said, "Well, I suppose I am a pretty stupid old woman about such things." Mr. Urmson arched his eyebrows.

"The parson," said he, "is even more envious than stupid. I hope he may live to outgrow it; and if Miss Golightley had not made me forget myself by giving me a text, I should not have provoked him."

"But tell me, Uncle Golightley," said Madge, who sat between him and Garth, "is it certainly true that the Indian is buried under the threshold? Has nobody ever looked under it, to see?"

"People who look under gravestones," observed Garth, as his uncle did not immediately reply, "are apt to find a curse buried there, if nothing else."

Besides the seven persons whose shadows were flickering about the fire-lighted kitchen, there was an eighth present—a silent, self-contained, stoical individual, wrapped in a dark shawl, and smoking a short cutty pipe. It was old Nikomis, the cook, who had sat and smoked thus for the last ten years, and who, it appeared, was not to be frightened away by unusual company. She was so far removed within the chimney corner that, although the wrinkled coppery skin of her broad grim face received the intensest glow of the fire, no shadow was cast into the room beyond. She sat with her arms folded, and the pipe stuck in the corner of her mouth, and from pipe and mouth alike jets of smoke issued at stated intervals; but for this she might have been a statue or a mummy, so far as any sign of life was concerned. Hitherto she had neither taken part in the conversation, nor even seemed to be aware of it. But at Madge's idle question she partly turned, and pushing aside with one dark knotted talon the swath of grayish-black hair which hung down beside her face, fixed her narrow black eyes upon the fresh and lovely girl.

Garth, sitting between, observed these two women with an artist's eye for contrast. While marveling at the breadth of a human nature which could include two such diverse beings under one category, the fantastic notion occurred to him, whether any imaginable freak of destiny could ever cause their several thoughts or desires to run for one moment in the same channel. Madge, it was true, had been known to entrap Nikomis into something like conversation, and even

to effect an entry to the old Indian's wigwam in the garret, which was closed against every one else. But this must have been due rather to their intense dissimilarity, mental and spiritual as well as physical, than to any direct sympathy between them. The notion went and came in a breath, and then Garth made his rejoinder to Madge. Nikomis thereupon gave vent to a guttural "Ugh!" and, turning again to the fire, resumed her impassive smoking as before.

"The old lady agrees with you, Garth," remarked his father—for Nikomis's habitual silence had for years brought her to be spoken about in her own presence as if she were deaf or out of the way—"I have always believed that the murdered warrior, as well as the old original sachem, was an ancestor of hers, and this confirms it."

"My good fathers! Mr. Urmson," cried Mrs. Tenterden, with an accent of anxiety, "what—why—I shouldn't think it would be safe! at least," she added, lowering her voice behind her fan, "the Indians down in Virginia are perfectly awful."

"Oh! Mildred," murmured Golightley, letting his hand fall softly upon hers, "you are simply the most delicious woman in the world — isn't she, Cuthbert? Oh, it'll be charming to watch you two."

"Nikomis stays here, Mrs. Tenterden," said Cuthbert, entirely unmoved, "because the place belongs to her. I wish to atone for the wrong my forefathers did hers. She is a lady, and appreciates my motive; and even should justice require my scalp at her hands, no personal feeling would be engendered either on her part or mine."

The idea of Mr. Urmson being scalped by his cook caused Mrs. Tenterden to fold her statuesque arms with a shudder.

"But why do you think she is one of those Indians instead of any other?" she asked.

"It saves so much trouble. . If I believed she was some one else, how could I believe I was repairing my ancestors' misdeeds?"

The good-natured attempt which Mrs. Tenterden made to catch the drift of this remark put the scalping out of her mind; and, before she could recur to it, Golightley had taken up the conversation at the point where Garth had left it.

"By-the-by, Garth," he began affably, "aren't you laying down the law rather broadly as regards that matter of opening graves? My notion was that an old tomb was one of the likeliest of places for stumbling on some forgotten treasure in."

"If there's a fortune under our doorstep, it can't be meant for us," returned the young man. "We should probably stumble on some proof of our never having had a claim even to such fortune as we possess."

"Oh, then let us not look!" exclaimed Madge, with a *naïveté* that drew forth a general smile. "Besides — there are the ghosts. Are there any ghosts do you think, Miss Elinor?"

"It seems as if there might be to-night," said Elinor, with a half-playful apprehensiveness of eyes and tone, and a slight nervous shrugging of the shoulders.

"Ghosts? to be sure there are!" affirmed Uncle Golightley. "I wonder, now, whether I ever told any of you a ghostly experience of my own, which happened to me in this very house, when I was a mere boy—thirty years ago? I don't believe I ever did. Well, now, this is just the place' and time for a ghost story—let me see if I can remember it!" .

CHAPTER XXVIII.

GOLIGHTLEY'S DOUBLE

THERE was a general movement of attention, and Golightley began:

"Yes—I was between twelve and fifteen years old then. Cuthbert, you were away in Europe at that time, and I was living here alone with the captain, and being about as unhappy as I knew how to be, I suppose. I was much in the garret, partly to be out of the way, and partly because I enjoyed rummaging over the old chests of papers — It's curious, as I was remarking to you this morning, Garth, what an attraction that garret has had for our family one way or another."

"I recollect I used to haunt it before you

were born," remarked Cuthbert; "but I never saw the ghost."

"He appeared first to me," rejoined Golightley, stroking his face; "but there's no reason, so far as I know, why he should not appear hereafter to other people. Well, one day—one day, Miss Margaret, with your black eyes—I had staid in this garret until near dusk, and was just going to shut up the chest and depart, when my eye happened to light upon a document folded in triangular shape, which I couldn't remember having seen before. It was a parchment, very worn along the folds, and crumpled at the corners, and discolored in several places, as if it were either very old, or had been carried about a great deal in somebody's pocket. I took it to the window—for it was getting pretty dark, you know—and found some half-erased writing on the back—I could make nothing of that, and said to myself, 'I'll look inside.' But, on trying to open it, I found it was carefully sealed along the edges with seven wafers—four blue and three red ones.

"I was thinking whether or not it would be wrong for me to open it, when all at once I felt there was some one in the garret with me! I was scared for a minute: I was standing with my face to the window, and the idea of turning round was disagreeable, I can tell you! However, I had to turn at last, and sure enough there was somebody squatting down beside the chest of papers I had just left.

"I looked at him, at first, only in surprise. There was not much light to see him by, and he had his back toward me, still I fancied there was something familiar about him. Gradually I noticed that he appeared to be about my own age and size; not only that, but the clothes he wore were just like those I had on. His hair—as nearly as I could make out—was about as long as mine, and curled in the same way. And, by George! his way of pulling over the papers and holding them up to look at them, was so like my own way, that I could hardly believe he was not me! For all that, there was something devilish about him, as if some evil spirit was amusing himself with mimicking me. After I got over my surprise a little, I began to feel —not frightened, exactly, but indignant!

"I didn't move or say anything, but stood watching him; and, though it grew darker, I saw him more clearly in the darkness than in the light. He continued pulling over the papers and peering into them, until at last he brought out—what do you think it was, Mildred?"

"O Golightley, don't!" exclaimed Mrs. Tenterden, with one of her shudders. "I declare it's awful!"

"As soon as I saw it, I knew I had to deal with nothing human; and another thing—I became immediately conscious of what was going on in my *Doppelgänger's* mind, or perhaps it would be more accurate to say, I felt his mind as if it were my own, and the thoughts he had seemed to be my thoughts. Though I saw him, and knew that I was something distinct from him, yet I knew that I was possessed by him, in the same sense that people used to be in the witch-days. And though I felt, so far as I had any feeling of my own left, that he was hideous and repulsive to the last degree, still I couldn't help sympathizing with him, and looking at things from his point of view, and agreeing, as it were, to everything he proposed. But the worst of it was, that I knew I was guilty of whatever wickedness he might meditate: I must consent to his crimes, and that was the same as to commit them myself. He had power over me!"

"Why didn't you down on your knees, lad, and pray God to succor you?" boomed the venerable parson, at this point.

"I didn't think of it, I suppose, until it was too late. It was part of the ghost's infernal cunning, you see, to make me forget everything except him and what he was doing. Well, the thing he brought out was a discolored old parchment, folded in triangular shape, and very much worn and crumpled along the edges. He turned it over, and I saw, looking through his eyes, that something had been written on the back, and partly scratched out. Then I felt him think —'I'll open it!' and when he (or we) made the attempt, we found it was sealed along the edges with seven wafers—three red and four blue."

"Why, it was something like the one you found, wasn't it?" murmured Mrs. Tenterden. "How strange there should be two of them!"

"A coincidence," remarked Cuthbert, "is often the strangest feature of adventures of this kind.—Proceed, brother!"

"The sight of those wafers," continued Golightley, who was sitting erect, with his elbows on the arms of his chair, and accenting his narrative with the impact of one long forefinger against the other—"the sight of those seven wafers, so far from making me hesitate about my right to break them open, gave me (through the depraved heart of the *Doppelgänger*, you understand) a thrill of delight, because here was something unlawful to be done. And yet, somehow, it didn't seem wrong either, but a particularly pleasant kind of right. At all events, when I saw him begin breaking the seals open, I approved and rejoiced exceedingly, and accepted the deed as my own. We violated them one by one, and, when the parchment lay open before us, we had a complacent little chuckle together."

"The Lord be merciful unto you a sinner!" rumbled Parson Graeme, whose venerable mind had lost the elasticity whereby to distinguish the impress of a skillfully-told fiction from that of a true tale. Fortunately, he was a Universalist, and had hopes even for so depraved a soul as Uncle Golightley's.

"But tell me—what was in the parchment?" demanded Madge, with a piquant intrepidity that caused a corner of Cuthbert's mouth to move slightly, and him to turn a quiet glance on the questioner.

"What was in it, my dear child?" returned Uncle Golightley, taking her hand caressingly in his own; "why, writing—nothing but writing!" The body of the writing was in an old-fashioned but easily-legible hand; but across the top of the page was one sentence in a different character. We read that first, and it gave us such an appetite for what was to follow, as only a warning to read no further could have done.

"However," said the story-teller, after an interval of silent gazing at the fire, which, reflected in his glasses, seemed to give his eyes a red, demoniac glare—"however, I am not going to tell you what was written in that document—I promised my *Doppelgän-*

ger I wouldn't, and it's a promise I haven't the courage to break. Luckily, the story does not need that I should; in fact, its peculiar interest would be greatly impaired were I to do so. It is enough to say that it was a potent spell, and that its effect was to endow us (under certain penalties which I can appreciate better now than I did then) with a peculiar and irresistible power; a power, too, that could be exercised invisibly, and whose very existence would be unsuspected by most people. Not only that, but it was, in a certain sense, a perfectly legitimate power; no one could have condemned me—us—for using it; no one, except ourselves, could have divined the secret sin that lurked within it; in fact, the sin was nameless, intangible—so subtile that it vanished altogether beneath a direct look, or appeared only in the likeness of a virtue. And to tell the truth," affirmed Uncle Golightley, leaning back in his chair with a dry laugh—"to tell the truth, my good people, I'm more than half inclined, to-night, to think that there really was, so far as I was concerned, more of right than wrong in the matter, after all! The devil had a finger in the pie, I admit; but it's my opinion that he simply played a practical joke on my common-sense; and that, if he had kept out of the way and had left me to deal with that seven-sealed affair alone, I should have come off without singeing a hair. It was the doubt—the damned, haunting, casuistical doubt—that betrayed the cloven hoof! That *Doppelgänger* of mine—he tries to persuade me that he's the best friend I have; and most of the time I believe him, but sometimes—when I have a headache or an influenza, for instance—sometimes I don't!

" Well—but this is getting to be rather a metaphysical ghost-story, isn't it.—Come, wake up, Mildred, and hear the end of it.—As for you, Cuthbert, old boy, I see you remember my philosophic and analytic predilections of old.—Well, and so, my little Margaret, the ghost and I read to the end of our naughty parchment, and then we folded it carefully up, and sat down to think what we would do next. We didn't need the parchment any more—that was pretty plain to us—but neither would it do to destroy it,

or to let anybody else get hold of it. It must be put away somewhere, where it would remain both safe and secret. After a few moments I felt it coming into the ghost's mind where the hiding-place should be ; and I agreed to it immediately, and we had another quiet chuckle over our cleverness. I saw him put the papers back in the box and shut the box up; the triangular parchment with the seven violated seals he thrust into his bosom—I still seeming to be the real doer of all he seemed to do. He got up and stole away on tiptoe down the garret-stairs; it was then quite dark, but, as I said before, I could see him all the better for that, and I stole along with him. It was so dark that, when we came to the first-floor and met Captain Brian on the broad landing, he passed without seeming to see us. Since then I have often wondered whether, had he seen us at all, he'd have seen two of us or only one ? and which one ?

" Down we went to the kitchen—this same old kitchen with the embers of a fire upon the hearth. There was light enough there to throw a shadow on the opposite wall, but yet there didn't seem to be enough to cast two ! One only could I see stealing along beside me. Either the ghost itself was the shadow—or else, in spite of its overmastering reality to me, it had not material stuff enough to intercept the dying firelight. We went to the dresser—the same one, I think, that stands beside the wall there now—and laid hold of an old pewter plate with a double bottom, used for keeping buckwheats hot. We unscrewed the false bottom, slipped the triangular parchment inside the plate, and screwed it up again. Then we took an old hatchet from the corner where it hung and went down the cellar-steps.

" It must have been pitch-dark, but I saw my pet cat sitting on the head of an apple-barrel. She had always been fond of me, after the selfish· manner. of cats; but now her back was up, her eyes glaring, and her tail almost as big round as my arm. As we came nearer, she gave the most hideous, despairing, miserable yowl I ever heard, and dashed past us up the stairs. It could not have been the sight of me that had thrown her into such a fit, and I leave it to any one familiar with ghost-stories like this to guess what else it could have been.

"The cellar-door flew shut with a bang, closing us in. I was ordinarily rather a timid boy, I believe, and I remember wondering why I didn't feel frightened then, for I was as bold as a lion. Probably it was because I existed only in sympathy with the ghost, and, of course, a dark cellar was the most congenial sort of place for him. We kept along and soon brought up against that part of the wall which is just underneath the front-door of the house. On the other side of the wall, and beneath the threshold-stone, lay the bones of the two legendary Indians. The wall was of brick—the same bricks that Neil Urmson had built up there two centuries before. I saw the ghost take the hatchet and begin loosening some of these bricks and taking them out. I had known he would do this ever since I felt the purpose enter his mind up in the garret, and now I approved again, and seemed to help. In a short time there was a hole through the wall, and a little cavity had been dug out beyond. It seemed to me that we had dug right into the skeleton of the murdered Indian; and when we had taken the old pewter plate with its contents, and thrust it far into the hole, I peeped in through the ghost's eyes, and saw it lying in the mouldering cavity of the ribs, just where the heart used to be!"

Here Mrs. Tenterden began to laugh rather hysterically; remarking brokenly that it seemed such a funny thing for a skeleton to have a pewter plate for a heart.

"Ay, see how a man is led on from one thing to another!" growled the ancient parson. "If he hadn't broken open the seals and read the parchment in the first place, he'd never have been tempted to make away with his father's warming-dishes afterward!"

"Well, I'm nearly at the end of my catalogue of crimes," returned Golightley, laughing affably, and not at all put out by the interruption. "By George! I ought to feel complimented—eh, Cuthbert?—at the flavor of reality I seem to have contrived to give to this extempore little *jeu d'esprit.*—Let

me see, where was I, my dear little Margaret? Oh, yes, we had got the parchment safe into the hole. Well, then we filled the hole up, and replaced the bricks as they were before. And then came the most disagreeable part of the adventure to me.

"The ghost had hitherto kept his back constantly turned toward me, and I had never thought of his face—whether it resembled mine or was different from it, or how it was. I had only seen him from behind, and had no more curiosity as to his features than as to my own. But, when the last brick had been settled in its proper position and there was no more work to do, the ghost turned quietly about and stared at me!

"He certainly did resemble me very closely, but it was a ghastly likeness, brimming over with infernal malice. It was a face that copied mine throughout to a hair, and yet, instead of being an innocent, boyish face, it was a face that had lived in hell, and was familiar with all its wickedness. And another thing—wicked as it was from the core outward, I could see nothing in it which I could not imagine true of myself. We were essentially one, and among all the legions of devils there was not one who could have represented me as this one did. In him I saw all my good turned to bad, and all my bad made worse. He was a visible prophecy of what I might at last become, and had just taken the first step toward becoming. You mustn't expect me to describe the face; but if any one of you, when you get to heaven, grow tired of singing psalms and thrumming on your harps—just look down over the edge for a minute and call for me!

"Now, as I said, so long as the ghost had kept his back toward me, and so concealed the full blast of his deviltry, I had been bold and jaunty enough; but when he confronted me eye to eye, and forced me to realize what it was had supported me and led me on, I began to sicken and tremble. At the same time, though, I felt that whatever strength I had now depended on him, and that, hideous as he was, I could rely on no other support than his. I would have given the best half of my life never to have seen him at all, but, since that was past helping, I was ready to give the other half to keep him with me forever thenceforth. But the worst of that kind of friends is, they are so apt to take leave of you on the wrong side of the scrapes they get you into; and I knew, as soon as he turned about, that he was going to desert me in that dark cellar. The last moment, I remember, was an indescribable whirl of all sorts of strange sights and thoughts. I imagined this fellow dogging my steps ever since I was born, sometimes coming near enough to touch me, sometimes dropping behind again, then catching up once more, and, on this fatal day, fairly getting the best of me. And that was not all: I saw him cropping up at unexpected junctures throughout my future life, always bearing the same devilish resemblance to me, always, by means of the spell, helping me to gain some advantage, fair in outward seeming, but which in my own secret heart I knew was dastardly.

"So by degrees he vitiated my soul, surely, yet so subtilely that even to myself I would not admit my guilt. At last the fifth act of the tragedy came; the spell had been used for the last time—it had succeeded, as it always must, but my time was drawing near. In one of the concluding scenes I made a sort of half-hearted effort to retrieve myself, but it did not avail. Suddenly I saw a body that I knew was mine, lying in a familiar room, bleeding inwardly. Friends were standing round it, and some enemies were not far off; but, searching everywhere, I could nowhere find the demon. For an instant I felt a thrill of triumph, thinking that after all I had escaped. Then the last breath came, and the soul left the lifeless corpse and paused for a moment beside it. As it turned away to depart I saw its face, and it was the face of the demon.—There, my little Margaret, is not that a nice ghost-story?"

CHAPTER XXIX.

A KISS AT PARTING.

I NEVER knew, brother," said Cuthbert, after no one had spoken for a time, "what a dramatic genius you had. Upon my word, I would not dare venture either into the garret or the cellar to-night."

"My good fathers!" ejaculated Mrs. Tenterden, folding her arms with a shudder, "I should think not, indeed!"

"But that isn't all!" exclaimed Madge; "how did you get out of the cellar? And did you ever see the ghost again?"

Golightley laughed, and drew his hand down over his face caressingly. "I see I shall have to confess," said he, "or you'll all be looking upon me as a hideous criminal, taking this means to make a clean breast of it, without getting compromised.—Why, don't you recollect, Cuthbert, that old volume of Italian romances, translated by a certain John Reynolds about the time our family left England, and brought over here, I suppose, by old Captain Neil himself? Well, I got the idea of my yarn from one of those infernal old histories of his; and, by adding local tints here and there, I made it into what you heard. Bless me! I thought some one of you would have found me out before I was half through."

"If John Reynolds could have told the story as you told it," observed Garth, with a long sigh, "we should have remembered him even after two centuries. There's truth in it, more or less, for everybody!"

"I don't like to think so," murmured Elinor, with a slight frown and contraction of the under eyelids.

"What! all a make-believe?" grumbled old Mr. Graeme, standing up and kicking a shower of sparks out of the red-hot log with his huge foot. "Humph! shouldn't make believe about serious things like that, Golightley, my lad. However, since it's over and done, it's better to have it make-believe than truth—no doubt about that, eh?—haw, haw, haw!—Nikomis, what do you think—why, where is she?"

It was now observed for the first time that Nikomis was no longer one of the circle. On reflection, however, Garth thought he remembered having seen her depart about five minutes previous—shortly before the close of the story, and Madge affirmed that she had gone off in the direction of the back-door.

"Your metaphysics were too much for

her, brother," said Cuthbert; "the next time you tell the story, you must flavor it with scalps and tomahawks, for her sake."

"I told it altogether too well ever to venture on repeating it," returned Golightley, laughing and turning away. "By George! I almost humbugged myself for the time being."

"Nellie!" said Mrs. Tenterden, who had just crushed a yawn, "isn't it time our wagon was here?—I declare, Golightley," she added, good-naturedly, "all this excitement has made me dreadfully sleepy!"

Garth looked out of the window and reported that the wagon was at the door. It was thereupon arranged that Elinor and Mrs. Tenterden should come the next afternoon to visit the studio, while Madge, who was sitting as a model to Garth in one of his pictures, was to appear in the morning. Meantime, the minister, with ponderous gallantry, stood ready to escort the three ladies home, looking, in his vast cape-coat, like some genial old mountain with snowy summit. The ladies put on their shawls and hoods, for it was colder than ever, and all the seven friends came out upon the door-step, and paused there a moment to see the wide valley sleeping beneath the moon, and Wabeno watching over it like a shadow.

"Is this the threshold-stone you all were talking about," inquired Mrs. Tenterden, "that has the Indians under it?"

"Yes," replied Cuthbert; "and it is here that the pewter buckwheat-plate reposes."

"Now, grandfather, if you'll put Mrs. Tenterden into the wagon, I'll hold the horse," said Garth.

"Uncle Golightley," said Madge, softly, as they stood observing the parson's manœuvres with his charge, "I can tell you where Nikomis went."

"Can you, my dear?" he responded, laying his hand affectionately on her shoulder. "Well, where did Nikomis go?"

"She went down-cellar," said Madge, looking up in his face.

Uncle Golightley made no reply.

"She's a funny old creature," continued Madge, "but not half so stupid as she looks. She used to be considered a sort of witch, I believe, before she came here. I think I am better acquainted with her than almost any one, and she has told me some very curious things. I think you would be interested in her."

"All in?" called Garth, from the horse's head.

"In a moment!" cried Madge.—"Thank you, Uncle Golightley! Good-night!" She gave his hand a little pressure, and whispered in his ear: "I liked your story very much; but I shall make you tell me the rest of it some time!"

"All right?" called Garth, again.

"Yes, yes!" they all said.

As he came round to the side of the wagon, Madge stooped down, and held out her mouth for a kiss. He kissed her; and the wagon drove off before Uncle Golightley could decide whether or not it were incumbent on him to claim a salute likewise.

CHAPTER XXX.

THE STUDIO.

"On, my Garth," exclaimed Madge; "I am so tired!"

"Rest, then," he answered, lowering his paint-brush and leaning back in his chair.

"I didn't mean in that way," rejoined she, availing herself, nevertheless, of the permission, to stretch her arms and alter her position. "I'm tired of seeing you sit there so long moving a little brush up and down. Tell me, do you love painting better than you love me?"

Garth looked at her, with his chin upon his breast, but made no reply.

The studio occupied the northeastern corner of the attic, an area about six paces square being divided off from the rest by rough partitions. The naked beams and boards of the angled roof, sloping steeply to the floor on the north and east, gave a rude vitality to the aspect of the room. The brown bareness of the walls was partly veiled by festoons of sombre or vivid drapery, and partly by studies of human heads or bits of landscape, tacked up here and there. An ottoman across one corner of the room was covered with the hide of an Indian tiger; in the recess behind, a cast of the Venus of Milo was bound as to the temples with a blue-silk scarf, whose fringed ends rested on her left shoulder. In the opposite corner stood a suit of early seventeenth-century armor, reflecting in its polished surfaces, with an added depth of tone and grotesquely distorted, the manifold forms and colors of the surrounding objects. Scores of canvases were stacked against the walls, some with their brown backs turned to the spectator, others revealing more or less of their painted faces. An antique bronze candelabrum depended from a hook in the great beam traversing the angle of the roof. A small iron stove was set up on the hearth, and above the fire-board were grouped some of the old pikes and battle-axes which Captain Neil Urmson brought with him from England, in 1647, together with a couple of Revolutionary muskets and a pair of cutlasses, trophies of the late captain's warlike achievements. The studio was lighted through the roof, a section of which to the north had been removed, and its place supplied with coarse glass, across which wired shades were made to slide back and forth. In the shadow beneath this window lurked a tall, mysterious mirror.

Of the pictures to be seen here, not the least striking, perhaps, was the studio itself, with the artist and his model posed in the strong light and shadow. She, clad for the occasion in an antique, long-waisted gown, ruffles at her wrists and a quaint ruff standing out round the open neck, a heavy chain falling from her shoulders to her waist, and an aigrette of feathers in her puffed and frizzed hair, was seated negligently in a high-backed, oaken arm-chair, her crossed feet outstretched beyond the stiff hem of her embroidered petticoat, and her right cheek supported on her hand. Over against her the artist at his easel, again in his red boating-shirt, the sleeves turned up to the elbows of his dark, muscular arms. Masses of deep brown hair stood up all over his square-built head; while the white light from above showed the depression in the centre of his rugged forehead, and cast swarthy

shadows beneath the irregular level of his shaggy brows, and brought sharply out the strong curves of the under lip, and the cleft in the chin. When he was seated, the massiveness of the young man's chest and shoulders, and the noble set of his head upon his stalwart neck, gave promise of imposing stature; and it was an odd surprise, on his standing up, to find that he was below middle height.

Madge, after a pause, during which she twisted the links of her necklace between the fingers of her left hand, spoke again. Her tone was half plaintive, half wayward; but the girl was so thoroughly good-natured, so prone to humorous mischief, and, above all, so beautiful, that it was always difficult to forecast either her words or her acts. The eye of analysis was dazzled by her charms, while the subtile fluctuations of her moods compelled it to be continually focusing itself anew.

"You loved me better when you loved me first," said she, "and you used to say then that you hated painting—well, at least, you said it was wicked, and you hate everything wicked, you know. Now that you've come to care for painting, you'll begin to hate me!"

"How am I changed, Madge?"

"Oh, don't I remember how you used to blaze at me with your eyes sometimes, and make me quiver all over! You're always quiet and grave and old, now; and I'm getting old, too! But painting crawls so, that a year seems no longer to you than a week does to me."

"What a silly girl to be jealous of painting! Were you jealous of my mother? she was my first love. Sit here beside me," he continued, in a more tender voice. "My girl, other loves can only teach me how to love you better."

Madge, having seated herself on a camp-stool at her lover's side, had taken one of his hands in her lap, and was stroking it lightly with her finger-tips.

"You have the handsomest, strongest hands that were ever seen," murmured she. "You might do anything with such hands."

"I'll make you a fortune with them."

"Will you?" said she, glancing at him

sidelong. "Is that all you paint for—to make me a fortune?"

Garth hesitated, half smiling.

"Are you always thinking of me when you paint?" she went on, holding up her finger. "No; and I believe you often forget me even when you're doing my portrait!"

"You're too near me to be seen or thought of distinctly," returned he, reddening a little; "but you must be at the bottom of all I think or do."

She nodded her head, and smiled to herself without looking up. "I'd like a fortune," said she, lightly; "the biggest in the world; but I'd want some of the world with it!"

Garth waited to hear more.

"I wouldn't paint pictures or write books, or do any of that stay-at-home sort of work, if I were a man! because, however well I did them, it's they would be famous, and not I my own self. Instead of sending things off to make money for me, I'd go and make money my own self, and have everybody see me make it; and I'd make it *with* my own self, because I was so brave or strong or beautiful or something! If I were a man, I'd be a famous soldier, and conquer the whole world; or a terrible robber; or at least a great minister or statesman, to make everybody do and think what I pleased —one day one thing, and another day the opposite thing, if I chose it! Yes, I would Mr. Garth, if I were a man!"

"Humph!" ejaculated the artist, clutching at his back-hair, with a smile; "better be a prize-fighter or an acrobat."

"I'm only a woman, you know," continued Madge; demurely, though with a peculiar glance into her lover's face. "But even women can do something besides stay at home and spend money, if they have it; and, if not, grow old and be poor both. I can't sing and play on the violin like Miss Golightley: but I could be an actress, and have all the men in the world in love with me. I'm not afraid of them, and I'm beautiful enough: and I know how to make myself seem even more beautiful than I am. What do you think of that, Mr. Garth?" she demanded, with a sudden soft laugh that

prevented him from knowing exactly what to think. He gazed at her, but, though she met his gaze, he could not penetrate the laughter-sparkles dancing in her long, black eyes.

"What put that in your head?" he asked at length.

"It isn't in my head, it's I!" returned she, laughing still. "Do you remember that night when you canoed the rapids? Well, if you hadn't done it, sir, I'd have disappeared that same night, nobody knows where."

"I didn't tell you about it till next day," said Garth, shaking his head.

"Oh, I'm a witch! didn't you know? Nikomis taught me. I was flying over the tops of the trees, on my way to a witches' meeting on Waheno, when I saw you shooting the lower fall; so I alighted on the pine-knoll, and left the other witch who was with me to go on by himself. He was angry, but I told him that a man who was brave and skillful enough to run those rapids was better than a witch who could fly about on a broomstick. Since then, every once in a while, he's sent me invitations to attend witch-meetings all over the world; and several times, Mr. Garth, I almost went; for you haven't done any brave, splendid things for ever so long; and you were away from me in Europe for years and years. Tell me, did you think I'd rather stay here than travel about with you? Would you have been astonished if you'd met me in London, or Vienna, or Paris, or some of those nice places, leaning on the witch's arm? Well, I think it was very good in me to resist his temptation, and wait for you to come back. But now you only sit and paint, as if people lived forever, and Urmhurst was the best place to live in. I wish I were a man!"

Garth turned in his chair and took both her hands in both his, with a gentleness which was at times peculiar to him, and more impressive than any ordinary vehemence.

"My dear girl! my dear little girl," he repeated in a low, inward voice, such as the listener seems rather to feel than to hear. In a few moments he rose abruptly, and began to pace up and down the studio slowly, his hands clasped behind his head. "I've done you wrong, Madge; but poverty is the trouble—we live from hand to mouth. Would you have married me any time in the last six years?"

"Listen, my Garth," returned she, springing up to walk beside him, folding her hands round his arm and speaking close to his ear. "I would have married you the day you left college. You should have asked me, sir! Then we would have been rich and famous before now."

"It takes as long for a married painter to make a reputation as for an unmarried one; and meanwhile—"

"Oh, always this painting!" cried she, stamping her foot. "Garth, you are asleep; ever since you've had an easel and palette you have been asleep. Be all warm, and awake, and fierce, and splendid! Make me afraid of you a little, please, dear! Yes, I am jealous of painting; I want you to love me—me, more than anything in the world! Do you?"

"Yes," said Garth, pausing in his walk and looking at her.

She put her quick arms round his neck with a little exulting cry, and they kissed each other.

"If you had married me when you left college," resumed Madge, softly, looking down at the dainty pointing of her toes as they walked on, "it wouldn't have been by painting that we should have made our fortune. Ah! you don't know what I can do, even if I wasn't a witch. You don't know me, dear, though you love me better than anything in the world. But if you'd married me, you naughty boy, you would have found me out long ago—and found yourself out too."

"Do you know what you are talking about?" exclaimed Garth, half laughing, but with a hint of passion in his tone.

"Look there!" said Madge. She pointed to the dark corner where the mirror stood, now reflecting the faces and figures of her lover and herself. "Are not those two people handsome and well-matched—eh? and they have brains, which is more important. The man looks his brains: you might think the woman only beautiful, but I

shouldn't wonder if she had as much sense as the man; at least, she can use what she has more easily. I believe those two people could do anything they pleased: only, they must always please to do the same thing. They could do or be anything—a king and queen, if they chose. I wish the man was taller: however, his face makes him seem taller than other men's bodies make them look. He and his wife are just of a height .... oh, she isn't his wife, is she?"

This latter turn was so demurely given, that for an instant Garth missed the point of it, and for the next instant doubted whether Madge saw it herself. But there was a sparkle in the corner of her eye to rebuke his slow wits. There could certainly be no question as to her intelligence; and some of its manifestations made Garth, in spite of his years in Europe, half believe himself her inferior in worldly wisdom. She was self-possessed to a degree extraordinary in a village maiden, unless her own theory as to witchcraft were to be accepted.

He paused a while before speaking. It was hard to be self-contained under the influence of this young woman. She made darkness seem light, and the impossible easy, and, witch or not, she was bewitching.

"What do you want?" he demanded at length. "If I'm not a painter, I'm nothing!"

"You don't know what you are. You are a man; I love men, and the best man best; and I've never seen a better man than you. Most good men are fools, and most bad men are cunning; but you are not cunning, and you're not a fool; you are good, and yet you have all the strength that bad men have."

"Madge, if Sam Kineo had beaten me in that fight of ours, would you have loved him instead of me?"

She looked sidelong at him, and gave his arm a soft pressure, but the next moment said, waywardly: "Why not, sir, if he'd beaten you fair, and been in the right? He told a falsehood about me, to be sure; but if he'd made it good against you . . . there's no telling, it might have turned out true."

"Is strength all you care for, then?"

"What is better worth a man's having,

I'd like to know? women don't fall in love with weak failures. You cannot use your strength in painting."

The artist stopped in front of his easel, and gazed frowningly at the picture. Madge, her cheek resting on his shoulder, embraced his relaxed arm and hand. Her eyes were toward the picture, but she was watching her lover, and feeling his pulse; being still, perhaps, a little afraid of him.

"My best does that," he said at length, nodding at the canvas; "and so the highest part of me doesn't satisfy you."

"No part of you satisfies me: I want the whole! Men must have bodies to their heads. Painters aren't manly enough for you to be one. You should do things, not sit down and imitate them."

"Great painters are great men; you don't know what you're saying, Madge. The 'whole' means evil as well as good: my art has helped to keep my evil down."

"Why do you call it evil? strength and power are not evil, my Garth. I believe a great deal is lost from the fear we have of being called bad, by weak people and fools. Let them call us what they like, so we get the better of them."

"Hush, my darling! You never talked like this before. I shall begin to believe all you said about witches and robbers."

Madge relinquished his arm, and walking listlessly to the model's chair sat down in it. "Well, paint me, sir," said she; "you love my picture better than me. But it can never be to you what I would be, and you can never be to it what you might have been to me."

"Heaven and earth!" burst forth Garth in a sudden blaze, "what would you have me do?"

The woman's eyes filled with tears, and she hid her face in her hands. "I only want you to love me!" quavered she.

"Love you! Would it be loving you to give up painting? Oh, I've had my temptations! without knowing it, you have sometimes been my tempter. Asleep? but I'm doing my best: don't wake me in that way! But it's hard and dull for you . . . but, Madge—"

Although Madge had hidden her face,

and filled her eyes with tears that were at least half honest, she had not closed her eyelids; for Garth, while thus passionately delivering himself, was worth looking at—with hot face and flashing eyes, and hands now clinched, now thrown open, as was his way in vehement moments. But with the utterance of her name his fierceness melted, and his voice was charged with the masculine tenderness which, however self-possessed, she could never hear without a quickened heart-beat. He came near, and drew her hands from her face, dropping to his knee beside her chair.

"Madge, I'll confess: I thought you tired of me. We were too long apart, and misunderstood each other. I've not done all I might with painting—not tried to make money from it, as if I'd been sure of you. I got bound up in my pictures, and stingy of them. But now, I'll sell everything; I'll paint to sell, and to be famous. It's a grand profession, more than I can do justice to; I musn't give it up. But no more dullness and slowness, my girl. Come, we'll finish this picture, and then wait no longer. Marry me, dear: be my wife. You shall see the world, and be happy your own way—every one at your feet. Come, I trust you—trust me!"

She leaned back luxurious, with half-closed eyes and parted lips. This was something like a wooing! Truly, when Garth was in this vein almost might a statue have throbbed responsive; and Madge, despite her clear head and firm fibre, was exquisitely sensible to the luxury of love: possibly, indeed, her appreciation outdid any man's power of ministering to it single-handed. Be that as it may, she was soothed and pleasured now, and had the wisdom not to let her present failure to enforce her will regarding her lover's profession distress her. Suffice it that, after long apathy, she had kindled anew in him some of that passionate fire which she had almost feared was quite extinct. Yes, he could still be splendidly impetuous, still bring agreeable flutterings to her heart, and stimulate blood to her cheeks and tears to her eyes. He was lovable still; a hero not likely to be given up, painter or no. And though, in his strong moods, he swayed her judgment and magnetized her will, she was nevertheless self-conscious of a subtiler, more persistent power, likely in the end to get the odds in her favor.

"How can I help trusting you, when you're so kind to me?" murmured she with a happy sigh. "I must wait till you're cross again before knowing what to do." Presently she looked and leaned toward him, and said with curious earnestness: "Garth, tell me, you are really more than other men? I've thought a great deal, but I've seen very little. You never met any one, in Europe or anywhere, that you were afraid of? but no, no!" she added quickly, putting her hand over his mouth, "don't answer me—never answer me when I ask such silly questions: I don't want to hear, and you don't know what I mean either. Let us be happy, and think of nothing. There! now go and paint me: I won't be tired again."

CHAPTER XXXI.

THE PICTURE.

THE sitting was accordingly resumed, Garth working at first mechanically, but gradually increasing in fervor, till he began to emit the occasional long sighs which denoted profound absorption. "I wish your lodgers weren't coming to-day," he muttered, at length, "I might finish this head."

"If I'd been Miss Golightley, I'd never have left Europe," affirmed the model. "I'd have gone on the stage with my violin, and made a bigger fortune than Mrs. Tenterden lost."

"You're not cold-blooded and *blasé*, but beautiful and energetic," replied Garth, with rather less than his customary impartiality. "How do they get on at your house?"

"They don't know how to be poor at all," said Madge, laughing; "but they are very pleasant. I hope they'll find who stole their money. Mrs. Tenterden said a detective was after it—not a regular detective, but some one who had been acquainted with them before; a Mr. Selwyn—the same name as your friend."

"Ha!" muttered Garth, to himself; "what if it should be Jack! it would be like him to turn detective for a while—and be a good one, too."

"Your uncle Golightley knows nothing about the detective," Madge remarked, after a short silence. "He doesn't believe in detectives, Mrs. Tenterden said, and told her it would be no use employing one. But this Selwyn offered himself in a friendly sort of way, and Mrs. Tenterden consented without telling your uncle, because, she says, he's been so kind and helpful that he would feel hurt if anything were done against his advice."

"I should think Mrs. Tenterden was in the right," said Garth. "Turn more to the left, and look at the battle-axe over the fireplace."

"Your uncle is very rich now, isn't he?"

"I know nothing about it; he didn't appear to be two years ago."

"If he is, do you think he'll give you back any of the money your father has been sending him?"

"He might make the offer," said the artist, with a smile. "But, you know, there's a mystery about that which nobody understands, except, perhaps, Uncle Golightley himself."

"He is rather mysterious," she responded, meditatively. "What a strange story he told us last night!"

"Father says he was a morbidly imaginative boy."

"Such vivid imagination seems like reality to me. What do you suppose was in that paper that he hid in the cellar?"

"You're turning to the right again," said the artist, shaking his head.

"Do you think it could have had any connection with the mystery about the money?" persisted the model, who seemed mischievously determined to prove her lover's patience to the utmost. "Let me tell you, sir," she continued, as he pursued his work in silence, "that you have no head for affairs. You would let yourself be robbed as easily as poor Mrs. Tenterden. And if ever something happens that you pretend you wish should happen, Mr. Garth, it must be on condition that every bit of the business be left to me! do you hear?"

"God bless your clever little heart! you shall do your worst with me and with everything belonging to me," exclaimed he, laying down his palette and brushes, and clasping his hands behind his head, with a smile. "Only you must promise to let me paint you at least once a year without asking me a single question about the connection between bank-accounts and ghost-stories. There they come!"

In fact, there was a multitudinous tramp upon the attic-stairs, and the indistinct murmur of voices; then three authoritative raps on the door.

"Come in," said Garth, throwing on his coat and passing his hands through his hair. In stepped, accordingly, first Mrs. Tenterden in black, somewhat out of breath, but smiling and greeting the artist with perfect good-nature; then Miss Golightley, in gray touched up with scarlet, coldly civil and undemonstrative; close behind her, Uncle Golightley, striding magnificent in a purple-velvet smoking-jacket, with his head in the air; and, finally, Mr. Urmson, senior, in a long dark-brown dressing-gown, bound round the waist with a cord, giving him the appearance of an ascetic and reverend monk.

"So different from the studios abroad, Nellie," remarked Mrs. Tenterden, in an undertone. "I should think it would be better on the étage below."

"Ah—ah! Garth," exclaimed Uncle Golightley, coming forward and expanding himself, "so this is your workshop—ah! and this is the model.—Good-morning, Mistress Margaret; well, you're enough to make a house-painter turn Raphael." He laid his white hands tenderly on the young girl's shoulders, and was about to bestow upon her an avuncular salute; but she, with perhaps an excess of maidenly reserve, evaded it at the critical moment by stooping suddenly to pick up one of Garth's paint-brushes. "Well, well," laughed Uncle Golightley, recovering himself, "you're bent on breaking my heart, I see that.—But let's have a look at this work of yours, Garth. Cuthbert tells me that you are painting the family history, as he is writing it. H'm! . . . yes

. . . . by George! . . . . h'm!" with these words, and holding his hands arched over his eye-glasses, the child of æsthetic culture settled himself in front of the canvas; the rest of the company (with the exception of Garth, who stood behind the easel, with his eyes on Miss Golightley), grouping themselves on either side of him.

The picture represented five figures relieved against a depth of sombre background. The central personage was a man of grim aspect, whose dark frown strangely contrasted with the grin which twisted his lips from his clinched teeth. From a deep gash in his chin the dripping blood spattered on his steel gorget, and trickled over his polished breastplate. The chief light in the picture was created by the smoky flash of a pistol, leveled by him against a cavalier in the foreground, whose form showed black against the glare. The latter had just received the bullet; a battle-axe was slipping from his grasp, and he was on the point of falling heavily on his face. A soldier in a buff jerkin had started forward, and grasped him by the arm and shoulder.

Of the two remaining figures, one was a young woman, nobly formed, who clung to him of the pistol, while her eyes fastened on the cavalier in a stare of terror and anguish. Her left hand, lying across her bridegroom's breast, was red with the blood from his wound, which had likewise sullied the purity of her golden wedding-ring. This ring, judging from the presence of the minister, whose colossal outline loomed in the background, had but the moment before been fitted to its place. Into the midst of the bridal-party, murder had thrust its ghastly visage, illumining every face of the group with an infernal gleam, and writhing their features into some likeness to itself. Here was depicted the fatal consummation of a sinful history—a consummation which might well be the starting-point of a yet gloomier history of retribution and remorse.

"Oh, what a dreadful picture for anybody to paint!" exclaimed kind-hearted Mrs. Tenterden, with a gesture of aversion.

"I hope it may not rekindle ancestral heart-burnings," said Mr. Urmson, who was standing at her side. "It's a scene from our family history, you know, in 1646. He in the black coat is Sir Reginald Golightley, and the black-browed gentleman who has just pistoled him is his ex-bosom friend, Captain Neil Urmson."

"What a shocking thing! Why did he do it?"

. "Ah, I know the story—I know the story!" murmured Uncle Golightley in an absent manner, still spying at the picture beneath his arched hands.—"But go on, Cuthbert—you're the historian—you can give it more effect than I could, I dare say.— Really, Garth, this is very good indeed!—By George, you surprise me! Figures in the foreground still unfinished; but—h'm!"

Cuthbert went on to inform Mrs. Tenterden of the main points of the story, and explained to her how Sir Reginald had got beside himself with fury at being compelled to witness the marriage of Lady Eleanor to his rival.

"I should think he would!" cried Mrs. Tenterden, indignantly. "If I ever heard of such an outrageous flirt, to worry the poor man so! I declare, she was as bad as any of them—worse!"

"I hope," said Cuthbert, quietly, "that she knew nothing of the plot against your ancestor until she saw it consummated. It came very near having a different upshot from what Captain Urmson had intended; and, for my own part, I must confess that I have sometimes wished Sir Reginald had fairly succeeded in splitting his old friend's head open; it would have saved the Urmson descendants all the trouble in the world!"

Mrs. Tenterden had perhaps been on the verge of uttering a similar wish; but finding herself half disarmed by this forestallment, she was content to remark, with gentle gravity, "But there wouldn't have been any descendants in that case, Mr. Urmson, would there?"

"O Mildred!" murmured Uncle Golightley, in a sort of dreamy rapture, "you are delicious—delicious!"

"You are right, Mrs. Tenterden—the captain had no brothers," said Cuthbert, with his usual presence of mind. "But that is all the story, so far as they were concerned."

"But not the whole story!" added Golightley, with a melancholy shake of the head. "Ah, no—that isn't ended even yet!"

"Dear me, what dreadful creatures they were in those days!" sighed Mrs. Tenterden, as she turned away. She walked to the sofa, and sat down with evident satisfaction; and, Madge taking a seat beside her, the two entered into a friendly conversation. The elderly lady had taken a great fancy to the ingenuous village beauty, and had already been moved to make her a confidante in many matters whereon speech was perhaps more pleasant than politic. But Madge, in spite of her ingenuousness, had about her an air of security and good sense which inspired trust; and, as a matter of fact, she had kept more than one secret in her life with such inviolability as might have justified even more confidence than she received.

CHAPTER XXXII.

A CUSTOMER.

ELINOR GOLIGHTLEY, all this time, had been standing without words, and almost without motion from the first, gazing at the picture; and the artist had the pleasure of seeing the very essence of the tragedy which he had portrayed reflected in her face. It was a face remarkably susceptible of tragic expression, and withal possessed of a subtile mobility which rendered it especially available for artistic purposes. By-and-by, Miss Golightley moved away, and, without taking any notice either of the painter or the rest of the company, began to pace slowly, with her arms folded, up and down the little studio.

Garth came out from behind the easel, and apparently became absorbed in the picture himself. Something in it no longer pleased him. He glanced frowningly from the canvas to Miss Golightley, and from her to Madge, and then back again to the picture. His preoccupation was finally invaded by his uncle, who laid an affectionate arm across his shoulders, and asked him what he meant to do with those two figures in the foreground.

"That fellow in the buff coat—who is he to be? You must have him a portrait, you know, as well as the rest. It's well, my dear nephew, to observe the laws of harmony even when a departure from them would escape critical detection. That's a great secret of power! Now, here we have Parson Graeme—an excellent likeness, too, though how you persuaded that jolly old phiz of his to put on the necessary expression of alarm and horror, is beyond me! Then, there's yourself—very powerful that; and, by George, not a bit flattered either! ha, ha! And there's your Miss Margaret," added Uncle Golightley, lowering his voice; "but she's the jewel of the picture—puts all the rest of you out of countenance. Garth, that face ought to make your fortune, if you painted nothing.else all your life. II'm!—what was I saying?"

"I mean to make the others portraits," said Garth. "The soldier shall be Jack Selwyn, a descendant of the Selwyn who came with Captain Neil from England, and left him because of their quarrel about the right to disturb the old sachem's grave. Most likely he was really present at this scene."

"There was a young fellow of that name whom we met abroad. I couldn't quite make him out. Reckless, devil-may-care chap—seemed to have brains, too; but devilish independent and inquisitive. However, what are you going to make of the cavalier?"

"I don't know; but, since his back is toward us, it doesn't much matter."

"Besides," said Cuthbert, "he evidently cannot live long, whoever he is."

"Look here," said Uncle Golightley, drawing himself up and caressing his cheeks, "what do you say to putting in a likeness of me? By just turning the head a little more to the right, you'd show the profile; and, for all you know, I have every bit as good a profile as Reginald had."

The artist looked hard at him for a few moments.

"Cut off your whiskers," said he, "and you'd have a good cavalier's face;" and, after a pause, he added, "you'll do very well."

"You are very modest," remarked Cuthbert, "to desire to stand in the shoes of a jilted lover—with a bullet through him into the bargain."

"Ah, you mustn't judge too much by appearances," returned Golightley, with a languid smile. "Now, if you observe that young woman's face closely, don't you see that she appears to care quite as much for poor Reginald as she does for that black-haired savage with a bloody chin? By God, Garth! that gold ring and the bullet are in the way, to be sure, but, give her a fair show, and I believe she'd choose the other man, after all."

"If these portraits are going to rake up all the dead and buried jealousies of the family, I advise Garth to take all his faces from his imagination," said Cuthbert, arching his eyebrow; and with this caution he walked away, and, joining Miss Elinor, began to discuss with her the pictures and sketches which were dispersed about the studio.

"Uncle Golightley," said Garth, "I think that face of Eleanor's spoils the picture."

Ilis uncle, who had again become absorbed in admiring contemplation of this very face, absolutely started. "My dear nephew, you evidently have painted better than you know."

"Madge was not the right model for it," continued Garth. "Her face is too beautiful, and has no tragedy in it. You were talking about the law of harmony—don't you see that face can never harmonize with the tone of the picture?"

"Now, Garth," said his uncle, putting his arm through that of the young artist as they stood together, and beginning in a tone of good-natured amusement, "just listen to me for a moment. I'm an older man than you, and I know by heart all the good pictures that ever were painted. I tell you frankly, between you and me, that what you have done there is, in some respects, as good as any man ever did. It has power, it has truth, it has originality—that's a great point—it has something in it that nobody else could have put there—something inimitable and indescribable—you understand what I mean. And I tell you frankly, that that face of Madge's, or Eleanor's if you will, is worth all the rest of the work (good as it is) put together. Now, don't touch it," he went on, emphasizing his appeal with his long forefinger; "my dear boy, don't touch it. As for harmony, beauty *is* harmony; it is, as Ralph Waldo Emerson says, its own excuse for being. I feel the greatest interest in your success, you know; you have genius —undoubted genius; but I see you have some of the infirmities of genius too; you don't recognize your own happiest touch. Yield to my judgment—yield to my experience. By-and-by, all in good time, you'll acknowledge that I'm right. Take my word for it."

"I could take your word for it," replied Garth, after pulling at his hair awhile, "on any other point better than on this. I can be advised in technicalities and still be an artist in my own right; but the soul of the picture must be my own. Michael Angelo might conceive it better, but I'm Garth Urmson."

Uncle Golightley patted his nephew on the shoulder. "Did you ever hear of a young fellow named Hafiz, who wanted to pull down this tiresome old sky? you remind me of him. But you must build up where you pull down: now, what are you going to substitute for this face?"

Garth made no reply to this question, though words seemed to lie behind his lips; and his uncle, who really appeared to have the matter at heart, was encouraged.

"You've bothered over this until you're a bit crazy—that's all. Go quietly on and finish up the odds and ends, and cover Lady Eleanor up till all's done. I'll risk my reputation as a connoisseur on your finding her as satisfactory as I do, in the end. I shall have something more to say to you, then. By-the-way, as to art *versus* profit. Is there anything of a market for good pictures in this great and free country?"

"I shall do my best with this thing, at all events; I want money."

"By George, I want you to have it! That picture, with its present Lady Eleanor, is worth its weight in gold, and I am much mistaken if you don't make a small fortune by it. Have you thought of any particular price?"

"No," said Garth, rather shortly; for he thought his uncle unnecessarily curious.

"Because," continued the latter, produc-

ing a cambric handkerchief from his purple-velvet pocket, and hastily wiping his eye-glasses with it, "if five thousand dollars will buy it, it's going to be mine. Of course, a richer man than I might offer more, and still get it at a bargain; and you mustn't oblige me merely because blood is thicker than water, and all that. In fact, I tell you frankly, I think the picture—as it stands—is worth infinitely more. But five thousand is as high as I can go just now; and, between you and me, four-fifths of that is for the very part you don't appreciate—you barbarian! Well, think it over, my dear boy, and take your time. As long as you give me the run of the studio, you know, I can afford to be patient—ha! ha!"

Garth, for some time after hearing this speech, was afflicted with a species of mental dizziness, which prevented him from taking conscious note of what was going on around him. He walked or sat, answered questions, or volunteered remarks, apparently as usual; yet all was automatic and slipped from his interior recognition like water off a duck's back. He was awake only in an Aladdin's vision of wealth, and of what he would do with it. Five thousand dollars was ten times as much as he had expected for his picture; and wonderful were the changes which the consideration of this sum introduced into his plans and prospects. The world now lay submissive, inviting him to go whither he chose, and do whatsoever he pleased in it. Without more ado he could marry Madge and carry her abroad—not with a penurious and uneasy eye for economy, but generously and with flourish of trumpets.

In reviewing his past life he marveled at the torpid indifference—for such it now appeared—which had suffered to pass away so many barren and irrevocable years. He began to arrive at an understanding of what Madge must have endured throughout his dreary season of delay, and could not enough admire her long-suffering affection and patient cheerfulness. She might have married when and where she pleased during the past few years; yet had she not only remained true to her first love, but never, until this very morning, had dropped so much as a hint that he was doing less than his utmost duty by her. This argued her no less lovable than she was lovely and loving. Such women were rare, indeed; and Garth accused himself of having valued her at less than her true worth, and heartily thanked his stars that she had been spared to him till what time his eyes began to recognize his fair fortune.

But, though self-convicted of having been, as Madge had expressed it, asleep, Garth was still a prey to doubts as to what was the soporific! He could not think it painting, which had been the means of raising him out of sleep to the present happy waking. Nor was it the lack of public recognition which had bedrowsed him, since he had never fairly sought it, still looking upon himself as in the artistic chrysalid, unripe to canvass the world's suffrages. How, then? was he the victim of hypochondria? or had he but passed through a disagreeable though necessary phase of development?

"At all events," was the young painter's conclusion, "I'm in no danger of a second hibernation!"

"I didn't know before," said Miss Golightley, with an irrestrainable gush of laughter, "that you Northern people ever did really hibernate!"

In becoming for the first time actively aware of her presence, Garth was likewise aroused to an obscure consciousness of having been for an indefinite while in conversation with her. Looking about him in some bewilderment, he found himself alone with the young lady in the studio, apparently engaged in piloting her through a large portfolio of drawings and studies, which lay open on the sofa before them. Hereupon her laugh, which had the rare charm of untrammeled spontaneity, proved wonderfully contagious, and the artist responded with a heartiness of mirth that surprised himself.

CHAPTER XXXIII.

A CRITIC.

"I HAD no idea you ever laughed," said Miss Golightley, becoming sober, while the pink flush rapidly died away from her clear face. "Why do you?"

"Because you helped me catch sight of my own absurdity; I suppose nothing else is ridiculous enough. Thank you. So you can laugh too?"

"Yes, but never at my absurdities; only at my solemnities, sometimes."

"How long have we been at this portfolio, Miss Golightley?"

"Ever since your father handed me over to you, and took the rest of the people down to the orchard. If I had known you were hibernating—"

"Have I done anything outlandish?"

"Nothing but seem indifferent to your own sketches, and, when I asked you whether you were never afraid of the use of models lowering your ideal, you made that singular remark—or, after all, perhaps it was profound?"

"Talking of models," said Garth, with a more serious air, "I was thinking, a little while ago, what a good face for tragedy yours was. But I believe your laugh is still better. It's perfectly funny, and yet there's a kind of pathos in it. The dimples that come on your cheek-bones are good, too, and unusual—I'm only being artistic."

"Oh, I've been talked to by artists before," returned the lady, with a little disdainful quiver of the mouth.

"You think," said Garth, after a pause, "that my picture there would be better without the portraits?"

Miss Golightley colored slightly, but had the courage of her opinions.

"Only one of the faces is really a portrait. The murderer has your features, but the expression comes from his own character—I think you must have imagined that, not copied it. But your imagination seems to have done nothing with the woman's face. It's very lovely, of course, Mr. Urmson, and very well painted; but it has no more to do with such a tragedy as that than your cousin herself has."

Garth sat frowning at the wall before him, and said nothing. Miss Golightley, supposing that she had seriously offended him, determined to define her position, as clearly as she could, and then leave him to his ill-humor.

"I was thinking, when I asked you about

models, how some of the greatest painters seem to have made their models their ideals. They would fall in love with some beautiful woman, and paint her in their pictures; and get so blinded by their natural affections as to persuade themselves that she was above any ideal that their imaginations could conceive."

"Why might she not have been?"

"I don't think that is the point," returned Miss Golightley, coldly. "A great artist has a divine gift, and he dishonors it if he only copies or adapts Nature, instead of recreating it. He ought not to allow any human being to be the limit of his inspiration, even if she were more beautiful than anything he could create."

"What imports, then, is not what he paints, but what he tries to?"

"It seems to me he should keep his art sacred from everything else—not even run a risk with it. As soon as he finds himself hesitating whether to make his model an end instead of a means, he should never paint her again. Models must have no souls or characters of their own, but give themselves up to be made over in harmony with the spirit of the picture. Otherwise the artist will by-and-by begin to make the spirit of his picture in harmony with them; and then, though his picture may be lovely—lovelier than if he had aimed higher—the divinity will be out of it. Are you smiling because what I say is commonplace, Mr. Urmson?"

"No—at the poor pegs of models. But I don't feel like smiling. Say more."

Miss Golightley having, perhaps, been piqued into saying so much as she had done already by Garth's supposed antagonism, was embarrassed at his unlooked-for acquiescence.

"I only meant," said she, doubling and undoubling the corner of one of the drawings, and gradually becoming pink from forehead to chin, "that persons who have genius should be particularly careful—the dearest, most intimate companions of their life may become the worst enemies of their art, if allowed to influence it in any merely personal way. Their love and their art might serve to counterpoise each other, I should

think—each be the recreation from the other—but never interfere."

"A bad business, I'm afraid," Garth muttered gloomily to himself. "There is one thing about my picture, however," he added, looking Miss Golightley in the face, with a self-compassionate smile, "though I hadn't the power to annihilate my cousin's individuality, and give her one to carry out the design of the picture, at all events, I didn't bully the design into correspondence with her individuality. As you said, they have nothing to do with each other. Well, you are an honest woman, and I thank you. Do you consider my uncle a good critic?"

"I should suppose he had very correct ideas. Why?"

"Why," said Garth, digging his hands into his coat-pockets, "he likes Lady Eleanor, and advises me not to alter her on any account. You see, I'd had my own misgivings about her, and you have confirmed them. But . . . after a while I shall want to ask you one more question. Meanwhile," he went on, pulling an old piece of pasteboard out of the pile of drawings, "here is the first portrait I ever painted."

Miss Golightley looked at it at first with a smile, but soon with a softened and sympathetic interest. Despite grotesque errors of both drawing and coloring, the characterization was effective and powerful. It represented the head of a mild, serene woman, whose hair was beginning to blanch beneath her immaculate white cap, though her wide, level eyebrows still retained their youthful darkness, and the whole face, albeit marked and worn by the advance of age, still seemed to retain—just below the surface—the sweet and tender spirit of pure young womanhood. Such a face, be its years however many, can never really grow old.

"Is this Mrs. Urmson?" asked the young lady, in a voice low almost to timidity.

"Yes—my mother. I did it up here by stealth, believing I was committing a sort of theft. The paints are some that Nikomis gave me, and I laid them on partly with my fingers, and partly with an old pair of scissors. But I don't think I could do it so well again. My second portrait is on the other side. Both are done from memory, without models; but I think I caught the spirit of the faces all the better."

Miss Golightley could not help smiling at this remark, and it was a shy, girlish smile, not cold and cynical. She turned over the piece of pasteboard.

"Oh, this is your cousin—it's very funny —I should think it might have been very good."

"I showed it to her, for the first time, the other day; but she doesn't appreciate it. When I was doing it, and making a profound secret of it, I remember how guilty I felt one day, when she said she would like to have some one take her portrait. I didn't go near my paint-box after that for several years. But since then my cousin has lost her faith in painting, and I have found mine."

"Do you mean that you didn't care for painting when you did these things?"

"I liked it so well that I thought it must be wrong. My grandfather used to tell me that whatever boys liked to do was pretty sure to be bad for them. In one sense I think he came very near the truth—for men as well as boys. Too much doing what they like makes doing what they don't like harder. And they have to do what they don't like once in a while."

To this profound remark Miss Golightley made no rejoinder, and they turned over the contents of the portfolio for a while in silence. Garth was well aware that he had been unusually talkative, and that he was talking merely to gain time; though what he was gaining time for he had but an indistinct idea. From his recent vision of happiness and ease, he had abruptly waked to find himself neither easy nor happy. The alternative forced upon him was as disagreeable as it was simple—it was the old question between honor and profit. But profit in this case meant more than the ostensible five thousand dollars. The providing Lady Eleanor with a new head to correspond with the emotions which were supposed to be agonizing her heart, would not only involve the forfeiture of his uncle's offer, but, as the immediate consequence, all present chance of getting married. And, if he missed this chance, what right had he to suppose that

8

Fortune would procure him another? Madge would lose faith in him, and perhaps marry some one else. At all events, she would be doubly offended: first, that he should prefer for his picture any other face than the lovely organization of curves and colors which she called her own; and, secondly, that for so impertinent a whim he should voluntarily and indefinitely postpone their already tardy happiness. An impertinent whim—that was what she would consider it; and really, for the matter of logic, what was it more? A disinterested woman like Miss Golightley, who had received a life-long artistic training, and possessed cool and fine discrimination, might perceive its profound inward significance; but Madge, ingenuous, affectionate, wayward, unsophisticated, would only feel the slight to her beauty and her love; and who could blame her if she resented it?

Garth turned the matter over and over in his mind, but could get no satisfaction out of it. He wished that the bargain with his uncle had been irrevocably completed before this misgiving about Lady Eleanor's physiognomy had entered his own head. He wished that Miss Golightley, the sight of whose face as she looked at the picture had suggested to him his first doubts, had staid down-stairs; or at least had gone down with the rest, and not remained to poison his dream of felicity with her dose of unanswerable remonstrances. But what an ignoble mood was this! in very truth, he wished none of these things; and was conscious of a wholesome, hearty respect for the young lady who had been kind and resolute enough to tell him what he ought not to have waited to be told. All the same, it was open to him to regret that Uncle Golightley had not set his heart on some other part of the canvas than that appropriated to Lady Eleanor's features, so that honor and profit might have fraternized at last, and rung his wedding-bells for him side by side.

But might he not hope, after all, to effect an honorable compromise? What if his uncle, when he saw the alterations, were to come to his senses and discover that he liked the picture better than ever? Or, what if Garth were himself to discover an unsuspected capacity for tragic expression in Madge's face, and by a few telling touches so bring the same to bear as to enhance the value both of the portrait and the design at once? It was true that, upon Miss Golightley's theory, the power to do this would argue him but an indifferent lover; nevertheless, he was inclined to believe that, given the power, he could safely afford to let the theory take care of itself.

Supposing the worst to come to the worst, however, he reflected that, save for the disappointment, he would be really no worse off than he was before. It was always possible that he might still find another buyer for his picture; and, although not five thousand dollars, nor anything like it, was to be looked for, it was not too much to anticipate five hundred, or even a thousand, which would enable him at least to get married, if not at once to set forth on his wedding tour. Meanwhile he would be careful to keep Madge from all knowledge of Uncle Golightley's offer—his uncle himself would surely abstain from all premature allusion to it—and thus, if the affair turned out badly, she would at least be spared any further mortification than that of seeing some other set of features take precedence, on this occasion only, of her own. She need never know how near she had been to affluence, and so the silent surrender of the opportunity would not affect her. These consolatory reflections pretty nearly exhausted Garth's list; one loop-hole, perhaps, remained in the background, through which it might be found practicable to effect a not dishonorable escape; but on this point he felt rather insecure, and had avoided putting the question to the issue until the very last moment.

"That is the end," said Miss Golightley, laying down the last drawing. "I am very much obliged to you."

"Not at all," returned Garth, abstractedly, closing the portfolio and tying up the string; "the obligation is on my side."

"I don't know what made me say all that," remarked Miss Golightley, with a faint smile glimmering around her mouth and eyes; "somehow I felt better acquainted with you than I am."

"It was the laughing, I suppose, that surprised us out of our customary behavior. I wonder when we shall laugh again? Before you go, come and take another look at the picture."

They arose and came round in front of the easel, and both looked, resting a hand on the back of the low chair. Presently the artist said:

"I'm inclined to think the whole thing a failure. Do you?"

"I don't know how to blame or praise it technically, Mr. Urmson; but I never saw a picture that made me feel so sad. It ought to make the world better—it makes evil such a fearful thing. And yet your—Lady Eleanor seems to be making fun of it!"

"You think, then," said Garth, turning his eyes with a kind of vehemence on his companion's pale face, "that the picture has merit enough to make the alteration of that part of it worth while?"

"I'm sure of it!"

"Well," rejoined he, drawing a deep breath, "that is saying a good deal! But I am glad you have said it."

They turned away, and walked to the door.

"We are going to stay to dinner," observed the lady, pleasantly, "so I suppose I shall see you again."

"Yes. Come up here often, Miss Golightley. I have other things to show you."

"By-the-way," said she, with her hand upon the door, "you said a little while ago that you were going to ask me a question."

"So I did," said Garth, smiling, "and you answered it!"

He escorted her to the foot of the garret-stairs, and then returned with measured steps to the studio. After sitting inactive for a few moments before the easel, he lazily took up his palette and mixed some dark-brown paint upon it, whistling softly to himself the while, and tapping his foot upon the floor. When the tint was ready he dipped his brush into it, and prepared to apply it to a certain part of the canvas.

"It may be against history, Lady Eleanor," he muttered, between a smile and a frown, "but off comes your head nevertheless."

A noise as of some one running upstairs caused him, however, to suspend the act of execution. It was Madge; she burst into the room, all breathless and sparkling.

"O, my Garth! — dinner is ready—but O, Garth, dear, isn't it splendid!"

He got up, letting brush and palette fall to the floor. She was flushed and joyous, and her dark eyes were glistening with happy tears. She stood before him with her hands clasped, full of light, life, and eagerness, yet touched with a shade of maidenly timidity that rendered her quite irresistible.

Garth tried to say something, but no words came; all at once he took her in his arms.

"Uncle Golightley has told me," she murmured on his shoulder. "O, Garth, think of five thousand dollars! and all because my portrait was in it! If you had left out the picture, perhaps he would have given more! My dear, darling boy, how happy we shall be! But dinner is ready—shall we go down together?"

"Yes; take me down with you," replied Garth in an oddly jocose tone. "Keep your eye on me, Madge. I'm not fit to be trusted alone with five thousand dollars in my pocket."

"Oh, I'll take care of it for you, sir," she rejoined; and hand in hand the happy lovers left the studio: so Lady Eleanor was reprieved.

BOOK V.

GRAPPLING.

CHAPTER XXXIV.

CURRENT OPINION.

THE Danvers' cottage was old-fashioned and rather small, but well built and comfortable, and as clean as any in Holland. Mrs. Danver, though chronically ailing in one way or another, was morbidly neat in her ways and ideas, and since the death of her husband (who, whatever his inventive genius, had made no claims to nicety either in temperament or habits), she had ridden her hobby with free rein. The rooms glistened with cleanliness, and the household furniture of all kinds was kept at a nervous tension of immaculateness almost oppressive to behold. Mrs. Danver's infirmities, though they prevented her from doing much work herself, did not hinder her from rigorously overseeing the "help" which she employed, and which, thanks to the steady income yielded by the mysterious "patent," and regularly paid in by Mr. Cuthbert Urmson

as executor, she was well able to afford. As for Madge, it was undesirable, for many reasons, that she should be bound to any drudgery whatever. Her position as Garth's betrothed wife required a gentleness of breeding and a refinement of occupation which fortunately the patent proceeds did not suffer her altogether to lack. And it would have been a pity, in any case, to have dimmed her beauty and dulled her spirits by subjection to ignoble toil.

It must not be inferred, however, because she allowed herself the enjoyment of help and of a few other luxuries, that Mrs. Danver was a bad economist. The late Mr. Danver had, indeed, been rather an extravagant man, ever ready to borrow largely of the future; but this trait of his had confirmed his spouse in the opposite tendency, and now that he was gone, she set to work to recoup herself in some degree for the lavishness of the past. She was understood to be well off, comparatively speaking: the more that she made no display of wealth—

indeed, rather affected a genteel - poverty style of conversation. She had never been able to understand, she was in the habit of saying, why her income, being derived from a patent, did not augment from year to year, as by all law and precedent it should. Her mind sometimes misgave her whether Mr. Urmson was doing the best possible by it. She had made bold to hint as much to him once in a while, but he had only smiled, and said that, when the country grew richer, it was to be hoped she would too. Well, she hoped so; but, of course, her poor dead husband having left all the management in Mr. Urmson's hands, there was nothing to be done—no, and, she dared say, nothing to complain of either. Only it was queer, and a small increase, year to year, would have been very encouraging.

Mr. Urmson was a literary man, and not over-robust at all lately, since poor Mrs. Urmson was buried, and of course it was but natural he should accept the reports of the agents just as they were given in, not making any inquiries such as a pushing, active business man might have made—not without results, who could say? But she was not one to complain, unless for poor Maggie's sake, who had shown a patience in waiting all these years which, with such a face and figure as hers, not the best man in New England was worth. And she might have the best quick enough if she wanted him. But no, none but Mr. Garth; and when Mr. Garth was ready, and had sold pictures enough, why, Mrs. Danver supposed that, if poor Maggie was not grown old and dead by that time, there might be a wedding. And she did not complain, only if that was the way it was going to be, why, that was all about it.

Thus Mrs. Danver, with a gradually rising intonation. But poor Maggie, despite the proffered facilities for being dispirited, had got along remarkably well. Partly by good luck, partly through her connection with the Urmsons, but more than all by dint of the force, acuteness, and tact of her character, she had gained a sort of ascendency in the village. The foolish gossip that had been current about her a few years previous had gradually died away; though

no one could boast of being in her confidence, yet she repelled no one, and no one could prove any harm against her; and mere surmise, however plausible, can never, in the long-run, make head against palpable good report. During Garth's long absence abroad her name had grown to be almost a household word among the dwellers in Urmsworth, and a flavor of romance attached to her, as if she were a merrier sort of Evangeline. She charmed mankind; and her betrothal and demure discretion healed the jealousies of her own sex. She had great mental as well as physical activity, and was forever busy about something. She acquired solid repute by teaching a Sunday-school twice a week, under favor of old Parson Graeme, who had never wavered from his early allegiance to her; and she insensibly took the lead in all dances, picnics, boating expeditions, sleighing and skating parties, that came off in the Urmsworth neighborhood. On such occasions she overflowed with life, laughter, and happy suggestion. The people were proud of her; and if she was something of an enigma, the more of such enigmas the better for the world's weal!

Therefore Garth, when he returned home at last, was rather begrudged the possession of her, especially as he was found to hold aloof from village merry-makings, withdrawing himself, and Madge, of course, with him, into the seclusion of his studio or of the forest. Nor was his unpopularity amended by the continued delay in the anticipated nuptials, to which every Urmsworthian had been looking forward with much interest. The affair was canvassed among the astute and honest villagers, and great sympathy was felt for the Danvers. Of course, no one was called on to interfere, and people must manage their own business; but that a girl like Madge Danver should be kept on tenter-hooks, merely because Garth Urmson had got back from Europe with some grand notions in his head, was simply a sin and a shame. If he thought himself too good for her, why didn't he step out of the way and give some honest fellow a chance? Why, there was that chap Sam Kinco, whom nobody had seen for ten years, but who was believed to be doing well somewhere—he would have married her, and had half a dozen children by this time, if the Urmsons hadn't clubbed together to get him out of the neighborhood. It was a high-handed business altogether.

Thus the villagers. The sudden appearance in their midst, however, of Golightley Urmson and the two ladies turned the current of discourse in a new direction. Golightley was generally approved of from the beginning. It was remembered that he had been an intelligent and affable youth, and that his father, the old captain, had been very harsh and severe with him, and inordinately indulgent toward his half-brother, Cuthbert. He had finally obtained leave to go abroad, where he had evidently amassed an enormous fortune, and was now come home to spend it for the benefit of his old townspeople, whom he had not in all these years once forgotten. Golightley Urmson was a philanthropist, with the means to carry his philanthropy into effect. He would build them a new grand hotel, he would erect the long-talked-of mills and mill-dams, he would endow the poorhouse, establish a library, and drain the great meadows below the lake. It was to be hoped that he would assume his proper position as master of Urmhurst—a position which was now suspected to have been his from the first, though he had consented to forego it in favor of his half-brother. Cuthbert Urmson was very well in his way, but he was getting old and infirm, was a recluse and a student, out of accord with the spirit of his countrymen and of the times, and, in in short, by no means the person to occupy the most prominent position in the county. Garth, with his artistic follies, was, of course, out of the question entirely; whereas Golightley, with his knowledge of the world, affluence, and energy, might easily aspire to the State Legislature, and even to Congress, where he might impress upon the country the merits of Urmsworth, its wants and its wrongs. Or, if he preferred it, it would be an easy matter to raise so prominent a personage to the position of most honor and authority in his own State; and as Governor Urmson, of New Hampshire, his name, with

that of his birthplace, would go down with ever-increasing glory to remote posterity. It was a splendid dream, although inspired by somewhat less than a full knowledge of the past life, opinions, position, prospects, and desires, of the individual principally concerned, and therefore not certain to be prophetic. Meanwhile, as I have said, it created a new subject for gossip.

As for the two ladies, opinion concerning them was suspended for the present, but they were watched with curiosity, and when they took up their abode with Mrs. Danver, a great deal of casuistry was brought to bear upon the problem why they had chosen her house in preference to any other. Mrs. Danver herself was sounded by her friends upon the subject, but, inasmuch as the only reason she could have given was that Parson Graeme had recommended her to the ladies, she very wisely shook her head and shut her mouth, thereby intimating that there was a mystery in the affair, which nothing should induce her to reveal. This reticence on her part had one good effect, for which the ladies, had they known anything about it, would probably have been thankful. It got Mrs. Danver in the habit of keeping to herself such information with regard to her boarders as chance from time to time threw in her way: and thus it happened that the curiosity of Urmsworth society as to a purely imaginary question created a barrier against itself in matters of actual import.

Mrs. Tenterden and Miss Golightley occupied two snug and cozy rooms on the upper floor of the little cottage, on opposite sides of the passage-way, and they also had undisputed monopoly of the parlor whenever they wished it. Mrs. Danver's parlor, boudoir, and dining-saloon were, and had always been, comprised within the four walls of her kitchen, the "best room" having been locked up, as a rule, and only opened on high days and holidays, when the ancient newness of its smell and aspect, the immitigable stiffness of its chairs and sofa, the gilded glitter of its mantel-ornaments, and the unsunned brilliance of its carpet, were enough, without the aid of the hair-picture of a tomb and a weeping-willow which hung over the fireplace, to frighten away any ordinary intruder. When the ladies were first introduced to this virgin grandeur, and informed that it was at their disposal, Mrs. Tenterden burst into a hearty laugh, to the great astonishment of Mrs. Danver; while Miss Golightley, with a perfectly grave face, walked across the room and back once, and said that it was very nice, but that they had not been accustomed to that sort of thing, and would probably confine themselves to their bedchambers. "But you must let us dine with you in the kitchen," said Mrs. Tenterden, who had now recovered her composure, and was wiping her eyes; "we must dine with you and Margaret in that lovely clean kitchen;" and Mrs. Danver, who had been in doubt whether or not to be offended about her parlor, decided not to be, and replied, with one of her hungry, melancholy, stiff-moving smiles, that she should be quite pleased to have the ladies take their meals with her and Maggie, if they pleased to do so; and thus harmony was established. Mrs. Tenterden, however, had an incorrigible habit of laughing at the most inopportune moments, merely because something happened to tickle her sense of the ludicrous; and, as Miss Golightley often told her, it was impossible, under such circumstances, to count upon any one's good-will for ten minutes together. But Mrs. Tenterden, as a sort of counterpoise to this bad habit, could never be persuaded that her laughing hurt the feelings of anybody; and the genuineness of this, her conviction, often impressed itself on those she laughed at, and made them grin and bear it more good-humoredly than they themselves would have believed possible.

CHAPTER XXXV.

FAITHFUL ENEMIES.

A few days after the visit to the studio, Mrs. Tenterden, in her morning-gown, and with her little bag of tatting in her hand, entered Miss Elinor's room. That young lady was sitting in a large horse-hair-covered rocking-chair by the window, her violin and bow lying idle in her lap, her mouth very resolute, and her eyes very open, as was her way in reverie. When the door opened, she set the chair in motion with her foot, and handled her violin.

"Daughter," began the elder lady (for they mothered and daughtered each other, though in reality owning no such relationship), "I have some news at last. Margaret tells me they're going to have a picnic somewhere up in the woods to-morrow, and wants us to come. This lovely weather—they call it Indian summer, you know. Golightley and all of them seem to be going," continued she, sitting sumptuously down, and proceeding to open her tatting-bag.

Miss Elinor put on a very cold and uninterested expression, and only said:

"Well, what did you tell her?"

"Oh, I just said I'd speak to you, of course—it's nothing to me," replied Mrs. Tenterden, in flat defiance of what she knew to be the truth. "Margaret says that before young Mr. Garth went to college there used to be a picnic regularly every Michaelmas, and that old Mr. Graeme, the minister (think of that man being ninety-five years old, dear; I declare he looks as if he'd outlive poor Mr. Urmson now)—that he used to manage them, you know. But lately they have been falling off, and I think she said this was the first one young Mr. Garth would have been to for ten or twelve years. He was in college, you see, and afterward in Europe."

Miss Elinor took up her bow, and let it wander lightly over the strings.

"Young Mr. Garth is going, then, I suppose?"

"Why, yes, indeed, since Margaret's to be there," returned Mrs. Tenterden, with a genial little laugh. "He may be going to paint a picture of us all. Nellie, did you know that Golightley had bought that picture—that shooting-scene of his? Five thousand dollars. Splendid, isn't it, for the young man? I declare, though—such a thing as that—it would give me the nightmare! I can't think what Golightley bought it for—he has such a fine taste for all that sort of things you know; but I tell him," she went on, laughing—"I tell him I believe he only wants that portrait in it of Margaret; and he says he does—confesses it. I told him I didn't know what you'd say to that, or Mr. Garth either. I must say, though,"added Mrs. Tenterden, more soberly, "the portrait's the best thing in the picture—in fact, it looks to me as if it didn't belong there, somehow."

"It isn't supposed to belong there," said Miss Elinor, who had already heard from Madge the news of Garth's backsliding; "but young Mr. Garth is not such a fool as to let art stand in the way of money; he's like all other Yankees, I suppose. Only I do wish he'd leave out the art altogether; not add insult to injury!"

"Why, how uncharitable you are, daughter!" exclaimed Mrs. Tenterden, reproachfully. "I'm sure—this wild idea of yours about playing and singing in public, and I don't know what all!—why shouldn't he poor young man sell his pictures as well!"

Miss Elinor executed a spasm of refined contempt upon her violin.

"Certainly the poor young man may do as he likes; only if I find him disagreeable—How would you like me to do my playing and singing in ballet-costume?"

"Well, I think in my heart, daughter!" cried Mrs. Tenterden, scandalized, but laughing in spite of herself. "Nellie, how can you?"

"If it brought me five thousand dollars, who could blame me? I can tell young Mr. Garth one thing, though," added she, sitting erect in her chair and growing pink and haughty; "when I dress as a ballet-girl I'll throw away my violin and my voice, and dance as a ballet-girl too. I reverence my art; but he—may do what he pleases with his, of course;" and she set herself rocking again, pale as before.

Mrs. Tenterden was not enough conversant either with the principles of art in the abstract or with the merits of this particular case to understand the analogy; nevertheless, and though she had been unable to appreciate Garth's picture or to make much out of himself, she was never without a word for the down-trodden.

"Besides, daughter," she began, after some meditative tatting, "you know they're

so poor. Here was Margaret telling me that she and Mr. Garth couldn't be married all these years because they had no money, but that, since he was to have five thousand dollars for his picture, they would be, immediately, and go to Europe; and the dear child seemed to think it was boundless wealth. I declare, it was quite touching."

"Oh!" murmured Elinor abstractedly, gazing out of the window—"oh!"

"I must say, though," resumed Mrs. Tenterden, after a pause, "I can't think where all the money goes to. I'm sure Golightley, when we first became acquainted with him, was always saying how poor he was—though there was plenty of money in the family—because he was giving away three-fourths of his share of the income every year to support his nephew and his brother Cuthbert, and keep up the honor of the house as he called it. But, for all I see, Cuthbert has been poorer than Golightley. One would suppose they would be—Mr. Urmson and his son would be—very well off now at any rate, because, since Golightley has made this large fortune of his own, of course he would give up the whole of the other fortune to them. Seems as if the money just vanished away, doesn't it?"

"It's none of our business," returned Elinor, coldly; "it's enough to know that your brother has supported them for twenty-five years."

"Oh, no; I don't mean that they haven't done all right about it," exclaimed charitable Mrs. Tenterden, "only it seems so queer. That young Mr. Garth doesn't look at all dissipated, or anything of that kind; that can't be the matter. Indeed, from what Margaret said, I should think he had rather too little—spirit, you know. However, it's none of our business, true enough."

A considerable silence followed, during which Elinor drew some airy arabesques of melody from her tempered instrument. The elder lady, who cherished good-natured sentiments toward music, serenely listened for a while, but at length interposed between two bars.

"Golightley has certainly been very generous, hasn't he? Seems to show the old Golightley blood in that," she said, with complacent pride. "But what a fine face Mr. Cuthbert Urmson has, Nellie! He doesn't look to me at all the sort of man would consent to be dependent on anybody, nor his son either. But I suppose the fact is, the poor man has no health and strength, and can't go into enterprises and speculations like Golightley. He looks as if he suffered a great deal of pain, though his manner, you know, is so cheerful. I wish he'd let me give him some of my medicine."

"I've learned not to depend on faces," observed Miss Golightley. "I never saw a man's face I liked more than Mr. Urmson's, and I liked even his son's pretty well after —a little talk we had that day in the studio. So far as appearance goes, I should certainly have thought it was they who supported your brother, rather than he them. But the more we find out about them, the more contemptible they seem to be—at least Mr. Garth Urmson. I wish we had never come to this place."

"Mercy, child! they are very pleasant people, I'm sure, and related to us besides. And I must say I'm quite captivated with Margaret. That young man is certainly very fortunate in having such a beautiful creature attached to him."

"More fortunate than he deserves," said Elinor; "I wish she would marry some one else."

"Well, Nellie, what will you say next, I'm sure!" exclaimed Mrs. Tenterden, laughing. "Whom else should she marry, dear?"

"Mother," said Elinor, after some moments' pause, the transparent pink again stealing into her grave face, "one reason why I have learned to distrust people's looks is because of your brother. When I first saw him, I couldn't help believing him false and mean; and even now, though I know how good and noble he really is, I cannot trust him when I'm face to face with him or hearing him speak, but only when he's out of the way. I can't reconcile what he seems with what he is and does. If he could exchange heads with his brother Cuthbert, it would be just right for both of them."

"Well, Nellie, what a scandalous way to talk of poor Golightley!" remonstrated Mrs. Tenterden, with an imperfect effort to be serious. "Why, I always thought he was very good-looking, and I'm sure he thinks so. Well, my dear, what made you let him ask you to marry him if you can't bear the sight of him, poor man?"

"I would have prevented it if I could. I don't think he asked me because he loved me," said Elinor in a low voice. "And I told him I didn't love him."

"For mercy's sake, daughter, if he didn't love you, why should he ask you? It wasn't till after Mr. Tenterden lost all his money that he made you the offer; so it couldn't have been for your fortune."

"Do you suppose I think him capable of so paltry a trick as that?" said Elinor, with indignation. "You do not know half how noble he is yourself. He asked me to marry him because we had lost our fortune, and Mr. Tenterden had helped him when he was poor, and he saw that to marry me would be the best way to repay his obligations. He doesn't love me. How should he? I know how disagreeable I am; and, besides, I'm young enough to be his daughter. I ought to care for him. I despise myself for not caring for him, and that only makes it worse. I hardly know sometimes whether I am angry with myself or with him. I hoped I should get used to him in time by thinking how generous he was; but I believe his being so generous is one reason why I—can't." Her mouth quivered a little.

"Ah, let me tell you, my dear," said Mrs. Tenterden, shaking her head and laughing wisely, "men don't marry penniless girls whom they don't love just to make them rich: don't you believe it! not Golightley nor the best of them. What makes you imagine he don't care for you? You should hear the way he speaks of you to other people! Marry you to make you rich? not a bit of it! He waited till he was rich before asking you to marry him. As to gratitude or obligations, I, for my part, don't know of any. John let him have a thousand pounds—I think it was about a fortnight before our robbery—and Golightley paid it back in a week; that's all about that. It may have happened to turn the scale of the speculation, or whatever it was, that Golightley made his fortune by; but that was just as it happened, you know. But you are such a strange girl, Nellie Golightley. I declare it seems sometimes as if you hadn't a bit of heart, or didn't believe anybody else had any. Young ladies weren't so in my time—mercy!"

Miss Elinor drew down the corners of her mouth in a cynical smile, picking at the strings of her violin with her finger-tips. "At least you can't say I ever pretended to have a heart," she remarked at length. "I don't pretend to have one, and I don't want any one to think I have. If your brother ever asks me to marry him again, I shall tell him that; and then if he wants to have me, since I never can love any one, it would be better (for me at least) to marry him than any one else. He might have a bad time of it, but it would be all the same to me, not having any heart; I should be as happy as head could wish. Very amusing, neither of us loving the other, and yet marrying on general principles, as it were!"

"Oh, well, if you choose to talk that way!" returned Mrs. Tenterden, a little provoked at this young-lady-like perverseness. "As to a heart, I believe nothing would make you confess you had one, not if you were dying of it that minute. Of course I, for my part, don't want you married, my dear. But I am an old woman, and shall probably die soon; and what's to become of you then I don't see!"

"When you are angry with me, you always revenge yourself by talking about dying; but, now I am going to tell you a secret that will put you in good-humor. There is one beloved object in the world—not your brother—which makes me feel I have a heart, which I love, which I want to marry, and which will bring me a fortune, and which I should be broken-hearted to be parted from—even I."

"My good fathers, Nellie!" exclaimed Mrs. Tenterden, dropping her tatting in her lap. "Whom do you mean, child? tell me, quick! Not surely that—that young Mr. Selwyn?"

"Young Mr. Selwyn! I mean my violin—my own sweet little violin," said Elinor, laying the graceful instrument against her cheek, with a little laugh. "My violin and

I can be happy together, in spite of everybody—can't we, dear?" she added, addressing it with a sad, tender playfulness.

Mrs. Tenterden was fairly surprised, and driven back on her good-nature. "You do beat all I ever saw, Nellie Golightley," she declared, with a sigh. "I can't make you out. I don't know at this minute whether, if Golightley asked you to marry him again to-morrow, you'd say yes or no."

"Well, now, I'll tell you another secret," said Elinor, smiling faintly, her cheek still pressed against the violin. "I think he might marry Margaret. I've thought so, and hoped so, ever since we first met her. I'm sure he admires her, and would love her if he didn't think I stood in his way. They would get on together delightfully. She is just the girl who would enjoy society and wealth, and all that, and he would enjoy showing her off. If he would give a thousand pounds merely to have a portrait, he would give his whole fortune, and everything else, to have her. I would certainly give anything, except my violin, to see them married. She likes him a thousand times better than I ever could, already."

"Well, I do think in my heart!" asseverated the old lady, quite outdone. "Did you know, my dear, that Margaret is engaged to marry Mr. Urmson, and that they're head and ears in love with each other, and will be married this winter? To hear you run on, any one would think—well!"

"Such a person as Mr. Garth Urmson has showed himself to be, will never be head and ears in love with anybody but himself," rejoined Miss Golightley, with contemptuous emphasis; "and there might be a chance of his becoming a better artist if he didn't marry. And Margaret wouldn't care for him, I know, if she realized what he was. I should think his having kept her waiting so long was proof enough he cared nothing about her. And then—I might be alone with my violin—and you!" and, rising quickly, the girl caught Mrs. Tenterden and the violin in one embrace, and hid her face on the former's soft, ample shoulder.

This method of winding up discussions, and enforcing arguments, has advantages

which can never attach to the dry pro-
poundings of mere logic; and Mrs. Tenterden attempted no further expostulation. She
returned Elinor's caress with all her heart,
and, then, having picked her tatting from
the floor, and smoothed her collar, she resumed her placidity.

"There's no reason, of course, my dear,
why you should be either married or trained
for a concert-performer just yet. What,
with the money we got by selling our furniture and things, and those investments
of yours in Boston, that have never been
touched, you know, for ten years, there
must be enough to live along on, at least, as
well as we are doing now. By-and-by, perhaps, we may be able to move down to Virginia, and be comfortable. Then there's
Mr. Selwyn: he may succeed in finding out
who robbed us, and getting some of it back.
It would be a good joke, wouldn't it?" said
the good lady, shaking gently with subdued
chuckling—"Golightley's astonishment. He
hasn't an idea that anything's being done
about it."

"I never could understand," observed
Elinor, meditatively, "why Mr. Selwyn,
who seemed to be quite rich, should have
interested himself in that affair, or why
your brother objected so strongly to his
having anything to do with it. It almost
seemed as if he suspected Mr. Selwyn of
knowing more about the loss of the money
than he had any right to know."

"Good gracious, daughter, what an idea!
A gentleman like Mr. Selwyn! I should as
soon think of suspecting Golightley himself.
No, the truth is, my dear—what I, for my
part, think—Golightley was just a little bit
jealous. Mr. Selwyn is rather too handsome and clever to be a safe acquaintance
of the young lady one is in love with. And,
what's more, I think Mr. Selwyn was jealous
of Golightley—so that was a pair of them:
and, if you must know everything, I think
that had something to do with Mr. Selwyn's
being so obliging about managing our business for us, and so anxious that Golightley
shouldn't be told. So now, miss, you see
what you are responsible for! I declare I
had quite a turn just now, when you began
with that nonsense about your violin—I was

really afraid, for a minute, that he had made
an impression."

A smile had drifted across Miss Elinor's
face while the other was speaking, but it
ended in a half sigh. "I am getting very
callous and bold, seems to me," she said.
"I can listen to talk about falling in love
and marrying as if I were—I don't know
what. Heartless people must be more or
less indelicate, I suppose. Heigho! Well,
why shouldn't he have made an impression?
He was handsome and clever, with fearless,
straightforward manners that I liked; I
even liked the way I heard him swear once.
Dear me! he is profane and very dissipated,
I suppose; and there's Mr. Garth Urmson,
with a face like Beethoven's, who never
drinks or swears, and is false and mercenary
to the core; and there is your poor brother,
whose soul Heaven has made so good and
noble, that there was nothing left to keep
his body from appearing as small and contemptible as Mr. Garth's character. There's
no such thing as a Man in the whole great
world!"

"Mercy! there are only too many of
them, I'm sure," exclaimed Mrs. Tenterden.

"If you will show me one, I'll worship
him," said Elinor, in a low voice. She
turned as she said it, and gazed out of the
window at the horizon-line; but in a moment rested her arms upon the window-sill,
and laid her face upon them, while Mrs.
Tenterden went on with her tatting in
sumptuous serenity. What a good, lovable,
sensible woman she was! taking life as easily as pale, vexed Elinor took it hard.

"By-the-way, my dear," said she, replacing her work in the bag, and rising—for
the primitive Urmsworth dinner-hour was
one o'clock, and it was time to dress—
"about the picnic. You'll go, I suppose!"

"It makes no difference to me whether
I go or not," replied Elinor, sitting up in her
chair, and setting it monotonously a-rocking
as before. "It will be disagreeable to meet
those persons; but, since we must be here
all winter, that can't be helped, and it will
be better out-doors than in."

Mrs. Tenterden laughed in her jolly, re-
proachful way. She always laughed where
other people would have compromised for a

smile. "I declare, you ought to be ashamed to talk that way, daughter. Well, then, if you want to go, I suppose we must. I told Margaret that would probably be the way, though, of course, I don't care anything about it myself. You'd better be getting ready for dinner, dear." And so she took her stately, comfortable departure.

CHAPTER XXXVI.

BOOTS AND EYE-GLASSES.

THE next morning was even warmer than is usual in the Indian-summer weather. The atmosphere, especially near the horizon, was dim with tender haze, and the south-westerly breeze, mild from the fortunate courts of the great Indian deity Cantantowwit, stirred the crimson and gold woods with indolent breathings. So impressive was the dreamy splendor of the valley, as seen from the southern windows of Urmhurst, that Golightley was more than once, in the intervals of his toilet, beguiled from his looking-glass to behold it, and he could scarcely have paid it a higher compliment. The toilet was with him a religious ceremony. He was in sad earnest about it always. The aspect of the man when newly risen from repose—if the disturbed grapplings with slumber which for many months past had been his nightly portion could properly be called by that name—would scarcely have prepared us for the gracious transformation brought about in him by these devotional exercises. Could orthodox religion effect such palpable improvement in its votaries, we might look forward to a significant deepening of the general piety. This toilet conscience of Golightley's was a typical trait in him. So far was he from being a reckless person, or indifferent to appearances, that he might be suspected of sometimes sacrificing the plain reality of good to the good-looking semblance thereof. And the nervous disquiet which in temperaments like his is apt to wait on such transactions may have had something to do with his uneasy nights. His hair having been duly anointed,

parted, combed, and brushed; his triple beard thoroughly groomed; his teeth, hands, and nails, duly purified, perfumed, and polished; the ample folds of his neck-cloth artistically composed, and a suitable waistcoat of figured satin selected, Golightley next turned his attention to the question of boots. There were at least a dozen pairs to choose from, all exquisitely made and in perfect repair, and it was a noticeable peculiarity that most of them were fitted with brightly-polished steel spurs. The natural inference would be that the owner of such gear must be proud of his feet and fond of riding; nevertheless, the facts were quite otherwise. If Golightley's boots were his strong point, it was because he knew his weak point to be his feet, and summoned every resource of the cobbler's art to solve the problem how to make what is flat and shapeless appear high-arched and shapely.

The result was very creditable, and probably deceived everybody except the maker and the wearer; the latter unfortunate gentleman, however, was never at ease (either literally or figuratively) in even his newest boots, but constantly tormented himself with the fancy that the fatal secret of his instep had been found out. The devil could not have been more solicitous about his cloven hoof than was Golightley to disguise the plebeian ugliness of these wretched extremities. As to the spurs, they were but an additional device to distract the observer's eye, and at the same time to lend a sort of martial dignity to the tread. It was a pathetic circumstance that, among so large an assemblage of boots and shoes, there should not have been so much as a single pair of slippers. The worst of acting a false part before the world is the dread it begets of ever dropping the mask for a moment to take breath. I will not assert that Golightley Urmson absolutely slept in his boots lest he should be found dead some morning with the secret revealed; but it is not too much to say that he suffered as much mentally from having them off as he did physically from having them on; and I submit whether moral corns are not, in the long-run, full as unendurable as material ones.

The boots having been drawn on, he walked up and down the room in them twice or thrice, scrutinizing their fit and general appearance. All this time he had been without his eye-glasses; he now paused in front of the mirror to put them on, and the change for the better which this small addition made in him was almost startling. It was like a magic touch, smoothing away premature wrinkles, brightening the sallow complexion, lending vivacity and pungency to the expression, and an aspect of refinement and prosperity to the whole man. Golightley stuck to his eye-glasses with almost as much constancy as to his boots, and with quite as much reason. We have already had a glimpse of that unlucky squint of his; but, even had this sinister deformity been absent, the glasses could hardly have been spared. Not that his eyesight was infirm; but his eyes, heavy-lidded, haggard, with curious little furrows surrounding them like a network, produced an effect altogether at variance with that which their owner thought desirable. There was no life in them, and yet they told tales. But the glasses—although, as a matter of fact, there could have been no more real life in them than in the eyes — had nevertheless a sparkling semblance of vitality which age could not dim nor emotion disconcert, and which, if superficial, possessed the redeeming quality of being impenetrable. They could never droop, swerve, or falter; neither, it must be admitted, could they convey love, anger, nor command; but only a very confident nature, perhaps, would deliberately exchange a condition of inactive security for the risky freedom of unprotected activity.

When Golightley was quite ready, he drew a long breath, straightened his shoulders, stamped sharply with his foot, smiled, bowed, and lightly kissed his finger-tips to the image in the mirror, and turned to go down-stairs. His glance, however, happened to light upon the collection of time-stained trophies which in this, as in most of the other rooms, hung above the fireplace, and he staid a moment to look at them. An old horse - pistol, nearly two feet in length, seemed chiefly to attract his curiosity, and he was on the point of taking it down to examine it more particularly, when a knock was heard at the door, and Cuthbert's voice summoned him to breakfast.

CHAPTER XXXVII.

UNFAITHFUL FRIENDS.

"By George, old chap, how delightful all this is, eh?" cried he, as arm-in-arm with his brother he entered the kitchen, where breakfast was set out. "This country hush, these exquisite autumn tints, this air of balm! Ah, what earthly gold is so precious to the soul as the yellow glory of that old elm? Old Urmhurst, too—the quaint old rooms and furniture and customs! I begin to think my exile's life has been a sad mistake, after all. Yes, you're a happier man than I am, old chap, because you're a wiser man and a better man—though I mean to do some good, if I can, before I go to chaos. —Good-morning, Nikomis. By the Great Spirit, madam, these buckwheat-cakes are light enough for the happy hunting-grounds! —By-the-by, Cuthbert, isn't that venerable deadly weapon over my fireplace the identical one which our forefathers used to annihilate their best friends with?"

"Yes," replied Cuthbert; " and its portrait is among the others in that intended purchase of yours in the studio. Five thousand dollars, I understand?"

Golightley waved his fork deprecatingly.

"The boy has genius. Five thousand dollars won't hurt him; oil the wheels a bit, and get his name up. By-the-by, where is he this morning?"

"He has been irregular the last day or two; it may be his company that has upset him. But as to this picture—you had better change your mind about buying it."

Golightley laughed, but he was a little puzzled.

"Of course," said he, "there is no absolute value to a work of art; it's a matter of fashion, scarcity, whim, and so on. Now, I honestly consider the picture worth the sum I named, looking at its merits of color and composition alone; but, to be frank with you, I shouldn't be buying it but for that—"

"That portrait of our pretty friend Margaret," Cuthbert interposed, quietly. "Well, it's precisely on account of that portrait that I say you'd better change your mind about buying the picture."

Golightley knew something of his brother's eccentricities, but this took him by surprise. He had expected that his bargain with Garth would be considered eminently creditable to both parties; if it was also recognized as a splendid compliment to Madge, why, so much the better all round! He thought Madge one of the beauties of the world, and was not averse from ingratiating himself with her. That she was soon to be married did not annoy him; beautiful women had been married ever since the time of Helen of Troy; and Helen, at least, had not let her marriage spoil her for the rest of the world. Madge would doubtless create a sensation in society so soon as she came out, and Golightley imagined a handsome gentleman, just past the prime of youth, who passed his long white fingers through his hair and replied to a respectful *coterie:*

"Little Margaret? Ah, yes; found her in the backwoods; saw what might be made of her, so set to work and did what I could. By George! the dear child got so fond of me that— Well, I was obliged to marry her off to my nephew there. Yes; ha! ha! Oh, I got him to paint her portrait for me, and for a quiet man like me that does quite as well as the original, you know, and may be just a leetle bit better.—You take me, madam, I see. Ha! ha!"

If this were not the whole future to which Golightley looked forward in his relations with Madge, at any rate it came as near being so as it suited his present convenience to own. Of course there might be unsuspected elements involved, which would claim consideration in due season. There was a great deal in Madge besides her beauty; she was very shrewd and intelligent, ambitious, and possessed of a subtile kind of audacity. Moreover, unless Golightley's diagnosis were at fault, she had, or believed herself to have, a secret and particular lien upon himself. It was not easy, therefore, to foretell how they might ultimately stand toward each other; "and meanwhile,"

thought he, "let things take their course up to a certain point, so that I may be freer to act on the spur of the moment, and less apt to compromise myself meanwhile."

But he had not been prepared for Cuthbert's objection, and he could only conjecture its probable upshot. He would have liked to retort upon his brother with some neat epigram, but he could think of none at the moment, and, indeed, he seldom did himself justice in that quiet, penetrating presence; his genius was rebuked, as, it is said, Mark Antony's was by Cæsar's.

"Ah, Cuthbert," said he, "I sometimes think it's a pity you are not more ill-natured and cynical than you are; you'd make such a devilish good satirist. Now, what are you up to? The only safe thing with you is to treat your utterances like those of the old oracles, and give them any signification but the most ostensible one."

"Well, expound what is hidden, if you suspect anything."

"Seriously, you know, my dear old boy, I might be a bit hurt. You forget that I'm the lad's uncle. I explained to you the other night that since my late business enterprises had done so well, I want the family to enjoy the good of it. You're not as frank as I've always been with you. When my affairs were in suspense, I knew you felt the same interest in keeping me up as if the need had been your own, and I took what I required, as a brother should, frankly and freely. I don't say—I never did say—that either one of us had a better right to the property than the other. Blessed be the Great Spirit, that's a question that need never be entered on now. I simply acted, as I always wish to act, like a gentleman—a—and a brother."

"Is your meaning a hidden or an ostensible one?" inquired Cuthbert at this point.

"It isn't doing me quite justice, you know," continued Golightley, shaking his head, with a somewhat melancholy smile, but not otherwise noticing this interruption. "You'll never know—no one can ever know —I speak frankly to you, dear boy, as I could to no one else—ever know what a life of self-abnegation mine has been. You don't know how constantly you've been in my thoughts. Damn it, you know, Cuthbert, I

give religion and all religious virtues a wide
berth—a man like myself necessarily out-
grows that sort of thing; but I have a code,
and, frankly, I consider it none the worse
that it's not dependent on superstitious nonsense: well, what I mean to say is, a man
of my principles could not but have the wel-
fare of you two in view in whatever he did.
I was obliged to draw heavily sometimes, I
dare say; sometimes, perhaps, I didn't realize, in the absorption and excitement of the
moment, how comparatively small the income of the estate really was; but I never
hesitated, because I knew your interests
were as mine, and—"

"Nikomis," said Cuthbert, with the deference which he invariably observed in his
intercourse with that dusky personage, "be
kind enough to give Mr. Golightley some
more buckwheats."

"It amounts to just this," resumed Golightley, taking this second interruption in
very good part, and giving his long forefinger an expository up-and-down movement—
"just this: I've had my innings, and now I
want you to take yours. I suppose you
won't deny that there's Urmson blood in all
of us? If I'm rich, I've a right to make you
and Garth rich too—and Mildred and Elinor
into the bargain. And it did me good to
hear that Garth was a painter, because that
gave me an avenue, you know—"

Perceiving that he was understood, Golightley threw up his finger and continued
his breakfast.

"But," observed Cuthbert, after a pause,
"all this does not touch my objection."

"See here: it isn't possible—you know
too much of the world, my dear brother, if
not of me, to suspect me of any rivalry? It
would be entirely out of the question. Of
course I'm not so insincere as to deny that
were I to enter the lists against a boy like
Garth, he could have no chance; but it's out
of the question, for twenty reasons. The
girl is devilishly attractive, but for a man of
great social experience like myself, the position of husband, of all things— To tell you
the truth, Cuthbert," continued Golightley,
resuming his finger, confidentially, "Madge
Danver—Madge Danver is nothing but a
country-girl to-day; but, unless all signs fail,

and I am greatly mistaken, the opportunities—you understand—of fashionable life
and the world will develop that country-
girl into a—Circe! and a man like myself—
a social Ulysses, so to say—doesn't entangle
himself with Circes. I tell you frankly, my
dear Cuthbert, I consider my nephew a bold
man: he shows all the intrepidity of youth;
but, by George, if I were in his shoes, I'd
tie Circe to the bed-post. She's clever
enough as it is, and if ever she comes to
know her own power—look out!"

"What you say doesn't make me any
less in love with her than I was before," returned Cuthbert, as he pensively stirred his
tea; "and I cannot suppose Garth to be
any more open to reason on such a matter
than I am. However, I don't presume to
question the accuracy of your insight any
more than the reality of your self-abnegation. But if you happen to wish to put
both beyond the possibility of cavil, I can
tell you how to do it."

Golightley stroked his mustache with the
tips of his fingers, and brought forward his
temple locks over his ears, but would not
further commit himself.

"Pay your addresses to Miss Margaret
and take her to Europe, and hand Garth
over to Miss Elinor."

Golightley paid the dryness of his brother's humor the tribute of an arch "Ha! ha!"
Then, still caressing gently various parts of
his countenance, he spoke dreamily: "Nellie, sweet Nellie—ah, there's the woman for
a wife, if a wife there must be! Gentle
blood, high breeding, culture, accomplishments. Nature full of tenderness and passion, if you can only arouse it; that cold-
ness, pride, high-mightiness, merely superficial you know—the feminine shield to
screen the feelings she dare not discover.
Dear child, she idolizes me: too good for
me, of course; but I owe a duty to her and
to Mildred. I owe them a duty—I owe
them a duty. An exquisite reserve and refinement about Nellie."

"Her manner toward you shows it. How
long have you been betrothed?"

"Eh? Well, that's a matter—that shows
the kind of girl Nellie is. I speak to you,
my dear old chap, with perfect unreserve.

I proposed to her, you see; I proposed to her the week after poor old John Tenterden's death. The circumstances were a bit peculiar. John had just lost his fortune—or rather he had just lost Mildred's: the money was all hers. And very singularly, I had just been successful in—a—a large speculation, which put me in possession of funds enough, as I just said, to make the whole of us comfortable for the rest of our lives. Well, of course, that turned the tables completely for Nellie and me, and she, with her refined sensitiveness, you know, felt it. She'd have taken me at half a word while I was poor and she was rich, but as soon as it was the other way she drew back. She said to herself, 'He's acting from a feeling of charity; he sees we are poor and alone, and he asks me to marry him as being the only way of securing us his wealth and protection.' So what does she do but refuse me? By George! I was really—really touched. Such refinement, such high breeding: risking the loss of me, you know, rather than compromise the integrity of her independence. Oh, it was very fine! And she went on and talked about earning her own living as a concert player, and all that; and, of course, understanding just what was in her mind, I humored her, and proposed coming over here until business matters can be arranged, and allowed the whole question of our marriage to hang fire. It suited me better, too; for I shall have to look about for a residence, and find out what climate suits her best, and, between you and me, school my mind to bid farewell to bachelorhood—ha! ha!"

"Insight is peace," observed Cuthbert, quietly. "If all men were like you, the course of true love would run smooth. But I fancy Miss Elinor has her share of insight likewise. Did she not come pretty near the truth in her conception of your motives?"

"Well, *you* have insight too!" admitted Golightley, with a smile. "But I do care for the dear girl, and she's of a kind that wears well. Do you know," he added, after a moment, "I was really delighted when poor John's fortune left him, and came, as it were, into my pocket. I'll tell you why. You see, he was a man totally devoid of administrative and business ability. By George, Cuthbert, that child Nellie understood ten times as much about business as he did. Well, he had the greatest dependence on my judgment, and so on, and wanted me to manage everything for him, and insisted on telling me what he had done or thought of doing, and asking my advice; and I would say to him, 'John, I can't take the responsibility of managing all this infernal great property of yours: I'm a man of no wealth myself, and if you were to lose anything by my advice, how could I replace it?' 'Replace it!' says he; 'if you'll assume the position of my steward, I shall no more think of calling you to account than if the money was your own.' I used to joke with him about that, and, one day, about a month before the crash came, said I, 'Look here, John, the money belongs to Mildred, and she and I are brother and sister; what do you say to deeding the whole of it over to me, and then all of you coming to live with me as my guests?' 'Say?' cries dear old John, in that hearty way of his, 'I say come on! get ready the deed, and Mildred and I will sign.' Well, I had a great laugh at him, you may be sure; but I thought then it would have been better all round if it could have been so. I never saw a man so worried about financial questions; he was so devilishly conscientious about his duty, and was always afraid he wasn't doing the right thing by Mildred's legacy as he called it. Probably we didn't imagine, at that time, how soon our mutual position would be reversed in earnest. I've forgotten whether I ever told you the circumstances, dear brother."

"I have forgotten it, if you have," returned Cuthbert, fixing his eyes on the other's face.

"The coincidence was so curious. From some confused statements of poor John's I fancy most of his investments were in South American stock, which was thought to be very good at that time. In fact, it stood so high that I was tempted to dabble a little in it myself. I happened to hear of a good opening, and in I went with every penny I had. This was not long after that talk with John. One morning I went on 'Change and found there was a corner. Unless. I could buy a thousand pounds' worth within two hours, I would lose all I had; if I could buy, I stood a chance of making seventy-five to eighty thousand sterling. There never had been such a grand opportunity known. Well, I hadn't ten pounds ready money to my name. I thought a minute, and then I went straight to John. 'Lend me a thousand pounds,' said I. You see, I was certain of not losing, and I knew how glad dear John would be at having been the means of making me a millionaire. He wrote a check on the spot. By George, Cuthbert," exclaimed Golightley at this point, " he was as good and kind a fellow as ever lived on this earth, and if there is a heaven he's in it now."

" We will assume there is a heaven," said Cuthbert. " Go ahead."

" Well, not to make a long story of it, I used that check just where it was needed, and a week afterward I paid back to John the thousand I owed him, and had left to my credit, all told, just eighty-three thousand pounds sterling. I didn't tell him then; merely said I'd made a good thing, thanks to him, and turned the conversation. I meant to surprise him afterward. Poor John! five days after that, we knew that everything he had was gone; and what was devilish strange, considered as a coincidence, I mean, was the fact that it had gone in the same crisis that had made me. I tell you, Cuthbert, it made me feel very queerly. Who can tell, you know — who can tell whether some of poor John's property may not actually have passed into my possession? I assure you, my dear Cuthbert, I almost felt as though some infernal fatality had brought to pass, in this way, precisely that 'transfer' that we had been joking about a few weeks before. Poor John! he never suspected; but that notion crossed my mind, and has bothered me ever since. Who knows? Somebody must have lost what I gained, of course, and why not poor John as well as anybody else? Well, it decided me on one point—I made a vow that day that I would never gamble in stocks again as long as I lived."

" You're as wise after success as before. Such good luck could hardly be repeated,

certainly. But do I understand you to say that the amount of Mr. Tenterden's loss was the same as what you won?"

" Oh, much greater; John must have lost a great deal over one hundred thousand, at least. But the reason I've bored you with all this, dear boy, was so you might comprehend my attitude and feeling toward Mildred and Elinor. I felt, by George, as if all I had belonged to them; and the thought that that thousand pounds which John lent me may have been the means of losing him everything he had—well, you can imagine, better than I can tell you, the way it was with me."

" But Mrs. Tenterden seems to think there was a robbery, or some sort of foul play."

" Dear, good Mildred! I've sometimes had half a mind to tell her, right out, that if anybody is to be apprehended on that count, it might just as well be me as the next man! Poor dear Mildred! She's a clever woman in many ways, too, and delicious all through; but you know how unreasonable women will get now and then; no doing anything with them. Yes, she had some wild idea that there had been a conspiracy and fraud and forgery, and I don't know what not; and it was all I could do to prevent her setting a detective at work, at ten pounds per diem, to hunt down the guilty ones. Dear, good soul that she is! Well, I hope to make her more comfortable than she could ever have made herself."

Cuthbert sat eying his brother in silence, and seemingly in a fit of abstraction, until at last the latter, having finished his breakfast, rose from the table and turned toward the fireplace. There sat old Nikomis in her corner, apparently fast asleep: as well she might be, under stress of so much powwow that concerned her not. Golightley, who had perhaps quite forgotten her existence for the time being, stood scrutinizing her for a moment, and then strolled to the window.

" It is nearly time to be under way for the picnic," he remarked. " What can have become of that boy of yours, old chap?"

" Before he comes," said Cuthbert, rousing himself and passing his hand up over his forehead with a sigh, "I want you to listen to a few more enigmas about the picture."

"Make haste, then, for here he is!" Golightley exclaimed, from the window-seat.

In a minute Garth's forcible step was heard through the house. He flung open the kitchen-door abruptly, and, seeing his father seated alone at the table, came forward with his cap still on his head, and his face flushed and frowning. He sat down opposite his father, and pulled a letter out of his pocket, the envelope of which bore a foreign postmark.

CHAPTER XXXVIII.

UNCLE AND NEPHEW.

For some days Garth had been under a cloud: a certain sweetness generally perceptible beneath his most rugged manifestations had been almost entirely obscured. A man of his temperament can easily become the most disagreeable companion imaginable. Stripped of the silent kindliness and geniality which should redeem stern features and reserved manners, he soon grows intolerable. To attempt to conciliate him is like putting your head in a lion's mouth, and it needs more than average nerve and audacity to bully or ridicule him into good-humor. The best part of him at such times is his morbid tendency to keep out of the way.

Since the morning of the reception in the studio, Garth had scarcely spoken a pleasant word, or done a kind deed. He had moved sullenly about, his under lip grimly pursed up, his rough brows lowering over his eyes. He rambled off in the forest after dark, only returning in the small hours of the night. He had avoided his father, stared his uncle out of countenance, and had conducted himself toward Madge with an odd mingling of rudeness and impulsive tenderness. The only person he had fraternized with was Nikomis; he would sit opposite her in the roomy fireplace for hours at a time, neither speaking nor spoken to. Her dusky companionship suited him better than that of any pale-faces; and he appeared to regret

9

that he had not been born and bred a full-blooded Indian, with a copper-colored skin, a wigwam, and a collection of smoke-dried scalps. All this time he touched neither pencil nor paint-brush.

Such having been his history of late, the impetuosity of his manner as he entered the room on this morning of the picnic was something of a surprise. Golightley, who had withdrawn to the window-seat, escaped his notice at first, and he sat down opposite his father, conscious only of him and of the letter in his own hand.

"Father, I must read you this," he began; "it's from—"

"Good-morning, Garth," said Cuthbert, in a low, sarcastic tone, which he used but seldom. "You might take off your cap and say good-morning to your uncle; and perhaps, if you ask her properly, Nikomis may give you some buckwheats."

Garth rose, putting the letter in the side-pocket of his coat, but leaving the envelope on the table. He understood that his father had desired to warn him that they were not alone, and he thanked him with a look.

"I want no breakfast," said he; "besides, it's time we were off, uncle.—Father, you're coming with us?"

"No; I find I must keep my study to-day. Besides, I think I've eaten too many buckwheats. Make my excuses to the ladies."

Garth paused a minute, eying his gray, pale, emaciated, bright-eyed father wistfully.

"I'll see you this evening, then—late," he said at length.

"Off with you, then, and may the nuts and grapes be plentiful; though, for my part, I think buckwheats are a great deal nicer, and quite as indigestible. Good-by."

The uncle and nephew accordingly made ready to depart, each of them, perhaps, wishing he might have had Cuthbert's private car a while longer. Golightley, however, was too affable to manifest any discontent: he gayly donned his hat, threw a precautionary shawl across his arm, glanced at his spurs, and professed himself eager for the woods.

"*Addio, fratello mio!*" he cried, turning

on the threshold, and airily kissing the tips of his fingers; and so preceded Garth out of the room.

Mr. Urmson took up the envelope from the table, glanced at the handwriting and the postmark, and finally put it in the pocket of the dressing-gown he wore, with a sigh. Then he turned to the old Indian.

"Nikomis," said he in a feeble and rather dejected tone, "I find my pains are going to come on again. This will be a bad day for me, I apprehend. I've been doing so well for the past week or so that I suppose I must pay for it. Can you have the medicine ready in about half an hour? I shall be overhead in the study."

Nikomis only grunted in reply; but, as Mr. Urmson prepared to leave the room, she got up from her seat, and, hobbling after him, threw open the door, took him gently but effectively under the arm, and so moved beside him down the hall, and slowly up the stairs. Mr. Urmson's face looked pinched and bloodless, and in mounting the stairs he pressed his lips rigidly together, and once or twice his eyelids quivered and almost closed. Arrived at his study-door, however, he turned, with something like his customary smile, and said:

"Thank you, Nikomis; you are a very kind old lady."

Meanwhile Garth and Golightley were on their way to the village, the latter, according to his persistent custom, having linked his own through the former's unwilling arm. Golightley was probably a believer in the magnetic influence of one human being upon another, and fancied that, if he could but contrive to handle his companion enough, he would be thereby enabled to make a corresponding moral impression. Doubtless there are many persons who do enjoy being stroked and patted, and who are more or less liable to pur under the operation; but Garth never purred in any circumstances, and was as averse from being touched indiscriminately as though he had lacked a skin. Nevertheless, he had never openly resented the tactics of his uncle, toward whom he was, perhaps, the more doggedly determined to show liking, because instinctively holding him in disfavor. Garth

had a powerful imagination and more than enough sensibility; but along with these qualities he possessed a sturdy rational faculty, which was continually collaring its more refined associates, and asking them what they were up to.

His uncle, as they left the house, had entered upon a discussion of Mr. Urmson. "Cuthbert, your dear father, Garth," said he, "is a man you might call ἄναξ ἀνδρῶν—a chief of men, as old Homer has it. By George, he is a fine fellow! I really knew him very little before I went to Europe; he was away himself, you know, during most of my big-boyhood; and being so much older than I, of course—and, then, having different mothers, too, I suppose—we weren't so intimate as we might have been otherwise. But I always knew—bless you, I knew just as well!—that there was the making of a grand friendship between us two, if ever we got a fair show. But I'm bound to confess that there's more to dear old Cuthbert than even I had given him credit for. I only wish he didn't look so confoundedly like his own ghost sometimes. I remember he used to be rather delicate, and, of course, I knew that years would have their way with him, as with the rest of us! but, by George, I wasn't prepared for such a change as this!"

To hear his father eulogized made Garth restive, even when convinced that the eulogy was sincere. But the mention of ill health merged this petty emotion in a deeper one.

"You spoke of that once before," he said, looking at his companion, "and I heard Mrs. Tenterden say something about it, too. My father is getting old, and the last few months has had pain sometimes—rheumatism, I suppose; but he cannot be seriously ill."

"Ah, my dear boy, you see, you are with him from day to day, and his debility wouldn't come on you with a shock, as it did on me. He has hardly a remnant of the vivacity and sparkle that I remember in him. I still catch a glimpse occasionally of that old subtile, ironical humor that can never quite die out of him; but the elasticity, the mischievous glance—ah, dear old

Cuthbert! I fancy your dear mother's death must have shattered him a good deal?"

"He bore it so much better than I," murmured Garth, speaking less to his uncle than to himself, "that I almost forgot he had anything to bear." He was silent for some moments, but finally said, heaving a deep sigh: "Yes, I can see now that my father is not the same man since then. No doubt it struck him deeper than it did me. But he never shows what he feels—hardly ever—either joy or sorrow."

"Ah, yes, that's Cuthbert: a great deal of the Indian stoic in him. But a loss of that kind will wear a man down, you know, give it time; and, no doubt, it may have impaired the recuperative power. Doesn't he consult a physician?"

"No—yes; Professor Grindle (a college professor of mine, who used to practise medicine) was here last spring; perhaps my father consulted him. He has letters from him once in a while."

"Oh, we must get him a regular live doctor!" exclaimed Golightley, enterprisingly; "see what's the matter with him, and cure him up. I dare say, now, this little variety of having me with him, and seeing Mildred now and then, and so on, will be of the greatest benefit to him. I hope to do wonders, my dear Garth, in the way of raising his spirits and making everything easy and comfortable for him. Bless his heart! he's had plenty of anxiety and trouble, I don't doubt; so have I—we all have had; this uncertainty and restriction regarding money-matters, you know, and all that sort of thing; but that's done with now, thank Fortune, and I mean to have us all easy and comfortable from this time forth. As for you, you have genius, and are bound to make a fortune of your own. However, I should be glad to think that I'd given you a bit of a lift at the start—eh?"

Garth was silent for some time. At last he said:

"You have given me such a lift that I shall never want another."

Golightley's recent conversation with Cuthbert had put him somewhat on his guard as to Garth's possible sentiments on this subject, and he had already made up his mind what was the proper thing to say.

"Now, my dear young nephew," he began, engagingly, "I can't let you forget that I am your uncle, and have a right to take avuncular liberties with nephews and nieces whom I love. I see what's in your mind, and I like you the better for what I see; and, to prove it, I mean to be perfectly frank with you. There's a little bit of professional pride and jealousy at work in you. You want your picture to sell entirely on its own merits, and not—"

"If you did not see what is in my mind," said Garth, taking advantage of his uncle's hesitating for a suitable expression, "I should feel like telling you."

"Ha! ha! Well, now, my dear boy, you must consider, you know, how deep and genuine my interest in you is. Why should not you prefer to see your picture—which, as I have often said, has intrinsic power and originality enough to make your reputation without me—to see it in the hands of a warm friend and relative rather than of a mere disinterested connoisseur? When you come to think it over, I know, without your telling me, that that consideration alone will give you more satisfaction than the mere price, more or less, that goes in your pocket. Why, it's a mutual pleasure and gratification to both of us."

"Why do you tell me this, Uncle Golightley?" demanded Garth, with an air of grave curiosity.

"Ah, my dear Garth, because a rather sad experience has taught me the wisdom of perfect frankness between those who would be friends. And I want you to feel how great my interest is, not only in your artistic, but in your domestic future. I'm so glad you're going to marry that sweet, lovely girl, Madge!. It's such a good thing for a young man like you, of sound, high principles, just entering on life, to have such a charming creature as that always at your side, helping you over the rough places, and beckoning you up the heights. Ah, Garth, what a different life I might have led, if—But no matter. No doubt it's better as it is. H'm! where was I?"

Perhaps Garth did not know; at all

events, he did not tell, but callously left his uncle to find out for himself.

"Well, what I'm coming to is this: I spoke just now of professional jealousy. Now, I know what it is to be a hot-blooded young fellow, and I know that there's more kinds of jealousy than one. And I tell you fairly, Garth—I hinted it once before—that the portrait which you have incorporated with your picture in such a masterly manner, and which is a masterpiece in itself—that portrait, and the associations which will always cling to it, have mainly influenced me in this little transaction of ours. But, I'm sure, after what I've said about that charming girl, that you cannot misunderstand my attitude toward her. I admire her, you know, in the æsthetic sense. I might say, impersonally, but that I feel myself too much bound up with you all on other grounds to call it that."

Uncle Golightley seemed likely to go on yet further in this earnest vein, but at this point Garth interrupted his solemn discourse with a laugh, which, despite the elder's insight into the workings of the artist's mind, seemed to take him by surprise.

"I'm afraid I'm not a hot-blooded young fellow, Uncle Golightley," said the nephew. "I never had a misgiving on Margaret Danver's account, and it doesn't matter to me what the picture is bought for, so long as it's bought. That is the unpoetic fact. I hope you admire Margaret—or her portrait—at least as much as you say you do, because otherwise you would be, from an artistic point of view, a fool to spend a cent upon the picture, not to speak of a thousand pounds. But I told you my opinion on that matter at the time."

Uncle Golightley was seldom so much put out as not to be able to rally quickly, and he now recovered himself with great good-humor.

"I remember, you young Vandal; and, by-the-by, I wish you'd explain how you came to put that wonderful face into your composition, only to utter blasphemy against it afterward."

Garth shook his head.

"I forgot the picture," said he, "while I was painting the face."

"By George, well you might! Ha! ha! You rascal! So you're not afraid of a rival well up in the forties—eh? Ah, well, I don't blame you; and I see we understand each other very well. But it struck me you were a trifle in the blues lately, and I feared I might have unwittingly trod on your corns in one way or another."

"I truly believe," said Garth, after a minute or two, "that the only person I'm quite safe in distrusting is—this!" indicating himself by a slight contemptuous gesture. "Do you know, whenever I dream of you, you appear as a scoundrel! The discredit is mine, not yours. And I disliked your ways—your free way with women. I beg your pardon for it. It was because I haven't the strength or the goodness, or whatever the virtue is, to do innocently what you can do. I'm in a bad way, it seems."

"See here, my beloved nephew," cried Uncle Golightley, with a half-laughing, half-apprehensive glance at his saturnine companion, "have you gone melancholy mad, or are you dreaming awake? I never heard you in this vein before."

"Have no anxiety," returned Garth, shaking his shaggy head again, with a brief, unmirthful smile. "It must be an eccentricity of genius—and that will soon pass, Heaven knows! There are the wagons."

CHAPTER XXXIX.

LOVER AND MISTRESS.

In fact, the forest had now thinned away and they were within sight of the Danvers' cottage, which stood on the hither outskirt of the little village. Before the front-gate of the garden inclosure stood a roomy but rather primitive rustic vehicle, consisting of a platform mounted on four wheels and fenced round with half a dozen uprights—in short, an old-fashioned hay-rigging. To fit it for its present employment three or four stout boards had been fastened horizontally to the uprights, at a suitable height above the flooring, by way of seats; and a number of baskets of provisions had been securely stowed away forward. Two wiry farm-horses were harnessed to the shafts, and a group of persons, among whom were Mrs. Tenterden, Madge, and Mrs. Danver, was collected hard by. Madge was feeding the horses with handfuls of hay, while Mrs. Tenterden seemed to be examining the rude conveyance with some misgiving at its lack of springs, and confiding her apprehensions to Mrs. Danver.

As Garth and his uncle drew near, the latter stepping jauntily along with his beard in the air, the former butting forward with downward brow, Golightley, in the exuberance of the moment, took off his hat and waved it in the air, uttering a view-halloo. Mrs. Tenterden straightway began hunting in her pockets for a handkerchief to wave in response, but did not find it until the gentlemen were so close at hand as to rob the act of its propriety. Madge left the horses and advanced to meet the new-comers, looking like an incarnation of the rich and lovely day.

Golightley was on the point of greeting her with all his customary gallantry of manner, but happening to remember his companion's crotchets on the subject, he forcibly constrained his cordiality to a mere gentle pressure of both her hands and a fatherly compliment on her appearance and costume.

She laughed, and looked so provokingly kissable that poor Uncle Golightley sighed, and passed on to wreak his tenderness upon sister Mildred, leaving Madge to her lover. She stood in front of him, holding on to a button of his coat, and twisting it as she spoke:

"I saw you pass twice this morning, from my window, and you didn't look up. Tell me, dear Garth, have I done anything wrong? Are you sorry, or glad—or angry?"

"I've been growing wise during the last few days, that's all. You have done nothing wrong."

"But why should growing wise make you sad?"

"Because it shows me what a fool I have been until within the last few days. But I shall get over it soon, and be as merry as I am wise."

"Tell me what you have been growing wise about?" demanded Madge, with a quick, scrutinizing glance.

"About marrying you. I ought to have married you years ago instead of going to Europe. By this time we should have been a well-to-do farming couple, with something tangible to do and think of—crops and hogs and markets."

"Hogs and markets! You funny boy! I am thinking about fine people and society."

"It is all the same what you call them; I think hogs and markets sounds the best. That is my wisdom. When I was a fool, I should have preferred something abstract and ideal. A fool, Madge, is a person who talks and thinks about things above him. When I first fell in love with you, I ought to have made up my mind never to busy myself about anything more above me than you are. I never saw you looking better than you do this morning; but," he continued, taking both her wrists in his hands and griping them hard, "there's nothing abstract about you—or ideal either! and there sha'n't be in my life from this time forward."

"Do, Mrs. Tenterden, look at those two sweethearts, without a word for anybody but their two selves!" cried Mrs. Danver. —"Maggie, we're starting, child!—Well, wouldn't you think she was deaf, ma'am?"

"It's a very delightful kind of deafness, I'm sure," said Mrs. Tenterden, laughing; for she was not so old as to have forgotten the time when she suffered from a like infirmity. "It makes one forget all about matter-of-fact things and people."

"Ah!" sighed Golightley, caressing his cheek, as he turned his tinted eye-glasses on the lovers. "When boys and girls are in love, it comes to the surface in every look and gesture; but when we get a little older, Mildred, it may show less, but it makes more havoc with our insides. Where's Elinor?"

"She's always the last one to be ready, you know," said Mrs. Tenterden. "But there she comes."

"All in gray and scarlet, like fire and ashes. *Buon' giorno*, fair lady! the last, best gift of Heaven to man!" He took her hand and kissed it. "Come, Garth, show your public spirit enough to get us in the wagon. You and I must act as derricks for these four nymphs.—Mrs. Danver, let us begin with you."

Mrs. Danver, who was entirely captivated by Uncle Golightley's attentions, was accordingly hoisted on board, and Mrs. Tenterden, a much heavier weight, and the heavier for her laughing timorousness, followed. Then came Elinor, who, as she gave her hand to Garth to be lifted up, expected him to say good-morning to her, and had the answering greeting on the tip of her own tongue; but he turned his face away and said not a word, upon which the proud, self-contained young lady flushed pink to the ears. Madge was the last, and she bounded up with such unexpected lightness that Uncle Golightley lost his balance and fell backward, to his great chagrin, especially as the mishap unseated his tinted eye-glasses. However, he immediately jumped up again with a great laugh, and declared that Madge was the first young lady who had ever got the better of his understanding, and defeated his upright intentions.

By this time the two or three other wagons which had been waiting, full of picnickers, at the corner of the adjoining road, were beginning to rumble away toward their destination, amid much noise and merriment. Garth, who had taken his place as driver, was preparing to follow them, when Mrs. Danver, with a sudden shriek of recollection, reminded him that it had been arranged they should call at the parsonage for Mr. Graeme, whose age and position entitled him to that attention. The horses' heads were therefore turned in that direction; but before they had proceeded many rods, the hoary patriarch's colossal form loomed into view, somewhat bent and stiffened beneath his vast, invisible weight of years, but still sturdy enough, as it seemed, to bear half a generation more. While yet at a distance he uplifted his voice, mighty in spite of the cracks and quavers that occasionally sounded through it, and began a jovial monologue.

"Hullo, folks! Why, I began to think you'd forgotten me, I'm such an inconsiderable young man — haw! haw! haw! So there's Master Garth! is he actually going to a picnic at last? Well, I've lived to some

purpose, now that I've seen that come to pass; no mistake about it—ho! ho! Why, the other day, when he was a little chap about up to my knee-buckle—he's not much over that now, either—the other day—well —eh? what was it happened the other day? I was just going to say something, but I do believe I've forgotten it, though I've got a wonderful good memory; no mistake about that—ha! ha! ha!—Whoa, Dobbin!—Good-morning, boys and girls.—Young man, if you'll lend a helping hand—I'm not quite so spry in the joints as usual this morning—once more! Thank you, sir.—I don't know your name, but—Golightley? Maud Urmson's boy that went to London five-and-twenty years ago? Got back? Why, lad, we're all heartily glad to see you again. I do believe—though, now I think of it, I saw you yesterday—or was it day before yesterday? Yes, yes; but it's the hair on your face that bothered me. You're the first Urmson ever wore side-whiskers! but there was always more of Maud than of Brian in you, anyway. You had a show of the split in the chin, but not the jaw—not the eye, either. Garth's the man—Urmson all over, like his grandfather and his great-great-great-grandfather before him. They didn't any of them paint pictures, though— eh, Garth? I always said you ought to give that up; you will, too, I guess, one of these days, and take to soldiering or privateering, as an Urmson ought—haw! haw! ho!— Madam, good-morning—Mrs. Tenterden? Yes, yes; I know you all now—Maud's little girl that we heard of, but never saw. Do you know, madam, you came very near not being born at all? Why, if Maud hadn't been told that Brian was dead, and if he hadn't been told that she was dead, they'd have been made man and wife in the year 1781; and then where would you and Cuthbert have been, I want to know?—ho! ho! where would you have been, Cuthbert, lad? Why, where is he?"

"He said he must keep to his study to-day," Garth made answer.

"Ay, working on his history—a history of the United States, Mrs. Tenterden, incarnated, so to speak, in the Urmson family. The family, madam, has been here pretty nearly from the start, and borne a hand more or less directly in all the chief events; but never, if you observe, ma'am, aiming for the top places—no commanders-in-chief or Governors or Presidents among 'em; they represent the heart more than the head of the people, you see, Mrs. Tenterden; though as for Garth there, it isn't easy to say what he represents. Cuthbert would make him out the full body corporate, I suspect—ho! ho! But I tell him no Urmson ever took to paint and canvas before—though Garth has a fist for other things as well, ma'am, when the time comes. Why, last Michaelmas-day —haw! haw!—he gave such a licking to Sam Kinco as scared the chap out of the village—that was five or ten years ago, and he hasn't been back here since. And all on Miss Madge's account. But she's a little witch; and some day, when Garth gets big enough, I'm going to try a tussle with him about her myself. I believe she loves me better than she does him now."

So saying, the venerable Titan drew Madge, who happened to be sitting near him, on his gigantic knee, and kissed her on both cheeks. The love-making between him and this young woman had never undergone abatement or eclipse from its beginning to the present day. Madge, to do her justice, had been as true to him as he had been to her. Possibly she appreciated the moral support which his countenance and affection afforded her in a community where the parson was still able largely to influence and direct public opinion upon all social questions. Moreover, his unswerving and outspoken belief in her may well have had the effect of moulding in some degree her own estimate of herself. Although too clear-headed not to be aware that in this or that particular respect the genial credulity of the old giant palpably overrated her, she would nevertheless think better of her deserts from a comprehensive point of view; and thus, in deceiving him, she would be indirectly compassing a self-deception. Parson Graeme had never, perhaps, been a person of very profound intelligence: and, during the last few years, such mental faculties as he had had been gradually becoming clouded and untrustworthy. Madge, however, though

possessing no small talent for demure ridicule, was never known to exercise it at the expense of her hoary admirer—a piece of self-restraint which becomes easily intelligible if we suppose her to have recognized his value as a moral ally; for who but a simpleton would think of discrediting the pillar of his respectability by chalking caricatures upon it? Although, moreover, the good minister could hardly have boasted such personal attractions as would be likely in themselves to captivate a young woman of Madge's tastes, yet did she seem to find a peculiar pleasure in clinging about him in every affectionate attitude, caressing and caressed. I would by no means deny the possibility of her having detected in him qualities so superior to all merely external attributes as to sink the latter beneath consideration; but, be this as it may, it was patent to the dullest eye that the contrast between the warm grace of the lovely, blooming girl and the frosty ponderousness of the age-smitten parson was vastly picturesque, and, so far at least as Madge was concerned, certainly most politic. However, the wisest policy is not necessarily self-conscious, and Madge might have been a politician unawares. It is not easy to look upon such a woman and judge her severely, or even impartially. She appeals to something in man more potent than any merely judicial or logical weapon that he is apt to have at command.

CHAPTER XL.

Soon after leaving the village the wagon got into the rough woodland ways, and jolted horribly, much to the distress of Mrs. Tenterden—one of those women who seem especially fitted by nature to grace a smooth-rolling carriage, drawn by pampered steeds, and attended by liveried footmen, but who are quite out of their element in a New England hay-rigging, or in any other situation involving physical unease and awkwardness. She clung to the wooden upright on one side, and to Golightley's arm on the other, in manifest discomfort and alarm.

"Don't you think you'd better walk, daughter?" she said to Elinor. "This jolting will be sure to give you one or your headaches; and I'll come with you, so as you won't get lost."

"No, I enjoy jolting," replied Elinor, with a malicious smile; "besides, what if you should find you had forgotten the way to the picnic-ground yourself?"

"I think that's very mean of you, Nellie," cried Mrs. Tenterden, laughing at the detection of her own duplicity. "Well, I hope, at any rate, there are no eggs or brittle things in those baskets, or there'll be nothing left of them."

"Oh, dear me, ma'am!" said Mrs. Danver, shaking her poke-bonnet, with its immaculate starched frill, "when you've been bumped about as much as I have, you'll never notice this at all—though, too, I've got aches and pains in all my poor bones, and have had many years, ma'am—yes. But you always being able to live in luxury, as I might say, it is but natural you should find it come a little hard at first."

"Oh, I know all about country-life," returned the other lady, who had too much spirit to submit to any such assumption of superiority. "I was brought up on the plantation down in Virginia, and ran wild all over the place till I was seventeen.—But I must say I don't know where you get all your endurance from, Nellie; you were such a puny little thing when we took you, after Mr. and Mrs. Golightley died; and then we all went over to Europe, and lived there ever since—in luxury, as you would say, Mrs. Danver," she added, with her good-natured laugh.

"Elinor has the old Cavalier spirit," said Golightley, "and minds jolting no more than one of Prince Rupert's horsemen."

Elinor seemed inclined to resent being made the subject of personalities in mixed company, and she would have withdrawn into herself with all the haughtiness of her twenty maiden years; but at this juncture Parson Graeme put his enormous finger in the pie.

"Is miss a Golightley?" he asked, in his time-worn rumble. "Why, I thought, madam, she'd been your own daughter. A

real Golightley! Cuthbert and I had been thinking they'd died out. Let's see: there was Rupert, Brian's friend, was killed near Jamestown, when I was no older than Garth is now. But, to be sure, he had a brother Charles—ay, that's the man! We knew Charles had a son, but we never heard of a daughter.—Miss, we're right glad to have you among us—eh, Cuthbert? Why, where is the lad? He'd rejoice to see Charles Golightley's daughter."

This was certainly tiresome and foolish, especially since something similar to it had taken place once or twice before; and Uncle Golightley wore a compassionate sneer, while Mrs. Tenterden looked as if she might have laughed. But Elinor answered him with a gentleness which she could not help feeling for the decayed old patriarch, with his recollections of seventy years ago, and his forgetfulness of the passing hour.

"Charles Golightley was my grandfather, Mr. Graeme," said she; "his son James was my father. We have not quite died out yet, you see; but I am the last of the Golightleys."

"You have a sweet voice, my lass," said the venerable minister, gazing at her with his ancient eyes; "a sweet voice, that tells of a true soul and a pure heart. Take an old man's word for it."

His own voice, as he spoke, abated somewhat of its ruggedness, for he was susceptible as a child to certain superficial impressions. The next moment, however, he reverted, with a child's inconstancy, to his customary noisy joviality.

"When that boy yonder was born, ma'am," he began, addressing Mrs. Tenterden, and pointing to Garth, "we were looking about to see whom he was to marry. Cuthbert was always for historical compensation—something of that sort—ho! ho!—and he said the Urmsons had treated the Golightleys so shabbily, it ought to be made up somehow: if there was only a little girl Golightley, Garth might marry her when they grew up, and settle it that way. 'Better hunt her up,' said I, 'before he gets ahead of us, and falls in love with the wrong girl.' Haw! haw! haw! However, miss," continued this old *enfant terrible*, "he grew up such a bashful chap, he was always hiding away by himself, and we couldn't get him even to go to the picnic till he was quite a lad; and then he shinned up a tree before any of us got there, and never came down till we were all out of the way again. But, sure enough, that same night he was punching Sam Kineo's head because Sam had—What was it he did to you, Madge, my lass?"

"Nothing, grandpapa, dear," replied that young lady, with a covert glance at Garth, who had turned partly round as if trying to relieve her from her supposed embarrassment by commanding the eyes of the auditors to his own flushed and darkening visage.

"I beg the company's pardon," said he, "for having to rake up the story; but Sam Kineo said he had done what he had not."

Good Mrs. Tenterden, whose own good humor not seldom betrayed her into inadvertently exasperating the raw places of less happily constituted persons, hereupon began to chuckle and shake her statuesque shoulders, at the same time casting arch glances at poor Madge, evidently with the intention of presently uttering some unforgivable innuendo about the coquettishness of pretty girls and the unsuspecting credulity of young men. Elinor saw the impending peril, and was impelled, despite her declared hostility and contempt for Garth Urmson, to make an attempt at turning the conversation.

"We met a gentleman abroad who, I believe, was a friend of yours, Mr. Urmson. His name was Selwyn."

"Yes," said Garth, involuntarily putting his hand in his coat-pocket; "he was with me in Europe the first year, and afterward studied law in Germany. A very different man from Kineo!"

"He was a very intelligent person," observed Mrs. Tenterden. "We all got to like him very much. At least," she added, recollecting herself, "I thought him very clever and agreeable.—You didn't, Golightley?"

"I'm glad to hear it," Golightley hastened to say, settling his eye-glasses and bringing forward his hair over his ears—"very glad to hear, Garth, that Jack Selwyn was a friend of yours. Of course, one

who has seen so much of what strangers on the Continent sometimes turn out to be, has to exercise great caution in admitting people to too great familiarity. H'm!—You mustn't say I disliked him, my dear Mildred; but I felt it would be unadvisable to consult a man whose respectability we had no means of establishing, upon a matter like the recovery of your lost property, you know. Besides, it was perfectly impossible to recover anything. I—h'm—I believe I never mentioned it to you before, my dear, but for several months I employed the first detectives of London and Paris, and nothing came of it."

"My fathers! Golightley, did you really?" exclaimed Mrs. Tenterden.—"Well, if that isn't the funniest thing, daughter! Well, to think of our not knowing it!"

"Selwyn," began Garth, and hesitated for a moment—"Selwyn," he continued, "is one of the most upright and keen men I know. He has traveled over the world ever since he was a child, and knows men better than most men do.—You were mistaken in not trusting him, Uncle Golightley. I believe he would know a thief or a scoundrel as soon as he looked at him."

"Ha! ha! a sort of moral touch-stone of humanity. Well, it's really a pity we hadn't been better introduced to him. But I'm interested about this Kineo, Garth. What was he, and what became of him?"

As Garth did not at once reply, old Mrs. Danver interposed her thin, faded voice. "He was just one of those half-breed Indians, Mr. Golightley, and I suppose that's about all anybody does know about what he is. He first came here, just a little baby, with Nikomis, now the cook up to Urmhurst, where you've likely seen her, sir. She called herself his grandmother. But the best I can say is, I never did take to either of 'em. I was really quite glad when Garth put him down so, for I do believe he might have troubled Maggie, though she always laughs when I say it."

"A half-breed, was he? Light or dark?"

"Well, seems like he was pretty light for a half-breed," said Mrs. Danver. "I recollect we used to say, when Garth was more tanned than usual, there wasn't much to choose but what he was as dark as Sam. We did use to say, too, now and again, that there was a likeness to each other between them other ways, though Sam was taller than Garth, and his hair was straight, and he hadn't eyes like Garth—I'm sure of that —and his nose and mouth were different. Fact is, I don't know just how it was, and I am not a good hand at putting likenesses, anyway."

"Are there any half-breeds in Europe?" demanded Madge. "Perhaps he stole Mrs. Tenterden's money."

"Ha! ha!" laughed Uncle Golightley. "Then we must get Garth to give him another thrashing. Ha! ha!" .

"How lonely you must have been, Margaret, dear, when everybody had gone to Europe and left you behind! If I were you, I would make Mr. Garth give a pretty strict account of his acquaintances while he was abroad. I, for my part, think it's very suspicious when a young man stays away so long from the lady he's engaged to," said mischievous Mrs. Tenterden. .

"By George, Garth, that's a fair suspicion!" cried Golightley, entering loudly into the spirit of the fun. "Come, who knows but what you have a full-fledged Don Juan under that red shirt of yours! Let us constitute ourselves a committee of inquiry."

Garth, who had been giving his attention to the horses during the latter few minutes, faced about again at this attack.

"Be careful," said he; "for if you guess the truth, I shall confess it."

"This is getting serious," observed Golightley. "Perhaps, in deference to the feelings of some of those present, we had better let this unfortunate matter rest."

"Well, I was down to the post-office this morning," said Mrs. Danver—who, although not chargeable with any quick appreciation of the humorous, was happy to be able to contribute her item to the discussion—"and Mr. Stacy said to me there was a foreign letter come for Mr. Garth Urmson."

"I declare, Mr. Garth," cried Mrs. Tenterden, laughing, "that does look very— very— Do you admit receiving foreign letters?"

Garth again put his hand in his pocket, and pulled out a fold of blue letter-paper. "Here it is," said he.

"The letter is in evidence, and should be read," affirmed Uncle Golightley, in his self-assumed character of Madge's counsel.

"I have read it," rejoined Garth, with a smile; "but that must suffice for the present. You will all probably know the contents hereafter." And he thrust the fold of blue paper back.

Hereupon the Rev. Mr. Graeme, who had been sitting in seeming oblivion of external things for some time past, began to chuckle inwardly. At length, when every one's face was more or less set working by the contagion of his stupendous mirth, he found utterance as follows:

"Ho! ho! Foreign letters don't come as often as they did a while ago, when Cuthbert, poor lad, used to hear from Europe four or five times a year, telling him he'd been drawn on for a thousand dollars and odd, and signed—haw! haw! haw!—'Your af—'"

What the signature was will never be known; for, before it could leave the forgetful old gentleman's lips, the wagon suddenly swerved violently to the left, and Garth shouted, in a voice that might have done credit to the stentorian parson himself in his best days, "Look out for your heads, everybody!"

Everybody crouched instinctively, and the overhanging branch of a tree swept close above them. The horses, taking advantage, as it seemed, of their driver's carelessness, had shied off the roadway, and hence the accident. Everybody escaped except Uncle Golightley, whose hat was taken off; but such was his agility that, almost before any one else had remarked his mishap, he had vaulted from the wagon and was running toward the place where it had fallen, laughing loudly at the adventure; and when, having picked it up and clapped it jauntily on his head, he had overtaken the others, his amusement at the adventure was still unsubdued.

Garth had halted his horses, partly out of consideration for Mrs. Tenterden, who, like most of her sex possessing ample physical development, was timorous as a rabbit, and who now needed time to convince herself that neither she nor any other member of the party had actually been deprived of life; and, when that point had been settled, she was moved to expostulate with Garth for his recklessness in putting so many lives in jeopardy.

"Now, just suppose we'd all been killed! I'm sure its providential."

"Yes, it was an escape," responded Garth, gravely, eying Uncle Golightley as he spoke. "But a hat is no great loss, especially when it can be picked up again. We have but a quarter of a mile to go. Jump in, sir."

"Since we're so near, I have a mind to stretch my legs a little along this charming forest path," said Golightley. "*Au revoir*, though I'm a quick walker, and shall probably keep you in sight most of the way. By-the-by, I wonder if Miss Elinor would consent to keep me company?"

Elinor had not uttered a syllable since the accident, but had turned more than usually pale. While Mr. Graeme was speaking, she had looked point-blank at Golightley; after that she paid no more attention to him until he spoke her name.

She then stood up, and began to make her way to the end of the wagon, Parson Graeme, with elephantine gallantry, lending her a helping hand over the seats, while Mrs. Tenterden and Mrs. Danver pursued her with exhortations and advice. Golightley stood ready to receive her at the end of her passage, but she sprang quickly to the ground without touching his offered hand.

"Good-by," cried Madge, smiling, and kissing her hand. "Now you are going to talk secrets."

Golightley gayly beckoned a parting salute with his uplifted finger-tips. "We're only in quest of an appetite. Don't eat up all the nuts and grapes before we get there."

"Shall we carry your hat for you?" inquired Garth, as he gathered up his reins, "or do you think you can risk wearing it yourself?"

"Ha! ha! ha! ha! I believe I won't trouble you," was the reply. "You know, I can keep out of the way of branches better on foot than in your old hay-rigging."

Garth spoke to his horses, and the springless vehicle trundled off, bouncing along the uneven wheel-ruts, and was soon lost to sight round the bend of the lane. The two pedestrians were thus thrown upon their own resources for mutual entertainment. They advanced at a leisurely pace, side by side, but not arm-in-arm, and conversing with earnestness and animation.

BOOK VI.

LOVE-MAKING AND FLIRTATION.

CHAPTER XLI.

CAPTIVE.

ELINOR was angry: the delicate color which rose and fell in her face, and the tone of her voice, showed that plainly enough. At such moments she stood revealed as preeminently of an emotional temperament. Her customary disguise of cold indifference became transparent, and could never again mislead. The feeling that was in her frankly and pungently expressed itself; it tingled forth through every avenue of gesture and aspect. Like a child, she would forget herself in the generous vehemence of her utterance, though never overstepping that which lay deeper than consciousness itself—the innate, vital law of ladyhood. Not that this subtile restraint would render her indignation less formidable. Bitter is a woman's tongue; but the tongue of a lady can prick like an envenomed needle!

But Golightley was not disheartened. He had a well-grounded confidence in his strategical and persuasive ability, and in his knowledge of Elinor's temper. He had no doubts of his ability to explain things. Moreover, he was versed in the ways of women enough to know how not to exasperate them—a rare accomplishment. Elinor pointedly avoided touching him, for with her a mental or moral antagonism was inevitably carried into physical manifestation; but although he was particularly fond of laying his hands on people, especially if they were young and pretty women, he took not the least offense, but maintained his gentlemanly hilarity at its full height. He prattled on engagingly about the woods and the weather, the freedom and simplicity of country-life, and the happy prospects of the present party, and met all Elinor's stabbing little rejoinders with an artless mildness that showed no wound. At length she turned upon him with dilated eyes and fell intent.

"Mr. Urmson, I should like to know what you think Mr. Graeme was going to say when he was interrupted?"

"My dear Elinor, I didn't interrupt him. Why didn't you ask him, or the horses, or perhaps our friend Garth, who made most of the noise?"

"I thought it would be fairer to ask you. I'd been looking at you, and it struck me that you were most concerned in it, and that Mr. Garth knew it."

"What most struck me," observed Golightley, comically, "was the branch of that confounded tree that took my hat off. Now, Elinor, don't be cross, but tell me frankly what's the matter."

"It was the way you looked," she exclaimed, with an impulse of shame and resentment at being forced to explain herself on so ignoble a matter. "Any one might speak against you; but I couldn't be mistaken in what your own face said. If what you have told us about the way things stand between you and your brother is not true, Mr. Urmson . . . how could you dare to do it? You looked so frightened at what he was going to say—oh, dear me!—and when that interruption came, you looked so thankful, and you were in such a hurry to get out

after your hat, that it came into my mind the name Mr. Graeme would have spoken was yours. Well, that's all I have to say."

"By George! it would serve you right if I were mortally offended," remarked Golightley, stroking his beard musingly, and wrinkling his forehead. "I wish I wasn't so good-natured. Here is Miss Elinor telling me that I've been begging all my life of my brother, instead of giving him money, as I pretended, and that I was so afraid of detection that I jumped out of a hayrigging and ran away! And she insinuates that Garth—a good-looking fellow, much younger than I am—improvised the accident to save my credit! I am too good-natured—by George, I am."

"Do I wish you to be good-natured?" exclaimed the young lady, with contemptuous lips. Golightley wiped his forehead with his handkerchief and sighed. "And, oh! how you have made me wrong your brother!" she continued, vehemently. "Tell me what is the truth, quick, Mr. Urmson! I can't bear this."

"Now, my dear Elinor," said Golightley, in a large tone of charity, "you are making a great to-do about nothing, and you will be very sorry before long. You dear child, what a terrible puzzle and fume you have got yourself into, to be sure! Let me see if I can't clear you up and make you all happy again. I'm not sure I'd do it merely on my own account; but my brother Cuthbert is one of the best and noblest of men, and I must put him in a right light, come what come may."

This honorable exordium might have made more impression upon Elinor had not the inward turmoil of her wrath muffled her ears, and disordered her understanding to such an extent that she scarcely heard what her companion was saying. She walked along with her teeth set edge to edge, and an expression which she meant should be impassive, though, in fact, it was very far from being so. But Golightley was sure of his ground, and proceeded with all his customary self-possession:

"If there were only a recognized law of the Medes and Persians, which changeth not, about primogeniture in this country, I dare say it would be a good thing in some ways. I believe it's still in some vogue down South; but we Down-Easters go in for equal rights in our families as well as in our politics. But the Urmson family—either purposely or accidentally—have always settled the bulk of the property on the eldest son, and packed the younger ones off with a few dollars in their pockets to get along the best way they could. It was as much a matter of course with us as it had been before we emigrated; although, mind you, it was perfectly free to us to change the order of things whenever we pleased."

By this time Elinor's mind had a little recovered its poise, and she was able to pay some heed to what followed.

"Well, now, Cuthbert being the eldest, it was an understood thing that the estate went to him: I never thought of questioning it, for one; and besides, you see, there was the old captain's will, dated after his first marriage—that is, dated before ever I was born or thought of—distinctly bequeathing everything to him. All I could expect would be a codicil giving me something to begin the world on. As it happened, though, there wasn't even a codicil for me; though there was a provision made for Eve or her descendants, in case any of them should turn up. The truth is—ha! ha!—I wasn't much loved by my good father, and, my mother dying so early, there was no one to take my part."

Elinor's face softened at this indirect appeal: she could not but sympathize; for though Mrs. Tenterden loved her quite as much as if she were her own daughter, yet it was not with the love of the mother Elinor had lost, and the difference was such as a girl of Elinor's disposition would be specially alive to.

"Now, my dear," continued Golightley, repressing a strong desire to take Elinor's hand, and contenting himself with smoothing forward his hair on his temple, "it is enough to say, as regards Cuthbert, that this will is the only one he ever saw or knows anything about; consequently, he always has believed, and believes now, that the entire property, except the provision made for Eve's possible descendants, belongs to him."

"But you told mother and me that you had been supporting him ever since Captain Brian died. What! were there two wills?" she added quickly, with a searching, half-distrustful glance at him.

Golightley caressed himself musingly for a full minute before replying. "When I made that assertion to you and Mildred," he said, slowly, "I was thinking of facts. We weren't thinking of coming here then, and, of course, I never contemplated having to explain matters on poor, dear Cuthbert's account. It wasn't likely that the particulars would interest you, and I never was much given to tooting my own whistle. And, even now, my dear child, I sha'n't make any direct assertions in self-vindication. I haven't kept silence all my life to break it now. If you are bent on damning me on the evidence of my changes of countenance, and Garth stopping a wagon, you probably wouldn't really wish me to bring forward better evidence in my defense. However, I can put a few things to you hypothetically, as it were, and so leave the matter in your hands. Now, I have good reason to believe that, though I didn't please my father, my mother really did love me, and it's fair to suppose that she would wish me to be well provided for; and, since my father was entirely devoted to her, it's fair to suppose that her wishes would have the greatest influence on him; but she died when I was a baby; so that, supposing my father had been persuaded to do anything or everything for me, you see he had a score of years or so to think better of it in, and go back to his first purpose."

"But her dying wish!"

"Well, but to go on with our hypothesis. You suggested a second will just now. I don't say there was one, but you see how there might have been one, and also why there might have been an intention to destroy it. And, then, not being at all a methodical man, he might easily have mislaid it, or thought he had destroyed it, perhaps. Then, by-and-by, you can imagine an inquisitive boy, left pretty much to his own devices, ransacking the old garret, for lack of something better to do, and coming across— By-the-by, my dear Elinor, don't you remember a very tiresome ghost-story I was trying to amuse you all with the other night ? "

" Oh !" murmured Elinor, raising her hand to her forehead, and then letting it fall, abruptly. Such impromptu side confirmations often carry conviction more surely than ordinary demonstration. " Why don't you speak straight out ? I'm feverish with this 'supposing,'" she exclaimed. " The truth can be trusted."

"Ha! ha! I don't know about that; the truth is about the only wild beast that nobody has been able to tame. But I will trust you, my dear, and I won't bother you any more. There isn't much more to it. My father sent me to England with a couple of thousand pounds, and nothing was said about lost wills on either side. I made up my mind to fight my own way, and hold my tongue. Cuthbert had a wife, and, of course, would need a settled property more than a flighty, unencumbered bachelor like me. Cuthbert behaved like the gentleman he always has been, and offered to go halves with me; but I told him if ever I needed a trifle to help me out of a scrape, why, I'd apply to him; but I couldn't consent to anything more. The devil of it is," said Golightley, pulling forward his hair, and glancing at Elinor, "that I have been obliged to apply to him pretty often. I met with such a confounded lot of ill-health and ill-luck as brought me high and dry more than once. Oh, I don't set up for a saint at all; still, you see, I might have been worse."

"O Mr. Urmson!" was all Elinor found to say. She bent her head, and her arms drooped at her sides.

" I had the best of poor Cuthbert, didn't I ?" continued Golightley; " not only had the pleasure of helping him without his knowing it, but the pleasure of giving him the pleasure of being generous to me. It was just as generous in him, you know, as if the means had really been his. To be sure, I had to put up with some people's thinking me a sponge, and with one young lady's thinking me both a sponge and a story-teller; but I'd do more than that for dear old Cuthbert; and, now that I've got my little pile all safe, I hope to do at least

as much—and for Master Garth, too. By-the-by, as to that wagon-accident, I'm afraid I did the dear boy great injustice. My first idea was that the venerable parson was alluding to his letters home for remittances, and that Garth, naturally disliking to have the subject ventilated in public, stopped the venerable tongue in the only way he could. But it occurs to me, on second thoughts, that Garth, ten to one, supported himself during his travels—portrait-painting, and so forth ; and so I am really the guilty one, after all. And Miss Elinor doesn't consider me fit to be spoken to."

Elinor turned to him with as sad a smile as ever glimmered in a young lady's eyes. " If you consider me fit to be shaken hands with, will you do it ?" she asked. "Oh, you don't know how much you have to forgive!"

Nor did he seek to know, though the inquiry might not be uninteresting. For it is perhaps to be feared that her extraordinary suspicion of Golightley could hardly have taken such sudden and vigorous root in a reluctant or even impartial soil. The truth probably was that, disliking the man instinctively as much as she was forced to esteem and admire him on principle, she had snatched at the mere shadow of a dishonorable appearance in him with the half-despairing hope of proving it a substance, and thus justifying her blind intuition, and freeing herself forever, at this latest moment, from a union to which she was painfully averse.

The issue was a double punishment to her sinister desire. Not only was she rebuked by Golightley's vindication, but she was shamed by the revelation that his seeming falsehood pointed to an even greater nobility of conduct than he had yet been credited withal. He was verily a paragon of generosity and self-sacrifice, and now her defeat left her with neither strength nor purpose to contend longer against whatever might be his wish regarding her. She had but one offering to make in requital of her injurious thought, and, if he chose to demand it, she must not refuse. No wonder, therefore, if her smile was dismal and her gesture spiritless.

Golightley, on the other hand, brimmed over with the milk of human kindness and self-satisfaction. He understood his victory and its value; he felt himself distinctly in love, and inclined to press his advantage. In spite of his worldly experience, he was, under certain conditions, a susceptible man, and even an impulsive one; and there were few things that suited him better than giving expansive utterance to warm and caressing sentiments. He took Elinor's sad, shrinking little hand between both of his own, then lifted it to his lips, and finally tucked it away tenderly under his arm.

"My sweet Elinor," he began, "I must not let this crimson and gold path come to an end without asking for one golden hope. A year ago I broke in upon your mourning too abruptly and heedlessly; I was full of my own selfish hopes and desires, and longed to preserve you and dear Mildred from feeling the pressure of the straitened circumstances—"

"Yes, yes, that was—my misgiving," interrupted Elinor, who was now pale to the lips. "I am proud, Mr. Golightley—I'm sure I don't know what for—and so I answered as I did, because I couldn't believe that any one who knew me well enough to care for me could find anything in me to care about, but only to pity; and I was too proud to be pitied; and I'm sure you can't care for me."

If Golightley had not persuaded himself beforehand that Elinor was at bottom quite as ready to marry him as he her, the beseeching tremor that shook this last sentence could hardly have been misinterpreted. Being thus prejudiced, however, he accepted it as a tender hint to proceed, and gallantly complied with it.

"Ah! my dear little girl! I see you have plenty to learn on some subjects, and it must be my privilege—lucky dog that I am!—to spend the rest of my life in teaching you, by practical example, how to appreciate yourself. I will only say now that you are the only entirely lovely and admirable creature I have met. I don't pretend to be worthy of you—what man is? But there's a sort of poetical compensation, isn't there? in our coming together in this way, a healing up

of the old legendary feuds, reconcilement of Cavalier and Puritan, eh?—ha, ha! Now, my dearest child, if you think you can ever come to put a value on the devotion of an elderly chap like me, who has sown his wild-oats, such as they were, why, you know how long it has been yours!"

After a moment Elinor stopped in her walk, and, pressing her forehead against Golightley's arm, burst into a fit of tearless sobbing. Her companion's words had smitten her with a sense of desolation and exile. Youth cannot easily be reconciled to the sin-born divorce between physical and spiritual beauty or ugliness. Had Golightley, indeed, been indictable merely for a rude and ungainly outside, Elinor might soon have schooled herself to endure or even to love this for the sake of the inward loveliness. But her quarrel lay deeper. Golightley was comely and graceful with the refinements of society and culture, and her aversion grew from an instinctive perception of some impalpable, indescribable quality in him which had as little to do with ordinary physical repulsiveness as had his virtues with his good looks. In short, if his beauty were mainly spiritual, his ugliness would seem to be wholly so. What malicious perversity of Nature was this?

Elinor had dreamed her virgin dreams of ideal love, wherein all was harmony and most interior satisfaction. Was the fault in her or in the world, that the realization was so dreary? If this love were heaven on earth, what must heaven be? And why were human beings endowed with longings and intuitions which there was nothing in heaven or earth to appease and justify? This marriage would be like a taking of the black veil, with the tragic difference that, instead of consecrating her to a mystic and impersonal union, it would subject her in absolute self-surrender to a being of flesh and blood. Yet if she could not surrender here, what place had she in the world, where a worthier love—one built on less selfish foundations—was to be looked for? She was bewildered, and so forlorn of help and sympathy, that she was clinging to the very man of all others who was the cause of her forlornness. There was nothing left to her but him; and perhaps God, in requital of her sacrifice, would either so open or so shut her eyes that she might love him with heart as well as mind.

"Why these untimely sobs, dearest lady-love?" cried Golightley, putting his arm round her waist, encouragingly.

Elinor freed herself in a moment, and stood before him with quivering, breathless mouth and piteous eyes, rubbing her hands round each other and intertwining her fingers.

"I think the best thing would be for me to die, but I will be yours if you want me—if you think you ought to have me. Seems to me I wasn't made to love as other people do. If I must live, I suppose you are best for me. I wish I were more like other girls. Perhaps I shall become better by-and-by."

"Now, my sweetest little Elinor—"

"Don't speak to me so!" she broke in, with a sudden, startling change of tone and expression, clinching her hands and setting her teeth. "Why are you always so soft and kind, humoring my foolishness and petting me and complying with me? Why don't you show the strength that must be in you? Be strong and commanding with me! You must be like an iron man. Never be weak and yielding to me. Mr. Urmson, I believe there is a devil in me that would tear you to pieces if it thought it could master you. I want strength and laws, and a will over me like Fate. You are too good—never let me get the advantage of you by finding out how good you are."

To this passionate outburst Golightley was able, at the moment, to oppose nothing better than a somewhat unmeaning smile. He was not one of the rugged, hammer-and-anvil sort of men, and could not pretend to be. His conquest of women had always been accomplished, not by main force, but by finesse, and by taking cunning advantage of feminine weaknesses. Although a little daunted, however, he was not seriously disturbed. He thought he understood the power of soft methods better than Elinor did; and, moreover, he could not suppose that this strange mood was other than transient. She would soon calm down, and take her new happiness as a sensible girl should.

Doubtless it would require tact to manage her just at first; but who had more tact than Golightley himself? He had not lived upward of forty years in the world for nothing.

"Take my arm, my dear," he said, quietly; "we shall soon learn to understand each other. You have made me the happiest of men, and I am not going to ask anything more of you till you are ready to give it.—Ah, we're coming to the end of our golden path, I see; and hark! there is no mistaking that 'haw, haw, haw!' We must be close upon them."

In a few steps more they would pass the edge of the wood, and come in view of the merry picnickers. Elinor suddenly tightened her hold on Golightley's arm, and looked up at him. "Kiss me!" she said, in a low, imperious tone that had more fierceness than love in it; "not my cheek—kiss my lips!" He knew not what to make of it, but he obeyed. She drew a long tremulous breath; and after a moment said: "It can never be undone now." Golightley, for his part, did not altogether regret that their *tête-à-tête* ended simultaneously with this remark.

CHAPTER XLII.

DANCING AND FIDDLING.

HALF a dozen wagons were drawn up side by side on the edge of a shallow hollow. Overhead vast trees spread their burly branches, and sent their yellow leaves, one after another, wavering earthward, carpeting the glade as with the dying sunshine of the dying year. At the farther end of the stretch of turf rose a granite rock, apparently composed of three separate fragments, so united as to present the semblance of the roughest imaginable chair or throne, with a low seat and high encaverned back—such a throne as Hiawatha might have held his woodland state in. The forest in the immediate neighborhood was so thinned out that the place might almost have been considered a pasture, yet it was wilder-looking than where the growth was denser. Knots and ribs of rock emerged here and there above the uneven surface of the ground; wild-apple trees crooked their fantastic limbs on the knolls and ridges; crimson clusters of huckleberry-bushes sprouted on all sides, and straggling, unpruned grape-vines, heavy with thick-skinned purple clusters, coiled round tree and bowlder or wriggled prone along the earth. The tract lay high; at a short distance roundabout the forest thickened, and billowed away on all sides over unmeasured leagues, while far southward, at the farther extremity of the distant, unseen valley, Wabeno just showed the crest of his dusky mane.

The ancient parson was bustling about with ponderous decrepitude, overseeing the unloading of the wagons. Garth had freed his horses from the shafts, and was leading them away to a comfortable spot by the neighboring brook-side. Madge was assisting Mr. Graeme, or rather taking charge of him—deftly righting his wrong doings, and guiding and finishing off his right ones. Mrs. Tenterden had mounted a small hillock, whence, with her gown gathered about her in one hand and her parasol open in the other, she was contemplating the scene in a solid, majestic sort of way, as though she were the genius of the place. This, however, was but a vain appearance, inasmuch as she was really, despite her vaunted youthful experiences of country-life on the plantation, infinitely less at home than any one of the company. But she had at least escaped from that dreadful jolting hay-rigging, after which anything was home-like.

As the two pedestrians drew near, Elinor, to Golightley's renewed surprise, sent forth her voice in a long, loud trill—a throbbing scream of vehement melody, which overtopped all the buzz and tumult of the party, and drew upon her universal attention. No one but Elinor knew what a sore burden went out on the wild music of that scream. Garth's horses, on their way to the brook, threw up their heads and pranced, more like battle-steeds at the sound of a trumpet than the sober-sided old farm quadrupeds that they were; and Garth himself felt his heart bound and his brows lift, and anon was visited by a reminiscence of that other

10

outburst at the lake, and was angry, he knew not why. Meanwhile Golightley, not to be outdone, swung his hat, and was delivered of a well-rounded huzza; to which the whole band of picnickers, led by the reverend Stentor, bellowed and screamed a noisy response. Mrs. Tenterden rashly waved her parasol; caught by the breeze, it overcame her balance, and she came tottering down from her perch with desperate steps, and threw herself, with an involuntary gesture of passionate *abandon*, into the arms of the mighty minister. Hereupon uprose a huge volley of many-toned laughter, so confusedly echoing from every side that it seemed as if all the rocks and trees, and the wagons and the babbling brook, took part in it. In the midst of this mirthful uproar Elinor and Golightley came up, and stood the centre of the hilarious assemblage. Every eye was turned upon her with a new interest. She seemed to have advanced at one step from the position of a silent, unnoticed, somewhat stiff-mannered young lady to the rank of a leading social favorite, rivaling Madge on her own ground, besides being mistress of another to which Madge was a stranger. There are sometimes epochs in a life when the reserved soul comes flushing to the surface, feels its deep brotherhood with humanity, draws recognition and sympathy therefrom, and for an hour is and does that which shall in the retrospect astonish itself and its companions, though seeming at the moment more true to Nature than Nature's self. So Elinor, in the reaction from her passion of loneliness and repulsion, sprang abruptly into an intense and homely fellow-feeling with her kind, knew herself one with them in each intimate trait of soul and body, felt their warm, racy life flowing through her fine blue veins, and was conscious thereby of a new unbounded scope of power and freedom. She forgot her frigid misgivings, and became instinct with quaint, genial delights. How easy, sweet, and many-sided was existence, with joys like daisies and buttercups, as numerous, as humble, and as simply gathered! She saw how flimsy were the barriers of aristocracy: longed to be of the mass, to act and think and play with them, to hide from herself behind their wholesome vulgarity, and plunge over head and ears in safe depths of commonplace. Withal and beneath all, she sadly knew this humor could not last, that her half-baffled identity was on her track, and soon would hunt her down, and, therefore, she yearned to taste the full flavor of the flitting time.

"What shall we do first?" she asked looking smilingly around upon the smiling faces. "Let's play hide-and-seek, or blindman's-buff, or let's have a dance! Oh, yes, a dance—shall not we, Margaret? because we can all enjoy that together."

"Oh, but there's no fiddler, miss," answered half a dozen voices; "the fiddler's sick, and couldn't come. Old Dave's got his rheumatics, and had to stay back. Have to give up dancing to-day, I guess."

"Oh no, we sha'n't!" cried Elinor, blushing and laughing. "I'm so glad I brought my violin! and I'll fiddle for you as long as you like. Yes, I can, really, just as well as Dave—can't I, Margaret?—Come now, ladies and gentlemen, take your partners.—Mother, you must dance—you must dance with Mr. Graeme; I'm sure you can't refuse him. Well, but what is the dance to be?"

"Dear life!" cried Mrs. Tenterden, between bewilderment and amusement, as the minister made her a mammoth obeisance, and presented his arm; "if I ever thought of anything like this!—Why, Nellie, I declare you're a perfect captain!"

"The Virginia Reel, boys and girls," proclaimed Mr. Graeme; "in honor of our Southern visitors. Bustle about now, lads, and choose your lassies!—Here, my little lady, let me help you to the choir-box—there you are! I never saw you before, my dear lass, but I like your face right well. Ay, the fiddle—where is it?—there, in the box! All ready now—hold on! where's Garth? where is that boy? climbed up the chestnut again? Ho! ho! ho! Down to the brook—no, here he is back again.—Hullo, Garth Urmson, you're late! no partners left."

Garth, sauntering moodily up, with his hands in his coat-pockets, might have seen a pretty picture had his eyes been open to it. Elinor, violin in hand, was standing in Hiawatha's throne, whose hollow canopy rose high above her head, while the rugged and weather-worn texture of the rock picturesquely contrasted with the delicate complexion and clear-cut features of the slender and stately young musician. Down the glade in front of her were ranged the dancers in two lines facing each other, the men on the left and the women on the right, headed respectively by Parson Graeme and Mrs. Tenterden, Golightley and Madge standing second. The misty sunlight slumbered over this scene; the great trees cast tender shadows across it, and made it rich with tributes of golden leaves; the mighty sky impended infinite above all. Amid such large surroundings, the full-grown company of human beings might almost have been taken for a band of frolic elves, joyously preparing to cut fantastic caprioles to the music of Titania's bow. The spot was precisely such a one as imagination would have fixed upon for a fairy meeting; and the sunshine was so moderated and mellowed by its journey through the Indian-summer atmosphere that it might easily take the place of the enchanted moonlight of elf-land.

"Never mind," said Garth, "I'd rather look on than dance." Accordingly, he threw himself down at full length on the slope of the little hollow, clasped his hands beneath his head, and so composed himself for the spectacle.

"Turn out your toes now, children—best foot foremost. Let drive now, my lass!" boomed the parson; and with the word Elinor waved her bow and let it caper across the strings, and the reel began.

Never, certainly, since picnics began had such dance-music been heard as this. It inspired each awkward village boy and girl and dame and elder with the nimble spirit of sylvan nymphs and fauns. Nobody could keep still. Those who were legitimately engaged in the figure naturally threw off all restraint, whirling, bounding, and gallopading as if all laws of gravity, both physical and metaphysical, were at an end; but the many whose turn had not yet come, and upon whom it was incumbent to keep steadily in line, found it a task beyond their most resolute powers. They jigged up and down and to and fro in their places, waving their arms, swaying their bodies, and tilting their heads this way and that, like so many heathen dervishes. The madcap tune set their blood dancing in their veins, their eyes dancing in their heads, and their souls dancing in their bosoms. Old people and young were there; yet all seemed young alike, for it was odd and pleasant to see how the boyishness and girlishness latent in the aged ones cropped out under the magic influence of the violin, as fresh as ever in itself, albeit sadly thwarted by the load of crusty old years which had been silently hardening over it. That in them which danced was the same now as ever in childhood, only the fleshly instrument was not quite so handy.

Parson Graeme had in ancient times been a most Titanic performer, dangerous to be within reach of when the fit was on him; and though of late years he had hardly attempted to do more than hobble through a turn or two, and then back to his seat, today he seemed to cast from him a score or so of his supernumerary winters, and to recall in some degree the heroic achievements of his mighty youth. If the enormity of his gambolings was somewhat subdued, the portentousness of his enjoyment was no less than of yore. As for Mrs. Tenterden, though almost young enough to be his granddaughter, she was less than a match for him on this score; her best exertions served only to keep her inevitably in the way of the rest of the dancers, where she revolved slowly, first in one direction and then another, laughing, breathless, bewildered, and perhaps not a little astonished at finding herself hail-fellow-well-met with such a number of the commoner sort of people.

Madge and Golightley meanwhile represented the refinements of the art. Golightley was master of its æsthetics and scientifics, and entered into the fun of the thing with a kind of cultured yet humorous vigor, which contributed greatly to the popular enjoyment. But Madge danced with a grace and poetry of motion such as she alone was capable of. She danced with complete self-surrender, spontaneous and care-free as the sparkle of a fountain. Here was an end to which she was created; here was fit exercise for her. Faultless and unweariable were her flying steps. She made dancing seem something worth being born and living for; she was the matchless embodiment of the matchless music. Golightley, though his acquired and educated proficiency could not rival her inborn genius, was at least the worthiest partner she could have chosen. Madge had never liked him half so well before, nor, on the other hand, had she ever appeared so fascinating to him. This was a ground on which they could meet with utmost mutual cordiality, and from which they might proceed, perhaps, to still more interior and significant degrees of sympathy.

But Elinor, by whose skill all this merry enchantment was wrought, had so identified herself with the spell she was weaving that by-and-by she could no longer distinguish between herself and it. It seemed to her as if these creatures were thus gesticulating and coming and going solely in obedience to a fiat of her will, and without any volition of their own. They moved in harmony with the wild fancies that gamboled through her brain, and were, in fact, nothing more than mystic incarnations thereof—a sort of visible expression of her fantastic mood, a palpable reflection of her mind! This quaint notion so worked upon her imagination, and thence upon her violin, as to elicit a yet crazier development of the hurrying tune, immediately responded to by an increased fury on the dancers' part; and it occurred to Elinor that, if she should happen to go mad, the whole company of caperers would have no choice or alternative but straightway to go mad likewise.

CHAPTER XLIII.

A COUPLE OF INNOCENTS.

ALL this time Garth was lying on the slope of the hollow, precisely as he had at first disposed himself, except that his eyes, after wandering abstractedly from one to another of the Virginia Reelers, had at length settled upon Elinor, and did not again remove. His complete physical repose was in such utter contrast to the frantic unrest of the others that he appeared to exist in a different world, or rather, as Elinor fancied, only he and she had real existence at all; the rest were mere shapes of the imagination, whose sole use, little as they might think it, was to interpret between her and him. And what was it that she would communicate to him? Nothing describable; nothing that words could convey; nothing, surely, of the slightest practical moment. Nor could it be aught susceptible of being hereafter recalled and brought into relation with matter-of-fact and normal conditions. Garth, as he existed in the matter-of-fact world, was anything but congenial to her. What sympathy could she have with a man capable of selling his artistic honor? But in this ecstatic state something like a one-sided sort of communion appeared not only possible, but inevitable; and hence a conceivability, to say the least, that the artist of form and color might, in some primitive and paradisiacal form of being, have met and held fruitful converse with the artist of sound. The transcendentalism of this idea made it harmless, and at the same time rather enhanced its attractiveness. The entire fabric of it must vanish the moment the violin-strings had ceased to quiver; therefore let its evanescent perfume be enjoyed to the full. Was Garth, on his side, conscious of it? Never might that be known. Yet he lay so still, and withal so subtilely awake, it seemed as though he alone could comprehend and translate the inner meaning of that whose outward effect was but to inspire a score of queer phantasms with an antic frenzy. The vibrations which whirled them in idle circles like dead leaves, breathed to his soul, perhaps, the vague, unutterable secret of a virgin's heart.

In this manner it came to pass that Elinor, when the Virginia Reel had spun itself out, found herself in an apparently quite other mood than when it began; nevertheless, the last was an orderly outcome of the first, or was possibly the first, more intimately apprehended. How the dance ended, or wherefore, or why it did not happen to go on forever, she could not have told; but at length it was all over — the world no longer obeyed the laws of harmony; the

dream-shapes relapsed into the vulgarity of flesh and blood; and the pale musician stood, with her violin folded in her arms, wondering, like the rest, whence the late enchantment had come, and whither it had gone. Garth still preserved his supine immobility, and made no sign.

The dancers were all very warm, especially Mrs. Tenterden, who had, however, exerted herself less than anybody. They gradually wandered off, singly, or in pairs, to seek coolness and repose in this or that shady nook; the big minister crawled under the largest of the wagons, and instantly fell asleep; and Mrs. Tenterden spread her parasol and wandered hither and thither, exclaiming, panting, and declaring that she had no idea an Indian summer was so hot. Golightley stood fanning himself with his hat, and wiping his forehead with his scented pocket-handkerchief, sending the while occasional inquiring glances toward Elinor, who, however, seemed wholly unconscious of him and of everybody else. Madge, as the result of some little reconnoitring, discovered a similar insensibility in Garth; and thus it happened that the late partners found themselves thrown back upon one another— a state of things which neither, perhaps, altogether regretted. The lady proposed a short stroll in the direction of the tawny belt of woodland on the left, and, the gentleman assenting with gallant alacrity, they presently walked off together.

When they had threaded their way for a few minutes through the living pillars of the forest, Madge took Golightley's arm with an innocent confidence that charmed him.

"How beautifully Miss Elinor plays!" she said. "How happy you must be, dear Uncle Golightley! Mrs. Tenterden has been telling me a great deal about how you were in Europe—how kind and helpful you were to them, you know. What a delightful coincidence, wasn't it? that you should become rich just at the time they became poor!"

"Ah," said Golightley, putting on his hat seriously, "those things that we call coincidences, Miss Margaret, are a mystery; they are providential."

"Oh, do you believe in providence?" exclaimed she, softly. "I'm so glad! because, if you do, surely everybody can—you are so wise, you know. But how funny providence is sometimes! One would think it was hardly worth while to take the money out of poor Mrs. Tenterden's hand only to put it into yours; because, you see, you use it to take care of Mrs. Tenterden and Miss Elinor, just as he did. However, I dare say, you have a better right to it than he had—I mean, you understand better what it's worth."

"H'm! what I should have preferred, of course, would have been that poor John should remain affluent, whatever the state of my fortunes."

"Of course," assented Madge. "But I suppose," she added, reflectively, "there's only a certain amount of money in the world, and what one loses another gets. And it's particularly providential, to be sure, this time, because Mrs. Tenterden is the daughter of your mother, and it was from your mother that the money first came."

"Eh? What a clever little head you've got, Miss Maggie!" said Golightley, with an avuncular smile. "But I believe you're a little beyond me now."

"Now you're making fun of me, Uncle Golightley. I know how stupid I am," rejoined Miss Maggie. "All I meant was that since it was only by a sort of accident that your mother got separated from your father, after their first meeting down there in Virginia, it is a sort of accident, too, that Mrs. Tenterden ever was born, and so it's another accident—now don't laugh at me! —that all the money didn't belong to you; and not only all your mother's, Uncle Golightley, but all your father's, too; because, you see, it's just as much an accident that your brother Cuthbert was born as that Mrs. Tenterden was."

Golightley threw back his head and laughed loudly. "By George! Why, what a little casuist you are! Ha! ha! I don't know what Cuthbert and Mildred would say to being told that they were nothing but a sort of faux pas—eh? Ha! ha! He glanced narrowly at her from underneath his blue glasses; she was stepping along with her finger on her lip, which seemed to pout a little, as if she were childishly resentful of being made fun of; but the broad brim of her hat so overshadowed her lovely face that he could not be certain whether he read her expression aright. He fancied at one moment that she partly returned his glance from the corner of her long, dark eye.

"Oh, there's a good grape-vine!" she exclaimed, suddenly, pointing to a huge oak-tree, which had died in the grasp of a vine which seemed almost as old as itself, though abounding with fruit. "What a splendid bunch that is! Oh, thank you! But here's too much for one person to eat; you must therefore go shares with me, Uncle Golightley."

"Ah! with pleasure. I can never refuse to go shares with you in anything, Miss Margaret," said Uncle Golightley, with an indulgent smile. "These grapes, though," he added, after eating a few, "are not worthy of the occasion. Ah! if you could have eaten grapes with me in Italy and France! Well, who knows but we may all meet there one of these days? Garth, of course, being an artist, will steer for Rome and Florence as soon as he can weigh anchor here; and, as for me, I fear it may turn out that I've been an exile too long to take kindly to my native soil at this late day."

"Tell me why you came back here at all?" demanded Madge, abruptly, resuming his arm and peeping brightly at him from beneath her shadowy hat-brim. "Mrs. Tenterden says it was decided on so suddenly that she had hardly time to pack up. I'll tell you what I think was the reason, shall I?—you won't be angry?"

"Nothing that you can say, my dear," affirmed Uncle Golightley, affectionately patting her hand, "can make me angry."

"Well, then," she continued, with a peculiarly mischievous smile, "it was because you were frightened away by your ghost. Ah! you were just a tiny bit angry, after all."

"What has got into your little head? My ghost! Why, I'm not dead yet."

"You know very well, sir, that isn't the ghost I mean. I mean the same ghost that you saw up in the garret at Urmhurst, and went down-cellar with. The one that opened the triangular parchment, you know, which was dated in 1781, and was signed— you won't be angry if I tell you how it was signed?"

"Look here, Miss Maggie," said Golightley, dropping his voice, and looking cautiously about him, "what the deuce have you been up to? You didn't hear anything about dates and signatures from me, nor from Mildred either. Ha! ha! Well, here I am, talking as if my ghost-story had been a true tale."

"You didn't know, I suppose, Mr. Golightley, that I am a witch," returned his charming companion, tossing her head. "I know all sorts of strange things about people, and I could tell you everything that was in that parchment, though neither I nor Nikomis can imagine why the ghost should hide it away in the grave of Nikomis's ever-so-great grandfather."

"Nikomis's ever-so-great grandfather, was it?"

"Yes; but that's a secret, and you must not tell anybody. You see, I tell you all my secrets, because I know you can keep secrets better than most people, especially such ones as I tell you. And then Nikomis is a terrible witch, and if she were to hear that you had spoken about her to any one, she might get angry and burn you up, or change you into somebody else, or somebody else into you."

"Dear me! and how would she manage that?"

"Oh!" laughed Madge, evidently enjoying her own grotesque and absurd fancies, "by muttering some spell over the triangular parchment, I suppose."

Golightley echoed her laugh, though in so preoccupied a manner that it was plain he must be thinking of something else. The two walked onward for a considerable distance in silence, for Madge, perceiving that something had given his meditations a serious turn, had too much good-breeding to break in upon them with any further unfolding of her fanciful conceits. At length, however, Golightley spoke, and himself led back the current of talk into the former

channel, as though the quaint humor of it had taken his own imagination captive.

"How long, may I ask, have you been in the witch-business, Miss Maggie?"

"Oh, ever so long," she replied. "I remember Nikomis gave me my first lessons when she lived in her wigwam in the woods, before coming to Urmhurst. But the time I studied most in witchcraft was while Garth was abroad. There was nothing else to do, hardly, all those years. I learned a great deal. In some ways I got to be even more of a witch than Nikomis; for she doesn't know how to read, you see, and I can read in two or three languages, and that is very useful in some kinds of witchcraft."

"But you never read anything," pursued Golightley, "either with or without a signature, that gave you grounds for believing that I had been frightened by a ghost in Europe? Nikomis doesn't keep a European witch correspondent, I fancy—eh? Ha! ha!"

"Well," began Madge, hesitatingly, and paused—then suddenly brightened up again, and went on. "Yes; we have a correspondent who travels all over the world, and in Europe as well as in other places. He sends us messages every once in a while, and then Nikomis and I get inside our magic circle, and I read them to her. And there was something he wrote us about a year ago that I couldn't quite make out; but, since you told us your ghost-story, I see the meaning of it. So you see, Uncle Golightley," she added, with an arch glance, "you betrayed yourself."

Uncle Golightley shook his head and smiled. "And what sort of a chap is this correspondent of yours?" he asked; "and what may his name be?"

"Oh, he's a very strange creature indeed," said Madge, mysteriously; "he's half red and half white, and, if you strike him with a sword, fire comes out of him."

Had Madge, after making this extraordinary speech, happened to look at her companion's face, she might have seen a singular expression come into it and immediately pass away again. In a few moments he spoke in his usual tone.

"Which do you like best, my dear Margaret — blind-man's-buff, hide-and-seek, or being my partner in the Virginia Reel?"

"I like being your partner, I think—you dance so well. And then I like going shares with you in the grapes."

"You're a witch, and of course you can beat me at dancing," said the other, with a short laugh; "but, I dare say, we shall suit better after having had a little more practice together. As for the grapes, I see you have some of the bunch still left. I suppose that lucky dog, Garth, will get those?"

"I suppose so," assented Madge, with a sigh; "though I don't think he cares for them so much as I do. He never will take the trouble to pick them for himself; but if I put them into his mouth, he might probably consent to eat them."

"I think very likely," responded Golightley, dryly. "I offered him a rousing good bunch the other day, and he swallowed it without winking. But, by-the-by, my dear, aren't we getting pretty deep in the woods?"

"Oh, we sha'n't get lost," she answered, with a smile. "Keep to the left. I was brought up in the woods, you see, and can always find my way."

They kept to the left accordingly, and are lost to our sight amid the falling gold of autumn.

CHAPTER XLIV.

THE OTHER TWO.

GARTH and Elinor, meanwhile, on emerging from their respective brown studies and looking about them, had found themselves virtually alone together. Garth raised himself on one elbow, stared at Elinor until she was forced to return his glance, and then threw himself to his feet and walked toward her with a superfine set grin on his face, the cynical grotesqueness of which would have made her laugh had she not been both irritated and secretly startled. What did he want with her? She could not doubt that she must be as disagreeable to him as he to her; and the last thing she would have anticipated was a malice-prepense conversation

between them. It is true that she did not despise him quite so much as before Golightley's explanation: and the discovery that she had wronged him on one score, perhaps mitigated her sternness on another. On the other hand, she might have reflected that previous to his artistic self-degradation the charge against him of indolent dependence had not disturbed her in the least. Probably all she did think of at this moment was that his approach was unwelcome, and that she would be rid of him as soon as circumstances would admit.

"We must not appear singular, Miss Golightley," began Garth, bowing with punctilious politeness. "We aren't asleep, so we must take a stroll. I'll help you down —jump!"

"I don't care to walk, thank you,". said Elinor; but she had already "jumped" at his bidding, and now, in spite of her disclaimer, kept beside him as he sauntered toward the brook on the right. She meant to turn back after a few steps; but it did not appear necessary, or even very easy, directly to withstand a man of this kind.

"Since we're in different walks of art," he resumed, "I may safely praise your proficiency. Such genius certainly should be published. There was an undercurrent in that tune you played which might have sold at a high price."

"I don't look forward to playing in public," replied Elinor, coloring high with indignation at what seemed to her, fresh from her dream, a most ungenerous and injurious speech.

"No? Well, selfishness is pleasant when you can afford it. But, where's your vanity? Think of enrapturing thousands of people! Art, you know, has three recommendations: it can minister to your private, selfish enjoyment, and it can get you money, and flattery. But I should soon be tired of painting pictures merely for my own amusement. I need admiration and good pay to keep me going."

"I have no right to suppose you are not in earnest in what you say, Mr. Urmson; but I must say it seems to me strange that Art should reveal so much of her beauty to —one holding your opinions. And it's hard to understand, too, how any one who can see so much of her divinity should find it possible to speak of her as a drudge and a convenience."

"I suppose this is meant for praise concealed under a thin veil of reproof. Between your praise and my uncle's money, I ought to be very happy. Do you recollect our profound conversation in the studio a few days ago? I've been afraid you misunderstood something I said then. I fully agreed with your criticism on the picture, but of course the alteration suggested was out of the question. My uncle had already offered a large price for the picture as it stood. Highly as I honor art, Miss Golightley, a check for a thousand pounds is worth all the ideal scruples in the world."

"You are really very frank. But how have I deserved this confidence?"

"No confidence at all; only it's pleasant to feel you are understood. There's a sort of inverted analogy between your case and mine, thanks to one and the same individual —that is, if I may construe your remark about not playing in public as hinting at your betrothal to my beloved uncle. I congratulate you. His affection for you, you see, has freed you from the necessity of doing that to which his affection for me compels me."

"There could never possibly be any likeness or sympathy between you and me, Mr. Urmson. Excuse me, I must turn back now."

"No; you can do more good here than anywhere," returned Garth, his sardonic expression darkening into something less unnatural but more lowering. "Come, come, Miss Golightley, you'll have to put up with me sooner or later; and there's something I wish to find in these woods. Besides, you were an old friend of mine long before you knew of my existence. After that first meeting in the Green Vaults I followed you—inadvertently, of course—all over Europe. At last, to break the spell, I took your portrait. That answered for a time; but here we are again, you see."

"It is easier to take such a liberty than to resent it, sir; but—"

Garth laughed. "Liberty? A cat may look at a king; and, to be honest, I put your face on canvas only to free my memory of it. A liberty! Why do you wear a face? If there be a liberty, it is on your part."

"I am glad you can speak to a lady in this way," said Elinor, with her iciest haughtiness; "I may have been mistaken in thinking well of your pictures; but after this I can never be mistaken in you."

"Say more like that!" exclaimed Garth, grinning with a kind of savage delight. "I like to hear you say what I am. Consistent, am I not? a charlatan in art and a charlatan in character! I told you you could do more good here than anywhere."

"I must consider myself as well as you, Mr. Urmson," said she, stopping short in her walk, and turning her face aside.

"Yes; but don't go back—don't!" he repeated, in a tone of such strange entreaty as made Elinor's heart beat quicker, in spite of her best resolution. Half involuntarily she moved on. "Think what a dramatic situation!" he went on with a hurried impetuosity of utterance. "You detest me for what I am, and I hate you for what I'm not, and we are saying what we think! Appreciate your privileges, Miss Golightley; you might search the world for charlatans, and not find another like me."

"Let me go," said Elinor, speaking low lest her voice should tremble.

"Do you know why?" he continued, not heeding her. "Because I was meant for a gentleman. I'm no common man. My mother was a most pure and sweet woman; and there's no nobler, gentler, braver man than my father. You understand that?" he demanded, suddenly, frowning at her with glowing eyes.

Elinor drew her breath and said, "I am willing to believe it."

"Yes. Well, they're in me, both of them," he said, motioning toward himself with his chin. "And, against that, I've made myself what I am. You mustn't forget, either, that I'm an only son, and the last of the Urmsons; and that all the honor of the race, and all the life-long hopes and prayers of my father—he has devoted his whole life to me—end in me."

It seemed to Elinor that the last three

words were as if he had struck so many blows on her heart. She drooped inwardly, and kept her body erect only by a conscious physical effort. She no longer thought of turning back, however, though to go forward was now even more painful than irksome.

"Hear more, since you're so condescending," resumed her companion, after a short silence. "You must excuse my egotism, but I have reason to be proud of myself. To realize my merit, you should have heard what my father said to me when he sent me to college, and once before, when I was a boy; and you should have known the fine resolutions I made after my mother's death. I tell you I'm no common man. Then you should know in what a religious, reverential way I have talked and thought about art. You needn't trouble yourself to disparage the good in my pictures. There is good in them, and power in me, but that I choose to be a charlatan, to paint pictures as great as any in the world. Excuse my laughing; but when I remember the doubts and anxieties I used to suffer as to my genius— But I recognize my genius now, and I've no doubt I can make myself rich by it. It was only while I thought of consecrating it to lofty ideal ends that I had any misgivings about it. Such a blessed peace and security as I enjoy now, Miss Golightley!"

"Oh, what are you throwing away!" muttered Elinor. "It weighs me down."

"Not that tone, after my pains to be explicit! With all my complaisance—no sentimental sympathy, if you please. Show me how bitter you can be."

"You could not be so bitter if you were what you would have me believe. Think of the girl who is to be your wife, Mr. Urmson."

"I care only to talk of myself, Miss Golightley. I haven't talked so much in ten years as I have talked to you. I'm dumb enough to people who love me, but detestation loosens my tongue. You bring the worst in me to the surface, and so put me at my ease; but my admirers misunderstand me, and torture me by probing after imaginary good. Our relation can be of great mutual benefit. Love is sugar, but hate is salt. Haven't I made out my case yet? Think again of a man knowing the good that I know, and having such reasons to be honorable as I have, who nevertheless gives it all up for a paltry thousand pounds. I admire your gravity. In your place, I should laugh till I cried."

"Mr. Urmson," began Elinor, hurriedly, "I am alone in the world, with no father or mother, or brothers or sisters. Seems to me it would be safer to die than to believe what you ask me to. Your uncle wishes to marry me, and I think him a good and noble man; but he could not help the harm this would do me. But, if you are so base, how can you wish to marry a girl without money, like Margaret? There is a contradiction somewhere — an impossibility. I used to think my life had been sad in some ways, but how am I to endure this?"

"Take care! there's danger of my hating you in a different way—a worse way."

"Nothing is worse than this," she said, with a slight shudder.

"Come, let us be wise, and make the best of our position," said Garth, smiling. "I like recognition for my sins even better than for my virtues; and you happen to be the only person qualified to give me full measure. I've taken special pains to bring my moral state clearly before you, and you have naturally less charity and tenderness than any woman I know of. Let me feel secure of your constant and thorough detestation—if you would be so kind. Put all your available contempt and venom into every word you say to me, and then I shall have a real pleasure in meeting you. In the natural course of things, we must often meet; but, I tell you fairly, if you try any other method with me, you'll be sorry for it. I won't put up with any gentleness or relenting from you, Miss Golightley. If you falter, you may stir up seven devils in the place of one."

The latter sentences came in a growl, with latent fierceness underlying it; but anything like a threat kindled Elinor's courage.

"You ask me to become a devil myself!" she exclaimed, vibrating with excitement.

" What have I done that gives you the right to speak to me so? "

" You would not like to hear. You have played on your violin there, for one thing, and I've heard your voice in singing. Why did you stay to talk with me in the studio? What have you done with the violet I gave you down by the lake? it was not meant for you. Oh!" cried Garth, with an impetuous gesture of his arms, "don't refuse my request on any plea of conscience! Keep your conscience for something else. For I solemnly assure you, whatever might appear, you would be doing an angel's work, not a devil's."

Elinor made no reply. All this time they were pressing onward through the woven forest, hurriedly, as though driven by some swift necessity; he mechanically putting aside the branches for her to pass, and aiding her to protect her violin from a chance blow or scratch. After this silence between them had continued for a few moments, he looked at her, and saw tears running down her face. She herself hardly seemed conscious of them, so intense was her painful preoccupation.

He continued to fix his eyes upon her, until she felt them, and their glances met. Almost immediately he spoke, in a quiet, indifferent tone:

" We must not get lost, Miss Golightley. Keep to the right. I think the lane is not far off. There are some strange things in these woods; but I have not found what I came out for, and I beg your pardon for bringing you. Selfish people like myself are always getting into such scrapes. I beg your pardon for leading you so far out of your way."

" I'm not used to the woods," returned Elinor, who had hastily wiped her eyes. " I like some sort of path; this seems a wilderness."

" It is a wilderness; even the paths don't go far; the longest only leads from one wilderness to another. However, the lane is not far off. Hark! "

They stopped and listened, each with a sensation oddly compounded of chagrin and relief. In a moment it came again — the sound of voices, a man's and a woman's,

easily recognizable, though the speakers were still too distant to be descried between the trees.

" This is the end," muttered Garth, with the mingled smile and frown that sometimes appeared on his visage. " We're in the world again, Miss Golightley. Doesn't it seem to you, now that civilization is within hail, that we've been making a great ado about nothing? My dear uncle, I guess, would poke fun at us without mercy. After all, how can we do better than to adopt the world's views? Kindly oblige me by looking upon me as an upright, sensible young gentleman, with too just a perception of what is due to himself and to those connected with him to throw away fortune for what really is, when you come to examine it rationally, the most purely fanciful crotchet imaginable. Recollect, too, that even if circumstances force me to go a little beyond my conscience in one instance, I can, and no doubt will, pay back debt and interest on the very next opportunity. You wouldn't give a man up for one trumpery little genial, venial fault? I beg to take back all my morbid and ill-tempered self-abuse. I'm a very nice sort of person."

" I'm not sorry we took this walk, Mr. Urmson," said Elinor, glancing at him with a timid humility in the expression of her eyes and mouth, which lent them a new charm. " We seem to have come to nothing; but I don't think I shall ever feel so— so much in the right again. How should I judge? how can you, even? " .

" Oh, let it go! " growled Garth, with a gritting of his teeth. " What are judgments to me? I've insulted you with a lot of weak rubbish, and you fitly punish me by taking it kindly. But I'm in such a perverted fix, Miss Elinor, that the kindest kindness helps me less than none at all. I'll hail those two people."

" Please wait a moment! " said she, hurriedly, coming in front of him as he was on the point of raising a halloo. " Just let me say that I know you will do right, whatever happens." As she spoke, flushing and paling almost at the same instant, she held out her hand as a pledge of her sincerity.

As Garth faced her, she fancied that,

from his short, massive figure, his shaggy head and dark brows, his glowing eyes and grim mouth, suddenly came forth an influence of tenderness and manly sweetness so powerful that it affected her almost as a physical touch. He also made a motion to take her hand in his own; but, ere he had done so, the gentle impression vanished as abruptly as it had come; he thrust his hand doggedly into his coat-pocket, and turned aside.

"Be offended or not, as you choose," he said, gruffly; "I can't touch your hand, nor justify your expectation; it's as foolish as it is well meant!" With this, and without again looking at Elinor, he hollowed one hand beside his mouth and gave a whoop, which instantly put an end to all confidential disclosures on the part either of himself and Elinor, or Uncle Golightley and Madge. In another minute all the four friends and lovers were standing together in the lane.

CHAPTER XLV.

THE VEIL AND THE LETTER.

"It's fortunate that our respective moral and social reputations are without spot or blemish," remarked Uncle Golightley, with a humorous glance and smile; "otherwise this might be an awkward meeting for all of us—eh, Garth? Ha! ha!"

They walked onward in a group at first, as if shy of pairing off again; but soon a sort of neutral division was effected, Garth and his uncle going in advance, while Elinor and Madge followed on behind. Golightley alone, however, seemed to be in the vein to talk. He was in a most affable humor, and did his best to make the others as pleasant as himself.

"I say, old fellow," he cried, banteringly addressing his nephew, but talking over his shoulder for the benefit of the ladies, "I'm afraid you're a gallant, gay Lothario!—You must look after him, Miss Margaret. If I were in your place, I wouldn't be letting my young man receive mysterious epistles in the morning, and go off on secret expedi-

tions with young ladies in the afternoon, without instituting a pretty strict inquiry. Eh?"

"Why, then, I think you must be his confederate, Uncle Golightley," retorted Madge, cleverly; "for it was you who carried me off, and left him free to do what he liked.—But I sha'n't be anxious about him so long as he chooses you for a companion," she added, with affectionate diplomacy, to Elinor.

After proceeding a little farther, the party came to a fork of the path, marked by a clear woodland spring, which bubbled up at the base of a large rock-maple, and so slipped sparkling and tinkling away into the heart of the golden forest. The source was set in a margin of large rounded stones and pebbles; but the bottom of the little basin was strewed with soft, white sand, which the ebullition of the crystal water caused to curl and gyrate in curious palpitations. The maple had already lost most of its foliage, the earth round about was strewed with it, and two or three leaves swam like great drops of blood on the surface of the spring.

"By George!" exclaimed Uncle Golightley, as he caught sight of this refreshing spectacle, "I didn't know till now how devilish tired and thirsty I am! Let's play we're four little children, and all lie down on our stomachs and have a good drink. Come!"

They sat down on the smooth stones, and every one of them owned to being more weary than they had supposed. Elinor took off her hat to arrange the veil which had got torn from its fastenings during her passage through the wood. While hunting for a pin, she laid the veil on a stone by her side; and, being a light, gossamer thing, the southwesterly breeze caught it, and wafted it upward. Garth saw it go, and sprang for it, but was too late. It floated and swung through the air, now sinking, now rising, and, at length, just as it seemed on the point of starting on a long flight northward, it was caught and held by a forked twig on the tip-top of the very maple at whose base the party were seated.

"Now's our chance to prove who's the best climber, Garth," exclaimed Uncle Golightley, intrepidly rising to his feet and advancing upon the tree.

Garth laughed, threw off his coat, and measured the maple with his eye. "Give me the first chance," said he; "if I fail, your success will be the brighter."

"Please, don't either of you go up," said Elinor. "No one needs a veil in the Indian summer; it is more trouble than use."

"Oh, yes, do let him go!" Madge exclaimed, clapping her hands; "I want you to see how beautifully he climbs."

Uncle Golightley retired, laughing, while Garth clasped the trunk with his arms and knees, and prepared to swarm upward. In so doing he found himself face to face with a rude inscription, or perhaps it was a natural irregularity in the surface of the bark; at all events, it bore a distorted resemblance to four letters, M. D., G. U., the last two inscribed below the first two, and all four surrounded by a circular incision. In a moment he both recognized the inscription and the occasion on which it had been made. It was on that day, ten or a dozen years ago—the day of his first picnic, when he had paused here to drink and to muse over his untold love, and to dream of a temple built on this spot to Love and Peace. Yet here, a few hours later on that same day, he had half murdered Sam Kinco, and hence had fled with the terror of blood-guiltiness upon him. It was a spot, therefore, where the evil omens overpowered the good. Even these letters, straight and shapely as they had once been, had now grown into distorted ugliness and malproportion.

"Dear me, Garth, are you never going to move?" exclaimed Madge, impatient for the exhibition to begin.

"All right," he responded, and forthwith began the ascent in earnest.

"Oh, you careless boy!" cried the young lady the next moment—"look if he hasn't thrown his coat right into the water!"

The careless boy was by this time too far on his way to remedy the mishap, nor was it necessary he should do so, for Madge herself had snatched up the garment, and, after giving it a good shake, threw it cloak-like over her own pretty shoulders. The whole action was very graceful and feminine. In many girls, lacking the requisite ingenuous artlessness, it might have seemed in slightly doubtful taste to put on a lover's coat; but there was such an unaffected, childlike spontaneity about Madge as transformed the slight impropriety into a refined and charming, because innocent and impulsive, act of affection.

All eyes were now fixed upon the climber, who made his way uninterruptedly to the lower branches, from which point his progress was too easy a matter to excite much interest. As ill-luck would have it, however, at the very moment when he was balancing among the topmost boughs and reaching upward for the veil, an eddy of the breeze lifted it lightly from the forked twig and bore it once more aloft, amid a general wail from the on-lookers. This time it did not linger aimlessly about, but set off at a steady, business-like rate, and in less than a minute was hopelessly out of sight. Garth retraced his steps, and, swinging from the lower branch, dropped to the ground.

"Your efforts were well meant, but of no avail," said incorrigible Uncle Golightley.

"If you hadn't waited so long, just at the beginning," observed Madge, "you'd have caught it before the wind did. You're not so light as a zephyr, poor boy," she added, with a half-mischievous, wholly-admiring glance at his sturdy shoulders. "Come, let me help you on with your coat. It didn't get very wet, after all—only the sleeve a little."

The party now resumed their walk, and about a quarter of an hour later arrived at the picnic-ground. They must have been absent much longer than they had supposed, for the picnic, so far as the meat and drink part of it was concerned, was over. Nor were they destined even to partake of the broken remnants, for poor Mrs. Tenterden, shortly before their arrival, had been seized with a bilious attack, consequent, in part, upon her exertions in the dance, and partly from having eaten a little too much *omelette aux fines herbes*, exquisitely prepared by Mrs. Danver, and was now reclining in the shadow of Hiawatha's throne, surrounded by a sympathetic throng, while the gigantic parson tenderly supported her head, and fanned her with his hat. Meantime her groans and sighs were distressingly audible, and several of the less experienced of the spectators had already made up their minds that she was about to breathe her last.

"O Elinor, child, where have you been?" gasped the good lady, as the girl hastened up. "I thought you were lost. Ah! I declare I believe I am going to die. I declare I think you mightn't have left me all alone here. Oh, dear! I never was so sick in my life. You must get me back home somehow. I won't die out here in the woods, you mark my words."

"Can we have one of the wagons to go back in?" asked Elinor of Garth. "There's no danger, but she is so seldom ill that anything makes her think she will die."

The wagon was soon ready, and Mrs. Tenterden was lifted into it, and made as comfortable as possible on a couch of shawls and wraps. Elinor, Madge, and Golightley, got aboard with her, while Garth drove as before, the minister and Mrs. Danver remaining behind to see that the rest of the picnickers got into no mischief. It was now late in the afternoon; the dry, golden haze which had more or less pervaded the landscape all day began imperceptibly to increase, and the sun sank earthward slowly, like a great red Chinese lantern. There was little or no conversation among the party, all efforts in that direction being resented by Mrs. Tenterden as a disregard of the solemn fact of her approaching dissolution, and she accordingly bemoaned herself with very slight interruption during the whole journey.

At last, after driving for what the invalid declared to be hundreds of miles, the Danvers' cottage was reached, and she was safely disembarked. Garth and Golightley gave her each an arm into the house, and afterward lingered a while on the steps with Madge, Golightley delivering himself of his parting pleasantries, while Garth stood by silent, with his hands in his coat-pockets, and a rather unamiable smile on his face. But all at once his expression changed; he felt in all his pockets, one after another,

and finally demanded, in a disturbed tone, whether either Golightley or Madge had seen him drop a letter.

"How now? the *billet-doux* lost?" cried his uncle. "Ah, my dear boy, see the imprudence of carrying such treasures to picnics and forest-walks! — By George! it serves him right, Miss Margaret; and I shouldn't blame you if you'd picked his pocket of it."

"It was a letter of importance," said Garth, impatiently, still searching his pockets.—"Have you seen it, Madge?"

"I was trying to think," said she, with her finger on her lip, and her eyes fixed apprehensively on his face. "O my dear Garth, don't be angry! I'm afraid I do know where it might possibly be; at least—"

"You have seen it? Where?"

"Dear me! you know, when you threw down your coat, I picked it up and shook it to get the water off; and I'm afraid, dear, it must have got shaken out of the pocket. Which pocket was it in?"

"In this side-pocket. That was up by the spring, I shall find it there.—I'll go back at once, if you'll take the horses round, uncle."

"I'm sure I hope you will find it, dear; but I'm afraid—O Garth, had it an envelope?"

"Yes—no; I left the envelope at home."

"Well, I believe I saw something I thought must be a leaf, but I guess now it must have been the letter, floating off down the little rivulet from the spring. I was so excited in your climbing the tree that I only just glanced at it, and then forgot all about it. You don't think that could have been it, dear, do you?"

"I'm afraid it was; and it may be in the brook, or even in the lake, by this time. Well, I must look for it. Luckily there's a moon.—Tell father not to sit up for me, Uncle Golightley. Good-by."

He walked away, but in a few moments heard a swift, rustling step behind him, and there was Madge, rosy and panting.

"Say you'll forgive me, dear Garth— and kiss me, won't you? I'm so sorry! Good-by, dear. I do hope you'll find it."

He kissed her, and left her standing in the twilight road—rosy, sparkling, and lovely. "There never was such a woman!" he said to himself; "and am not I the luckiest and happiest of men?"

CHAPTER XLVI.

COLD COMFORT.

As Garth walked on toward the forest, his steps quickened, and his down-turned face worked silently. The moon hung low over the valley—pallid, still, but promising sumptuous brilliancy anon. The wind was veering to the north; it came cold across the young man's cheek, with a prophecy of the Indian summer's departure and winter's onset. Already the slumberous gaze was melting out of the air, and the rims of the ghostly moon showed sharp and clear. The twilight woods were full of solemn grandeur, more impressive than the sunlight and glow of noonday. But Garth was not attuned either to beauty or to grandeur. The day had gone ill with him; he seemed to tilt against the might of Fate—he could not prosper, and his best efforts helped against himself.

He had gone forth that morning with the intention of doing Elinor what he presumed would be a service. The idea of her being united to Golightley had always been distateful to him—not that he admitted caring for her himself; but, with the fastidiousness of an artist, he was averse from seeing her fine, pure tone impaired by association with a perhaps good-hearted and enlightened, but not profound nor truly delicate person, like his uncle. He did not believe that Elinor really loved this man; more probably she would accept him mainly out of consideration for the well-being of Mrs. Tenterden. But this would involve a sacrifice of art to convenience, as deplorable in its way as Garth's own mercenary transaction regarding his picture. There was need of a *deus ex machina* to set matters right.

Now, precisely such a divine deliverance was provided in the news which Garth had found in his letter that morning. It would enable Elinor to act without reference to anything less than her own highest impulses. The news must, indeed, be kept secret for a time from every one except Cuthbert; but Garth had seen his way to dropping such hints to Elinor as would put her on her guard against prematurely entangling herself. A word or two, when opportunity offered, would doubtless suffice, and the picnic could scarcely fail to afford such an opportunity.

But, alas! the opportunity had come too late. When the outpouring of Elinor's voice in that musical scream of hers fell upon Garth's ears he felt a premonition that the mischief had been done, and this premonition she had subsequently confirmed. It only remained for him, therefore, to keep his news to himself, and inwardly to denounce the folly and precipitation of womankind. Not, he was careful to repeat, that he felt the least direct personal concern in the matter; but it was disagreeable, on general grounds, to see a refined young lady throw herself away.

This disappointment had aided to becloud the day for him, and now the loss of his letter bade fair to give him an uneasy night. It was of great importance that the letter should be found—for, although Garth was familiar enough with its contents, their publication might bring about much trouble. In spite of what Madge had said about its falling into the water, he still hoped it might be lying on the margin of the little spring. He resolved, however, to begin his search at the upper mill-dam, and so work upward to the junction of the mill stream and the rivulet, and thence along the rivulet to its source beneath the maple-tree. A less imaginative man would have gone to the most probable spot first; but Garth loved hope better almost than its gratification, and chose to move in the direction of the best chances rather than away from them.

Three or four hours later he arrived at the spring, and after casting a keen and anxious glance about, he flung himself down with a groan on the grass beside the margin. He was weary and haggard; he was wet from wading in the stream, and his hands and face were scratched by the brambles. His search had been unsuccessful, and it was useless to think of pursuing it further. The letter was lost, and Garth could only hope that it was as much lost to everybody else as it was to him. He had done what he could.

He lay on his back, gazing upward at the purple sky. The moon, now riding high and clear, shone with great brilliance. On every side uprose the penciled shadow of the trees, and at every breath of the northerly breeze their dark leaves forsook the boughs whereon the pleasant summer had been spent, and swam zigzagging earthward through the air. Without sound they fell, continually, like dusky tears, into the bosom of the earth. The great forest was steeped in overwhelming silence; the liquid bubbling of the spring, which in the daytime was almost inaudible, now resounded clearly through the stillness. How ghastly white the lifeless moonlight lay!

It lent a death-like pallor to Garth's face as he reclined motionless and with shut eyes on the turf, his arms thrown out each side, and one knee drawn up. Slight shiverings passed through him from time to time, but he was scarcely conscious of cold or even of hunger. He only felt overpowered by invincible drowsiness.

CHAPTER XLVII.

A FORGATHERING OF FOREFATHERS.

At length he fell asleep, and had a singular dream. It seemed to him that he was possessed by the spirit of each one of his ancestors in succession, beginning with the first emigrant. Taken separately, they were more or less one-sided versions of one central principle; but, as a whole, they formed a nearly symmetrical individual—an individual more nearly akin to Garth himself than was any one of the component types, kindred though these were. Or, in other words, Garth was realizing the various phases of one life in its progress through half a dozen generations; and often, so intimate was his sympathy with the ghosts of the past, he seemed almost to be but remembering old experiences of his own. Yet,

through all, that mysterious something, which we call personal identity, asserted itself, and made him know that he was Garth, and not another.

First he grew instinct with the spirit of an ambitious, haughty, but not ungenerous man, whose stern and headstrong temper was mitigated by deep-lying veins of tenderness. His effort was toward freedom and honor; but the immitigable pride and self-will that nothing could subdue, ever tended to hamper and pervert his fairest purposes. At last the noble friendship, which might have elevated and purified him, was by jealous love poisoned into hatred and treachery. Yet, in the moment when the murderer stood with finger on trigger, taking his fatal aim, he felt a thrill of horror and relenting, and half intended to forbear. But it was too late; the deed was done, and was become a part of the past and of the doer, and crowded out remorse. He had made his choice between good and evil; and his descendants, in order to their redemption, would have the burden of his sin to deal with in addition to their own.

"I have felt this before," thought the dreamer; "this spirit has been in me from the beginning, and has his battle to fight over again in my life."

The influence became indistinct and ebbed away, and a new one entered in its place. Garth's heart beat faster and his blood seemed burning hot. The soul that now possessed him was like the last, but endowed with more fire and less light, with fewer waverings toward good, and with more downright lust for ill. His look was intolerant, his temper dangerous and passionate. But he, too, could win men to love him, and loved he was with all a true friend's heart. And once more a woman—this time a guilty woman—came between. There was no misgiving on the husband's part; he frankly trusted his wife with his friend and his friend with his wife, and thought no evil. But temptation came secretly, and yielding; and worse followed, for the sinful union must needs be sealed with the husband's blood. Verily, the land of iniquity was becoming unwieldy!

Garth stirred in his sleep and breathed

more heavily; he owned a fellowship with this dark spirit not less than with the former one; the possibility of a like crime lived in him, if he did not strangle it. The secret sympathy with sin lies nearer to the natural heart of man than sympathy with virtue, and an evil influence affects him more positively than many good ones—for he recognizes more of himself in it. Good, nevertheless, if the man acknowledge in it not of himself but of God, may outweigh all the evil in the world: and at all events it was doubtless well for Garth that his next ghostly visitant was of a different complexion from the preceding ones. There was need of an interval of health and sanity.

Here was now a purer and quieter phase of life; an organism in which the hot blood of the race might cool itself a little ere flowing further; a personality, grave, thoughtful, and silent; one who followed the sea, and traveled widely, and looked much at men. But as the stamp of lineage was less distinct in him than in the others, so was his influence upon the dreamer less powerful, and the sympathy between them less interior. The state was a passive rather than an active one; space was given to draw breath and to reconsider, but little actual advance was made. There were no grievous sins, but neither were there any great struggles or victories; and save in so far as rest and freedom from loss are themselves a sort of gain, the tale would have to be resumed at the next step, pretty nearly at the point where it left off before. Pass on, however, inoffensive soul, and may he who follows be the stronger because of thee!

The visionary succession was now approaching the present daylight, and the mystic presence which next held sway came into closer union with the sleeper's being than did any of those who had gone before. He was vehement, adventurous and lawless; with great capacities, energies, and silences; passionate in his affinities and fatal in his hatreds. Withal a strange faculty of secrecy and reticence—a kind of rugged cunning, compatible with rough outspokenness and stalwart courage; and joined to a strong picturesqueness of aspect and manner. He was formed to quell men and to master women, and in all ways to be at battle with the world. It was fitting that he was born to an age of war and anarchy. He, too, is destined to turn against those who love him, and to shed blood; but his sins are not without remorse, and perhaps his worst-seeming errors are the result rather of recklessness than of ill-intent. Not the less do they remain as pitfalls for posterity; and the prospect has never looked so dark as at the moment when this last turbulent spirit fades away.

The dream is near its end, for the dead have declared themselves, and he who still lives must influence the dreamer otherwise than through midnight visions. Yet Garth, between waking and sleeping, has borne in upon him a perception of his father's sphere. Lofty and refined though it be, it is too little allied with the passionate weaknesses of its predecessors to work their regeneration. Such a man puts evil to flight, not takes it up and transforms it into good; whereas the enemy must be fought and conquered with his own weapons, if the victory is to hold. Such a man can only raise the battle-field to a higher level, where the contest will rage with a more comprehensive intensity — where there shall be no forces in reserve, nor any avenues of retreat, and where the issue, however it fall, will be final. But happy for Garth that such a man watched over his youth, not too much interfering or fault-finding, and ever obliging the wrong to work out its own correction! Deprived of such wise guidance, doubtless worse things would have befallen him than had been the lot of his ancestors. Even as it was, his plight was critical enough. Tingling with the traits and impulses of six generations, he walked with unsteady balance between light and darkness. He followed a vision of beauty through all forms of life, and would fain quench his thirst with no drink less noble than the true elixir of life; but how many a poisonous draught sparkles and tastes as well! The future was ominous: unholy shapes lurked beside the pathway, plotting to overthrow him. Oh for some beneficent goddess to shed a radiance about his footsteps, and shield him from harmful clutches in the folds of her enchanted veil!

Garth opened his eyes. His sleep had brought him no refreshment; rather it seemed as if the weight of two centuries were heavy upon his shoulders. As he gazed upward, a sort of floating film intervened between his eyes and the large star which twinkled in the zenith. Now it hovered almost within his grasp, swaying upon the light northern breeze. It sank yet lower, and at length settled gently on his face. A faint, delicate fragrance eminated from it. What was it? Garth put up his hand doubtfully, and grasped Elinor's veil. He had missed the thing he came to seek, but this filmy truant, which had eluded him before sunset, had returned with the veering wind and descended upon him like a fragrant benediction while he slept.

The young man rose stiffly to his feet, with hot head and shivering limbs, and set off homeward along the ghostly forest lane, his inky shadow silently keeping pace with him, like an evil memory. As he stumbled onward, it crossed his mind how he had fled down this same path twelve years before, leaving what he believed a dead body outstretched on the same spot whence he had just now arisen. He had looked forward to the gallows; and had rushed, instead, into the soft embrace of Madge. What more pleasing disappointment could have been imagined? And yet, might not the honest hug of the hangman's noose have saved him many a trouble, against which even Madge's loving arms could not protect him? Was his outlook now less sinister, on the whole, than that which had confronted him on the terror-stricken night of boyhood? A child's troubles grow out of the earth, and may generally be uprooted and trampled down; but in after-life they seem to descend from the clouds, and are not so easily managed.

CHAPTER XLVIII.

A POWWOW.

It was a good deal after midnight when Garth reached Urmhurst, and paused a moment under the porch before entering. The wind during the last half-hour had waxed greatly stronger, and whistled shrewdly

round the northeast corner of the dark and massive old house, and rattled the rose-vine which climbed over Eve's window, and rustled through the dried oak-leaves of the porch. It was a cold sharp night: winter was hurrying down from the Arctic Ocean, and would be here by morning. From the valley came the white gleam of the lake and winding river, looking as if the frosty gusts were already beginning to shiver them into ice. The valley itself was bleak and desolate, its brown woods and meadows gradually paling to gray, until Wabeno lifted its shadowy, dim-gleaming barrier against the farther world. Many an Urmson—all those old fellows whose dust lay in yonder graveyard, but whose lives Garth had gathered up into his own that night—had stood where he stood now, and gazed across the bleak, moonlit valley till that immemorial mountain stopped the way. The stern Puritan, in his jack-boots and steel breastplate; the black-browed, handsome, reckless soldier, who followed Phipps to Quebec; the blue-eyed, swarthy mariner who had traded in the East Indies and in Arcadia, and had traversed all the world between; the Revolutionary captain in blue and buff, broad-shouldered, grim, choleric, and reticent—each one of them had leaned with folded arms against this stunted oak-trunk, and had frowned at Wabeno as at the symbol of an irremovable bar in the way of his success. But not one, Garth fancied, had borne so heavy and unquiet a heart as he; for they, at least, had been forth to wrestle with the world, and had done something, good or bad, that had had a flavor and a fashion of its own, and was not, at all events, insignificant. But he, the descendant of them all, had done nothing; had only vexed his soul with doubts and broken beginnings and marrowless compromises. Yet he was the heir of their qualities as well of their name. What was the clog in his machinery that prevented his bringing all this accumulated energy to bear? Were scruples and conscientiousness but an artful device of the devil? If he could pluck something out of his breast and fling it away forever, would not the world lie at his feet? If Christ, when he went up into that high place whence he overlooked all the

11

kingdoms of the earth, had chosen to comply with his companion's moderate condition, would not his name have been better known and celebrated to-day than it actually had come to be?

Garth ground his heel against the stone, and it was wedged in the cleft of the granite threshold, so that an effort was needed to pull it out. The fancy suggested itself that the old Indian underneath had put forth a skeleton gripe, with the intention of dragging him down into the grave, and taking revenge upon him for the injuries perpetrated by his forefathers. But this scheme of retribution did not meet Garth's views; on the contrary, it brought him to a sudden recognition of the immense value of life, and of the inestimable possibilities which were within his power to realize. If he could but fasten his hold firmly upon something definite and continuous, he felt that he could climb upward to the stars, even though the sins of twenty generations were piled upon his shoulders. Were not the worst of his difficulties, after all, imaginary? Had he not been a little insane of late? or, at least, might he not be visited presently by some luminous inspiration of genius, in comparison with which ordinary perception was mere purblindness? He passed his hand over his forehead, and was startled to feel how hot it was; and yet, how chilly was the wind! Heaven forbid that he should be taken ill at a time when something more than common good health was to be wished for!

He opened the heavy green door and entered the house. The kitchen-fire was alight, and Nikomis sat smoking in the chimney-corner. On the table stood a joint of meat, and though, in spite of his long fast, Garth now felt little positive appetite, he managed to swallow somewhat, and then, instead of drinking the tea which Nokomis had ready for him, he asked the old lady whether she could not find him any whiskey.

Being an Indian, it was entirely beneath Nikomis to manifest any surprise even at so unprecedented a demand as this. As for whiskey, no house in New Hampshire, except the meeting-houses, was ever known to be without it; and Urmhurst was no exception to the rule, although the only member of the household who was in the habit of consuming it was Nikomis herself. Golightley, indeed, occasionally took a glass, embellished with a little hot water and a lump of sugar, but neither Cuthbert nor Garth was inclined to keep him company. To-night, however, the young man was sensible of a pervading shiver such as only a draught of fire could allay. He had taken cold, and so potent, because unusual, a remedy could hardly fail to check its further progress.

Nikomis grunted, and laid down her pipe. The liquor was not far off; in truth, she forthwith drew from her pocket a battered pewter flask which proved to be half full of it. She poured some into a tumbler, added a little water from the teakettle, and a few other ingredients, stirred it up, tasted it, and then handed it to the young man with a grunt of emphatic recommendation. He sipped it, shuddered, sipped again, laid down the spoon, and resolutely drank off about half of the mixture.

"There's something very genuine about that, Nikomis," he said, with tears in his eyes; "I dare say I might get to like it in time."

"Ugh!" responded Nikomis, relighting her pipe, and gazing at the fire; "dare say —dare say!"

As was usual after supper-time, the kitchen was unlighted save for the flickering firelight, and even this had now subsided to a ruddy glow, which served to illumine hardly more than the cavernous fireplace. Garth drew the antique oaken chair far up on the hearth, and held his hands toward the embers, while his dusky companion puffed at her pipe, and the slowly-emitted smoke hung and swayed in fine clouds until it came within the draught of the chimney, which whisked it suddenly upward and out of sight. It was a snug old place, this chimney-corner, and just now it seemed to Garth to contain the only bit of human life that was left in the world. Here sat Nikomis and himself, types and compendiums of two hostile peoples, literally hobnobbing together in the most amicable manner imaginable. All the bitterness of a traditional and hereditary enmity had simmered down to yonder pungent noggin of punch, or was vanishing into oblivion along with the fumes from the Indian's pipe-bowl. But this was only because they were the last of their race; all the rest had been exterminated on both sides; and, Nikomis and he, having before them the alternative of either scalping each other, or of making up all grievances over a feast of whiskey and tobacco, had wisely decided upon the latter course, and had thereby become aware, at this late day, what pleasant company they had been denying themselves during the latter centuries.

"What a good thing it would have been, Nikomis," said Garth, "if that old sachem of yours and my contemporary ancestor could have come to an understanding as cozy and sensible as this, instead of pitching into one another with blunderbusses and tomahawks! I wish you had been sitting here two hundred years instead of ten. But two hundred years ago you would have brewed me a cup of poison instead of a glass of grog."

The fire in the old lady's pipe-bowl glowed and dulled again, but she said nothing. Garth took another sip from his tumbler, and continued:

"Nikomis, if you really represent the posterity of the old sachem, as my father says, we owe you much more than bare house-room. But, if, as I suspect, your people were the kidnappers of my aunt Eve, the account between us may be considered balanced. Now, tell me honestly, was it not so?"

"Nikomis old squaw — know nothing," grunted the Indian, after a pause. "Why you ask, Garth? What you think we do with Eve? Think we scalp—um?"

Garth shook his head. "It isn't likely you would have come to Urmhurst if Eve's scalp had been among your collection," said he. "But, if she lived to marry one of your tribe, Urmhurst and a legacy would belong to her children."

"Why you talk that way, Garth? Nikomis old squaw; papoose all dead; tribe all dead. Why you talk so—um?"

"I talk of what I wish were true," returned he, grasping his hair with both hands, and resting his elbows on his knees. "I can conceive of nothing better than to leave this blood-stained old Urmhurst to a descendant of your side and mine. It isn't your sachem, but we Urmsons, who have really been buried underneath this great heavy house all these generations past. No good will come to us till it is either got into other hands or burned down."

"Ugh!" assented Nikomis, with smoky utterance. "Big house —big curse—ugh!"

"A wigwam is much better," continued Garth; "better even than a grave, at least so far as other people are concerned. A grave is a selfish luxury, apt to make a quarrel among survivors. Only the last man—supposing him to have dug his own pit beforehand—can drop into it with the certainty of not causing a spirit of strife to rise up out of it. Nikomis, do you know that I'm going to be married?"

He raised his head as he made the inquiry, but his interlocutor answered only with a puff of smoke; so he resumed his former position, and continued:

"And, since my wife wants to see the world, we shall probably leave Urmhurst to my father and you. You must take care of him till we come back."

"How long-a-that?" demanded Nikomis.

Garth gave a gruff, short laugh. "A year or more—as long as the whim lasts."

"Cuthbert dead in a year," observed the sibyl, smokily. "Nikomis too, maybe."

"My father dead in a year!" repeated Garth, with a momentary sinking of the heart. He sat upright in his chair and looked hard at the wrinkled bronze statue that smoked so impassively in its sombre niche. He took the tumbler from the hob and slowly drank what was left of the contents, then cleared his throat, and said, very gently, "My father is not an old man, Nikomis." But the old Indian, having committed herself to an assertion, was evidently resolved that it should stand unaltered, right or wrong. Meanwhile her ominous words, whether justifiable or not, sank, during the few minutes' silence that ensued, so deeply into Garth's centre of existence, that the outward effect was the same as if they had altogether passed out of his memory. He made no further allusion to them; he could not talk—could hardly think—so far below the surface as they lay. Nevertheless, they could tinge every drop of blood that coursed through his veins. The only ostensible result, however, took the form of a resentful impulse against his uncle and Mrs. Tenterden. "Meddlesome fools!" he whispered, setting his teeth hard together; "they've been babbling their nonsense here, and she got it from them."

"That was a good punch," he remarked, presently; "I believe it's gone to my head, and made me talkative. Suppose you let me have a pull at your pipe," he added, observing that Nikomis was knocking out the dead ashes preparatory to refilling it. She recharged it, still silently, and handed it to him. It was an old red-clay pipe, curiously chased about the bowl—such a pipe as the sagamores might have smoked in the time of Columbus, or earlier. As Garth took it, and set it going with a brand from the fire, it occurred to him that it was one of Nikomis's most precious possessions, and had never, so far as anybody knew, been seen in another mouth than hers since her appearance in Urmsworth. Her present surrender of it, therefore, must be looked upon as a really extraordinary piece of condescension. "The calumet of peace, Nikomis," he said, with a smile, as he puffed out the first gray cloud. "This ought to complete my cure."

The swarthy sibyl took a dry stick of wood from the oven and laid it on the glowing embers. It quickly caught fire, and flooded Garth's face and figure with dancing light. She studied him for a moment with her wrinkled eyes, and then asked, abruptly:

"How you like Sam—um?"

"I ought to like him, since I gave him a thrashing," replied the young man, meeting her look with a glance of momentary curiosity; "but, I think that white rascal, who was said to be his father, spoiled him. But I dare say he's improved since he was here. Have you heard of him lately?"

"Ugh! he great man now: very rich. Come here by-'n'-by. Ugh! very rich."

Garth was aware that Nikomis had received occasional intelligence of Sam ever

since he went away; but this was the first time she had ever volunteered any information about him; and, Garth, not having potent faith in his old associate's manly worth, had delicately forborne to push his inquiries beyond the bounds of formal politeness. But the idea of Sam in the character of a great and wealthy man came as an amusing surprise.

"I'm glad to hear it," he said, in his deep, kindly tones. "And has he a family along with his other riches?"

"No squaw yet," rejoined Nikomis, with her characteristic grunt. "Sam get squaw here. He live here; not go 'way. Great man."

"And who is his squaw to be?" inquired Garth, pleasantly.

"Madge his squaw," replied Nikomis, with the most phlegmatic composure.

Garth stared a moment, but, on second thoughts, laughed very good-naturedly. He was not so used to conversation with this fantastic old personage as to be always prepared for her peculiar and unheralded flashes of humor.

"But, I thought Madge was to be my squaw," he said. "Does Sam mean to fight me for her again? Will no one else suit him?"

"He take Madge—you take Elinor!" grunted the sibyl, as composedly as before.

"You're not a good match-maker," returned Garth, growing grave again. "It's a more complicated business with us than with the red people. But I'll make this bargain with you," he added, smiling once more—for he was in a singular mood of profound shallowness, and more or less defiant and reckless withal—"if Madge tells me that she prefers Sam to me, and if, then, Miss Golightley offers me her hand, I'll take it."

"Ugh! ugh!" assented Nikomis; and, as if to ratify the agreement, she stretched out a dark talon for the calumet. "What-a-good-a-have wrong squaw—um? Sam rich man, take Madge; you picture-man, take Elinor. Tell you what, Garth, you not very wise. You think Madge care for you?" Here Nikomis made a sound in her throat like a crow cawing under its breath, at the same time shaking her head slowly. "You not very wise."

These deliberate attacks upon the very roots of his hopes and happiness might have irritated him, coming from any other mouth than Nikomis's, or dismayed him, but that he believed unalterably in Madge's affection. As for poor Sam, if Garth could have accepted the idea that the vagabond half-breed was really capable of loving her, he would have felt some compassion and even a little respect for him. But he saw in old Nikomis's grotesque utterances only the half-cunning, half-senile attempts of a tenacious but narrow and decaying mind to realize a long-cherished though hitherto unacknowledged purpose. And—his mood to-night being, as I have said, somewhat reckless and defiant, owing either to the whiskey, or to the peculiar effect upon his brain of the chill he had got while dreaming in the woods beneath the moon, or to the stress of things in general—he chose to amuse himself by humoring the ancient squaw's whim. He felt free to converse with her in a strain of fanciful extravagance such as he could have permitted himself with no one else, and which, just at this time, was especially comforting to him. He was grateful to her for being precisely the strange, unorthodox, half-savage creature that she was, and would not have exchanged her company for that of the most charming civilized woman in the world. He was aware of the stirring of something unorthodox and savage within himself, which rendered a contact with the Indian's nature congenial and stimulating.

"I can understand your knowing Madge's heart, Nikomis," said he; "you were intimate with her all the time I was away. But are you as sure about Miss Golightley? If she were to refuse me, after Madge had left me in the lurch, I should be obliged to take your Sam's scalp."

The idea of a woman's refusing a man who had made up his mind to have her seemed to be beyond Nikomis's primitive conceptions. What her own romance might have been is unknown: perhaps, after a good stand-up fight, she was knocked down with effectiveness enough to satisfy her maidenly scruples, and so borne off to her husband's wigwam; although the North American Indians usually manage these matters rather in a mercantile spirit. At all events, the wooers where Nikomis was brought up had evidently been in the habit of carrying their point, one way or another; and when Garth suggested the contingency of Elinor's refusing him, she replied with a grunt of uncompromising contempt for so paltry an objection.

"Then you make her!"

"You are a true sibyl!" exclaimed the young man. "You're much wiser than civilization, Nikomis! Of course—make her! Why wasn't all the world born Indian?—all warriors and squaws and wigwams? I might have felt as if I were alive then. Or beasts! why aren't we bears and lions, instead of pottering about between heaven and earth, afraid to say what we think, or do what we wish? I want to roar, and have no soul, and tear my enemies to pieces with my teeth and claws, and eat them raw! ha, ha, ha! No right and wrong, and duty and law—only instinct."

This rhapsody was uttered in Garth's customary low but powerful bass voice, and with such savage zest as might have stirred Nikomis's wild old blood better than a war-whoop would have done.

"Ugh, ugh!" quoth she; and after an interval again, with confirmed approval, "Ugh!"

"But we are forgetting my uncle," resumed Garth, after a short silence. "If I don't take Sam's scalp, I must· have his. He thinks Miss Golightley belongs to him!"

"Caw! his scalp no good," said Nikomis, with a motion of her hand, as if throwing away so pitiful a bauble. "You take her—he do nothing! Caw! he nobody. Nikomis put him-a-fire 'nd burn up! You take her; me fix him."

"Let's get him and put him in the range now," suggested Garth, rubbing his hands and chuckling. "He'll keep us warm while we're drinking another glass of punch. Shall we take him whole, or split him up into kindlings?"

"No need a-that," replied the other, gravely; and then, peering at Garth through

her cloud of smoke, "you think-a-make fun
—um?"

"Yes; fun worth making. What, you
mean 'make-believe?' No, no! burn him,
and the house with him, if you like. That
might be the best plan."

"You not wise, Garth," repeated Nikomis, with something of the pride of superi-
or faculties in her manner. "Me burn him-
a-not—see him—not touch him. He go Boston—go London: Nikomis sit-home in kitch-
en 'nd burn him all up. Ugh!"

"Witchcraft!" exclaimed Garth, becoming suddenly enlightened; and truly the appearance of the old lady at this moment,
bending forward from the shadow of her
niche into the red glow of the firelight,
which kindled up her dark, bronze features,
the wrinkled eyes, the prominent cheek-
bones, the great hooked nose, and the wide
thin lips, and flickered upon the grizzled
lengths of coarse, straight hair that hung
down on each side of her furrowed cheeks—
her aspect certainly was as witch-like as
ever woman wore—"witchcraft! Nikomis,
I had forgotten. You'll make a wax image
of him, and melt it before a slow fire; or
write a spell on a piece of paper, and light
your pipe with it! Why, a witch is better
than either an Indian or a wild beast.
Have you got the paper with you—or the
image?"

Before Nikomis could answer, the conversation had a sudden interruption. There
was a sound of low, steady knocking, whence
proceeding Garth could not at first determine. It seemed to come from the air round
about them. Nikomis, however, immediately pointed upward. Cuthbert's room was
overhead, and evidently he was awake and
knocking on the floor. Garth sprang to his
feet.

"Is my father ill? Has he been?"

Nikomis also had risen, and stood half
revealed in the glimmer, like a grotesque apparition which the next moment would vanish altogether. After listening an instant,
she quietly resumed her seat in the chimney-
corner.

"He all right," said she; "powwow
wake him up, maybe. You go see, Garth;
maybe he want you."

Garth left the kitchen with quick, heavy
steps, and bounded up-stairs. His father's
door was ajar; and, as he approached, it
opened wide, and he saw his father standing
in his dressing-gown, with a lighted lamp in
his hand.

———

CHAPTER XLIX.

PUTTING THE CASE.

GARTH looked anxiously at Mr. Urmson's
pale, composed face. Under the rigorous
oppression of a heavy fear, his late half-de-
lirious mood had been suddenly quenched,
as fire is smothered by ashes. "Is anything
the matter, father?" he asked, in a low
tone.

"So I began to think," replied Mr. Urmson. "Come in out of this cold entry."
He led the way into the study, and set the
lamp on the table. "How's this?" he continued, standing in front of his son. "You've
been smoking Nikomis's tobacco, you villain, and drinking her whiskey too, I believe!"

Garth could not repress a smile of relief
at hearing himself called villain—a term of
endearment which recalled the boyish days
when he was always either villain, troglo-
dyte, ragamuffin, sockdolager, Hottentot, or
whatever else his father's gift for bestowing
grotesque epithets could devise, and which
likewise seemed to intimate that his fears
had been premature, since a man sick unto
death would not be apt to indulge in playful
banter. The two sat down, Mr. Urmson in
the rough-hewed, but indestructible old black
oak chair, upholstered in figured green vel-
vet, which was said to be a good deal older
than Urmhurst itself, Garth in the broad
window-sill on the other side of the table.

The study was large, furnished with massive and antique simplicity; the floor was
brown and bare save for a few rugs; the
walls above the dark wainscot were picture-
less and unornamented. At one end of the
room was a deep alcove fitted up with book-
shelves, and containing the whole of Mr.
Urmson's practical library—a somewhat remarkably small one for a literary man. The
writing-table was the most modern piece of

furniture in the study, large, convenient, and kept in good order. The fireplace, although smaller than those on the lower floor of the house, was yet of ample extent; and a log of wood still glowed and flickered, lying athwart the brass-headed fire-dogs. A serene, ascetic, yet mellow and pleasant atmosphere pervaded the place, and Mr. Urmson himself, in his long, sober-colored dressing-gown, looked like an enlightened and humanized acolyte. Since his wife's death he had become more and more secluded in his habits, not as if repelling the world, for the essential kindliness which underlay his superficial manner of demure satire was never obscured; but as failing by mild degrees to find a certain sort of mystic sunshine there familiar to his youth.

Garth, being seated, and his immediate anxiety appeased, allowed an odd humor of dullness to possess him. He leaned his elbow on his knee, and his chin on his hand, and stolidly beheld the still-running sands of the old hour-glass which stood beside his father's desk, its crystal sides uncracked by more than ninety years of use, though one of the four ebony columns of its frame had given way beneath the weight of the countless hours that it had undergone. Mr. Urmson, quietly but keenly observing him, curved the fine corners of his mouth with a subdued, humorous smile. Almost immediately, however, the smile passed away, for Mr. Urmson's smiles of late years, though they came nearly as readily as of yore, and were no less pleasant than ever, were yet much shorter-lived than formerly, the sunshine that called them into existence seeming inadequate to their long preservation. We can remember when they used to play thoughtfully about his clear face, subsiding and silently brightening again for minutes, but now they appeared to share the infirmity attendant upon nearly seventy not altogether unshadowed years. Some old men smile chronically, with the vacant, sly happiness of idle senility; others suffer their features to stiffen into wrinkled and hoary harshness. Cuthbert Urmson's spirit was too wholesome and too strong for either feeble alternative, but perhaps it had grown a trifle weary of its life-long burden of earth, and impatient of the labor of urging a cloddish, incomplete response to the transcendent inner movements.

After red sand enough to fill a thimble had flowed from the upper into the lower bulb of the primitive timepiece which Mr. Urmson preferred to any modern innovations, he said, tapping his chin with his forefinger, and moving his foot forth and then back beneath the table: "You seem to be ripe for bed, old gentleman; we can talk to-morrow; I only wanted to know whether you'd found your letter."

Garth passed his hand across his forehead, as if brushing away troublesome cobwebs, and paused, apparently for the purpose of gathering his wits together before replying. "I should have come up at once if I'd known you were awake," he said. "The letter is lost; it was from Jack Selwyn."

"So I thought, from the envelope."

"The amount of it is," continued Garth, rousing himself with another effort, "that Jack has found out something about the Tenterden money."

"Has he got it back?"

"What?—Oh, he knows who robbed them."

"Who is the robber?" demanded Mr. Urmson, in a tone low but ringing, and with a sudden gleam in his eyes.

"He doesn't say. He will be here in a few weeks. Some mystery or other. That is why I wanted to find the veil. If any one else were to— What did I say? I mean the letter. But it must have got dissolved at the dam."

"Have you spoken about it to your uncle?" asked Mr. Urmson, after a pause.

Garth shook his head. "There's something wrong between Jack and my uncle. Jack was disrespectful, probably. No, he said no one was to be told. I might have told Miss Golightley, though, but that—it turns out to be of no consequence. She won't need the money when she gets it."

Mr. Urmson moved his eyebrows inquiringly.

"She is to marry my uncle," explained Garth, shortly.

His father leaned back in his chair and held his chin musingly between his forefinger and thumb. "They are engaged, then," he murmured; and added, after a pause, with an arch lifting of the brows: "Why, I don't see how Golightley could have done better. What is your objection? Shall no one marry except you?"

"It's a shame," said Garth, seeming at length to get the better of his stolidity. "But she did it for Mrs. Tenterden's sake."

"Oh, then you imagine her to be not in love? Why, your uncle seems to me a very fascinating as well as clever fellow: and highly-educated young ladies like Miss Elinor are apt to admire men a good deal older than themselves. I suppose, at any rate, there's no doubt about his being in love with her?"

"Anybody might love her."

"To tell the truth, this surprises me a little; it had got into my head that, if he were smitten by one person more than another, it was by Madge. And, Garth, if you are seriously opposed to this match, I am still inclined to think that you might stave it off by presenting him with Madge as a substitute."

Garth remained sullenly silent to this suggestion; but his father, seemingly determined to prick him through his sullenness, continued on in the same vein:

"To be sure, there are difficulties in the way; in some respects it seems like a game at cross-purposes. Miss Elinor, by your notion, marries to enrich Mrs. Tenterden; and Golightley, as he tells me, owes his whole fortune to some lucky help that Mr. Tenterden gave him at a critical moment. So he may be marrying from a sense of duty or gratitude too. Really, it looks as if they ought to be spoken to. There's no telling what troublesome and absurd embarrassments an overgrown sense of duty may lead people into."

"H'm!" growled Garth, moving his head assentingly.

"But then," proceeded Mr. Urmson, "even supposing this sense of duty done away with, there remain further difficulties. Madge herself might object to being transferred; or, if she could be persuaded, the objection might possibly come from you. It's a pity you can't gird on sword and shield

and settle the matter, as your forefathers would have done, by hacking and thrusting. But in this age I fear there's no hope of that kind of rescue."

"I have no hopes," was Garth's moody rejoinder.

"Besides," added his father, following out his train of thought without heed of the interruption, "if it were morally right to cut off your uncle's head or run him through the midriff, it would still be a rash and impolitic act. He hasn't yet paid you for your picture, has he? and your very marriage seems to depend on his doing that."

"Father, I have had a dream, and a strange talk with Nikomis, and my head feels queerly. I'm in a bad humor, and I can't pretend otherwise. If Uncle Golightley pays me for my picture, I shall never paint again."

"Why not?" asked Mr. Urmson, with a quiet look.

"Madge doesn't care for painting," said the other.

"What shall you do instead?"

"I don't know. Be a farmer."

"Does Madge dislike painting so much as to like poverty better? If you go on as you have begun, painting would make you richer than farming. Does she fully understand that?"

"It's hard to tell what she really wants. I ought to be Julius Cæsar and Cræsus made into one. But farming is my only alternative."

Mr. Urmson leaned his thin cheek on his hand, and appeared to meditate. "I don't understand, from what you say, whether you give up art and culture for digging and planting to please yourself or her. If it's a whim of hers, which you know to be unwise, might it not be advisable to say no to it?"

"It is my whim," said Garth, with something of a savage effort, raising his face. "I thought you would have seen through it, father."

"When you were a boy, I remember you used to be afraid of painting, or ashamed of it—"

"Well, painting is ashamed of me now."

"Oh! But let us see, old gentleman. If you have compromised with your conscience for the sake of getting married a little sooner, but intend by way of penance to give up what is, to say the least of it, your best means of livelihood, don't you write yourself down even more an ass than a sinner? Would not Madge rather wait than marry a poor, stay-at-home farmer? You'll make a very poor farmer. I should think, by a little waiting, you might in this case eat your cake and have it too."

"But that is not all—" began Garth, and broke off feverishly.

"Is it on your own account that you are in haste?"

Garth got to his feet, and stood, with suppressed excitement, beside the table. "Yes," he said. "I'm not safe till she's my wife. I must be chained down and locked in."

"When you were a boy— Here, do you remember this?" asked Mr. Urmson, opening a drawer of the table and taking therefrom an ancient birchen rod, which he switched through the air once or twice, and then handed to his son. "When you were a boy, you once volunteered to chain down and lock in yourself. Now, it seems, you need a wife to do it for you."

Garth took the rod and examined it, as though it were some great natural curiosity, turning it over and about, and slowly drawing it from one hand to the other. It recalled to him the past years of childish passion and struggle and conquest, which had seemed a fair promise of greater conquests afterward. Yet what his father said was true: he was more manly then than now. But on the other hand, a whipping with a birch rod was a simple and palpable matter, whereas the course of discipline or castigation to be enforced in the present case was far from being so. There is an incorrigible distinction, and difference both, betwixt childhood and puberty. It sometimes seems as if a human being's enemies multiplied out of all proportion to the development of his power of fighting them. Garth laid down the rod and looked at his father gloomily.

"You have not told Madge of this? She might not relish the profession of jailer. But what particular enormity are you in danger of committing?"

"I haven't told myself what," returned Garth, gruffly.

"Why, I always took you for a pretty honest fellow. I had relied on you to help me out with the peroration of my history. But if you really mean to betray your art, and to marry a wife under false pretenses, without fairly giving yourself a reason—"

"Father, there is more the matter than I am responsible for. Every way is the wrong way. I must take the way that wrongs myself rather than the way that wrongs other people. There's no help; and I can't laugh about it."

"No; the best help one man can give another is the opportunity to feel and use the strength that God puts into him. I have always tried to do that much for you, old gentleman. But methinks that must be a very ugly knot which has no loose end at all. Now we have always behaved to one another like decent Yankee gentlemen, who prefer letting their hearts be guessed to turning them inside out at once. However, once in a great while—not oftener, perhaps, than once in a lifetime—it is worth while to drop our points for a moment, and be a little unceremonious. Old boy, I used to tell your mother—sometimes, when she asked me very hard—that maybe you were not altogether a bad person. And, to be quite candid, I don't like to see you brought to your wits' end (however far that may be) without wishing to lend you as many of my own as I may happen to have to help you along."

Garth's face changed somewhat for the better at this beginning, and his father went on:

"Well, as to this picture-business, which seems to have arisen on purpose to give you trouble, though it may not turn out so badly —the only strictly honorable and healthy course seems to be to have your own way with it, come what will. And the first consequence would be to delay your marriage. I don't take into consideration any possible Providential interference, because that would be unpractical. Your marriage would be delayed, your uncle no doubt disappointed, and Madge hurt and perhaps offended, the more because she knows it was in your power to fulfill your engagement, and would not be likely to appreciate at their full value your reasons for not doing so. Still, so far as that goes, and in spite of appearances, you would have done right and not wrong both to yourself and others. And you would have the advantage of being able to paint on."

"Yes, father; but that is only the beginning."

Mr. Urmson here took his penknife from the tray of the inkstand and began to whittle, in default of a better subject, the shaft of a quill pen. He had a way (said to be a trait of the Urmson race) of fixing his eyes steadfastly upon those of the person to whom he was speaking. Some people liked this sometimes; others did not; but few, perhaps, found it pleasant at all times. And Mr. Urmson, at the present juncture, anticipated having to touch upon delicate matters, and provided this means of keeping his eyes averted, and thus relieving, so far as might be, the listener's embarrassment.

"If I were some fathers," said he, "I might tell you that a good end cannot excuse a wrong act; or, if I were some others, that you were a fool to risk your happiness for a shadow, and still more to abandon your profession for having once disgraced it; and I might say all this as though it were an original discovery of my own. But since I left the birch rod in your keeping when you were a boy, I sha'n't assume the responsibility of this sort of metaphysical birching now. But as an outsider, who may as such have his faculties of perception and reflection in better working order than yours can be, I'll ask you a few leading questions. You needn't answer them to me, but you will to yourself; and so I may help you indirectly to get some light thrown on this difficulty. You were in Europe a long time; Madge is a beauty, but beauty does not wear so well through absence as some other qualities; it pays, in that way, for being so powerful at close quarters; and perhaps your absence, in spite of all you could do, taught you as much."

Garth gave a great sigh, but, before he could say anything, Mr. Urmson, smoothly paring off a long white strip from his quill, continued:

"In that case, I venture to take it for granted you would feel the more bound to keep your word to her; and you would naturally, from a very proper feeling of self-reproach, and also, perhaps, from a prudent distrust of your own strength, wish to keep it as soon as possible; and so it would be harder to forego the means your uncle offers you: and wrong would look uncommonly like a higher sort of right."

"You are making this too easy for me; I ought to say it myself," interposed the culprit, with heaving and uneven utterance. But Mr. Urmson shook his head and smiled.

"No; every man to what he can do best. These things should be said, because, once a trouble is reduced to words, it is reduced to its least harmful terms too; and I say them, because I have a much readier gift of the gab than you, and don't wish to sit here till breakfast-time seeing you stumble where I can run. As to making it easy for you, you'll find it hard enough, I doubt, to satisfy your tenderest conscience before you are quit of it. I can see nothing easy about it, for my part. Well, now, old boy, I can imagine another thing. You are much improved in the way of taste and judgment and cultivation generally by your experience abroad; and it is fair to infer that you learned how to appreciate finer degrees of harmony and form than you could before you went away. You may have met with an incarnation of this loftier ideal, and felt drawn to it by what seemed the loftier part of your nature, although in opposition to commonplace morality. You may have thought that in giving it up you would be giving up all your better possibilities, and folding your talents in a napkin. And this would bring about rather a curious complication. That ancient friend of yours, the old Adam, would not miss the opening to observe that if you really thought you ought not to accept that thousand pounds, here was something to console you for refusing it. You would remain unmarried another year or so, but meanwhile you would be entitled to more freedom of thought and fancy than if you were a husband; and in a year or so what might not happen? In this case, you see, old Adam, though no doubt arguing for his own ends, would have the very truth and right to back him which were your own best weapons against him; and in my opinion you would be in a very awkward fix. At all events, a candid observer cannot help admiring the skill and ingenuity of old Adam."

"I seem to be made of glass," muttered Garth, leaning back against the window-sill, with his hands in his coat-pockets, and gazing at the pale, keen, gentle, firm-hearted old man.

"You might have given me credit for seeing through something less transparent than glass," rejoined the latter, who had now whittled away all the feathery half of his pen, and was beginning on the quill proper. "However, the fact is that you gave me the key to my discoveries by saying, a few minutes ago, that every way seemed to be the wrong way. But I tell you again that I don't see any smooth way out of this scrape; you have got to catch it heavily one way or another. All I can do is to put your alternatives clearly before you. I have got you now so that you can neither marry without dishonoring your art, nor forbear to marry without seeming to court a dishonorable passion, which, nevertheless, seems to be your only opening to a higher life. And I don't see any present use in going farther, old gentleman. Only, I hope it may comfort you a little to remember that I have been with you, at any rate, so far."

"I begin to know you at last—to know I know you, rather."

"And after a fellow has done what he can, Providence is not a bad thing as a background. Meanwhile we must go to bed."

"I remember when mother died you met me before I knew about it, and talked quietly and cheerfully for half an hour until the others came in; and afterward I thought how plucky you had been, and I was ashamed to give in. It's the same now. Most men are brave enough if they are so for themselves; but you can help other people to be brave."

Mr. Urmson stood up in his long monastic gown and yawned. "Did you find Nikomis good company?" he asked.

"She said some strange things. Is she a daughter of the sachem, father? and does she mean to do us good or evil? She is a witch, I know."

"Well, I have found her a very valuable acquaintance. She knows things I would be glad to know. I shall think just as highly of her whether as friend or enemy. The worst thing I ever knew her to do was letting you share her whiskey-bottle. You have not been quite in your right mind, old gentleman."

"It is not that," said Garth, putting his hand to his head. "I have been cold and hot and topsy-turvy ever since my nap in the woods. Maybe I'm in for a fever."

His father felt the shaggy young man's pulse with his pale, sensitive fingers. "Now your tongue," said he. "Well, it's proper enough that your spiritual struggles should have their projection in the body—if that will be of any comfort to you. You are not in a very desirable condition, certainly; and, if you have a fever at all, you may make up your mind for a pretty severe one. However, you shall have nurses enough, and homœopathic medicines."

"Is nothing the matter with you, yourself?" demanded Garth, turning about and facing his father at the door. "Everybody has been saying lately that you were looking ill; and Nikomis said—"

"What? her opinion is always worth hearing."

"She said you wouldn't live another year," said Garth, intending to speak it lightly, but ending with ignominious solemnity.

Mr. Urmson laughed in his quiet, inward way. "After all, I see, Nikomis is less than omniscient. I have not speculated as to the day of my departure, but I hope to live as long as is good for me, and to die to some good purpose. Good-night, my good old reprobate!"

BOOK VII.

DISCORD AND HARMONY.

CHAPTER L.

CUTHBERT.

Had he been essentially a practical man, it is not likely that Garth would have got much solid encouragement out of this interview with his father. Ostensibly, indeed, there might rather have seemed to be reason for greater dejection than before. Instead of making light of his difficulties, or suggesting a feasible way out of them, Mr. Urmson had deliberately counted them up and set them in order, denying its full weight to none, and sparing not to admit the multiplied menace of all combined.

Nevertheless, and despite his increasing bodily discomfort, Garth, ere he fell asleep, was in better spirits than for several days previous. That the evil of his plight had not been extenuated was implicitly complimentary to his ability for getting the upper hand of it. If his father had thought him craven, he would scarcely have been at the pains of frightening him; and, on the other hand, what more poignant way is there of suggesting heroism than to warn of heroic obstacles? A hero delights to battle against odds; and, if Garth knew himself for less than a hero, he was yet near enough akin thereto to feel the inspiration of standing in a hero's shoes.

To be understood, moreover, is to be twice one's self, and his father understood him but too well. To find that another mind than our own has analyzed our position and entered into our doubts, is armor against danger and assurance of sanity. Hard is it for man to be alone in trouble. He blenches, partly from ignorance, and in part because in his loneliness he is not afraid to blench. And though God be forever present with every man, yet were mankind created for mutual sympathy, and through that sympathy is it that God indirectly seeks to impress his love upon us. Garth was far from being an infidel; but he had fallen into the shadow, and perhaps at this stage was better helped by a friendly human hand than he could have been by dint of abstract religious faith. There might come a season, however, to him as well as to others, of want whereto no merely human aid could minister, and well would it be for him in that time if he had recognized the Divine inspiration of all human charity.

Cuthbert Urmson heard the door of his son's room close, and then he sat down again in the old chair, leaving the study-door ajar. The aspect of cheerful composure which he had maintained during the interview now began to fade out of his face, and in a few minutes he looked many years older. He leaned his head heavily on his hand, and his shoulders bent forward. The lower lids of his eyes were contracted, his lips set together, and occasionally he fetched a long sigh, like a man enduring wearisome physical pain.

By-and-by he turned himself toward the table, and began, mechanically and with exaggerated accuracy, to put in order the papers and other things which lay upon it. The scattered parings of the quill pen he brushed slowly together in a heap with his fingers, and dropped them into the waste-paper basket. Then he closed a drawer which was standing open; but the action reminded him that he had taken the birch rod out of it, and he looked across to the other side of the table for it. It was not there. It had fallen to the floor, then? Cuthbert rose and walked round the table. But no; it had disappeared entirely. Garth must have taken it with him as he went out. It was a good omen. The young man, in his usual silent and undemonstrative fashion, had put himself upon his honor; and that was so far significant as to show, at all events, that he did not consider himself to be hopelessly beneath a flogging. "And the best of sinners," thought Cuthbert, with the faint smile playing about his mouth, "could hardly come into a healthier state of mind than that!"

Clasping his hands behind him, he stood on the hearth with his back to the fire, swaying his body with a slow motion from side to side and forward and backward, after a fashion peculiar to him during solitary meditation. The deep stillness of the night and of the sleeping house seconded the grave abstraction of his thought. In glancing back over his life he saw himself, perhaps, as a man who had hoped well, if not too wisely, and had thus kept a modest light of happiness and serenity burning secure throughout a great deal of unpropitious weather. A fretful, selfish, impatient man would hardly have reached even Cuthbert's moderate age without stumbling or altogether falling by the way. But Cuthbert's roots grasped beneath the surface-loam of existence, and drew their essential nourishment from subterranean springs. He had taken a wife whom few persons of his intellectual rank would have looked upon as a fit helpmate in the wearisome endeavors of earthly life; but he, being wise as well as intellectual, had seen her in a more searching light than that of the understanding, and found in her all he needed. In fact, he had reverenced and looked up to her from first to last in a way which must have seemed akin to infatuation to those whose judgments of human worth are made solely from the standpoint of the brain. Cuthbert, however, constantly felt her superiority to himself, and this perception charmed while it humbled him. He used to say to himself, or to Professor Grindle, who was a sort of masculine other self to him, that Martha was so much better than himself in all vital respects as to be above the reach of envy, which could not have been the case had she condescended to meet him on his own ground. He would admit her inferiority on one point only—the power, namely, of being as much

delighted with him as he was with her; but for this failure there was the all-sufficient excuse that he was incomparably the less delightful person of the two. Professor Grindle had never attempted to impugn his friend's position in this matter; but the latter never knew that one reason, at least, of this forbearance lay in the fact that the learned, brusque, kindly man of classes had himself been in love with Martha, at the time when Cuthbert stepped between from foreign parts and married her.

Martha's unexpected death had been precisely the deadliest thrust that her husband's philosophy could have met with. In a sense he had not survived it. A great part of him had died with her. She had left him at the time when he was most dependent upon her comforting companionship. While she lived he had been able to look upon the gradual decay of his worldly affairs with a composure that almost amounted to amusement; for he enjoyed the privilege of knowing that the ill luck which so beset him was not of his own making, and meanwhile he possessed the inexhaustible consolation and refreshment of a beloved and loving wife, whose value each fresh slight of Fortune rendered but the more conspicuous. As year by year Golightley's speculative æstheticism ate up the family fortune, until at length there remained nothing except the annual produce of the farm and the earnings of Cuthbert's pen, he smiled his whimsical smile, and held himself wealthy in the ownership of a comfortable dressing-gown and slippers, and of a wife who could mend holes, darn and knit socks, and superintend the cooking of a wholesome dinner. Professor Grindle, to whose prudent care Cuthbert had intrusted the management of the fifty thousand dollars of Eve's legacy, had more than once counseled him, during some severer pinch than usual, to mortgage Urmhurst for at least some part of its value, since it was not to be supposed that Eve or any descendants of hers had any existence, even at the time Captain Brian's will was made, except in that willful old gentleman's imagination. But at this Cuthbert would shake his head gravely, and reply that Nikomis had always appeared to him a mysterious personage, and that until her mystery was entirely cleared up he would try to get along on the produce of the Urmhurst farm and on the interest of the fifty thousand dollars—both of which sources of income the terms of the will had left him at liberty to use. Indeed, it was solely through drafts on the latter revenue that Garth had been enabled to keep at college. Professor Grindle would grumble out something uncomplimentary to the sagacity of the old captain, and sarcastically ask Cuthbert what became of that part of the three thousand or so dollars of interest which was not included in Garth's expenses; whether Cuthbert bought cigars and champagne with it; and, if so, why he never offered any to his guests. Mr. Urmson generally affirmed that he spent it for lottery-tickets, or in Paris dresses for Mrs. Urmson.

"Then I shall tell the Danvers," the professor would retort, "that you've no head for business, and that they'd better make over the agency of that famous patent affair to me."

At this and similar threats Cuthbert would only arch his eyebrow, and the professor would be forced to console himself with the reflection that the old captain had, after all, done better than he had intended, since, if the Eve legacy had not been set apart, Golightley would long ago have squandered the whole of it. But neither the professor nor anybody else could prevail upon Mr. Urmson to regard this matter in any other than a humorous light—so long as Mrs. Urmson was alive.

In Garth, again, a less securely grounded faith than Mr. Urmson's might have seen much to be disturbed about. The boy's most ostensible traits had been ruggedness, reserve, and self-will that could easily become obstinacy. The finer, gentler, nobler qualities that lay behind would soon have been irrevocably choked off by any but the most skillful and ingenious treatment. Some persons—among them, as we know, the Reverend Graeme—had been of opinion that Mr. Urmson had grossly neglected his paternal duty in not imposing his own will and judgment upon his son, instead of leaving the lad (as he appeared to do) entirely to his own devices. But, though Cuthbert never

would defend himself from this reproach of negligence, neither would he pretend reformation. "I sha'n't exactly introduce Garth to the devil," he once said to Professor Grindle, whose ideas on education more or less agreed with his own, "for that would be taking an unwarrantable liberty; but if Garth insists deliberately upon forming the acquaintance, it would be taking a liberty still more unwarrantable to lock the door on him. He must do—I won't say as he likes, but as he chooses. I don't pretend to be wiser than my Creator, and he saw fit to give me free-will. Children are new wine; they must be let ferment freely, or they will never become clear, strong, and full-flavored."

"They may talk about desperate gambling," remarked Grindle, rubbing his smooth bald crown and wrinkling his forehead; "but what gambler ever played such stakes as you, or with so steady a hand? To be sure, the prize is worth the risk, and, as you say, may be unobtainable in any other way. But—I hope the boy'll take to something soon."

Perhaps Garth's entanglement with Madge had caused his father more doubt and anxiety than any other thing. Mr. Urmson mistrusted everything about Madge except her beauty and her intelligence. He was a man who, though rationally opposed to antipathies, was by nature prone to them; but reasoning failed to get the better of nature in this instance. The fact that Mrs. Urmson shared his unfavorable judgment no doubt tended to confirm it, though Cuthbert always made a point of disputing with her on the subject, and arraigning her for uncharitableness. Martha, who was charity itself (tempered with a wholesome dash of feminine prejudice), generally yielded a nominal assent to his arguments, as a wife should do; but, unluckily for Cuthbert's peace of mind, he never had contrived to convince himself. He had to content himself with hoping that his insight was at fault; or, if not so, then that Madge, being bad, might vouchsafe the redeeming iniquity of breaking faith with her lover at the last moment. When Garth went to Europe it had seemed as if Providence were about to promote the latter alternative; and Cuthbert, then groping in the fresh shadow of his wife's death, had blessed his son's departure as a ray of light in the prevailing gloom. But when Garth came back, though it was soon manifest to his father that his devotion to Madge was no longer so blind and ardent as before, she, on the other hand, seemed perversely determined on being more inviolably constant than ever. In fact, it was impossible to doubt her sincerity. A woman who would remain faithful to a man for years without being married to him, would hardly fail to be a model of wifely faith when they were united. "I don't know," sighed Cuthbert to himself; "perhaps I was wrong, and she will make Garth the best wife he could have. If my Cotton Martha were here, she could mend my dull wits. The boy seems to care for no one else, unless that portrait sketch he showed me is a sign of something."

The first months of Garth's return had passed uneventfully away, and matters seemed inclined to adjust themselves with stupid, inert impunity; there was to be no tension, no crisis, no catastrophe, good or bad. There was a tameness in the prospect that might have dissatisfied Cuthbert some six years previous, but now he acquiesced in it with a corresponding tameness and inertia. If the grim, sinister history of two centuries were destined to die away in an uneventful country idyl, with no glimpse of struggle and temptation, no flashing out of poetic justice and retribution, why should not a quiet, elderly gentleman, whose main object in life ought to be to get out of it as quietly and decently as possible, rejoice and thank his stars thereat? Let Garth, an able but not as yet transcendent artist, marry his pretty and clever and worldly-wise wife, and gradually work his way to a respectable, if not foremost, place among his fellows. Let Golightley wisely invest and temporately spend his newly-acquired fortune, paying his debts or not as he thought fit, for Urmhurst could get along with the nothing it had very comfortably. Let the mystery which had brooded beside Captain Brian's death-bed, and overshadowed the relation of his descendants to each other, remain unsolved forever. Let Nikomis pass away unshriven, and Eve's posterity prove a

dream, and Urmhurst stand firm upon its blood-cemented foundations. In due course let the legacy revert to Garth, and enable him to take his wife on a pleasure-trip to Europe, and by that time, surely, Cuthbert might hope that for himself the long, secret, incurable physical anguish of life would be over, and gentle Cotton Martha visibly at his side once more. Let these things be. He had hoped much, and hope, even if it be delusive, has a kind of unearthly wisdom in it, and brings a kind of happiness of which any realization must fall short. Surely, now, at his journey's end, he might be content without earthly realizations. Moreover, crippled as he was with age and disease and poverty, what front could he oppose to events of moment, even if they came? It was better as it was.

Nevertheless, as the old man stood tonight, on the ash-strewed hearth, with his hands clasped behind him, and mused upon the developments of the last few weeks, he could not but admit that, whether he had strength to meet it or not, the crisis was at hand, and wore a threatening aspect. He knew what Golightley had done, he understood Madge's position, he saw Garth's danger, he divined Selwyn's mission. He perceived, likewise—what they could not—their respective relations one to another, and knew, withal, that they knew not of his knowledge, nor suspected it. Yet there were certain points which still remained obscure to him; and others, perhaps, there were which came not near enough his range of vision even to be speculated about. However, the general winding-up could not be far distant, when all things should be made clear. Cuthbert felt that he had a part to play in what was to come, and one rather fitted for a man in the prime of his years and powers than for him, whose flesh was weak, and whose spirit, however willing, might well partake of the frailty of his bodily condition. Nevertheless, as he stood there solitary and unsupported, and thought of what was to come, the blood entered his face and showed faintly through his cheeks. He drew his feet together, and stood a little taller and more erect. He had never been burdened with self-esteem, and now for the first time did he fairly realize that he, too, might be of importance in the old Urmson romance. Yes, they could not do without him; and with the conviction came the gallant flush of courage and resolution which assured him that he would not be found wanting.

A muffled footfall on the staircase informed him that old Nikomis, who always wore moccasins, in spite of the civilizing influences of her latter years, was coming up to bed. The hour-glass had just run out; he turned it, and then went forward to the door, where the Indian met him. ·

"Garth looked feverish," said he; "will he be laid up?"

"Ugh! do him good! He too much well; never been sick; fever one month—two month—do him good. You better go to bed," she added, raising her candle and scrutinizing Cuthbert's face; "you more account than Garth."

"We must take care of him, though," answered he, with a smile. "By-the-way, Nikomis, is it certain that Mr. Kineo is coming here?"

"So his letter say," replied she, with an affectation of indifference.

"And Madge knows of it, I suppose—yes, for she must have read you the letter. So he has made money? Does he mean to settle here?"

"Nikomis know nothing," said the old woman, looking glum. "He stay—he go—me know nothing. Caw! me poor old squaw."

"But he is coming back to see you, Nikomis—not for any other reason. If he were poor, you might have suspected his motives. I'm glad he has prospered. He must live at Urmhurst while he is here—that is, if he doesn't object. We'll put him in Eve's room, and put Mr. Golightley in Garth's old place. Will that be agreeable to you?"

Cuthbert spoke with a smile, yet in a tone that seemed to invite Nikomis to declare her mind to him. Outwardly considered, the proposal he had made was rather a singular one; for Sam Kineo, so far as Urmsworth had had knowledge of him, was not exactly the kind of person likely to be sought after in drawing-rooms.

It was fair to suppose, however, that his experience in the world had rubbed smooth his original savagery, especially since he had succeeded in life from a money point of view. But Cuthbert, though doubtless hoping that such might be the case, would not have been apt to base his invitation thereon. During the years which had elapsed since Sam's first departure from Urmsworth, Mr. Urmson had grown to be more and more of opinion that the young man's interests were intimately connected with those of the Urmson family. He had not attempted to conceal this opinion from Nikomis, albeit conveying his intimations in such a manner that, if she were unprepared to meet them half-way, they would appear unintelligible. Nikomis, on her side, had been as discreet as only an Indian, perhaps, can be. Not that Indians have more intellect than white people: it is tolerably certain that they have not nearly so much; but their instinctive prejudice in favor of keeping their own counsel often serves them in as good stead. Nikomis admitted little and denied less; she appeared to know a great deal, yet could not be proved to know anything. Animals do things, and perhaps think about doing them, but they are not often overheard talking about their doings. Indians—and Nikomis as an Indian—probably more nearly resemble animals in this respect than do their white brethren. They have their powwows, it is true; but they are incitements to action rather than intellectual deliberations.

On the present occasion the swarthy old woman did not immediately reply, but gleamed at Mr. Urmson out of her narrow, black eye-slits as pungently as if she were expecting a reply from him. "Sam do very well," she said, gruffly, at length; "he rich—he buy house, if he want. What Sam do here—um?"

"Nobody knows so well as you what he wants, or where he should go; I must leave it entirely to you, Madame Nikomis. If you bring him here, he shall be welcome. Well, I ought to be getting sleepy. Good-night."

After she had creaked on up the garret-stairs, Cuthbert stepped across to Garth's room and looked in upon him. He was tossing and muttering in his sleep, his face hot, his lips dry, his hair in a black tangle. His father turned the pillow for him, and smoothed out the twisted sheets and blanket. In doing so he caught sight of a piece of fine bluish gauze, of silken lustre, which appeared to be tied about the fevered man's throat. He attempted to take it off, but, finding it impossible without risk of awakening the sleeper, he presently withdrew to his own chamber.

CHAPTER LI.

FOUR TEMPERS LOST.

THE following morning was the coldest of the season thus far; there had been a great change since yesterday. Long, shaded folds of gray cloud lay along and across the heavens; a chilling, business-like wind was abroad, and had already done miracles in the way of stripping the forest of the remnants of its gaudy finery. Mrs. Tenterden, who, in consideration of her hard jolting in the bay-rigging and over-indulgence in omelet, had felt herself entitled to exceptional luxury, took a late breakfast in bed; and afterward, wrapping herself in a stately *négligé*, reclined on the sofa, while Elinor paced up and down the room with her hands behind her, bending her brows at the carpet, and replying somewhat coldly to the elder lady's questions and remarks.

"Well," exclaimed the latter, laughing comfortably, without interruption to her speech, "all I have to say is, I never thought anything could make up for that knocking about I got yesterday; but if you're really engaged to Golightley, Nellie, I declare you might have knocked me about for a week without my saying a word. Of course, I knew it must be; I could see well enough that you cared for him, in spite of all your to-do about it. Well, now, I suppose you'll be so taken up with each other I sha'n't see anything of either of you. I shall be quite *de trop*, I suspect."

"You shouldn't say that, mother," said Elinor, pausing in her walk to fix her strange, unequal eyes upon Mrs. Tenterden's good-

humored countenance. "If I become his wife, it will certainly not be with any thought of getting rid of you."

Here there was a tap at the door, and Madge came in, with a soft, blooming face and a pretty white apron. She had already that morning served Mrs. Tenterden with her breakfast, and spoken sympathizingly about her indisposition, and now she was bound on a new errand of mercy.

"If you would let me comb and brush your hair for you, dear Aunt Mildred, I should be so glad! You have such lovely hair! And perhaps it might make your poor head feel a little easier. May I?"

Mrs. Tenterden's head felt perfectly well, but she was ready to believe otherwise for Madge's sake. "Bless your heart, my dear, you may do just as you like!" she exclaimed, pleased and flattered. "How kind you all are to a poor old woman, to be sure! Mercy! who can that be?—Why, Nellie, did you expect— I declare, I believe it is Golightley, sure enough! Hark!—Quick, Maggie, that cap on the dressing-table; oh, and my slippers—dear me! where are they? —Did I leave them in your room, Nellie?"

"You'll have to do without them now, at any rate," returned Elinor, a mischievous smile brightening through the midst of her seriousness. "Curl up your feet under your *peignoir*. There—but remember, you mustn't move!"

Golightley knocked and entered, bending at once beneath the weight of his news, and of the delicate compliment of being admitted to a lady's bedchamber levee. He was grave, sympathetic, subdued, and fascinatingly at his ease. He seated himself on a low cricket beside the sofa, and, taking Mildred's hand between his own, patted and caressed it while he talked to the younger ladies and to her.

"How delightful you all look here! By George! what a lucky fellow I am to know three such women all in a bunch! I'd like to know who wouldn't envy me now—Garth, or anybody else. Oh, by-the-by, so sad about dear old Garth, isn't it? You know, he was out late last night, looking after a letter or something, and not finding it, and getting wet and worried and falling asleep in the

12

woods, and one thing and another, and now the poor boy's come home with a bad fever, and delirious, and so on and so on, and I told Cuthbert, Mildred, that I knew you'd like to send him up some of your medicine. —There, now, Margaret, dear child, don't you be frightened. I've told you the worst all at once, because I thought that was the best way. Don't be frightened, because he's going to get well again, you know, and be better than ever."

"Good gracious alive!" cried kind Mrs. Tenterden, sitting up in genuine concern, unconscious that her bare white feet were visible below the hem of her morning-gown. "Why, the poor young man! I declare, I'm so sorry for him! He ought to have had aconite the first thing. What sort of a fever is it, Golightley?"

"Is it contagious?" demanded Madge, at the same moment, rousing herself from a brief trance or fit of abstraction caused by the ill news.

"Well, we hardly know what it is yet; it may turn out contagious, or it may not. I wouldn't advise any of you dear people to go near, anyway; it wouldn't do to have you taken down too, Margaret—delirium and all —no, no! We must keep your little head straight, whatever happens. But as for Cuthbert and me and Nikomis, we're case-hardened old veterans, and we aren't afraid of it. But I thought I'd better tell you, you know, for fear it might leak out in some other way and make you anxious."

Golightley addressed himself to the company generally, but Madge had an impression that he was talking at her and covertly watching her. These two had conversed with somewhat unusual frankness—to use an agreeable word—the day before, but had not prolonged their interview far enough to arrive at any distinct and practical basis of action. Consequently they were still a little wary of each other, and prepared to make the best of whatever chance advantage. Golightley, perhaps, had not come out of the late encounter with quite his usual sense of superiority; for Madge, while displaying an alarming acuteness of apprehension as to his own weak places, had given him no corresponding purchase against herself—none, at least, that he could use without more disconcerting himself than her. But he was not yet ready to admit that no such handle was discoverable; and Madge, recognizing this, was old enough to know the wisdom of avoiding even the appearance of evil.

"You are very kind," said she; "but he —belongs to me, Uncle Golightley, and I must be with him, however it is." There was a slight tremulous cadence in her tone which touched the heart—her own, maybe, as well as others. Women often beguile themselves better than any one can do it for them.

"No, no, Maggie dear!" exclaimed Mrs. Tenterden, getting up with energy. "What do you know about nursing, and what would young Mr. Garth say to us if we allowed you to catch the disease from him? Just let me go over there; I know how to manage, and nothing can hurt me. The idea of nobody but that Indian creature to take care of him! I declare it is perfectly dreadful!"

Here Mrs. Tenterden interrupted herself with a small scream, at the same time bundling back on the sofa. She had set her heel upon a crooked hairpin, which had reminded her of her unshod and exposed condition, and for the moment put all her Good-Samaritanism out of her head. But the mishap served its purpose in inducing a less flurried and headlong view of what should be done. Golightley was presently sent back to Urmhurst with an homœopathic medicine-chest under his arm, and a message to the effect that Mrs. Tenterden would follow so soon as the inertia of earthly conditions could be overcome.

Madge waited until Golightley had passed by the windows on his way homeward, and then she retired to her own room, and began mechanically to put on her boots and otherwise array herself as for a walk. But before her preparations were half completed—in the act of tying on her hat before the looking-glass—she lapsed for the second time into a trance, and was so found some time afterward by her mother, who came with the information that Mrs. Tenterden was ready to set out for Urmhurst.

"Well, what are you doing, Maggie girl, and she waiting, and Garth down with the typhus?" expostulated Mrs. Danver, in a complaining monotone. "Sitting half-dressed and staring into a looking-glass — it's real unthinking."

Madge caught her mother's eye in the mirror without turning round, and after a moment deliberately untied her hat and laid it down on the table.

"What ails the child?" cried Mrs. Danver, heightening her tone. "I guess Mrs. Tenterden isn't going to be sitting waiting all day with her things on, either. Do, now, Maggie, have done and come along!"

Madge was accustomed to treat her mother without much ceremony when they were in private; but she had never yet allowed herself to forget the consideration due to persons of more importance. Now, however, she said curtly, "I'm not going with Mrs. Tenterden."

"Well, I should think you'd had more manners, Maggie; let be what Garth 'll say when he comes to and hears you've not been near him. Of course there's nobody expects you to go in his room and catch the contagion, child. Goodness knows there's plenty to do, this side of running risks; but seems to me, if he was my young man, I wouldn't risk strangers being round and me staying home like I didn't care for him: let be Garth's not the kind that seems over-eager for marrying, either."

"Is Miss Golightley going over?" asked Madge, after a pause.

"Well, I don't see what *she* should be doing there, that I *must* say!" returned Mrs. Danver, tartly. "Maybe she will, though, if you don't, just to bear Mrs. Tenterden company, if no more."

"I sha'n't go," said the beautiful young woman, finally, turning and facing her mother with a hard look. "I don't like his being sick in this way, and delirious, just as if he were some old woman. It isn't manly. Men such as I care about are never laid up in bed with fevers, having medicines given them, and not able to take care of themselves. I don't like Garth for it, and I never shall like him so well again, even if he gets well. Garth sick with a fever! Pah! I wouldn't have believed it."

These sentences were uttered in Madge's customary soft tone, or, if there was a metallic ring in them, it was very subdued. Nevertheless, the half-resentful contempt which they expressed was conveyed likewise by a certain subtile inflection of the voice: there could be no question that she was speaking sincerely. Mrs. Danver was quelled, and could say not a syllable. After a short silence, Madge turned back to the glass, as if to address her reflection therein, and added:

"I would rather have a fever myself than think that he has one. Do you suppose I'm afraid of the contagion? I'm a woman, and sickness couldn't degrade me, and, if there's to be any sickness, I should have had it and not he. Think of my Garth, who canoed the rapids and beat Sam Kinco, lying helpless, with a set of doctors and nurses round him! I'd be ashamed to get well, if I were a man."

"There, now, Maggie, I do think you've said enough," put in Mrs. Danver, partly scared and partly scandalized. "I've often found you hard and bitter, goodness knows, but I did think you cared for something, anyway."

"I do care for something; but I don't care for feebleness and disease. If he were wounded half to death in a duel or a battle, I'd give the blood he lost out of my own veins to make him strong again. Well, I won't go to him; you may tell what you like to Mrs. Tenterden."

"Maggie Danver, you was always an uncertain child to do with," said Mrs. Danver, with solemnity. "Times when one might look for you to be cross and ugly, you'd come out soft and smiling as an ear of corn; and times again, for no cause ever I could see, you'd turn as uncomfortable as a hailstorm. And goodness knows it's I that gets the worst of it; it's not Mr. Graeme, nor the Urmsons, nor the folks at the picnic and the sewing-bees that hear of it. What I say is, I used to think you had a bad side to you, Maggie Danver, as might be the case with others, no more, no less. But to hear what you've said this day, one needn't go far to believe you're just bad clear way through. Ah, maybe you don't pay much heed now," continued the aggrieved parent, in a strained quaver—for, to tell the truth, Madge had been quietly walking about the room during the greater part of this harangue, laying away her things and humming softly to herself, as though in profoundest solitude and abstraction—" but the time will come, Maggie Danver—"

At this juncture Mrs. Tenterden's voice and step were heard in the passage, and the next moment her imperative knock sounded on the door. Madge's mother stepped aside, with a pantomime to her daughter, as much as to say, "How are you going to get out of it now?" But Madge's spirit was fully up, in its own peculiar way, and there can be little doubt that she would, at that moment, have asserted herself in the face of any odds, come what might of it. She walked quietly to the door and opened it.

"Margaret," said Mrs. Tenterden, in a good-naturedly authoritative tone, "you mustn't think of coming with me, dear. I'm so forgetful, I asked you to go without thinking, just after we'd been talking about the contagion too! Just you stay quietly at home, and we'll send you news of him. Oh, I don't suppose it's anything serious—just he caught a cold and got a little feverish.—O Mrs. Danver, you here! Keep her at home, and don't let her get all nervous and worried. Oh, I shall find my way; Nellie's going out for her constitutional now, and she'll accompany me part way, so as I won't get lost." So spake the good lady, busily drawing on her gloves and shaking out her skirts: she much enjoyed the importance of all feminine affairs. "Good-by, dear!" she added, and stepping forward took Margaret's hand and kissed her on the cheek, the young lady submitting to the caress with unusual nonchalance; but Mrs. Tenterden was too much preoccupied to notice it. With a nod and a smile to Mrs. Danver, she bustled off, and soon she and Elinor were on the road to Urmhurst.

Elinor had listened to the news of Garth's illness with an apparent apathy which would have struck an observer as being distinctly uncomplimentary to the invalid. While the others were conversing about it, she had turned away to the window, and stood drumming absently on the pane with her slender finger-tips. After all had gone out, and Mrs. Tenterden was stepping briskly hither and thither, getting ready for her expedition, Elinor left the window and dawdled listlessly to the sofa, upon which she threw herself with an expression of gloomy *ennui.* She made no reply to the elder lady's interjections and scraps of remark; only upon the latter's asking her to run and see if Margaret was ready, she had replied, with a slight yawn: "Of course, she mustn't go with you, mother. It would be better that I should take the fever than that she should." And again, more decidedly: "Of course, she'll want to, mother; but what difference does that make? As to your missing the road, I'm going out myself by-and-by, and I'd as lief go in that direction as in any." Mrs. Tenterden was in the habit of yielding to Elinor's will and judgment in all questions pertaining to social and practical conduct, reserving the right to disagree with her on subjects moral and theoretical. Hence the worthy lady's countermand to Madge, and Elinor's unpremeditated "constitutional."

As they walked along, Mrs. Tenterden, as usual, assumed the laboring oar of talk, conning over, as talkative people will, all the possible and impossible aspects of the affair, trying back for causes and explanations, and prophesying all that would or might or could not result therefrom. At length, however, she became aware that her companion was not paying even her customary tribute of "Yes," "No," and "Oh," but was moving beside her absolutely silent and inattentive, fixing her eyes on the ground, and making thrusts at the earth with the point of her umbrella.

"You don't seem to hear any more than if you were deaf, daughter," she cried, in some pique. "Don't you feel well? Mercy alive!" she added, laughing, "I hope you haven't taken the fever by sympathy. There's no telling but it may have been in the air last evening, and then every blessed one of us might get it."

"There would be some fun in having a malignant case of typhoid," remarked Elinor, with one of her odd, one-sided smiles; "you'd feel you had a right to ask all your best friends to let you alone. I believe I'll take it."

"No, Elinor; I don't think it's right to say such things; it's like tempting Providence," said Mrs. Tenterden, with religious gravity.

"Providence tempts us," returned the girl, with a slight laugh. "It goes by contraries. Either Garth Urmson or I might have had the fever, and, because it would have suited me, he had it. I haven't even an excuse for catching it from him, as Madge would have."

"It seems a very strange time for you to be talking this way, daughter, just when you ought to be most contented—with your fate settled in life, and everything."

"What a funny thing fate is!" remarked Elinor, who seemed to be in a moralizing mood this morning. "People can have only one fate in their lives, and yet they can't have that the way they'd like it. I wonder if they are sorry afterward? Because, after all, they might do as they please, if they only would. Imagine having used up all your life in doing what you are told is your duty, and then finding, after all, that you had only wasted and spoiled yourself, and been made a fool of! Then—I should feel that Providence was evil. You needn't be shocked, mother; I could say a great deal worse things, if I chose; I do very often to myself. Unluckily, it makes no difference what I think or say. I feel sometimes that, if I were to have two lives, I should be unspeakably wicked in the second one, out of revenge; oh, more wicked than— I never could be wicked enough."

"I declare, I think you're quite wicked enough as it is, Nellie," exclaimed Mrs. Tenterden, thoroughly angered by this uncalled-for wantonness of impiety. "I beg you won't speak to me again; I've a right to my ears, I suppose, and I won't listen to it. I don't see who has less right to find fault with the way she has been treated than you have. What have you ever known of any hardships, I should like to know? and everything has always been just as you wanted it. You're a spoiled child—that's what you are. I'm sure John and I did everything; I'm sure I never asked or expected any return—I wouldn't demean myself to take the least thing. You can never

say that against me. I declare, I think it's very unfeeling and ungrateful of you, Nellie, to do—the—way you—do! And just when you've got Golightley to marry you, so as—you—can do without me." Here Mrs. Tenterden began to sob resentfully and forlornly. She belonged to a class of persons who must ever be the despair of logicians.

Elinor stabbed a tuft of grass with her umbrella, and halted. "The house is right round this bend," she said, with her coldest tone and glance. "I had better not go any farther. I suppose your brother will come back with you. Good-by." Mrs. Tenterden stared a few seconds at the stern, pure young face with a cross-eyed glance that characterized her when embarrassed or offended. Then she wheeled about, and walked off with short steps, her head thrown up and slanted toward the right—likewise signs expressive of indignation. Elinor also turned, and set forth in the opposite direction; but before she had gone a dozen yards she stopped again, and, hastening back, overtook Mrs. Tenterden.

"Mother, will you forgive me? I suppose I think I have hardships, and that is as bad as really having them, or worse. But, don't say I was taking advantage of my—of your brother, to be ungrateful. Mother—oh, not ungrateful, am I?" The girl's face, always so susceptible of delicate shades of expression, was touched for a moment with an angelic light. Her mouth trembled, trying to smile, and longing to weep. Her eyes grew large and tense, till tears entered them. Her hands unconsciously reached forward as if she would have fallen on the other's neck, to try and kiss and be forgiven. But who are so implacable as those who cannot tell how they have been injured? Mrs. Tenterden's wrath had not had time to subside. With an air of insulted resignation she held up her cheek for Elinor's penitential salute. Elinor shrank back as from an invisible buffet, looking aged and hardened in a breath. "Well, never mind," she said, lightly; "no doubt I shall be properly punished, at last."

So they parted, being none the better for this attempted reconciliation. Mrs. Tenterden proceeded to Urmhurst, supported by a lively sense of the disparity between her deserts and her allowances; and Elinor walked like one in the wilderness, alone and without hope of companionship.

CHAPTER LII.

OPINION AND PREJUDICE.

GARTH's fever seemed to fasten its grip upon the brain; he lay muttering unintelligibly and tossing about; his eyes generally closed, his lips dark and cracked, he knew no one, but he was particularly sensitive to sound and to the tones of various voices. His delirium sometimes became violent, and then only his father might come near him. From his boyhood up Garth had reverenced his father almost more than he had loved him; and now, in the confusion of his reason, he would still listen and yield when the old man spoke. He commonly endured the ministrations of Nikomis indifferently well; but Mrs. Tenterden, in spite of her truly kind and warm-hearted intentions, had an unfavorable effect upon his nervous system, apparent whenever she entered the room. Her talk—or rather her whisper, but it amounted to nearly the same thing—her would-be cautious manner of moving about, the very sphere of her presence, seemed to discomfort him: at least so thought everybody except good Mrs. Tenterden herself, who could never be brought to suspect it. Outside of the sick-room, indeed, she was a useful assistant, but the ever-instant problem was how to keep her outside. Cuthbert, who was constitutionally prone to become genial under the pressure of active misfortunes, was in the mood to derive a good deal of secret enjoyment from the planning and carrying out of the numberless subtile schemes whereby his fair fellow-nurse was beguiled into keeping her distance, and blinded to the fact of her beguilement.

As to poor Golightley, there was no opportunity for smoothing over matters with him. It may be recollected that Garth, in his first interview with his uncle by the lakeside, had conceived what is called an instinctive prejudice against him, owing to some unprepossessing quality or other in the inflection of his voice. This prejudice, so long as the young man's impulses remained subject to will and reason, had been kept in abeyance; but it now asserted itself with distorted emphasis. When his benevolent relative, therefore, duly fortified by fumigation, stepped soothingly up to the bedside, and, laying a gloved hand on the sick man's shoulder, exclaimed, "Why, Garth, my dear boy, what is the meaning of this? Come, you must get well at once—I can't allow you to be breaking all the young ladies' hearts by any such devices"—the unbridled Garth howled like a wild beast, and raised himself up in bed with such a formidable aspect as plainly declared his enmity. Golightley took this ugly reception very good-humoredly; and, though, of course, he made no further attempt to heal the distemper by personal magnetism, he grudged no pains to be serviceable and considerate at second-hand.

When fever gets hold of a strong and hitherto healthy man, it seldom minces matters with him, but puts forth its full strength and virulence. Garth, who since the measles had never known sickness, seemed bound to make up for lost time now. He plunged into the disease as if he loved it and could not get enough of it; it was hard to say whether he possessed it or it him, but it was a perilous intimacy either way. The homœopathic medicines, though possibly keeping matters somewhat within bounds, did not immediately check or even visibly alleviate the complaint. Mrs. Tenterden, who had seen yellow fever at Charleston, and consequently thought her opinion upon sickness in general to be entitled to the first consideration, began after a day or two to lift her eyebrows and depress her mouth, and affirm, with a shake of the head, that Garth was a very sick man. Golightley hem'd and ha'd at this information, stroked his face and scrutinized his boots dejectedly, and, walking to the window, stood puffing cigarette-smoke against the panes. Nikomis received it with wrinkled and swarthy impassiveness; had she been chiseled out of the bricks of the chimney-corner in which she abode, she could not have displayed completer apathy; nevertheless, she always took care to have the invalid's food and drink ready and good, and she further vouchsafed one or two dishes of pure Indian parentage—mysterious concoctions of certain herbs—which seemed to suit him better than any other part of his diet.

When Garth's illness became known to the general public of Urmsworth, and it was understood to be something really serious, they all constituted themselves his biographer, giving one another abstracts of his career from infancy up to the present time; throwing especial light (gratuitously provided by the brilliance of their imaginations) upon the more obscure and questionable episodes; weighing his good qualities against his bad, and generally shaking their heads over the result; forecasting sagely what might have been his future, and pointing out, with a cadence of warning melancholy in their tones, the causes leading up to his present overthrow and approaching dissolution. So the old Urmson family was doomed to die out? Well, like as not it had run on about long enough. No call to suppose it would have grown better than it had been; and, speaking honestly, the Urmsons were never a growing, progressive lot; had not gone ahead with the times, but stuck in the same place, pretty near, that they were in two hundred years back. They weren't the kind to do their neighbors much good, and, worse than that, they wouldn't let their neighbors improve them. Aristocracy was not recognized in the American Constitution, but somehow the Urmsons had always acted as if they were an inch or two bigger than anybody else. Golightley Urmson—well, there was some excuse for him, and he might do something yet; but the rest had about as well go. Urmhurst was a first-rate site for an hotel, and an hotel was what the village wanted; Garth would likely be buried this winter; the old man would hardly stop above-ground many months after him; some enterprising chap might purchase the estate, put in a few additions and alterations to the old shanty, paint it white, and cut down the big trees round about, and who knows but what—well, say, a year from next spring—there might be as spruce an hotel standing there as could be found in the State? Say a year from next spring at the outside.

The Rev. Mr. Graeme, on first learning the news, set out for Urmhurst with the intention of bringing to bear upon the invalid his three hundred pounds avoirdupois of religious cheer and consolation. But the road was longer than it had been in the good pastor's younger years, and by the time he had reached his destination he had quite forgotten the occasion of his coming. It was therefore with renewed concern that he heard of his grandson's indisposition; but, having in the course of his walk traveled backward into time some twenty years or so, he bethought himself to remark that, after all, Garth was barely five years old yet, and could only be suffering from some one of the complaints incident to childhood. "Where's Martha?" he added, looking around.—"Ay, you are here, Mrs. Tenterden; and very hearty you are looking, ma'am; but the child ought to have its own mother—nothing like its own mother.—Eh, Cuthbert? ha! ha!" Then, after a silence of a few moments, he looked again at Mr. Urmson, and said: "Ay, boy, she's dead, poor girl! It was I read the service over her; and Garth, to be sure, is a man now; so he's done with that fever you were telling me of—done long ago. Well, well, it seemed but just now I was starting up from the village to comfort ye all about him.—I forget things here and there, ma'am, sometimes, I believe. —I came to tell you, Cuthbert lad, I'd preach again on Sunday. I'll preach from the blessed Lord's healing the sick; and we'll have prayer for Garth, and for ye all, that ye may be comforted concerning him.—Come and hear me, lad, and you'll feel all the better for it. God bless you and prosper you!— You've been a good husband, Cuthbert, and you'll be a happy father.—God bless yo all!"

So the benignant old giant went back to the village. His heart was as true and sound as ever, but the strings of the mind had grown slack and out of accord, so that it was no longer possible to get coherent music from them. Whether the minister ever wrote out or composed his proposed sermon must remain a matter of doubt; at all events, he duly appeared in the pulpit (where he had rarely officiated of late), and gave out the text as he had announced it a few days before to the circle at Urmhurst. But when he began to preach, the congregation rubbed their foreheads, and consulted the text over again. The sermon was logical, connected, and able beyond all expectation; but it had nothing whatever to do with the subject specified. The preacher's delivery was more forcible and like old times than had been the case for years—on that point everybody agreed; but not a word did he let fall about healing the sick from beginning to end. Probably the solution of the mystery would never have been discovered to this day, had not Madge Danver been in church; she had always been noted for her good memory, and by the time the discourse was half over she had seen through the whole matter.

"It was one he preached about ten years ago," she said to Elinor, as they walked home together. "I remember it very well, because it was the only time Garth was ever at church. I suppose the poor old man, in thinking of Garth and of preaching at the same time, got possessed somehow with his old sermon, and imagined the world had gone back to that same memorable Sunday."

"It was a good sermon," said Elinor.

"I remember, when he preached it before, people said it was the best he had done; but it wasn't very appropriate for this occasion, was it? It was meant, you know, to give advice and encouragement to some one just beginning life, as it were; and Garth, perhaps, is very near the end of his life now."

Elinor turned and looked full at her companion, who had uttered this sentence in the same soft, even tone in which she had been speaking all along. Was Madge a miracle of resignation? or was it possible that she was indifferent? As the question presented itself to her, Elinor suddenly blushed. Could Garth be dying, and this girl not care—this lovely, sweet-tempered, *naïve*, charming creature, who had seemed to love him so devotedly—could she actually not care? It was not to be believed. Yet, with a renewed shock of misgiving, Elinor recollected her first secret surprise when Mrs. Tenterden

had succeeded in persuading Madge not to run the risk of visiting Urmhurst. It was true that Elinor herself had argued against it, and had hitherto not permitted herself to harbor a suspicion against Madge's true-heartedness. But now, venturing for a moment to imagine herself in Madge's place, she could not help thinking that nothing short of physical force would have availed to restrain *her* from tending the bedside of a man she loved. It might be unreasonable, rash, selfish—anything; but she felt that she would have gone, and trusted to love to take care of her. Had Madge felt thus, and yet let herself be held back, yielding, too, with so little apparent difficulty, and now alluding to a possible fatal end with so strangely quiet a demeanor? Why, that was not to be believed either!

Elinor was almost severely straightforward, and she was at first on the brink of directly asking Madge in so many words to resolve her doubt. But a second thought made her pause and change her intention. For more reasons than one she could not speak with her companion on this subject, and she blushed again as she admitted it. But the episode produced a deep effect upon her, one that would not easily wear away. From this time forth she watched Madge with a singular kind of impersonal jealousy, and her own situation became fraught, to her mind, with many fresh difficulties.

CHAPTER LIII.

A VOLUNTEER.

THE third week of Garth's illness was marked by great prostration, only occasionally varied by delirium. Whereas in the first week it had been necessary to lower the preternatural unrest of the patient, it was now requisite to prop him up with every kind of stimulant. Nikomis stolidly but actively asserted her faith in the virtue of pure brandy, and administered it with a freedom which somewhat awed squeamish Mrs. Tenterden. But, in the teeth of all remedies, Garth continued to sink, the mischief appearing to concentrate more and more in the brain. A secret dread began to grow in Cuthbert's mind lest, even should Garth fight his way back to health, his reason would be lost in the struggle, and he began to pray that his son might rather die. After so stern a prayer, the faded old gentleman, lying wrapped in his dressing-gown on a sofa near the sick-room, would sometimes indulge in one of his subtile, unaccountable smiles. Was he amused at this ignoble end of the haughty Urmson family? or could he, defeated and thrust down to the lowest pit of fortune, yet so far sympathize with inscrutable Destiny as to reflect her ironic grimace?

Long, blank silences ebbed themselves away, Cuthbert sitting or lying motionless, but for the most part unsleeping; for a physical not less than a mental anguish dwelt in his breast, and left him small leisure for repose. The only nurses besides himself were Nikomis and Mrs. Tenterden. The village doctor, who had tended the case up to the last week, had then had the misfortune to be thrown from his horse and break his leg, and he had been confined to his room ever since. Cuthbert thereupon had determined upon sending for Professor Grindle, and Golightley had volunteered to go to Bowdoin College to fetch him; but they had not yet been heard from. It was a critical and anxious time. Garth, as he lay muttering on his bed, was an unprepossessing thing to look at. His bony forehead and shaggy brows, his great cheek-bones and gaunt jaws stood forth almost fleshless; his sunken eyes were like dull embers at the bottom of caverns; his swarthy hair rose erect about his head, a black jungle of inextricable tangles; his hollow cheeks were rough and savage with a three weeks' growth of beard. Through all his prostration, however, he was singularly alive to certain seemingly immaterial things, such as the influence of certain spheres, and harmonious or discordant sounds. No one but Cuthbert could approach him with impunity, though, except when he was irritated, or, more rarely, soothed, he appeared unconscious of everything around him. By-and-by even his father felt that his power over him was on the wane. Garth disregarded his voice, and resented his touch. Good Mrs. Tenterden, who, helpful though she had been throughout, could not forego her prerogative of discussing painful matters with the wrong persons, once let fall to Mr. Urmson something about keepers and asylums, thereby occasioning him a momentary awful sinking of the soul. Anon summoning his strength from some hidden source (there was no sign of any in his meagre, bowed figure), he made shift to answer with a sober cheerfulness of tone that must have cost him dear. But again that night, after Mrs. Tenterden had returned home, he relapsed to an inward agony, and, for the first time in his life, Amen stuck in his throat. Toward morning he prayed that, if there were anything in the world which might save his son, it should be made manifest at once; if not, might the worst declare itself without delay! With this petition on his lips, he stood with folded arms by the bedside of the gaunt invalid, and gazed yearningly upon him. "Garth, dear old curmudgeon, what a good-for-nothing father I must seem to you! It's hard I cannot help you now."

A bird, the latest lingering of the southward-departing tribe, alit for a moment on the bare bough of a tree by the window to warble a golden bar of farewell melody. It seemed to reach Garth's ears. He partly turned his head toward the window, and moved his hand; the haggard harshness of his face softened somewhat. "If I could cage that bird, its song might help him," went through Cuthbert's mind. But the next instant the bird flew off, and soon was miles away, sailing southward over the frost-nipped valley, and aiming onward toward Wabeno and far beyond. It was like the flight of a last hope. Cuthbert turned round, pressing his hand on his breast, and uttering a low sigh of pain. Nikomis was standing in the doorway, looking like a grotesque heathen idol carved out of mahogany.

"Cuthbert, you come go to bed," she said, gruffly. "You die too soon enough anyway. Garth all right; he better soon; me take care. Come!"

"I suppose I ought to outlive him, for decency's sake, being his head nurse," answered Cuthbert, with a nervous twitching of the corners of his mouth. "And I believe I'm in for a bad hour or so, sure enough. If I shouldn't be better by ten o'clock this morning, you must look out for Mrs. Tenterden with the new medicine. She expected to be up from the village by that time. And be sure you understand the directions she will give you. However, I shall have to be up, anyway, for no one but I can follow out the directions even when they are known. So call me when she comes, Nikomis."

But it so happened that Mrs. Tenterden did not arrive at the expected hour. On reaching the Danvers' cottage the night previous, she had gone to bed complaining of indisposition, and declaring that she believed she had caught the fever at last, and only wondered she had not done so long before. Elinor, after some examination, was pretty well satisfied that the matter was not quite so serious as the elder lady supposed, and the sequel justified her diagnosis. Nevertheless, Mrs. Tenterden contrived to pass a tolerably bad night, and by morning it was a settled thing that she must keep her bed during the day.

"If anybody could take my place!" complained she. "But that's the worst of it. Poor Mr. Urmson's as sick as can be himself, but he and I together might manage; but he can do nothing alone. There's Golightley gone over to Brunswick to see that Professor Grindle; but he'd be no good, anyway. It's no use, the poor young man must die, and that's all about it. I declare, Nellie, I shouldn't be surprised if I died myself. You've no idea how sick I am!"

The breach between these two had till now remained unhealed; but the presence of disease and worry seemed to influence the kind old lady to forgive and forget, and Elinor was disposed to meet the hand of reconciliation half-way. She had never felt so alone as during these latter days—not even when her father and mother lay dying in Charleston, and she knew not where to find a home beyond their grave. It is not reverent nor necessary to inquire too closely what thoughts and impulses, what resolves and fears, had visited her in the cheerless period of her late solitude. Their only outward effect upon Elinor was to render her unusually gentle and forbearing, as one might be

who had secretly determined on making a long journey, and wished to leave tender recollections in the hearts of those she left behind.

"Couldn't you at least send some one to the house with the medicines, mother?" she asked. "Would not Mrs. Danver—or ought not Madge to go? If he were to die for want of some help that Madge might have given him, what would become of her? I think we have no right to prevent her from having a free choice about it, one way or the other. Shall I tell her?"

"Seems as if it would look rather hard to have him just dying up there, and she knowing nothing about it," groaned Mrs. Tenterden. "She can't do anything, though, and it would be just tempting Providence to go into that house with the contagion. I know that to my cost. And it's more apt a great deal to catch young people than old ones. Besides, it was I prevented Madge from going when she wanted to at first, and there's really no more reason for it now. Poor young man! I wish he was in better hands. Of course, Mr. Urmson is very kind and careful, but he really doesn't seem to care much about him; I'm sures he smiles and makes jokes as if he expected him to be well to-morrow. And the poor young man has got something twisted round his neck. Nikomis says he's had it there ever since the first morning; anyway, it's twisted so tight that I wouldn't be surprised to hear he'd strangled himself with it at any time."

"Why isn't it taken off?"

"Yes, you don't know, my dear. It would be as much as anybody's life was worth to take it off. Of course, it can't be untied, and if you were to use a pair of scissors or a knife, it would be the death of one or both of you. I tell you he's as jealous of it as if it were some great treasure. I thought," added Mrs. Tenterden, chuckling faintly, in spite of her general misery, "maybe it was something of Madge's she'd given him, and he remembered was hers all through his delirium, poor boy."

"What was it?—a handkerchief, or a scarf—"

"Mercy, child, I don't know," said Mrs. Tenterden, rolling over on the pillow. "I didn't see distinctly. It looked gray and silky. Maybe it was a scarf, or an old veil, or something. But you mark my words, if he don't strangle himself if it isn't taken away from him."

Elinor felt her heart beating and her hands growing cold. She walked to the window and looked out, trying to quiet herself. But she could not be quiet. She walked back to the bedside. Mrs. Tenterden, with her back turned, seemed to have fallen into a doze. After a moment's hesitation Elinor went softly out of the room, and, running down-stairs, entered the kitchen.

"Mother won't be able to go up to the house to-day, Mrs. Danver," she said. "There is some medicine which should be taken there immediately. Will Madge go with it?"

"Well, Miss Golightley, I suppose likely the child would take it, and gladly," Mrs. Danver replied, speaking with hesitation, however, and avoiding Elinor's eyes. "To be sure, it has seemed as though folks was working to keep 'em apart, and those who hadn't so much call was taking her place. It's not for me to speak, and . Garth he's near to me as my own son, goodness knows, though I do think he might have been a little more spry, and not have kept my poor girl waiting while he was painting his pictures and living in Europe, and not making much out of the business, either, if 'one might say so."

"She won't go, then?"

"Really, well, I don't see any call to be so sudden, Miss Golightley," said Mrs. Danver, panting. "I'm sure there's a good long time gone by, and nobody thought of asking her whether she'd go or not. Not but the child would go, and gladly, if it hadn't seemed as if folks was keeping her away. But now I think of it, miss, I don't know where Maggie is just at the present. She went out about an hour since without dropping a syllable, and when she'll be back is more than I can say. Likely she's run up to the house without waiting for an asking. I couldn't say."

"And you yourself could not leave the house, I suppose?"

"Well, really, miss, you come so sudden. I'm sure I'd go, and gladly, and have gone any time the last three weeks, but Mrs. Tenterden seemed to think it belonged to her, being a relation, I presume, and it wasn't for me to speak. But I'm such an invalid, and my hip comes on so badly these last cold days. Though if Mr. Stacy could lend his wagon, perhaps I might. I'm sure I care for Garth dearly as my own son, though it . seemed hard of him to keep Maggie waiting so long."

"Don't you think it would be better for me to find some one to take up the medicine, without need of your troubling yourself about Mr. Stacy's wagon?" suggested Elinor, involuntarily putting her hand over her heart. "No doubt one of the village boys would be glad to run up with it. You might be within call of Mrs. Tenterden, if she were to need anything while I'm away. Will that do?"

Mrs. Danver seemed to think there were no insurmountable objections, and Elinor returned up-stairs, trembling, but glad in a subdued, exalted way. She hastily put on her hat and warm winter jacket, scarlet, with lining of soft, gray fur, and then noiselessly reëntered Mrs. Tenterden's chamber. The packet of medicine was lying on the table, and she put it in her pocket. She stepped up to the bed, and, bending over the sleeping woman, lightly kissed her on the cheek. She started down the stairs, but, before reaching the landing, she returned in obedience to a sudden impulse, and, going to her violin-case, took out her instrument and bow, and slipping them underneath her jacket, finally left the house.

CHAPTER LIV.

A SOPHIST.

WITHOUT wasting any time in making inquiries after errand-boys, she struck off from the village, and took her way swiftly toward Urmhurst. She walked with her eyes on the ground, wholly preoccupied, but there were a freedom and good-will in her motion which showed that she was going whither her deepest inclination led her. And, now that the Rubicon of her purpose was safely

overpassed, and there were no more obstacles or hesitations in her way, her heart
moved at ease, her fingers were warm, her
breathing quiet, and her cheeks slightly
tinged with pink. A man in her place
would have been grave and stern, or astir
with nervous anxiety; but Elinor was
sweetly conscious of an inward lightness and
satisfaction, contrasting with the gloom of
the past weeks as a summer day with a winter night. An older woman, or one who
tasted the sweet and bitter flavors of life
with less intense an appreciation, might
have lent an ear to the demurs of conscience, questioning her right to put health
and life in jeopardy by interference in matters which concerned other persons (from
the social point of view at least) more nearly
than herself. But it must be confessed that
Elinor made little account of conscience
when conscience came in collision with emotion. She trusted her intuitions, being unable to believe that what they seemed to
justify could be other than right; and a
young woman's intuitions are simply the
voice of her heart. Elinor's heart would
doubtless never suffer her to do anything
unwomanly or base, however far it might
occasionally lead her from the path of orthodox morality; but her example is none
the less indefensible, until all young women
shall have hearts as pure and upright as hers,
and a great deal calmer and wiser.

At the time when the events of which
this history treats took place, the disease
called typhoid fever was popularly believed
to be contagious. Probably not a few country doctors, a quarter of a century ago, were
more or less partakers of the current delu-
sion, and it is not to be wondered at if un-
professional persons believed in it. As for
Elinor, she never entertained a doubt upon
the subject; indeed, her persuasion as to
this point had not a little to do with the
strangely gladsome sense of exaltation and
relief wherewith she had embarked on her
present enterprise. It is not enough to
say that she fancied she was about to imperil her life; it must be added that she
faced the supposed danger rather as courting
than braving it. During her dark hours we
may imagine her to have thought, on some

girlish insufficient ground or other, that life
was not so desirable a thing as it was generally credited with being. When such a notion had once gained possession of her, she
would not be long without an occasion for
humoring it. Some array of circumstances
would be sure to arise—romantic, pathetic,
peculiar—fatally enticing her to take her
fate in her own hands, and seeming to justify her in the deed. To welcome death,
when it lies in the path of love, of despair,
or of womanly self-devotion, is not the infirmity of ignoble minds; the subtile selfishness and irreverence which underlie it escape
the eye of the person most concerned,
though they be revealed to the disinterested
critic. And Providence, being perhaps as
wise and just as most of us, may sometimes
take such wanderers under its especial protection, and either forgive their error or
gently prevent their attainment of the end at
which they so crudely aimed.

It was scarcely ten o'clock when Elinor
set her slim foot upon the threshold-stone
of Urmhurst, and knocked at the great
green door. Upon twice repeating the summons, and obtaining no response from within, she turned the latch and stepped into
the broad, dark hall. The kitchen-door was
ajar, and, peeping through, she saw a fire
burning in the fireplace, and for a moment
fancied she heard a step in the passage-way
at the farther extremity of the great room;
but, after listening awhile in vain for any
repetition of the sound, or for any other
signs of a human being, she went up-stairs
without further ceremony. It was not until
she had reached the upper floor that she met
Nikomis, coming out of Cuthbert's chamber.

The old Indian's face was as inscrutable
as usual, but she stopped short on seeing
Elinor, and uttered a grunt of inquiry. She
had evidently expected to meet some one
else, and waited for an explanation. Elinor,
who had never felt so serenely uplifted in
spirit as now, or so instinct with all the
tender potency of womanhood, spoke briefly
of Mrs. Tenterden's indisposition, and of her
own purpose to take that lady's place for
the time being. "Is Mr. Urmson with his
son?" she added. "I should like to see
him first."

Nikomis fixed her small black eyes upon the girl, as if to find out what sort of stuff she was made of; and Elinor met her glance with an inspiration of curiosity on her own part. These two women, though they had often before been in each other's company, had never till now happened to think of taking each other's measure. But at a moment like this some such mutual inspection was natural and inevitable. Are you like me, or different from me? Have you good for my good, or evil for my evil? These are the unspoken questions which eye asks of eye. Persons of the same race and general condition may read the answers with comparatively little difficulty; but, when the new comes in contact with the old, the invader with the aboriginal, civilization with savagery, then does the inquiry become complicated.

The Indian might, indeed, perceive at the first glance that Elinor was of a refined and straightforward nature; but she would wish to probe her more deeply than this before admitting her to favor and confidence. Elinor, however, had in Nikomis a problem that might have posed anybody.

"Cuthbert very bad," said the old witch, in answer to Elinor's inquiry. "You can see him 'f you like—in there." She motioned with her head toward the chamber.

Elinor passed before her and went in. A slender, gray-haired figure in a brown dressing-gown was lying on the bed, with one hand over its breast, its eyes closed, and its face entirely colorless. Elinor went close up to it, but could perceive no motion or sign of life. There was a peculiar, faint odor in the room, which the young lady instinctively disliked to breathe. After a few moments a tingling, numbing sensation seemed to creep through her body from head to foot, and she felt, with a fluttering of the heart, that the form which she looked upon would not respond were she to touch or speak to it. She stilled her own breathing in order to see whether the body breathed; but it lay awfully still. She now became aware that Nikomis was standing just behind her, and, with a shock, the thought entered her mind that perhaps this grim, inscrutable old savage had dealt foully

with the lives committed to her charge. She recollected hearing certain things from time to time about Nikomis, which hitherto she had disregarded or taken in jest, but which now sharpened her suspicions. It seemed more than probable that Nikomis had had motives to crime, and had waited so many years only for fit opportunity: and what opportunity could have been more fitting than this? The horror of the situation so wrought upon Elinor as to lift her above the region of selfish fear. She did not think of herself at all, save as a voice and instrument of retribution. She looked round upon Nikomis, who stood dark and portentous at the foot of the bed, and, at the same time, grasped with one hand the sleeve of the prostrate figure's garment, as though at once protecting and seeking protection from the dead.

"Have you done this?" she asked.

The Indian's eyes glittered, and she threw up one arm above her head: there was in the gesture a revelation of savage and untamed power. The wild, lawless strain, usually concealed beneath her stoical exterior, seemed now on the verge of breaking forth. The furrows about her mouth and forehead, and the harsh, stern features, bore witness to the cruel and inhuman deeds told of her race.

"What you do here?" she demanded, in an imperious, guttural voice. "Nikomis belong here. Garth, Cuthbert, Urmhurst—all mine."

"They are not yours. They are mine—for I love them!" Elinor exclaimed, her slender figure seeming for the moment to dilate and heighten. She wore an expression impressive to see on the face of a girl. Suddenly, she came forward and stood so close to the Indian as almost to touch her. The latter's eyes blinked under so near and passionate a scrutiny. Some time passed—it might have been half a minute—before Elinor spoke, in a new tone, from which the unnatural huskiness had vanished. "You were not so wicked—you have not done it," she said.

Nikomis made no reply.

But Elinor returned to Cuthbert, and, bending over him, laid her delicate cheek beside his. It was not so warm as her own, but it was not cold; and presently a barely perceptible movement of breath whispered past her ear. She rose, smiling and tremulous from the recoil of passion. "O Nikomis, he isn't dead," said she. "What is it?—you have given him an opiate to make him sleep! I am always distrusting and wronging people." She spoke with her eyes full of tears.

Nikomis turned sullenly away. Did the strange old creature really half regret not having been so criminally revengeful as Elinor had fancied her? Certainly, if she had come to Urmhurst with the intention of paying off on its occupants the ancient grudge of her tribe, she had good grounds for feeling dissatisfied with herself. As an Indian, the inheritor of a traditional policy of retribution, she had not acted up to what was expected of her; and she was not to be consoled by imputations of charity and forgiveness. Elinor's suspicion had perhaps suggested to her the idea of masquerading for a while in the guise of a wickedness not actually her own, and thus stealing credit for that which she had lacked gall to make a reality.

The girl now took up her violin and bow, which she had put down on the bed, and repaired to Garth's chamber. There lay he with whom her thoughts had dwelt much of late. Mrs. Tenterden's account of him had not prepared her for such a spectacle of helplessness and decay. A feeling of sharp distress made her mouth quiver, and contracted the lower lids of her eyes. But, again, he was alive, and evidently had received every care of which the case admitted. The bed and the room were spotlessly neat and fresh. Garth was lying with his haggard face turned sideways on the pillow, his eyes dull and partly closed, an intermittent, unintelligible muttering moving his unshaven lips. The fingers of one hand were fumbling strengthlessly at a gray twist of silky material which tightly encircled his neck. Elinor knew her veil at once. She drew nearer, and stood between the sick man and the light; but he muttered on as before, and did not seem to notice her.

At this juncture she became conscious of a profound change which had taken place within herself during the last few minutes. She had set out for Urmhurst believing that she was about to imperil her life, and meaning to make that peril as inevitable as she might. But the searching though rapid experience she had passed through since her arrival had put her in a new mood; and she now recognized the unworthiness of her former one. She had pictured herself ministering to Garth, and winning him back to life at the same moment that she herself declined from it. Whether he lived or died, life would be equally a blank to her; but she could imagine a happiness in dying with the thought that but for her he might have died also. She had seen herself loosening the veil from his neck, and drawing it, poisoned as it was, across her face, pressing it to her lips, and at night folding it in her bosom. In the morning she would awake to a dreamy languor, which again should lapse into the fever that by sure and fatal degrees must bring her toward her death. Each friend who had cared for her should have a word—a token of remembrance. Garth Urmson would not be among those friends; but Golightley should have something—her violin, perhaps—which might utter to his ear in harmonious chords all that its mistress would fain have felt for him, but could not. But Garth would expect nothing from her; he did not care for her; it was with a quaint, grave pleasure that Elinor told herself this. And he was nothing to her—save in so far as he had made all other men and women in the world less than nothing. By no earthly possibility could they ever have become anything to each other. Nevertheless, she had learned from him one thing—that God had not seen fit to make the man with whom she could have been happy. For, had such a man existed, he would have looked like Garth, and spoken as he did, and shown like traits of temper and disposition; and still would have been some other than he. But since it was evident that no man who was thus at once Garth and not Garth could exist, the unavoidable inference was that she, Elinor, was out of place in this world. They were nothing to each other; yet through him she had acquired the conception of an ideal man. For that she thanked him; and was content to acknowledge the obligation by spending a healing, fatal hour at his bedside.

To some such effect had Elinor communed with herself while on the way to Urmhurst. But, since entering there, her mind was changed. She had till then viewed her purpose mainly from the imaginative and, as it were, æsthetic side; but afterward she had found herself in the grasp of appalling realities. She had been made to know that the death which comes not in the strict course of nature is a hateful thing, and that those who inflict it, whether upon themselves or others, are abominable before God and man. Elinor was perhaps more apt than the generality of people to do right when once she had clearly convinced herself what right was. She perceived that the romantic circumstances wherewith she had ornamented her intention were a mushroom growth of false and unwholesome sentiment; and, when these were stripped away, the thing which they had masked stood forth in frank and naked ugliness—cowardly self-murder, neither more nor less. Elinor blushed, as at a suggestion immodest and indelicate. She faced life again; and if she saw nothing pleasanter therein than heretofore, she had at least the sad satisfaction of knowing that there was no honorable alternative against it. But, indeed, at this moment, by a kind of instinctive wisdom, she forbore to dwell upon the future at all, and looked only to the duties immediately in hand.

The situation in its new aspect was not without its perplexities; for, though her mind was changed, her peril from the supposed contagion remained unaltered, or nearly so. To leave the house without having done what she could for the invalid was out of the question; but, though she might take every precaution, only the mercy of Providence could secure her from harm. Thinking this, Elinor was moved to do something which not every young lady of her age and experience of life would have deemed it worth while to do. She left the bedside, and, walking to the window, knelt down there and clasped her hands on the broad low sill, and turned her face toward the cloud-flecked sky, as a child might have done; for there was a precious element of childlikeness at the core of her grave, reserved, and haughty appearance. She said no words, but simply opened the petals of her heart, and willed that the living God in whom she believed should see into it, and do his pleasure with her. Anon she rose and looked round with a downcast timorousness that would have surprised persons who had only met Miss Golightley in society.

But no one had seen her, and in a few moments she took her place in the world with renewed confidence. The dreamy exaltation of the earlier morning had passed away; so, too, had the violent revulsions of feeling which had followed it; and now she felt both inspired and practical, as those do who have been able to pray earnestly and unreservedly. She took the medicine-box, and in a skillful and self-possessed manner proceeded to administer the prescriptions, and otherwise carry out the instructions which the doctor had given. She had the power of self-concentration, and in fact could not help becoming so utterly absorbed in anything that interested her as to be blind, deaf, and dumb, for the time being, to everything else. It would have charmed a physician, amused Cuthbert, and scandalized Mrs. Tenterden, could they have seen this cold-mannered, fastidious young lady busy with her whole soul in care of the unconscious invalid, herself more unconscious than he, pink and serious of face, light and effective of hand. She did not remember Garth, until she had done with him. Few men (in a like position) could so completely have sunk the what they were in what they did.

By-and-by she drew breath and paused, and the patient became a person once more. He had taken his treatment so unresistingly thus far that Elinor thought she might achieve the second part of her mission (which was to relieve him of that silken necklace that he had come by so unaccountably) as readily as the first. Accordingly, though now with some little hesitation and shrinking, because the wearer of the necklace was at this moment less a convenient parcel of impersonal symptoms than a personal and inconvenient Garth, she bent over him anew, and began with wariest fingers to search for the knot. But immediately, and as if he had known what was intended, the invalid moaned and feebly bestirred himself, obstructing as best he might Elinor's already timid efforts. She was not long in coming to the conclusion that nothing could be done while he remained in that crossgrained condition; but neither was she so infirm of purpose as to yield until a certain original expedient of her own had received fair trial. The idea might or might not be worth anything; it had occurred to the young musician without premeditation just before leaving the Danvers cottage; at all events, she was disposed to put faith in it. Should it succeed, there would be for her a poetical beauty in the success which would render it doubly dear.

CHAPTER LV.

A QUACK.

SHE took her violin and retired again to the broad window-sill; for Elinor always liked to be within hail, as it were, of the sky when she was doing anything that involved the deeper energies of her nature; and, after a little musing over the strings, she began to play. At first she kept her eyes toward Garth, to mark the effect upon him; but as the music grew upon her, she surrendered herself to it, and heeded only the harmonious visions which her bow created. The chamber sang with wholesome melody; within the sphere of such fresh sounds it seemed impossible that any wrong or infirmity should exist. The discord of disease must surely be silenced and brought to health at the command of chords so finely potent and inspiriting. The knotted and disordered fibres must relax and gently reassume their right arrangement; the fever and the anguish must slink away, powerless to hold out against the sane and attempered onset of measured strains and tuneful cadences. That which is beautiful, in a word, must prevail over that which is opposed to beauty; and

no kind of beauty so inwardly and vigorously affects the condition of most people as the beauty of sound. Garth, as Elinor knew, was peculiarly susceptible to musical impressions, and she believed it within her power to unlock the sinister distemper of his brain and body with the golden keys of harmony. Possibly, too, she counted somewhat upon a vein of personal sympathy on the æsthetic side between her and him, existing despite their incompatibility at other points—a sympathy enabling her to choose such concords as should medicine him best, and him to employ their virtues to the utmost. A person with less reverence for her art than Elinor might have dallied with so novel a project, but would have lacked the childlike confidence and constancy actually to attempt it. To Elinor, however, the divine efficacy of music was not questionable, and, if she felt a doubt, it was only as to her own ability to do rightly what could be done.

To look upon music as one of the healing arts, if it be a heresy, is, after all, entitled to respect on the score of its primitive antiquity; and no doubt Elinor was quite enough of a classical scholar to have read the story of Orpheus, and drawn her own conclusions from it. I have called her idea original, and in its practical and particular application it was so; but most probably its germs had long been present in her mind, biding their time to blossom into definite form. Nor can I venture, in face of the magic doings of modern science, to deny its power so to analyze disease and melody as to match one against the other on definite fixed principles, and prescribe precisely the sort of tune most suitable to rheumatic cases, or pronounce what overture or symphony should be exhibited to sufferers from heart-disease or consumption. Beethoven, Bach, and Mendelssohn, would then be hailed as among the great physicians of humanity; every doctor would keep his violin or flute in the same case with his pills and ointment, or even exclude the latter altogether; and medical students would divide their time between thorough-bass, pathology, counterpoint, and physiology. Whether or not this dream be ever realized, to Elinor must belong the credit of having been bold and simple-hearted enough to apply the theory as well as to believe in it, without waiting for the tardy experiments of science. Boldness must not be left out of the account, especially if we regard the matter from Elinor's standpoint. Garth's life was at a low ebb, and whoever held the opinion that the right music would do him good, must also accept the risk of seeing him made worse by a wrong selection or a false accord. Yet Elinor's only guidance here was again her intuition.

Of false accords there certainly were none, and each fresh movement seemed to be a more subtile, persuasive, and unanswerable argument than the last, to forsake sickness and become sound and whole. Not a mere argument either, but a charm, able to effect that which it advocated. As she played on, feeling herself more and more at one with her instrument, a moment came, as once before at the picnic, when she seemed to herself to rise above the crabbed conditions of flesh and blood, and to address Garth immediately, in a comprehensive and transcendent utterance; and he and she seemed the only realities in a world of shadows. With this fantasy came a sense of the inadequacy of any hand-made medium—even of a violin—to transmit or interpret the all of what she meant; and forthwith she relinquished it, as one forgets a thing outgrown, and merged, like a blackbird weary of its artificial accomplishments, into a full tide of native song. Now at last she knew herself at the height of her power, and did not think of doubt or failure. She journeyed on through happy realms of melody, at ease, untrammeled, and secure. Garth the invalid, gaunt, feverish, and feeble, had vanished from her apprehension; he was well again, with activities and capacities larger than before, at once the reader and the inspirer of her harmonies. Perhaps it is unwise to attempt to paraphrase in words the strange, unconditional vagaries of a young woman's musical ecstasy. The best success can be but an obscure suggestion, which the charitable imagination of some few of the initiates may enable them to supplement. Be it rather said in simplest speech, therefore, that Elinor sang her fill, and stopped: and suddenly the ecstasy was gone, and the room

13

and the invalid and the singer quivered back like a smitten harp-string into the unresponsive, staid rigidity of common life. The singer slid from the window-sill to her feet, and pressed the tips of her fingers to her temples, as though bewilderment were throbbing there. Presently she looked up, smiled, sighed, and anon slowly approached the bed, with a shy inspection of the bony, unshorn visage that was reposing on the pillow.

Garth's eyes were open, and for the first time Elinor saw in them a steady and intelligent light. Decidedly there was an improvement, though whether due to the doctor's remedies or to the musician's, the latter troubled not herself to inquire. She stood still for a minute or two while he looked at her and accustomed himself to the idea of her presence. There was no wonder in his regard—he had been brought too near the verge of life for that; it was a far-off gaze of solemn contentment; hardly the gaze of a living, material man, but suggesting the notion that a departed spirit had come back to earth for a moment, and was glancing at this life through the windows it had been wont to use while in the body. Elinor was slow to speak, lest it should vanish, after the manner of departed spirits, upon being addressed. At length, however, it seemed natural to say, in a subdued, fluent tone, as though they had previously been conversing together:

"You will feel better after I have taken the veil off your throat."

There was a long pause, as if the spirit were essaying to incarnate itself once more, and found some difficulty in making use of its fleshly instrument. Meantime the eyes kept up their look of inaccessible, contented gravity. Finally, after a trial or two, the voice came, slow, hushed, and intermittent:

"Yes. I—kept it—for you. It—came back to me—in—my dream."

Elinor also waited awhile before replying, not because her voice was sluggish, but from an idea that such a leisurely mode of talk would best suit his invalid condition. "I shall have to cut it," said she. "The knot is too tight."

She felt in her pocket for her penknife, and brought out along with it a pair of gloves, which, mindful of her new purpose to avoid contagion as much as possible, she proceeded to draw on. But by the time she was ready, Garth had found his tongue again. "No," said he, with the quiet, unreasoning perversity of a helpless man; "untie it."

Elinor knew better than to argue the point with him, and even fancied she understood something whimsically complimentary to herself in his unwillingness to let her veil be summarily dealt with. She put up her knife, therefore, and set to work with her gloved fingers upon the compact intricacies of the knot. Neither the light nor the position of things was favorable, and Elinor labored for some time, bending down her pure face close to Garth's without accomplishing much. All the while she was wondering with a still feeling about her heart, whether this idle whim of his would cost her her life, and, if it did, what he would think when he came to know it. Garth, for his part, was probably too near the balancing-point of existence to feel the same sensations as he would have felt in health; but the nearness of that face, with its lines as clear as flower-petals', could not but have been grateful to him. Meantime her gloved touch was doubtless more or less objectionable to him, and had speech been easy he might have remonstrated. As it was, he lay voiceless and motionless; and when at last Elinor conquered the knot and softly drew away the veil, he breathed an infantile sigh of satisfaction, which contrasted comically with the gaunt ruggedness of features that disease had made to look much older than before. His glance rested for a moment on the veil, which Elinor was now holding in her hands, uncertain what to do next; then, to her no small relief, his eyelids drooped and closed, and almost immediately he was deeply and serenely asleep.

She walked with a meditative step to the window, drawing the veil backward and forward through her fingers, and then unfolding it to its full breadth. It was wofully creased and soiled, and there were half a dozen rents in it. Needless to say, it could never be presentable as a veil again. Never-

theless, Elinor felt a strong, unmanageable desire to keep it, to treasure it, to hide it away in some place as near to her as remote from the rest of the world. Her former temptation came back to her, somewhat modified in kind, but even more urgent than at first. She leaned her shoulder and head against the window-frame, and looked out, folding her arms and crossing one foot over the other. The sun, half-way up the cold, blue sky, was steering his course through bevies of broken clouds, and Elinor's oddly attractive countenance, with its small nose, low, sharp-cut brows, high cheek-bones, and finely resolute mouth, was alternately lighted and shadowed by their flight. She leaned there many minutes, wholly rapt in serious musings. The bleak, wide landscape met her eyes, and may have rhymed with her mood, but she was not actively aware of it. It was the vision of her future that possessed her. How more than bleak it was! It did not seem possible to her, as a modest and honorable girl, to fulfill the destiny that awaited her. A month ago, ignorant of her own nature and capacities, in a fit of cynical, self-contemptuous passion, she had pledged her word and surrendered her lips, and had felt and said, "It can never be undone." The month—or was it the last hour? —had taught her so much that, were the past revocable, not all the world could have prevailed upon her so to dishonor herself again. But now, what relief was there? Life was full of such hasty errors and late regrets. If it were unwomanly to submit, to resist was despicable. There was only one escape, but, oh, how easy and alluring! —wrong, perhaps, but surely there were greater wrongs. What use and good were there in death, save as it was a refuge from life's fatigue and bitterness? Might not one say, "Let it come," and yet be pardonable?

It is vain to seek answers to these arguments; they are based upon appearances, and cannot be refuted from their own standpoint. Pagans cannot refute them at all; but, fortunately for the peace of Elinor's conscience, if not for the health of her body, she was not a pagan. When she had reached this crisis in her meditations, she stood erect, looking up, and twisting the veil into a ball between her hands. Grasping it tightly in one slender fist, she went to the fireplace and laid it carefully on the red-hot centre of the half-burned log. Afterward she pulled off her gloves and threw them in heedlessly among the ashes. She did not remain to watch the burning, nor stay in the room at all; but with a glance at Garth to assure herself that he was still sleeping, she passed out of the door, and, with the business-like air of a professional nurse, betook herself to Mr. Urmson's chamber.

He was lying much as Elinor had left him; but, after observing him for a while, she was of opinion that the effect of the opiate was wearing off, and that he must soon awake. She sat down beside him in a low, leather-covered easy-chair, leaning back her head and folding her hands in her lap. Now that she had come to a stopping-place in her morning's labors, she began to realize how greatly they had exhausted her. Her body felt as weary as her mind; but the fatigue was not of a painful sort, but such as made repose a luxury. She wished she might sit in that comfortable chair for a whole year, with nothing to think of, and nothing to do.

Had she been in a less worn-out condition, the revelation of Mr. Urmson's ill case must have kept her thoughts busy. She had known him to be in delicate health, but had thought of nothing worse than the rheumatism, neuralgia, and dyspepsia, to which any gentleman of his age and habits of life might be subject. His habitually composed and cheerful air had seemed inconsistent with the presence of any acute disease; and Elinor, in common with most other people, had too much enjoyed the playful humor, which derived an added charm from his bodily frailty, to ask much about his complaints. But as he now lay pallid and unconscious, without the power to beguile or parry the observer's eye, the lines of suffering worn into his face showed very distinct, and the fact that they could ever have been kept in the background seemed more than ever strange. Elinor contemplated the refined, sharp-featured visage in a fit of dreamy preoccupation; but at length it occurred to her that a person so reserved as was this gentleman, and so sensitive to scrutiny, would be sadly discomposed at the idea of being stared at when the veil of his voluntary self-control was withdrawn. Therefore she chivalrously closed her eyes; and with the purpose in her mind to have an explanation with Mr. Urmson, so soon as he should awake, touching the nature of his malady, she quietly dropped asleep. Thus it happened that, in spite of the trouble which seemed a while ago so dominant at Urmhurst, a stranger entering unheralded would have been first of all struck by the prevalent tranquillity.

Minute after minute passed away, however, without the stranger making his appearance. Garth, in his chamber, was breathing his prosperous way through the first refreshing slumber that had come to him since the beginning of his illness. Cuthbert, by an occasional movement of the mouth and eyelids, or a slight change of posture, showed that ere long he would emerge from his stupor; but Elinor, whose face had the rare charm of looking more lovely in sleep than in awakening, dreamed as sweetly and profoundly as a baby in its cradle. These three might have passed for the sole occupants of the house. Nikomis, if she were within-doors at all, must have retired to her den in the garret; and we have no warrant for supposing the presence of any other person besides her. Nevertheless, had one of the three sleepers happened to wake up and listen intently, a dull, intermittent sound might have been heard, as of voices conversing together in some corner remote from intrusion. Voices, was it? and not rather Nikomis humming to herself the burden of an Indian chant? or even the wind rumbling in the chimney and sighing hoarsely in the attic overhead?

However that might be, at all events there were none to listen. Sleep, which has something sacred in it, and through which mankind pass from one day to another, and from the old to the new, and from darkness into light, and from weariness to refreshment—sleep brooded over these three harassed persons, and perhaps brought them visions of a serener state of things to come.

So sound was their repose, it would have needed more than a distant murmur of voices, or the complaining of the wind, to have aroused the least rapt among them. They had surrendered their own self-guardianship, and lay helpless and exposed to whatever danger menaced them. But angels, it has been said, watch with especial jealousy over those who sleep, and perhaps the most fortunate thing that can happen to the unfortunate is to sink down in unconscious slumber at the moment when they have done whatever they could do, in vain.

The sun had passed the highest point that he would attain that day, before this peaceful condition of affairs seemed likely to be disturbed. But soon after noon there was an alert, firm step upon the threshold of Urmhurst, and a brisk knocking at the door. The knock, like Elinor's earlier in the day, was unanswered, though the murmurs of the wind in the chimney seemed to have been startled into silence by it. Like hers, it was presently repeated, more emphatically than at first; but, albeit the sharp echoes traveled through the old house from top to bottom, visiting every darksome nook and corner, and even finding their way into Garth's long-neglected studio, where the tragic picture of Lady Eleanor's wedding stood dusty on the easel, no one came forward to open the door and give the visitor, whoever he might be, a hospitable Urmson welcome. Cuthbert, indeed, sighed uneasily, and half opened his eyes for a moment; but no one else stirred; and Nikomis, if she were not asleep as well as the rest, was strangely neglectful of her duties. By-and-by the visitor, who seemed to be of a bold and impatient disposition, threw the door open, entered, and closed it again with a reverberating bang. He paused a moment in the hall, and then began an exploration of the rooms on the lower floor. Finding nothing there, he bounded up-stairs with the light activity of youth, and, after another short pause at the top to listen, he turned to the right, and walked directly into the room where Mr. Urmson and Elinor were reposing.

CHAPTER LVI.

AWAKENING.

On seeing the sleepers the young stranger doffed his hat, and holding it against his hip, stopped short, and ejaculated below his breath, "Deuce!" Presently he came forward, stepping lightly, a rather quizzical smile stirring the corners of his golden-brown mustache. He halted again in front of Elinor's chair, and looked down upon her with the full glance of a pair of bright hazel eyes. His smile gradually forgot itself in a more tender and wistful expression. Then a sudden resolve flashed into his face; he stooped quickly but gently, and, for half an instant, his mustache touched a little brown mole upon the upper part of the young lady's else immaculate cheek. She received the salute with disconcerting equanimity. Had her admirer been a fly she could not more superbly have ignored the liberty. Her serene eyelids quivered not, nor did the faint color deepen in her face. Indeed, the young man looked much the more disturbed of the two.

"It was a devilish contemptible action!" he murmured to himself. "By the saints, though, I've a mind to do it again!"

But a low voice behind him said, "Wait, young gentleman. That lady is private property."

He turned with a start. Mr. Urmson was awake, and was eying him with an aspect partaking, after all, rather of perplexity and inquiry than of severity. The stranger immediately approached the bedside, and took the elder's thin hand in his own warm, white one. "Selwyn—you remember me?—old Garth's Jack," said he, speaking with a touch of embarrassment, but frankly and heartily. "I took this for the Sleeping Palace in the fairy-book; and when I came on the Beauty here, I imagined myself the Prince, predestined, you know—But something must be the matter, Mr. Urmson? Anybody ill?"

"Garth is ill," replied the other, raising himself on his elbow and drawing his brows together in the effort to collect his ideas. "You haven't seen Mrs. Tenterden? How long has— Do you know how this young lady came to be here?"

"My good luck must have had something to do with bringing her, I should think; but doesn't she belong here? I landed in Boston only day before yesterday, and came right on. Seen nobody but you, and know nothing. Old Garth—he ill!"

"I'm afraid Nikomis has been giving me one of her famous herbal distillations," said Mr. Urmson. "Excuse my not sitting up just yet—I'm none the less glad to see you, Jack. What's the news? You look well; growing older seems to have done you more good than it has the rest of us. Garth got your letter; but he lost it again the same day, and has had typhoid ever since."

"Devil!" rejoined Selwyn, sympathetically. "And you and Mrs. Mildred been nursing him? Poor old genius! Don't you think, though, he needed something of the sort to thin him a little? he was such an infernally heavy lump, mind and body, he couldn't budge himself nor be budged. Terrible fellow for slumping into holes and crawling in grooves! But about the letter, Mr. Urmson," continued the young man, drawing a chair to the bedside and seating himself. "Garth read it you, didn't he?"

"Suppose you turn your back to Miss Golightley; you'll be less apt to awaken her," said Mr. Urmson, a little maliciously. "Besides, I want to look at you, Jack. So you are turned detective? Speak low."

"I like to match my head against a clever rogue's; but— Oh, I'm no detective myself. I hit upon a lucky suggestion or two that put my dogs on the scent, but—"

"Why, what was it to you whether Mrs. Tenterden got back her money or not?"

Jack dropped his eyes with a half-smile, but raised them again immediately. "If you hadn't waked up just when you did, I might have lied to you about that," said he. "Well; I may never be able to kiss her again; but I shouldn't have done it at all if I hadn't meant to try and get leave to do it all the rest of my life, Mr. Urmson."

"In that fairy-tale, if I remember aright, the Beauty was awakened by the kiss of the true Prince. Miss Golightley seems to be still asleep. I fear the omen's a bad one for you."

"Omens be damned!—or no, I beg pardon; been trying to break myself of that habit since— I'll risk my chance with the other fellows."

"She is already engaged to be married," Mr. Urmson continued.

Selwyn's face seemed to grow older; he leaned forward on his knee, biting his lip; took his breath to speak, but let it forth again in a short sigh. "Garth, I suppose," he said at length. "Dear old fellow, I'm glad it's he!"   •

"It's a yet more eligible match than that —Mr. Golightley Urmson."

The blood flew into the young man's face, and he sat up erect, as if he had been pricked with a lancet. "Then," exclaimed he, smiting his knee with his clinched hand, "he'll never marry her!"

"Why not?" inquired Mr. Urmson, gravely. Jack was forced to recollect himself.

"That's the second time you've seen me make a fool of myself. I had no business to make any such assertion. I don't happen to like your brother—your half-brother, Mr. Urmson. Miss Golightley will marry whom she likes, of course. Well, I'm glad I didn't know it before. Are you fond of your half-brother?"

"Why, I wish him well. We have always been on the best terms."

"He's staying with you, I suppose?"

"He took a room in the village while Garth is ill. At present he's in Brunswick, to get an old acquaintance of yours, Professor Grindle, down here."

"Old Grindle—how he used to 'dead' me! But he'll put life into Garth, if anybody can. But Garth's not one of the dying kind; he'll live till he's tired of it. I want to see him. Where is he?"

"He was in this world at five o'clock this morning; but his stay seems rather uncertain, in spite of what you say, Jack. We'll go in as soon as I get my house-legs on again. If you have any business to talk, though, you had better trust me. Garth has been delirious for the last two or three weeks."

"Poor old Garth—dear fellow! I do

hope he won't die, Mr. Urmson," said Jack, his voice husky with earnestness, and his sensitive face darkening. "I'm just like a woman about him--always have been since a shaking he gave me in college. But I know he won't die. Think of having her to take care of him! By—Jove, if I were Golightley, I'd keep her out of the way! Unless— Is that Danver affair on still?"

"It was when he caught the fever, I believe; but the shadow of death may hold such matters in abeyance for a while," answered Mr. Urmson, with the glimmer of a smile. "Yes, Jack, if you came here for love, methinks you are too late."

Jack tossed his head. "Well, business first, and love afterward, Mr. Urmson. I haven't told you about our success with the thieves. To begin with, we haven't got either of them, and we have found out that one of them has spent most of his share of the money."

"Oh! then there are two of them? Do you know who they are?"

"We know who one of them is, and I have my suspicions of the other, though my detectives don't know that I have yet. We followed the first one to Liverpool, and there lost sight of him. His name is Flint. We are pretty sure of coming upon him sooner or later, and then he will tell us how to get hold of the other one, who is the chief sinner, and an infernally clever fellow. The way they contrived the robbery it was almost worth the money they stole to see. And the other one managed so well that nothing short of Flint's evidence could convict him, even if we caught him."

"Who do you suspect him to be, Jack?" asked Mr. Urmson, taking pains to meet the young man's eyes with his own penetrating glance. "From your letter, it should be some one in this neighborhood. Is it any one I am likely to know?"

Selwyn caught up his knee and set his hat upon it; the hat fell to the floor, and he stooped to pick it up. "Knowing is an ambiguous expression," said he, with a smile. "You might think you knew him, but, if he turned out a thief, you'd think you hadn't known him, after all. Anyway, though, it would be unbusiness-like of me to blab my

suspicions. They might be wrong, in the first place."

"But that's too unlikely a supposition, Jack. What in the second place?"

"You might receive and comfort him, Mr. Urmson," returned the other, smiling again. "You'd do that for a near friend or relative, wouldn't you? Most men would."

"I am not a bigot in the cause of human methods of justice," said the gray gentleman, holding his chin musingly between his thumb and forefinger. "I should probably let my action be guided a good deal by circumstances. However, your second supposition doesn't apply, either; for the only man of the kind for me is that poor half-brother of mine—your successful rival, young gentleman. He has lately been in Europe, you know, and has come back with some money. But a thief who should rob a lady for the sake of making himself an eligible match for her would be *sui generis*, to say the least of him."

"Well, I shall hold my tongue, or you will begin to think me a poor detective. If Golightley is to be the first villain, you'll say nobody short of Garth ought to play second. But, joking aside, I don't believe she can love him; and when it comes to the point, she won't marry a fellow she doesn't love."

As Jack made this assertion, he caught a peculiar expression in Mr. Urmson's face, such as caused him to turn abruptly in his chair. Elinor was still reclining in the same position, with her hands clasped in her lap, but her eyelids were unmistakably open, though still heavy with slumber. Jack rose at once and made his bow. His bow was somewhat noted in society for its easy grace, but this time it scarcely justified its reputation. His self-possession was impaired by the necessity for wondering how much of the late conversation the young lady had overheard, and by the attempt to recollect precisely in what words it had been couched.

"I only came in to tell you he was better, Mr. Urmson," said Elinor, sitting up and putting her hands to her hair. "I didn't know you were busy.—Mr. Selwyn! oh, I think I must have been asleep."

"It was my cursed bellowing waked you up; though I thought we were whispering,"

Jack interposed regretfully. "Is—a—Mrs. Tenterden well, I hope?"

"Oh, not at all! I left him asleep—Yes, she felt a little feverish this morning, so I came up with the medicine.—I hope my playing didn't disturb you, Mr. Urmson?"

"That spell which Nikomis wrought on me has left its influence in the air, I think," said he, looking pleasantly on the young lady's face, and making a determined effort to get up. "Everything you do and say is music, Miss Elinor, and would cure me of being old and good-for-nothing, if anything could. As for Garth, I don't wonder that he's better. Come on; let's all go in and have a look at him."

As he stood erect, the young people placed themselves on either side of him, each supporting an arm; and so they advanced, a well-united trio, toward the door. But at the same moment a lightsome step sounded along the passage-way, and a charming figure of womanly youth and grace, with high color and sparkling eyes, appeared at the threshold. The trio paused with one accord; but the new-comer, after a brief hesitation, just long enough to give the beauty of her presence its full effect, came straight up to Mr. Urmson and kissed him on the cheek. Elinor looked hard at her, and did not offer any greeting; but the other took her hand with a kind of joyous freedom, and said: "You dear Elinor, I've seen him! I dared come, because Mrs. Tenterden's in bed, and is not to know. How thin he is! but I like his beard—it looks like a pirate's."

Unless one positively hated Madge, it was nearly impossible to withstand the fresh onset of her glowing loveliness when she was bent upon being agreeable. All previous doubts and criticisms must for the moment forget or rebuke themselves; or it might even seem that such a woman was better worth believing in than any cut-and-dried distinctions between right and wrong. Elinor, who had studiously avoided associating with her since their conversation after church a fortnight previous, and had even indulged in unspoken disparagement of whatever she had seen her do or heard her say in the mean while, now felt a twinge of remorse—a misgiving lest, after all, she had misunderstood

and done her less than justice. For here stood Madge, where Elinor had uncharitably believed her afraid to come, and spoke of Garth in such tones as she surely durst not have used had she been indifferent to him—which Elinor had suspected her of being. The words were nothing; it was the loving tone that was unmistakable. On the whole, therefore, it seemed likely that poor Madge had really acted from the most lofty and disinterested motives up till to-day; and to-day, in breaking loose from her self-imposed restraint, she had betrayed just that trait of loving womanly weakness which made the charm of her character complete. So, not for the first time in her experience, Elinor found herself obliged to do homage to a virtue which her reason rather than her intuition acknowledged.

All this time Madge had paid no direct attention to Selwyn, though the corner of her long, oval eye had no difficulty in taking sidelong note of him. Jack, on the other hand, made little effort to disguise his admiration of Madge, whose developed beauty quite beggared his anticipation. "It's sad to be forgotten, Miss Danver," he said, with an independent toss of his head sideways; "but it seems I must remind you of your pirate's right-hand man—Jack Selwyn, at your service."

"Truly, I knew you very well, only I never thought you would remember me," returned Madge, naïvely giving him her hand. "I can never forget any one who loves my Garth."

Selwyn gave Madge a keen look, and before he let go her hand he pressed it gently, but so significantly as might justify her in supposing that he wished to establish a tender private understanding with her. Under the circumstances, it was an audacious act, to say the best of it; yet, with the perverse luck that seems so often to attend audacity, it met with no open rebuke. Madge, perhaps, thought the best way to discourage flirtation was not to make too prudish a resistance to it. At all events, she kept a demure countenance, and withdrew her soft fingers only in time to avoid attracting remark.

"Did you see Nikomis when you came

in?" asked Mr. Urmson. "I begin to think that Sam Kineo must have come back unexpectedly and carried her off."

"Oh, I don't think she expects him now," Madge hastened to say, veiling another side-glance at Selwyn beneath her dark lashes. "He doesn't care much for the poor old thing, I'm afraid; besides, it must be so much pleasanter to stay in Europe than to come back here."

"Sam Kineo—isn't that the fellow Garth thrashed?—Queer name, Mr. Urmson. And I remember a Mount Kineo, somewhere north of us, so called on account of the number of flint-stones found there. Probably Sam is a pretty hard case."

"You have a talent for analogies, Jack; but the world is full of flints," remarked Mr. Urmson, a little ironically. During their somewhat disconnected colloquy the group had been collected just within the doorway. As the old gentleman spoke, he drew Selwyn a few steps onward across the threshold, leaving the two girls behind. "We are forgetting Garth," he continued; "but we're too large a party to visit him all at once.— Madge, you might take Miss Elinor down to the kitchen, and fumigate yourselves in the chimney-corner.—Do you come with me, sir. I presume your cigar-case will be a sufficient protection to us both. Come along; and, after we've made our call, we'll rejoin the ladies by the kitchen-fire."

CHAPTER LVII.

A FRESH FACTOR.

THEY entered the sick-room accordingly, and shut the door behind them. Mr. Urmson approached the bedside, and, after touching Garth's pulse and laying his finger-tips on his forehead, he said, "Well," with a long sigh, and then below his breath, "God bless her!" The invalid breathed on in seemingly dreamless sleep. Selwyn, standing motionless and in silence, observed him for a long time, afterward walking moodily to the fireplace and leaning there, with his shoulders against the side of the chimney-piece

and his hands in his pockets. Mr. Urmson had taken a seat over against him.

"I had no idea of this," Jack said at length. "No mere fever has done that to Garth; there's been hell in his mind. And you may call me a fool if you like, Mr. Urmson, but I know one thing that's been the matter."

"Be as wise as you please; I sha'n't mind."

"Well, look here. I love Garth, and I don't care who knows it: that's one thing. And I know a cheat when I see it, no matter if it's as pretty as Madge Danver. I've seen women enough, good and bad, but never her equal, either for beauty or deviltry. If I were Mephistopheles and Caliban mixed half and half, there might be a chance of her getting suitably married. No wonder Garth got the fever!"

"I don't know your sources of information, but, judging by appearances, their engagement has been remarkable for the good faith and constancy shown on both sides."

"Good faith and constancy are life to scoundrels, but death to honest men. I don't pretend to fathom Madge Danver, but there's no mystery about Garth's share in the business. When we were in Europe together, Mr. Urmson, he lived like a man who felt that he was at his best and happiest, and knew there must soon be an end of it. But often, after we'd had a particularly fine time somewhere, and had got home again, he'd begin to tramp up and down the room, with that scowl of his, and his hands in his pockets, talking about Madge. By God, it was pitiable! He'd set his teeth, and growl out that she was the loveliest, sweetest, purest—that whatever good or great thing he did would be her doing—you can imagine the kind of stuff it was: always the same thing, and a lie from beginning to end. Once he came near killing me, for the second time in our acquaintance, because I told him he didn't care a damn for her, and knew it. He swore she was all he lived for, and that he had come to Europe only to make himself worthier of her. I told him I believed he lied, and then he took me by the throat. I hope I'll never get such another look as he gave me for a couple of seconds. If he'd only look that way at Madge once, I could almost believe she'd be true to him ever after; for she'd see that Garth had a bigger devil in him than she had. It wasn't two seconds before he let go of me, and put his hands down by his sides; but I'd made up my mind to be murdered, and almost wished he'd go on and finish me. Then I saw another thing I don't care to see again—I saw him cry. I never meant to tell this, Mr. Urmson. He's a terrible fellow."

Jack took a chair and sat down, fixing his eyes on the fire, his face moving with suppressed excitement. Mr. Urmson folded his arms, and was silent.

"At all events," Jack went on, advancing his chin and using a steadier tone, "that was the last I heard from him about Madge Danver. He went home some months afterward, and I must say I never imagined he'd find her faithful to him. But all I knew of her then was the glimpse or two I got of her before we started for Europe. She's clever enough to cheat with honesty. She has her own reasons for not letting him go till she's got her other strings in proper order."

"You have a clear head, Jack, and something better than that, maybe. I agree with you that Garth ought not to marry her. You know him well; but Madge you do not know. You have penetrated further than most people are able to do; you see the subtlety and perverted principles beneath the beauty and fascination, but you've taken no account of the goodness and sincerity that are mixed up along with them. That is what makes Madge hard to deal justly with. I have reason to believe that she has loved Garth at times as much as she can ever love anybody, and that she would rather love him than any other man. She might have married twenty times while Garth was abroad, and the reason she didn't was that she feared to find out, when it was too late, that Garth was her true match, after all. Her love seems to come and go like the tide; but, in fact, it is her opinion as to the identity of the man with her ideal of him that varies. She would be perfectly happy if Garth would assert himself so powerfully as to drive all doubt and wavering out of her

mind. She doesn't enjoy fickleness for its own sake."

"That's just what she does do, I say," interposed Selwyn. "What sort of an ideal has a girl like that got? What she likes is to feel the contact of a peremptory, masculine nature with her own. But she wouldn't be satisfied to find all the qualities she likes collected in one man. She'd rather have them distributed among half a dozen or a hundred, and so have the fun of going to a different man for the enjoyment of each quality. Fickleness is the breath of her life. I beg your pardon for disputing you, Mr. Urmson, but I believe what I say."

"I quite believe you believe it; but I'd rather be too lenient, Jack, than over-harsh; and maybe, when you have lived long enough to find out how little good the best-disposed people can do, you'll think lenient opinions the wiser."

"Yes, but no fellow can hoist himself by his own waistband. I take myself as I am; God only knows whether I'll ever be any wiser. Look here. When Madge first came in just now, she was as full of the devil as she could hold. She has been up to some mischief or other this morning. Garth had nothing to do with her coming. That sentimental talk about him was humbug, and—"

"How do you know that?" inquired Mr. Urmson, beginning to smile.

"Because in the next breath she encouraged me to make secret love to her. Yes, I'm set down for a place among the happy hundred already. Was there ever anything between this Sam Kineo and her?"

"There may have been; but Sam hasn't been in this part of the world for the last ten years or thereabouts, and I'll admit she may have been fickle enough to forget him."

"But she'd remember if she saw him. And what if she had seen him, and he were in the house at this moment?"

"And what if he should turn out to be the Mr. Flint whom you lost sight of at Liverpool—who, of course, is a half-breed Indian, known to have received letters directed in a feminine handwriting, and postmarked New Hampshire? That would be rather curious, in spite of its probability;"

and Mr. Urmson took his chin meditatively in his hand. Jack was not fully satisfied whether the other's mood were wholly ironic or partly earnest; but at all events he seemed to resolve, after a little consideration, to let that particular subject drop for the time being. There were several other questionable matters.

"How about this nursing, and medicine-bringing, and music-playing?" he demanded, rising to get the violin, and returning with it to his seat by the fire. "Yes, this is Miss Elinor's instrument. But how came she, and not Madge, to act as Mrs. Mildred's substitute?"

"That is one of the few things that I don't know. I was asleep. Madge, you will be gratified to hear, has not visited Garth at all until to-day. It seems strange that she and Elinor should have come separately and apparently in ignorance of each other. I must say I was more surprised to see Madge here than Miss Elinor."

"It's all cross-purposes now," said Jack, biting his under lip; "but there seem to be about as many good people as bad mixed up in it, so it ought to come out right in the end—as right as things in this world are likely to come.—There's somebody."

A wagon had driven up to the door, and there were voices in the hall below. The two men sat looking at each other, listening. Madge's voice, with its elastic rise and fall, soft and yet penetrating; the magniloquent superiority of Golightley's organ; and then a short, forcible rumble that caused a smile to chase away the pugnacious expression which had just darkened Selwyn's face, and Mr. Urmson to rise to his feet with a breath of relief. Professor Grindle!

"We'll meet them down-stairs," Mr. Urmson said, leading the way; and arm-in-arm they descended and entered the kitchen, whither the whole party had betaken itself.

"Ah, my dear Cuthbert, I got him, you see, in spite of the prince of the powers of Bowdoin and all his angels. But the dear boy's on the mending hand already—so our little Margaret tells me—and all Elinor's doing, eh? Ha! ha! H'm!"

This latter interjection, with an accompanying change of expression from gay to grave, was elicited by Jack Selwyn, whom Golightley had not till then happened to see. Feeling an authoritative tap on the shoulder, however, he turned his head, and had the sensation, which, whether agreeable or the reverse, was manifestly unexpected, of beholding within two feet of him a face he had supposed to be distant at least three thousand miles. Jack's hazel eyes seemed to find their way through Golightley's tinted glasses, and there was no avoiding a recognition. "Ah, you must be Selwyn—Jack Selwyn, I think. Let me see—studying law in Vienna, aren't you? How-d'y'-do?"

He held out an amicable, if somewhat patronizing, hand, which Jack looked at curiously, without moving his own from behind his back. "I keep an eye on the law," he said, while Golightley endeavored to ignore the rebuff by ostentatiously unbuttoning and removing his kid glove; "but speculation is my hobby just now. You ought to be able to give me a hint about South Americans, if any man can."

"Yes, I'm sure of that, Mr. Selwyn," said Madge, who had been observing the encounter of these gentlemen with an arch expression of mischief. She came up to Golightley as she spoke, and put her hand affectionately within his arm. "He made all his money in South Americans—didn't you, uncle? But then, you know, poor Mr. Tenterden lost all his in them; so you mustn't be too precipitate and positive, Mr. Selwyn.—Now you needn't laugh, Uncle Golightley, because you know you taught me those words yourself."

Uncle Golightley had not laughed, nor even betrayed an inclination to do so; but after Madge had spoken, he seemed to think it as well to draw back his mustache and wrinkle the corners of his eyes in what might have answered for a spasm of polite merriment. At this juncture Elinor came up and touched his other arm, with a gesture implying both reluctance and the determination to overcome it.

"Won't you have some lunch?" she asked. "We've been getting it ready, and you are come just in time. You must have something to tell me about your journey."

"My sweet Elinor!" he exclaimed, turning quickly and raising her hand to his lips. It was, perhaps, as honestly affectionate a salute as he had ever given a woman.

"Come, then," said she, blushing and drawing him away.

Jack looked after them rather blankly; but he bit his lip with chagrin on finding that his discomfiture was being secretly observed by Madge.

"They are ever so much in love with each other," she remarked, as soon as their eyes met. "Don't you think they will be very happy?"

"I think she ought to be," Jack replied, after a pause, solacing himself with the ambiguity of his phrase.

In fact, however, Madge must have been as much suprised as he that Elinor should so far break down the barriers of her maidenly and constitutional reserve as thus deliberately to seek out her lover. Only Elinor knew how, during the last few hours, she had sadly but resolutely bound herself to be to Golightley, in deed as already in word, all that a woman may be to a man. He, for his part, had herein a new experience before him, and one which, in the present aspect of his affairs, was likely to occasion him a good deal of unpremeditated emotion. For it should be said of him that if hitherto he had been practically a stranger to the more noble and unselfish kind of love, he had also never happened to meet with a woman at once capable of rendering him the like tender and refined observance, and willing to do so. For the present the change in her bearing flattered and titillated him only; but a time might come when it should influence him more importantly.

CHAPTER LVIII.

PICKLES AND CIGARETTES.

"LET us have luncheon, too," Madge proposed, with a dash of demure convivialism in her tone which made her appear delightfully jolly. "I know where there are some pickles, and I think maybe Nikomis

might let you have a little brandy. And then you'll smoke a cigar over me, won't you? so as to drive away the contagion."

"Contagion!" echoed Jack, as he followed his beautiful entertainer to the pantry. "Everybody here seems to think typhoid contagious. It's nothing of the sort."

"Oh, isn't it? How clever you are! Well, I don't care whether it is or not, for I know I shall never die of a fever. That's the pickles, I think. Can you reach them?"

"These are infernally good pickles, Miss Madge. Suppose we sit on these two water-pails and eat our lunch off the flour-barrel. I suppose I mustn't tell you how much in love with you I am? besides, you know it already."

"Oh, I'm engaged to Garth, Mr. Selwyn," said she, very gravely; "so you may tell me whatever you please."

"You are as logical as you are lovely. Well, I admire your genius for finance. Perhaps you can tell me something about South Americans?"

"Now you are making fun of me. Why should you come all the way from Europe to this pantry to ask such a question as that?"

"All the wise people don't live in Europe; but, after eating these pickles, I'm prepared to expect almost anything of this pantry. I'd give a thousand pounds for trustworthy information about South Americans."

"Oh, I dare say; then you'd go off and make eighty or a hundred thousand. I'd give five times as much as that, Mr. Selwyn, if—I had it in my pocket."

"But the better way is to find out for yourself, without asking anybody, and then you could put the hundred thousand in your purse; and if any fellow came along, and offered you five thousand for information, you could turn up your nose and look virtuous and say: 'Go away, you naughty man. I don't know what you mean!'"

Madge laughed heartily, though not loud. "I like you ever so much," said she. "It's so pleasant to be perfectly silly once in a while! Aren't you going to eat any more? Oh, I suppose you want your brandy."

"Thank you, Miss Madge, I always carry the creature with me," replied Jack, producing a small traveling-flask from his pocket. "Nikomis's might be too strong, you know. But this will keep us just at the right point of silliness. You must take a little."

"I will, if you are sure it's good for contagion, Mr. Selwyn; and perhaps I ought to smoke a cigarette too, if you have one. Thank you. South American ladies smoke cigarettes, don't they? Let's pretend we are there."

Jack struck a match and handed it to her; she lit her cigarette, inhaled the delicate smoke, and breathed it forth again through her nostrils, her dark eyes sparkling at him through the fragrant haze. "Do I do it right?" she asked, innocently.

"Yes; and all you want now to make you perfect is a little refined swearing now and then; only you must be careful always to do it in a low, quiet voice, and with a very distinct enunciation. Let me instruct you."

"No," said she, with a sigh; "I sha'n't be perfect till I have a fortune. What was that we were talking about? Oh, finding out about things for yourself. But, even if you had, there might be so much trouble in the way of turning it into money, that you would prefer to let the other fellow pay you for informing him. Shouldn't you think so? Because I'm sure anybody who couldn't make a fortune out of five thousand pounds might as well stay at home and forget all about South America."

"You'd have to convince the other fellow, though, that your information would lead to something, else he might prefer to find out for himself too; and then where would you be?"

Madge touched her lips to the brandy, gave a little shudder, and set it down; then the ash of her cigarette fell on her dress, and she shook it hastily off with a merry pretense of dismay. She was evidently in the highest spirits, yet thoroughly under control of herself. Jack was by no means sure that he could read her thoughts, yet he felt it to be highly probable that she read his; and whether or not she was decided what to do, had, at all events, no special

anxieties. She comprehended the bearings of the case, and meant to profit by her knowledge in one way or another. So much seemed likely enough; but how she got her knowledge Jack was unable to conceive. It could hardly have been by dint of pure mother-wit; and, on the other hand, it was incredible that any criminal in his proper senses would spontaneously confess himself to a woman, be her fascinations what they might. Was it possible, then, that Madge really knew nothing, and was audaciously attempting to bluff him into giving her a clew? These speculations passed through Jack's head while he was biting off the end of his cigar and striking a fresh light. He leaned back on his water-pail till his shoulders came against the side of the meat-safe, and in this position awaited what his charming companion might say next. It ought to be something to the point. But there was never any forecasting what Madge would say or do.

"I wish you'd teach Garth to smoke and drink and swear," she began, dropping her festive air for one of thoughtful gravity. "He does them once in a while, of course, but not smoothly and as if they were nothing. He would be shocked if he saw me— this way." With the words, she crossed one knee over the other, and fell into a beautiful parody of Selwyn's careless attitude. He smiled satirically, and said, "After a ten years' courtship, that's odd."

"Oh, there's a great deal about me that Garth doesn't know, and wouldn't if he were to court me ten years more. I don't behave to him as I do to you, Mr. Selwyn. Garth isn't a detective; and he says straight out what he means and what he wants, as a man ought to do. There's nobody like him, I know. I don't want there to be."

"If I teach him to smoke and drink and swear, there wouldn't be any Garth at all. Is that what you want?"

"You teach him anything!" exclaimed she, with a pungent accent of angry contempt, though still the tone was low. "You think you know me, Jack Selwyn. You've found out that I didn't visit him while he's been ill, have you? And you say I don't love him. You are an honorable gentleman, of course, and can tell women how they should behave and think; and you can see through them, can't you? *You* teach my Garth anything! Ha! ha! ha! I do love him! I do—do love him!"

"Do you?"

"Yes, I love him. And yet I can tell you all you would like to tell me, if you weren't too—polite. I didn't go to him when he was ill, because I didn't care to; and I didn't care whether he died or not. I don't care now. And you may tell that to everybody you meet: I dare say you will. But rather than see him get to be like other men, with their airs and lies and little vices, I'd die myself. So I love him. I don't want to die; I like to live, and I never want to die; but I'd sooner die than see him like you, or like—the man who's engaged to marry Elinor."

"You are very acute, Miss Madge," muttered Selwyn, conscious that he had winced. "Would you be willing to take me on your detective force?" asked she, with an angry smile, resting her firm round arms on the barrel-head, and bending her bright face toward him. "It must be such an interesting profession, if a handsome, fashionable young gentleman goes into it just for fun—or no, it was because he had a noble, abstract hatred of wrong, and love of justice! And now that he finds somebody is going to marry Elinor, how much more abstract his hatred of wrong becomes, and how much harder he will make his detectives work! And he means to get people to help him without their knowing it themselves; he sees through everybody, and manages them so cleverly!"

"You are letting your cigarette go out, Miss Madge."

"Thank you; I know what you mean. You don't want Garth to marry me; I wouldn't make a good wife for him. Perhaps he don't love me, because we have waited so long? But then you know that he'd marry me, whether he loved me or not, because he's said he would; so you want to make him believe that I'm not faithful to him. Do you think I didn't understand why you began to flirt with me the first minute you saw me, and why you proposed to sit in here, and gave me brandy to drink and tobacco to smoke? You thought you'd get

evidence against me, and tell Garth I was immodest and false, and would betray him for the sake of the first fop that came along. That was honorable and like a gentleman, wasn't it? And how self-sacrificing of you to flirt with a pretty girl in the cause of abstract right and justice!—only you wouldn't tell Garth that part of it. Tell him all, if you like; you'll find he loves me enough to kill you for it. What right have you to meddle between us? If I ran away from him with another man, what would you think?"

"I should wonder what had been the object of all this talk."

"Ah, Jack Selwyn, what a quick-witted man!" She paused abruptly, and for a moment Jack thought she was about either to laugh immoderately or give way to a passion of tears; it was uncertain which. But after a few irregular breaths, she regained control of herself and did neither. She went on in a less rapid tone than before, though there was now a jarring metallic ring in it.

"I'll tell you, because I know you can't understand, and wouldn't believe if you did. If I ran away from him, it would be because I loved him too much to stay and marry him. I know what he needs, and what I am. He needn't feel jealous of the man I run off with, nor of anybody in the world. What is love? Can you tell me? Do you think there could be a woman who honored it so much as to turn her back on it?—Well, have I kept you entertained, Mr. Selwyn? Have you enjoyed your lunch?"

"Yes; I never had a spicier one," returned he. He spoke, as he had done ever since she had launched into this unexpected and bewildering tirade, in a cold, cynical tone, not because he felt cynical, but as an instinctive defense against being quite overborne and vanquished by the passionate hap-hazard subtilty of her attack. So soon as the stress was removed, however, he could venture to take a more genuine attitude. And now he owned to himself that he had taken this young woman's measure quite too heedlessly, and had fairly laid himself open to the taunts and ridicule she had dealt out to him. The interview had greatly modified his idea of her, yet in such a manner as to stagger all expectation of easily finding her out. What she had said was one thing, and something of a puzzle in itself; why she had said it, and whether she meant it, were other questions which Jack felt his inability to answer. He did not know whether she meant to marry Garth or not. Had she made up her mind to desert him, and was she trying to justify her fickleness by calling it fine names? Or was she (feeling herself insecure) striving to shame herself into honesty? Had she spoken from deliberate forethought or from unpremeditated impulse? It had sounded very like the latter; yet, on going over what had passed, Jack could not find that she had anywhere given him a practical handle against her. She had said some apparently very reckless things, yet nothing really irretrievable, that she might not interpret to her own advantage. On the whole, the main impression left upon his mind was that Madge was more of a woman, in every sense of the phrase, than he had given her credit for being. And though Jack was not given to fear of either woman or man, he was frankly willing to congratulate himself that his destiny was not bound up with that of this beautiful and brilliant girl.

"I'm sorry to have made you angry," he said; "but you ought to consider that no one but you would have been keen-witted enough to take offense. Take my advice for what it's worth—don't marry Garth: marry some old fool. You were born to set the world by the ears, and Garth would be terribly in your way, I can tell you."

"Thank you. You would not dare say that to me if Garth were here."

"I'll repeat it before him where you choose. Why should I varnish words with you, Miss Madge? You have given me the right to say what I think to you, and I shall use it henceforward. What would be the use of my declaring that I had a profound reverence for your candor and constancy and moral and religious fastidiousness, or that I believed in the guileless innocence of a girl who had just outwitted me? Yes, I admit you've outwitted me. I know no more about South Americans, for instance, than I did before; but then, Miss Madge, I know as much; and probably that will be enough for the purpose."

Madge got up and set her foot upon the water-pail, resting her elbow on her knee and her chin upon her hand, while her dark glance wandered over the brown boarded floor. "I'm glad you have treated me as you have done," said she. "I have looked forward to your coming, and I might have helped you, and you me; but I shall feel better to do without you, and to hate you. Do your best to take Garth from me," she added, looking up at him with a sudden gleam of enmity. "He won't thank you in the end, and I will have my way in everything in spite of you all."

"And I'm to clear out?" said Jack, rising also and going to the door. "Well, good-by. It's worth a man's being born to quarrel with you; but he'd better die than love you."

He went out, closing the door of the shadowy little pantry behind him. Madge, when she felt herself entirely alone, reseated herself on the bucket, and staid long in still-eyed reverie, one arm thrown across the top of the barrel, while the fingers of the other hand pinched little creases in the skirt upon her knee. At last a change came over her; she began to pant and tremble; suddenly she turned and pillowed her forehead on her arms, and then for a time she wept from her very soul. Could Garth have come to her then, he might have gained a blessing both for Madge and for himself. But the time passed, and she got slowly to her feet, feeling that she had done with tears. And, after all, the blessing might have grown into a curse.

BOOK VIII.

LEAVEN.

CHAPTER LIX.

THE PHYSICIAN.

THE meeting between Mr. Urmson and Professor Grindle had not been outwardly effusive. The professor's bald pate had reddened a little as he strongly griped his old fellow-student's hand, and he had said, "How do, Urmson?" in his usual abrupt, bass tones, perhaps made a little more uncompromising than usual to keep up the good old Anglo-Saxon traditions of unfeelingness. Mr. Urmson had replied, "How do you do, professor?" and after the exchange of a few questions and observations of no less momentous import, the two elderly gentlemen left the younger people to themselves, and proceeded in total silence up-stairs, Cuthbert leading, and the professor tramping sternly after him. In silence they entered Garth's chamber, and there the professor stood for a moment, motionless but observant, by the bedside. Then, without having touched the invalid, or emitted so much as a single professional grunt, he stepped back to the door, and beckoning to his companion, they went silently out into the hall again.

"Let him sleep," said the professor. "Lead on to your chamber, Urmson. Must smoke a cigar and toast my toes after that drive. The winter's upon us; you'll catch it up here sooner than we shall. Ay, I see; not much desk-work for you nowadays. Nursing. And Mrs. Urmson not here to help." Since Mrs. Urmson's marriage this old lover of hers, who had never told his love either to her or to any one else, had refrained from speaking of her by her Christian name; and this not from any unworthy jealousy, but because he derived a stern, unselfish pleasure from the thought that the only woman he had loved belonged to

the man whom he loved best, and chose to keep that fact before his mind by always giving her the name she was married to.

"Heaven is too near us, I sometimes think," Cuthbert answered. "The people we want most are so apt to slip into it out of our reach."

"'Tisn't that the boy needed her," said Grindle, taking a brand from the hearth and lighting his cigar with a series of short, rapid, whiffs. "He'll do very well—a strong grip of life, sir. 'Twas you I referred to more particularly, Urmson. You're not looking as I'd like to have you. You have that in your face, my man, that—none of your late communications had prepared me to see there. Now as your physician, I'll ask you a question or two. Your mother was a Danver, was she not? What was her constitution?"

"Take off your spectacles, Tom," said Cuthbert, coloring slightly; "you'll be sharp-sighted enough without them. I didn't get you here for this. However—No, nothing was developed in her, God bless her! It came, if anything, from her mother, who belonged to another stock—a poor one. She died of it."

Grindle took off his glasses and rested his elbows on his knees. "Ay, ay," he said slowly, gazing into the fire. "And that has always somewhat posed me, Cuthbert. That old curse—why did the Lord pronounce it against his creatures?—'The children's teeth shall be set on edge.' How often does the children's suffering accomplish the erring parent's reformation? It never can. What knows or cares that dead and buried and forgotten woman—or it may have been her father or mother—that you sit there hand-in-hand with disease, who might have been a vigorous man still, full of health and power?

Such a curse seems only to revenge; not to restrain, nor to requite justly."

"I suppose you must have a personal interest in such problems before you can expect to tackle them, Tom. What I have felt is, that the curse may smite the body and pass through to bless the soul. For, after all, I wasn't a perfect man when you and I used to argue the universe in college; nor afterward, even—quite. Some complaints you were in the habit of making anent the evils of a too ironical and self-complacent disposition, if my memory fail not. My grandmamma has very likely not cured me of those imperfections—not even bettered me, perhaps; but I'm self-complacent enough to believe she has kept me from intensifying them, and ironical enough to hope that she is none the worse off herself for having done so."

"Inform me how long this has been coming on you, my man."

"More than a year—a good deal more. Slow, but knows how to make itself felt."

"Where?" demanded Grindle, after a long puff at his cigar, still keeping his eyes upon the fire. Cuthbert's only answer was to put his hand for a moment over his breast. Then the two friends looked at each other. The professor, whose face during the past twenty-and-odd years had not been trained to the expression of tender emotions, wore an aspect of gloomy severity, as though he were reproving some delinquent for a grave misdemeanor; while Cuthbert's pale and slender visage had rather an arch and demurely unrepentant look, as if defying the other's sternness to do its worst.

"Had you acquainted me with this promptly, Urmson—" Grindle began. But he did not finish his sentence. He replaced his spectacles, leaned back in his chair, and continued his smoking. His large-boned but not fleshy figure, high, bald forehead, and massive Roman nose were silhouetted against the brightness of the window at the other side of the room. He was still a strong and able man, though somewhat Cuthbert's senior in years; and, while the silence lasted, the latter was indulging in the quaint speculation whether, in the next world, his friend would exhibit a spiritual excellence corresponding to his present physical superiority, or whether he would take rank by his mental qualities alone. But the settlement of the question was indefinitely put off by the interruption of Grindle himself.

"I'll not speak to you as a physician, then," said he. "Some alleviation may be practicable; but you don't require me to tell you, Cuthbert, what the end must be. Now, however, since I must leave you to-morrow, it would be advisable to go through with our business affairs and get them finally settled. When we may meet again, no man knows. I shall try to come up during the Christmas holidays; but *quid sit futurum cras fuge quærere*. Your brother Golightley, I presume, is at least independent of you?"

"Yes, so far as money goes, and for the time being."

"I forbore questioning him on the subject, though he once or twice hinted toward it. I own to disliking his physiognomy and the ring of his voice: twenty years of college-boys have made me over-critical, no doubt. Has he suggested reimbursement?"

"I fancy we can do without that," said Cuthbert, with a slight nervous movement of his shoulders and hands.

"You have the produce of your garden and orchard," returned Grindle, puffing uncompromisingly at his cigar, "and nothing else. The interest of Eve's legacy amounts to less than twenty-five hundred dollars this year, and, when Mrs. Danver's 'patent' annuity has been paid out of it, and the other regular and incidental expenses met, there'll be about one hundred left over. That's your year's income, sir. There's not a poorer man than you in the village. How do you pay your butcher?"

"Why, we pelt him with apples. But you forget Garth's canvas, and my pen and paper. Moreover, Golightley is ready to pay his board. We are doing first rate!"

"Well, well, sir, that's your own affair. And there's this to be said—if you have reason to be ashamed of your own improvidence, you have still greater cause to congratulate yourself on the way Providence makes it up for you. If you had not, years and years ago, consented to your father's laying an embargo on that fifty thousand dollars—a proceeding, sir, against which every principle of prudence and economy seemed to protest—"

" You protested, if I remember rightly, Tom," interrupted Cuthbert, arching his eyebrow; " but the economic principles were rather on our side. So soon as poor Golightley's drafts began to be a matter of course, I, with my unfailing sagacity, foresaw the future up to this very day, and perceived that, unless the legacy had been put out of reach in that way, it would have been drafted away with the rest. Then I informed Golightley of the exact amount at my disposal, and explained to him the worse than uselessness of overdrawing. And he never did overdraw."

"Ah, he had no lien upon Eve's rights, whatever he may have had upon yours. Captain Urmson had that fact in mind, I apprehend, when he executed the codicil. He never really believed but that the girl was tomahawked; but he had a presentiment that Golightley would make trouble, and so used Eve's name to secure you at least half the property. It may almost be called your own now, the allotted term of years is so nearly out."

"Five or six years hence seems a long 'now' to a fellow in my condition," remarked Cuthbert, with a smile.

"You have got the same erroneous impression that I had till lately. 'Tis true, the codicil was executed some years later than the will; but, whether by accident or design, the date of the will governs the provisions of the codicil; therefore, unless the persons therein mentioned appear within the next few months, their claim will be antiquated. Ay, ay, you are providentially favored so far as that goes, and Garth will have something to get married on."

"Unless the persons therein mentioned do appear," Cuthbert murmured, half to himself, and he added, aloud, "Did you speak of this to my brother?"

"No, sir," said Grindle, with emphasis. "As I said, he does not inspire me with confidence. By-the-by, he made some remarks on Madge, who seems to have grown into a lovely young woman; he volunteered some

14

reflections on her which I can hardly reconcile with my own impression of her. Do you like the match?"

"It has been a long engagement, you know," replied Cuthbert, with some hesitation, "and one might suppose that if there were any incompatibility, it would have come to the surface before now. Nevertheless, I think it would be juster to both parties if this discovery of yours about the codicil were kept private for a time. However ardent Madge's affection for Garth may be, I fancy money would inflame it still more; and though in process of time she might find Garth a little wearisome, I'm sure she would remain constant to—Plutus."

"Oho! Cuthbert, I'm sorry to hear this—heartily sorry. Your brother's insinuations, had I been inclined to accept them, might have prepared me for it. No; Garth is no fit rival for Plutus. But is that lovely girl . . . . ?" Professor Grindle mused a moment and sighed. His interviews with Madge had been brief and far between, yet enough, apparently, to render this new light thrown upon her character something more than a disappointment to him. Under ordinary circumstances, he would uncompromisingly have rebelled against any depreciation of her; but Cuthbert, unlike most people, was accustomed to say less than he meant, and only to say that upon grave occasion. "Have you hinted of this to Garth?" Grindle added.

"I have always allowed Garth's opinions to correct themselves, Tom. He is often wrong; but, when he is right, he knows why. I may as well unburden my soul to you: I hope they won't marry; and, if Garth can manage to stay poor awhile longer, I don't believe they will. The situation is a peculiar one. She likes him well enough, all but his artistic phase; and he, if he would abjure his art, would love her fiercely with all that remained—that is, with the less noble part of him. He partly understands that, I think, and dreads it the more because, at the same time, he feels it a temptation. You can understand, Tom, how Madge might tempt a hot-hearted yet undemonstrative young fellow like him."

"Ay, very well," said Grindle, nodding

his head slowly. "And, being betrothed, honor would seem to throw its weight into the wrong scale. 'Tis an awkward knot for the boy to untie, indeed. But, if Madge has made up her mind for riches, she will untie it for him."

"She must not be depended on either for good or ill. I believe her capable of making a great sacrifice, if her feminine perversity be inflamed. Jealousy, or pique, or a sudden impulse of admiration for his physical manliness, would be likely to drive her straight into Garth's arms, though it is quite as likely that she would repent the day afterward. She is a good deal more or less than mercenary. But her attackable point is her self-esteem. She would hardly believe that Garth could tire of her, or esteem her second to any other woman; and, feeling no anxiety about the security of her power over him, she naturally values him the less. Besides, I fancy his illness has rather cooled her regard than warmed it; she is like a beautiful animal in her inability to sympathize with physical suffering."

"Don't tell me she hasn't been at his side through it all, Urmson! What did your brother say about her having played him to sleep this very morning?"

"Not Madge. That was Elinor."

"That cold, silent girl? Elinor—hardly saw her, sir!" Grindle took his short beard in his hand, and crossed his leg emphatically toward his interlocutor. "Hey? Elinor— Is that another complication, Urmson? Unless my recollection's at fault, it was to an Elinor that your brother told me he was betrothed. Hey?"

"The engagement has been made public, and need not further concern us," returned Cuthbert, with one of his quiet looks of dismissal. "Elinor took Mrs. Tenterden's place for to-day, that's all; and Garth seems to have improved more by an hour with her than by what the rest of us could do for him in three weeks. She has the nursing talent, which Madge lacks, and seemingly she didn't fear contagion."

"Typhoid contagious!" said Grindle, grimly chuckling.

"So say many; and I have thought it as well not to combat the prejudice. Mrs. Ten-

terden, though most kind and helpful downstairs, would be a little tremendous in a sick-chamber; and Madge, since she seemed inclined to keep away at any rate, would be none the worse for a pretext both for justifying her resolution and making her stick to it. 'This only is the witchcraft I have used.'"

"You are a more subtile man than Othello—but always in an honest way, too," observed Grindle, slowly settling back into gravity. "Well, well. If music physics him best, and neither Madge nor Golightley objects, the experiment is worth prosecuting. Cold, she seemed to me—impassive. Not handsome either, though refined. Must look at her again. But, by-the-by, how came Madge, your beautiful animal, to put herself in the way of sick-rooms and contagion to-day? Is she returning to humanity?"

"If it were not Madge, I should lay it to Elinor's having come first; but I can't account for it. She was in a rather remarkable mood. Something must have happened, I think, which has put her out of her usual course. There's no use in speculating about it; but, once kindled or goaded into full emotional and intellectual activity, Madge would be a very interesting and unconventional object. Come, Tom, throw away your cigar, and let's see whether the sick boy is awake yet."

"He'll come out of it, sir," said Grindle, getting to his feet, and standing for a moment with his fists upon his hips, gazing into the fire. "All he needs is care, patience, and eating. Let the young lady play to him once in a while, if he likes it. Must have a word with her, by-the-by, before I go. Lead on, lead on."

CHAPTER LX.

NIKOMIS'S LODGER.

MEANWHILE, it is no less than the due of so respectable a personage as Nikomis that some inquiry should be made into her doings on this somewhat eventful morning. The old lady was a notable "medicine-woman," from an Indian point of view; and, in her own opinion, Garth's recovery, if it took place, would be mainly owing to what she had done for him. Her chief concern, however, had all along been rather for Cuthbert than for him. Toward Cuthbert her sentiments had, during the past ten years, undergone some important modifications, the full significance of which may appear later on. But it may be mentioned in this place that something like a feeling of mutual respect had grown up between the two; and this had ripened latterly into a peculiar confidential relation, unsuspected by any third person, not only as to its nature, but in itself. Among other matters, Nikomis had been made acquainted with the character of the disease from which Cuthbert was suffering, and which, in all human probability, must sooner or later make an end of him. It might, however, be alleviated, and to this good end the Indian had taxed the best resources of her knowledge and experience. But the anxiety of mind and bodily exhaustion brought about by Garth's illness had hastened the progress of his father's trouble, and Nikomis, while nursing both invalids with tolerable impartiality, could not free herself from a shade of resentment toward the younger man for sapping, however unconsciously, the springs of the elder's life.

When Cuthbert, therefore, went to lie down early that morning, leaving Garth in her care, she resolved that he and not Garth should get the first benefit of her ministrations. She had already prepared a narcotic, famous in her Indian pharmacy for its soothing and restorative virtues, and possibly had enhanced its efficacy by distilling it under certain aspects of the moon, or muttering over it spells which made it worth all the unbewitched nostrums in the world. Be that as it may, she now poured a sufficient dose of it into a wineglass, disguised its flavor with a little brandy, and got Cuthbert to swallow it between waking and sleeping. Then, leaving the glass upon the table, she hobbled grimly off to Garth's chamber—as unprepossessing a herald of health, perhaps, as ever did her best for two human lives. Garth having been made as easy as might

be, Nikomis betook herself to the congenial kitchen, intending, no doubt, to spend an hour or so over a pipe and a tumbler of grog. Ere she could establish herself in her wonted corner, however, her attention was caught by a scratching sound, alternating with a low, whining whimper, which seemed to come from outside the back-door that opened upon the orchard. An ordinary listener would have supposed that some vagabond dog, chilled by the night air and emboldened by hunger, was trying to gain admittance to the warm hearth and the hospitality of a bone. But Nikomis was not an ordinary listener; she had the ears and instincts of a savage, and so seemingly commonplace a sound as this had for her a meaning as definite and clear as the most straightforward utterance of sentences could have conveyed. She stood rigid, with her head thrust forward and her breath drawn. The noise came again; she took a few quick, moccasined steps forward, and pausing close to the door, gave vent to an answering whimper, ending in a muffled bark. There was a brief pause, and then the door was cautiously opened, and a tall man, carrying a heavy, oblong box strapped to his shoulders, and a stout, smooth cudgel in his hand, appeared on the threshold.

"All alone, granny?" he asked in a rapid, sliding utterance, still holding the door-latch in his hand, and peering round and beyond her as he spoke.

Nikomis gazed at him intently—so intently that the faculty of speech seemed temporarily lost to her; but on the tall man's repeating his inquiry somewhat impatiently, she made a gesture of assent with her hand, still keeping her black eyes fixed upon his face. After yet a moment's hesitation, he came in, with a step rapid and sliding, like his voice, though at the same time there was about his bearing a something half defiant, half jaunty, which indicated a man whose satisfaction with himself had outlived his faith and reliance on most other matters. He was dressed in a dirty velveteen jacket and torn felt hat; his black hair hung in straight black masses about a swarthy face, which might have been handsome but for the disfigurement of a pair of green spectacles with heavy brass bows to them. Altogether, he had rather an Italian aspect; and the heavy burden upon his shoulders, which on a nearer glance appeared to be a hand-organ, might have confirmed a stranger in assigning him that nationality. It was ten to one that he was a Neapolitan organ-grinder in very needy circumstances.

"What you staring at, granny?" demanded he in a whisper, putting his hand briskly on the old woman's shoulder. "Glad t' see me, eh? Why don't you say so, then? Here," he added, "help me off with this damned old box, granny, and carry it up to the wigwam for me. Got wigwam up in the garret, eh?—I know." He slipped the broad leathern strap down from his shoulder and swung the organ round against Nikomis, who helped him lower it noiselessly to the ground. "That feels good," said he, expanding his chest and giving his shoulders a shake. "I've carried that thing all the way from Boston, granny. You get it up to the garret right off. Wait a minute!" He took her abruptly by the arm again. "Sure all safe here—what? no harm in th' house—what?"

Nikomis put up her hand doubtfully and took the disfiguring green spectacles from the man's nose. The black eyes thus disclosed were handsome and penetrating, but evasive. But to Nikomis they were dearer than her own. "Sam!" said she, fastening her long knotty fingers on his tall shoulders, and looking up at him in a kind of spasm of grotesque delight. "You at home now. This all safe—your home. Nikomis bid you welcome." With the last words she straightened herself and made a waving gesture of greeting with her hand, as though she were an envoy come to present a palace to a monarch. Sam laughed—an almost noiseless laugh, covering his teeth with his lips and ducking his chin down to his breast.

"You very grand, old woman! My home—I know; but there's some little things to be settled up first, you know. Let's see, now—Garth sick, is he? But where's the old man?—he sick too?"

"Cuthbert sleeps," returned the Indian. "Why you come this way?" she added, noticing for the first time the significance of his disguise. "Why you make look so poor,

Sam? You not rich any more? Anybody you're afraid of?"

"Oh, well, that's a long story; tell you all about it directly, granny—too damned hungry for any powwow now. Show me where I can get something to eat, first thing; and take that old organ-box up-stairs—d'you hear? Got all my things in it—mustn't be where anybody can find it. I'm going to keep dark for a while, granny—d'you understand? Come, now, show me where the meat is."

Nikomis, although accustomed to exact and receive ceremonious treatment from all pale-faced mortals, seemed ready to accept with meekness any amount of this dark-skinned vagabond's cavalier behavior. She set a plentiful meal before him, and then, returning to the box, contrived with difficulty to mount it on her venerable back, and so to lug it slowly and uncomplainingly up to her wigwam. Arrived there, she seated herself upon it and spent a few minutes in regaining her breath, both physical and metaphysical. Rising at length, she made a few alterations in the arrangement of the place; and when all was ordered to her satisfaction, she hobbled silently down to the kitchen again, where Sam was leaning back in his chair and enjoying the luxury of appeased appetite. The beef and bread, and still more the flattering unction of a glass of brandy, had evidently won him to a more genial mood.

"There you are again, granny! So the old thing didn't break your back, after all—what? Oh, I knew you wouldn't mind it. Didn't you lug me on your shoulders when I was a papoose, and your cursed old knee was out of joint? Hobbling still, are you? That's right. So you remember the signals we used to have ten years ago, 'nd let in your little Sammy that had been away so long! He been through great lot of things since he saw you last, granny. Come along up to th' wigwam, 'nd he'll tell you about it."

Nikomis signified her willingness to lead the way, and Sam, having slipped off his travel-stained boots, followed her up to the first floor. The door of Cuthbert's room stood ajar; the half-breed peeped in, and, seeing how soundly the inmate slept, he glided stealthily up to the bedside. Nikomis, who had remained at the entrance, saw him stoop down and listen to the old man's low-drawn breathing. Then he drew a straight, narrow-bladed knife from an inner pocket of his coat, and made a pass with it toward the sleeper's heart. Nikomis uttered a guttural exclamation, loud enough to have waked Cuthbert but for the sleeping potion he had taken, and clutched forward vehemently with both hands. Sam had turned the point aside just as it arrived within a hair's-breadth of the other's breast; but at Nikomis's cry he uplifted the knife again, while his feat-ures took on a more sinister expression than they had yet worn, and for a few moments he stood in position to strike, watching if Cuthbert's eyelids trembled. But he lay as quiet and untroubled as though the breadth of the world had interposed between him and violence. Sam now threw a glance of jeering defiance toward the door, turned the knife in his hand, and, with a rapid motion of the wrist, made a pretense of taking Mr. Urmson's scalp. Then slipping the weapon back into his pocket, and laughing one of his silent laughs, he came away.

"What made you yell out, you old fool?" he said, as he rejoined Nikomis. "What should you care 'f I stuck him? I'd 'a done it 'f he'd waked; 'most sorry he didn't. Him and Garth, too, curse 'em! Where is Garth? Never mind, never mind; I'd cut his heart out 'f I were to see him—couldn't help my-self. All right, all right; we'll be even with 'em some day. Come on, granny."

They creaked up the attic-stairs together, and entered Nikomis's apartment. It was at the corner of the garret opposite to Garth's studio, partitioned off from the intermediate space by a rough boarding, and lighted by two small windows cut in the northern and western walls. But Nikomis ignored wood-en walls, and had fitted up the interior in such a manner as vividly to recall the abo-riginal wigwam. Seven or eight bean-poles were fixed at the circumference of a large circular space on the floor, and leaned toward one another until they met in a clump just below the ceiling. Around this framework were draped a number of old skins and blankets, so that the whole formed a rude tent, quite dark within, save when the loose flap that served as a door was fold-ed back. When this was done, however, and the eyes had had time to get used to the gloom, the floor was seen to be carpeted with dried sweet-fern; and the bed or mattress at one side was formed of a thicker layer of the same heathery shrub, covered over with a threadbare rug. Around the sloping sides of the structure might be dimly discerned various savage implements and trophies, while strings of colored beads, charms, med-icine-bags, and a number of quaint utensils, such as only an inveterate old witch like Nikomis could have imagined any use for, glimmered duskily here and there. But perhaps the most impressive sight, albeit the one least likely to be discernible to prying eyes, was the row of questionable objects dan-gling from a string which stretched from one side to another of the wigwam, at about a man's height from the floor. They resembled bunches of dried sea-weed as much as any-thing, or small clots of turf, with long, fine tufts of grass depending from them. In fact, however, they were no such innocent mat-ter: they were an assortment of old, smoke-dried scalps, cut from their enemies' heads by Nikomis's forefathers, and by her jealous-ly preserved and prized, together with the bloody legends belonging to each one of them. In her more pensive moments the old lady may be supposed to have derived as much consolation from a view of these ghastly mementos, dully illumined by the lurid glow from the bowl of her tobacco-pipe, as would a more civilized personage from the gold-mounted miniatures of her de-ceased grandparents and uncles, with locks of their hair braided neatly into the backs of the frames, and covered over with glass.

Into this retreat did Nikomis introduce her tall companion, bidding him make him-self at home there. He glanced about some-what discontentedly, and would plainly have preferred more commodious quarters, even at the cost of a good part of the aboriginal flavor. But there was no present oppor-tunity of improving matters, and he was fain to content himself with such solace as lay in a pipe. His hostess's rank old clays failing to suit his taste, which a residence abroad

seemed to have rendered fastidious, he unlocked his hand-organ and rummaged among
the medley of clothes, toilet-articles, skates,
perfumed letters, and other personal furniture which it contained, until he laid hold
of a finely-colored meerschaum. This he
filled with some fragrant tobacco from an
oil-skin bag, and then, laying himself at
length upon Nikomis's sweet-fern mattress,
he began a leisurely account of his adventures.

CHAPTER LXI.

CHANGES.

To judge from his own version of them,
they reflected great credit upon his physical
address and intrepidity, upon his cunning,
and upon his freedom from moral prejudices.
Probably he described his ideal self, and no
doubt he occasionally ornamented the events
to match the hero of them. Nevertheless,
the main thread of the story must have co-
incided more or less closely with the truth,
and it certainly indicated a career of considerable vicissitude. After leaving Urmsworth, Sam, as we know, went to Newburyport, where Cuthbert supported him for upward of a year as an independent apprentice
at the gun-making trade. But the young
fellow had altogether too much ambition to
think of settling down in life as a gunsmith.
About the time that his tedium was ready
to drive him into some ill-advised escapade
or other, a lucky accident occurred to him.
It was the year of the robbery of the Newburyport Bank. Neither in the deed itself
nor in the plotting of it did Sam have any
hand; but it so happened that a pistol,
whose stock he recognized as his own handi-
work, led him on to the discovery of the
criminals; and so coolly and astutely did he
manage matters as to compel their purchase
of his silence at the price of no less than
five hundred dollars. Possessed of this vast
sum, he felt that the world lay before him,
and he was resolved to lose no time in
making trial of it. Ere setting forth, however, he bethought himself that it would be
a pleasant thing to have the society of an
agreeable and clever companion on his trav-

els; and he made a secret expedition to
Urmsworth in order to persuade the person
of his choice to join him. She hesitated
and wavered long, but finally yielded; and
it was in Nikomis's former wigwam, on the
borders of the forest, that the arrangements
for the elopement were made. It was on a
Saturday evening, about the middle of March,
and the flight was to take place the night
following. All went well, and the fugitives
had got safely to the borders of the lake,
and were almost on the point of embarking
on Sam's boat, when the unexpected apparition of Garth, stripped to his waist, and
shooting the rapids in his canoe, changed the
young lady's mind. After a brisk dispute
with her would-be abductor, the pair separated, she stealing quietly back to the little
cottage on the village outskirts, while Sam
rowed across the lake alone, and five days
later sailed out of Boston Harbor in a vessel
bound for Liverpool.

Over the first five or six years of his
European life he passed very lightly, and it
is not improbable that he may have looked
back upon them with something less than
pure satisfaction. His money was soon spent,
and he set himself to get some more. At one
time he was a member of a circus *troupe*,
and by his own account achieved vast success as a bare-back rider. Later he engaged
as groom in the family of an English nobleman connected with the turf, and by taking
advantage of "private information," he contrived to land a large sum on the Derby of
that year. From this he might have gone
on and made a fortune, had he not unfortu-
nately persuaded himself, with cause or without, that his employer's daughter, whom he
was in the habit of attending on her rides,
was in love with him. In the midst of his
hopes he received a summons to his master's
presence, when the latter handed him his
wages and then fell upon him with a horse-
whip. Sam resisted: the nobleman was
worsted in the fray; and the upshot was, that
Sam was heavily fined for assault and battery.

He now left England and crossed over
to the Continent. Establishing himself at
Baden-Baden, he cut a considerable dash
with the remains of his Derby winnings,
gambled with a good deal of success, and

was accounted a personage of distinction. One of the stock countesses of the place, however, induced him to enter into a partnership. At the critical moment the outraged husband made his appearance, picked his quarrel with Sam, and demanded satisfaction. This he received—though in an irregular way. Sam, having accepted the challenge for the next morning, provided himself with a whip and a pistol, surprised the countess and her accomplice at their rooms that night, forced the woman to gag the man and tie him, half-naked, to the bedpost; then himself did a like service for her, and grasping his whip, set to work with a will upon both his enemies, nor held his hand until both hung fainting and bloody before him. In that situation did he leave them, locking the door upon them and carrying off the key in his pocket. The next evening he was safe in Paris, though with only a hundred francs in his purse, and the clothes he wore. This episode Sam related with relish, nor did Nikomis withhold the applause of glittering eyes and sympathetic grunts.

But there can be little doubt that for a long time thereafter the adventurer experienced almost unmitigated ill luck, and made acquaintance with very low depths of life indeed. He dodged about from one great city to another, trying his fortune at cards, billiards, thimble-rigging, acrobatism, or whatever else would put a little money in his scrip. About this period he began to be aware that by a sort of continuous coincidence he kept meeting a rather good-looking, stylishly-dressed gentleman, who seemed to have no more settled residence or occupation than himself, but who uniformly associated with conspicuous personages lived luxuriously, and fared sumptuously every day. Sam never had any communication with this gentleman, never knew who he was, and seldom got near enough to him even to distinguish the sound of his voice. But he thought he remembered catching a glimpse of him on the day of his landing in Liverpool; he believed he had once distinguished his blue eye-glasses among the spectators at the circus, and he was sure he had seen him make a bet at the Derby, and afterward drink a

glass of water at the spring in Baden-Baden. By degrees, therefore, he came to regard him as somehow connected with himself—a repetition, in a higher sphere and with distinguished fortune, of his own vagabond personality. This superstitious fancy affected Sam differently at different times. Now he felt a sort of irrational attachment to the man who played so well the part in the world which it was his own ambition to play; now he hated him for being so like and yet so hopelessly above him. At one moment he hailed him as an omen and prefigurement of what he himself was destined to become; at another, he cursed him as a tantalizing ideal which he never would attain. Sometimes he hoped to raise himself to his level; sometimes he longed for the power to drag him down to his own. Occasionally months would go by without their meeting; then, again, they would seem to dog each other week after week. Sam wondered what the issue of it all would be.

He was now about twenty-two years old, rather striking in appearance, with manners smoothed by contact with mankind, yet retaining enough individual flavor to be noticeable. His faculties were alert and keen; his passions violent yet cold; his bodily vigor and versatility were much beyond the average. His native stock of cunning had been considerably enlarged, and he had rid himself of all such moral and social prejudices as would be likely to impede him in the struggle for existence. He desired the good of no living creature but himself, and he was ready to believe evil of anything or anybody. On the whole, his chance of getting ahead of circumstances was worth backing; but what he desperately needed and could not obtain was a secure and respectable footing from which to act.

One day, in Vienna, after an unusual run of luck at billiards, which had enabled him to deck himself out in better raiment than ordinary, he strolled into a handsome café to get a glass of brandy and a cigar. From his table he could see through a half-open door into an inner private room, where four gentlemen were playing cards. Three of these Sam knew by sight as persons of consequence in the city — wealthy men, either connected with the government or prominent in finance. The fourth, who sat nearest the door, he immediately recognized as his man of destiny. The sight occasioned him no surprise, though he had not before known that the mysterious being was in Vienna. Their fates were intertwined, although they might never come into direct contact.

The game was one which Sam held in especial favor, perhaps because he had devised a simple but exceedingly ingenious trick which made winning almost a certainty, while detection was next to impossible. All that was required in it were three prepared cards and a fair amount of manual dexterity. As the swarthy and saturnine adventurer moodily watched the play, he cursed the luck that prevented him from taking a hand at such a table. What was the use of sleight-of-hand and ingenuity if one had only shabby fellows, with coppers in their pockets, to practise upon? One hour in the chair now occupied by his unknown other self would be worth ten years' swindling of empty pockets. What he lacked was a word of introduction. Once established on a footing with good society, his fortune thenceforth would be secure. But how, in the name of Beelzebub, was that word of introduction to be had?

The game proceeded with varying results, only the stakes became higher and higher. All at once Sam had a sensation. Unless his eyes deceived him, he had seen his man perform precisely the trick which Sam knew to be his own private invention. He rose quietly from his table and walked to the door of the inner room, when a glance at the cards convinced him that he had not been mistaken. The latest and strangest coincidence had taken place, and it had brought their long correspondent careers finally into collision. Sam returned to his table, drank off his brandy, again returned to the private room, and entered it boldly. He knew, and did not let slip, his opportunity.

The play was over; the four gentlemen were standing up, talking and laughing, the winner carelessly folding up and placing in his pocket-book a dozen or so of hundred-thaler bank-notes. Sam took him familiarly by the arm and grasped his hand.

"Act as if you knew me," said he in English. "I saw you do that trick. You have three prepared cards in your pocket. I can have you searched here before everybody, and kicked out of society. I'll do it, unless you present me to all these men as your particular friend Mr. Flint. Come, now!"

The man, upon perceiving Sam's drift, partially recovered his disturbed equanimity, and shook hands with simulated cordiality. The ceremony of presentation was then punctiliously performed, and the disreputable half-breed was a member of the best society. After the usual compliments had passed, Sam bade his sponsor enlarge upon their early intimacy, and allude to him as a young gentleman of vast wealth and highly connected. The command was obeyed, and, as in a fairy tale, the beggar was transformed into a prince. The Baron von Stecknadeln invited him to dine; Kriegsrath Pickelhaube hoped to be honored by his presence at the reception on Sunday evening; the banker Groschenlieb would feel hurt if he did not drop in at his reading-rooms the next morning. Mr. Flint gravely bowed his acknowledgments. Before the company separated, he turned again to his involuntary benefactor and requested him for his card, remarking that he must make a note of his address. It was given accordingly, and Sam read upon it the name of Mr. Golightley Urmson.

In a few minutes more they were alone.

"I want six hundred thalers," said Mr. Flint.

"You may go to the devil!" said Mr. Golightley Urmson.

"Come, now, we'd better be friends, Mr. Urmson. You're all right for this time, but you'll be wanting to play that same game again some day, and then I'll be there, you depend. No use, Mr. Urmson, old boy! You're no better than I am, 'nd you needn't pretend to be. Come, now, I don't want to hurt you; 'f I get something to start on, I'll do the rest for myself. Or we'll make a pair of us, if you like, 'nd do business together. Six hundred thalers, old boy! You wouldn't want me to discredit your introduction, would you?"

Mr. Golightley Urmson straightened himself, curled forward his side-locks, and made his tinted eye-glasses glisten overawingly. He explained that he was not what Mr. Flint took him for; that this had been the first and would be the last time he ever cheated at cards; that he had done it only to relieve a temporary embarrassment, and that so soon as his remittances arrived he intended giving the gentlemen their revenge. "You are an impudent rogue," he added; "but you happened to detect me in an action which I regret, and I am willing to regard your impudence as a timely retribution for my—ah—fault. I don't mind giving you some money as a free gift—a self-inflicted penance. Understand, I am not in the least danger from you, nor would I consent to be intimidated if I were. This is a free—ah—contribution." Here the orator magnificently drew forth his pocket-book, took out of it with the tips of his long fingers a fold of bank-notes, and, averting his eyes, held them superciliously toward Mr. Flint. "Now go to the devil!" he repeated, turning away.

"Now you look here, old boy," said the other, stepping quickly in front of him; "I know you 'nd all about you. I know what part of New Hampshire your remittances come from, and who sends 'em. I've watched you for five years 'nd more. You're no better than I am, except for luck. I knew we'd be even some day, whether I went up or you went down. You've kept up very nicely, haven't you, and know all the fine people? Very well. I'm even with you now, and if I go down, you'll go with me. The same devil for us both, old boy! I shall do all right without you for a while; but if I ever get in any scrape, I shall use your name to get out of it again. Maybe it'll get worn out sooner with both of us using it, but it'll be worn out for you 's well as for me. So maybe you'll want to keep me out of scrapes —what?"

"I cannot consent to be intimidated," Golightley repeated, still fingering his side-locks with an air of superiority, and beginning to walk off. Mr. Flint allowed him to get some distance away, and then called after him, in a tone so loud as to attract the notice of every one in the *café*, "Hi! Urmson, hold on!"

Golightley looked over his shoulder and paused. "Something wrong about this money," called Mr. Flint, not moving from his easy position on the end of the table, and shaking the notes in the air. "You've cheated me out of—"

Golightley came hastily back. Mr. Flint had spoken in German, and the tenor of his remarks did not promise to be such as the public ought to be made privy to. Golightley came up pale and a little tremulous, either with fury or, despite his disclaimer, with fury mingled with fear. Mr. Flint ducked down his head and laughed. "There's only five hundred here," explained he, so soon as he had recovered his gravity. "Come on, now —another hundred, old boy!"

The other hesitated. No doubt that, for a moment or two, he meditated rebellion at whatever cost. He looked into Mr. Flint's keen black eyes, and knew that he had to deal with a man more unprincipled and more desperate than himself—a man who had gained a most unlucky advantage over him, and who, moreover, had in some inexplicable manner become possessed of a knowledge concerning himself and his private affairs which already went far enough, and might, for all Golightley knew, extend much further. Of Mr. Flint, on the other hand, Golightley knew nothing; but, as he looked at him, he fancied he recollected having met with that swarthy, sinister, impenetrable face often before; it had haunted him for years past, like an evil genius, and now, at last, had fastened its ugly hold upon him. To defy an unknown, unscrupulous, hostile power like this was certainly rash, and might be fatal; nevertheless, the momentary impulse to do so was almost irresistible. A man's freedom, when it is first threatened, seems better worth preserving than honor, reputation, wealth, or any other thing. Yet it so happens that, in perhaps nine cases out of ten, freedom is sacrificed in the end. In the present instance Golightley had greatly weakened his position by yielding to Mr. Flint's first approaches: had he resisted from the outset, all might have been well; but he had been taken too utterly by surprise to weigh the matter, and the first demands made upon him had seemed to be such as it could do no great harm to grant. By so doing, however, he had crippled his independence, and to retrieve it now might be ruin. He hesitated for nearly a minute, while Mr. Flint silently but guardedly watched him. It is hardly too much to say that during these few seconds Golightley suffered as much anguish of mind as it was within his scope to feel. Suddenly drops of sweat started out on his forehead and ran down into his beard. He hastily took out his pocket-book, thrust the note into Mr. Flint's hand, and hurried away. The strength seemed to have slid out of him. He stumbled once or twice before reaching the street, and did not keep his chin uplifted as usual.

Such, in effect, is the version of this occurrence which Sam confided to Nikomis. Perhaps he exaggerated the ease and completeness of his own victory, and understated the prowess of his antagonist; yet there can be little question that the final result of the contest was much as he represented it to be. At all events, his worldly standing underwent a transformation forthwith. He rose at once to the higher social strata. His Indian strain rather helped him than the contrary in his intercourse with polite circles; his foreign appearance was a distinction, the more because no one knew from what nationality he sprang; and he had tact enough, and a sufficient smattering of languages, to satisfy tolerably well the demands of fashionable society. He lived by his wits as before, but the opportunities and the gains were far greater; and he used so much caution in his operations as for the most part to escape even suspicion. With Golightley he wisely interfered as seldom as possible; although, whenever his own resources waned, he never hesitated to demand, or failed to receive, assistance. By degrees the relations of the two men became less hostile; they drifted into a half-explicit partnership. Either Golightley's moral fibre continued to deteriorate, or he tacitly confessed himself a greater rogue than he had at first pretended. Be that as it may, he

accepted Mr. Flint's coöperation in several shady strokes of business. But the more closely their actual interests were identified, the further did they retire from visible intimacy. The breadth of Europe was more often between them than not; when necessary, they corresponded through the post, and once in a while they had an interview. Life went on with them pretty comfortably, and Mr. Flint at least greatly enjoyed himself. His physical accomplishments aided to render him somewhat conspicuous: as a horseman, a hunter, and a swordsman, he was in high repute; and once, after skating before Czar Nicholas of Russia, that potentate personally expressed to him his satisfaction, and gave him a diamond ring, which Sam still retained— less, perhaps, out of sentiment than as a resource in the hour of adversity.

"Why you make look so poor now, Sam?" demanded Nikomis, at this point, recurring to the question which had puzzled her at the outset; since, for all he had said thus far, there seemed no reason why her grandson should not be as affluent as at any period of his career.

"Oh, well, granny, Golightley's here, isn't he? S' long as he's rich, I sha'n't stay so very poor—he! he! he! Madge says he's going to be married, and I s'pose," added Sam humorously, "he'll like having me best man at his wedding."

"You seen Madge?" asked Nikomis, a little jealously.

"Seen her this morning; mighty pretty girl she is now, granny—mighty nice! She told me something I didn't know before," he continued, after a pause, throwing a sharp glance at the old woman. "I knew who your daughter-in-law was before, granny; but you never told me how kind my grandpa had been to me—what? Oh, no, I'm not so very poor, after all, granny."

"What you going to do with Madge?" asked Nikomis, passing over these allusions.

"What d' you want me to do?"

"Ugh! marry her," said Nikomis.

Sam knocked the ashes out of his pipe and laughed silently to himself. "She mighty pretty girl, granny," was all his reply. After refilling and lighting his pipe, he said: "Old Golightley's got ahead of me this time. They can't touch him till they've caught me. No evidence against him, 'less I give it. Tell you what, though, I don't care. I spent all my share, 'nd if they track me down, I'll peach on him. Damn him, he had more 'n half the money, anyway, 'nd I'll do it, 'less he gives me half what he's got."

"You stolen money, Sam?—stolen money right out? Whose money—um?"

"What you looking so glum about, granny?" returned Sam, with a passing scowl. "What do you care whose money it was? It was Golightley's stealing, anyway; he put me up to it, 'nd then covered all his own tracks, curse him!"

"Nikomis sorry you a thief, Sam," said the old squaw, with a grim solemnity of manner different from her hitherto submissive and fond demeanor. "Nikomis never been a thief. You might have had my money. Me sorry you came here 'fraid to show yourself. Nikomis never 'fraid to show myself."

"Never mind, granny, Garth 'nd Cuthbert can't deny the legacy—that's safe, anyway."

"Don't know 'bout that," said Nikomis, shaking her head. "Maybe Golightley spent all that. Besides, how you going to make show it's yours?"

"You've got the papers, haven't you, to prove who I am?" exclaimed Sam, jerking himself suddenly up on his elbow. "Damn you, you haven't lost them? Madge said you had 'em. Come, now, granny, no nonsense!"

"Ugh! Madge. You better ask her for 'em, then," retorted the Indian, with a gleam of sullen resentment. "Maybe she got 'em."

"By the devil, you old hag," said Sam, sitting up with a threatening look, "didn't I tell you, no nonsense? What you done with those papers, now? I want 'em."

"You cut my heart out, Sam," was Nikomis's reply, sitting grimly impassive before him. "Maybe you find the papers inside me."

The other threw himself back on his mattress, with something between a snarl and a snicker. Plainly his grandparent was not to be intimidated, and since she alone could establish his claim to the Evo legacy, he had made a mistake in trying to bully her. She must be cajoled into good-humor; though, as to the probable cause of her sudden perversity, Sam was quite in the dark.

And, indeed, such waywardness might well appear singular. During many years Sam had been the old woman's hero. She had seen in him the instrument of retribution upon the traditional enemies of her tribe. In his absence she had adorned him with every stern or subtle quality that answered in her savage code for virtues, and had looked forward to his return as to the proud consummation of her life; she was no squeamish moralist, and her decalogue had little in common with the Mosaic one. Nevertheless she owned her prejudices, and next to cowardice disdained vulgar theft. A man might conquer men by open violence, or by superior craft if force were unavailing; but tamely to steal was beneath the dignity of a true Indian, descendant of mighty sachems.

In short, deep-seated and long-suffering though Nikomis's affection was, it could not stand the strain of her contempt; and Sam's shameless avowal of his shame had fortified her scorn. Moreover, the thought that enriching him meant impoverishing the Urmsons bore weightily against him. For, although theoretically hostile toward Garth and his father, their charitable and kindly conduct toward her throughout the past years had not been without effect; insomuch that at this crisis she found herself, not a little to her own surprise, taking their part against her grandson and herself. It was a strange transformation, albeit by the logic of circumstances inevitable. Revenge, if put off too long, is apt to become an irksome affair, the realization of which would bring more disaster than its defeat. Yet it might be rash to credit Nikomis, on the strength of her quarrel with Sam, with an abandonment of all sinister designs against the Urmsons. Her nature was a dark and involved one, and she was probably capable of shielding her foe from an unworthy tomahawk, only in order to butcher him herself with proper respect afterward.

Meanwhile, before Sam could reopen the conversation upon a more conciliatory basis, Elinor's knock at the outer door of the house put an end to the interview for the time being. Nikomis, who supposed the visitor to be Mrs. Tenterden, prepared to go down; and the half-breed, with his pipe still between his teeth, turned on his side and composed himself for a nap. Nikomis, at the door of the wigwam, turned round, with the flap in her hand, and looked within. There lay Sam, the darkest object in the darkness, as he was the least heroic in her regard. With a grunt the old Indian let the flap fall over the opening, and so made the darkness uniform and complete. Then she turned away, and slowly hobbled down the garret-stairs. She had blotted her grandson out.

CHAPTER LXII.

MADGE'S VICISSITUDES.

ALTHOUGH Nikomis had opposed a tolerably impassive front toward her degenerate grandson, her heart was secretly bitter with its unsunned wrath, and she retired in a mood to avenge herself upon friend and foe alike. Had she, at this juncture, encountered Mrs. Tenterden instead of Elinor, the former's constitutional timidity and want of tact, acting upon the sardonic and exasperated temper of the Indian, might easily have brought on a catastrophe. But after her brief and vehement altercation with the younger lady, the old witch withdrew in a state of such composure as often results from the meeting together of two strenuous mental atmospheres. Yet the storm may have been rather postponed than dissipated, the exciting causes remaining. Nikomis might yet find occasion to relieve her soul.

Madge, after her interview with Sam in the small hours of the morning, had returned to her chamber glowing with pleasurable excitement. Lying upon her bed, her hands clasped between her cheek and the pillow, and her dark, sparkling eyes looking into the darkness, she had meditated until dawn. At an early hour she left the house and betook herself to Urmhurst, which she entered noiselessly by the kitchen-door. A few minutes afterward she was standing (as Sam had stood two or three hours before, and as Selwyn was to do not long afterward) by Cuthbert's bedside.

"He looks dead," she thought to herself. "What if he and Garth were dead—it's all so silent here!" She shook her head. "I shouldn't like it; I don't want it to be so. Death is disgusting; besides, then, everything would happen because there was no help for it, and there would be no chance of changing one's mind, nor of having one's way in spite of difficulty. I like uncertainty. I would not murder anybody; death is hateful; but for death the world would be good, because there'd be time enough for every one to get what he wanted out of life. No one is really wicked—only some have to do more in order to enjoy themselves than others. If Mr. Urmson, for instance, wanted to do all I mean to do, he'd have to be more wicked than I expect to be. But he is clever! he's the only man who ever came near understanding me. If my poor Garth were half so keen—"

As the thought of Garth entered her mind, she slowly moved toward his chamber; but on reaching the door she opened it brusquely. The face upon the pillow lay with its hollow, half-opened eyes turned toward her, while the lips moved in indistinct mutterings. Madge's warm, brilliant visage at first expressed aversion, but soon curiosity seemed to become dominant. She drew near and laid her white hand, firm and tenacious, despite its softness and dimples, on Garth's bony wrist, and tried to catch his unrecognizing eye with her own.

"What an unlucky fellow he is!" ran her thoughts; "I wish he were not; but that has always been the trouble with him. I could never get on with unlucky people, because I don't mean to be unlucky myself. I wish disagreeable people might be the only unfortunate ones, and all the agreeable, lucky! See what a man Garth is, in spite of his troubles! Any one else would look effeminate and silly after such an illness, but he seems only older and manlier. I like that coarse, black beard. He suits me—Garth, you suit me, on the whole, better than any one else. Why won't you be what I want you to be? But you won't, and if you did I suppose it would spoil you somehow—how provoking! I love him for not being what he must be if I'm to marry him! Dear me! what will become of me? I wish I knew what had become of some woman who was like me, and had felt as I do when she was a girl. . . . People here will be surprised when they hear of me, years from now—shocked, too, I suppose." She laughed under her breath, stroking Garth's unresponsive hand with hers.

"And what will you think, my Garth?" she whispered, bending over him. "O Garth, you mustn't die! I shouldn't half enjoy anything afterward—I should be thinking that perhaps I might have been happier with you. And so I should be—if there weren't so many ways of being happy! I should like to try them all, and then come back to him. No—dear me! I don't know what I do most want, and that's the worst of it. I don't want Golightley; and Sam. . . ." She rested her forefinger on her smooth cheek and meditated for several moments. Suddenly rousing herself, she drew a long breath, glanced toward the door, and then crouched down till her face was on a level with her lover's, and his feverish breath mingled with hers.

"Never mind about Sam, Garth dear," she whispered. "You are the best, no matter what happens. They may say I don't love you—but feel this, dear!" She pressed her mouth to his parched lips, and more than one heart-beat passed ere she removed it. "Do you think I would have done that for Sam?" she asked, smiling. "Have you poisoned me, my Garth?" Again she kissed him, deliberately as before, and afterward yet a third time. "Shall I have the fever and die? Let them say I didn't love you now, if they dare!" She sprang to her feet. "Good-by, Garth," she said, waving her hand, her face and figure radiant with life. "If I have poison on my lips—Sam shall be poisoned too! and you won't be jealous, will you?"

From Garth's chamber Madge descended to the kitchen, and, building up a fire there, proceeded to cook herself a comfortable breakfast. By the time this was eaten it was nearly ten o'clock, and she was preparing to go up-stairs to the wigwam when the sound of knocking at the outside door made her pause, and conceal herself in the alcove: for she did not wish her presence at Urmhurst to be known just at present to Mrs. Tenterden (whom she supposed the new arrival to be). But when, after entering the house, Elinor walked into the kitchen with her violin under her arm, Madge, in her surprise, stepped on a creaking board, and Elinor's eyes at once turned in the direction of the sound. The next moment, however, all risk of discovery was over ; Elinor left the kitchen and went up-stairs. Madge listened, and soon heard the sound of voices in dispute ; then ensued a silence ; and finally the old Indian came hobbling down and was received by Madge with an engaging smile.

The two exchanged a few words together —affable on Madge's part and sulky on that of Nikomis—and then the former made her way to the garret. As she passed Garth's door, the sound of music from within made her pause a moment. What right had Elinor to play to Garth? Madge had never yet found occasion to be jealous, but it did now occur to her that here was an infringement of her proprietorship. Should she go in and protest? No—she desired no present outbreak with Elinor; moreover, to assert exclusive rights over her lover would tend to cripple her freedom of action. She passed on, therefore; but the episode had its effect : a woman like Madge knows how to use a provocation both as a handle against an opponent and as a justification of wider liberties on her own part.

"Come in, Madge," said Sam, with a yawn, rolling himself over on the mattress at the summons of her voice at the wigwam entrance. "Come in—all at home!"

"Come outside immediately, Sam Kineo," retorted she, with dignity. "I wish to speak with you."

"By the devil, you can order a chap round!" muttered he, crawling out on his hands and knees and looking up at her. "Hi! she is a beauty, sure enough."

"That'll do for compliments," said Madge, in a tone of decision; "and be so kind as to use proper language when you speak to me. Are those your best clothes?"

"Good enough to lie in a garret with, aren't they? I've better in the box when the time comes."

"I wish you to come to the village with me this afternoon, and be introduced to everybody; so you had better put them on soon."

Sam chuckled sardonically. "I think I won't appear in society this afternoon, thank you," said he. "Some people might be too glad to see me."

"Afraid of the police!" exclaimed Madge, scornfully; and added, with a favorite phrase of hers, "If I were a man I'd never be afraid or ashamed to face anybody."

"Oh, you can talk about police; but how is a chap to face the United States army?" demanded Sam, sulkily.

"If you'd had any sense, Sam Kineo, you would have got all you wanted without interfering with the law at all."

"Gently now, Madge, that's a little dear. If you'd been with me, it would ha' been all right, no doubt; but you wouldn't come when I asked you."

"What do you mean? I am to marry Garth Urmson. I've nothing to do with you."

"Marry Garth—eh? curse him! If you'd said that last night, I'd have cut his heart out for him this morning."

Madge laughed. "You haven't forgotten how he thrashed you when you were boys. But you mustn't think I'm so foolish as I was in those days. Do you suppose I'd run away with an escaped robber when I might stay at home and marry a prosperous artist?"

The half-breed fastened his narrow, level glance on the young woman's blooming face. "You look here now," muttered he; "I'm not so foolish now as then, either. You've fooled me twice in my life, and that's enough. You may call me an escaped robber, but I'll be an escaped something else before I'll see you and Garth come together!"

Madge drew nearer her companion and rested her hand on his arm. "What fun!"

said she. "It's quite romantic to hear you talk that way. Do it some more, won't you?"

"No need of that," returned the half-breed. "You know what I mean."

"How stupid you are! I thought you would be at least as entertaining as Golightley; but he is ever so much better than you are."

"Golightley Urmson is no better than I am," returned Sam, moodily; "and I'll make him feel it before I'm done with him. Maybe you didn't know that he and I were pals?"

Though there were few things which Madge knew better than this, she chose to express proper surprise, and so drew from Sam the same story which he had just told Nikomis, together with some further particulars which Nikomis had not heard. An hour or two passed away in the narration, when it was interrupted by a loud summons rapped out upon the house-door below.

"That sounds like a policeman!" exclaimed Madge, maliciously.

She rose as she spoke; but to her astonishment Sam caught her wrist and violently dragged her down again. "If that's the police," whispered he, between his teeth, "it's a bad day for you, Madge Danver!"

"I hope it is the police," she cried, passionately, struggling to free her wrist.

By a rapid movement, Sam pinioned the girl, and pushed her back against the hand-organ box. She struggled desperately, and, being exceedingly strong for a woman, would probably have escaped from a man less powerful than Kineo. But he gripped her like a vise, and his fingers sank deep into the firm flesh of her arms. At length, with short breath and cheeks afire, she gasped, "If you don't loose me, I'll scream."

"Then I'll cut your throat," he hissed in her ear. "Curse you, I can hate easier than love you. You little jade! think you could bully me?"

"Sam, let me go!"

He gripped her tighter, and snickered. "Want to marry dear Garth, do you? You little liar! How'd you like to see that pretty scalp of yours hanging there with the others—eh?"

"Sam—I'll never be false to you."

"Wait till I cut your throat, my little dear—then I might trust you. Think I forgot how you lied about me to Garth ten years ago? I'd not trust you out of reach of my knife for all Golightley's money and Mother Eve's legacy put together!"

"What have I done?"

"We'll see, my little dear. If you've set the police on me .... hush!"

Madge Danver, full of life as she was, would rather have died than endure the suspense of the minute that followed. A man's step, resolute, and vigorous, was audible on the lower flight of stairs. Who could it be? Had some hideous fatality actually brought the police to the house, at this moment of all others? If that vigorous step kept on up the garret-stairs, Sam would murder her, in the belief that she was an accomplice against him. He held her rigidly down, though she had ceased struggling, and they were both listening intently. As she lay there, her memory reviewed all her past relations with this man, and she fancied that, beneath her uniformly arrogant bearing toward him, she had always harbored a secret fear—nay, had even foreseen the present crisis, and herself at his mercy. She was conquered, perhaps in the only way that such a woman could be conquered, by sheer physical force and brutality. And as she panted in the grasp of the man who had conquered her, and who might the next moment become her murderer, she felt a strange and new satisfaction in him. He was the incarnation of power, irresponsible and irresistible; and he could not have hit upon a better way of wooing this wayward creature. She might be quicker-witted than he, but his muscles had forced her to the brink of eternity, and the superiority was a real and substantial one.

Meantime the steps had paused on the bedroom-floor, and there was a low murmur of voices. Was the officer showing a search-warrant, and demanding information? As the two strained their ears to listen, it suddenly came into Madge's mind that of course the enigmatic stranger could be none other than Jack Selwyn. Instantly the painful tension of her mind and body relaxed, she broke into a faint, tremulous laugh, and murmuring, "It's all right, Sam—I'm so glad!" her head drooped over sideways, and she fainted away.

CHAPTER LXIII.

POISON.

SAM loosed his victim with a grunt of surprise, and saw her topple over toward the right and lie limp and insensible on the floor. Before he could make up his mind what to do next, Nikomis had entered. At sight of Madge she stopped short; then fixed her eyes on Sam. "You fool!" she exclaimed, gutturally, "you killed her?"

"Not I!" replied the half-breed; "she's fainted, that's all. Who came?"

"No one t' hurt you," grunted the Indian, stooping over the girl.

It was not long before Madge began to gasp and sigh, and the color to flow back to lips and cheek. Anon she upraised herself giddily on one arm, and put her other hand over her heart, afterward holding up the fingers, as if to see whether they were bloody.

"I thought you had stabbed me," she murmured with a shudder.

Sam felt ill at ease; the glow of his ferocity had cooled, and it did not occur to him that Madge could be free from resentment at his treatment of her. He had probably been carried beyond his original intention by mere savage excitement; but he was alarmed to think how narrowly he had missed committing a crime objectless in itself, and sure to have been fatally disastrous to him.

"Come, now, forgive and forget!" said he, sitting down by Madge, and assuming his most agreeable manner. "What's the use of you and me bearing malice, Madge?"

Madge gazed at him thoughtfully for a while, saying at last with a sigh: "You are a real devil, Sam, aren't you?—No, don't mind my saying it. I think a real devil is what I need. I shall never forget how you looked. . . ." Here she shuddered again. "No one but you would have treated me so —I am so beautiful. Any one else would have relented. But what can you be made of?"

"Flesh and blood, ain't I?"

"Well, perhaps!" She eyed him curiously. "Can you really be my hero? I ought to hate you. It isn't quite pleasant to have been conquered, after all."

"Oh, I wouldn't have hurt you," affirmed Sam, reassuringly.

There was a gleam in the young woman's eyes as she answered: "If I believed that, I would despise you as well as hate you. But it's false; you meant to do it!" She raised her hand and laid it on his shoulder appealingly. "Don't you disappoint me, too! I have tried so many things; I'm tired. Don't speak any more about it; you don't understand me; you'd only say something stupid."

It was true that Madge was a mystery to the half-breed; yet he was shrewd enough to perceive that his violence had somehow not wholly displeased her. Perhaps the right way to win a woman's heart was to threaten it with a bowie-knife. However evil are a man's deeds, he may generally be persuaded that some involuntary virtue is mixed up with them; and, however bad he may be, the virtuous persuasion flatters him.

"It was Jack Selwyn who came," remarked Madge, after a pause. "A friend of Garth's; they were in Europe together. Did you never meet him?"

"Selwyn?—hold on! a slender, sharp-eyed chap, always dressed well? By the devil, shouldn't wonder if I did know him, after all! Selwyn. You knew he was going to be here—eh?"

"Yes. Does he know you by sight?"

"Not he! knows Golightley, though; Golightley thought he suspected something."

"At all events, Selwyn knows all about the robbery, and I think he's after you." She was speaking in a faint, listless tone, and Sam sat motionless, his dark face set in malevolent abstraction. Nikomis had retired into the wigwam some time before, and both Madge and Sam had forgotten her.

"Think he's brought any one with him?" inquired the half-breed after a while.

Madge shook her head.

Sam reflected a minute and then asked,

"How did you come to know 'bout this affair of ours before I told you?"

"From Mrs. Tenterden, and from Golightley, and from a letter," replied Madge, nonchalantly. Then, noticing Sam's surprise, she added with a smile, "The letter was from Jack Selwyn."

"He writes to you—eh?" hissed the other, with a momentary return of the savage.

The young woman smiled again, somewhat defiantly.

"Got him after you, too, eh?—by the devil! How does he begin, then?—'Madge dearest,' or 'My sweet mistress,' or what is it—eh?"

"Ah!" cried Madge, angrily; for a woman will endure bullying far more submissively than coarseness. "If you know how it began, you may find out what was in it!"

Perceiving that he had made a mistake, Sam would again have attempted an apology; but Madge impatiently stopped him. "Never mind—never mind. The letter was written to Garth, but I read it, without Garth's knowing."

"I see!" nodded the other with a glance of crafty significance. "You . . . . eh?"

"I found it in the woods," said Madge, hastily.

Sam still nodded significantly, as much as to say that the finding was wonderfully opportune. "So Selwyn's the chap's been tracking me down!" he muttered, presently. "Did you show this letter to Golightley?"

"No—nor to any one else. Don't suspect me, Sam; if I chose to deceive you, I could do it without your suspecting. I didn't wish to frighten Uncle Golightley away, nor to let him know how much I knew about him. But you can do me neither good nor harm—except bodily harm."

There was a sincerity in her tone which was pathetic, because, in her, it betrayed so much inward stress; and Kineo could not but feel some sense of her forgiving disposition toward him. "I've been shabby to you, my little beauty," said he, "and I'm sorry for it—by the devil I am! Tell you what, Madge, if you 'nd me pull together we can fool Jack Selwyn 'nd all his gang. Just you get round Selwyn 'nd find out how much he knows, and if he suspects I'm here, just throw him off the scent—d'ye see? You've got brains, 'nd, if you do the best you can for me, I'm satisfied."

"I should think you might be, Sam Kineo," she answered, quietly. "But what shall I get in return for it? How can you help me? Uncle Golightley is too clever for you. If he marries Elinor, don't you see he's sure of the money whether he's found out or not."

"Not a bad notion—marrying the woman you've robbed!" assented the other. "We ought to stop that off, somehow."

"When do you mean to see Golightley?"

"Oh, soon enough. And look here, Madge Danver—if that chap Selwyn's in love with Elinor as well, he'd bear easy on the man that could prove his rival a thief—eh?"

"What do you think of me?" asked Madge, abruptly.

"Sweetest piece of flesh ever I came across! what more d'you want?"

She gave a short, hard laugh. "Nothing, I suppose. But I mean, you seem to think I would stop at nothing. I've never done anything very wicked, yet."

The half-breed ducked his head in noise-less cachinnation. "Yes—you look innocent enough, 'nd that's the wickedest part of you. I know you—you love devilry just for its own sake, 'nd you can't keep your fingers out of it."

"It isn't true!" cried Madge, getting to her feet excitedly. "I like good people and good things—only—"

Sam had risen too, and, catching her hands in his, he peered with a penetrating grimace into her eyes. "No you don't—no you don't—no you don't!" he repeated, shaking his head slowly. "No use, my little dear; should have liked good things before that picnic that you and I and Garth went to. Too late now—the devil's got you—better give in to him!"

She flushed, and tears filled her eyes; then she grew pale and smiled. Immediately Sam threw his arm around her waist and kissed her, not reverently, upon the mouth; kissed those lips which were poisoned now, if never before.

15

She partly freed herself from him, and at the same moment they both, by a common impulse looked toward the opening of the wigwam. There appeared the grotesque visage of Nikomis, swarthy and framed in darkness: and her black eyes seemed to gleam approval of what had been done.

———

CHAPTER LXIV.

COUNTERMINING.

THE arrival of Golightley and Professor Grindle, shortly after the episode just described, brought to an end that parallel movement of events whose progress has been indicated from the earliest hours of the morning. Madge returned with Elinor to the village in the afternoon, and Selwyn undertook the care of his friend Garth during the ensuing night.

The next morning Professor Grindle, finding Garth still on the mending hand, bade farewell to the household and set off through the woods to the village. It was a gray, cold day, and the professor resentfully anticipated an early and severe winter. "The young folks will enjoy it, no doubt," muttered he, as he gathered his old-fashioned top-coat more closely about him, and stepped sturdily along the frost-hardened pathway; "but after a fellow gets to be forty, he should move a degree nearer to the equator every year, and allow the sun to restore the caloric which old age takes away. I don't know, though; if all the graybeards lived in the south, and left the youths and maidens to their own devices up north, the world would go to rack and ruin very soon. Ay, and what would we poor duffers do without them, to remind us of what we once were, or hoped to be?—Hullo! there she is."

At the end of a long, leafless vista an erect and slender figure, equipped in fur-lined jacket and muff, had come into view. As they neared each other, the old gentleman lifted his hat, exposing his bald pate to the icy breeze, while Elinor, whose face was pink with cold and exercise, smiled and became pinker still.

"Good-morning, young lady," he called

out in his strident, kindly tones; "I wish I had such a nice muff to keep my old fingers warm! May I ask your permission to walk back a little distance and chat with you?"

"I'd rather go with you, Professor Grindle, if you don't mind," replied she, turning. "How are your patients?"

"Garth'll get well; Cuthbert won't," said Grindle, sternly.

"I know Mr. Urmson very little, I suppose," said Elinor, after a pause; "but I can't help feeling that I love him."

"Ay, ay, Cuthbert stands high in our Yankee peerage, as an honest, enlightened, tender-hearted man. May his son prove worthy of him!—I think he will."

"They are very unlike," was all Elinor's answer.

"Ay, that they are. Well, young lady, like or unlike, I leave them in your care. I've left all necessary prescriptions in writing, but you don't need to be told what the errands of mercy are."

"Thank you, Professor Grindle. I've never been useful to anybody; I shall be glad if you will teach me how to begin." This was said with earnestness, tempered only by the reserve which rendered most of Elinor's utterances apparently mere society-talk. But Grindle, in addition to his native penetration, had heard enough about Miss Golightley during the past twenty-four hours to enable him to estimate her more accurately than most of her acquaintance. There was a cordial glow in his resolute old eyes as he looked upon her.

"You'll give the sick people music from time to time," said he. "Harmony and melody are valuable commodities in this world, and those who can produce them deserve the world's thanks."

"I like to think that music may do more than merely amuse people," remarked Elinor, looking up shyly.

"Urmhurst is a fine field for a purveyor of harmony, just now, my dear young lady. You apprehend me—I don't speak strictly by the letter. Your violin is the symbol of something deeper and better."

"But you must not think that I am like my music; I have no such power."

"Well, well, we'll not quarrel about that," said Grindle, smiling. "Now, you'll pardon me if, in speaking of our patients, I take you a bit into the family confidence—and after all, you know, you're a cousin. Cuthbert is a man who cannot live long; but peace of mind, though it won't cure him, is his best medicine: and I find that this match between Garth and Maggie Danver causes him great anxiety—he thinks they don't really care for each other."

"Does Mr. Urmson wish me to hear this, sir?"

"Telling you of it is my own idea entirely. 'Tis the old story, you perceive, of a boy and girl falling in love, and growing up to repent it, and yet, for one cause or another, failing to break it off. Now, interference in these affairs, unless delicately managed, is quite as apt to tighten the knot as to loosen it. An honorable man, so long as he believes his mistress true to him, would chop his right hand off sooner than deny her. But if there were evidence that she wasn't true—the case would be altered. Are you intimate with Madge Danver, Miss Elinor?"

The intonation given to these words explained their significance. Elinor flushed suddenly. "I would rather not have suspicions," said she.

Grindle gave a grimly humorous smile. "Wrong should not be suffered, my dear young lady," said he, "through disinclination on the part of honest people to take counsel against it."

"I think we are more apt to wish our suspicions true than to find them so," returned Elinor, shrinkingly.

"Ay, ay," assented Grindle, with his uncompromising nod. "But should the career of a young fellow who might do good in the world be spoiled by the selfishness of a pretty girl, who, however she may wish her own advantage, would most likely ruin him without securing it?"

Elinor took one hand from her muff and let both hands fall at her sides; her figure drooped, and the light faded from her eyes. Grindle, looking at her, had a new impression of her personality. Her face had a charm easily missed by an unsympathetic observer, but which, once recognized, was fascinating forever after. It was a face in which nobleness and severity were singularly blended with tender human irregularity: it contained a discord analogous to that by which great composers elicit their most poignant harmonies. She had spent her life without finding a fit opportunity for parting asunder the veil which hid her inward ardor and impetuosity. Professor Grindle half doubted whether he would be justified in urging these latent forces into action. To cut a leash is a less revocable proceeding than to apply a spur.

"What right have I to meddle between them?" she demanded at last.

"The universal.human right to support a good cause," answered the professor, with great gentleness. "Besides, there's no one to take your place. Cuthbert has begun to stagger under his responsibility: your young shoulders may relieve him, if you will. You are a heroine, Miss Elinor, if you'll let yourself be one."

"I'm afraid I could not be impartial," said she.

"Glad to hear it!" cried Grindle, heartily. "Be heart and soul on the right side, and don't mind about giving quarter till all's over. And now I've said all I need say, Miss Elinor, so I'll only add good-by." He stopped and held out his hand, Elinor putting her own frankly within it.

"I'm glad we met, Professor Grindle," said she, with a smile and a look that made the hackneyed phrase valuable.

"God bless her!" muttered Grindle, more than once, as he tramped toward the village. "I might have had a daughter like her!"

When Elinor came in view of Urmhurst she saw a gentleman with a cigar in his mouth approaching from the direction of the farm-yard. He was sauntering meditatively along, holding his cane behind his back with both hands, except when, from time to time, he took the cigar from beneath his mustache and filliped away the white ash. He did not seem aware of Elinor's approach, and she had leisure to remark the slender, vigorous grace of his figure, the manly, keen-eyed comeliness of his face, and even the excellent fit and good taste of his apparel. The shadows of life seemed to abate somewhat of their gloom in view of this handsome, energetic, and independent young fellow, who could dress so well and puff his cigar so composedly through them all.

As he caught sight of her he took off his fur cap and made a bow—gracefully enough this time—and exclaimed cheerfully: "Good-morning, Miss Golightley! How's the old lady?"

Elinor smiled in spite of herself at this rather irreverent paraphrase for Mrs. Tenterden; but Jack Selwyn was not like other people, so she only replied that the lady in question was doing rather better.

"That's all right," observed Jack. "Garth had a tip-top night, too, as I know to my cost; he'll be out skating by Christmas. Mr. Urmson's asleep in celebration of his son's convalescence. Golightley's got the dyspepsia from too many buckwheats, and even I have been obliged to smoke an extra cigar and take a run over the farm-yard. Ever been in the barn, Miss Golightley?"

"I never was in any barn, I don't think."

"Deuce! wish I might have the luck to introduce you to many a better enjoyment. Come on, and know what you've never known till now!"

She went beside him, smiling occasionally as he chatted about the weather and the country, until he lifted the broad, wooden latch, and ushered her into the fragrant, brown-shadowed interior. He then pulled out the old sleigh to the middle of the floor, and arranged a comfortable seat in it with the buffalo-robe.

"This is very jolly," said Elinor; "how good the hay smells; and nothing can be sweeter than cows' breath!"

"Oh, yes, there can!" Jack longed to retort; but he repressed himself, and said instead: "So you like New England savagery? Do you mean to live here?"

"I believe my mother and—Mr. Golightley Urmson think of living in New York."

"To tell the truth and shame the devil, I don't adore Golightley myself, and am not going to congratulate you on his having the right to dispose of you. Are you angry?"

"It's the devil who ought to be offended, I should think," said Elinor, lifting her brows a trifle.

"I hope he may be, before I'm done with him!" muttered Jack, setting his teeth. "Well—but look here; about that money-business of yours."

"Mrs. Tenterden's? She will be very much obliged to you."

"Oh, damn her obligations—no, no! I mean it's very kind of her to let me be of some use. She'll recover probably two-thirds of what was stolen—say eighty thousand pounds."

Elinor sat still and gradually became very pale; the announcement had taken her by surprise, and seemed to produce anything but a pleasant effect upon her. "It's too late now," she said, at length, rather bitterly. "All the good things in life wait until you don't need them before they come. What should a girl on the eve of a wealthy marriage want with eighty thousand pounds? But it was very kind of you, Mr. Selwyn."

"Oh, that's all right!" returned Jack, very cheerfully. "Yes, Golightley has just about the same sum we hope to recover for you—eighty thousand. Funny, isn't it?"

"Yes," murmured Elinor, abstractedly; but all at once she turned and said, "What do you mean?"

"Nothing; only it's funny, you know."

"Where is the man who stole the money?"

"Under surveillance. But it's the accomplice we're after—want to get State's evidence out of him. We believe he's hiding somewhere hereabouts."

"State's evidence? Does that mean betraying the other?"

"It's this way. The accomplice has in his possession letters or proofs of some kind, which are necessary to the conviction of—a —the chief scoundrel. And the accomplice has spent all his share of the booty. Therefore, his evidence is worth more to us than his person, and if he'll sell it in consideration of escaping prosecution, we'll agree to the bargain."

"That is, you punish one thief for keeping what he has stolen, and pardon the other for having dissipated his part?"

"Oh, we'll be down on both of them with all the pleasure in the world, if it can be managed," said Jack, smiling.

"Does the principal know that he is under surveillance?"

"Rather imagine not, Miss Golightley."

"He lives openly—isn't hiding, as the accomplice is?"

Jack nodded, not certain whither this swift questioning tended.

"He lives openly—as you and I and Mr. Urmson do—here in our neighborhood?"

"Hold on! what put his being 'in our neighborhood' in your head?"

"You said the accomplice was without money, and hiding hereabouts. He could only come here to get money from the principal, and so the principal must be here as well."

"You are deuced clever," said Jack, smiling upon her admiringly. "I must tell you though that it's very evident you know nothing at all about this affair; and, since I have charge of it, and it isn't finished yet, I sha'n't let you know anything."

"I don't wish to be told anything," replied Elinor, with one of her point-blank looks. "But I don't like your consenting to such a piece of meanness."

"Hullo! why, what?"

"Encouraging one of these men to betray the other."

"But, look here—if we can't touch the chief scamp in any other way—"

"Then don't touch him at all!" exclaimed Elinor, with a glance and a tone that made Jack's eyes sparkle; and, rising as she spoke, she bade him good-morning and walked out of the barn, and thus ended the conversation.

"She can't really care for the blackguard, you know," said Jack to himself afterward, reviewing her words and behavior. "But does she suspect Golightley of being the blackguard? If not, why take blackguard's part? Hum—why take it any way? As to scruples against State's evidence—inadmissible, of course; though it does seem mean, as she says. What a divine, glorious creature she is, now! Compare her with Madge. By-the-way, I must make friends with Madge again, and see whether she can't tell us anything about that accomplice. I wish this damned business was settled, so I might attend to my own! She doesn't care for me yet, but she may at last! God bless her, whether she does or not!"

CHAPTER LXV.

HOUSEWORK.

THE current of affairs at Urmhurst now flowed on with that smoothness vulgarly supposed to be of ill omen. Garth rapidly grew better, but there was a change apparent in him such as may often be noticed in new convalescents, but which generally fades away with the full return of health. To lie in the same bed with death purifies a man, at least for a time. With Garth, an ugly knot seemed to have been loosened at the centre of his spiritual life, setting free his nobler energies.

It was a rule of the sick-chamber that no painful topic should be discussed in it; and thus Garth's bedside became a sort of moral oasis in the midst of a wilderness of conflicting interests and passions. Here did the world put on its most smiling and light-hearted aspect; and if anybody during the day thought of anything agreeable to be said or done, such word or deed was reserved for the court of his majesty King Convalescent. An unimpassioned observer (were such a monster possible) would have admired the change wrought in the bearing, and seemingly in the very nature, of some half-dozen rational human beings, when they stepped across the threshold of this enchanted chamber. It was analogous to the difference of colors in light and shadow. Garth's august infirmity forbade the impertinence of gloom.

"Nothing like the typhoid for putting a moody, sulky, crack-brained brute of a genius in a good-humor," remarked Jack Selwyn to his friend one day. "But hurry up and get well, man, and come out skating, that the world may benefit by your improvement."

"When I go skating, Jack, there'll be an end of this peace and good-will we're all making so much of. I've not been ill for nothing—and I won't get well for nothing, please God!"

"Oh, damn your holiness! It's because you couldn't help it, in both cases."

Garth laughed.

"Well, what do you think you've been ill for?"

"I did some strange thinking. I imagined I was going through a great spiritual experience. I was in a fight between devils and angels—and, what seemed odd, they had the voices of members of the family and acquaintances! At last, when I was at the very bottom of the pit, I was lifted out by a divine angel of harmony."

"The first sane word you've said yet!" cried Jack. "Elinor Golightley is a divine angel of harmony. The rest is bosh."

"No it isn't," returned Garth. "When a fellow has been knocking about in chaos for what seems thousands of lifetimes, he doesn't come out feeling quite so selfish and impudent as when he went in."

"I think I'll try your recipe, if you haven't patented it. Get my fever, go to bed, dream and gibber my way through chaos for three weeks, and then jump up and prate about my spiritual vicissitudes—and pose as a saint ever afterward!"

"Confound you, Jack Selwyn, how dare you exasperate me when I'm ill? I'll tell Elinor Golightley!"

"Don't!" cried Jack; "I'd rather you'd punch my head." He tossed the end of his cigar behind the fire, and rested his elbows on his knees. "This has been a jolly fortnight, Garth, old fellow. We'll not see such another soon."

"Where do you suppose we'll be ten years from now?"

"Ten years! Say ten weeks. I'm none of your Parson Graemes, or Methuselahs even!" said Jack, getting impatiently to his feet. "Hark! there comes Miss Golightley with your dinner. Good-by; I'm going to the lake to see if the ice bears."

Elinor, having arranged Garth's dinner for him, took up her favorite position by the window, whence she could gaze out upon the frosty sky, and the bleak valley beneath it. This young lady had during the last two weeks become the governing spirit at Urmhurst. For the first time since gentle Martha Urmson's death, Urmhurst had found a mistress. Elinor was by no means averse from taking a human interest in lowly affairs; her scope was broader than that of the mere lady of culture and refinement. And the duties she performed reacted upon herself: she was less frigid and haughty, and her eyes were brighter and her voice cheerier, than before her houskeeping began.

"When I was a boy," observed Garth, "my mother handed over the housework to me for nearly a year. I did everything, from sawing wood to making pudding. Do you do as much as that?"

"Almost. You should have seen my hands a week ago: there was a great blister on this finger, and a sore place inside the thumb, and a scald on the wrist. But after all, you know, I have the Danvers' char-woman to help me. She is very amusing. She said yesterday she didn't like scrubbing and rubbing about an old place like this; it was like cleaning and laying out a corpse ready for burial!"

"Is poor old Urmhurst so near its death?" muttered Garth.

"I told you to make you laugh," said Elinor, reprovingly. "Another time, when we were brushing the cobwebs from the great beams in the ceilings, she said it was cruel to strip the poor things of their coverings, just when winter was coming on."

"What is Nikomis doing all this time?"

"She is such a strange old creature—she grows stranger every day. Lately she has taken to wearing beads and old feathers, and such things; and once she appeared with her face painted in blue and yellow stripes. She doesn't work herself, but sometimes she watches the charwoman and me with a kind of smile—if you can imagine her smiling!—as if the house were hers, and we her servants. And once, when we had gone to put the cellar in order— If you've done your dinner, I'll take the tray out."

"No—I must hear the rest first."

"Well," resumed Elinor, smiling, and growing pink, "the amount of it is that we were given to understand that the cellar was her exclusive property, and no one was to trespass in it. For, when we got to the bottom of the stairs, she suddenly rose up before us, throwing up her arms and motioning us back. She looked like the spectre of the old sachem that Mr. Urmson says is buried there."

"Yes, there's no telling what awful secrets may be hidden in that cellar. Have you ever been in her wigwam, up in the garret?"

"No, indeed. But sometimes I hear a rumbling sound, as if she were talking to herself there: and the two tones are quite different; it reminded me of the chanting of the priests in the Roman Catholic churches."

Here Elinor took up the tray, and, remarking that she must go down and make the coffee, she departed in spite of Garth's expostulations.

It was doubtless fortunate for Elinor that this pressure of alien duties and interests kept her from brooding too much over her own destiny. Her housework gave her wholesome bodily exercise and fatigue, while her mind was busied with the difficult and delicate enterprise of searching for the clew to the problem intrusted to her by Professor Grindle. A main obstacle in the way of success was the necessity of working in silence and unaided. A feminine intuition restrained her from seeking the help of Jack Selwyn, and there were equally good reasons against taking counsel with Cuthbert. For, clear-brained and honest though she was, Elinor lacked the authority which wifehood always confers in emergencies of this kind; and, in the present instance, her embarrassment was perhaps increased by the fact that the person whose marriage prospects were in jeopardy happened to be Garth.

Meanwhile, time dragged along very irksomely with Sam Kineo. The fact that he was comparatively safe so long as he staid in the wigwam, only made abiding there more dismal to him: there was not even the excitement of uncertainty and suspense.

"Tell you what, Madge," he grumbled out one day, as she stood at the door of the wigwam, looking down upon him, "I'm going to see Golightley now; get this thing over, one way or 'nother. You tell him I must see him to-night."

"You'd better leave me to manage him; he'll get the better of you, somehow. And I sometimes think, from the way he goes on, that he has done something already to make himself safe."

"I've got something to make him safe!" growled Sam, tapping the breast of his coat.

"If you mean that old bowie-knife of yours—"

"Knife?—it's his handwriting I'm talking about. No, no! no use knifing Golightley yet awhile. I'd like to knife that chap Selwyn."

"He's the only man I ever met that I couldn't make in love with me," remarked Madge, thoughtfully. "But that's because he's so infatuated with Elinor Golightley. I can't make out, though, why she doesn't marry him instead of Golightley."

"Oh, no telling 'bout women!" muttered Sam, contemptuously. "Most likely she's in love with Garth, and jealous of you."

"In love with Garth!" repeated Madge, sharply; then she smiled incredulously. "Poor Garth! nobody was ever in love with him but I: and he never loved any one but me. I've never had the fun of being jealous."

"You just wait," returned Sam, chuckling maliciously. "Going? Fill my pipe for me first, there's a little dear; and don't forget about Golightley."

On leaving the wigwam and its loutish occupant, Madge descended wearily to the bedroom floor. It was quite dark; from Garth's chamber came sounds of light-hearted talk and laughter. Suddenly the door opened, and Elinor came forth, her whole bearing eloquent of alert and cheerful composure. Madge drew noiselessly aside and saw her, herself unseen, pass down the broad staircase. A sphere of purity and wholesomeness seemed to invest her as she moved. Madge gave a short sigh, and passed her hand across her forehead. After a few moments' hesitation she advanced toward the door which Elinor had just closed, and laid her finger on the latch. But her purpose, whatever it may

have been, faltered: she drew back, and went wearily on down-stairs. In truth, it was a long way from the wigwam to Garth's chamber.

CHAPTER LXVI.

A NEW NEPHEW.

AFTER supper that night, the audience being assembled as usual in the convalescent's room, Elinor took up her violin and made ready to play. Whereupon Uncle Golightley, who had been making himself highly entertaining for the past half-hour, got up and caressed his cheeks and settled his eye-glasses.

"Now I'm going to be impolite," said he, stepping to Elinor's side and taking her hand lightly in his. "Instead of listening to your music I'm going to retire to my room and see whether I can't get rid of a confounded headache that's been dogging me all day. By-by! pray that I may reappear sound and whole at breakfast." He raised her finger-tips gallantly to his lips, waved his hand with a smile to Garth and Cuthbert, and departed.

Among many odd specifics for the cure of headaches, Golightley's was certainly one of the oddest. Having shut himself into his room, he slipped a pair of India-rubber over-shoes over his boots, washed his hands carefully, brushed his hair and beard, and ended by putting on a jaunty traveling-cap and a pair of lemon-colored kid gloves. After surveying himself in the glass, he took from a corner of the room a handsome gold-headed walking-stick. Pressing a spring in the handle, he drew forth out of its hiding-place a long, blue, needle-pointed stiletto. He examined the blade closely, tried the point upon his thumb, resheathed it slowly, and remained for several moments with the cane balanced across his hand and his eyes fixed doubtfully upon it. At length he seemed to alter his mind as to the expediency of taking the weapon with him, and, replacing it in its corner, he stepped out of the room and noiselessly ascended the garret-stairs.

The person who admitted him to Niko-mis's apartment closed the door after him and fastened it. The room was lighted only by the small oil-lamp which was burning inside the wigwam. Golightley, having removed his eye-glasses, was able to discern a tall, athletic figure standing close beside him. "Mr. Flint, I presume?" said he. "Is your respected female relative present?"

"Just you 'nd me alone together, and the door locked!" was the somewhat menacing reply. Apparently the host meant to intimidate his visitor before dealing with him.

"I've no doubt you're right in thinking we're alone, Sam," rejoined the latter, easily, replacing his eye-glasses. "Still, you know, *humanum est errare.* I'll trouble you to bring that lamp out of the tent, and let me have a look for myself. Elderly men, you know, get fussy about small matters.—The lamp, if you please!" he repeated in a louder but still affable tone. "Or shall I call downstairs for one?"

"Oh, take a look 'f you like," said Sam, with a sneer. He brought out the lamp, and Golightley, taking it from his hand, stepped back and surveyed him attentively from head to foot, smiling blandly the while.

"The face is the face of Samuel," he remarked at length ; "but the toggery is the toggery of—where *did* you find those garments, my young friend? singular eccentricity in a fellow with fifty thousand pounds in his pocket!"

Mr. Flint gave a snarl, and stepped quite close up to his interlocutor, as if to emphasize his own superiority in height and brawn. "I don't want that sort of talk," said he. "My money's gone, 'nd you've got to make it up to me."

"See what comes of wearing shabby clothes! Your pocket, I suppose, had a hole in it?" As Golightley made this laughing reply, he held the lamp close to Sam's face, which wore at this moment a most unamiable expression. "Take it," he added, "it's soiling my gloves; and I'll excuse you from hunting after eavesdroppers this time. Will you lead the way into your boudoir?" They entered, and the visitor threw himself down on the mattress and looked about him. "Ah! so this is the abode of the noble savage!" said he, as he drew off his gloves. "And— one, two, three, four—by George! do you

mean to say the old lady lifted all that hair herself?"

"If 't hadn't been for Nikomis," answered Sam, who had squatted down just inside the wigwam-door, "my mother's scalp would ha' been there too."

"Really? And may I ask who your mother was?"

"You know, but I don't mind telling you. She was your father's daughter."

"That's interesting," murmured Golightley, producing a cigarette. "And what may have been my sister's married name?"

"I've got the papers. All safe, 'bout that."

"It's to be hoped they're drawn up in proper form," rejoined the other, as he struck a match. "If it's your ambition to share with Garth the honor of being my nephew, you must be careful not to tell lies, you know. However, taking the papers for granted, what next? Have you any plans?"

"Oh, I know what b'longs to me!" said Sam, nodding his head.

"Eve's legacy, eh? Well, now, Samuel, I'll speak to you for argument's sake, as if you were the nephew you profess to be, as well as the thieving vagabond that you are. —There, there—don't get excited! Try one of my cigarettes. Now keep your eye on me!"

Here the speaker sat erect, and spreading out the long fingers of his left hand, accented his discourse upon them with the forefinger of his right.

"Assuming, then, the lawful heir to have arrived armed with the proper credentials, we have first to consider certain irregularities of his, evidence of which is in the hands of the police, and which constitute him a felon. This fact, we may suppose, would make him feel a certain delicacy about proclaiming himself, as it were, from the housetops; he would be more likely, perhaps, to hide himself in the top of the house—ha, ha! Well, but let us suppose that this legacy was not his only resource; that he had another, by which he might benefit without being obliged to declare his identity. Let us suppose, in short, that the uncle of this individual possessed a fortune of a good many thousand pounds."

"What's the use of all this powwow?" interrupted Sam, surlily. "Twenty thousand pounds is my figure, 'nd low enough, too. If you don't pay up, I'll turn State's evidence—that's all about it!"

"The value of State's evidence, my dear Samuel," rejoined Golightley, still unruffled, "depends upon its being obtainable only from one source. Now, in the present case, without questioning your possession of sufficient evidence to convict me, I must inform you that, if you decide upon giving that evidence, it will be at once forestalled, and thus rendered valueless. In other words, rather than put you to the pain of swearing your uncle into jail, I would swear myself in! See the point?"

Golightley was evidently enjoying his command of the situation, and the humorous sententiousness of his statement of it; while Sam could not but feel that he had been to some extent outwitted. He reflected, however, that although Golightley might, by surrendering his booty, and giving himself up to justice, nullify Sam's own attack, he must still be willing to pay liberally for the assurance of Sam's silence. What other propositions he might have in reserve, the half-breed could not divine; so he waited sullenly for developments; and his patience was rewarded.

"It amounts to about this," said the elder man. "You have, or are supposed to have, two things which I am willing to buy of you. The first thing is the bundle of my letters and memoranda relating to our little transaction abroad. The second thing is the certificate of your mother's marriage, and your own birth. I'm disposed to be generous. How much?"

Sam was neither a saint nor a person ordinarily sensitive about his honor; yet the idea of selling his birthright struck him unpleasantly. He had, all his life, had occasion to lament the disadvantages of obscure birth; and having only within the last few weeks come to a knowledge of his true parentage, he was not disposed lightly to surrender the proofs of it. True, he could make no practical use of it at present; but every human being has something which, to him, is above being bartered for on any

terms: and in Sam's case this priceless treasure turned out (somewhat to his own surprise and annoyance, perhaps) to be his birthright. He was perplexed, and a little ashamed, but he could not help it.

"I don't want to be hard on an old pal," he said, in his rapid, undertoned way. "Give me a check for ten thousand pounds, 'nd you may have your letters."

"Ten thousand for the letters?—modest, upon my word! But I suppose you throw the certificates in?"

"Not a bit of it! I mean to keep those."

"Keep them! You're crazy; what can you do with them?"

"Well, I'll just keep 'em."

"Now, Samuel, no one knows your merits better than I do; but I've only a moderate capacity, and I can't swallow more than one nephew. Those certificates can never be worth a penny to you, and yet I'll pay you well for them. It's a feeling I have— you, very naturally, can't understand it— that the line must be drawn somewhere; and I draw it at your nephewship. Come, what will you take?"

"You're my uncle," said the half-breed, sullenly, "and you've got to say so. I'd go to the gallows sooner than give it up. You'll not get those certificates, Uncle Golightley."

Luckily for Sam, his unwilling relative did not know that not he but Nikomis was the actual possessor of the certificates in question. As it was, the position of the men toward each other was changed, and now the nephew had the best of it.

"I'll take the check for your letters," observed the latter, as Golightley smoked his cigarette in silence. Golightley looked up, and the eyes of the men met. They were at bay; but the elder had the most to lose; and after a moment he spoke with the manner of a man who accepts the inevitable with the best grace possible.

"Well, since you insist upon being one of us, you ought to look at things from a family point of view. I'm to marry the woman to whom this money belongs; not only that, but I should never have laid a finger on the money if I hadn't had that marriage in view. It wasn't a robbery in the ordinary sense of the term—only a sort of family arrangement."

"You're as much a thief as I am," was Sam's gracious interruption; "and I'm as much of a gentleman as you are."

"It would be spoiling two good things for you to insist too much upon the gentleman. However, my point is this : In paying you hush-money, I rob her—my future wife—and defeat the object for which I engaged in the transaction at first. You've had more than a fair share already. Will you take five thousand ? I appeal to you as a thief and a man of honor."

Sam perceived Golightley's irony, though he could not perceive his object in being ironical just at that time. He answered doggedly :

"Ten thousand is what I'll have, Uncle Golightley, 'nd more afterward, if I need it. Whichever of us has it, it'll be in the family all the same, you know ! And if I go to the devil, the rest of you shall go along with me."

"You drive a hard bargain, Samuel," remarked Golightley, looking at the half-breed with a curious expression of amusement. "Recollect how the last straw broke the camel's back, and be careful to stop at the last but one. Well, I'll write you the check. You know our bankers, and how to manage the affair with safety to yourself. How long do you propose to remain in your present quarters ? "

"That's my own lookout; just you write out the check."

"Perhaps you'd like a little ready money to start on ? If you travel in that costume, with a check for ten thousand pounds in your pocket, it might prove awkward for you, and so for me." He took out his pocket-book. "I've a thousand dollars in gold and bank-notes here; you'd better take them and get yourself an outfit."

Sam took the money and examined it closely, being naturally suspicious of such kindly thoughtfulness on the part of his new-found uncle. But both notes and coin were genuine, and the half-breed pocketed them with the self-satisfied grimace of a scamp who has got the better of his fellow.

Golightley now arose and stepped forth from the wigwam, and began putting on his gloves again. "I shall see you once more, then," said he, turning upon his host, who stood like a black pillar against the smoky light that glowed within the wigwam. "Perhaps, by that time, you'll have thought better about those certificates. I sha'n't mind writing that check double if you do."

"Good-night, uncle ! " was all Sam's reply.

"Au revoir ! you're a sharp fellow," returned the other, and went out. On the landing below he heard the sound of Elinor's singing. Moving softly to the door, he leaned against the jamb, and listened there until the song ceased. Then he stole back to his chamber, and was seen no more that night.

CHAPTER LXVII.

CRAFT.

EVER since his quarrel with Madge Danver in the pantry, Jack Selwyn had been asking himself whether or not her information regarding the robbery was extensive and particular enough to be of value : and Madge, on the other hand, had amused herself with mystifying him to the utmost of her power. He had pretty well made up his mind that the accomplice of whom he was in search was named Sam Kineo ; but, assuming such to be the fact, he was at a loss to imagine why Madge should hesitate to expose him. He knew that the two had been acquainted in childhood ; but, even supposing an attachment to have existed between them at that time, it was not credible that it should survive a separation of ten years or more. Neither could he believe that her reticence was merely whimsical, for he had offered her substantial inducements to break it. And finally, if she really knew nothing, how was she able to appear so knowing ?

One evening, when she was preparing to return from Urmhurst to her own home, Jack offered to accompany her, and his escort was accepted. It was a cold, bright night, and as the two young people paced arm-in-arm together beneath the leafless trees, they might have been taken for a pair of lovers. Indeed, Madge, glancing at Selwyn's manly face out of the corner of her long, dark eye, may have sighed to think what a charming wooer he would make; and Jack, as he felt the light pressure of her shoulder, and caught the outline of her glowing cheek, might have mused how sweet would be the wooing of her. But it did not happen to be their destiny to love each other. The conversation proceeded in an unromantic and even uninteresting strain, until Madge exclaimed, slipping her hand from his arm and stepping aside:

"Do be more agreeable, or witty, or something! Why did you come with me? I can find my own way home perfectly well."

"I've been wondering, then, how you got hold of my letter to Garth, and what use you made of it?"

"That is neither witty nor agreeable, nor even polite. If you have reason to suspect me of knowing anything about it, you should know how I came to know; and, if you suspect me without reason, you are insulting!"

"If it would be politer to believe you a witch—that's my only alternative."

"That is to say, a woman with brains must be either dishonest or a witch. Perhaps there are other ways of finding out things than through your letters, Mr. Selwyn. If you were not so busy with your suspicions, maybe you'd see more. Tell me now — of what do you suspect me?" She bent forward and looked smiling in his face.

"Of not seeing your own best interests."

"Yes; women must always be thinking of their best interests—that's men's idea! —and the lower the interest, of course the more they think of it."

"No, Miss Madge. Some women are disinterested—"

"Elinor Golightley, for instance—because you are in love with her. But if she should happen to marry the gentleman to whom she's engaged, maybe you wouldn't except even her. What right have you to

treat me as if I were not a lady?" she went on, angrily. "You know nothing against me. What are you? Do gentlemen try to get on the right side of women when they want to steal something from them, and are not clever enough to get what they are after fairly?"

"All right, Miss Madge; I'll be plain with you, if you wish it. It's true that I undertook this job chiefly for Elinor Golightley's sake; but that is nothing to the present purpose. But it's true, too, that I do suspect you—of intending to play false with Garth, and turn all this trouble to your own advantage."

"But how I'm going to make it turn to my own advantage is more than you can imagine—eh, Mr. Selwyn?" she interposed, banteringly. "I can guess your thoughts. You believe that Mr. Golightley Urmson has done something very wrong, and that I, somehow or other, have found it out; and that I meant either to marry poor Golightley or to blackmail him, and then run away to Europe and be happy. And yet you were puzzled at my being such a goose as to receive stolen goods, knowing them to be such; and you wondered why—if money was what I wanted—I didn't take your reward and tell all I knew. Am I correct so far, Mr. Selwyn?"

"At all events, you guess well," said Jack, with a smile.

"Well, perhaps you'll tell me the rest of your suspicions yourself."

"I'm sure you can do it better than I could."

"You promised to be straightforward, and instead of that you are sarcastic. Well, I'll play my own part and yours too. Did you never hear of Sam Kinco?"

"I've heard of a Mr. Flint—"

"Oh, yes, and Mr. Flint is Mr. Kinco—that's easy enough. Well, he and I used to be great friends. He was in love with me, and . . . a great many things might have happened, only that I became engaged to Garth, and thought it to my interest (as you would say) not to break with him. Of course, I wasn't true to Garth, because I loved him, you know; I shouldn't think of trying to make a clever man of the world like Mr. Jack Selwyn believe such an absurd thing as that."

"What do you want me to believe?"

"Only what you can't help believing; but please don't be so cross! Well, Sam Kineo has written to me several times since he was abroad; and several months ago he wrote me that he had made a great deal of money, and wanted—me!—to help him spend it. But my best interests, as usual, prevented me from accepting his offer. Then, only a little while ago—since you came here, in fact—he wrote me that he was poor again, and—"

"He wrote you since I have been here?"

"Don't get excited, Mr. Selwyn, please," said Madge, quietly resuming his arm.

"Where was his letter dated from?"

"Oh! I'm not sure that I remember that!"

"I have reason to think that Sam Kineo is concealed somewhere in this neighborhood. Perhaps you'll let me see his letter?"

"It wouldn't be right, I'm afraid, without his permission. Besides, if he's in this neighborhood, the letter must be a forgery, so it would be of no use to you."

"Look here!" exclaimed Jack, impatiently, "damn this hide-and-seek game! I'll admit I'm not your equal at it. If you've anything to tell, out with it, in your own way! You know whether or not it will be worth your while. But if you only want to amuse yourself—be amused, in the devil's name!"

"I am amused, thank you," said she, with a low laugh. "But I have something to tell you too. This Mr. Flint, as you call him, had a plan which he wanted me to help him in. The police, it seems, after trying to catch him for a long time, and failing, at last gave him to understand that if he would come forward of his own accord and give evidence against a certain person who was implicated with him, he should receive a free pardon for himself."

"He was right, so far," remarked Selwyn.

"But, you see, one reason of his receiving such a kind offer was, that he had lost all his money, so that nothing except his evidence could be got out of him. Well, he

thought the offer over, and by-and-by it seemed to him that he could do better."

"He thought so, did he?"

"Yes, and I think he was right. This—certain person, you know, could be convicted only on Mr. Flint's evidence—there would be no use in arresting him without that; so it was probable that he would be willing to pay Mr. Flint a good deal—several thousand pounds, perhaps—to destroy all evidence against him. And this letter that I received asks me to find out how much money this certain person will give for the evidence-papers; and if the bargain is made, I am to hand over the papers to the certain person, and carry the money to Mr. Flint. Isn't that a good plan? and don't you think it would be to my best interest to help in it?"

"I don't know what to think."

"Oh, then it's no matter; especially as I have given him my answer."

"Given him your answer?"

"I wrote him to send me the papers, and I would get the money for them."

"Gracious God!" muttered Jack, and plunged into a silent tumult of thought. Could it be that this girl, so far from scheming dishonestly for her own advantage, had actually contrived to bring both thieves to justice by her unaided ingenuity? If so, what a long and painful apology Jack owed her! But it was his instinct to distrust her, and even yet his faith was weak. "Have you got the papers?" he asked.

"I shouldn't give them to you, Mr. Jack Selwyn, if I did have them."

"What the mischief are you going to do, then?"

"Well, you see," replied Madge, folding her hands demurely in her muff and looking up at him, "it wouldn't be nice to have people we know arrested and sent to prison, no matter what they had done. I'm sure Mr. Cuthbert Urmson wouldn't like that, nor Miss Elinor Golightley either. So I thought I would tell the certain person that I had the evidence against him, but that if he would give back the money to the person from whom it was stolen, I would destroy the evidence; and nothing more should be said or done about it."

Jack mused for a while, twisting his mustache and rubbing his chin. "It's true enough," said he, "that the recovery of the money is the main thing, and that arrests may be very disagreeable to all concerned; but, for all that, we have no right to compound a felony. Why should you shield these two scamps? You don't really care for them?"

"I care for the honor of the family," replied Madge, after a pause.

"The honor of the family has suffered all it can already; punishing those who've dishonored it won't make matters any worse. Put us on the track of this fellow Flint, or Kineo, and let justice take its course."

"Are you quite sure, Mr. Selwyn, that you'd be so anxious justice should take its course, if its doing so would not clear a rival out of your way?"

"The thief would be known to those most concerned, whether he were publicly convicted or not: it would be the same to me in either case."

"If I loved a man," exclaimed Madge, quickly, "I'd stick to him all the closer if he did wrong and got into trouble!"

"I dare say you would. But, since you don't love such a man, let's understand each other. Your plan is to destroy the evidence-papers, after having used them to compel the restoration of the stolen money to its owner. But have the papers actually been handed over to you?"

She appeared to hesitate, and finally shook her head.

"I thought not: and it isn't likely that Kineo would be such a fool as to let you have them until he got his fingers on the money. But, look here. If we know where he is, you can safely pay him the money, and we'll come down on him after he's received it, and bag money, papers, and all. That's the only sure way."

"If Sam Kineo would trust me with knowing where he was, he would trust me with his papers. I can deceive him about the money, for that belongs to some one else; but his liberty belongs to him; it wouldn't be fair to help you take that away from him."

"Oh, for mercy's sake, my good young friend, don't let yourself become sentimental about such a blackguard! If he trusts you, depend upon it he trusts you to be a fool: he would take your scalp any moment if he thought he could get five dollars for it!"

"Do you really think so?" murmured Madge, gazing guilelessly up in her companion's eyes. "Is he such a villain as that?"

"I'm afraid he is, Miss Madge," replied Jack, shaking his head.

She appeared to hesitate awhile, but finally said: "Don't you think, after getting the papers from him, you might make that certain person give up the money without sending him to prison, or having any more trouble?"

"It isn't for me to decide. But, if you think it would make you feel better, I'll do what I can to bring it about."

"Well, then—but maybe you won't believe I'm telling you the truth?"

"Good Lord! Nobody lies without an object," cried Jack, who was quite at the end of his patience.

"And since you see no object in my telling lies, you are willing to believe me? You are always so polite!"

"If you care for my apologies, Miss Danver, you shall have as many as you want, with all my heart. But you yourself helped me to misjudge you."

She put her hand reluctantly in her pocket. "Do you know Sam Kineo's handwriting?—Very well, then, this letter will tell you all I know. I don't believe you'll catch him, mind! The address is not very precise."

Jack took the letter, and, holding it in the moonlight, glanced hastily through it. "The deuce!" muttered he; "in Canada!" Madge watched him with a peculiar sparkle in her eyes, but said nothing. "I shall leave here to-morrow," continued Selwyn, after another examination of the letter. "If we succeed, it will be owing to you. Of course, you won't speak of this to any one. A careless word, you know, might do as much harm as you have done good."

"I shall be very prudent, Mr. Selwyn," returned Madge, demurely. "You needn't come any farther with me—there is my house. Good-night."

"I managed that well," said Jack self-approvingly to himself, as he slammed the door of his bedchamber half an hour later, and set about packing his valise. "But I'll be hanged if I can quite see through that girl, yet!"

Sam Kineo, awakened from his doze in the garret by the noise of the door, muttered a curse on the world in general, and rolled up his head in the blanket.

BOOK IX.

FERMENTATION.

CHAPTER LXVIII.

LADY ELEANOR.

One afternoon Elinor took it into her head to have a look at the studio. No one had entered this room since the occasion of the little party's assembling there in the autumn, to see the unfinished picture. After standing a moment or two on the threshold, she went in.

A gray film of dust had gathered over everything, deepening the feeling of solitude and desolation which the studio inspired. The intruder stepped lightly, as one who fears to awaken a sleeper. Each object that met her eyes seemed entranced, awaiting the moment when a spell should be broken, and the frozen stillness change to genial life. It was a bitterly cold day, and the skylight was arabesqued with frost. Glancing toward the fireplace, Elinor saw a small pile of wood, the remains of last year's fuel, standing behind the stove. She kindled a fire; and soon the frost on the skylight began to liquefy, the air to smell faintly of heated iron, and the dreary influence which heretofore had brooded over the room to yield to the benign influence of flame.

An old duster of peacock-feathers was hanging from a peg beside the fireplace. She disengaged it, and was about to whisk it across the surface of the dust-veiled picture on the easel. On second thoughts, however, she left this untouched, and contented herself with dusting the other objects in the studio. As she did so, the recollection of that October afternoon returned upon her with circumstantial distinctness. There was the very sketch upon the wall which Mr. Urmson had pointed out to her, and commented upon so humorously. Yonder, in front of the easel, had stood Golightley, his hand upon Garth's shoulder, and speaking to him in an undertone, while the artist leaned against the back of the chair, with lowering brows, biting his lip. On the sofa, Madge and Mrs. Tenterden laughed and chatted together. Later, when the rest had gone, Elinor sat on the same sofa, the portfolio lying open between her and Garth, who was so preoccupied that only her involuntary outburst of laughter had aroused him. She smiled again at that recollection. And here was the same sofa, and the portfolio just as they had left it so many weeks ago. She sat down in the old place, and thought over all that they had spoken together, until she could almost believe that he was once more beside her. . . . No! she was alone.

Having furbished up the neglected studio, Elinor, after the wont of benefactors, conceived a kindness for it, and thenceforward used it as her boudoir. She had not much leisure; for, though Garth was now quite convalescent, his father seemed to be failing rapidly, and it was Elinor's sad pleasure to be his nurse. When occasion served, however, she would quietly mount the garret-stairs, and, having made her fire in the little stove, sit down to read or ponder over the portfolio, or play upon her violin. No one ever disturbed her here, or even seemed aware of her retreat. Even Golightley never sought her out; but his manner toward her had, during the last few weeks, undergone a welcome change from flippant gallantry to unobtrusive observance. As for Jack Selwyn, he had some time since departed on a journey—whither or with what purpose was not declared.

As she was reclining one day on the sofa, shaping out dreamy forms of melody on her violin, the door opened, and Garth came in.

"So this is where you go?" said he. "I've heard mysterious music for the last week or two. The old studio looks comfortable."

"You shouldn't have come up," exclaimed Elinor, blushing a little. "What if you were to have a relapse! You must lie down on this sofa."

"No relapses or sofas for me! I'm going to get to work again at my old picture. Go on with your playing."

"I was going down in a few minutes."

"Don't—I shall work better to music. Stay a little while."

He sat down in front of the easel. He was far from robust-looking; but the fever seemed to have filed away an incrustation over the true man, leaving the spirit in him more free and powerful. His expression had lost its former sullenness, and there was something really beautiful in his smile.

"You didn't touch this," he remarked, nodding toward the picture. "I'm glad you didn't—no one but I can make it clean!" He seized the palette-cloth as he spoke, and rubbed it over the canvas, which glowed forth once more in the sombre brilliance of its coloring. Then, leaning back in his chair, he gazed at it long and steadfastly, as he might have gazed at an enemy who had fought him to the death. At length he took up his palette and brushes, and began mixing some fresh tints.

"It was here we had our first talk—do you remember it? The first, and the last, but one! The other was at the picnic; and now here we are again. After all, it's less than a dozen weeks, altogether. But we must forget each other now, and set to work. You play me something, and I'll paint it."

After some little wandering prelude, Elinor rose by degrees to the full height of musical possession, and played as she had never played to any one but Garth. Like all profound musicians, she penetrated to the soul of facts and incidents; she saw the story of her life translated into large meanings, and with subtile bow and faultless fingers she gave the vision utterance. Art is the duct through which divinity reaches man, and there are moments when the duct becomes a river, and the artist prophesies with a voice greater than his own—the creative voice that harmonizes all things. But insomuch as every interpretation smacks of the interpreter there was so much of Elinor's personality in her music that Garth, inspired with it, was in truth inspired with her. He painted rapidly and vehemently, and yet in a kind of trance. It was the emotional side of the man that was at work; his intellectual and material parts acted merely as instruments.

At length Elinor lowered her bow, and Garth his brush, both with a sense of exhaustion, as after intense albeit unheeded exercise. Drops of sweat stood on Garth's forehead, and his hands trembled. After a few moments he got up, and, walking with a heavy step to the sofa, sat down there wearily.

"You see, you were not strong enough," Elinor said, with an upbraiding smile.

"Yes, I was; for it's done."

"I'm very glad," said she, with a long breath.

"So am I!" rejoined he; and there was a happy look in his deep-set eyes.

"May I see it?"

"Yes—in a few minutes. I don't know myself what I've painted yet. The music did more of it than I."

After a pause, he continued: "In fact, it's been your doing from the beginning. You first set me fermenting that day up here; then you shamed the devil out of me at the picnic; and you saved my life in the fever."

"I should like to think I had helped you. I was useless before I met you."

"You sha'n't find it useless to have helped me."

They had fallen unawares upon a region of emotion which was perilous, yet hard to escape from. There was much that they might say to each other.

"A man can only begin to be happy when he sees that happiness is not good for him. It is hard to take things to heart and yet keep tender-hearted—isn't it?"

"I suppose we live here so as to become strong enough for heaven. It takes strength to bear worldly happiness; and eternal happiness—"

"If I become strong enough to be your friend, I shall be satisfied."

"Then be satisfied!" said Elinor, smiling, but with tears. Garth took her extended hand, and held it for a breath or two, meeting her eyes the while. The world seemed far off, but whether joy or pain were mightiest in their hearts, they knew not. But they knew that in the last few minutes they had lived.

It is the profoundest emotion that soonest veils itself. Garth presently stretched up his arms, clasped his hands behind his head, and said, with a smile:

"I shall be a great artist, after all—an old master! I feel immense confidence in myself! Other artists have not had my inspiration. The world ought to know that my best pictures were painted with a violin."

"I like better that the violin should be hidden in the pictures," said she, tremulously.

"Well—as the soul is hidden in the body. But the soul outlasts the body; so you will get your deserts at last."

"Oh, I have them now!"

"Let us see what I have been doing here!" exclaimed Garth, abruptly, rising from the sofa. "The light will be gone in half an hour more."

At this juncture, however, Madge and Golightley climbed the garret-stairs, knocked and entered.

"Didn't I tell you so?" laughed the former, glancing at her companion. "Dear me, how cozy everything looks!—It was so kind of you, dear Elinor, to think of bringing that poor black-and-white creature up here for a change!"

Golightley stood by in silence; his usual volubility and self-importance seemed to have deserted him of late. Garth explained laconically that he was an intruder in the studio, not a guest.

"But music and painting belong together, as we all know," returned Madge, lightly. "I suppose you inspire one another."

"I have kept you waiting a long time for your picture," remarked Garth, turning to his uncle, "and now I have no picture for you. Come and see."

They all moved in front of the canvas. Garth was himself the first to break the momentary silence that ensued. He glanced at Elinor and murmured:

"It was a real inspiration!"

"What?" demanded Madge, sharply, setting her small, white teeth against her under lip.

"H'm—yes—I see!" muttered Golightley, adjusting his eye-glasses, and bending forward. "You've painted Margaret out and Elinor in. An inspiration, sure enough!"

"Of course, the alteration puts an end to our bargain. I preferred to follow my own judgment.—But I'd no idea I was painting you, Elinor! it's strange!"

"I don't think it looks much like me," Elinor said.

"Not pretty enough, of course," began Madge.

"I mean, it's idealized too much to be called a likeness," interrupted the other, with one of her point-blank looks.

"But at least you think it better than mine?" Madge continued, the blood rushing into her cheeks.

Elinor turned upon her again, and said, coldly:

"It is better than yours, for the picture."

"Garth, you said just now that our bargain was off," observed Golightley, laying his hand on the artist's shoulder. "By George! so say I, too. The picture, as it was yesterday, was a fine picture—worth a thousand pounds to me, and more to a richer man. But, as it·stands there at this moment, Garth Urmson, it's worth ten times that—a hundred times that! With those few rapid touches you have wrought a miracle; and I believe, from my soul, that you have painted the greatest picture of its kind that there is in the world! By George, Garth, I mean what I say!"

Indeed, it was very evident, both from the tone of Uncle Golightley's voice and the workings of his countenance, that he was unusually moved. Everybody was surprised, not only at his emotion, but at his words. The greatest picture of its kind in the world! They all looked again at the canvas. The light was already fading, but the face of the new Lady Eleanor gleamed forth with marvelous power. The greatest in the world! Was it not so, indeed?

"I'm afraid Uncle Golightley won't have money enough to pay for it," remarked Madge, dryly. The light had faded quite out; the spell was broken. The picture had lived its moment. But if it had touched the top of art, and found appreciation, a moment was long enough.

"By-the-by, my dear Elinor," said Golightley, as they turned away from the casel, "Mildred sent me up here to find you. She wants to ask you something about Cuthbert's medicine. Shall we go down?"

CHAPTER LXIX.

WHEN the two had taken their departure, Madge threw herself down on the sofa and burst out laughing, holding her handkerchief before her mouth and biting it with her teeth. Meanwhile she watched Garth with an angry sparkle in her eyes. She looked as dangerous as she was beautiful. Garth had remained in front of the picture, but his face was turned toward her. Suddenly she stopped laughing and exclaimed·

"Do, pray, look somewhere else. Isn't the greatest picture in the world better worth studying than I am?"

"I wasn't looking at you as an artist."

"Oh, no, I suppose not. I'm not good

enough for pictures. You were only looking at me as a lover—a true, devoted, passionate lover—ha, ha, ha!"

"I expected you to be angry."

"What! angry because I caught you flirting with Elinor Golightley? My own sweet Garth, you were never more mistaken! Did you imagine I haven't seen what's been going on between you two from the first? I understand it—it's an artistic affinity, that's all!"

A flash of resentment crossed Garth's face, and he turned away.

"I want you to listen to me," said Madge, in a low, smooth voice, leaning forward toward him with an undulation of the neck and shoulders, as of a tiger creeping to ambush. "Come and sit by me, please."

He drew up a chair and sat down before her. "Try not to say what is disgraceful, Madge—for your own sake."

"Or for Elinor's sake—which? You are an impostor, Garth Urmson! I don't care how wicked a man is, if only he lets it be known, and isn't afraid. If you had said, long ago, 'I'm tired of you—I'm going off with another woman!'—if you'd strike me, now, for saying what I'm saying, instead of sitting there with your hands in your pockets, pretending you're shocked and grieved—ha, ha, ha, ha!"

Garth lowered his eyes; he made no reply. Madge was drawn up on the sofa, resting her check on her clinched white hand; she kept one position, yet a subtile, continuous motion vibrated through her body and limbs. There was a look in her eyes which Garth did not choose to meet. Such looks are harder to forget than the most poisonous words.

"You may find that you'd better have sold your picture as it was, instead of taking all that trouble to insult me. Golightley won't buy it now, for all his talk; and I'd have let you go and welcome without your throwing away a thousand pounds. You think Elinor can make it up to you; but what if she didn't get back her fortune after all? Do you suppose she could make you as rich as I could have done? I wish you were worth being jealous of—but I can live as I like in spite of you! What do you know of how a woman may love a man? I wish I did love you—for an hour—so that I might show you what love is, and then leave you to want me forever! I wonder that there's a single good woman in the world! I don't believe there is, unless she's a fool!"

These wild sentences followed each other rapidly, with low-toned, malignant emphasis. Still looking down, Garth said, huskily:

"How came such thoughts into your mind?"

"They are the truth."

"They are false!" said he, in a voice that made her shrink. He raised his eyes, and such was the light of indignation in them, that the expression of the woman's face was quenched. Though she knew that Garth would never harm a hair of her head, she felt the thrill of absolute fear. Something he would do!

"What makes you beautiful?" he asked, sternly and sadly. Other words seemed about to follow, but he held them back. That one question was pregnant enough. It entered into Madge's soul, and made her know that all power of her physical fascination was thenceforth at an end with him. If she would regain him now, it must be by other means. But what other means had she? She had worshiped her beauty, conquered by it, risked her future upon it. If it were despised, what was left her?

"Make me ugly, then!" she whispered, setting her teeth; "strike my face! crush me!" She was half beside herself.

"I could give you no other beauty instead of that."

She caught a tone of compassion in his voice, and the idea that he pitied her drove her mad. She sprang up with a wild look, and the thought, "I will kill myself!"

Glancing about, her eyes lighted on the rusty cutlass that hung above the fireplace. She glided round Garth, leaped up with a sharp cry and caught it down. Awkwardly, but with good-will enough, she aimed a sort of thrust at herself. Garth was in time to turn the blow aside; then he struck the weapon from her grasp. She screamed with rage, and sprang for it again. It had fallen at the foot of the easel; as she rose with it in her hand, the picture confronted her.

Instantly she plunged the blade through the canvas, cutting and stabbing until every vestige of the new Lady Eleanor was destroyed, and the entire painting was a mass of tatters. This done, she looked round for Garth.

The excitement of the afternoon, culminating in Madge's desperate attempt against herself, had been too much for the convalescent, and, the moment after disarming her, he had fainted away. Madge saw him lying face downward on the floor, and felt her blood thicken with horror; for her first idea was that he had been wounded by the cutlass in the struggle, and was dead. She got on her knees beside him, took him in her arms, and, with the unconscious strength of excitement, rose and fairly carried him to the sofa. Then she searched for a wound or a blood-stain; but there was none to be found. It was only a fainting-fit—with a sob of relief in her throat that assurance came to her at last. She herself was worse used than he. Her dark hair hung loose upon her shoulders, the bosom of her dress was torn open, the wrist which he had struck was bruised, and there was a thin cut across her left palm.

She lifted his powerless hand to her lips and kissed it; then put it in her bare bosom and let her heart beat against it. "Do I not love him?" she asked herself. "I would die for him. But I can't get up to him; and now he doesn't care that I am beautiful."

The fainting man gave a sigh; she took his hand from her bosom and stood up. "If I only had some cordial!" she thought; and in a moment an idea struck her, and she swiftly left the room.

Sam Kineo, moodily smoking on his pile of blankets, was startled by her sudden entrance and sprang to his feet. "What's the matter now?" he whispered; "police?"

"Give me your brandy—quick! Garth has fainted."

"Garth? bah!—let him faint."

"Sam Kineo, you must give it me."

"Must, eh? I see, you're making love to him again! Now, don't get excited, my little dear; the brandy's safe in my coat-pocket. But, before you get it, you'll have to give me a kiss. Come, now!"

"I will never—"

"Then you don't get the brandy."

"O Sam, don't ask me now—only not this time! I'll come back afterward— Oh, any time but now!"

"Any time won't do. Tell you what, my little beauty, I won't stand this dodging about—plensant's pie-crust in the morning, 'nd flustering up in the evening! You'll just give me a nice, affectionate kiss, and then you may go to dear Garth with the brandy."

Madge felt that she must submit. She had put herself in the way of evil with her eyes open, and had ere now discovered that it is not so easy to play fast and loose with evil as with good. The spirit of darkness stretched out its arms, as Sam did now, and forced her to yield him tribute.

"Very well; do as you like," said she, in a hard, hopeless tone. Sam chuckled, and, having exacted full payment for his brandy, suffered her to take it. At the door she turned and said, "You will be sorry for this all your life." The half-breed only laughed his noiseless laugh, and she came out. But her returning step had lost all spring and lightness, and on the threshold of the studio she faltered, shamed and wretched, and half-minded to steal away again. Nevertheless she entered, and found Garth already in part recovered. The brandy was not needed, after all. "I wonder if he'd thank me," thought the girl, "if he knew what I paid for it!"

"I've not done much good to-day!" was Garth's first observation.

"That's a thing one soon gets used to," she rejoined, with bitter lightsomeness.

"Madge—with all my heart I want to be good to you," said he, gently. "I'm partly answerable for what you said and did, to-day."

"No, no, no! It would make no difference to me to be answerable for much worse things."

"That alteration in the picture was not the insult to you that it seemed to be. It's the first thing I have done to make me worth an honest woman's marrying."

At the mention of the picture, it occurred to Madge that probably Garth had not seen her act of vandalism. She stepped to the easel and moved it so that he could behold the tattered canvas. He gazed straight at it for an appreciable time, and asked—

"Did you do that?"

She nodded.

He clutched his hair and laughed so pleasantly and unexpectedly, that Madge brightened up for a moment as if sunshine had fallen on her.

"Well, I'm glad it's done," said he. "The old picture has served its purpose, and was destroyed at the most fitting moment. My girl, let us annihilate our past in the same way—the bad and foolish part of it, I mean. This shall be our last quarrel."

He tried to take her hand, but she drew it away. "Don't think I'm angry— Or think what you please! There's blood on my hand—it's a bad omen. I've been naughty; I'm not good enough yet. Perhaps—to-morrow!"

"Did you cut yourself?"

"Only a little scratch: I'm sure it might have been much worse—or better! Yes, why did you interfere? You'd have had your picture safe and me out of the way by now."

"Nothing would be safe for me without you, Madge."

"Don't speak so! If I don't laugh, I shall cry—or go mad again! Don't touch me. I tell you I'm not ready."

"Only say we shall be married soon."

"So that you can say, 'I kept my promise to her!' You don't love me. Why don't you tell me the truth about Elinor Golightley?"

"There are some things a man had better not put too plainly even to himself. At least, Madge, I have never thought of marrying any one but you. My fever has given me time to think, and I believe that if I ever wanted—something, it was because I knew I could never have it—not because it was the thing for me to have."

After a long pause, Madge said: "I didn't hate the picture for being altered. But why did you put her in my place?"

"I did it unconsciously."

Madge sat a few moments as if preoccupied, then rose with a tired look. "Thank you for telling me all this," said she. "Of course, I don't understand much of it— You can't expect me to understand things by sympathy, as some people do. But you are very kind to tell me."

"You'll understand when we're married."

"Perhaps I'd better not understand. But we'll talk about being married some other time, when you are stronger, and I'm in a better humor. The fire has gone out, too, and Elinor would scold me if I kept you here in the cold."

CHAPTER LXX.

DATES AND INITIALS.

AFTER Garth and Madge had left the studio that evening, and Madge had gone home, he remembered that he had left the door unlocked; and since it seemed inadvisable that the summary fate of the picture should become known just then, he mounted the garret-stairs again, shortly before going to bed, in order to make all safe.

At the head of the stairs a gust of air blew out his lamp. He groped his way toward the studio, found the door, and entered. It was dark, save for a slight glow of red through the draught-holes of the little stove. It seemed to Garth, however, that he was not alone in the room. He stood quite still and listened intently, but there was no sound. He moved toward the stove to get a match from the box on the wall beside it; his leg struck the chair, and it fell over with some racket. A moment afterward he fancied he heard a step, light and stealthy, in the passage outside the room; and then—unless his ears deceived him—a door closed softly—the door of Nikomis's apartment. Had she been in here before he came? If so, for what purpose? and why had she stolen away so stealthily?

He now struck a match, lit his lamp, and looked about him. Everything appeared much in the same condition as he had left it a few hours before. There stood the tattered canvas on the easel; on the floor lay the cutlass; and the other evidences of Madge's outbreak and his struggle with her were present. There were no signs of any foreign disturbance. Possibly his senses had deceived him; at all events, Nikomis

was welcome to enter his studio if she wanted to; only, why should she have been at such pains to get away undiscovered? After some reflection, Garth dismissed the subject from his mind, as of no possible importance; and having locked the door, and put the key in his pocket, he returned downstairs.

During the next ten days the artist was content to lay his art aside, and to devote himself exclusively to the business of regaining health and strength; and they returned to him with extraordinary rapidity. It seemed as if the false Lady Eleanor had been the bar to his recovery, if not the cause itself of his illness; and now that she was annihilated, the sick man might arise. Garth was light-hearted, energetic, and serene. He walked, sleighed, or skated, day after day, breathed deep of the clear cold air, and ate enormously. He was even sociable, was seen often in the village, and became known and liked there as he had never been before. Everybody remarked the change in him for the better, and congratulated him upon it. Mrs. Tenterden merrily supposed that it must be the prospect of being so soon married that was bringing him round; and Garth did not deny it. In fact, it was his determination to be married in the ensuing spring, and he spoke much with Madge about their future, and urged her to use all due dispatch with her preparations. And Madge seemed to be more than usually active with her needle, though she could hardly have expected to manufacture an entire trousseau herself. She was not so full of bright talk as usual, but often fell into long silences; and when, occasionally, she allowed herself an outburst of vivacity, a certain hardness was apparent in her voice and manner, seeming to indicate an absence of genuine feeling, and suggesting a latent bitterness. In her ordinary conversation, she betrayed a curious and almost morbid interest in her own condition and prospects. She put hypothetical cases and worked out imaginary situations for herself. But such eccentricities are not uncommon with young women for whom a great change in life is imminent; and Madge's odd behavior gave anxiety to no one.

Garth made himself especially agreeable to poor Mrs. Danver, who had been seriously ill of late, and did not seem likely to survive very much longer. He visited her every day, and she became deeply and favorably impressed with him : insomuch that so far from carping at him, as had heretofore been her custom, she now took to extolling him in and out of season. She declared—what, indeed, was the truth—that she'd never had the chance to know him for what he was before; and glad she was, and didn't care who knew it, that Madge was to have a husband who was a gentleman, and a clever, sober, kind-hearted man, what was more ; for she would like to know how many there were like him that would come and sit an hour or two every day beside a poor, sick, complaining woman, who'd never had much sympathy nor consideration that ever she could remember; which it wouldn't have been her fate to say, as say it she must, if there'd been more people, young or old, like Mr. Garth Urmson. And all that troubled her now was, that that strange child Maggie didn't at times more than half seem to appreciate her good fortune; not that she supposed that there would be much fortune, leastways at first, in the worldly point of view : though there was the Eve legacy would likely be coming round to those the Lord properly intended it for one of these days: but money was not everything, though times there were she almost feared her Maggie took that view ; and, if she did, all Mrs. Danver could say was, it wasn't from her mother that the girl got such worldly notions, nor would she ever cease to raise her voice against it. These declarations were generally made to Mrs. Tenterden, who laughed incredulously at any exceptions taken against the beauty who had won her own heart, and affirmed that two young people more in love than Garth and Madge she had never seen—unless it were Golightley and Elinor.

About a week before Christmas, Garth was visited with an idea, which, after he had turned it over in his own mind for a while, he resolved to communicate to Madge. Accordingly, he took possession of her as soon as she arrived at Urmhurst, and carried her up to the studio.

"You must help me look over the sketches," he explained, "and pick out those which would be most likely to sell. I shall take them to Boston and sell them to some picture dealer. They ought to bring four or five hundred dollars, at least."

"What could you do with four or five hundred dollars, Garth ? "

"At least I could buy a wedding-ring with it," he answered, smiling at her.

"Do you really want me for your wife ? " she asked, glancing at him sidelong.

"If you were at the other side of the world, I'd leave everything to bring you back."

"But suppose, after all, I wouldn't come with you ? "

"If I found you, you would come."

"Well, perhaps ! for you are very strong. But, then, I might not let you find me, you know ! "

Garth put his arm round her waist with a masterful air. "I have you," said he, "and it will be my fault if I let you go ! "

He unlocked the door of the studio, and they went in. The chill and disorder were in unfavorable contrast with the snug aspect of things when Garth had last entered the room, and discovered Elinor on the sofa.

"Oh, how cold ! " was Madge's exclamation. "No one has been here since we went out—that's evident ! " As she spoke the last words, she gave him a covert look, quickly averted.

"Yes, I came up here to lock the door that same night: and, by-the-way," he added, turning to her, "I imagined some one was here when I came in. My lamp had gone out—"

"You saw nothing, then ? "

"No; I only had the feeling that I was not alone. Afterward I heard a sound in the passage, and a noise like a door shutting."

"Dear me ! what do you suppose it was ? "

"Nikomis, no doubt : either she, or my imagination. I didn't follow up the adventure, and had forgotten it till now."

"Sha'n't we have a fire ? "

"Yes; I mean to burn whatever we don't pick out for sale, beginning with the five-thousand-dollar picture. Next year we'll start fresh, with no relics of the past to drag with us. Sit down there, and see whether my paintings can't make you warm and comfortable for at least an hour."

Madge crouched down beside the stove as he bade her, and Garth tore the strips of canvas off the frame, and with them and some billets of wood soon created a fine blaze, quite sufficient to keep his beautiful companion's fingers from getting cold. Then he collected together all the sketches and studies in the room, piled them on the sofa, and began making his selections, appealing from time to time to Madge for her opinion upon a doubtful specimen. The condemned ones he passed over to her, and she put them in the stove, for the most part without looking at them, and with an air as if her thoughts were elsewhere.

At length, however, she summoned together her wandering thoughts, and asked Garth to give her a pile of sketches to look over and decide upon for herself. He placed a portfolio full beside her, with the permission to burn them all if she liked, and then returned to the sofa.

She took up a handful of them, listlessly looked them over, and fed one after another of them into the red-hot little maw, that always roared the more insatiably the more it was filled. These gone, she gathered up a second supply. The first drawing that met her eye was a study of the steel headpiece which Captain Neil Urmson had once worn, and which had been reproduced in the picture; this was allowed to add its quota to the now genial warmth of the studio. The second scrap represented Madge's own cottage on the verge of the forest, with a glimpse of the village beyond. After a minute's hesitation, she gave this to the flames also. The third sketch caused her to concentrate her gaze into sudden intensity, and to set her teeth against her lip. After the first look she glanced round at Garth, to see whether he were watching her; but he seemed absorbed in some discovery of his own. She returned to the sketch, which she scrutinized long and curiously. Considered as a work of art, it hardly merited such attention; it was merely a rough and hasty rendering of a woman's head, and neither the features nor the coloring were such as Madge considered beautiful. Nevertheless, she must have been impressed, for her own expression underwent a marked change during the short time she was examining the portrait. In the lower left-hand corner was a date—1845—and the name "Dresden." It had then been painted some years ago, while Garth was abroad: he had never shown it to her, nor ever said anything to lead her to suppose that such a thing could have existed. Why had he kept such a secret?

The incident was, in itself, as unimportant as it could well be; but circumstances, inward and outward, gave it no little weight to Madge's mind. She put herself in Garth's place, with a result not entirely creditable to him; for it is not always charitable to judge others' motives by our own. The effect upon Madge in the present instance was to make her conclusions cynical. But, since she was not in the habit of giving her thoughts frank and immediate expression, and since, moreover, it may have better suited her convenience to be cynical than explicit, she kept silence upon her discovery.

"Madge!" said Garth.

She slipped the portrait into her pocket, and said, without looking round—

"What?"

"Do you remember, the last time we were up here, giving me some brandy?"

"Oh—when you fainted away? Yes."

"Where did you get it?"

"It was Nikomis's, I believe. I got it from her room."

"This flask isn't hers, is it?" He held up a silver flask mounted in Russia leather, and handsomely chased. "I found it under the sofa," he added. "It has the English mark upon it; and a date and initials besides."

"Let me look at it," said Madge, getting up and coming to the sofa. She took the flask and examined it; on the bottom had been scratched the letters "S. K.," and the date 1845. A few moments' reflection showed her that to prevaricate in this matter would be more perilous than to confess.

She had anticipated the finding of the flask, but had not been aware of the existence of the initials and date, which made all the difference. It was a situation in which presence of mind was worth more than anything else, and presence of mind was a virtue which Madge had always cultivated. In a wonderfully short space of time, therefore, she took her decision, and the sequel evidenced its soundness.

"I will tell you all I know, Garth," she said, returning his inquiring glance with perfect frankness. "Perhaps I should have told you before, but I did what I thought was for the best: and, at any rate, I'm glad not to have the secret to keep any longer. Sit down here and listen."

The conference lasted for an hour or two. At the end of it Garth said:

"I'll write to Professor Grindle to-night. You could not have done more kindly or wisely than you did."

His look and tone caressed her with a tenderness so deep and masculine as wellnigh to impel her to the utterance of those few further words which would have left nothing to be said. But she remembered that little sketch of a woman's head—and turned away unconfessed.

CHAPTER LXXI.

CHRISTMAS PROSPECTS.

WHEN Christmas was still three days distant, there was again a gathering around the broad kitchen-hearth of Urmhurst. Mr. Urmson was able, for the first time in three weeks, to leave his room and join the group; he sat in the centre, the high, dark back of his chair rising above his clear, pale face, which seemed to grow more transparent and spiritual-looking day by day. But the brightness of his eyes, and the indomitable cheerfulness of his bearing, whenever he let himself be seen at all, did much to counteract the effect of his bodily frailty. People are mostly taken at their own estimation, especially if it be such as to let us off easily on the score of sympathy.

Elinor sat beside him; then came Go-

lightley, Mrs. Tenterden, and Parson Graeme. The two latter had lately contracted a genial partnership with each other, the chief aim of which was to discuss the people and the events of years long gone by. The parson, whose memory of the past seemed to gain in clearness in proportion as his notions of the present grew confused, executed really portentous feats of historic reminiscence; while Mrs. Tenterden came in with a flowing embroidery of minute and detailed information, such as only a lady of much leisure and natural curiosity could ever hope to get together.

On the opposite side of the fireplace sat Madge and Garth, both somewhat taciturn. In fact, as Mrs. Tenterden was just observing, the young people, who had every reason to be chatty and lively, were sedate and laconic as a Quaker meeting; and thereby, she supposed, designed to bring upon herself and others the reproach of senile garrulity. "However, daughter," she added, "I've got something to tell you that I reckon will set the tongues of all of you a-going. I suppose I oughtn't to tell now, though, because it's for Christmas—there! well, since that's slipped out, I might as well say the rest. It's what Christmas-present I mean to give you. Or maybe I'll let you all guess!—that'll be best of all!" and the good lady chuckled comfortably and folded her statuesque arms.

But never, apparently, had so poor an assemblage of guessers got together round a New England hearth as this. No one had the enterprise to hazard a failure, except the parson, who instantly proclaimed the answer to be a wedding-garment! and thereupon exploded into stentorian mirth.

"Well, you're nearer to it than the others, parson," said Mrs. Tenterden indulgently, as soon as she could make her voice heard.—"I never saw such a stupid set as they are all to-night.—Well, then, Nellie, I'm going to give you whatever money is got back from our robbers, whenever they're caught! You'd have had it for a wedding-present, if you'd been married before Christmas, and the money had been got in time; and maybe I'd better call it a dowry, anyway; only, as life is so uncertain, I thought

I'd speak of it now, so as you might know in case anything happened."

Several members of the company appeared to consider all this more impressive than amusing; but Elinor answered, with heightened color:

"Thank you, mother; but I shouldn't have minded waiting, though life is so uncertain. A Barmecide fortune is as good one time as another. However, if any one pays me the money before Christmas, I'll consider I have the right to spend it immediately, without referring to you."

"What a pity the robbers, or one of them, couldn't have heard you, Aunt Mildred!" remarked Madge. "I'm sure he'd have gone straight off and brought you the money."

"My good fathers, Margaret!" cried Aunt Mildred, glancing over her shoulder with a shudder, "why, I'd rather never have the money than have the awful creature himself bring it here!"

"Even robbers — especially repentant robbers — are a kind of men," said Cuthbert.

"If one of them could have heard you say that, my dear brother, he'd have thanked you!" was Golightley's observation.

"Since Aunt Mildred has been so munificent," said Cuthbert again, "I may as well inform you, Garth, that Eve's legacy belongs to you in default of the other claimant; so unless he puts in an appearance some day or other, you will be pretty well off!"

Madge laughed. "If we could only manage to prove that the claimant was one of the robbers," said she, "he could be shut up in prison, and then both Garth and Elinor would have their fortunes?"

"I don't know that I should care for the claimant's money any more, because he happened to be a convict," said Garth. "But talking about Christmas-presents, I propose to propose which we may all give ourselves —a skating-party on the lake on Christmas-eve. It shall be a great affair: all the village, besides ourselves, shall be there, and we'll build the biggest bonfire that ever was seen. The moon is full on that night; and, if the ice is good. we ought to have a better picnic than any of the parson's."

This suggestion met with general approval.

"As to that about the ice, though," said Golightley, leaning forward and caressing his mustache, "is there reason to suppose that it is what it should be in view of such an occasion? Anybody been down there lately?"

"This snow fell before the lake froze," replied Garth. "But we can go and find out."

"Happy thought, by George!" exclaimed the other. He sprang up and went to the window. "Ah! what a superb night. Now what do you say to some of us wrapping up warm and going down to-night? Just look at that moon!"

"Mercy, Golightley, you'd all catch your death!" cried Mrs. Tenterden.

But some of the others favored the idea; and finally the four lovers, as the good lady called them, made up their minds to start. While Madge and Elinor were putting on their wraps, Garth went out and harnessed the double sleigh, and filled it with buffalo-robes, blankets, and hot bricks. Then the party got in, and they drove off with much noise and festivity. The moon, shining on the snow, made the woods light as day; and the road had been worn by the sledges of the wood-cutters sufficiently to render the sleighing good. They reached the lake without accident; and when Garth had tested the ice and found it safe, they drove forth upon it toward the little islet at the mouth of the cove.

"By George—black ice, too! That beats my experience—eh, Garth?" said Golightley. "It's like driving on air. You might see the stones on the bottom."

"How thick is the ice?" inquired Elinor.

"About nine inches."

"Where is the bonfire to be?" asked Madge.

"On the nose of the island," Garth replied, "so that it can be seen all over the broad part of the lake. If it were in view of the meadows, it would be hidden from the place where most of the people will be. I believe there's a shed on the island which was used by the ice-cutters last year. We can stable the horses in that; and by clearing away the snow a little, we can cook and eat our dinner in the midst of warmth and comfort."

" How is it about fish ? " asked Golightley. "Any chance for a chowder ? "

"Nothing easier. The lake is full of trout and perch; the women shall catch them through the ice, and I'll cook them."

"It's a paradise on ice ! " Golightley declared.

They came to the islet, and passing round the promontory, the panorama of valley, lake, and river, lay before them. The river was dammed lower down, and had overflowed its banks to an average breadth of half a mile; and this polished pathway, like a black mirror twenty miles long, glistened lonely and silent in its white setting of snow, farther than the eye could trace it. But farther still, Wabeno showed his dim outline against the sky, like the ghost of some traditionary mountain, the material substance of which had long passed away.

"I wished I'd brought my skates! " Madge exclaimed. "The ice is perfect now. Day after to-morrow may not be so fine as to-day."

" Can you skate, Elinor ? " asked Garth.

"Hardly at all; but it seems as if I could do anything to-night! "

" And I—since nobody will have the good manners to toot my horn for me—I am the fortunate purveyor of all this delectation," remarked Golightley. "Remember it in my favor, friends, if ever you should have occasion to think ill of me."

"One cannot be expected to carry a December night about in one's mind quite all the time, Uncle Golightley," returned Madge, maliciously.—" But I'm sure you must know how to skate, Elinor; at all events, you have a lovely skating-suit, and I have been all the last week making one to look exactly like it."

"Aha! so that you may be mistaken for one another, and one of you, perhaps, escape to parts unknown, while her accomplice in the plot delays pursuit until it be too late! I scent mischief," laughed Golightley.—" And by-the-by, Garth, à propos of mischief, what has become of your friend Jack Selwyn ? Is his business so pressing that he can't postpone it for a treat like this ? "

"There he goes, now! " cried Madge, suddenly.

They all looked where she pointed, and saw a figure, faint and far away in the moonlight, skimming across the meadow-ice half a mile below. In a minute or two the figure gained the shadow of a clump of pines on the right, and was lost to view, only the low reverberation of the ice bearing testimony to the reality of the vision.

" It might have been he; he's mysterious in his movements," said Garth. "But I don't know his address. Professor Grindle, though, sent me word this morning that he should try to spend Christmas-day with us. He may get down in time to join us here."

They sat silent for a while, looking at the scene. " Ah, it seems a shame ever to leave this," murmured Golightley at last. " Why can't we be changed into moon-elves, and dance here all night long? Who knows when we shall be so well-tuned again? I declare, I believe I'd walk home if I thought I could get anybody to go with me! "

He glanced at Elinor as he spoke; but she made him no answer. "It seems a pity to lose this so soon," repeated he.

"But we must," said Garth, "since we're sensible people, and not moon-elves, or even lunatics! " He turned his horse with the words, but the animal slipped, and, in recovering itself, struck the forward sleigh-runner with its hoof, and snapped it.

"That horse has a soul," said Golightley, when the nature of the accident was known. "He heard me mention walking home, so he just put down his foot and said, ' You shall do it ! ' "

"One of us can still ride," observed Garth.

"Why not two of us ? " said Madge.— "Have you got your spurs on, Uncle Golightley ? "

"No, no! I wouldn't ride an animal that has shown himself such a Christian as Dobbin ! You three must fight it out between you."

" I shall walk," said Elinor.

"All right," said Garth, after a pause.— "Madge, you and I will ride. It won't be the first time we have been on a horse together."

He slipped the horse out of the shafts, and drew the disabled sleigh under the shed on the islet. Then they all walked across the ice to the mainland, Garth leading the steed. Arrived there, he mounted, and Madge, taking his hand, rested her foot on his, and sprang up behind him; then clasped her arms round his waist, and they galloped away through the glimmering forest. It needed only the parson and the shining armor to render the parallel to their childish exploit complete.

CHAPTER LXXII.

CONFESSION.

ELINOR took her companion's arm, and for a while they walked on in silence; for Golightley was not so imperturbable a wooer as he had once been, and his audacity seemed even less when he and his mistress were alone together than in company. This subdued bearing of his had been very grateful to Elinor; yet it was of a kind rather to lead her to suspect him of an increase of affection toward her than the contrary. For, though never obtruding himself upon her, or attempting anything in the way of personal magnetism, as he had not spared to do in the earlier stages of their acquaintance, he now had a way of silently watching her when he fancied her unaware of his observation; of divining and fulfilling her wishes while they were yet in the germ, and of receiving her words with an undemonstrative reverence, that was flattering because evidently sincere. Nay, he was even a trifle too subservient for her taste, for she was not one of those natures that feel it delightful to condescend; and often she found herself trying to force him into a manlier and more independent attitude toward her than he was himself inclined to assume. She was doing her best to like him, by dint of resolutely shutting her eyes to whatever might tend to reflect discredit on him, and by magnifying and dwelling upon everything that made in his favor. Such honest effort on her part would scarcely fail, in time, to attain something like success. She was ever ready to defend him against detraction; and

when, unwittingly, he had spoken or acted in contradiction to what she considered his better phase, she hesitated not to take his part against himself as well.

At length he broke silence by saying, with some signs of nervousness in his voice and laugh, "By-the-by, what an odd idea was that of Mildred's about your dowry, wasn't it?—the Barmecide dowry—ha, ha!"

"It may turn out a reality."

"So it may, Elinor—so it may! Stranger things have happened. What should you say, now—but this is only one of my eccentric fancies, you know, such as I'm famous for—what should you say, now, if some strange chance were to bring you that dowry, and at the same time were to—ha, ha!—were to—"

"Were to what?"

"Well, say, were to leave me a beggar!"

"How do you mean?"

"Well, let's put it this way. What if I were a beggar now—by my own voluntary act—and you were the possessor of eighty thousand pounds?"

"I'm not sure that I understand you—unless you mean that you think of settling your fortune on me when you marry, which I should not like at all. But I forget—you were only joking!"

"Ah, my dear Elinor, there's many a true word spoken in jest! And supposing I were to do—or had already done—such a thing as you mentioned, don't you see how it might rather be an act of justice—of conscience—"

"Don't let us waste this beautiful winter moonlight by supposing anything foolish," interrupted Elinor, with something of apprehension underlying the brusqueness of her tone. "There's something I want to ask you. You have never told me where you were going to take me after we are married!"

"I sha'n't have the right to direct our movements, my dear Elinor. I shall be your dependent, living on your bounty—"

"Now, you must attend to my questions!" she interrupted once more, with an affectation of playful rebuke. "I was thinking, if you liked Europe better, I should prefer it on some accounts, too. We could come back afterward, you know, if we found it didn't suit us. Don't you think so?"

"Elinor, I— By George, I love you too well! If I cared for you now only as I did at first, I might—it might be better for both of us! If you could believe how I repent—if I could feel that you forgave me—there's nothing else I should mind!"

"Is it such a crime to love me?" said Elinor, laughing sharply, and turning her eyes away from the spectacle of his manifest agitation. "I don't know what you are talking about, I'm sure. I wish you would answer my questions about Europe. Don't you think mother would like it better?"

"My God! don't make it so hard for a poor devil. You'll never forgive me, and that's why you won't listen to me! It's my only chance—if I don't tell you now, it will be too late, and you'll think even worse of me than I deserve. I have repented—by George, I have!—and made what restitution I could—"

"Wait a moment—stop!" She clung to his arm and pressed her forehead against his shoulder. She was tense and quivering with excitement; he was relaxed and tremulous. In a few minutes she steadied herself by main force. "Now will you come home quietly?" she asked. "Remember," she added, beseechingly, "we are going to be married! I have not asked to have anything told me. But if anything were said, it could never be unsaid . . . . I will walk home alone if you please! I think you must have been—drinking!"

It was an appeal—a final, desperate expedient for remaining deaf and dumb. But, intense as was her will not to hear, Golightley was by this time too much unmanned to be restrained. What was in him to say, must out! and when Elinor heard his nervous laugh at her impugnment of his sobriety, she felt the vainness of further struggle. She quitted his arm abruptly, and moved onward, haughty and cold.

"If I could get you to realize what my life has been—how one phase has developed into another, without my seeming able to control it!" said Golightley, walking beside her in his wretchedness. "It has seemed, by George! as if destiny was always against me. I've always meant well—I can say that! But it has really seemed as if my very gifts —my peculiar fineness of perception, and all that—had helped lead me wrong. If I'd been formed of such clay as other men, I should have done well enough!"

"Do not speak as if I knew anything," said Elinor, with an almost labored distinctness of enunciation. "I know nothing. Say what is the matter in as few words as you can, since you have begun. Remember—I would not have listened to it from anybody else!"

But it was hard for him to speak plainly and succinctly, now that it had come to the point. The crookedness of a lifetime made itself felt. He could not help hesitating and temporizing on the verge of his gulf, though longing to plunge headlong.

"Ah—you know what a gift I have for finance? of course, everybody knows that. But it was a gift with a curse on it, like the others; I could make anybody's fortune but my own. Well, then—where was I? Oh, when I got acquainted with poor, dear John and all of you—you know how highly he thought of me, Elinor, how thoroughly he believed in me? And the good he saw in me may have been there, you know, though with evil mixed with it, of course. Well, I wouldn't take charge of the money—the investments and all that—though dear old John besought me to do it, time and again; and though I knew, too, that the property being actually Mildred's, and she my sister—"

"I know all this; I think you did quite rightly and prudently not to interfere. Is that all you had to tell me?"

"It was just so that you might see things from my point of view. The way I looked at it was, that even if I had taken the management, and the property, by some—some accident or other, you know, had passed into my own possession, still it would have been in the family all the same, and none of you would really have lost anything—in fact, you would have been the gainers, since I could place the investments where they'd realize a fourth as much again as under poor dear John's management."

"Do you mean to say that anything of this sort happened?" demanded Elinor, slowly.

"Ah — that was the principle of the thing, as the moralists say; and if you only eliminate the accident—it wasn't strictly accidental—"

Elinor stopped and faced him, though her eyes were downcast. She spoke with manifest pain and effort. "Did you—steal—the money?"

He glanced up at her with a blanched, wretched look, his hand feeling about the sidelocks of his hair, and wandering down over his beard.

"It seems a terrible thing to put it that way!" muttered he. "But, frankly, I've never had a moment's peace of mind since then. But I haven't explained to you the—ha, ha!—what the lawyers call the extenuating circumstances. There were extenuating circumstances, Elinor—by George, there were! It was that scoundrel Flint, or Kinco, or whatever his name is, that got me into it!"

"You stole your friend's money — he loved and trusted you so! What must I believe next? Ah, dear me!" She still spoke with painful, lagging utterance, and the last words were a heavy sigh. Then, though with almost unconquerable repugnance, she raised her head and compelled her eyes to rest on him. Such a look, it was more agony for her to give than for him to sustain. For he had not appreciated the full ugliness of the crime he had committed. He saw in it an offense against morals, against good taste, and, worse still, against respectability; he was miserable at the loss of his prestige in the eyes of Elinor and of the world; and he was poignantly affected by the shame involved in the process of confession. But if everything had turned out comfortably, if his guilt had never been brought to light, and he had been able to enact the part of benefactor and philanthropist with the proceeds of his roguery, it may be open to question whether either his heart or his conscience would have been disturbed. At all events, it had never occurred to him that the knowledge of his degradation might cause Elinor deeper shame and suffering than he himself was capable of feeling.

"I had expected," said he, at last—"I had expected you'd at least have given me credit for speaking out before we were married. If you knew what my love for you has grown to be, lately, you would give me some credit. I didn't know, frankly, what my capacities for love were until within the last month; and yet I risk the loss of you—by George!"

Elinor began to kindle with indignation; the man had absolutely no thought but for himself. "What credit do you expect?" she asked. "You were a coward to tell me all this! You should sooner have died than insult me with the confession of your deformity! If you had been faithful even to evil, I might have had a kind of respect for you! But there is no manliness in you! You confessed only when you knew you must be found out at any rate. It was dastardly and insulting! You were afraid I should listen to gossip against you—you thought I was as treacherous as yourself! But you have thrown away the only trust that any one will ever have in you. I would have believed no evidence but your own!"

"Destiny is against me, or this would be none of it!" said Golightley, with an hysteric sort of bravado.

"I ought to thank you, though," Elinor continued, not heeding him in her passionate preoccupation. "At least, I can believe myself, now! I was right in detesting you when I first saw you. You are as contemptible as you look—that is my comfort! I am glad you are a criminal—I am glad!"

"O Elinor, can't you care for me a little still?"

She turned upon him with that strange, uneven glance of hers, which was yet so direct and disconcerting, and with a smile on her lips that made Golightley feel his degradation as no frown could have done.

"That is not reasonable. You are not lovable. How can I care for a man who has spoilt my life, and deceived me into believing evil good, and good evil? I know why you asked me in marriage. After you had stolen your friend's money, you thought you would steal me for your wife, so that you might say, 'No such great harm was done, after all!' I have no very high opinion of myself, but I will not be the balm of your evil conscience!"

"It isn't merely to make me happy, you know," he said, twisting his hands together. "It would be saving a human soul. Only you could do it, Elinor; and I'm not too far gone to be saved!"

The expression of sarcasm passed from Elinor's face and voice, and sadness took its place. "I have a soul, too!" said she. "You have taken away the freshness from it already. If we had been married, it would have lost whatever else in it is worth preserving. Loving me cannot save you, nor my loving you; you must love truth and honor."

Golightley shrugged his shoulders, and laughed his short, empty laugh. "Oh, well, so be it! When it comes to fearing the Lord and keeping his commandments, I may account myself done for! So be it. I'll disappear. You may think less despitefully of me some day, my dear Elinor, when things come to be known that are not known now."

"Who will pity him if I do not?" thought Elinor, compassionately. But her sense of justice was too true and keen to yield overmuch to the gentler sentiment. Yet she felt that the very fact of having suffered indignity at his hands, had given him a sort of claim upon her. Providence had ordained that their paths should cross; ought she not therefore, so far as might be possible, to turn the meeting to good?

"I shall never be what I might have been if we had not met," said she; "but I will not think despitefully of you. I will hope and care that you may do well hereafter, if that will be any help to you."

"I am a beggar, my dear Elinor, too poor even in my deserts for respectable folks to concern themselves about me. All I shall ask of your condescension is that you enjoy your fortune none the less because of the evil hands it has passed through. I anticipated Mildred in her generosity—ha, ha! It is all paid in to your credit in the Beacon Hill Bank—all my share that is to say. What the—ha!—the other scoundrel had, is gone past redemption."

"Has he proofs against you?"

"Oh! you've heard that? He will probably surrender them in consideration of my check for ten thousand pounds."

"How can you offer him that, if—"

"Well, the fact is—though I hadn't meant to trouble you with details—that the check will not be paid when he presents it."

"You mean to cheat even your accomplice!" exclaimed Elinor, with irrepressible disgust.

"You can deliver me up to the majesty of the law, if that will make you any happier. I deserve it, of course. But my being devoured won't save my friend the accomplice."

"You need not misunderstand me so!" said Elinor, blushing sadly. "I wish no harm either to you or him. But there shall be no more cheating! You have not yet given him the false check?"

"It still lacks my indorsement. When he hands me my letters—"

"If they can be got in no other straightforward way, he must be honestly paid for them. Since the money is mine now, I shall pay him."

This proposal took Golightley by surprise, and changed his recklessness into an emotion that brought tears to his eyes. "My dear Elinor—my dear Elinor!" exclaimed he; "I—no, no! my safety is not worth that sacrifice."

"Money is not what I most care for," returned she, a little coldly. "You asked me to sacrifice myself a few minutes ago. I do this on your sister's and brother's account as well as yours. They would not wish to have you—in prison!"

"If you could have but said it was partly for your sake too! But no—let it go! No one will care. I'll refuse Flint the check, and he may keep the letters and do his worst. I have a grain of pride somewhere about me, still, by George! I won't accept your noble and generous offer."

"I shall never be likely to ask another favor of you. You have no right to refuse me this."

"If you'd only say it mattered a snap of the finger to you what became of me!" he broke forth, with real passion. "You are so cold to a poor devil that loves you! You make him know he has affections, only to freeze him when he's at your feet. A drop of warm human charity would give him life to feel your justice better!"

Elinor began to tremble and catch her breath. "I do not wish to be cold and uncharitable," she said, brokenly. "I am all alone; there is no one to be 'strong for me. I must defend myself in the best way I can. I try to keep the soul God gave me pure and good. It is because I am so weak that I seem so hard. I would be kind, and help people, if I could."

Golightley passed his hand across his face and groaned.

"I begin to feel all I've lost," said he. "Be cold again, Elinor; by George, I can't stand that!"

"I may do it, then?" she asked, quickly and timidly. "Where is he?"

After some pause and hesitation, Golightley said:

"He can't be got at, just now. Selwyn and his detectives are on the lookout for him, and he's obliged to keep dark. But I was to have met him in about a week, and then it might be arranged."

There was something so constrained in his manner as he made this speech, that Elinor was not free from misgiving. "You do not promise!" she said.

"Ah—well, the truth is, I—ha, ha!—I was afraid you might not—"

"I will believe your promise."

"Upon my soul, I thank you, Elinor!" He cleared his throat, and strove to recover the jaunty air which he sometimes affected. "Be the oath recorded! Given life and liberty, your commands shall be obeyed! Of course, if I should turn up dead and buried within the next six days, you'd let me off, eh?—ha, ha!"

"I shall believe you," she repeated, gently.

They were standing facing each other, a few paces apart; and now there was a short silence. It was broken by Golightley.

"I must stay hereabouts till all's settled," said he, clearing his throat again; "but I presume there'll be no more *tête-à-tête* for us, so I'll say 'addio' now. Good-by, Elinor Golightley; may I have been the only pitfall in your path!"

Elinor's sad lips could utter no words; but she drew her slender hand from her muff and held it toward him. He stepped quickly forward and took it between both of his. But he did not offer to kiss it.

In a few moments he relinquished it, and, walking onward, left Elinor alone. As she followed in the same direction, she caught occasional glimpses of him at the turnings of the path, where he waited to see that she did not lose her way. But when the forest became more open, he disappeared, and she reached home solitary.

CHAPTER LXXIII.

NEXT MORNING.

NEVER before had Elinor so greatly felt the need of some friend to whom she might tell her trouble, and who would sympathize with her and counsel her; and never had she been so isolated. Mrs. Tenterden, Cuthbert, Garth, Madge—all were alike impracticable. Whether or not any of them knew or suspected the truth about Golightley, she could not tell; but she felt that she must wait unshriven till the end came, when and whatever that might be. Meantime her thoughts gave her no rest. The night passed almost sleeplessly, and, when at length the day confronted her, it came as something to be endured rather than lived through.

Though she had never loved the man who had so disgracefully failed her, yet he had occupied the lover's place, and, whatever gentle emotions had visited her heart, she had felt in duty bound to train toward him; striving with faithful desire to render her observances so generous, that in time they might become spontaneous and sincere. Thus had Golightley represented something real to her, though himself a sham; and when he abruptly ceased to exist (so far as her intents and purposes were concerned), she was as a vine robbed of its support, which, though it was perhaps but an infirm wooden post, had nevertheless stood her in the stead of a marble column. The delicate tendrils of her affections grasped instinctively after something that might take the place of what had been lost. It seems a mistake to suppose that those whose feelings have undergone rude treatment are less susceptible of fresh impressions immediately than long afterward. The forlornness of recent abandonment calls out for comfort more urgently than that which time has inured to its condition. Elinor, possibly, had never been in a mood so accessible to the influence of a true and ardent lover as when, on the morning following her rupture with Golightley, she walked out to take the medicines of air and exercise.

The road she happened to follow led toward the mill-stream, and thence along the bank to the lake. After walking a mile or so, Elinor came in view of a little hut, roughly constructed of unhewed logs and roofed with pine-bark. Smoke was issuing from a primitive sort of chimney aperture at one end; and before the doorway a man was standing with a cigar in his mouth. Upon hearing her step on the snow, he turned quickly, and immediately began to make gladsome gestures of greeting. As Elinor got nearer, she perceived that the man was Jack Selwyn.

"Good-morning, princess!" exclaimed he. "Permit me to rejoice that you have dispensed with your retinue this morning. You were out in force on the pond last night."

"How did you know we were there?" asked she, surprised.

"What! didn't you see the lonely skater? I recognized Miss Madge's voice, I'm sure; and Garth's. And my intuitive perceptions informed me of your presence!"

"Why didn't you join us, then?"

"Oh, five are almost as poor company as three, you know," replied he, smiling.

"Why do you stay here? We thought you were hundreds of miles away."

"I've only been here a day or two. Will you come in and take a look at my winter palace? I have always looked upon you as the princess in the fairy-tale, and longed to be the fairy prince who rescues you from some danger, and does the polite generally. I found you asleep once! But come in! it's quite jolly."

The shadow on Elinor's face lightened somewhat as she followed him into the hut; he had the happy faculty of raising people's

spirits without reason given or required. The tiny interior smelt of pine-resin; a log of hemlock was crackling in the fireplace, and Jack, with great ceremony, offered his guest a seat on the wood-pile.

"This spot is historic," he remarked. "Here, many thousand years ago, a youth called Garth built him an enchanted canoe, of birch-bark, wherein, when it was completed, he seated his august form, and sped away down yonder rapids to the lake. Death, having failed to catch him on the journey, gave up the pursuit permanently; and thus it happens, dear princess, that this same Garth is yet alive. The place has been improved from a mere open shed to a hut, since the era whereof I speak. I find it mighty comfortable. A splendid retreat to study the nature and habits of snow and ice in!"

"Why don't you come to Urmhurst, Jack?"

"Well, for reasons. Changes are in the wind. But ere long, if it please your highness, I shall have strange tidings to impart."

"Oh, don't talk so about it!" said Elinor, suddenly becoming piteous. "I know it all—even more than you do!"

Jack rested a hand on either knee and stared. "What do you know?"

"About the robbery. Golightley himself told me, last night. And he has given it all back—all he had."

"Golightley told you? Given it back, has he?" repeated Jack, taking up one of his knees thoughtfully, and biting his mustache. He glanced sharply at Elinor, to see what temper she might be in.

"You mustn't feel too much cut up about it," he said, cheerfully. "I wasn't sure whether I ought to let you into the secret, long ago, or not. I did give you a sort of hint about it once, you know: I half thought you suspected. But do you really know quite what a scamp the fellow was? Did he remember to inform you, for instance, that the thousand pounds he borrowed of John Tenterden were the means that enabled him to commit the robbery? and that—"

Elinor colored. "I didn't ask him; I'd rather not know."

"Oh, but you'll have to know some time; and, in my opinion, it's only justice to your-

self and other people that you should know.
If you go off with the notion that, although
he did weakly allow himself to be ensnared
by evil counsels, still he might have been
worse, and a good deal could be said in his
favor, you'd simply be wasting valuable compassion, much better bestowed elsewhere.
Now, the fact is, that never was a meaner
or more treacherous theft committed than
this! Golightley took advantage of Mr.
Tenterden's confidential disclosures to him,
and of memoranda which the poor old man
had intrusted to him, to forge an order on
his agents, directing them to buy up the
whole stock of a certain mine. The purchase was made, and it took all Tenterden's
money to do it. Thereupon Golightley and
his partner—Flint by name, and Kineo by
nature — circulated the reports they had
ready, and down went the stock to nothing
at all. It was all contrived beautifully, that
must be admitted. Well, then these fellows
quietly bought it all in, at a hundred per
cent. discount, using for that purpose the
very same ready money with which Tenterden had just obliged them. That was an artistic touch, wasn't it? But all this time
the mine was not only good—there was nothing better; and as soon as the false reports
were proved to be false, up goes the stock
again like a rocket, and our two friends
realized at what figure they pleased. Luckily, Kineo was sharp enough to get some evidences of the forgery and conspiracy into his
hands, foreseeing that he might find them
useful some day. So now, you see, the
knaves have fallen out, and the honest men
—or women, rather—are coming by their
own again! "

Here Jack, who had spoken as fast as
possible in order to avoid interruption,
stopped, and tossed up his fur cap. I'm
glad that's off my mind!" he exclaimed.
"Many's the time my very bones have ached
with holding it in!"

"I was in no danger of thinking too well
of him," said Elinor, with a sigh. "But
they are neither of them to go to prison. I
am going to get the proofs from Kineo, and
burn them."

"The devil you— How, I mean?"

Elinor explained briefly, Jack listening

with keen attention. "You don't mean to
say," he exclaimed, when she had finished,
"that you're going to throw away ten thousand pounds on that—trash!"

"It will not be thrown away."

Jack bit his mustache, and frowned: he
had his own convictions on the subject.
He was wise enough to perceive, however,
that nothing was to be gained by a dispute
with Elinor, who would be more likely
either to dissent from him, or to impose
some restriction upon his action, than to be
persuaded by him: whereas, if he dexter-
ously changed the topic, he would retain
both her favor and his own freedom.

"Oh, that little villain of a Madge Danver!" he muttered, shaking his head. "What
a wild-goose chase she did send me on!"

"Then Madge has known—!" exclaimed
Elinor, and stopped.

"Bless your heart, princess! she has
been the arch-conspirator from the beginning. She took counsel with herself betimes as to whether Golightley, Kineo, or
myself, were more eligible for her. But she
quarreled with Golightley, and in me she
was disappointed; as for Kineo, his prospects will, at all events, be improved when
you have carried out your royal purpose of
buying the proofs of him."

"Oh—are you sure that—"

"I cannot myself believe," interposed
Jack, while his cheeks reddened a little,
"small as is my reverence for Master Golightley, that her hold upon him was anything more than a threat of exposure. There
must be a limit to the greatest human de-
pravity, you know!"

"But I meant—" said Elinor, coloring
also, "about Garth."

"Oh, we're safe in calling that match
off, I think. That whole affair of hers with
Garth has always been a mystery, though.
Mr. Urmson says that she loves him, after
a fashion of her own. Sometimes I agree
with him, and at other times I don't. But
whether or not she loves him, I'll bet she
won't marry him."

"Does he love her?" asked Elinor, in a
lower tone.

"Well, he's bullied himself into believing
it, as he has bullied himself into a great

many other things. But when she elopes and leaves him in the lurch, he will find himself face to face with a truth which I warned him of years ago, when we were at college—that he is married to his painting, and that any engagement outside of that would be bigamous!"

Elinor rose from the wood-pile, and stood for a few moments with her hands hanging folded and her eyes on the fire; then she moved toward the door.

"Madge must do no such thing!" she said, turning to Jack with a troubled look. "It would be too sad, after all that has happened. If she wishes to visit Europe, and see beautiful things and great people, she shall go with mother and me. She can be as gay and fashionable as she pleases: it's natural she should wish to be — she's so beautiful and brilliant. I'll speak to her to-morrow."

"You'll find this charity a more extravagant one than the other," ventured Jack, twisting his mustache and eying her gravely.

"Then I shall like it the better," said she, with a passing smile. "This money seems to have had a curse upon it, so far; I don't need it, and I would like to make it do a little good, after so much harm. I don't want to be rich; I should like to live by my violin!"

She stepped across the threshold, out to the sparkling snow and sunshine. Then Jack took his courage in his hands and followed her.

"Princess Elinor," said he, "why do you lavish all your bounty on the rogues, and leave the poor honest fellows out in the cold?"

"Only the rogues seem to need it," she answered, smiling again.

"No—because then I would be a rogue; and I'm not! I've been a good-for-nothing all my life, but I have always reverenced good women, and told the truth to everybody. Can't you give me something too?"

"I'm afraid I have nothing for you," said she, startled.

"Look here! I don't want ten thousand pounds, nor to be gay and fashionable at your expense. All I want is the greatest
17

treasure on earth! and that's you. I love you with my heart and soul. I always have loved you; and I never loved any other woman. Elinor—say you'll be my wife. I believe I can make you happy—I *know* I can!"

"I cannot—oh, I cannot!" she exclaimed, turning her face away. "I never can be married. I feel as if I should hate the man I married, even though I had loved him before—marriage has seemed such a gloomy thing to me, since I have looked forward to it at all. It seems like going to prison!"

"But to be my wife shall be coming out of prison! I know it was wrong to ask you so soon after this fuss; but I won't be impatient; I'll give you forever to think it over in! at least, I'll give you as long as that fellow in the Bible had to wait — seven — months, wasn't it?"

Elinor laughed ruefully, pressing the point of her foot into the snow.

"I won't try to persuade you on the ground of the difference it would make to me," continued Jack, "because that would keep me talking here all the seven months. But you should be as much mistress of the world as a man can make you who has seen the world and worships whatever part of it you stand on. After a while, even if you didn't find much of anything to admire in me, you would have associated so many jolly things with me, that at last you'd count me in as one of them—almost without meaning to! Do say, at least, that you won't begin with saying no!"

It was not easy wholly to resist this pleading—not the words so much as the manner of it. Jack was so immeasurably in earnest, so heart-and-soul in what he was saying, his face and voice expressed so much more than his sentences, and the vigor of his desire made itself so strongly felt, that Elinor, though she had been all no when he first opened the subject, could not at once say no when he had ceased. And why should she say it—at once? The ardor and utterness of his devotion touched her, coming, as it did, at the season of her greatest loneliness. No doubt but the marriage would give her a scope and freedom of life such as she might not otherwise easily attain; perhaps, too, it offered opportunities for generosity and unselfishness, which a solitary existence would lack. Why say no—at all?

Again, she was not called upon for an immediate or positive answer, either one way or the other. She was to be allowed time to question and scrutinize the new idea on all sides, and to pronounce upon it at her leisure. All that was asked now was, that she should not say no. She had always liked Jack, the impact of whose vigorous and manly nature was an unspeakable relief after the clamminess of Golightley. And Jack had — unconsciously — used one argument which sank more deeply into Elinor's heart than any of his deliberate ones: "Garth is married to his painting!" Then, what need for Elinor to be over-solicitous about her destiny?

All this while Jack's bright hazel eyes were searching her face, which was turned downward. When she lifted it at last, he drew himself up like a soldier in presence of the enemy. The color sprang to his cheeks. "But you do not know me!" said she, faintly.

"If we'd been married a century, I could not say 'I know you!' There would still be a thousand new—lovelinesses to learn! But I love you!"

"You say too much. I have nothing to give you. I don't love you, and I'm sure I never can. It would spoil a true friendship if you try to make it anything more!"

"Whatever you do, don't think of friendship!" exclaimed Jack, with great earnestness. "There never yet was a true friendship between a man and a woman! But just stand still and let me love you! Don't move!"

"I don't know that it's worth while for me to care what becomes of me—but that's an ungracious thing to say! I like you so much that—I feel sure we were not meant for each other!"

"But don't say no! whatever you do, remember that!" He came one entreating step nearer.

"I won't say it, then—now. But," she added, hurriedly, for the delight that leaped into Jack's eyes frightened her, "it will make it harder for you and me if I must say it hereafter. But at any rate you shall see me, and know something about what sort of a person I am; and then, perhaps, you'll thank me for not having said yes!"

"All I'm afraid for is, that one of us may die—for this is too good to be true! Elinor—Elinor—Elinor!— No, don't be scared! I mean to be as subdued and circumspect as a duenna. But a duenna may kiss the princess's hand just once!—Elinor, don't you think seven weeks is a very long time?"

"O Jack!" she said, panting and turning pale; there was genuine dismay in her eyes and voice. "Remember this is not a promise—not an engagement!"

"No, of course not, else I'd have—not kissed your hand! But it was only by accident that I said seven months. You know those Bible fellows lived hundreds of years, and we have left only forty or fifty at the outside."

Elinor could not help laughing, though there were tears on her eyelashes. And so they parted for that time.

———◆———

CHAPTER LXXIV.

TWO OLD CRONIES.

EARLY in the afternoon of the same day, Madge left the cottage, and set off toward Urmhurst. She walked along with a somewhat pensive mien; occasionally looking up and about, and then again falling into reverie. She was pale, but there was brilliance in her eyes extraordinary even for her; and such a deliberation and stateliness of movement as might indicate a great bracing-up and dilation of the spirit within. On arriving at the house, she mounted at once to the garret; for Garth, as she knew, was not at home, and there was no one else to question her proceedings. In the garret she remained for more than an hour. On her return down-stairs, Golightley met her in the hall. He had on his hat and coat, and accompanied her, with his usual affability, on her road toward the village.

"There is an enterprising air about you this morning, Miss Maggie," remarked he. "Are any fresh projects in suspense?"

"None that concern me, Uncle Golightley. But I believe Mr. Kineo would like an opportunity to say good-by to you, before he goes."

"Ah! I presume he desires to rid himself of those—ah—documents, does he not? Well, I shall drop in on him this evening, I think."

"From what I understood, I don't think he means to let you have them until after he is quite sure that they can be of no further use to him. His idea seems to be that, if you had the documents before he got his check cashed, and was on his way to Europe, something might happen to hinder his getting away."

"H'm! he doesn't expect me to—h'm!" Golightley caressed his cheeks thoughtfully, and murmured inarticulately to himself as he stalked along. "If our friend has become so cautious," he continued at length, "or has taken such cautious advice, Miss Maggie!—as to mistrust my good faith, the only result would be to defeat the prosperity of both parties. He must know that it would be impossible for me to draw that amount of ready money myself, for, in order to do it, I should be obliged to go to Boston; and just now there are guardian angels abroad, who might misinterpret my intentions in making such a journey. As to his anticipating any hinderance after our bargain is settled—anything of that sort, you know—he simply cuts his own nose off if he's ass enough to suppose it. And he certainly can't expect me to let him keep the documents until he has cashed the check and taken flight! With every respect for his sound memory and conscientiousness, that would—eh?" Uncle Golightley brought forward his side locks and laughed.

"I shouldn't imagine he would expect anything so unbusiness-like," returned Madge, composedly. "But might not some compromise be made? For instance, suppose he were to hand the documents to some third person, who would give them to you on receiving word from him to do so?"

"Ha, ha! an admirable scheme, my dear Margaret, with only one objection to it, which is—the difficulty of finding a *fidus Achates* of both parties; one whom I could

depend upon to hand me the documents when my honorable friend sent him the necessary permission; and whom my honorable friend could trust to keep them from me until the aforesaid propitious moment arrived! I must confess that I should be at a loss where to put my finger upon such a treasure of a confidant!"

"Yes; but I believe," said Madge, glancing at him from the corner of her long, dark eye—"I think such a person has been found!"

Golightley stopped caressing himself, and pressed on his eye-glasses.

"Who is it?"

"It's Garth, I believe."

"You believe it's—*Garth?*" He fetched a long breath and retained it for several seconds; then drew his brows together and threw up his chin. "Well, I don't!" he declared; and brought his hands together with an emphatic clap.

Madge laughed lightly. "I was afraid you wouldn't—that is, that it would surprise you at first. Poor Garth seems so innocent, and slow to see things. But the most innocent-seeming persons sometimes turn out to have been quite acute. At all events, Garth knows all about your affairs and Mr. Kineo's, and has known for some while. And he has called on Mr. Kineo at his lodgings, and they have made all arrangements. It was on his account that Garth got up the skating-party for to-morrow—so that he might be able to skate away down the meadows without any one's suspecting him. And it is Garth who will take charge of the documents for you, Uncle Golightley."

"When does Kineo propose delivering them to him?"

"Oh, Garth has had them several days."

Golightley paused to recover himself. "If that be the case," he rejoined, "I shall take the liberty to keep my money in my pocket! I begin to think it must be my honorable friend Kineo who is stupid!"

"Not quite so stupid as that!" answered Madge, laughing again. "Of course he didn't let Garth have the documents for nothing. Garth paid him fifty thousand dollars in bank-notes for them yesterday; and you are to give him the check you were to have given Kineo—and more too, I'm afraid!"

"H'm! upon my word, this is interesting! By George, Garth is coming out!"

"You see, Garth found out, among other things, that Sam was heir to the Eve legacy; so he wrote to Professor Grindle for it."

"But it strikes me," interposed Golightley, "that the professor is too good a business-man to give up that same legacy without proof positive that it belonged to the person in whose behalf it was applied for."

"That same thing struck Garth—wasn't it curious?" rejoined Madge, with a smile. "So, as I happened to know where the certificates of his mother's marriage and his baptism were, I got them, and Garth sent them on with his letter. Professor Grindle found them legal, and sent them back to us with the money. Only, that is a secret, because only Nikomis and I know where the certificates are kept, and I borrowed them without her permission."

"I think I could make it worth somebody's while to show them to me!" remarked Golightley, with a significant look.

"Oh, they are quite safe—nothing can happen to them; and Sam, I know, is very fond of calling himself your nephew; more so, I think, than Garth is!" said Madge, with an engagingly confidential air.

"Well, by George! I feel sat upon," exclaimed Golightley, with a rather ghastly attempt at a humorous grimace. "My projects don't look especially brilliant, do they? But I ought to thank you for the confidence you have shown in me in giving me such an amount of private information. Suppose, now, I had got a little bit nervous and anxious, and had gone and told my friends, the guardian angels, that a dear nephew of mine was starting for Europe on such and such a date, by such and such a route; but that he was apt to be very heedless and flighty, and would they please take care that he reached his proper destination?—What if I had been such a fussy old uncle as to do that—eh?"

"Ah, but I knew you were never fussy, Uncle Golightley," returned Madge, with an arch glance. "You never will be until you

have those documents of yours to take care of; and then your nephew will be beyond the guardian angels' reach!"

"Ah! belle dame sans merci! You don't leave me a loop-hole, do you? Not one, not one, not one! Well, now I suppose you will marry Garth, and settle down here quietly; happy and contented in the care of your hens and cows, cheerfully busy with the housework and cookery; and, in the evenings, bringing out your spinning-wheel or your knitting, and sitting with your lord and master before the kitchen-fire! A lovely idyllic picture—two souls possessing perfect confidence and satisfaction in each other! —I suppose, by-the-by, that Garth had no impolite questions to ask you, as to how you came to be so well informed on all these obscure points, and as to your reasons for not having confided in him until now? Nothing of that sort, eh?"

"There was no need for him to ask me such questions, Uncle Golightley," replied Madge, with dignity. "You speak almost as if I had anything to conceal from him! Of course Garth knows that whatever information I had came to me accidentally, through my intimacy with Nikomis; and that I had not told him about it at first, because he was ill, and because I had hoped that things might be arranged so that the family name need not be disgraced. But when I found that nothing could be done without his help, there was nothing left but to ask him for it. He trusts me perfectly; why should he not? Does not Elinor Golightley trust you?"

Madge could not have known what would be the full effect of this last stab; it may have determined Golightley to a course of action as to which he had hesitated until then. He made no reply, however, though his face twitched and grew whiter than before. But when, soon afterward, he had left her and struck off through the woods by himself, he murmured more than once, "There is one loop-hole, Miss Maggie; just one!"

————

CHAPTER LXXV.

MUTUAL COURTESIES.

His course now led him toward the point of junction of the mill-stream with the lake. Although he had never, thus far, been interfered with by any of those "guardian angels" whereof he had spoken to Madge, yet he could guess pretty accurately where they might be found, and doubted not that it would be easy enough (should he feel so inclined) to have speech of one of them. He may not, however, have been aware that Selwyn himself was already returned; and it was therefore an equal surprise to both of them, perhaps, when they presently met in one of the more secluded forest by-paths.

Jack was in such high spirits from his morning's interview with Elinor, that he would probably have greeted even the devil with magnanimity, had that personage happened in his way; and since Golightley had lost what Jack had gained, and was furthermore in a fair way to get full measure of retribution for his misdeeds, the younger man was disposed to be forbearing. Accordingly, he bowed with grave politeness; and, perceiving that Golightley had something to say to him, he stopped.

"A fine afternoon again, Jack; I'm in hopes this weather will keep on over to-morrow. I see you've returned from your trip in season to join our picnic on the ice."

"Well, I've not quite made up my mind whether to go."

"Ah, really? Your arrival seemed so opportune—"

"I hope it may prove so."

"The fact is, my dear Jack, I don't believe we shall be able to do without you! Have you heard—have you heard the latest developments concerning this robbery business?"

Jack looked at him attentively, wondering whether the man could be meditating some evasion even at this stage of affairs.

"I'm open to instruction," said he.

"It's a philosophic virtue, I believe," observed the other, "for a man to know when he's beaten; and I'm free to admit that I am a very good philosopher, as far as that goes. But I presume even philosophers have their weaknesses; and mine is, not to be philosophic on any one's account but my own. Now, to proceed to the point at once: our friend Samuel Kineo, *alias* Flint, who (as you are most likely aware by this time) is on a visit to his grandmamma in the attic of Urmhurst, proposes to leave for foreign parts to-morrow evening, with ten thousand pounds ready money in his trousers-pockets, to pay his traveling-expenses withal."

"I conceive you, sir!" said Jack, sarcastically. "Having given him that sum in exchange for the power he held over you, you are now desirous of defrauding him of his hard-won earnings. Very astute, and just what I should have expected of you! But are you correct in saying that he holds ready money, and not a check, which might or might not be worth more than the paper it's written on?"

Golightley laughed. "Well guessed—well guessed, my dear Jack! but you are out for once. Very likely I had intended something of that sort, but I've been forestalled. I haven't got the documents, and some one else—my nephew Garth, namely—has paid the ready money. That money, of course, is the Eve legacy, and is, or was, the last scrap of Urmson property left from my ravages. Garth, wishing to save the family honor, and all that sort of thing, dumps it into Kineo's pockets, gets in return the inconvenient documents, and then recommends my fellow-outlaw to be off as fast as his skates can carry him."

"That's news certainly; where did you pick it up?"

"From the young lady who, as I take it, contemplates sharing the rewards and perils of Mr. Kineo's future career—unless, indeed, she has contrived a way to outwit him, as well as the rest of us, which is always possible! She confided the secret to me, you understand, on the assumption that self-interest weighs a few ounces more in my balance than is actually the case. By-the-by, I may as well tell you that, some few weeks since, I paid into the account of the lady who was to have been my wife the sum of eighty-and-odd thousand pounds. It's all I had, except a trifle, to—keep me in gloves and cigarettes for a month or so!"

The tone and manner of this reference to Elinor smote Jack with compassion. In Golightley's preceding utterances had been perceptible only the jaunty bravado which strove to disguise, however flimsily, the shameful squalor of exposed rascality. But in mentioning her who, to him as well as to Jack, was the first and dearest of womankind, his voice had turned hoarse, and the haggard lines in his face had seemed to deepen. "If the fellow really loved her," said Jack to himself, "to have lost her is more than enough punishment for meaner crimes than his. Heaven knows I'm far enough from deserving her myself!"

"Look here!" he continued aloud, planting himself face to face with his interlocutor, "I don't see but what you deserve some credit for this hint. Of course I see that it gratifies your spite to block Kineo's little game, and of course you rely on Garth not to use the proofs against you, since you've already given up your share of the booty to the proper owners. Still, you do risk something, and I've no right to suppose that your chief motive is not to save your brother and Garth their fifty thousand dollars. And I'll be damned if I'm not sorry for you, any way! What do you mean to do with yourself, if you get out of this scrape?"

"Ah, well—absit odium, my dear Jack, but you must allow me to say that that would be my own business!"

"I know. But I had a reason for asking. —Confound it, look here!" said Jack, with some embarrassment, "I've got more money than I know what to do with—what would you say to my shipping you off to Australia? —my people have got a place of business there—and putting you in the way of making a good, honest living? You can make a new man of yourself there, in every sense of the word. What do you say?"

"It's kind of you, Jack, by George!" answered the other, indifferently. "But the fact is, I'd thought of a longer jaunt than that—or rather, I hardly think I'm up to that kind of thing now. You see I've given it a pretty fair trial—this campaigning about at other fellows' expense, you understand—

and I'm tired of it! I don't seem to have the stuff in me; talent enough, but it doesn't seem to work out in the right way. No—no, I'm afraid I shouldn't do your introduction much credit. I'm pretty well tired out —I'm pretty well tired out!"

"Oh, while there's life there's hope!" returned Jack; but he could not help acknowledging to himself that Golightley's words were true. Everything in the man's appearance testified to an exhaustion of moral and mental resources almost beyond hope of remedy. "Well, think it over," he added, "and we'll speak of it again next week. Probably we'll be able to let Kineo off in the end, after making him hand back the legacy, so he won't stand in your way. I should like to give you a lift if I can."

Golightley stood silent awhile, looking abstractedly first in one direction and then in another, and settling and resettling his eye-glasses on his nose. Then, appearing all at once to recollect himself, he lifted his hat to Jack and said:

"Till next week, then!—by-the-by, what was it? . . . . ah, yes—kind of you, very kind of you, by George! Till next week, then, Jack—Auf Wiedersehen! as we said in Germany." And, with a wave of his hand, he passed on.

Jack continued his walk in the opposite direction, pondering over the new aspect things had taken. "Poor old Golightley!" he murmured; "there doesn't seem to be much left of him, sure enough. His mind has taken to running on two or three subjects—and not particularly agreeable ones, I fancy—until he hardly hears or remembers what is said to him on other matters, even when they especially concern him. But that was a happy thought of mine about Australia, if he can only find the sense and pluck to take it up.

"But to think of dear old Garth, my genius, whom nobody ever suspected of the power to awaken from the reveries of imagination and idealism—actually making a practical man of affairs out of himself, and concocting a plot to bring things right without asking leave of anybody! Well, no doubt he might beat any of us at our own game, if he chose to put his mind to it. The plot would have worked beyond a doubt, but for the incalculable contingency of old Golightley's butting against himself. As for me, so far from turning out a success in my amateur detectiveship, I've simply been cajoled and bullied about like a raw schoolboy. I've found out very little that wasn't plain beforehand to anybody, and what I have found out hasn't helped me do anything. Then Madge must pack me off to Canada, like a political exile, with that hocus-pocus of a letter of hers; and there I might have been to this moment, hunting for phantom Kineos in snow-drifts, if an accident hadn't revealed that I was turning my back on what I was after. It's no thanks to me that the scamp didn't make off long ago; that must have been what Madge intended; but I suppose the rogues fell out, between the three of them, and let the opportunity go by while they were busy quarreling.

" Well, then, here are Elinor and Garth, both with their scheme all arranged independently of each other and of me, and Garth must actually have had an interview with his ruffian of a cousin—God save the mark! I expect he'll punch my head well for interfering with his plans; but it would never do to lose the legacy in that way. Besides . . . .

"Look here! of course, he can know nothing of Madge's rascalities? No—these geniuses who can see through stone-walls if they only will look at them, can be blinder than dead men when they choose not to see. She could make him believe what she liked about herself with half a word; and after all there's nothing definite against her; nothing to be sworn to—only sworn at! ha, ha, ha! By jingo, it's a shame for me to be giggling here about these things; but I'm so confoundedly happy on my own account, I should giggle at a funeral! Well, if Miss Madge will only start on an elopement to-morrow evening, it will at least have the good effect of averting Jove's anger from my own head, when I intercept and bring back the erring pair. . . . Hullo! behold him, in his habit as he lived! "

In fact, Garth was in view, walking rap-

idly with his head down, and making slashes at the snow before him with his stick. He was close to Selwyn before noticing him.

"Jack! I thought you were in Canada!" They shook hands.

"Who told you I was in Canada? "

"Madge."

"Did she tell you who sent me there? "

Garth smiled. "Well—it was to keep you out of mischief! "

"Just as I thought—she's been telling him a lie! " thought Jack; for his friend's light treatment of the matter was not otherwise explicable. "And no doubt she represented me as a busybody, which I am!—You'd like to have me back there, then? " he demanded aloud.

"No; you can save me trouble, since you are here. Sam Kineo is to escape to-morrow night, by way of the long meadows. You can take care that nothing gets in his way; and be sure you do it! "

"Ha! my lord is imperious. Will he deign to remember that I serve, not his interests, but those of his betters? "

"I have the means of unloading my unhappy uncle to the last farthing. I shall do substantial justice, without the injustice of publicity."

"Listen to the autocrat! Might your slave petition for a guarantee? "

"Take my word, Jack! "

"The sublime assurance! I wonder whether there is a single thing in this world which Garth Machiavelli Urmson does not know? Methinks, not one! "

"I know that you and I are of one mind on this matter—and that I am in a hurry! You'll be on the lake to-morrow? "

"I know that it's lucky for you I happen to be in an extraordinary good-humor. But I shall not appear on the lake to-morrow; if your new protégé is to have the bars let down for him, it is not in common decency that I should make myself personally conspicuous in doing him that service. And—hold on! I must tell you the occasion of my good-humor, lest you attribute my complacent behavior to poltroonery. Elinor Golightley has half promised—or maybe three-quarters—to do—what do you think? "

"I haven't the least idea."

"We have hit upon the one thing that he didn't know! and now he shall be told that also. Why, to be my wife.—Oho! interested at last, are you?"

The expression of Garth's face, and his entire bearing, had in a moment undergone a great though indescribable change. His lips parted; his eyes seemed to grow smaller; he leaned heavily on his walking-stick. But before Jack could speak again, he said, slowly:

"I never was more surprised. There's nothing for which I ought to be more glad." He held out his hand. "I didn't even know that she and my uncle were parted yet. Jack, I'm glad for you with . . . all my heart!"

With the last words he gripped his friend's hand so forcibly that the latter winced. "You've got your muscle back, if not your cordiality!" he said, laughing. "But as to that affair with Golightley—of course she never cared for him: and I, happening by good luck to come upon her at the right moment—O Garth, dear old curmudgeon and friend of my earlier days! I

am so happy! *absit inridia*, as poor Golightley would say, but you'll never be so happy, with all your genius. But I mustn't give you the idea that she has actually promised yet, because she hasn't, and thinks she never can, and so forth; and—mind you—I wouldn't have opened my head to any one in the world besides you about it; but you and I, you know . . . Oh, do be enthusiastic, can't you? I would for you!"

Garth laughed, stretched his arms and shoulders, and yawned! But when he saw a shade of disappointment on Jack's handsome face, he said, with the deep-toned tenderness which he rarely threw into his voice:

"I feel your happiness so much, Jack—that's why I don't say more. You know I was always a dumb beast. But you can't say so much for yourself as I can feel for you!"

They parted, each going his way. Jack was appeased.

"Can the same Creator have made that man and his uncle?" he asked himself, admiringly.

BOOK X.

G A R T H.

CHAPTER LXXVI

GETTING UNDER WAY.

GARTH was up early on the morning of Christmas-day, and went out to the barn to have a word with the cows and horses. Many changes had occurred in his world since that October morning of his last recorded visit; there were new friends, new enemies; but, after all, these animals greeted him with the same brute sincerity of kindness now as then. They did not sympathize with him; they did not pity him, nor

hope nor fear for him. They did not honor his pure resolutions, nor share his anxieties, nor respect his principles. Yet they did love him, after their own fashion and upon their own grounds; and the positive and palpable assurance of this fact gave Garth strong and deep satisfaction. He gazed in their calm faces with eyes as serene as theirs: there was no need to hide his trouble from them, and therefore his trouble took wings and flew away for a time. Peacefully they gazed at him, with just enough recognition of what he was, to be pleased with him; and he gazed back, until he could almost identify himself with the sweet, soulless animal nature. Blessed is it for the world that only man is dowered with a soul! If moral experience and responsibility descended below him in the order of creation, the earth would be a more intolerable purgatory than any that Dante or Swedenborg has told us of.

So Garth lounged amid the stalls and mangers for a luxurious hour or two, and thought that the longer he lived within the realm of kine-land, the more loath he should be to bid farewell to it. At last, however, it became necessary to get some breakfast, and prepare for the events of the day; and he reluctantly put on manhood again and returned to the house. Kinco had already been instructed as to the course he was to pursue and the precautions he was to observe, so there was not much to do besides packing provisions in hampers and baskets, getting fishing-lines in order, and heating indefinite numbers of bricks to the scorching-point for the benefit of tender feet and hands. When everything else was ready, he harnessed two horses to the double sleigh (which had been healed of its late wound), and leaving them at the door, with their blankets on, went up-stairs to bid his father farewell.

"I shall be thankful to have a day to myself," remarked Mr. Urmson, in answer to Garth's regret that he must be left solitary; "or, rather, to have the privilege of spending it undisturbed with the select society of the last two hundred and fifty years!" and he laid his thin, graceful hand on the piled-up manuscript of his history. "I expect to be amazingly refreshed by the time you return."

"You certainly look better to-day than you have lately," said Garth. "The professor will say so when he sees you to-morrow. By-the-way, since you will probably have fallen asleep before I get home to-night, I'll wish you a merry Christmas and a happy New-Year, now. Many of them, father!"

"Thanks, beloved Hottentot! But to tell the truth, I hope you'll keep the happy New-Year for yourself. I have had as many as I can hold—quite as many as are good for me. Although I am still the parson's junior by some few winters, it can be said

of me—when the time comes—'He died full of years!' It takes very much fewer years to fill some people than others; and Providence has made my capacity somewhat limited."

"No, no!" said Garth, speaking the words with an indrawing of the breath. He sat down beside his father; his throat ached and his eyes filled. "How I love him!" he thought. Then he looked enviously at the strength of his own youthful limbs and shoulders; with all his love, he could not give away an hour's use of them! How almost omnipotent is man's spirit; how impotent his flesh! Why were such unkind mates yoked together?

"I can do nothing for you!" said Garth. "I would do anything."

"Come, be a good boy!" exclaimed his father, with playful severity. "Else I shall think that I have been able to do nothing for you, though I have been willing to do a great deal!"

"I shall be—alone, if you go!"

"Who said I was going, yet awhile? I mean to live quite as long as you or anybody else can find a use for me. Didn't you just tell me that I was looking better? As to your being alone, I doubt whether Providence will have the heart to condemn you to such poor company; you don't seem to me so entirely depraved as to require such discipline. No, old gentleman, I believe you will find the New-Year a happy one, before you are at the end of it. I'll venture that prediction. Now get out, for there comes your grandfather's sleigh!"

"I wanted to tell you something," said Garth, pausing and looking at his father. "But I'll wait till to-morrow. You will be at leisure then?"

"Yes, I shall rest to-morrow. Farewell, beloved Hottentot! Give my love to Mrs. Tenterden and—Elinor."

When Garth got down-stairs, he found the Reverend Mr. Graeme in his sleigh, with Mrs. Tenterden, Elinor, and Madge.

"I won't keep 'em all, Garth lad," boomed the parson, with titanic glee. "You can take one of 'em; and fill her place with your best hamper.—Golightley," he added, as that gentleman made his appearance at the door, "I guess you'd better hop in with Garth—he's got a double team and I haven't. Don't be afraid, boy; we'll hand over your belongings to you when we get there—haw, haw, ho!"

As Garth helped Madge to alight, he noticed an unusual pallor in her face.

"You look tired," said he.

"I am tired. I was doubting whether I'd go."

"Perhaps you'd better not. You know the party is not for pleasure, though we pretend so."

"I've a great mind not to go!" she murmured, looking wistfully at him. "I'll leave it to chance! Let's pull straws: if you draw the longest I'll stay."

She held the straws, and Garth drew the longest.

"You stay!"

"It's absurd! I won't be kept back by a straw! I'll go!" she exclaimed, laughing.

"If you wish to come home early, I'll come with you."

"Oh, if I go I shall never come back!" was her answer.

When every one was seated, and the baskets and hampers securely stowed away, Garth gathered up his reins and asked the parson if he were ready.

"Any one else for the lake?" bellowed the reverend gentleman, directing his inquiry at the darksome front of Urmhurst.

"What a pity Mr. Selwyn didn't come!" exclaimed Mrs. Tenterden. "He'd enjoy it so, and he's so lively!"

"All the lasses are taken up, so far as I can see!" rejoined the parson, mirthfully. "The young man would be lonely, ma'am!"

Elinor felt a painful embarrassment. When changes have been rapid and violent, they appear dreamlike in the immediate retrospect. Was Golightley really forever disconnected with her future? Had she really listened to Jack, and half yielded to him? If so, why must the old appearances, now vacant of life and truth, still be observed? Why was it that the forms of the social world must always be under the control of the more shallow-minded and short-sighted? Mrs. Tenterden and the parson represented the conventionalism of society, before which

all individual tumult and emotion must be still. They saw according to the letter, not the spirit; and for their sakes all that was real and living must be disguised and stifled.

As they drove away, Elinor happened to catch Garth's eyes, and fancied she discerned a smile in them—though whether of sympathy or of irony, or of something else, she could not decide. Be it what it might, she flushed resentfully, and thereafter sheltered herself behind a haughty reserve; which, perhaps, was the best attitude of which the circumstances admitted.

Sam Kineo, who had heard the parson's stentorian query, and had mentally responded to it, crawled stealthily to the attic-window, and, peeping forth, saw the sleighs disappear amid the naked forest.

"I'll give them a surprise to-night!" he muttered to himself, as he gazed after them. "If they think I'm going t' sneak off with my tail between my legs, they're mistaken! Those village fools shall have a sight of Sam Kineo before he goes! If 'twasn't for that pretty little she-devil of mine, I'd let 'em have something more than a sight—curse 'em all! but she can't fight 'nd run, as I could: never mind! we got the best of 'em all; 'nd Garth 'll find I took the interest on my legacy, before he gets home to-night!" Solacing himself with these reflections, Mr. Kineo withdrew to his bower, and began the preparations for his departure. He felt that his star was once more in the ascendant, and longed to celebrate the occasion by doing something memorable. Had he not recognized that the success of his ultimate escape and immunity was dependent upon his forbearing to commit any intolerable outrage, he might have been tempted, in the gayety of his heart, to set Urmhurst on fire, or to take terrible advantage of the loneliness of Mr. Urmson. But he felt that such indulgences would be not merely foolhardy, but suicidal; especially as in Nikomis he had a suspicious and vigilant overseer. He had never succeeded in appeasing the resentment of this grim old witch, who might have served him so well; and it had been owing chiefly to her that his departure had been so much delayed. He therefore resigned himself to inoffensiveness, tempered by the determination to make up for it whenever circumstances should give him a chance; and in this mood he lit his pipe, opened his organ-box, and gave his attention to the selection of an outfit for his journey.

CHAPTER LXXVII.

QUESTIONS AND ANSWERS.

MEANWHILE the party arrived at the lake, it being then about noon, and found a multitude of the village-folks already in possession, and flying hither and thither over the ice in all directions. Having reached the islet and stabled the horses, Garth began the construction of the big bonfire, and sent a dozen or so of the younger gentry in quest of fagots and kindlings. They accepted the job with enthusiasm, one small boy, with a huge red tippet wound round his head and body, showing himself especially energetic and untiring; he was a member of Madge's Sunday-school class, and was perhaps stimulated to such exertions by a secret passion for his mistress. In a short time there was material enough collected to last throughout the day; and Garth, having built up a lofty superstructure of scientifically-adjusted twigs, boughs, and fragments of decayed stumps, took some paper and a match from his pocket and deftly set the whole pile on fire. "That ought to burn well: the kindling was good!" he muttered to himself. And it did burn gloriously. There was no wind, and the flame rose straight upward, until it ended in a thick column of smoke which might have been visible twenty miles away. The buffalo-robes and blankets were now brought from the sleighs, and seats were arranged for Mrs. Tenterden and the parson, where they might at once keep warm and have a view of all that was going on. Golightley, although he had brought with him a highly-ornamental pair of foreign skates, with some kind of patent fastenings, declined taking an active part in the amusement; he remained near the fire, replenishing it with fresh fuel from time to time, and responding to the sallies of his two companions.

Madge, as she had foretold, was dressed in a costume which closely copied Elinor's, insomuch that at a short distance one might easily have been mistaken for the other. Madge, however, was an accomplished skater, while Elinor could do little more than move about, with no attempt at curves and flourishes. Skating had not at that time such vogue among women as it has since acquired; but neither then nor since have there been many who could show such graceful mastery over the art as Madge. She loved it as she loved dancing, and it displayed her physical beauty and adroitness to at least as good advantage as did the latter exercise. Moreover, she was as tireless on her skates as she was skillful, and could keep in motion for hours at a stretch, without any appearance of fatigue.

Garth, likewise, had complete command over his motions upon the ice, and the compactness of his figure enabled him to perform evolutions which were the despair of many a longer-limbed rival. When he and Madge skated off together, therefore, there was a general disposition to applause among the beholders; and the small boy with the red tippet was generous enough to ignore unworthy jealousy, and give utterance to his unselfish admiration in a cheer. Not being, however, so familiar with the mysteries of poise and balance as with the exercise of the nobler emotions, his cheer whirled him over backward, and bumped his head unmercifully. When the throes of physical anguish had subsided sufficiently to allow of his sitting up and and taking conscious note of earthly things, he descried Madge far away, swinging in easy curves, regardless of his pain. His heart swelled within him as he gazed; from manly pride he had forborne to weep thus far; but there are bumps and bumps! As he tottered dejectedly to his feet, and scrambled away toward solitude, salt tears were freezing upon his cheeks, and his heart was embittered against the seductions of Sunday-school.

After Garth and Madge had made the circuit of the lake, they paused where, at its southern extremity, it merged into the river. Presently she said:

"Garth, will you take my hand, now,

and skate down there, away and away, as far as we can see—ever so far beyond Wabeno? and then get on board a ship and sail to Europe—O Garth! and live there? Will you do that with me?"

"If we had the Eve legacy, we might!"

"Well—what if I did have it, in my pocket, now?"

"If this were the first of the New-Year, instead of Christmas-eve, you might have had it—that is, if Kinco had not come. His right to claim it would have ended with this year."

"Then I wish he had never come! But Garth—it is not too late! Let him be taken —both of them! It would be right! and then we should be free! Will you, Garth Urmson?"

She spoke with a sudden flash of excitement, that made Garth's own blood tingle. What she suggested might be done, and public opinion, justice, and the law, would bear him out in it. And he and Madge needed freedom: how easy to grasp it! The world would lie before them—for a time, at least; all that was irksome in the ties that held them to each other would be forgotten in the warm flood of the life that they might live. Madge's hand was in his; her look was upon him; she awaited his decision. On his next words hung their future. He wheeled about; she saw the light in his eyes.

"You will do it!" she cried, in a low tone of triumph. "That saves me!"

He paused a moment; then the light sank back.

"I won't do it!" he said, harshly and abruptly.

The harshness was not for her, but for his own infirmity; but she could not know that. Their hands dropped apart: her vivid face darkened.

"You are a strange creature, Garth Urmson. You think every one has rights but me. Heigho!—Well, let us go back, then. It's time you were at work, catching your fish."

They skated back to the islet slowly and in silence; and for the next two hours Garth worked like a Titan. First, with the sharp ice-hatchet that he carried at his belt, he cut a score or so of holes through the ice, twenty feet apart, in straight rows. Beside each of these he set up a little rod, made of the twig of a birch-tree, with a line attached to it, whereby a baited hook was let down to the depths below. These preparations being finished, the fun began. Wherever a rod bent, the fisherman to whose charge it had been intrusted must grasp the line, and haul up whatever was at the other end of it. Women as well as men took part in this sport; even Mrs. Tenterden laughingly permitted herself to be established beside one of the holes, though she was too busy with being amused at the exploits of others to pay any attention to her own business. Fish were plentiful, and before long more than enough for the chowder had been caught, chiefly perch and trout. At length word was given to pull up all the lines; and it was not till then that Mrs. Tenterden was heard to complain that she thought hers must have got caught in something: the rod had been broken down, and only saved from being drawn under by falling across the hole, in which position it stuck fast. Garth took hold of the line, and perceiving at once that something unusual was the matter, hauled away with all his might. In a few moments out flounced a huge pike, three feet long, which snapped its horrid jaws at Mrs. Tenterden in so bloodthirsty a manner that the good lady sent forth a scream which brought everybody on the pond pell-mell to the spot. When the cause of her alarm became known, there arose a multitudinous roar of laughter; amid which Garth attacked and slew the "sockdolager," as the parson called it, cleaned it, and flung it into the chowder-kettle.

When the chowder was cooked, it was ladled out into tin bowls, and so handed around to be eaten with iron spoons. Garth took his seat by Elinor, and they chatted together about diverse indifferent matters, until he said:

"Jack Selwyn is the only friend I ever made, and he tells me secrets he would tell no one else. I saw him yesterday, and he told me what I was glad to hear, for your sake as well as his."

"He did not say that I—we—"

"No, no! he didn't magnify his hopes. You will find it possible to be kinder to him than you think you can be now. He loves you; and, when you know him better, you can't help loving him!"

Here there was an interruption, and Elinor was left to her reflections. That Garth should have congratulated her on the new step she had taken, affected her oddly. It was as if some one from whom, by a desperate effort, she had escaped, had suddenly appeared beside her, serene and kind, and given her joy on the success of her attempt. She wondered whether he would have spoken so calmly had he known what others knew about Madge: she wondered—even while taking shame to herself for so doing. Perhaps he did know: evidently he was aware of his uncle's guilt, and so why not of other things? But, again, what was said of Madge might not be true; the worst part of it, at least, might not be. She and Garth might fully understand each other. Who could say? and yet—Elinor could not bring herself to believe it!

At this point, however, she was reminded of the promise she had made to herself the day before, bearing upon this very matter. If Madge—supposing her to have formed any such scheme as Jack had imputed to her—could be persuaded to relinquish it for that which Elinor had to offer, might not all be well between her and Garth even yet, and Elinor the cause?

Ah! but the task was a hard and ungrateful one, and Elinor, now that she was face to face with it, could not help shrinking. She lacked the flow of persuasive speech which seems to render such intercessions easy to some people; and here she might hesitate on other grounds than those of personal unfitness. Not only would it in no way help Elinor's interest to meddle with Madge, but Garth (if the opinion of those who knew him best could be trusted) might be the worse instead of the better off were Madge secured to him. Was it not more reverent as well as more prudent to let Providence work out its own ends in its own way, without any impertinent interference?

Elinor would have been glad to have felt satisfied of this. But the more she strove

to be so, the more persistently did certain stubborn questions force themselves upon her. If Madge were ruined for lack of any argument or effort which Elinor could have used, would not the responsibility lie at Elinor's door? Did not all women owe a sacred duty to their sisters who were in peril? Was any earthly gain or loss worthy to be set against that duty?

Elinor got impulsively to her feet, and looked about her. Madge was at some distance upon the ice, teaching the small boy with the red tippet the mysteries of the outside edge. Elinor came up behind them and said to her:

"Won't you give me a lesson, too?" and took her other hand.

Madge looked surprised and on her guard, but offered no objection, and they skated off together, leaving the boy again forlorn.

"You see it's very easy," Madge observed; "but I suppose you don't have many chances to skate in Europe?"

"Not many. Would you like to go to Europe?"

It was several moments before Madge answered—

"I mean to go, some day!"

"But would you like to go soon—with us?"

There was another pause; Madge let go Elinor's hand and glided along beside her with a serpentine movement.

"Does your future husband authorize that invitation?"

"I meant with me and Mrs. Tenterden. I have not told you that we have got back most of our fortune. I shall not be married."

Madge swept about and looked in Elinor's face. "So Jack Selwyn has let out the secret, has he?"

"It was Golightley who told me, Madge."

"But what a funny invitation!" rejoined the other, with a soft laugh. "Is this to part Garth and me? or is Garth to be of the party? or—would not Garth do without me?"

Elinor flushed with indignation, and was half resolved to leave Madge to her fate. But her better will still overcame.

"I thought you might like to see the world before you were married. We could bring you to the things and people that would give you most pleasure. You should go where your beauty and talent would be best acknowledged. It would be better than for you to go in—in almost any other way!"

"But why do you ask me?" repeated Madge, coldly.

"O Madge! because you are a woman, and I am a woman: and no other woman knows what I know about you—what I found out by chance. I want to be a sister to you, if you will let me! I have felt what it is to be alone and in trouble—and in temptation! I longed for some one who would speak to me and be kind to me. And though I can do so little for you, Madge—still, if you will believe that I speak from no selfish motive, I might do something!"

Madge's expression abated somewhat of its hardness and incredulity, and she said more gently:

"You have never seemed friendly to me before."

"I know it—I was wrapped up in myself. And you never seemed to need a friend before. I do want to be your friend now!"

Madge cast down her eyes and was silent. But suddenly she looked up and asked:

"Ought I to marry Garth?"

Elinor hesitated: was Madge testing her sincerity? But even to gain her end she could not prevaricate.

"Not unless you love him," said she.

"Come!" said Madge, holding out her hand again. Presently she continued: "You do seem honest; and, if you are honest, you are very kind! But you mustn't think I would do anything foolish—put myself in any one's power. Perhaps I don't mean to marry Garth; but, then, I know now what I did not know a month ago—that he does not care for me! He would marry me from a sense of duty—which I hate! I don't expect to die of a broken heart about it; and yet I don't believe there's another man in the world so well worth loving as Garth Urmson! Don't forget I said that, Elinor! —But I'm not fit for him. He is all that I admire in a man, but he is so much more besides, that my part is crowded out of sight. So I should be happier with a lesser man—one more like Jack Selwyn, maybe!

only Jack happens to hate me (he has some reason to), and to be in love with somebody else. Can you guess with whom?"

She smiled as she put the question, and added immediately, "But don't have him, Elinor!" Then she pressed her hand a little closer and said, hurriedly:

"I will prove that I thank you for having wished to be kind to me. I will tell you a most precious secret. Garth Urmson loves you—he has loved you ever since he first saw you! You must do the rest."

As she spoke the last words, Madge curved aside with a graceful impulse, and was gone. Elinor stood overwhelmed with thick-crowding thoughts. She needed to be alone. But all at once a voice close behind called out:

"Miss Danver!"

Elinor looked round. It was the small boy.

"Oh, you ain't she!" he exclaimed staring. "I guessed you was Miss Danver! Want her to learn me some more outside edge!"

He scrambled away disappointed. Elinor now reflected that Madge had returned no definite answer to her proposal. Did she mean to refuse it? or was she revolving the question in her mind? Elinor looked across the surface of the frozen lake, glistening beneath the pink light of sunset clouds, but the beautiful skater was not in sight.

"She shall sit beside me as we go home," was her thought, "and then I shall know."

CHAPTER LXXVIII.

SONG AND FROLIC.

THE sun had by this time gone down, amid a splendid wilderness of crimson and gold, scarlet and green; and, though the moon had risen, dusk came on apace, for the sky to the east was clouded. The great bonfire was soon the centre of illumination; its red light gleamed along the ice, and the shadows of those who stood near it stretched out in dark rays, until they were blended with the outer gloom. And out of that gloom figures came gliding up swiftly, and away again; like strange beings from another world, making themselves visible for a moment in the light of this, and then vanishing for evermore. As the night still deepened, the surrounding darkness seemed to creep nearer, growing ever vaster and more mysterious to the imagination; so that the great roaring bonfire was none too great or too ardent, since it was the only source of life and warmth left to mankind.

At length Golightley made a request that Elinor should sing. It was almost the first time he had addressed her that day—a fact which Mrs. Tenterden had observed, and she had not spared to rally Elinor and him on what she called their lovers' quarrel. Nor did she fail laughingly to regard this request of his as the first step toward a reconciliation. But to Elinor it had another meaning. Golightley had always shown unbounded admiration for her powers of song; and now, at this last moment, as it were, of their being together, he was asking, for a parting gift, that only part of her which she need not hesitate to grant him. There was something pathetic to her in the petition; and as she prepared to fulfill it, what remained in her heart of bitterness toward him passed away, and womanly compassion alone was left.

She stood up beside the fire, and with her hands folded in her muff and her eyes upon the darkness, she began one of those sweet, pathetic ballads which delight uncultivated ears as well as those that know true music. As she sang, a semicircle of auditors collected on the ice before her, continually augmenting in numbers, until every skater on the lake was there. A wide, open space was nevertheless maintained between her and them; and every sound except the singer's voice was hushed. Presently Elinor noticed, in the front rank directly opposite her, the small boy in the red tippet, with his hands in his pockets and his mouth wide open. Golightley, she knew, was standing not far away on her right, his face shaded by his hand. The others of her party were behind her — save that twice or thrice, and on each occasion in a different part of the semicircle of listeners, she caught— or fancied that she caught—a glimpse of Madge.

The song came to an end; but, in the pause and silence which followed the last verse, a new and strange figure suddenly swept upon the scene: as wild in his aspect and movements as any night-goblin of fairy-lore. In figure he was tall, symmetrical, and athletic, and his graceful proportions were well set off by the close-fitting fur-trimmed suit he wore. Round his waist was twisted a scarlet, silken scarf, whose long, fringed ends waved outward as he moved; and there was a bunch of scarlet feathers in his cap. His black hair hung below his ears; his face was swarthy, and appeared, in the uncertain light, to possess a sombre and saturnine kind of beauty. Such an apparition had never been seen on the lake before; and the group of auditors, now changed to spectators, with one accord widened out, so as to leave him ample space in which to cut his strange, fantastic capers.

Certainly it can seldom be the lot of human eyes to behold such unearthly gambols as were here displayed. The mysterious skater seemed to be superior to ordinary physical laws. Freedom and boldness are not terms competent to describe the amazing recklessness with which he tossed himself to and fro, in and out, now backward, now forward, weaving inextricable patterns and wheeling out swift circles, all with as much inimitable poise, ease, and finish, as if he could lean upon the air and be supported by it. Meanwhile, the red firelight and the black shadow played over him so bewilderingly as to render any deliberate scrutiny of him impossible. To many who saw him he was a presence half supernatural, and no one seemed to know whence he came or wherefore.

"Good mercy, what is it?" exclaimed Mrs. Tenterden, at last. "I declare it looks like a wild creature!"

"It's the champion skater of the world!" replied Garth, who had been watching the exhibition with an expression of mingled annoyance and amusement. "Do you wish me to present him to you?"

"Good gracious alive!" cried the lady, drawing her ample shoulders together with a shudder of dismay; "it would just scare me out of my life! Why, I'd as soon think of being introduced to a mountebank in a circus!"

While this short conversation was going on, Elinor, who had remained standing precisely where she had first taken up her position, saw Madge press through the outer ring of on-lookers, and beckon to her with head and hand. Fearful of she knew not what, she slipped quietly aside, and, skirting along the exterior of the groups, came at length to the point at which Madge had appeared. But Madge was no longer there.

Just then the unknown skater, who heretofore had been as voiceless as he was mysterious, gave utterance to a wild, ringing yell, at the same time urging himself at dazzling speed round the limits of his arena. The unexpectedness of the outcry and action caused a kind of panic; the ring broke up in confusion; and almost immediately the skater was nowhere to be found. Elinor, however, had seen him a moment later than most of the others. As she stood alone a little way out upon the lake, looking vainly for some sign of Madge, she had felt her arm suddenly seized, and on turning found herself confronted by the swarthy, sinister, handsome face, with its red-feathered cap and long, black hair. Before she had time to feel alarmed, he had turned quickly behind her and made off; and, but for the impress of his long fingers on her arm, she might almost have taken the episode for a swift hallucination. Be it what it might, it did not lessen her anxiety on Madge's account, and she still continued her search for her, passing to and fro, sometimes coming within range of the firelight, and again returning to the shadow. Often it seemed to her that she recognized the familiar grace of the lost figure swaying in easy evolutions a long way off; but, when she reached the spot, either the appearance had vanished, or it turned out to be some other than Madge. Had Mephistopheles snatched her away with him into irredeemable darkness?

At length, after nearly a quarter of an hour's absence, she returned with growing apprehensions to the fireside. The parson was relating some humorous incident of seventy years ago, to which Mrs. Tenterden was listening with good-natured chucklings;

Garth had gone to the shed to give his horses a feed of hay, and what had become of Golightley no one knew.

"Why, daughter, I thought he'd gone off with you, to finish up the reconciliation," said Mrs. Tenterden. "I should have been after you myself, before now, if I'd known you were alone, and that wild creature rushing about!"

"I've been looking everywhere for Madge," returned Elinor, impatiently. "Have you seen her lately?"

"Maggie? why, yes, to be sure I have!" was the comfortable answer. "She was out there in plain sight not three minutes ago, and we've seen her, off and on, ever since that horrid creature went away."

Greatly relieved by this information, Elinor sat down on a buffalo-robe beside the fire, and began to realize, for the first time, how tired she was. The fear of danger being removed, she could rally herself on the folly of having admitted it. An air of comfort and security dwelt within the little circle of firelight, entirely inconsistent with any evil apprehension. Thus five minutes passed away. Then, all at once a thought flashed into Elinor's mind that brought her to her feet with a start. Garth had just left the horses and was coming toward her. She led him a little way out upon the ice.

"Have you seen Madge?" was her question.

"Yes—before I went to feed the horses."

"Who was that — who was skating here?"

"Oh—you mean the champion skater of the world?" said he, smiling.

"Was it Sam Kineo?"

Surprised by the vehemence of her manner, Garth admitted that it was. "He is gone now," he added, "for good! But it was to have been a secret, and had better be kept a while longer. It was a piece of his melodramatic nonsense, showing himself in that way. We had especially arranged for him to get off secretly."

"I'm afraid something has happened," replied Elinor, with a trembling which she could not repress. "Madge's dress and mine are alike—I'm afraid you mistook me for her. I looked for her everywhere, and could not find her. If—"

"Well, I guessed you couldn't be Miss Danver this time!" exclaimed a voice beside her — the voice of a small boy. "I guess even she couldn't skate quick enough to be back here 'fore I was! She was going t'other way, too!"

"Have you seen Miss Danver?" asked Garth, gently, of the small boy.

"Yes, but she's far enough off by this time, I guess," he replied, tucking his chin inside the fold of his tippet. "I see her; she was with that skater chap with the red feathers in his cap. They was goin' it, I tell yer! Way down there—way down 'long the river!"

He scrambled away. Garth had pulled on his gloves, and settled his cap upon his head. He and Elinor exchanged a look, brief and eloquent.

"Shall you take no one with you?" she asked.

"No: and do you say nothing. If I can't do it alone, there is no help. Get the people home soon. Good-by, Elinor!"

"Good-by; God help you, Garth!"

She stood listening to the ring of his flying skates until the sound was no longer audible, and he himself had long been swallowed up in the gloom. Then she returned to the fire, faint and sick at heart.

CHAPTER LXXIX.

GRIM EARNEST.

THE sky was overcast with great clouds, but at intervals the moon looked forth between the rifts, and filled the valley with cold radiance. Garth, as he swept with flying strokes toward the south, peered intently into the gray night before him; but the changes from shadow to light, and back to shadow again, were more perplexing than constant shadow would have been. It was unlikely that he would see those whom he pursued until he was close upon them; and, the overflow of the river having broadened it to nearly half a mile, he had to guard against the risk of passing them.

13

He moved with great velocity, what wind there was being behind him, and the ice perfectly smooth: but he knew that the conditions were as favorable for the fugitives as for him; and, besides their long start, it was certain that Kineo, if not Madge, could skate as fast as he. On the other hand, they might not expect the pursuit to begin so soon; and, since they must travel all night, they would be apt to spare themselves as much as possible.

In former years, Garth had often skated down this valley from end to end; and, as he now mentally rehearsed the route, he recollected that at a certain point, about nine miles below the lake, the dead level of the meadows was interrupted by a ridge, lying at right angles to the river, and through the midst of which the current had forced its way. Here, of course, the stream was narrowed to its original width, and flowed with such rapidity over a rocky bottom, that ice was rarely formed even in the coldest winters. At this place, known in the neighborhood as the Bite, there was a wooden bridge, the only one for twenty miles; and here, Garth hoped, there would be a delay, if not an actual stoppage. He was now, as he calculated, about three miles behind the fugitives: but, if he could maintain his present pace, there was some chance that he might come up with them either there, or a short way beyond.

As he sped onward, his mind involuntarily busied itself with a review of his relations with Madge from their first beginning. If, as it was hard to doubt, she was a willing companion of Kineo's flight, the plot must have been arranged, in one form or another, long ago. They must have been in communication, not only since the half-breed had been concealed at Urmhurst, but during all the years of his absence abroad; and that being granted, then their intimacy, even in childish days, must have been far closer than Garth had ever imagined it to be. In that fight of his with Kineo — which was the opening act of his long love-drama—must he believe that Kineo, and not he, had been in the right? Recalling each one of Madge's well-remembered looks and words on that night, they now wore a new aspect and sig-

nificance. Had she been false even then?
Had he been made a fool and a laughing-
stock all his life long? The blood burned
in his cheeks at the thought, and his eyes
sought fiercely through the gloom. The
hour of reckoning had come! He flew onward like the very spirit of retribution, and
the hollow ice resounded beneath his steel-
shod feet.

Hitherto he had not considered how he
would deal with the fugitives when overtaken: but now the question arose whether
Madge, having dared such a step as this,
would return at his command? or whether
Kineo would easily relinquish her? Garth,
however, was not in a mood nicely to balance doubts and probabilities. All the imperious, relentless temper of the hot-hearted
Urmsons was throbbing within him. Vengeance was his—he would repay!—or, if
God's, then was he God's chosen instrument! There should be no parleying nor
pitying; of that there had been too much
already. As for Kineo, he had come to the
end of his tether: his punishment should be
quick and final. Any other man than Garth
would have said, "Either I or my enemy
must perish!" But Garth did not admit
the alternative. The might of his passion
made him invulnerable and irresistible. He
could not perish until he had worked his
will. He felt in his belt, where hung the
small, sharp ice-hatchet which he had that
morning used for cutting fishing-holes. It
was his only weapon: but his purpose was
deadly enough without any weapon. Kineo
should die: and Madge—who had tempted
mercy until there was no mercy left—she
should not die; but she should be brought
back, and held up to the shame and scorn
which were her due. As Garth swept forward with heightened speed, he cursed these
miles of barren ice that hindered his revenge! But he would have it, soon or late.
Had not his forefathers defied Fate as he defied it now, and conquered?

But what had they conquered? or what
had the conquest gained them? Garth's
own father had warned him. In their victories they were cursed! Should Garth be
cursed so, likewise? Had he dreamed, that
night beside the spring, to no better purpose

than now to cast aside the grim lesson of
the Urmson generations, and stain himself
also, the last of his race, with blood? Should
that old murderous demon triumph over him,
as it had triumphed over the rest, and make
the blot which had thus far marred their
name, eternal? Were his mother's love and
trust to be thus justified? and had all his
boyish struggles and self-discipline brought
him to this—that he must stand before his
father to-morrow with murder on his soul?
—As he cleft his way onward through the
cold, still air, two spirits seemed to move
beside him, on the right hand and on the
left. One wore the mien and features of the
Puritan ancestor whose hands had set the
granite threshold-stone of Urmhurst above
the sachem's grave; the other spirit showed
the lineaments of Garth's mother.

Who could say that Madge, at the worst,
had been always and altogether false? Had
she never striven to be true? and if so, had
Garth been always blameless for her ill-success? Even that afternoon she had urged
him, with a vehemence which now he could
comprehend, to take her hand on that same
journey which, to-night, she was beginning
with another. Even so lately she had hesitated in her purpose, and had needed only
sympathy and encouragement to have drawn
back. But he had answered curtly and
harshly. And if he had been unsympathetic
then, how many times had he been so before? Those years of his in Europe—were
they guiltless of what was happening now?
And those long months of dullness and delay
since his return, when he was paltering between right and wrong, action and inaction
—during that time how many golden opportunities to woo and win her had slipped
away? Was he not man enough to be at
once all she desired, and all he desired for
himself? If not, was it strange that Madge,
vivid and restless, should have fled from one
so paltry, selfish, and one-sided? He had
worn her out and driven her away, at the
very moment that he was hugging himself
for his virtue in keeping faith with her when
his heart was elsewhere! Did he well, then,
to be angry because the cup himself had
filled was held to his lips?

Onward still he swept, and the pace

must have quickened, for the spirit of the old Puritan was now outstripped! Blessed were the barren miles of ice that had hindered his revenge! Nor were they barren, since they had brought forth this fair fruit in him. He loosened the hatchet from his belt, and swinging it from right to left, sent it thence whizzing and spinning far across the glassy surface. "I'll get her, if God pleases," he said, aloud; "let the devil's part go!" But Providence knows many ways of saving; and that which seems the speediest is not always so, where wayward human souls are concerned.

Nearly an hour had now gone by, and the moon, looking down through a cloud-rift upon the long-drawn icy surface, marked the shadows of three human figures hastening along it, two in advance and one pursuing: and the space between pursuers and pursued grew constantly less and less. At length the latter, being within about four hundred yards of the old wooden bridge, came to a standstill. The buckle of the man's skate-strap had given way, and he knelt to repair it. The woman, after restlessly watching him for a while, threw herself down on the ice near by, and gazed back toward the place whence she came. Suddenly she crouched low and laid her ear against the surface; then leaped to her feet with a low exclamation. She had heard the ring of steel, approaching fast. The man, too, arose with a curse, holding one skate in his hand.

"Give me the money—quick! it's you they're after!" said he.

"It is Garth!" said Madge, half in a whisper. She lifted her clinched hands to her face and pressed them against her cheeks.

As the pursuer emerged out of the gray shadow and saw his quarry, he struck the heel of his skate into the ice with a harsh, grinding sound, and brought up between them, breathing deep, his brow moist with sweat.

"I'm come for you, Madge!"

She stood silent, mechanically clasping and unclasping her hands. Kineo, after glancing up the river, took his stand in front of her.

"It's man to man here. We'll settle this, Garth, once 'nd for all. Let her stick to the winner!"

Garth seemed not to hear him. "Come, Madge!" he repeated. But as he moved round toward her, she retreated, silent, her eyes upon his face.

"Let her alone! she's always been my girl!" said Kineo, with an oath. "She only amused herself with you till I was ready for her!"

Then Madge spoke. "He tells the truth, Garth. He kissed me that day at the picnic, years ago, though I denied it. And that night when you ran the rapids, I was going with him—only seeing you changed my mind. But I sha'n't change any more: I shall not come back. You needn't be anxious about me, nor regret me. I'm glad you know me for what I am, at last! I liked deceiving you at first, but I'm tired of it now. I'm going where I can be my real self."

There was no passion in the girl's tone, but a fatal apathy, as of one with whom all moral struggle was definitely over. She did not avoid Garth's look, but rather sought it with a kind of listless directness that was appalling. The truth that she had spoken, ugly though it was, had the power inherent in all truth. Madge had never been stronger than at this moment of frank degradation.

Garth had no arguments: he could only put forth his will, of the strange force of which he himself was perhaps but partially aware. "Come!" he said to her with the quietness of intense resolve; and, though she still shrank back, he glided forward and laid one hand upon her wrist.

As soon as she felt his touch, all strength seemed to ebb away from her; she sank down on the ice and bowed forward, relaxed and nerveless. Her very eyelids drooped, as though heavy with drowsiness. Vigorous as she had been to escape, she was powerless to move one step in return. Garth could stop her flight, but his will could not compel active obedience. It could deaden, but not vivify.

He knelt beside her and strove to rouse her; but she only sank yet lower, averting her face. Kineo laughed jeeringly.

"You let that woman alone now, Garth

Urmson, 'nd get up 'nd fight like a man! or, by the devil, I'll brain you where you are!"

Garth turned, and looked grimly up at him, but said not a word.

With a sudden snarl of rage, the half-breed raised the skate which he had been holding in his hand, and dashed it in Garth's face. The steel blade struck his chin and cut a deep gash there. Madge started to her feet with a piercing scream. Kineo, staggering from the violence of his own throw, slipped and fell. In an instant Madge had stooped and snatched the knife from his belt, and put it in Garth's hand, as he still knelt on one knee, half dizzy from the blow.

"Kill him!" she whispered through her set teeth. But Garth stood up, grisly with blood, and flung the knife away.

"He had his grudge to pay," said he, frowning. "But I came for you."

It seemed as if she must yield, or drop before him lifeless. Kineo was getting to his feet again, but there was no help in him now. Garth was master.

All at once there was a shout, and the resounding of ice from the direction of the bridge; then other shouts, coming nearer. Madge held her breath to listen; she recognized Selwyn's voice. Quick as thought she turned to Garth.

"Don't let me be shamed before them!" she whispered, hurriedly. "Let me go back alone, and be there before you—then no one need know! Garth—may I?"

The men were near; there was no leisure to deliberate.

"Go!"

She lingered yet a moment. "Say you forgive me!"

He looked at her without speaking; his face was ghastly to behold; but she thought she saw what she had asked for in his eyes.

When Selwyn and his men came up, Garth and Kineo were standing there alone. Garth looked at Jack angrily.

"Is this what you promised?" he demanded.

"I took pains not to promise, old blood-and-thunder! But—is that the whole convoy?" He pointed to Kineo.

"That's all!"

"Why, then," exclaimed Jack, cheerfully, though not until after a moment's pause for consideration, "so much the better!—Truss him up, boys!"

"Let him go: I am responsible!" said Garth.

"I'm not going!" snarled the half-breed, with sullen malignity. "You've put up this job between you. You want to get rid of me now that the woman's cleared off with the money! But I'll let 'em hear who I am, 'nd what I know. You've got me, 'nd now you'll keep me!"

"Oh, anything to oblige you, if you feel sensitive about it!" returned Jack, with a laugh; and the prisoner was secured accordingly.

· · · · · · ·

Madge had skated northward a quarter of a mile; then she swerved aside to the left, and in a hundred yards reached some low clumps of bushes on the verge of the ice: behind these she crouched and waited. By-and-by a solitary skater came by; it was Garth, hastening to catch up with her. Even then, so profoundly had his determination swayed her, it was almost by main force that she kept herself from calling out, or following him. But he passed, and she had made no sign. She watched him with wide-open, straining eyes, until he had faded into the night, and out of her sight forever. After that a dull interval elapsed; the little group of the prisoner and his captors went by; but she had no eyes for them—her face was hidden in her hands. At last she arose, and fled swiftly toward Wabeno, and toward the world beyond, which she loved so well.

———

CHAPTER LXXX.

BROTHERS.

As soon as Elinor had ended her singing, Golightley, without waiting to thank her, or speaking to any one of his intention, had set out on foot for Urmhurst. There was a kind of solemn alertness in his bearing, different from his manner during the last few weeks. He seemed to take pains not to let any of the wintry beauties of the night escape him; several times he paused to watch the clouds drift across the moon, or to observe the black tracery of the branches against the sky. Once he picked up some snow, made it into a snowball, and aimed it at the trunk of a tree thirty paces distant, repeating the effort until he hit the mark. Occasionally he would pull off his hat, and let the night air breathe upon his forehead ; and at two or three points of the route he stopped to look about him, as one might do who wished to impress upon his memory a scene he expected not to see again.

At length he stood before Urmhurst, and looked up at its darksome front, which seemed to frown forbiddingly upon him with its overhanging brows. Two of the windows were alight—those of Cuthbert's study, and of the kitchen. Peeping through the latter, Golightley saw an oil-lamp burning on the table, but the room was empty. He passed round to the back of the house, entered with as little noise as possible, and, lighting a candle, descended into the cellar. The floor was the bare earth ; the sides were walled with brick, built in between ancient joists of oaken timber. He made his way between a medley of empty apple-barrels, superannuated farming-implements, and other rubbish, until he reached the southern end. He was now standing directly beneath the Urmhurst doorway, and on the other side of the brick wall in front of him was the sachem's grave.

He set down his candle, and with a broken trowel, which he found lying near, began to loosen the bricks from the square space between four intersecting joists. They came out readily, and, after about a dozen had been removed, he took his candle and peered into the black cavity beyond.

Nothing was there but some brownish, crumbling fragments, which might once have been bones ; and, arranged amid them, a number of quaint little objects of Indian origin—medicine-bags and other such mysterious votive offerings—none of which had been there when Golightley last inspected the place more than a quarter of a century ago. These were all ; the thing which he had come after was gone. Evidently, the same hand which deposited the medicine-

bags had carried off the sacrilegious pewter warming-dish, with its contents.

A month ago Golightley would not much have cared whether the triangular parchment were lost or not. But latterly the world had changed for him ; and he needed it, not as a power, but as an apology and a justification : and it seemed more desirable to him for the later purposes than it had ever been for the former. It was useless to think of hunting for it, however ; and equally vain to hope that the person who knew where it was would tell. Most likely, indeed, it had been destroyed. On that night, three months ago, when Golightley had told his ghost-story to the circle round the kitchen-hearth, he had been half minded to destroy it himself. Something that Madge had said to him, after the story, had suggested the idea that she had made a shrewd guess as to what the triangular parchment might be ; and several keen innuendoes which she had let fall since then had pointed the same way. But other matters of greater temporary importance had made him comparatively indifferent to this : and now it was too late. Viewing her hints in the light of this disappearance, it seemed manifest that they were the issue, not of conjecture, but of knowledge. Nikomis had found the parchment, Madge had seen it and read it ; but neither she nor Nikomis had known how it got in the grave, until Golightley's fireside narrative had explained the mystery.

"Confound my stupidity ! " he muttered to himself. "It's not destiny, though I've always said it was ; it's my own stupidity, by George, that's beaten me ! "

As this wholesome conviction entered his mind, he heard the door at the head of the cellar-stairs open. Some boards were leaning against the wall near at hand ; he crept behind them, and snuffed out his candle with his fingers. Peeping through a crevice, he saw Nikomis come hobbling along, holding the light above her head, and mumbling to herself. She stopped within two paces of his hiding-place, knelt on the ground, and, brushing away a layer of earth and rubbish, lifted up a square bit of planking which had been concealed there. Out of the hollow thus disclosed she took the well-remembered pewter warming-dish; and unfastening the false bottom, three papers fell into her lap. One of these was the triangular parchment.

The veins in Golightley's forehead swelled as the old witch took it up and turned it about between her dark, knotty fingers. Should he blow out her lamp (he could easily do it, for it stood quite near him), and then trust to the chance of being able to seize the parchment and make his escape in the darkness? To his relief, however, the Indian decided the question by replacing the precious document in the dish, and putting the dish itself back in the hole, which she covered over as before. The other papers she stowed away in the folds of the blanket she wore; and so got to her feet and hobbled away, her frosty breath showing mistily in the light of her uplifted lamp.

When all was dark and silent once more, Golightley lighted his candle and thankfully repossessed himself of his treasure. At another time he might have regretted losing the other papers, which were doubtless the same that Madge had yesterday mentioned having sent to Professor Grindle—without Nikomis's knowledge or consent. But, as it was, he was satisfied, and lost no time in getting to his chamber, where he found a cheerful fire burning, evidence of his brother's kindly forethought. He sat down before the fire, with the parchment in his hands.

After he had sat there for a while, stretching his chilled fingers toward the leaping blaze, a singular temptation came to him. He longed to burn the document which he had been so near losing, and had recovered only by so exceptional a chance. He held it out to the flame—then snatched it hastily back again. Presently he repeated the action, this time keeping it extended until one of the corners had become brown; but he could not quite resolve upon the sacrifice, and the parchment was withdrawn once more. Finally, as though fearful lest he should commit the deed by a sort of fascination, without intending it, he jumped up, walked to the table, and laid the parchment down upon it.

His hesitation thus disposed of, Golightley threw off his clothes, bathed himself from head to foot, dressed himself in elaborate evening costume, scented his handkerchief, beard, and hands, and finished by drawing on his neatest pair of patent-leather boots. This done, he seated himself at his table, took out writing-materials, and wrote far into the night.

Cuthbert had spent the afternoon in his study, looking over and putting in order the MS. pages of his history. The work, the labor of a lifetime, was incomplete; and no one who had beheld its author's emaciated countenance could have doubted that, so far as he was concerned, it must remain so.

"It's been a failure in the same way that my life has been," he murmured to himself at last, leaning back in his chair. "There are good passages in it, and the plan of it was not altogether amiss; but Heaven has not seen fit to furnish such odds and ends as alone could have rendered it an effective and intelligible whole. So, being a failure, it had better perish—the manuscript, I mean! Ah, me! why didn't I concentrate all my wisdom in some Æsopian fable about mice or chimney-swallows, which children might have learned by heart, and sages have quoted three thousand years from now? That had been a worthier fruit of sixty years, methinks, than a handful or two of ashes. Vain man, who didst undertake more than thou couldst accomplish! Well—here goes!"

He took the thick pile of MSS. from the table, and laid it—not without a certain half-playful reverence—amid the burning logs upon the hearth. Then, with his cheek upon his hand, and an occasional smile stirring the corners of his mouth, he looked on until the busy flame had mastered every page of the famous history.

"That was easily done!" said he. "I wish all human mistakes and shortcomings could be so simply and comfortably rectified! If free murder and suicide were not immoral, what a blessing they would be!"

After a long interval of still meditation, he continued:

"How funny it is that I, simple as I sit here, have remained all my life as unread as my history! I have been loved, and liked, and some people have been a little afraid of me, and a few, I trust, have positively disliked me; but no one has known me, heart and brain at once; though my Martha knew the one, and honest Tom Grindle does more than justice to the other. And sweet, haughty little Elinor has come very close to me. Still, I have been alone. Not willingly, Heaven knows! It is not that I am more nice than wise, but more odd than nice! I can't tell people how to get at me; and, if they don't hit the mark the first time, all my efforts to explain myself only seem to puzzle them the more. Most human beings were made in pairs, or quartets, or scores; but I am one of those unfortunates who were put together from the spare pieces, and must remain unmated.

"Yet my range of sympathies must be pretty wide, since I have made friends with two such diverse personages as Elinor and Nikomis! I suspect Nikomis of having made great sacrifices in my behalf, in addition to the grim devotion with which she has tended me through my illness. She meant us no good when she first came here; but, somehow or other, I have won that unspeakable old organ which serves her for a heart. She means to deny her unhappy grandson for my sake: I am to pass my last days in affluence at the expense of my nephew! But I will have a grand explanation with her this evening. How surprised she will be when I open upon her the vials of my omniscience! She will think that, during my long association with her, I must have found means to appropriate some of her witchcraft. But it has really been touching to behold her, and all the other good people, walking on tiptoe and laying their fingers on their lips in my presence, in order to spare me the pain and humiliation of discovering secrets which I knew before they did! And I solemnly accept my *rôle* of deaf, dumb, and blind. But I must reveal my duplicity now, since a week hence my nephew upstairs (though he were the most deserving young gentleman out of jail) would be too late for his legacy. Nikomis shall help me prepare a statement that may satisfy Tom's scruples: and to-morrow, when he and

Garth are both here, we will hold a cabinet council!

"The beloved old Hottentot! Methinks I see a possible way out of the woods for him. He shall not marry naughty Madge—in fact, I doubt whether she be quite naughty enough, or quite unselfish enough either, to let him do so. But when I shall have shaken the soul of that poor, shameful, pathetic brother of mine, Elinor will be free; and then, if Garth cannot manage the rest, he is more faint of heart than I believe him.

"But poor, vain, pathetic Golightley, with his mystery which has been, for him, the saddest of mysteries! what shall become of him? If my life could be of service to him, he were most welcome; but that's absurd; and he has used up everything else! Yet what a pity that—since the only thing I can hope successfully to achieve in this world is a speedy getting out of it—I should be unable to benefit any one by my departure. I have no fortune to bequeath—no forlorn hope to head; I'm not even in anybody's way—except my own!—But come, Cuthbert! no grumbling. I'll at all events minister unto my brother until this not too solid flesh has melted: I fear he won't find many to take his part after I am gone.

"So! there comes my stern friend pain again. What a rigorous guide is this which brings me to thee, my own gentle Cotton Martha! I wish this might be the last stage of the journey."

The hour of physical anguish which now ensued for Cuthbert was also the one which saw the departure from Urmhurst of Sam Kineo, after a not very genial parting scene with his grandmother. When, therefore, a few hours later, she and Cuthbert had speech of each other, the interview pointed to results somewhat different from those which he had anticipated. They did not hear Golightley come in; but the new light upon affairs had made Cuthbert so anxious to see him, that at length, by way of beguiling his suspense, he crossed the passage, and opened the door of Eve's chamber. Nikomis came behind him.

Golightley was standing in the centre of the room, his back to the door. He was clad in full evening dress. On the table

beside him were written papers, neatly arranged. In his hands he held an object
which Cuthbert was at first unable to discern; but instinctively he glanced up at the
wall above the fireplace. Captain Neil's
historic pistol was missing from its accustomed place.

Golightley, unconscious of the other's
presence, raised the weapon, his left hand
grasping the barrel, while his right was on
the lock. The muzzle was aimed at his
breast.

"Brother!" cried Cuthbert; and hurried
desperately forward.

With a great start, as of one whose
nerves had been wrought up almost to the
pitch of madness, Golightley turned partly
round. At the same moment his thumb
tightened convulsively on the trigger. The
pistol exploded; the ball grazed his own
shoulder, and buried itself in Cuthbert's
heart. And Cuthbert, with only a sigh, as
of a tired child dropping asleep, fell forward
on his face, never to suffer pain of mind or
body any more.

CHAPTER LXXXI.

THE VICTIM.

ELINOR and Mrs. Tenterden had driven
home from the lake in the parson's sleigh;
and he, after gallantly helping them to alight,
and wishing them a merry Christmas and a
happy New-Year in advance, had left them
at the door of the Danvers' cottage, and slid
away with jingling bells to his own dwelling.

Mrs. Tenterden had enjoyed her day
greatly, and even the unexplained disappearance of Madge and Garth had occasioned her
no anxiety. As for Golightley's equally
unceremonious secession, she had openly
quizzed Elinor about it, archly warning her
that she must not practise too far upon the
good-nature even of such a long-suffering
man as he. After they got back to the cottage, the good lady called her to her room,
to listen to an exhaustive and leisurely re-
capitulation of the day's doings, in the course
of which every incident that had come under
Mrs. Tenterden's observation was brought

up for judgment, and dismissed with a laugh,
in which it was taken for granted that Elinor joined. At length, when nothing was
left but to slay the slain over again, the
younger lady remarked that it was late, and
that she would go to her room. The elder
thereupon kissed her affectionately and bade
her good-night, with the assurance that
things would soon begin to look more cheerful for them all. In that persuasion she
went sumptuously and peacefully to bed,
and Elinor left her.

But Elinor could not rest. She waited a
long time in the hope that Madge might appear; pacing up and down her little room,
or standing in anxious expectation at the
window. But Madge came not; and the
white road, and the field and naked forest
beyond, looked lonelier and more lifeless as
the empty minutes passed. Unable, at last,
to endure inactive suspense any longer, she
put on her cloak and hood, left the house,
and set off at a swift pace toward Urmhurst.

Garth, arriving at the lake upward of
two hours after he had left it, and finding it
deserted, supposed that Madge must have
got there in time to accompany the others
home. The question was, whether they had
gone to Urmhurst or to the cottage. After
some consideration, Garth decided that he
at any rate would return to Urmhurst, and,
if Madge was not there, would defer seeing
her until the next day. Accordingly, he un-
fastened his skates, and struck off through
the woods in that direction. In rather more
than an hour, weary in soul and body, he
came in sight of the house and approached
the porch. Some one was standing beneath
it; was it Madge? It was not until he stood
within reach of her that he recognized Elinor. He took her hand; then both at once
asked the same question:

"Where is she?"

Garth's fingers relaxed their hold, and
his arm dropped to his side.

"You have been to the cottage?" he
asked at length, in a dull tone.

Elinor nodded. She could not say anything.

"O Madge! I trusted you: you asked
me to forgive you." His voice had lost all
life and depth; he leaned against one of the

stunted oak-trees that supported the porch, and breathed like a man exhausted.

Before Elinor could comprehend the significance of his words, a sharp, violent noise from within the house smote upon their ears. Garth raised his head slowly.

"Who is in this house?" he asked, with something akin to indignation in his tone.

"I've not been in," replied Elinor, faintly pressing her hand on her heart. "There can be no one but your father and Nikomis —and perhaps Golightley."

He stood erect again and manned himself. "Give me your hand," said he. "Will you come?"

She replied only by tightening her slender clasp. Garth threw open the heavy door fiercely, and they went in. Half-way down the hall they paused a moment to listen. The stillness was complete. "It may be nothing!" said he.

But, when they reached the foot of the stairs, an invisible, appalling warning met them—the faint odor of burned powder. Garth stopped short, and for several seconds his heart seemed to fail him: he gasped audibly, and his hand grew rigid and shook. Then Elinor's courage roused itself, and she drew him on, striving to make him feel her voiceless sympathy. They went up the stairs together, and stood on the threshold of Eve's chamber.

Nikomis was sitting on the floor, with Cuthbert's head on her knee, and was parting back the gray hair from his forehead with one hand. His eyes were half closed; Elinor and Garth knew at once that he was dead. Golightley, in his evening dress, half sat on the table, in an attitude which, but for the circumstances, would have appeared jaunty. His left hand held the pistol by the barrel; with his right he was tremulously adjusting his eye-glasses. The expression of his features seemed, at the first glance, to indicate stupid annoyance—hardly more than that. Stretched along the still air hung a thin veil of smoke.

Garth relinquished Elinor's hand and came forward a few heavy steps, fetching his breath with a slight scrape in the throat at each inspiration. He had not looked at the dead body, after his first glance at it:

his eyes were fixed constantly on Golightley, whose blank gaze wandered and shifted uncertainly. Garth faced him for a long time, without word or gesture. At length he extended one arm, and waved the open hand toward his uncle, as if mutely to command his attention.

Golightley stirred uneasily, and passed his tremulous fingers down his cheek. He moved his lips to speak, but could make no sound.

"How came you alive?" demanded Garth.

Again the other's lips moved, and at last there came a voice, which had no substance in it, and yet was not a whisper.

"The clumsiest thing! I hadn't oiled the lock. I was very nervous—and his coming in and speaking suddenly made me jump! I had dressed myself on purpose, and—arranged everything. But I missed myself, by George! and—"

At this point his wandering glance lighted upon the solemn whiteness of the dead face, and became riveted there. The pistol slipped from his grasp, and fell to the floor. He stood up, like a man awakened, and snatched away his eye-glasses, thereby revealing the haggard obliquity of his vision.

"It can't be!" he faltered, querulously. "Some mistake—eh? My brother, you know—the only man who would have forgiven me! Who is here?—by George, it's terribly like!—at least, so it strikes me. But there would be no one to forgive me. . . . O Garth, you here? Well, now look at that —you've got the artist's eye—look at that, and tell me if it isn't a likeness!—ha, ha!— eh? isn't it?"

"Garth, why you not kill him—um?" growled Nikomis. "He kill Cuthbert, and laugh! Why you not kill?"

"He tried to die—I cannot help him!" said Garth, gloomily. He turned from his uncle and knelt beside his father's body. "This is for me," he said, taking it from the old Indian's support.

Elinor had all this while remained where Garth had left her, near the door. She now came quietly forward to withdraw Golightley from the room. But his mind, which had for a time been shaken off its poise by the horror of his deed, was beginning at last to realize what had happened. He broke into sobs and moans, rubbing his hands over each other, and holding them out entreatingly to Elinor, to Nikomis, and even to Garth.

"My brother! he's dead! Let me go to him—I have a right to go to him, for it was I that killed him! I have no one but him—everybody will be against me! I shall never be forgiven if you keep me from him! Won't any of you relent to a poor wretch who'd have been dead himself, but for an accident?"

"You must not go to him now!" whispered Elinor. "Come away—hush! Oh, cannot you pray God to forgive you?"

Nikomis seized him roughly by the arm. "You come out, you Golightley!" she growled, pushing him along. "You kill—now you want scalp—um? Next time you want to die, you tell Nikomis: me help you —ugh!"

Before Elinor followed these two out of the room, she came and stood near Garth, who, lifting his darkening eyes, met a look of such divine sympathy as he never saw on any face but hers.

"Your father would have forgiven him; and you will forgive him, soon," said she. "Even I had something to forgive."

"Thank you!" he answered, replying to the spirit rather than to the words.

Her eyes brightened through the tears that stood in them; and thus she left him, without further argument, alone.

CHAPTER LXXXII.

SPECIAL PLEADING.

On the New-Year's-eve following, three friends of Garth sat round the kitchen-fireplace, discussing the events which had lately taken place. It was morning, breakfast had just been taken, and Garth himself was upstairs, making his final preparations for a journey.

"I don't mind telling you, professor," said Selwyn, taking up his knee between his clasped hands, "that I'm against it. In the first place, he won't find her; then, if he

does, she won't come back with him; and finally, if she did come back with him, it would only make them both worse off than they are now!"

"But he could never rest until he knew there was no more hope," observed Elinor. "And if he were to succeed, Jack, it must be for the best!"

"Ay, I'm of your mind, Miss Elinor," said Professor Grindle, folding his arms and nodding his thick eyebrows at her. "Let each do his best before saying, 'God wills it otherwise.' That was my dear friend Urmson's plan—and he was the worthiest man I ever knew."

"My friend Garth will be up with him before he's done!" remarked Jack. Elinor gave him a smile, which, after he had meditated on it for a while, cost him a sigh.

"If I were Garth, though," he resumed, "I should never feel anxious about that young lady. If she is not able to take care of herself, may I be—surprised! What could have been neater, for instance, than her management of Kineo? She made him give her his ten thousand pounds on the plea that, if they met with any interruption, it would be safer with her than with him. So it would have been, if she had been as much under his thumb as he fancied she was. But she meant to give him the slip from the first. She has played one of us against the other in a way that gray-haired diplomatists might envy. What a political intriguer she would make! That will be her career, too, if I'm not mistaken. She will set kings and emperors by the ears, and alter the map of Europe, before she's done!"

"I don't know that I'd so greatly object to that!" said Grindle, with one of his uncompromising smiles. "But speaking of Kineo—I understand there was no evidence to convict him on that charge?"

"No, for Garth lit the bonfire with the proofs of the forgery and conspiracy, and all that remained for Kineo was to be locked up a few months for some petty felony or other committed before the grand affair. However, I heard last night that he had taken matters into his own hands. He pitched into one of the jailers, day before yesterday, with an iron bar from his cell-window, and so mauled the poor fellow that his life is still in danger. If he dies, it's either murder or the next thing to it; if he gets well, it's only State-prison for ten years. But even that is something!"

"Ay, and enough, I trust, Mr. Selwyn. But 'tis strange how all the evil passions and wickedness called up during this long feud between the Urmsons and the Indians should have centred in this Kineo, who has the blood of both parties in his veins. He is the incarnate emblem of all the wrong done and plotted for two hundred years. May it find its end in him, likewise!"

"Didn't you say, Professor Grindle, that Mr. Urmson had left something relating to Eve—telling what became of her after she disappeared?" asked Elinor.

"It was merely some notes, my dear young lady, of a conversation had with Nikomis on the night of his death. Eve, you are aware, was a strange, reserved, adventurous child, idolized by her father and controlled by no one. A party of these Indians, lurking in the neighborhood, made friends with her, and at length enticed her away with them. She and one of their boys—a son of Nikomis—had become quite fond of each other; and Nikomis conceived the idea of having them legally married when they were old enough, and thus, in some undefined manner, compassing a more refined retribution upon the Urmsons than could be wrought by merely killing and scalping her. The plan was agreed to, and the pair were afterward married by a missionary residing thereabout; and, when the child was born, the same priest baptized it with the name of Samuel.

"That's all about Eve, who died a year or so later. But the tribe got to fighting with its neighbors soon after that; and at length, in a night-attack, they were nearly all massacred. Nikomis, however, escaped with the boy; and, though wounded in the knee, she got safe to Urmsworth with him and with the certificates. Just what she meant to do seems uncertain; most likely she had no definite plan, but thought to lie in wait, and effect whatever mischief circumstances might put in her way. However, circumstances are powerful things, as

we all know; and in twenty years they have transformed Nikomis from a foe to a partisan."

"A partisan with exceptions, though," interposed Jack, with a smile. "She has always had a wholesome hatred of Golightley, and even Garth hardly thawed her until very lately. Mr. Urmson was the circumstances!"

"He, and her grandson's delinquencies," rejoined Grindle. "It appears, I find, that she was not aware of the application made to me by Garth for the legacy. She had already refused Kineo the certificates, and purposed destroying them, and so, as it were, blotting him out of existence."

"Mr. Urmson knew nothing of the application either, did he?"

"No, sir: and when, on that last night, he opened the subject to Nikomis, and proposed that the legacy should be settled on Kineo in the form of an inconvertible annuity, so that it might, if possible, avert rather than hasten his destruction, Nikomis would hear nothing of it; and on his persisting, she fetched the certificates and burned them before his eyes. Of course, things being as they are, that makes small difference; and Garth tells me that she is to have sole possession of Urmhurst henceforth."

"Well, things might have been worse!" exclaimed Jack, after a silence. "I don't believe anybody except. Nikomis could be hired to live in this house, now, upon any terms. And as for the money part of the legacy, it must have inflicted a bitter pang upon Kineo's manly heart to lose it in just the way he did; and since ,Garth wouldn't have condescended to touch it under any circumstances, there's no great harm done as far as that goes. All that troubles me is, that the rogue who was really at the bottom of the whole misery should get off scot-free!"

"I think," said Elinor, "that he suffers more than all, and almost more than he can bear. For his punishment is not such as to harden his heart: it has made it sensitive beyond what it ever was before."

"Ay, his pain is great," said the professor, gravely. "Were it greater, the poor wretch's brain, which already betrays occasional unsteadiness, would collapse utterly; and that, I apprehend, may be the final result in any case. But God's ways are not our ways; and, strange though it seems to us, 'tis doubtless true—that if anything redeems Golightley Urmson's soul, 'twill be his having slain his brother at the moment when he sought his own life. And Cuthbert, I'm well assured, would gladly have laid down his life for such an end. Nay, it was a happy release to him in any case. The disease he had would have killed him, with lingering pain, after a few months more. But, as it was—just one heart-throb, and then—rest!" The professor's throat swelled, and his eye-glasses became him.

A few moments afterward Garth came in. He wore a long top-coat with a cape to it, and held a fold of papers in his hand. Standing by the fireplace, facing them all, his square, impressive figure and visage filled the eye of the beholder and satisfied it, as a portrait by Rembrandt might have done; only that Garth was no portrait, but a reality. His beard was gone, and a deep scar was visible on his chin.

"I've read what my uncle wrote in Eve's chamber, on that night," said he. "Before I go, I must tell you of it.—Elinor, you remember his story, that first evening we sat round this hearth? It was a veiled confession, characteristic of him. Did you ever think what that triangular parchment may have been?"

"He told me, once—at least, he hinted that it was a later will of his father's, leaving every thing to him."

Garth shook his head. "It was not that. It was the marriage-lines of Brian Urmson and Maud Golightley, dated at Jamestown in 1781. The marriage was a secret one: their second marriages, which each made in the belief of the other's death, were illegal; and the children of them—my father and Mrs. Tenterden—illegitimate."

"Ay, and so poor Maud's flight northward is explained," murmured the professor, grasping his beard and throwing one knee over the other. "It was her husband, not her lover, that she sought. But proceed, sir!"

"I tell it only for its bearing on my uncle. Maud and Captain Brian agreed never to reveal their secret, and thus discredit their innocent children. The captain had already willed his property to Cuthbert: Maud, when she disappeared from her home, left all she had to Mildred. But when Eve and Golightley were born—the first and only legitimate children—the captain changed his will; half the property was to go to Eve; the other half, less two thousand pounds, remained Cuthbert's: the two thousand was for Golightley.

"Long after Maud's death, Golightley found the marriage-lines in the garret, and learned that he was the only legitimate son and heir. He was not man enough either to confront the captain with the record, or to burn it up and say nothing. Instead, he hid it, and, without ever meaning to use it against his brother, he enjoyed the secret sense of power it gave him. He brooded over the injustice done him, and by degrees lost all habit of frank speech and thought, and grew sly and hypocritical. It's piteous to think of! for, after all, his intentions were good."

"But if ever a man paved hell with such things, he did!" muttered Jack.

"It was not until after he got to Europe, and fell into difficulties," resumed Garth, "that he said to himself, as he has written here: 'If I ask the captain for part of the money which should by rights have belonged to me, he will give it me rather than have Cuthbert know that his mother was not a wife.' And when, twenty years afterward, he met the Tenterdens, he said in the same way: 'This fortune ought to be mine; I was defrauded out of it.' It seems to me tragical! His sin, as he told us in his story, was so subtile, that the more it was reasoned about, the more like a virtue it looked: and his Doppelgänger, though secretly poisoning his soul, was ostensibly his best friend all the while."

"Well—there may be a clean spot left somewhere on his moral carcass yet—I hope there is, with all my heart!" exclaimed Jack. "But I should admire him even more than I do, if, when he contemplated endowing another world with himself, he had burned up the triangular parchment, and held his tongue."

"He did try to burn it, but his heart failed him," replied Garth. "He could not bear to die without having put his poor excuse before the world. He had found an honest way to be dishonest: there could hardly be a more perilous discovery. I don't think we ought to condemn him.— Well, I didn't mean to talk so much; but I couldn't be silent either!"

With these words Garth thrust the folded papers into his pocket, and met the glance of each of his three friends in turn; and in all he read the silent acknowledgment of his appeal for mercy. After a pause he said:

"Now I'm going!"

He shook hands with Professor Grindle, and with Jack, who, after the manner of deep-hearted men, tried to make the strenuousness of their gripe compensate for the barrenness of their farewell words. But Elinor, as she put her hand in his, remembered their former parting, in the firelight on the frozen lake, a week before, and said, "God help you, Garth!" as she had said it then.

As he stood on the porch a few minutes afterward, the venerable parson drove up in his sleigh. Although this reverend gentleman had officiated at the funeral the day previous, and had come this morning on purpose to see Garth off, he had become quite oblivious of both facts during his morning drive through the cold, bright air.

"What! Garth, lad, where are you off so early?" he bellowed. "Going courting, I expect—eh, ho, ho, ho! Well, you'll find her at the cottage, I suppose, though, now I think of it, I've not seen Maggie for the last day or two. But you'll find her, I don't doubt. Well, good luck to ye, dear lad, and a happy New-Year! Oh, ay, you young folks think all your years are sure to be happy ones: but I guess you'll be none the worse off for an old man's blessing, any way —eh? haw, haw, haw!"

With that laugh, mighty in spite of its occasional cracks and quavers resounding in his ears, and, as it were, driving home the godspeed which had preceded it, Garth started on his quest.

CHAPTER LXXXIII.

THE WAY OF THE WORLD.

NINE months later, as Garth was packing his trunk in a room of one of the smaller Parisian hotels, a card was brought up to him; and almost before he had found time to read the name it bore, the person to whom the name belonged made his appearance.

"Garth, dear old curmudgeon!"

"Jack!"

They shook hands; but the next moment Selwyn impulsively threw his arms round his friend, and hugged him.

"Are you packing that trunk or unpacking it?" he demanded.

"I am starting for Vienna this afternoon. How long since you have been on this side of the water?"

"Not long. But why to Vienna?"

"I've not found her yet," replied Garth, looking down, "but I heard—"

"I know you haven't found her!"

Garth looked up.

"Because I found her myself, yesterday," Jack continued. "I say, don't look at a fellow that way! I've done you no harm!"

"Does she know I am here?"

"Yes. Garth—she's been playing hide-and-seek with you from the beginning: she won't see you: she's afraid of you: you'll never meet her—and that's the long and short of it!"

"She need not be afraid of me," said Garth, with a deep tremor in his voice. "Where is she?"

"I promised her not to tell."

Garth's face slowly darkened: but Jack, with tears springing to his eyes, came and sat on his knee and put one arm across his shoulders.

"Just listen to me, will you? and don't break my heart by sticking that cursed obstinacy of yours in the face of God's Providence! There are some things no man can do; and this is one of them. Look here— the confounded woman is married!"

"Is that the truth?"

"Do you think I came here to lie to you, Garth Urmson? Of course she is married, man! She's not such a fool— As to who her husband is, that's of small consequence; some infernal German baron or other! She's living a life you'd as well not inquire into; but it might have been worse. She has got what she bargained for, and it's to be supposed she likes it. She's the finest woman on the Continent, past the ghost of a doubt: but—well, she wishes you to let her alone. She said you hadn't cared for her for the last four years at least, and, in proof of it, she showed me a sketch you'd made while you and I were over here together, of a certain young lady's face. I must say that rather floored me!"

Garth started and reddened. "Elinor's!" he murmured.

"Never mind, old boy!" said Jack. "I've had time to forgive you since yesterday, though she has not, but keeps the sketch always within reach—a sort of *memento mori*, you know. But all I meant to prove to you is, that you can't do anything—you simply cannot!"

Garth sat gazing straight before him, his hand twisting the hair that clustered on his head, as Selwyn had so often seen him do, when deep in thought, at college. At last he said, almost inaudibly:

"Well."

"I'll step out on the balcony," added Jack, getting off his friend's knee, "and smoke a cigar, while you're—unpacking that trunk again! Then I shall have something else to tell you."

"No," said the other, with a smile, "I don't need to be alone, Jack. I've done my best: now I give it up. May God bless her!"

"Amen!—though she is the devil!" muttered Jack.

"As to your other news, I can guess what that is," continued Garth. "You are going to be—or perhaps you already are—"

"Let me tell my own news, will you?— I'm engaged!"

"Is that your idea of news?"

"It is news, you'll find! I'm engaged— but not to Elinor Golightley!"

"I don't understand you!" said Garth, after a pause, his brows lowering somewhat.

"Let's look at him! is he entirely shocked, or secretly pleased into the bargain?—En-

tirely shocked, of course! Well, the name of the new young lady—you have heard of her: we used to read poetry about her in college—is Bellona, goddess of war!"

"Jack, tell me what you mean!"

"Well, I don't know as it's much to my credit," said Jack, with rather a sad laugh, "but it's this way: Elinor Golightley is beyond me. She strikes notes I can never reach, tiptoe as I may; and if the love I've felt for her can't make me reach them, nothing else can. So I give it up, as you say. She said to me nine months ago: 'You don't know me; but you shall have opportunity to know me, and then—' Garth, I should be a fool as well as a selfish brute if I married her. She is meat for heroes; by which I mean to say (though I'm not given to running myself down as a general thing) that she's beyond me, and beyond any man I know—except one!"

"I'm glad you spoke to me of this, Jack," said Garth, rising from his chair and going up to him. "I may be able to save you from making a great mistake. I don't know what has put these notions into your head— but it's all wrong! You love her so well that you think you can't be worthy of her— that's all. It's what every honest man feels about the woman he loves; and it's a true feeling; but, if we didn't trust to God to make us worthy, there would soon be no more marriages! Besides, you must think of her! Women don't love as we do; and certainly Elinor Golightley, with her shyness and haughtiness— Don't laugh, Jack, at my pretending to instruct you in these matters. When a man is in love, as you are, his friend may sometimes comprehend his position better than he himself can—even though that friend be ordinarily thick-headed!"

"My dear friend, I have long known that your thick-headedness is merely an appearance, artfully assumed to cover fathomless depths of guile. But I'm all the more obliged to you! By-the-way, what do you think of doing with yourself now? Go home, or become an exile?"

"I don't know!" said Garth, a little disconcerted.

"What do you say to coming down with

me to Italy, and joining Garibaldi? You could wear that old red shirt of yours, you know, and be quite in the fashion. But you must be ready to start in three days, for all my preparations are made. Come, I won't be jealous, even in the event of your rising faster and higher in the good graces of Miss Bellona than I do! Will you go?"

"You will not go, Jack."

"Now, by God!" cried Selwyn, the blood rushing to his cheeks, "I won't be bullied and dictated to by you! I'm no baby, Garth, to go babbling about without a purpose! I have learned a fact which, if I hadn't been a blind ass, I should have seen from the beginning; I come to you to ask your pardon and make amends, and you put me off with a long-winded, flowery speech, that has no particle of sincerity in it. . . . Well, no, I don't mean that. But it's no use, old fellow! I shouldn't have come to you if it hadn't been settled. The fact is, she loves you, and has always loved you; you love her, and have always loved her. You were born and grown for each other. Bless you, my children! This is irregular and premature, of course; and as Aunt Mildred would say, 'I'm perfectly scandalized, my good fathers, well I do think in my heart, did you ever!' But why should we dodge each other, Garth?"

Garth knew that, beneath this screen of gayety, his friend was rendering him the dearest sacrifice that friends can make: and he blenched at the thought of taking the bread of life from the mouth of this too generous recusant.

"You have no grounds for what you assume, Jack," he said, with a troubled voice. "Don't do what both you and she might regret forever!"

Selwyn again approached him and threw his arm round him. "Garth, do violets ever grow in New Hampshire so late as October?" he asked. "Ha! theatric start of villain detected in his guilt!—Because I saw one a few days ago—pressed, you know, on the blank leaf between the Old and New Testaments of a little pocket Bible—which I hope you may have the pleasure of perusing some time. And what with the violet and the sketch, and my own mother-wit and

wisdom, here I am, requesting the honor of shaking hands with you!"

"O Jack, I wish it had been my luck to do this for you!"

"Give me that old red shirt of yours instead, and I'll call it square," returned Jack, laughing lightly. "Well, good-by for the present. Of course, you know, if it would really inconvenience you very much to leave a card, any time during the week, at a certain suite of rooms in the Grand Hôtel—it's your own affair, and I shouldn't dream of forcing your inclination. I am off for my general's tent in Italy. A hero's death, or victory and no pay! Farewell!"

So one day Garth found himself in a large room, all mirrors, gilding, and French furniture, waiting for some one to appear.

She came in at last, with a wide throwing-open of the door which had always characterized her, and was not inconsistent with a nature in so many ways reserved and shy. Garth stepped forward to meet her, and they shook hands: her hand was cold, she scarcely smiled, and her face wore that distant and rather haughty expression which he knew so well, and loved because he knew it. Then followed some highly-commonplace conversation; and, at last, Garth bethought himself to inquire:

"Is Mrs. Tenterden well?"

"I believe so—yes, I mean, very well! She'll be down in a minute."

Elinor had taken her seat on one of those comfortless little gilded chairs which only a French mind could have originated; a chair which made her seem three times as unapproachable as she would have looked without it, and that is saying much. But a brave man is not to be defeated even by a French chair. Garth walked across the polished floor and stood beside her. She glanced up in fear—in that sweetest of all fears, which no pen can describe. He said:

"Then I have only a minute to tell you that I love you. I want to tell you with my whole life!"

It was not more awkward, perhaps, than most impromptu love declarations. He had an idea, but not the leisure or composure to present it in its neatest or most logical form.

Elinor drooped, and hung her head. Garth bent and kissed her cheek, which flamed pink as the kiss came. An instant later she had put her hand in his, and risen, and looked in his eyes. What were French chairs, or the world, to them?

Mrs. Tenterden did not make her entrance for fully a quarter of an hour; such, at least, was the testimony of the two clocks —the ormolu and the bronze one—which ticked at each other from the ornamental mantel-pieces at opposite sides of the room. But to Garth and Elinor it was a long time, because enough for them to be made all over new in it: and yet the least of times, because, probably, there was a taste of eternity in it.

Just before Mrs. Tenterden appeared, Elinor said:

"Dear Jack! I love him, Garth!"

Garth, strange to tell, kissed her for those words. But such is friendship, and such is love!

CHAPTER LXXXIV.

URMHURST STEPS DOWN.

THE August of the following year was a very hot one in New England; and, when Garth and his wife landed in Boston, their scheme of riding by easy stages to Urmhurst seemed by no means so practicable as it had done while they were still on the cool Atlantic.

"Wife, we must give it up!" said Garth. "The horses would be sunstruck even if we escaped."

"Perhaps it will be cooler soon?" suggested Elinor.

"Not for six weeks at least!" returned the husband, shaking his head. "Except at night!" he added. "You never experienced a New England summer."

"Show me an almanac," said the wife, after a pause.

"Here is the 'Farmer's Almanac,'" answered the husband, taking it from his pocket. "Sit down, and I'll show you. But I hope my wife is not so weak-minded as

to believe that these prophecies are trustworthy?"

"Garth, this is only an hotel parlor! Some one might come in!"

Garth took no notice of this irrelevant remark.

"This is the twelfth?" he asked.

"It is the eleventh," said accurate Elinor.

"Well, here is the twelfth, then!"

"O Garth! you know you meant what day of the month!"

"Men are not like women; they can mean more than one thing at a time!" returned the husband, with an unsympathetic laugh. "Well, look here—as Jack would say—'August eleventh'—"

"Dear old Jack!"

"We must get in the habit of calling him Lieutenant, Mrs. Urmson; for if his wound is well enough for him to meet us on the Nile next winter, he will stand upon his rank." Elinor thought in her heart that his wound would not be well enough, either then or thereafter; but she said nothing, and Garth went on: "'August eleventh—about this time expect warm weather, with occasional thunder-showers.' How do you suppose the man could have known?"

"Give me the almanac! That is not what I wanted to see at all!"

"It's no trouble for me to hold it for you."

"You promised me you would shave every day, and I am sure you have not done it! Tell me about the moon."

"The moon is round: it is like a cheese: it has two eyes, a nose, and——stay one moment; thirteen is an unlucky number, Elinor—Mrs. Tenterden says so!"

"O Garth! you have grown so silly since we were married—and so sweet! I always have to laugh at you now; and I used to be afraid of you, even after I began to like you! But tell me, really, when is there a full moon?"

"On the fifteenth, dear Mrs. Urmson."

"And how long would it take us to ride to Urmhurst?"

"Three or four days."

"Well, then, don't you see, my good but slow-witted husband, that we can also ride there in three or four nights, when there will be no hot sunshine, but only a cool, beautiful moonlight: and in the daytime we can have *siestas*, like people in the tropics—now, isn't that a good idea?"

"We'll try it," replied Garth, with an affectation of non-committal gravity. "At least it may save us something in mosquitoes."

That same night, accordingly, they set out, having previously dispatched a courier before them to prepare a halting-place for the next day. The experiment was a complete success; they rode leisurely onward, and, as the city was left behind them, there were only the inner voice of crickets and tree-frogs, and the clear hoof-tramps of the two gray horses to interrupt the deep moonlit stillness. The world seemed all their own—a grave, silent, beautiful solitude. It pleased them more than bustle and brilliance, for it seemed to press them yet more closely to each other, and to expound to them the full, ineffable delight of mutual love and dependence. Occasionally the front of a wayside farm-house, gray with the rains and suns of many years, or glistening white with new paint, would echo back the sound of the horses' hoofs; or a dog would bark watchfully, and be answered by other dogs far off and near. Sometimes tall elm or butternut trees flung their black shadows across the pale roadway; sometimes sweet odors of unseen flowers breathed forth a greeting. When a brook crossed their path, they would draw rein awhile to listen to its liquid volubility; and again, they paused long to catch the distant murmur of the Atlantic on their right. It was a journey of enchantment through a land of dreams. True, there were mosquitoes—a sharp-tongued, business-like race, who do much to mitigate the romance of New England summer nights; but even they were greatly baffled by the breeze of their victims' motion, and could scarcely do more than make the enchantment seem less of a dream and more of a reality.

Garth and Elinor talked but little as they rode; but for miles at a stretch they would go hand-in-hand; and sometimes, where the road was even and the pace a walk, the husband's arm would find its way round the wife's waist. At last, just as the dawn began to blanch the east, and the first bird launched forth its song, they came to the farm-house where they were to pass the day; and, while the haymakers sweltered in the noontide sun, they slept. In the afternoon they put on broad-brimmed straw hats and strolled forth into the fields and rocky pastures, and sat beneath the shadow of trees, or stained their fingers and lips with blackberries, and at night, after the farm-folks had gone yawning to bed, Garth saddled the horses and they set forth once more.

On the fourth night they started from a spot about seven miles south of Wabeno, purposing to be at Urmhurst by sunrise. The road mounted a long, irregular acclivity, and so found its way to a rocky pass which wound through the midst of the mountain. On arriving at the highest point of this pass, the whole valley suddenly lay disclosed before them, with the long curves of the river whitening beneath the western moon. But overhead a black cloud was gathering, and a distant rumble of thunder gave warning of a coming shower. The riders urged their horses beneath the low-spreading branches of a chestnut-tree, where the heaviest rain would hardly reach them; and there they waited, gazing out upon the broad prospect.

"I shall be glad to see dear old Urmhurst again—sha'n't you?" said Elinor.

"I shall be glad; but I am more glad that we are not to live there. It was a strange fancy our coming here even for a day. All the business might just as well have been done by letter."

"But we could not have seen Parson Graeme and Nikomis by letter! I hope he has remembered to tell her that we are coming."

"Our courier will have informed her, at any rate. She probably knows, even without witchcraft, just where we are at this moment."

"I wonder whether she will be glad to see us?"

"I sha'n't expect much cordiality. But, when she hears our errand, she ought to unbend a little. I have an idea of making a great picture in illustration of an ancient prophecy — did I ever tell it you? — about Urmhurst and Wabeno?"

"I remember! — when Urmhurst leaves its moorings, Wabeno is to roar—?"

"Well, I shall paint that. . . . How bright that light is growing!"

"Yes; and it must be very far off. Isn't that about where Urmhurst is?"

"Yes."

"Oh, how it blazes up! What can it be? — Oh, Garth—" She turned quickly to him, and put her hand excitedly on his arm.

"Yes," said he in a low voice, answering her unuttered suggestion; "it is that, Elinor; Urmhurst is on fire!"

As he spoke, there came a flash of lightning, instantly followed by a thunder-peal so loud that it seemed to shake the mountain. The horses started and trembled. Other peals followed in quick succession; it was as if Wabeno had suddenly awakened from his sleep of unknown ages, and were rousing himself to some great occasion with roar on roar. Meanwhile the flame of the burning house rose higher, and its glare was reflected from the smooth surface of the lake below, and a dark mass of clouds to the northward glowed dull red above. It blazed a mighty beacon to all the land. The wife and husband sat and watched, not speaking, but full of many thoughts. The ancient prophecy was undergoing fulfillment, and they were there to see and hear. They were witnessing the last act of a long and gloomy drama; it was a wholesome act; the beacon was of promise, not of despair. Urmhurst, whose foundations had been laid in violence and sacrilege, and which had held its position through more than two centuries of wrong and disaster, was now vanishing (like the castles of wicked enchanters in fairy-tales,, because the evil and lawless spirit which had called it into existence had been finally met and overcome. The spectacle was not therefore a lamentable one; and yet—there being so much in all human works, not mechanical, that appeals to human hearts— Garth and Elinor could not behold the annihilation of the strong old house unmoved. In this world, where nothing that seems

stable is really so, all partings that are final must be sad. Long sat they there watching, while the thunder rolled about the mountain, and from time to time passionate showers fell. When the storm was over, they rode forward, the glow of the conflagration still lighting the northern sky. But, as they drew nearer, the earthly fire faded, the clouds vanished from the heavens, and the sun rose clear. It flung the shadow of Urmhurst's eastern chimney across a low heap of blackened ruins; roof, walls, and porch, were gone; and even the granite threshold had been shattered by the heat into shapeless fragments. It was not known how the fire began, nor were any human remains found amid the ruins; but that old Indian witch, Nikomis, had disappeared, and was never seen again.

.   .   .   .   .

Some two or three years later a couple of swifts happened to meet on the top of that tall chimney, which stood the sole survivor of Urmhurst. One was an exceedingly ancient and decrepit swallow; the other was a bird of middle age, who had digested his wild-oats, and possessed judgment.

"It appears to me that changes must have occurred in these parts," twittered the latter. "Unless I am mistaken, there was a house here when I was young, and another chimney—an unsalubrious one."

"Yes, yes; you are quite right," piped the old one, garrulously. "There was a house, and a chimney, an unsalubrious chimney—a kitchen-chimney, in fact. 'Tis a singular fact, by-the-way, that kitchen-chimneys are always unsalubrious. I don't know whether any one has ever generalized the observation before me, but you may rely upon it as being a correct one."

"I have heard it before—when I was quite young—and, now I look at you, I believe you were my informant. Yes, it is a fact of general application, as you say. In my youth, it aroused my indignation, and I contemplated crushing out the abuse; but there are so many abuses! The world, one is tempted to believe, almost needs abuses; and besides, as one grows older, one moderates somewhat one's zeal for reform. Instead of suppressing abuses, one indulges in abuse!"

"Very justly put!" piped the veteran, wiping his bill appreciatingly.

"I was going to inquire," resumed the other, disguising his satisfaction at the compliment with an unconcerned flirt of the wing, "whether the colony has permanently taken flight? You are the oldest bird hereabout, and, I doubt not, the best informed. How is it?"

"You have applied to the right quarter, I assure you," replied the elder, highly gratified in his turn. "If any one can afford you information, I can. The fact is, then, that since the disappearance of the house, the chimney has become unfashionable, and not a bird has built in it. Now, is not that odd? There's as much room as there ever was, and no disturbance; and yet the place is deserted. The house was never a bit of use to us—rather the contrary, some would say!— and yet, since it has departed, so have we! Now, how would you account for that?"

The younger swift turned his head sagaciously, first on one side and then on another, but did not think it worth while to hazard an explanation. The old cock wiped his bill again, and sidled up a bit closer.

"The fact is," he piped confidentially, "in this world, it is the indirect causes that are the most efficacious! You can't put the fact into more explicit language than that, could you? The indirect causes are the most efficacious!"

"It does sound well, certainly; and now I think of it, I remember having arrived at some such conclusion myself, a long while ago. But is there no prospect of a new house being built here, in place of the old one?"

"No, no, no! The site will never be used again; though some, no doubt, think it a pity. But the owner has crotchets. However, I respect crotchets; and since there's no chance of the owner's living here himself, I don't know that I should care to have any one else. One doesn't usually pay much attention to men and women, of course, though they have their uses — their indirect uses, mind you! But Garth was perhaps more noticeable than some men; he was kind-hearted, patient, and gentle. To give you an example of this: I once had the misfortune to break this limb, and, in consequence, fell down the chimney. He happened to be below, picked me up, and set the fracture so skillfully that— eh?"

The other swift had flown away almost at the beginning of this speech, without the old cock's having observed the circumstance. The latter, when he found himself alone, was at first disposed to be indignant; but, reflecting that truth and wisdom remain what they are in spite of not being listened to, he smoothed his ruffled feathers, spread his wings, and set off toward the South. But the great chimney still stands erect and lonely, a landmark for many miles.

THE END.